UNLOCK THE MYSTERY OF THE HEART WITH

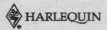

INTRIGUE

The place for
BREATHTAKING ROMANTIC SUSPENSE!

To introduce you to our expanded publishing lineup, we have collected stories from some of our outstanding veteran authors and paired them with brand-new stories from our most promising rising stars. In these four fantastic volumes, sample the best of the Harlequin Intrigue brand of excitement.

"Harlequin Intrigue gives readers
the best of both worlds—page-turning suspense
and sizzling romance.... Readers who love their
romance spiced with suspense need look
no farther for a thrilling read."
—*Romantic Times* magazine

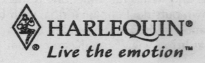

HARLEQUIN®
Live the emotion™

www.eHarlequin.com

JOANNA WAYNE

Joanna Wayne lives with her husband just a few miles from steamy, exciting New Orleans, but her home is the perfect writer's hideaway. A lazy bayou, complete with graceful herons, colorful wood ducks and an occasional alligator, winds just below her back garden. When not creating tales of spine-tingling suspense and heartwarming romance, she enjoys reading, traveling, playing golf and spending time with family and friends. Joanna believes that one of the special joys of writing is knowing that her stories have brought enjoyment to or somehow touched the lives of her readers. You can write Joanna at P.O. Box 2851, Harvey, LA 70059-2851.

SUSAN KEARNEY

Susan Kearney used to set herself on fire four times a day. Now she does something really hot— she writes romantic suspense. While she no longer performs her signature fire dive (she's taken up figure skating), she never runs out of ideas for characters and plots. A business graduate from the University of Michigan, Susan is working on her next novel and writes full-time. She resides in a small town outside Tampa, Florida, with her husband and children and a spoiled Boston terrier. Visit her at http://www.SusanKearney.com.

UNDER WRAPS

JOANNA WAYNE
SUSAN KEARNEY

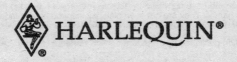

HARLEQUIN®

TORONTO • NEW YORK • LONDON
AMSTERDAM • PARIS • SYDNEY • HAMBURG
STOCKHOLM • ATHENS • TOKYO • MILAN • MADRID
PRAGUE • WARSAW • BUDAPEST • AUCKLAND

ISBN 0-373-83595-7

UNDER WRAPS

Copyright © 2003 by Harlequin Books S.A.

The publisher acknowledges the copyright holders of the individual works as follows:

JODIE'S LITTLE SECRETS
Copyright © 1998 by Jo Ann Vest

WHEN THE BOUGH BREAKS
Copyright © 2003 by Susan Kearney

This edition published by arrangement with Harlequin Books S.A.

® and TM are trademarks of the publisher. Trademarks indicated with ® are registered in the United States Patent and Trademark Office, the Canadian Trade Marks Office and in other countries.

Visit us at www.eHarlequin.com

Printed in U.S.A.

CONTENTS

FOREWORD
by Jasmine Cresswell

My grandparents lived in an old stone cottage in a tiny village in the picturesque Cotswolds region of England. Each summer, while my father stayed behind in our central London apartment, my mother and I would make the complicated journey by taxi, train and bus to spend two or three weeks with my grandparents in the country. The journey would take almost the entire day, although I realized once I grew up and learned to drive that during all those hours of travel we'd covered less than a hundred miles.

Once there, I was more or less left to entertain myself, which suited me very well. On sunny days I would search out some girlfriends from the village—the usual meeting place was the water pump by the old wooden footbridge—and we'd roam through the woods, take picnics to the abandoned stone quarry, swim in the local river and generally get up to what seems nowadays pretty low-grade mischief.

The quarry was a favorite destination. It hadn't been worked in over a hundred years, so it was more like a deep pond, surrounded by wildflowers, and we would clamber up and down the steep sides, cutting bulrushes and playing with the baby ducks and the moorhens, who were all amazingly tame. These days, if the quarry survives, I'm sure it's been fenced off as mortally hazardous to kids.

Rainy days were almost more fun than the sunny ones. I would retreat to my bedroom with books borrowed from my grandmother's secret stash of romances. Secret because she belonged to a generation that believed reading should be either educational or at the very least morally uplifting, and romances were way too much fun to fall into either of those categories.

The cottage dated from the eighteenth century and had thick stone walls so that the windows were at least two feet from the interior walls, leaving a window ledge that was big enough even for an adult to sit on, and plenty of space for a teenager. I would curl up on pillows pulled from the bed, close the drapes behind me and enter the magical world of Mills & Boon romances. At thirteen or fourteen, I'd never left England and I was enchanted as much by the exotic settings for some of the books as by the romance between the hero and the heroine. To this day, I have images of New Zealand sheep farms that are shaped more by the romance novels I read as a teen than by anything I've encountered since.

If I'd been growing up in the States instead of in England, I wouldn't have been able to read romances, because they didn't really exist on this side of the Atlantic until the seventies. Mills & Boon was still just a British publisher, not yet part of Harlequin, and paperback romances were almost unobtainable in the United States. American teenagers of my generation don't realize what a treat they missed.

Like a lot of people who become authors, I think I began to write as a way of extending and deepening the pleasure that I'd always found in reading. At the start of the eighties, many American publishing houses began to put out at least a few romance novels each month, and it was an exciting time for those of us wanting to write romance fiction. The genre was expanding to meet the tastes of contemporary American women; fresh, interesting ideas about plot and characterization were blooming in all directions.

Heroines in the romance novels that I'd read as a teen tended to be young, immature virgins who wanted a wealthy husband to solve all their problems. In effect, the Cinderella story told and retold. By the eighties, this had changed. American authors wrote about heroines who were smart, independent women looking for a soul mate to share their lives rather than a savior to rescue them. Heroes inevitably underwent a transformation of their own. Even if they were spectacular in the bedroom—and they always were!—they had to do a lot more than look sexy and have money in order to win the heroine's heart.

I really liked the new heroines, who were definitely much more my sort of woman than the fragile creatures of the past. And it was fun to create heroes who were sensitive, genuinely self-confident and yet endowed with enough macho spirit to stride across the pages of the story with an appealing swagger. Each book that I finished seemed to cover new ground and explore themes and subjects that hadn't yet been touched upon, so as I wrote there was a satisfying sense of discovery.

After a while, though, I began to feel a little frustrated. My heroine could pursue a career in almost any field. She could be an astronaut or a doctor or a world-famous sculptor. She could have a harrowing past, come from a distant land and have hang-ups about the way she looked, or anything else for that matter. She could fall in love with a hero who was the man-next-door, the president of a multinational corporation, or even the prince of a small European kingdom. But there was one thing my heroine could never do: she couldn't get involved in a crime or solve a mystery—not if I wanted the book to be published. Suspense and mystery, sadly, were not welcome in the world of romance.

All that changed wonderfully for the better twenty years ago, when Harlequin decided to step into unexplored territory and launch a line of romantic suspense novels called Intrigue. As soon as I heard about Harlequin's plans, I realized that I had found the perfect place to submit the stories I had always wanted to write: stories in which the heroine confronts danger, solves mysteries and sweeps from one adventure to the next. Best of all, while she faces her worst fears, chases down clues and escapes from deadly danger, she meets the man of her dreams and falls passionately in love with him.

My first book for Harlequin Intrigue was called *Undercover*, and it was published in 1986, when the line was more of a newborn infant than a toddler. Over the next few years, as the line grew up, I worked with a succession of wonderful editors who helped me to write several books that I'm proud of.

I'm writing for MIRA these days, but I still haven't changed my mind about the sort of stories I love to write—and to read. I'm delighted and honored to share in the celebration of Harlequin Intrigue's expanded publishing program. Romance fiction is great, but romantic suspense is even better!

Jasmine Cresswell

JODIE'S LITTLE SECRETS

Joanna Wayne

With special thanks to my wonderful editor whose encouragement and insight help me make each book special, and to my hardworking agent who keeps me on task. And to Wayne, always.

Prologue

There was no mistaking the signs. Jodie Gahagen had run away from him.

Hands trembling, the man reached down and picked up a pillow from her bed. He hugged it to his chest, burying his nose in the folds of cotton and goose down. The smell of her hit him in the gut, heightening his anger.

He dropped to his knees and rested his head on the pale pink sheets, sucking in the intoxicating fragrance. Two nights ago, the thought of Jodie Gahagen had woke him in the middle of the night. So strong, he hadn't been able to fight his need for her. He'd crawled from his bed and driven through the night to come to her.

Luckily, he'd found her that night, here in her bed. Alone. Her cotton gown had skimmed her flesh, waves of red hair spilling over her pillow, haloing her beautiful face and fanning her creamy shoulders.

The images crawled through his brain, like a video in slow motion. He knotted his hands in the bedsheet. That night he had watched while she slept, her breasts rising and falling, maybe against this very sheet. He could have taken her then, but he was a gentleman.

He could wait until she wanted him the way he wanted her.

The only sign he had left of his presence was the note, carefully tucked inside the crib of one of the twins. A reminder that he had been there again and that he would return.

After all, he was in love with Jodie Gahagen. She would love him, too, once she got to know him, the way she had loved the others.

And there had been others. So many men. No. The memories were running together. His mother, his unfaithful wife, the waitress who'd flirted and then laughed in his face when he'd asked her for a date. They had used men. They were not ladies, not sweet and honest the way Jodie was.

Familiar feelings washed over him, clawing at his insides, burning in his chest. Later, he would be strong enough to fight them into submission. Then his brain could take over, his cunning, logical brain that let him outsmart everyone, especially the stupid New York City cops. But for now, he pressed his head deeper in the pillow and longed for the day Jodie would be his.

A few minutes later he slipped out the door and into the darkness, a faceless blur in the maddening masses that was Manhattan.

Chapter One

Jodie Gahagen completed her hamstring stretches as the first sounds of a southern morning began their wake-up chorus. A bird's call, the splash as a turtle slipped from the bank into the Cane River. The sound of her own feet as they crunched into a pile of dry leaves. She and her sons had invaded a world that had been isolated from human contact.

Her nerves grew shaky at the thought. She'd never expected to be the only jogger on the trail this morning. But she shouldn't be surprised. After all, it was also six o'clock on Sunday morning, and the majority of the town's inhabitants were still snuggled in their beds.

Jodie yawned widely at the thought and stretched to touch her toes. Obviously, the sleepers hadn't been blessed with the dual alarm system she possessed. At thirteen months, her twin dynamos showed neither religious nor humane considerations for Sunday as a day of rest.

She tugged at her shorts and walked to the front of the stroller to check on them. Blair offered a smile, but Blake just stared at her over the plump thumb that was stuck in his mouth. ''Are you early birds ready to roll?'' she asked, brushing a wisp of red hair from Blair's forehead and dabbing at a spot of drool that dribbled down Blake's cute little chin.

Blair cooed a response and waved his hand like a frustrated traffic cop.

''Then let's get this show on the road,'' she said, giving the safety buckles of the double jogging stroller a final check. Movement behind her jerked her to attention and she spun around. A gray kitten stared up at her.

''A cat, just a cat,'' she whispered, steadying her breath and reaching down to run long fingers through his thick coat. Nothing to worry about, not here in the haven of hometown familiarity. Natchitoches, Louisiana, was a world away from New York.

Squaring her shoulders, she wrapped her hands around the handle of the stroller and started off at a brisk pace. In seconds, the world seemed to slide into order. The morning exercise ritual rejuvenated her, got her blood pumping and forced her mind into gear. The boys liked it, too, although the exercise for them consisted of swinging their pudgy arms and craning their necks to see any and every bit of action along the river route.

Trees, birds, tail-wagging dogs. They liked everything about their new hometown. Why not? Their unemployed mom was now home all day instead of only for rushed breakfasts in the morning and hurried dinners, baths and hugs at night. Besides, on the rare occasions she strayed from sight now, they had a doting great-grandmother jumping to supply their every want or need.

She was glad for this time with Grams. That was the one good thing that had come from the bizarre web that entangled her. Still, running away from trouble was not her style. If she'd had only herself to think about, she would have never given up, not as long as she'd had a heartbeat. But the night the lunatic had laid his murdering hands on her sons, the stakes had soared.

Now she and her boys were safe, but the man who'd turned her life into a house of horrors still walked the streets of New York City, and sooner or later his sick games would entrap another innocent victim.

An icy tremor shivered along her nerve endings, and she reined in her thoughts. Forcing body over mind, she picked up her pace, concentrating on the gentle strain to her muscles, the surge of pulse and power. The first mile rolled past, and the sun climbed over the tops of the brick storefronts, layering the town in heat and humidity.

A drop of perspiration slid down her forehead, and she whisked it away with her wristband. It was already November, but you'd never know it by the temperature. The weather was one of the fickle charms of north Louisiana.

Summer lingered into fall, then shocked the system with frigid cold fronts that swooped down from the northwest and plunged the temperature into the teens in a matter of hours. But until the icy winds blew in, she was going to enjoy exercising in the great outdoors.

A pickup truck rattled by on the street that wound up the hill from the river, and the driver honked and waved. Jodie waved back. She didn't recognize the man or the vehicle, but he undoubtedly knew who she was. *Miss Emily's granddaughter, visiting from the big city. The girl was married finally, with adorable twins. She was visiting for quite a long spell, too, already heading into the fourth week. And without her husband. Jodie Gahagen was the talk of the town.*

Fortunately, the hometown folks relied on speculation and their own imaginations to fill in the details. Jodie intended to keep it that way. Secrets secured the foundation of her new life, erected the barriers that kept her and her sons safe. As if in agreement, Blair waved his hand and giggled.

"You got it, tiger. Mommy won't let anything or anybody get to her boys."

Her boys. Hers and hers alone. The familiar tightness settled in her chest. Hers alone because she'd never told their father they existed. Until a few months ago, she'd been sure she'd made the right decision. Now she only prayed she had.

She rounded a curve, and her breath quickened. A man stood a good fifty yards ahead of them, half hidden in the shadows and overhang of a weeping willow. His shoulders were stooped, and an old jacket was pulled tight around him in spite of the rising temperature. Jodie's hand slid to the whistle in her pocket.

Head high, she gulped in huge helpings of air. This was exactly the kind of crazy, senseless fear she was forced to fight. But there was no reason for her heart to race here, in the middle of Natchitoches.

Still, she had jogged far enough for one morning. She slowed, steering the stroller into a 180 degree turn. Safely headed in the opposite direction, she twisted her head and stole a glance behind her. The man had disappeared.

Her feet flew now, eager to return to the homey warmth of Grams's house. Grams's world was timeless, slow and safe. Tall, white columns greeted you there, like protecting sentinels, ushering you into a world of cushioned couches, lacy curtains and dark, rich woods.

Grams and her unchanging world had sheltered and comforted Jodie when she had lost both her parents in a plane crash. She'd been only ten years old, frightened and alone, and wishing she had died with the people she loved most in the world. Somehow, Grams had convinced her that what her parents would want most was that she embrace life the way they had.

Now Jodie had returned to Grams's world, this time seeking safety for herself and her sons.

She jerked around as the sound of footsteps at her heels roared into her consciousness. The back left wheel of the stroller ran off the edge of the asphalt trail with a grinding bump.

"You better teach your mom to drive, kid." The voice was thick and husky. And shockingly familiar.

She kept her head down, praying to go unrecognized as the hulk of a sweating body dodged the stroller.

"Jodie Gahagen, is that you?" He stopped on a dime and changed directions.

She tried to answer. The words died in her throat, and all she managed was a nod.

"I can't believe you're out here at the crack of dawn." he said, matching his pace to hers. "Mind if I jog along with you and the kiddos?" he asked, after the fact.

Did she mind? Oh, yeah. So much so she could feel the cold sweat popping out on her body. In fact, next to the madman she was here to escape and the reincarnation of Jack the Ripper, she didn't know of anyone's company she minded more than Ray Kostner's.

"You can run wherever you like," she panted, her gaze straight ahead so that he couldn't see the anxiety he created. "It's a free country."

"I need to meet your tax man."

She felt his gaze all over her body, from the top of her clinging T-shirt to the bottom of her brief running shorts. Déjà vu? No. Everything had changed since she'd seen him last.

"You're looking great," he said. "Motherhood must agree with you."

Small talk. Nice and easy, give nothing away, not until she was in full control and calling the shots. "Thanks," she managed to reply. "It does. The same way bachelorhood agrees with you."

A puff of wind whipped a tuft of hair loose from her ponytail. She brushed the flying strands from her face, all the while aware of Ray's nearness and the fact that she couldn't afford to let down her barriers for even a second.

Two men had the power to hurt her, in different ways, but no less destructive. Ray Kostner was one of them.

"What are you doing back in Natchitoches?" she asked, determined to play his game of cordiality at the same level of perfection he managed. "Don't tell me you've given up the Big Easy quest for fame and fortune."

"No way. But Dad had a bypass last week."

"Oh, no." This time her response was genuine. Parker Kostner was a dear. He'd helped half the town out of one jam or another, whether they could afford him or not. His son was *not* a chip off the old block.

"Grams must have forgotten to mention it. Is he okay?" she asked, panting.

"Yeah. He's mending well, just ornery as ever. He's determined to get back to the office and take care of business. Mom is just as determined he's going to follow the doctor's orders."

"And she's recruited you for backup."

"That's about the size of it. I've settled into the spare office in Dad's suite while I help him out with a pressing case. If he comes near the office, I'm required to throw him out."

"I can't imagine anybody throwing your dad anywhere."

"I didn't say I was always successful."

"That's not what I hear about you."

"So, have you been asking about me, Jodie Gahagen?" His voice was low and teasing.

A sudden tingling feathered her skin, caressing her face and neck like a summer rain. Her grip tightened on the stroller handle until pain skittered her nerve endings and jolted her to her senses.

"No," she said, her voice shaky in spite of her resolve. "But you know how my grandmother likes to talk. Your name came up."

She slowed her pace to a near crawl, hoping Kostner would rebel at the lack of challenge and leave her behind. She was in no condition to one-up him in conversation or speed. The truth was she never had been.

Apparently the lack of physical exertion didn't faze him any more than her cool responses to his small talk had. He stayed at her side, stopping when she did at the corner where she'd parked her car.

"Do you need a ride back to Miss Emily's?"

"No, I have my car."

"Then how about a cup of coffee? We could—"

"I'm afraid not. The boys are ready for their cereal."

Ray stooped beside the stroller. "Cute kids," he said. "Bright red hair, just like their Mom."

"We have to go now," she insisted.

He didn't budge. He took Blair's hand, and the small pudgy fingers wound around Ray's. "Those dark eyes must have come from his lucky dad, though."

"No, neither of the boys looks anything like their dad." Her words were too caustic. If she kept this up, he would pounce on her inconsistent responses like the expert lawyer he was. But he had no right to do this to her. She wasn't a book he could pick up and put down whenever time or interest swayed him.

"Did I say something wrong?"

"No." She backed the stroller a few inches and maneuvered around him.

Undaunted, he followed her up the hill. "How long are you going to be in town?"

She looked up and faced his penetrating gaze, and her determination plummeted to the soles of her running shoes. "I'm not sure. Probably another week or so."

"Their dad must miss the boys." His gaze slid over her again, his eyes saying way more than she wanted to hear. "And if he doesn't miss their mom, he must be crazy."

She stepped to the side of the car and unlocked the door. "He can handle it," she said, picking up a wriggling child and buckling him into the car seat.

"Since we're both in town for a while, how about dinner tomorrow night? For old times' sake."

He smiled down at her, the same boyish grin that

had devastated her at fourteen and seduced her much later.

"I'm busy," she answered, turning away from him while her mind was still ruling.

"The next night then?"

"I'm busy tomorrow night and the night after and the week after that."

"I'd hoped we were still friends."

Friends? *A man who drove you wild with passion and then walked away as casually as if the week you thought was heaven had been a date for burgers and fries?*

"Friends usually return other friend's phone calls," she answered, her eyes on the stroller. "But I'm not mad, I'm busy, just like I'm sure you were. Besides, I'm not interested in reviving old times."

She quieted Blair with Cheerios as Ray bent and rescued Blake from the stroller. Wrapping his large hands about the small boy, he swept him into the air above his head. Blake, her usually slow-to-bond child, rewarded Ray's efforts with soft baby chuckles. He'd apparently inherited her weakness for bad choices in his bonding habits.

"The kid likes me," he boasted.

"He likes anyone who pays attention to him," she lied, all but yanking him from Ray's arms. Her fingers fumbled with the buckle on his car seat.

"No, I think he just has his mother's good taste. I can remember when she liked me."

"I still like you. Why shouldn't I?"

"Then why is a friendly dinner out of the question?"

"You have a short memory. I just told you that I'm very busy these days. I'm also married."

"Even busy, married women eat. Dinner and conversation. That's all. I promise I won't let you seduce me into any feelings unsuitable for dinner with a married woman."

"I don't think so, Ray."

His tone swung from light to deadly serious. "It never hurts to have someone to talk to when times are rough. Free legal advice is hard to come by."

"So that's what this is about. You didn't just happen to be out running at daybreak, did you? My grandmother put you up to this."

"Your grandmother cares about you."

"I'm fine. Just fine. But if I need your services as a friend or a lawyer, I'll let you know."

"Good. You call, and I'll come running. Just like always."

Exactly. Just like always. Ray Kostner and the NYPD. If a few meaningless words and halfhearted efforts could solve her problems, they'd take care of her.

"See you around," she said, with a quick wave of her hand. Seconds later, she jerked the car into gear and sped out of his sight.

JODIE WAS JUST beginning to relax again by the time Tuesday evening rolled around. There had been no visits or phone calls from Ray. Apparently he had taken her at her word that she had nothing to say to him.

At least not now.

One month ago, the story would have been different. She'd called him then, in the middle of the night, her hands shaking so badly she could barely dial the number that she knew as well as her own.

A woman had answered, her voice heavy with sleep, but still soft and syrupy. And Jodie had hung up and dialed Detective Cappan instead. The lanky, gum-chewing cop had rushed right over, but that time he hadn't been able to mask the anxiety that coated his empty reassurances.

She'd told him her plan, and he'd agreed to help, all but guaranteeing her she wouldn't be followed to Natchitoches if she covered her tracks the way he instructed. By all accounts, she was in California now, lost in the Wild, Wild West, a suitable backdrop for her world of lies.

First, a mad stalker in New York. Now Ray Kostner in Louisiana. A trip down the Amazon was beginning to sound easy.

Stooping, she rescued the last dripping, rubber duck from the tub. The twins were already bathed and fed and in the kitchen doing their final bit of entertaining for the night.

"What would you like for dinner tonight, dear?" Grams's voice echoed down the long hall.

"Whatever you'd like." A salad would have been fine with Jodie, but that would not be one of the choices. Full-course dinners were the way of the old South, and Grams was a bonafide follower of tradition. Words like *calories, fat content, fiber* and *cholesterol* were not in her vocabulary. Maybe at eighty-three, Jodie would drop them from hers, too.

Eighty-three. What a nice age. There had been several long nights during the last few weeks when her chance at winning the lottery had seemed a safer bet than reaching her next birthday. A sudden prickle of gooseflesh dotted her arms, and she massaged it away. The nightmare was behind her.

With quick steps she joined Grams and the boys in the kitchen.

"Okay, Grams, what can I help you do?" she asked, grabbing a flowered apron from the hook by the door.

"You could you get that bowl of purple hull peas from the refrigerator."

"Will do." She settled in for what was sure to be a monumental task.

Her grandmother saved everything, ladling spoonfuls of leftovers into plastic containers with colorful tops and tucking them haphazardly into every available corner of the fridge. Locating a particular item was similar to finding your size at an end-of-year clearance. You usually settled for close and were glad to get it.

The nearest thing to close this time was corn, cabbage or yellow squash. "Could you give me a clue, like what day you cooked these peas?"

"Don't you remember? We had peas and pork chops." Grams rubbed her temple, streaking it with flour. "It must have been Saturday. No, let me see, was it Friday?"

Jodie gave up the search. They'd had pork chops on Tuesday a week ago, with green beans and sweet potatoes. The cleaning woman had undoubtedly trashed the remains on Wednesday, but no use to burden Grams with details.

She never seemed to remember them in their exact state anyway. Her memory was fading with her eyes, in contrast to her desire to manipulate, which was keener than ever. The incident with Ray at the jogging trail had proven that.

"I must have accidentally thrown the peas out, but

I'll open a jar of the ones you and Selda canned this summer," Jodie offered. She opened the perfectly preserved legumes, dumped them into a saucepan and placed them on a back burner.

"How was your run this morning?" Grams asked, patting out a doughy biscuit.

"Fast, hot and tiring, like always."

"Then why do you do it?"

"It's good for me."

"It's bad for your knees. I heard that on 'Oprah,' or was it that new show with Rosie something?" She flipped a biscuit into a baking pan. "I guess you didn't see that Kostner boy again."

The question was thrown out as if it had just popped into her grandmother's mind. Jodie wasn't fooled. Grams had probably been searching all day for a way to bring Ray into the conversation.

But *boy?* The man was four years older than Jodie's twenty-seven, at least six foot two and reeked of power and manhood. "I didn't see him," she said, shaking a quick dash of salt and pepper into the peas. "I guess it was my lucky day."

"I reckon it was. You don't want to go getting mixed up with the likes of him. Confounded, money-grubbing lawyers. I don't trust a one of them."

"Ray's dad's a lawyer, and you like him."

"That's different. Ray's too big for his britches, running off to New Orleans when there's plenty of work for decent folks right here at home."

"You said the same thing about me when I moved to New York."

"Hmmph. I was right about that, too." She muttered the words under her breath, but not so low she didn't mean for Jodie to hear them.

"So is that why you had Ray look me up Sunday, so he could tell me I should move back to Natchitoches for good?"

"I didn't do any such of a thing. You know I gave up trying to mind your business for you years ago."

"Yeah, right." Jodie reached an arm around the bent and bony shoulders and gave her grandmother a quick hug. "I know you mean well, Grams, but I don't want or need Ray's help. I just have a few issues I need to work through."

Grams kept right on working. "Well, you're welcome to stay here as long as you want. That's what families are for. The fact is, I'm going to miss you and the boys like crazy when you leave. But don't let that influence you."

"We'll miss you, too. Next time we won't wait so long between visits."

"That's just why I'm concerned about you." She slapped a biscuit into the baking pan and wagged a finger at Jodie. "First, you don't visit me for nigh to two years, putting me off with all kinds of flimsy excuses, even with me begging to see my new great-grandsons. Then you show up on my doorstep unannounced and tell me you're going to be here for a while. And as far as I can tell, you haven't had one phone call from that husband of yours."

"I told you. We've agreed to an amicable separation until we decide what to do."

"It doesn't sound too amicable to me. Doesn't sound a bit natural, either. You didn't take his name when you married him, and what kind of father don't give a gosh darn about two wonderful sons?"

What kind indeed? The kind who didn't want a wife or children to start with. "You don't have to worry about me, Grams. This is the nineties. The boys and I will be just fine on our own.'' Jodie grabbed two stoneware plates from the shelf and started toward the kitchen table, praying she was telling the truth.

''I thought we might sit at the dining room table tonight,'' Grams said, taking the plates from her. ''It'll be a pleasant change. And we'll use the good china, the crystal, too. No use to let it go to ruin just keeping the shelf occupied.'' Her words were almost drowned in the melodic chime of the doorbell.

''Are you expecting someone, Grams?''

''Didn't I tell you? Ray Kostner's joining us for dinner.''

''You most certainly did not tell me. I would have made plans to be somewhere else. I just told you, I don't need his advice.''

''Well, then it doesn't matter that I forgot to mention it. He's coming over to give *me* a little advice tonight.''

''How convenient. You need help from the confounded money grubber. Sometimes you'll have to share with me how you choose your dinner guests and your advisors.''

The doorbell jangled persistently this time, and both Blair and Blake joined in the excitement, one clapping, the other swinging his pudgy fists and babbling.

''Now are you going to get that or do I have to do it myself?'' Grams said, dusting her flour-covered hands over the sink.

Shaking her head in surrender, Jodie answered the bell and ushered Ray inside.

''What a pleasant surprise,'' he said, stepping over

the threshold. "I was afraid you might already be away doing whatever it is that keeps you so busy."

She shot him an icy stare. "My plans changed."

"Good, I'm looking forward to catching up on your life. You've apparently been making a few changes since I saw you last. A new husband, twin boys."

"It's been a long time."

"Yeah. I guess it has." He leaned closer. "But that was one thing about us. We could go months, years even, without seeing each other, and still fall back into each other's lives like we'd never been apart."

"We're older now, I've changed. I don't fall into things anymore." Especially things like strong arms that belonged to a man who had the power to tear the heart right out of her if she gave him half a chance.

Ray started to follow her back to the kitchen. They both stopped when the doorbell rang again. "More guests?" he asked. "I didn't dress for a party."

"I don't know. I wasn't on the guest list committee."

"Lucky for me." He sniffed appreciatively. "And that smells like Miss Emily's pot roast. I'd have driven up from New Orleans for that."

Jodie walked back to the front door and peeked through the peephole. Roses, yellow ones, tucked in and between baby's breath and asparagus fern stared back at her. Her stomach took an unexpected lurch. Shaking, she eased the door open.

"Delivery for Jodie Gahagen." The teenager stepped from the shadows into the illumination of the porch light.

"Who sent them?" she demanded.

He backed up half a step and gave her a sideways glance. Frowning, he slipped the acknowledgment card from the pronged holder and placed it in her hands.

She ripped the envelope open and yanked out the card. *An admirer.* The words jumped at her like a vampire, sinking sharp teeth into the jugular and draining the blood from her body.

"Is something wrong?" Ray moved to her side and wrapped an arm around her shoulder. She didn't pull away. Trembling, she stared at the card, turning it over in her hand.

"See, I told you they were for you." The delivery boy stuck the flowers at her.

"I can't accept them unless I know who sent them."

"Well, ma'am, if you're Jodie Gahagen, they're for you, no matter who sent them. But I guess I could take them back to the shop if you don't want 'em." He flashed Ray a pleading look. "Miss Gloria won't like my bringing the delivery back though, not after she made me work overtime to get it to you tonight."

Ray fished in his pocket and pressed a couple of bills into the teenager's hand. "We'll keep the flowers," he said, taking the bouquet from him, "but tell Miss Gloria that in the future, Miss Gahagen likes her admirers identified."

Jodie heard the voices, heard the door close, heard Ray asking her what was wrong. She couldn't respond. The fear was overpowering, churning inside her with hurricane force, choking her breath away. Weak and disoriented she slumped against the wall.

"Hey, they're only flowers. We can toss them in the trash if they're going to upset you like that."

"No, I'm okay."

"Then you're a damn good actress. You're white

as a ghost and trembling like a kid on his first Halloween.''

Still shaking, Jodie continued to stare at the card, letting one finger trace the row of red hearts peeking from a border of roses. Red hearts, the unmistakable signature of a man who'd vowed to have her for himself or see her dead.

''Is someone harassing you, Jodie? Is that what this is about?''

''Yes.'' The whispered response worked its way through the cottony dryness that clogged her throat and lungs. Her mind swirled in fear and confusion. Still, one truth hammered through the whirlwind. She couldn't protect her boys by herself, not now that the stalker had found her.

Ray wrapped his hands about her waist and pulled her to him. ''Just tell me who's bothering you. If it's your husband—'' His face pulled into hard lines, and his muscles strained at the sleeves of his shirt.

''No. It's not my husband. But I didn't come to Natchitoches just to visit.''

''Your grandmother told me you were having marital problems. It's none of my business, but if the man is threatening you, I can make it my business.''

''Just listen, Ray. My grandmother doesn't know the real story, and I don't want her finding out. Promise me you won't tell her a thing about this.''

''You have my word. Now, what is it I'm not telling?''

''Someone was stalking me in New York. I've never met him, at least not that I know of. But he left me flowers and gifts and frightening notes.''

''You surely must have some idea who it is.''

''No. I only know he knows *me* too well. He knows

the color of the towels in my bathroom, the pattern of the sheets on my bed, the label in my nightgown.''

''That son of a…'' Ray's words trailed off and he gathered Jodie in his arms, gently rocking her against his chest. ''No wonder the flowers frightened you. But chances are they aren't even from him. And even if they are, he'll never follow you to Louisiana. Stalkers are almost always cowards who—''

Jodie's nerves tightened into frayed knots, and she jerked away from him. ''Don't give me statistics. I know them all, and none of them apply in this case. This is no ordinary stalker.''

''Ordinary or not, he won't get away with his perverted tricks in Natchitoches. The police will have him behind bars before his feet get southern dirt between his toes. You couldn't be safer.''

''Don't humor me, and don't fool yourself. I know better than anyone what the police can and can't do. It's myself I have to depend on now, but I need your help.''

''You name it.''

''I want you to take Blake and Blair and keep them safe.''

His eyebrows shot up. ''What did you say?''

''You heard me right.''

''I'll fight a madman for you, two if necessary, but no kids. I'm not the man for that.'' He stepped backward, a hand up as if to ward off blows.

''I know. You're a no-ties kind of guy. That's the way you've always wanted things, but this time you don't get a choice.''

''There's always choices. The boys need *you*. And they need their father, not some stranger they've never seen before this week. No matter how you feel about your husband, no matter what's happened between the two of you, you have to let him know his sons are in danger.''

"I agree,'' she said, her voice strong and dead level now that she'd made up her mind to do what she had to in order to keep her boys safe. "The boys' father does deserve to know the truth. That's why I just told him."

His gaze fastened on hers, his eyes demanding. "Don't play this kind of game with me, Jodie. I don't understand it."

"Think about it, and you will. A chance meeting between old friends. Chinese takeout and champagne. A rainy night that stretched into seven." The truth tore at her heart, shredding it into little pieces.

"No, if you'd gotten pregnant by me, you would have called and told me. And you would never have married another man while you were carrying my children. I know you better than that."

"So you do." She tilted her head to face him head-on. "There never was a husband, Ray. There was only you." She watched as every muscle in his body hardened to the consistency of solid steel.

His reaction didn't surprise her at all. He'd made it plain from the beginning, a wife and kids were not part of his game plan. It wasn't his fault her heart had refused to accept the truth. Or that the protection they'd used had failed.

"When this is over, you can ride off into the sunset in your flashy sports car, and I'll never try to stop you or ask anything of you. But right now Blair and Blake need you. And, whether you like it or not, *you* are the boys' father."

Chapter Two

No! No way in the world! The protest, silent but deafening, echoed in every corner of Ray's brain. He wasn't a father. He couldn't be. Fathers were nurturing. They read bedtime stories, changed dirty diapers, shoveled green, slimy baby food into yelling mouths.

Fathers were gentle, loving, caring. All of the things he wasn't, the things he couldn't be.

"There must be some—" One look at Jodie and the challenge stopped in midsentence. Fear clouded her eyes and powdered her delicate skin with a chalky whiteness that tore at his heart. He reached a hand toward her, his own doubts crushed with a sudden and suffocating desire to cradle her trembling body in his arms. His arms encircled her waist and he pulled her against his chest.

She stayed there less than a heartbeat before pushing away from him.

"I know you're afraid, Jodie, and I want to help you, but..." He trailed his fingers down her arm.

"Sure you do. About as much as you want to be run over by an eighteen wheeler. But, let's not make anything more of this than what it is."

"What's that supposed to mean?"

"It means you can wipe the panic from your face and cut the patronizing routine. This is not some ploy to catch a husband. When this is over, my sons and I will fly back to New York and you can run back to your life of Porsches and parties, and—"

She tossed her head back, swinging her shiny red mane into a tangle of curls that resettled reluctantly about her face and shoulders. "And whatever else it is that you do in New Orleans."

"I'd say what I do is my business."

"And it can stay that way. I don't give a damn about your choice of entertainment or your conquests. But like it or not, you are a father, and right now, your sons need you."

His sons. There it was again. But the accusation was only words, and saying them didn't make them true. Jodie was running scared, steeped in fear as thick and tangible as the worn Persian rug beneath their feet. She might claim anything to get protection for her boys. He didn't blame her a bit.

A shudder of relief coursed his body. That was it, of course. She was making up the whole paternity issue out of desperation. His brain reveled in the solution his frantic reasoning offered. Fatherhood was inconceivable. Defending beautiful women he could handle. Hell, he'd practically made a career of it.

"Why don't we step into the living room?" he offered, taking her arm. "That way you can fill me in on the details about your stalker."

"Does that mean you'll take the boys and keep them safe?"

"It means I'll do what I can to keep all of you safe. Me and the police and half the parish if need be. You're in Natchitoches now, not the Big Bad Apple.

Killers don't wander around the streets unnoticed. The truth is, nobody wanders around here after 7:00 p.m.''

"A new criminal in town might not know that."

"He'll turn into a believer if he shows up here."

"Will he, Ray? I guess we'll find out soon enough. He's either here now or on his way. The flowers are proof of that."

With an arm around her shoulders, Ray led her to a Victorian sofa made for delicate ladies half his size. He eased down beside her, his long legs fitting awkwardly in front of the low-slung coffee table. Careful not to topple the collection of crystal pieces that glared at him threateningly, he scooted the curved cherry legs of the table back a couple of inches, catching a crocheted doily on the edge of his watch.

Jodie unhooked the fragile threads with shaking fingers, and once again he felt the overpowering urge to hold her close. He grabbed her hand and encased it in his. It was cold as ice.

"This man really has you spooked."

"A man. Only a man," she said, her eyes cast downward. "I keep telling myself that, but in my heart I know he's a monster."

"He's a man." The assurance sounded good, but Ray wasn't sure he believed that himself now. Not after seeing Jodie like this. He struggled to assimilate the fear in her eyes with the images of her that lived in his mind.

Jodie in faded cutoffs, shimmying up the highest oak in Miss Emily's yard and dangling from a half-dead branch to save a wild-haired tomcat. Jodie in her first year of college, taking on the dean and finally the governor to right the injustices of campus housing policies.

Pain stabbed him in the gut as his mind considered the possibilities of just what it had taken to reduce her to this state of desperation. "Has this man touched you, Jodie? If he's laid a hand on you..."

"He's never touched me. He left packages and letters. I found them outside the door of my apartment or on my desk in the advertising firm where I worked."

"But he has been in your apartment in New York?"

"Yes, but only once while I was there. That night he picked up Blake and moved him into the crib with Blair. He left a note, a promise that he would return."

Ray felt the involuntary tightening of his muscles, and his hands knotted into fists. "The guy's a sicko."

"Exactly. And for some reason he's picked me to be the receiver of his morbid attentions."

"No wonder you were so afraid of him. It's just a damn shame a guy like that could get by with forcing you to give up a job you loved and make you run the length of the country to escape him."

"To *try* to escape him. Apparently I failed." Resignation tugged at the corners of her mouth.

"Not necessarily. Even though he hasn't identified himself, there's a good chance you know him, at least casually, or he knows someone you know. Either way he could have heard that you have a grandmother who lives in Natchitoches. He may have wired the flowers here on a hunch. Especially since Miss Emily is the only family you have."

"Then he's as good at hunches as he is at terrorizing."

"It looks that way. But I still don't think you need to panic. Wiring flowers from New York is a far cry from traveling a couple of thousand miles just to torment you for no good reason. There are millions of victims in New York he can switch his sick attentions to.''

Jodie stiffened her shoulders and sucked in a deep breath.

''That's my girl,'' he whispered, giving her hand a squeeze. ''You'll lick this thing.''

''I'm not your girl.'' She yanked her hand from his. ''I'm not anyone's girl. I'm a woman. And believe me, Ray Kostner, I've heard enough empty reassurances. I'm only asking one thing of you.''

''I'll do whatever I can.''

''Take the boys. I want them away from me entirely until this mess is over.''

He swallowed, but the choking lump in his throat didn't disappear. Getting involved with Jodie Gahagen again would mean breaking every promise he'd made to himself over the last two years. The woman was pure, unadulterated trouble to a man like him. And she was asking the impossible. But, she needed him, and he didn't have a chance in hell of convincing his heart to walk away and leave her alone and frightened.

''I'll help you find the lunatic who's stalking you. Count on it.''

''That's not good enough, Ray. It's not me I'm worried about.''

''I'll do everything I can.''

''I don't want everything. I've given up on expecting that a long time ago. I'm only asking one thing of you now. Either do it or stay out of my life.'' A lone tear escaped and slid down her pale cheek.

Ray brushed it away, his finger lingering on her

skin, his gaze locked with hers. "I can't take the boys. I haven't the slightest idea how to tend to kids. Even if they were mine—"

"*If* they were yours?" Accusatory fire leapt to her eyes. "If they were yours, you'd deny them to keep your precious freedom intact. Old good-time Ray Kostner. Free and easy." She met his gaze head-on, her lips drawn into thin, straight lines, the color returning to her face in shades of livid red.

"Well, don't worry, you're off the hook. You're right. They're *not* yours, and they don't need you."

"Take it easy, Jodie. I know you're upset, but we need to look at this stalker issue rationally."

"*We* don't need to do anything. The stalker is after *me,* and I don't need or want your advice or your brand of help. The fact is you've done way more than enough for me already." She stood up, her slim body hardened into fighter stance.

"You're taking this all wrong, Jodie."

"Forget it, Ray. Let yourself out. I'll explain to Grams why you couldn't stay." The words sliced the air as she turned on her heel and strode away without a backward glance.

JODIE PUSHED THE screen door open and slid through it, thankful the agonizing dinner for two was finally over and the kitchen was back in shipshape. Grams hadn't bought for a second her feeble story about Ray's suddenly remembering a previous engagement. She'd grilled Jodie like a piece of red meat.

Who did he have to run off and meet so suddenly? Why didn't he just telephone if he couldn't make it to dinner instead of coming all the way over? Why didn't he at least step into the kitchen and make his apologies to her? After all, she was the one who'd invited him for dinner.

Jodie had stammered and hemhawed with answers. Lying was not her forte, although she was getting better at it since necessity had made it a way of life. And the first set of lies all traced back to a rainy night twenty-two months ago. Her heart constricted at the memories, poignant and bittersweet.

She took a deep breath, consuming the scents of a southern fall. Damp leaves harboring fallen pecans, perfume from the clusters of blooming chrysanthemums that bordered the fence line. The wind picked up, shuffling the carpet of leaves and sending a cascade of new ones swirling to the ground.

She stood still, suddenly cold and shaking. It was as if she could feel someone's gaze crawling her body.

"I thought you might be out here."

The scratchy male voice came from nowhere. In a split second, her hands wrapped about the only weapon in sight. Twirling, she raised the flowerpot over her head.

"Sorry, Miss Jodie. I didn't mean to frighten you."

A giant stepped from behind the hedge that bordered the house and sheltered the backyard from traffic on the street. Breath escaped her body in a surge, leaving her so light-headed she leaned against the porch railing for support.

"Gentle Ben," she said, her voice quaking with relief.

"It sure is me. And I'd hate to know who you were expectin' to greet with that flowerpot."

"No one," she lied. "Just my big-city reflexes in top form." She sat the flowerpot back in its appointed spot and gave Ben a quick hug. Fifteen years of tending the yard and garden and keeping the fishing boat in good condition had elevated him to family status.

He stood back and gave her an appraising look. "Well, if living in the big city makes you that jumpy, you need to move right on back down here with your grandmother." He slid his hands into the pockets of a pair of new-looking overalls. "She pines away for you all the time. Worries about you, too. New York ain't the place for a pretty southern girl like you."

"Thank you. For the pretty part," she added, "but not the advice. Most of the time New York is the perfect spot for me." Jodie attempted a reassuring smile. "Besides, you know you're exaggerating, Ben. Grams is not the type to pine away."

"Maybe not, but she misses you just the same. We both do."

"From what I hear, you haven't been around enough to miss me. When did you get back in town?"

"Tonight. I called Miss Emily to tell her I'd be at work in the morning. That's when she said you were here. She said it would be all right if I dropped over to say howdy."

"Of course it's all right. Is your son better?"

"As good as he's ever been. He wasn't near as sick as he let on. He just had me up there waiting on him."

"He's lucky to have a father who cares enough to come running when he needs you."

"Yeah. 'Cept he don't know that." A dog's barking interrupted him, a growl that dissolved into a mournful howl. Ben got up and walked to the edge of the porch, staring into the darkness. "Full moon tonight. It riles the animals. People, too. Makes 'em restless and uneasy. Makes 'em do things they oughtn't."

Like send flowers, Jodie thought, wrapping her hands and arms about her body to ward off a sudden chill. Only some people didn't need a full moon to cause their darker side to surface. "Does the moon affect your moods, Ben?" she asked, more to make conversation than anything else, to shift her thoughts from her own troubles.

"Yeah." He nodded his head, still staring into space. "I guess maybe it does, seeing as how I feel right now. A little crazy, a little wild with fighting feelings I shouldn't have." He turned and gave Jodie a nervous smile. "I reckon it's a good thing full moons don't last too long."

Heavy footsteps interrupted Ben's words. Jodie's gaze flew to the corner of the house, but this time she didn't go for the flowerpot. She should have. It would have fit nicely on the top of Ray's head, and the dirt could have spilled deliciously over his shirt, streaking the snowy white with muddy gunks of earth.

She stared icily but didn't say a word while Ray and Ben exchanged greetings, offering a smile only when Ben excused himself and made his exit. And then the smile was only for Ben. The ice in her stare remained for her newest caller.

"What are you doing here, Ray?"

"Is that the way you greet guests in New York? It seems awfully unfriendly."

"Good. Then you got the message."

He dropped to the swing beside her. "I vote we cut the games, Jodie. We've been friends too long."

Friends. There it was again. All she had to do was forget they'd ever made love, that she had lain awake for nights afterward, reliving every touch of his hands, his lips, his body merged with hers. Forget that he hadn't returned her phone calls. Forget that he had fathered sons he wanted no part of.

"If you're here to renew an old friendship, you're wasting your time. Our definitions of friendship don't correlate."

"No, I came back because I'm worried about you." His hand closed over hers. "This terrorizing routine has got to stop."

"What a novel idea."

"Sarcasm doesn't become you, but I can understand it. Nothing is more frightening or frustrating than an enemy who won't come out in the open. It's a coward's way, but it works. I have a few ideas for stopping it."

"Your memory is short," she said, scooting to the far edge of the wooden swing. "It hasn't been two hours since I told you to stay out of my life."

"And when this madman is caught, I'll heed your wishes, if that's still what you want. But I'm not turning my back on you now, so you might as well accept my help." He leaned forward and planted his feet on the porch, stopping the motion of the swing. "How much do you know about stalkers, Jodie?"

"The typical profile information." Jodie got up from the swing and paced the porch, quickly realizing there would be no getting rid of Ray before he was ready to go. No wonder he had the reputation for being a barracuda attorney. Telephone solicitors were less persistent.

"And what do you consider typical?" He stood up and walked to the railing of the porch, leaning against it easily as if they were talking about the weather or the brightness of the moon.

"They usually follow a path of increasingly obsessive behavior. They're usually former lovers or spouses, but not always." She was quoting the literature now, the way the cops always did. "Occasionally they're total strangers who pick you out for some unknown reason. Apparently my stalker falls into that category."

The howling started again. This time she felt dark shadows of the madness Ben had talked about. It built and shivered inside her, pushing her closer to the edge of hopelessness.

"But my stalker always leaves a calling card."

"But not his name?"

"No. A red heart. Sometimes it's a cutout, sometimes a sticker or a printed pattern like the one that came with the flowers. More often, it's drawn with a red crayon." Her voice caught. Natchitoches had seemed so safe. Until tonight. "Sometimes he adds a message."

"What kind of message?"

"A warning. He tells me things that let me know he's watching me. He says I need to be a good girl, that he wants me to save myself for him. If I do, he'll continue to love me and make sure I'm safe. If I don't, I'll have to pay the ultimate price, like the others did."

Ray reached out and grabbed her arm, pulling her to him. His eyes bore into hers, penetrating her resolve. "What others?"

"He never says."

His hand tightened on her arm possessively. "You need to be more careful, Jodie. Stop jogging alone in isolated areas."

"You said yourself, just because he sent flowers doesn't mean he'll actually travel from New York to

Natchitoches. Besides, I left easy-to-follow clues that I would be in San Francisco. If he goes anywhere, he should go there.''

''If you believed that you wouldn't have turned into a shivering mass of nerves when the flowers were delivered. Just do what I say, Jodie. Don't go out alone, unless you're going to very public places, at least not until we know if this guy's in town.''

''So you think I should let this lunatic keep me prisoner and hope for the best. I certainly can't afford a bodyguard.''

''I can.'' The words were a hoarse whisper. ''And if it comes to that, I'll hire one. But right now, I'm in town and you can work your schedule of solitary errands around times when Ben or I can go out with you.''

''You're not my keeper, Ray. I'm not ready to trade one stalker for another.''

''Maybe not. But at least you know I'm not dangerous.''

Jodie met his gaze, and her heart settled like lead in her chest. Danger had many faces. So did pain. ''I can handle this. It's not your concern.''

He ran his fingers the length of her arms and back up again, sliding his arm across her shoulders, riding the strained lines of her neck with his thumb. Her pulse quickened, and she willed it to slow. But still she couldn't make herself pull away.

He leaned closer, his lips inches from hers. And then they met, soft and tickling, like the brush of a feather. So quick she had no time to stop him or the impulses that churned inside her. A touch and then he pulled away.

''Now go in and tell Miss Emily you'll be back in

a few minutes," he said, his voice suddenly hoarse. "Gloria Bigger is expecting us at the flower shop."

"Does she remember something about the man who ordered the flowers?" Her voice rose optimistically.

"Only that he called in the order, which means my theory about his still being in New York is probably right."

"Lots of people order flowers for local delivery."

"Not stalkers. When you order by phone, you have to give a credit card number. Mrs. Bigger said she's sure she checked the number out with Visa. That's the only way she accepts orders from strangers. If we have his name and the number of his account, we can identify him."

Jodie shook her head, doubts hammering away at the sliver of hope Ray offered. "He's smarter than that." But a surge of adrenaline rippled through her veins. The cops always said he'd make a mistake sooner or later. Maybe this would be the time. "I'll tell Grams," she said, "and meet you at Gloria's."

"We'll go together."

She didn't argue the point. Maybe it was the effect of the full moon addling her senses, or maybe she just didn't want to be alone. Whatever the cause, she was suddenly glad they were facing this thing together.

RAY SPUN THE steering wheel of his red Porsche, rounding the corner onto Front Street. It was eight-fifteen on a Monday night and the main street of town was all but deserted. The only visible sign of life was a couple of hand-clasped young lovers peering into the window of a store already filled with bright colored Christmas ornaments and a waving Santa.

The window display was a reminder of just how much Natchitoches would change in the next few weeks. When the light extravaganza was turned on along the river, visitors would flood the small town. The number of lights had grown steadily over the years. So had the crowds, especially for the first weekend of the popular Festival of Lights.

"How much did you tell Gloria?" Jodie asked, finally breaking the silence she'd imposed since climbing into his car.

He turned to face her. She was chewing on her bottom lip, the way she always did when she was worried. He would love to get his hands on the trash who was causing her this kind of grief. The last time he'd been with her she'd been—

He shook his head, pushing the memories from his mind once more, the way he had been trying to do ever since his trip to New York. "I told her the truth," he finally answered. "At least a partial truth. I said you were being harassed by someone and you wanted to verify the name of the person who sent the flowers. We'll get the credit card information and turn it over to the police."

"And I can hear them now. It is not against the law to send flowers, Miss Gahagen. Then they'll hand me hundreds of yards of bureaucratic tape and no action."

"That was New York. This is Natchitoches. There's not a hundred yards of tape in the whole town." Ray leaned closer, and the soft scent of gardenias washed over him, weakening his resistance and playing havoc with the promise he'd made himself earlier this evening. He was a friend helping out in an emergency.

He wouldn't make the same mistake he'd made in New York again, wouldn't give Jodie any reason to think of him as a man to hook her dreams of permanence on. They rode in silence until he pulled to the curb in front of the flower shop.

"Gloria must not be here yet." Jodie scooted closer to the passenger door but didn't open it. "The shop is pitch dark."

"Yeah, but that looks like her green sedan in front of us, and it looks empty. Wait in the car. I want to look around a minute."

"No." Her fingers dug into his arm, holding him back. "Something's wrong. I can't explain how I know. It's just something I feel, a dread that crawls across my skin when *he's* been around." Fear stole her voice, reducing her words to a whisper.

Ray wrapped an arm about her trembling body, pulling her close. Too close. His heart constricted and other body parts, ones far more traitorous, came to life. He struggled for control.

"Okay, Jodie, we'll go in together. Gloria's probably in the back of the shop going over the order slips as we speak. There's no possible reason for your stalker to show up at the flower shop. He couldn't suspect you were going to rush down here after closing to go over the records."

He eased open the driver's side door, one arm still about her shoulders. "Besides, like I told you before, the chances are slim to none the crackpot's traveled all the way to Natchitoches to make trouble."

Jodie pulled from his arms and swung open her own door. "I hope you're right," she said, rounding the corner of the front fender and heading straight for Gloria's car. "But I wouldn't make bets on it."

Chapter Three

Ray joined Jodie, peering through the windshield of Gloria's parked car. "See. The car's empty, except for a stack of papers and a McDonald's bag." He slid his hand over the hood. "And the motor's still warm. She must have beat us here by no more than a few minutes."

A sigh of what he hoped was relief escaped Jodie's lips in a whoosh. He followed her to the door, his gaze tracing the line of shrubs that bordered the side of the shop. For the first time since he'd arrived in Natchitoches, he felt the pangs of apprehension, the wariness of deserted places he'd learned to accept as commonplace in New Orleans.

But the shrubs were still and the only noises were Jodie's footsteps and the eerie rasping of the metal sign above the door as it caught the wind. He was letting Jodie's faceless fears set him on edge, and he couldn't allow that to happen.

He needed a clear head. If the suspicions rolling through his mind were true, Jodie was in real danger. The stalker she described had the earmarks of a serial killer, a man who chose his victims and then tormented them before leading them to their death. He'd have to walk a thin line, make Jodie ever cautious without scaring her to death.

Ray stepped in front of Jodie and banged his fist against the weathered wood. The door creaked open a few inches, then stopped. He pushed against it, but it didn't budge.

"What is it?"

"I can't tell exactly." Slowly, his eyes adjusted to the blackness of the room. He stepped inside, poking at the mass that blocked the door with the toe of his leather moccasin. A soft moan gurgled from the mass.

He dropped to his knees. Jodie draped over him and reached past him to grab the limp arm that lay across the cold tiles of the entrance way.

"Is that you, Ray Kostner?"

Jodie gave him no time to answer. She'd already squeezed her slender body through the partially opened door.

"Mrs. Bigger, what happened? Are you all right?" Jodie's voice rose to an uneven pitch.

"No, honey. Call an...ambulance and...tell them to hurry." Gloria Bigger's breath came in quick gasps, and her body jerked convulsively.

Ray managed to shove the door open a few more inches and squeeze through. His fingers searched the wall and found the light switch. Jodie dived for the phone, and Ray kneeled beside the suffering woman.

Illumination did not make the situation better. Gloria was white as a sheet, and her left hand clutched the material of her blouse at a spot over her heart.

He checked her pulse only to find that it was as weak as he expected. But at least she still had one. "We're getting help, Mrs. Bigger."

She coughed and tried to raise her head. "The flower order."

"Don't worry about that," he assured her, massaging her cold hands. "Don't worry about anything. We'll have you to the hospital in no time."

"The man..." She stopped in midsentence, whimpering in pain.

"Don't try to talk now. Just relax. Everything's under control." He gave her hand a gentle squeeze. After what seemed hours to him, Jodie hung up the phone and dropped to the floor beside them, brushing a tissue she'd found somewhere across Mrs. Bigger's sweating brow.

"I'm sorry," Jodie whispered, her voice shaking. "I didn't mean to drag you into this."

"Not...your fault."

Half of Mrs. Bigger's words were swallowed in a moan. But the expression on Jodie's face was proof to Ray that Jodie believed all of this was her fault. Hers and the stalker's.

Ray relinquished Gloria's hand to Jodie's as the cry of approaching sirens attacked the night.

"You'll be just fine after Dr. Creighton works his magic," Jodie whispered, her face close to the florist's ear.

Ray hoped the good doc had a double dose of the magic. The woman on the floor would need it.

JODIE GROUND HER TEETH and stared at Butch Deaton while he scribbled down notes on a pad of paper. It was about time he did something besides walk around the flower shop scratching his head.

She had known Butch ever since she'd moved to Natchitoches, even dated him a few times during her senior year in high school. Watching him tonight, she couldn't imagine what she'd seen in him. He was far more arrogant than sympathetic, and his competence, seriously in question.

"It looks like a routine emergency to me," he said, tapping his stub of a pencil on the pad. "The woman had a heart attack from natural causes."

"Papers and folders are scattered all over her desk," Jodie protested. "And the top drawer of the file cabinet has obviously been rifled through."

He leaned against the counter, one hand propped on the handle of the revolver that peeked from his holster. "I know the place is a mess, Jodie."

"Exactly. Because the man who sent me the flowers must have realized too late that he could be traced through his credit card information. He broke in here tonight to get the same records we were looking for. Only he beat us to them. That's why they're not here."

"Then Mrs. Bigger arrived unexpectedly and caught him in the act. He frightened her into a coronary." Butch finished her scenario for her, a patronizing smile splitting his lips. "I'm sure your theory sounds reasonable to you, but you don't understand police work."

"The theory sounds plausible to me, too, Butch, and I do understand criminal activity."

Butch stared at Ray as if he were a bug he'd like to stamp. "If the man was worried about being tracked down, he would have never called in an order and given a credit card number in the first place. Even a defense attorney should be able to figure that out."

"Maybe he didn't think about the card being used to trace him until after the fact."

"Sounds like a pretty stupid stalker to me."

"Or one who made a mistake. It happens. Surely even cops make mistakes occasionally." Ray stared him down.

"Occasionally." This time he directed his remarks to Jodie, stepping closer, putting a hand on her arm, invading her space. "We can't go jumping to any criminal conclusions, Jodie. I know you mean well, but you have to leave the professional decisions to the police department."

She backed away from him. "Then you really believe Mrs. Bigger trashed her own office?" Jodie's patience could stretch no further.

"It's not unusual. Fact is, it happens all the time. The family calls us in, sure someone's heart attack was provoked by a break-in. Later we find out that when the pain hit, the person kind of went wild for a minute or two, all panicky, slinging things everywhere."

"But Gloria Bigger wasn't even in the office when we found her. She was at the front door, as if she'd just arrived."

"Or trying to get help."

Jodie blew a blast of steam from between pursed lips. Arguing with Butch was useless. She should have known that from the moment she'd told him that she thought Gloria Bigger had been attacked by an unknown stalker who had followed her to Natchitoches from New York City. The way he had rolled his eyes at his partner had told her more than his feeble attempts to humor her. He thought she was a fruitcake.

"You don't need to worry, Jodie. I'll follow up on this. If Mrs. Bigger pulls through, she'll be able to tell us herself if she encountered somebody in the shop.''

''If she pulls through.''

''She has a good chance. In the meantime, you call me direct if you get any more flowers or see anyone suspicious looking hanging around the house.'' He pressed his business card into her hand. ''You can always reach me if you call the beeper number.''

''But you will get a team down here to check for fingerprints?'' Ray asked, reminding him of his earlier promise.

''Yeah, Kostner. I always do what I say I will.'' His gaze left Ray and sought out Jodie's. ''I can give you a lift to your grandmother's if you'd like. I'm going that way.''

''That won't be necessary,'' Ray answered for her. ''I'll see that Jodie gets home safely.''

He took her arm and urged her to the door. Reluctantly, she let herself be escorted out. The only real clue she'd located had been a stack of acknowledgment cards stamped with a border of red hearts, just like the one that had come with her flowers. Valentine leftovers, Jodie suspected.

But the heart cards had been in the back corner of the supply desk, and a larger stack of cards had been in the front, all decorated with fall leaves and pumpkins. Mrs. Bigger would have surely chosen one of those unless the caller had specifically requested something with a red heart.

The only thing that didn't add up in her mind was that the stalker had left red roses on her doorstep before, but never yellow ones. The shift in color probably had some symbolic meaning, but it was lost on her.

She was sure the stalker had sent the flowers. She had no admirers in Natchitoches. But did tormenting her give him such pleasure he would follow her all the way across the country? Had he been here, in this very office, frightening Gloria Bigger into a heart attack? Or was Jodie just the running-scared neurotic everyone took her to be?

By the time she reached the curb, her head was pounding. Ray opened the door for her and then climbed in on his side, settling under the steering wheel and firing the ignition. Seconds later, he pulled out of the parking spot, taking the curve at a speed that sent her flying in his direction.

"You told me earlier that this maniac you're so afraid of has never touched you. Were you telling me the whole truth?" Ray held a death grip on the wheel.

"I'm asking again, Jodie. Has this man ever laid a hand on you?"

"I'm not on the witness stand, counselor. And I don't have to tell you anything. This isn't your problem." Besides, she'd told him more truth than he'd wanted to believe already. And the rest of the truth...

Fear surged again, moving through her veins like ice water. The rest of the truth might be so gory even she couldn't bear to think of it. Only she could think of nothing else. Not since the night she'd been called to identify the body. And still the police hadn't believed her. So why would anyone else?

"Hey, wait a minute," she protested, realizing that Ray was heading in the opposite direction from her house. "I need to check on Grams and the boys, and I want to go home *now*."

"You can call them. Besides, you'll be home soon enough. I just need to make one quick stop."

"I should have ridden home with Officer Unfriendly."

"You had your chance."

"So, where is this stop you have to make?"

"My house. I need to pick up a few things."

"Like what?"

"Like underwear. A pair of pajamas, if I can find them. A shaving kit."

An unexpected lump gathered in her throat. She spoke past it, determined not to let anything Ray did bother her ever again. "Sounds like a slumber party," she quipped. "How fun. Too bad you had to keep the party hostess waiting."

Her attempt at uncaring sarcasm came out like the farce it was. She sat in silence, curses rolling through her mind like the blackest of Louisiana storm clouds.

But he was doing her a favor. Knowing he was heartless enough to throw his plans for being with another woman into her face was just the kind of reminder she needed to put him out of her mind for good.

"Actually the hostess doesn't know I'm coming." He picked up his cellular phone and punched in a series of numbers before sticking it in her hands. "Why don't you tell her she'll have a houseguest for a few days?"

Before Jodie could slam the phone into the side of his head, she heard Grams's voice at the other end of the connection.

JODIE PUSHED OPEN the screen door and Ray followed her inside, swinging a quickly packed duffel at his side. The house was dark except for the welcoming light in the hall. That could only mean Grams was asleep.

Of course Grams would have been up and ready to receive her guest with open arms if Jodie had given her the message he'd told her to deliver. But Jodie had no intention of frightening her grandmother or of putting her in danger. That left her only one choice and it did not encompass having a past lover move back into her life as a temporary bodyguard.

"Where do you want me to put this?" Ray asked, lifting his duffel a little higher.

She choked back her first choice of an answer. "Shhh." She placed a finger over her lips. "Don't wake up Grams. I told you I don't want her to know you're here."

"Don't you think she'll figure it out when I come down the stairs for morning coffee in my bathrobe?"

The image flashed through Jodie's head. Ray, clean-shaven with the hint of aftershave lingering in the air. Ray, his hair damp from the shower, his mouth minty fresh. Memories filled her mind, making her body weak but strengthening her resolve.

"Wait in the kitchen," she whispered. "I'm going upstairs to check on the boys. When I get back, we'll talk."

"It's pushing midnight, a little late for chatting."

"This conversation won't take long." She turned her back on him and hurried to the boys' room. She needed to see them sleeping safely in their beds. Needed to hear the soft sounds of their breathing and see their tiny chests rise and fall beneath their cuddly sleepers. Needed to feel that something was all right with the world.

The night-light glowed softly, illuminating her

steps enough that she avoided colliding with the wooden rocking horse and a stuffed tiger one of the twins had obviously tossed from his bed. Neither of the boys stirred from slumber as she tiptoed across the thick carpet.

Grams had chosen the perfect room for a nursery and then raided not only her attic but her neighbor's to find two cribs, the rocking horse and bright-colored paintings of Louisiana pelicans and sailboats. Only the mattresses had to be purchased.

The hasty exit from New York had forced Jodie to bring only necessary items. Clothing, photographs and a few of the boys' favorite toys had topped her list.

This time she'd have to travel with a whole lot less. Her heart constricted in pain at the thought of leaving her sons, but pain and heartbreak couldn't change what she had to do.

She tiptoed to the side of Blake's bed. Shadows from the teddy bear mobile danced along the pale yellow walls, and she shivered. The boys had been sleeping this soundly the night she had found the note tucked inside Blake's empty bed. The night the killer had been as close to her babies as she was right now. The night she'd vowed he would never touch her sons again.

Her fingers tightened around the crib railing, as she stared down at her firstborn son, her eyes adjusting to the faint light. Blake had kicked off the covers, and, thumb in mouth, was sucking away. She touched her fingers to her lips and then to his cheek before tucking the light blanket over him, knowing he would kick it off again before she made it back down the stairs.

The second crib was across the room, next to the window seat. Blair wriggled as she approached, his lips breaking into a smile as he slept. "Pleasant dreams," she whispered. "May you always have them, pumpkin."

The room was warm, but a sudden chill shook Jodie's body. They were not alone. A human-shaped shadow moved along the wall, and she jerked around in time to see Ray's back as he disappeared through the nursery door.

He'd intruded and then walked away. So like him. But the loss was all his. At least she was no longer tormented with whether or not she should tell a man who wanted no part of responsibility, of commitment, that he had two wonderful sons. Now it was he who had made the choice of denial.

A tear slid down her cheek as she turned from the cribs. It was time to let the past die. Today was more than enough to deal with. And dealing with it meant keeping her boys safe at all costs.

RAY STOOD at the kitchen door and stared into the blackness of a night that had started with bright moonlight and a heaven full of stars. Now dark clouds punctuated by ragged streaks of lightning pummeled the serenity.

And here he was back in Natchitoches, being sucked into a life he wanted no part of. Dealing with his disapproving dad by day, and now Jodie by night.

Jodie by night. The words had the ring of a song title, maybe even a romantic sonnet. Jodie, hot with passion, sex siren in a cotton gown, warming up a New York night with a blaze all her own.

Suddenly, heat suffused his body. He pulled at the collar of his shirt and went to the refrigerator. Retrieving a pitcher of cold lemonade, he searched the cabinets above the sink for a glass. Before he'd finished pouring, Jodie made her entrance, and the cold challenge in her eyes made a cool drink unnecessary.

He set the pitcher on the table. "Were the boys all right?"

"Sound asleep," she answered, playing along with him, pretending she hadn't seem him watching the tucking-in procedures from the shadows. "And so is Grams."

"As are most people in Natchitoches this close to the bewitching hour. I suggest we turn in, too. You've had a rough evening."

"Not nearly as rough as Gloria Bigger's."

"And none of that was your fault. The woman had a heart attack, her second according to the report we got when we called the hospital. And the last report said she was holding her own."

He took her hand. She pulled it away, as if his touch might defile her.

"It's possible you and Butch are right about the stalker not frightening her into a heart attack. It's also possible you are wrong. At any rate the flowers this afternoon were from the stalker."

"That's circumstantial evidence."

"Okay, I *believe* they were from the stalker. I also believe there's a good chance he is either in town or on his way. Call me crazy. I don't care. But this man is obsessed with me in some sick fashion. Obsessed enough to travel across the country to find me. I don't understand it. I just know it's true."

"I'm sure there have been many men obsessed with you, Jodie. I remember a few."

"Don't make light of this. You don't know the whole story."

Her eyes watered, dark depths of fear, and Ray fought the urge to take her in his arms. But comfort would not release the devils that were tormenting her. Talk might at least help him to understand them. "Go on, Jodie. You've been skirting the truth all night." He pulled out a straight-backed kitchen chair and led her to it. "Tell me the rest of the story."

She perched on the front edge of the seat, her eyes staring at a spot somewhere over the kitchen range, her hands on the table, clasped tightly. "It would be a waste of time. You wouldn't believe me any more than anyone else did."

"Try me."

"Okay." She took a deep breath. "I worked late at the office one night."

Her voice was hollow, as if she were delivering a memorized speech that had nothing to do with her. Ray listened carefully, his attorney's mind honing in on every detail.

"I had to finish up a presentation for a client. Max Roling, one of the college interns stayed to help. I told him I'd treat for dinner."

"And did you go to dinner?" he asked, when she appeared stuck in the mire.

"Yes, at a restaurant close to the office. It was late, past ten when we finally stopped to eat. We had a glass of wine. I guess the combination of zinfandel and fatigue got to me. I opened up for the first time to him about the stalker who was wreaking havoc on my ability to sleep or concentrate."

"What was his reaction?"

"No signs of guilt, if that's what you're thinking. He was surprised, and understanding. We finished the meal, and he hailed me a cab. I offered to have the taxi drop him off at his place, but he refused. He was supposed to meet a friend later, a waitress at a restaurant in the theater district.''

Pain hammered at Ray's left temple. He had a good idea where the story was going. ''I know this is tough on you, but tell me everything, Jodie. And be as accurate as you can.''

''I'll try. The facts are entangled with emotions.'' A frustrated sigh escaped her lips. ''Max hugged me tightly before I got into the cab. But instead of his arms, it was someone's gaze that I felt.''

She shook her head, rearranging the unruly curls that hugged her cheeks. ''I know. It sounds crazy. Several officers of the NYPD already assured me of that, in kinder words, of course. But *he* was watching us. I felt him, the same way I felt him tonight.''

''It's not crazy, Jodie. Survival is a sixth sense sometimes. You can't take it to court, but that doesn't mean it's not real.''

''I got a call in the middle of the night from the police department,'' she continued, a finger tracing the outline of a vine in the tablecloth. ''Max had my business card on him, and they needed someone to identify the body.''

''Oh, jeez! And you had to be the one they called.'' This time Ray's body refused to heed his own survival warnings. He rounded the table in quick steps and all but lifted Jodie from her chair, steadying her on her feet and cradling her in his arms.

''One week later, I woke in the middle of the night, shaking and afraid. That's the night I found the note tucked inside Blake's crib.''

Her voice dissolved into a shaky whisper. ''And

that's when I ran. Until today, I'd thought I'd made the right decision.''

''You did. You definitely did.'' Ray tightened his arms about her, and she swayed closer. She felt so good in his arms, so right. His brain went numb. His body grew warm.

When he'd left New York two years ago, Jodie Gahagen had been so embedded in his senses, it had taken months for him to even begin to get over her. Months before he could fall into bed at night without aching to hold her. Months before he had woken up in the morning without reaching for her.

Now it was all coming back, and he was powerless to stop the feelings that raged inside him. Her head was on his shoulders, her hair painting the front of his shirt with a tangle of bright red curls, her fragrance filling him like some exotic aphrodisiac.

It was all wrong. His brain whispered the warning. But his body shouted his need. He pulled away only enough to slip a thumb under her chin, to tilt her face upward. Her lips trembled, and he touched them with his own, softly at first, then harder, hungrily.

The world swam around them, and he was powerless to control the desire that choked away his will. Jodie finally did, pulling away, her eyes fiery, and her soft lips still swollen from his kiss.

''Why did you do that?'' she asked, meeting his gaze head-on. ''Why did you kiss me?''

''I don't know. An impulse.''

''A be-nice-to-the-scared-lady kiss?'' She walked to the other side of the table, putting a tangible barrier between them. ''I don't need that kind of comfort. The truth is I don't need anything from you. I want you to leave here, tonight.''

"I can't do that."

"Of course you can. You just pick up your bag and walk out the door. No phone calls. No cards and letters. You just leave and then nothing. You're good at it. I've seen you in action."

"If you're talking about New York, I had my reasons, Jodie."

"They don't matter, not now."

"Maybe not, but I'm not leaving until we know for sure if this lunatic of yours is in town."

"You have work to do. You can't be my bodyguard twenty-four hours a day."

"I won't have to. Ben will be here during the day. I'll be here at night. You and the boys will be safe, and if the man shows up, we'll nab him."

"He'll show up, but you'll never see him. No one will, until he wants to be seen."

"I'll stop him," he said, knowing that he had to protect Jodie, no matter what being around her every night did to him.

"You can stay here tonight, Ray. I'll make up some excuse to Grams as to why you're here. I'll have to tell her so many lies to make my plan of action work that one more won't matter."

"And what happens after tonight?"

"I'll be out of here," she said, her voice trembling.

"No way. You are not running away again. The chase has to stop somewhere, and it should be here where you have friends and family."

"And a policeman who gives credence to my story?"

"Butch said he'd check everything out. Besides, you can't keep uprooting the twins' lives trying to outrun a madman."

"The twins are not your concern. But you're right. I won't be taking the twins with me. This time I'll run alone and hope the stalker catches up with me. If I can see him, I can go to the cops with a description. I want this over, once and for all, one way or another."

"Now you're talking crazy, Jodie. I will not let you do this."

"Then you better come up with a hell of a way to stop me."

She spun toward the door, her hair flying. Ray thought hard for a comeback, but his mind drew only blanks while he watched her march her shapely little body out the door.

Chapter Four

The grandfather clock in the downstairs hall struck three. Jodie counted the chimes as she stared at the ceiling. Alone in the dark, memories played havoc with her determination and trounced on her will. Memories and proximity. Ray Kostner was in the next room, separated from her by a few feet and a wall. And an impenetrable barrier of regrets and denial.

She tossed again, mauling the sheets and wallowing in images that would be best forgotten. With all the complications in her life, all the hopelessness of running from a madman who wouldn't give up, Ray had still managed to slip back into her heart. She had learned nothing from years of mistakes.

As a teenager, it had been the relentless infatuation with the town bad boy. He'd always been a little bigger than life, more daring than the other boys in town, and far more exciting. He'd been the teenager who collected speeding tickets like baseball cards, ran away to New Orleans for a wild weekend when most of his classmates dared go no farther than Shreveport. He'd been the one kicked off the football team for ignoring the coach's orders and having his head shaved in Mohawk fashion, just to be cool.

He would have probably never made it through high school if his dad hadn't been the pillar of the community. Still, half the adolescent female population in Natchitoches had drooled over him since grade school.

Actually, Jodie had been a late bloomer. She'd been all of fourteen before she'd fallen under his spell. Ray had been a senior in high school then, and he had stopped by her house with her older cousin for a slice of her birthday cake. Too bad he'd liked Grams's coconut cake so much—he'd thanked the birthday girl with a kiss on the cheek.

The kiss.

Her first kiss. And it had to be from Ray Kostner. Not that it was much of a kiss. But she hadn't washed her face for days. She'd have waited longer if she hadn't gone up to Shreveport to the state fair and eaten that wad of sticky cotton candy. She'd waited for years for him to kiss her again.

God, she'd been stupid. Then she'd had youth for an excuse. Tonight she had only her own weakness to blame. She'd ignored every warning her brain had issued and asked for his help. Once again he'd torn her heart from her chest and stamped on it.

He'd denied his own sons.

She could live with his rejection, but as long as she had breath in her body, her sons wouldn't have to.

Jodie kicked her feet, entangling them even worse in a sheet that seemed to be fighting back. She gave up and attacked the pillow instead, pounding it into submission, and wishing for daylight.

She closed her eyes, for seconds, mere seconds. That's when she heard the noise. A cry of pure pain, and it was coming from the nursery. She jumped from the bed and raced down the hall. Before she was out her door, the second twin had joined in the wailing chorus.

Ray beat her to the nursery. "What's wrong with them?" he asked, from his position between the two cribs.

"I don't know. Maybe they don't like having strangers in the house."

"I'll introduce myself. The name's Ray Kostner. I'm here to help your mom."

Blake quit crying and stood, sinking his teeth into the top railing of the crib. He was all smiles now that company had arrived. Jodie nudged Ray out of the way and reached over the railing to check on Blair. He'd stopped wailing the second he'd caught sight of her too, but he looked none too happy. His lips were trembling, his eyes red from tears.

She let her fingers linger on his brow. "He has a fever," she said, picking him up and holding him close.

"I can drive you to the hospital."

"You don't rush babies to the hospital every time they have a fever. But I do want to check it. Could you get the thermometer for me? It's on the table over there."

Ray fumbled through the assortment of baby implements while Jodie changed Blair's diaper. "I don't see a thermometer."

"You have your hands on it."

"Really? Odd-looking contraption."

"Just hand it over." She took it and inserted it in Blair's ear.

"I thought you put those things in their mouth."

"Go back to bed, Ray. I'm not doing a class in Baby 101 tonight."

"If you're sure you don't need any help."

"I'm positive."

Relief eased the lines in his face. "I'll wait and see how high his fever is, though. High fever's not good for a kid. I do know that much."

"A hundred and one. You can go to bed."

"Does that mean you don't have to worry?"

"No, it means I don't have to panic. I'll give him something to bring the fever down and take him to the doctor in the morning. It's probably an ear infection. He's prone to those."

Ray backed to the door. Jodie settled in the rocker and cuddled Blair in her arms. Blake assessed the situation and figured he was the loser. He released a mournful wail.

"Do you think he has a fever, too?" Ray asked, slinking back inside the room.

"No. Probably just brotherly sympathy pains. Of course, he might need his diaper changed."

The look on Ray's face was one of pure panic.

"You could change him and see if that calms him," Jodie said sweetly, knowing she was scaring the wits out of the usually confident attorney and enjoying every second of it. "Staying here was your idea, you know. You might as well be useful."

Blake increased his volume level considerably when no one moved in his direction. "Okay, boy, quiet down now. You'll wake your great-grandmother." Ray stepped closer, his hands still at his side. "I...ah...I don't know how to change a diaper," he finally admitted.

"It's easy. I'll give you step-by-step instructions."

He looked doubtful. "What if I stick him with a pin? That would be a lot worse than a wet diaper."

"Diapers don't have pins anymore. Get one out of the package on the dressing table. You can change him in the bed. All you have to do is unsnap his jammies and take off the wet diaper. Slip the new one under and over his bottom and attach the tabs. Surely a high-powered lawyer can handle a simple task like that."

"We didn't cover changing diapers in law school."

No, she was sure they didn't. If they had, he would be an expert, like he was at everything else he did. She was the one who was a slow learner.

She watched his awkward movements as he changed the diaper of a son he'd never wanted and didn't claim, the amusement she'd felt initially dissolving into a lump that settled in her chest, choking her breath away.

In the morning she'd insist he leave the house. Gentle Ben would stay over at night if she asked him. He'd done it before.

"All done." Ray's voice interrupted her thoughts. "What do I do with this thing?" He held the wet diaper with two fingers, at arm's length, as if it contained radioactive material.

"Dump it in the plastic container in the corner."

"Disposable. I like it." The smile on his face forecast his pride in his dubious achievements. And either the dry diaper or the attention had worked. Blake was lying on his back, sucking his right thumb and kicking his legs contentedly.

"Do you need me to do anything else?" Ray asked. "No."

"You still look upset, Jodie. I'll call the doctor for you if you want."

"No." She placed her lips on her son's head. "He's cooler now that he's stopped crying. I'll rock him until he falls asleep."

Ray leaned on the door, watching her. She rocked faster, suddenly aware of the thinness of her nightshirt, the warmth in the room. "Go to bed," she whispered.

"Well, if you're sure you don't need me…"

"No, I don't need you." She almost choked on the words. She needed him. She couldn't lie to herself. But it was a need she would bury deep inside her, so deep she would forget it existed.

She closed her eyes, holding Blair so close she could feel the beating of his tiny heart as Ray turned and walked from the room.

THE SOUND OF a lullaby filled Ray's ears as he made his way back down the narrow hallway to the guest bedroom. What in the hell was he doing here? Two years ago he'd walked away from Jodie Gahagen, knowing he could never let her back in his life.

Tonight he was more convinced than ever he had made the right decision. She was the marrying kind, the type of woman who made love to you like there was no tomorrow and then had you planning a future of…of changing diapers and going to Little League games. The type of life he didn't want and couldn't handle.

So why was he here?

Jodie was in danger, that's why. *Pay the ultimate price, like the others did.* Even now the words settled like cold lead in his gut. If the man who wrote that note wasn't stopped, Jodie could wind up dead.

He couldn't let that happen.

Doubts rose inside him bitter as bile. He was nobody's savior. Ask his mom, his dad, his high school coach. Make demands, and Ray Kostner buckled under like an empty cardboard box.

Only in his professional life was he a man of might. And that's how he had to keep this. Impersonal. It was the only way.

He dropped to the side of his bed and flicked on the lamp, grabbing a pen and paper. He was wide awake now; he might as well work on the problems at hand. Number one: how to trace the identity of the man who was terrorizing Jodie. Number two: how to keep his hands and lips to himself when Jodie was around.

He closed his eyes as he heard the clock, praying he would get some sleep and not dream of anything that had happened nearly two years ago in New York City. Even he had his limits of endurance.

TENSION THICK AS a bowl of Grams's grits hovered over the kitchen table. The last thing Jodie had wanted was to pull her grandmother into this. But with the local police already calling the house, it was only a matter of time before she figured it out on her own.

"Why didn't you tell me this before, Jodie?" Grams fingered her coffee cup, running a bony digit around the edge of the delicate china handle.

Jodie reached a hand across the table and wrapped it around one of Grams's. "I didn't want you to worry."

"Well, of course, you didn't want to worry me,

child. But I'm family. It's my duty to worry." She got up, refilled everyone's coffee cup and then sat back down at the head of the table. "Now, Mr. Attorney, what are you going to do about this?"

"I'm—"

Jodie cut him off. "It's not Ray's problem, Grams. It's mine, and *I* can handle it."

"Pooh. If you could handle it, you would have done it already. Besides, you've got mothering to do, and Ray here doesn't do anything but run around town all day in one of those fancy starched shirts and neck-choking ties bleeding people dry with those confounded lawsuits. A little worthwhile work would do him good."

Ray's laughter filled the air. "You do know how to cut to the chase, Miss Emily." He stirred cream into his coffee and took a slow sip before continuing. "Jodie came to Natchitoches for help and we're going to be sure that she gets it. In fact, I'm going to get started on it right after you cook that bacon and eggs you've been threatening me with."

"Good." She pushed her glasses farther back on her nose. "What can I do to help?"

"Just keep everything under your flowered sunbonnet. The fewer people who know about all of this, the easier the hunt will be. I'll tell Ben, though. I want him to keep an eye on all of you during the day."

"And Selda. I have to tell Selda. The woman's been my next-door neighbor for thirty years. And you can't keep a secret from that nosy woman anyway." Grams was already up and busy, peeling off thick slices of honey-cured bacon.

"Okay, Grams. You can tell Selda, but no one else.

In fact, I'll go over with you after I've fed the boys their breakfast,'' Jodie offered.

"No need for that. She's already called. Said she had something she wanted to bring over for the twins, but I bet she already heard about what happened last night at Gloria's shop. She'll be over before the dishes are wiped to get an earful.''

The baby monitor on the counter buzzed with the sounds of wriggling movement and toddler babbling. "The boys are waking up,'' Jodie said, grateful for an excuse to leave Grams and Ray at each other's mercy.

"And I've got to eat and get back to those disgusting lawsuits,'' Ray said with a conspiratorial wink. "If I don't see you before I leave, I'll pick you up at twelve-thirty for lunch, Jodie.''

"I have plans.''

"Change them. I worked up a list of priorities last night, and I want to go over them with you. Also, I'll need information about everyone you came in contact with in New York on any regular basis. I'll need descriptions, when you've seen them last, anything unusual about the way they act around you. That type of thing.''

"You're not my attorney.''

"I'll take care of that,'' Grams said, cracking eggs into a pottery bowl. "I'll hire him.''

"I accept the assignment.''

Jodie shook her head in exasperation. She'd save her strength for a battle she could win. She'd handle Ray her own way, outside Grams's earshot. "I'll see you at lunch, counselor,'' she said defiantly before marching out of the kitchen.

LASYONE'S WAS BUSTLING at 12:30, tourists and locals alike crowded at the small wooden tables. Ray pushed through the door and then held it open for Jodie, ushering her into the spot he frequently referred to as aroma heaven.

The potent odors of hot spices drifted in from the kitchen where the miniature meat pies browned in huge pots of hot grease and oysters and shrimp danced on sizzling grills.

A waitress, blond and willowy and no more than twenty, flashed him a smile and wiped her hands on her apron. "Smoking or nonsmoking?" she said, sidling up next to him.

"Nonsmoking, unless there's a long wait."

She flashed her eyes flirtatiously. "I got a table just opening up in the back. It won't take but a minute to get it cleaned and set up."

"Sounds perfect."

They followed the sashaying waitress through ill-formed rows of tables, all covered in plastic cloths and most filled with huge helpings of red beans and rice, potato salad and the famous meat pies. A group of young men in jeans and work shirts looked up from their food as they passed. The waitress was prancing, but it was Jodie their eyes were on.

Ray didn't blame them a bit. Even in loose slacks and a cotton blouse, the figure beneath the mane of bright red hair was enough to make a man turn primal. He should know.

But the figure wasn't the only thing that drew men's attention. She wore the look of a challenge, forbidden, too self-satisfied. But Ray knew better than to buy the look. He'd kissed it from her face before, knew that beneath the cool exterior, there was enough heat to seriously threaten the polar ice caps.

Keep it cool. Impersonal. All business. The warnings flooded his brain.

He held a chair for Jodie and then took the one to her right, making sure his hand didn't brush her shoulder or tangle in her hair.

"Do you have a recommendation?" she asked, burying her head behind the well-worn menu the waitress had left.

"I've never had a bad dish here. Of course, I like my food spicy. Save room for dessert, though. The Cane River Cream Pie is the best in town, next to Miss Emily's, of course. I've been known to go for seconds."

"Everything looks good. Unfortunately, I don't have much of an appetite these days."

Ray studied the lines in her face. In most people, the kind of fear and worry she'd been living with would have drawn and drained their features, making them look tired and years older. It obviously didn't work that way with Jodie.

Her beauty wasn't at all diminished. If anything, the new seriousness made her more woman, more desirable even than the whirlwind of vivacious energy he remembered.

He smiled thankfully as the waitress returned with two tall glasses of iced tea. He was falling into the trap again. He wasn't sure who set the trap, Jodie or his own memories, his own needs and fantasies. All he was certain of was that he felt the clamps tightening every time he was around her.

But the traps would never hold. That's why he had

to remember that Jodie was off-limits. Friend in need, and nothing more. He owed that to both of them.

Bending over, he reached into the briefcase at his feet and pulled out a yellow legal pad. No use to put off the inevitable.

"I spent the morning on the phone to the NYPD," he said, looking over his notes. "It took some persistence, but I finally managed to talk to the detective who's investigating your complaints."

"Detective Cappan?"

"One and the same. Seems like a sharp guy."

"Not as sharp as the stalker."

"Maybe not. But he's out there trying. He thinks you did the right thing by getting out of New York. For the record, so do I."

"Right. We may as well make the stalker work a little harder at his tormenting business. Now, he, too, can give up his job and apartment, if he had one, and travel to beautiful downtown Natchitoches. Maybe we should put up a banner welcoming him."

"I wouldn't. We have no evidence Deaton wasn't correct in his initial assessment. Panic and pain caused Gloria to knock the files to the floor. The man isn't likely to travel this far from his home haunting grounds, not when New York City is overrun with replacement victims."

"No, and Cappan didn't think he would move beyond leaving notes. He almost had me convinced until Max Roling turned up dead. And all the poor man did to deserve losing his life was give me a comforting hug. Come to think of it, Ray, you may be treading dangerous ground yourself. I should probably come with a warning label."

The frustration in her voice tore at his resolve. He

battled the urge to take her hands in his, relying on words instead. "According to Cappan, Roling was murdered in a robbery attempt. The murder rate in Manhattan is down, but not extinct."

"I've heard Cappan's theory. It's old news. And wrong."

"You can't be sure of that." Ray ran his fingers up and down his glass, tracing a drop of condensation. "Stalking's a cowardly thing. In almost every case, the perpetrator waits until the victim is alone to act, just like yours has done. If there's no history of violence, the stalker usually doesn't escalate to that state."

"Thank you, counselor. I couldn't have quoted the police procedural manual better myself. It doesn't do a damn thing for bringing Max back to life though." She unclasped the napkin she'd been twisting and picked up her knife, spreading a layer of butter on a wedge of French bread and then wagging the utensil at him. "Besides, I doubt the murderer has a copy of the manual. Perhaps you and Cappan could send him one. It would make his life and mine a lot easier."

"We could have just left one for him in your apartment."

"What's that supposed to mean?"

"He came back, evidently the night after you moved out."

Jodie winced at his words and sucked in her breath, letting it out in a heavy sigh. "How do they know that?"

"Evidently the neighbor who purchased your furniture didn't get it all the first afternoon. When she came back the next day to pick up the bed and chifforobe, she found the door cracked open and the sheets on the bed wadded into knots, as if someone had slept there, or something. She was sure she'd left the door locked.''

''So it took less than twenty-four hours for the man to realize I'd run out. Fortunately, it took a month for him to track me to Natchitoches. Better than having him do it overnight. This way we know he's not psychic as well as crazy.''

''All we know is that he made a lucky guess about your destination. He could have talked to almost anyone who knows you and found out you were from here. At any rate, we have to put a stop to the harassment.''

''Not we, Ray. You have a short memory. *I* will put a stop to it.''

The determination in her voice caught him off guard. He met her gaze, and what he saw worried him even more than the fear he'd seen the night she received the flowers. The fight that burned in the deep recesses of her pupils now was the kind he'd seen in desperate clients, right before they'd ignored his counsel and taken matters into their own hands.

''You're no match for the likes of this man. Especially if it turns out he really is a killer.''

His words of caution were lost in the clatter of dishes being set in front of them. A huge plate of catfish for him, a shrimp salad for Jodie, and a bowl of fried okra for nibbling. He waited while the waitress gave her ''Anything else for you?'' spiel before continuing his lecture.

''When we get back to my office, I want descriptions of every man who's made a pass at you in the last year, even if you think it was totally innocent. I know a man in New Orleans who does unbelievably accurate drawings from verbal descriptions. I want to send them to Cappan and have him look through his mug books. Chances are this man has a record. Breaking and entering can get you time even in New York.''

''I've been through the suspect list with Cappan already.'' Jodie nibbled on a shrimp, taking her time chewing and swallowing, her eyes everywhere but focused in his direction. ''And I don't have time to go through it again today,'' she said finally, nudging a piece of lettuce with her fork. ''I have an appointment at three o'clock in Shreveport. I'm hiring a nanny.''

''That makes sense. Tending to those two would be too much for anyone.''

''No, they're not too much for me.'' She took a deep breath and straightened her shoulders, as if gearing up for a battle she hated to fight. ''But they'll be too much for Grams when I go back to New York.''

The bite of catfish stopped midway down Ray's throat. He coughed it loose, his body suddenly tighter than a spring. ''You are not going back to New York. Not until this thing is settled. For God's sake, Jodie, I just told you, the man was in your apartment the night after you left. If you'd been there…''

''Next time I will be there. It's the only way to stop him. If he followed me here, and I believe he did, he'll follow me back to New York. I'll let him know I want to see him, talk to him, find out who he is and what he wants from me. Then I can go to the police and have at least a chance of stopping him. But I have to do it alone. I have to protect Blake and Blair.''

''So you'll get their mother killed, or…''

''Or I could bring the nightmare to an end. You and Cappan both said the man is likely harmless. Besides, something has to be done. I can't just keep running. As it is now, I've put the boys and Grams in danger. And even you."

"I can take care of all of you."

"We're not your responsibility."

Ray put down his fork and wiped his mouth. Civilized dining was obviously over. He couldn't believe he was having this conversation, not with Jodie Gahagen. She'd always been headstrong, but in the past she'd at least been sensible. Now she was spouting pure lunacy.

What he wanted to do was just put his foot down and order her to do what he said. In the same breath he might order the Mississippi River to change its course or the sun to rise at midnight.

He'd have to think of something more democratic, and persuasive. After all, he was the top defense lawyer at Fowler, Glenn, Kostner and Grange. The top one in the south since the Greer murder trial if he gave credence to the press. He could damn sure argue a point. If he could find one.

The beeper at his waist vibrated. He pushed his plate back, leaving half a catfish. His appetite was suddenly shot to hell, but Jodie's had blossomed. While he stewed, she was cleaning her plate, evidently feeling much better now that her ridiculous plan was out in the open.

"I have to make a call. Will you excuse me?" he said, punching in the beeper and making a mental note of the number.

"Of course. I think I might try a piece of that pie you were talking about. Can I order one for you?"

"No, thanks. Just coffee for me. And if she has

some left in the bottom of a pot, tell her to warm that up for me. I need it strong.''

He opted to make the call from his car phone. It would be much quieter there, and if the beep was the one he was expecting he wanted to hear the caller clearly. He exited the restaurant and slid into the front seat of his unlocked car. Grabbing the phone, he punched in the number. The credit card administrator answered on the third ring.

''I have the information you requested about Mrs. Gloria Bigger's reported credits, Mr. Kostner. I hope this is helpful to her.''

''I'm sure it will be. And thanks for getting on this so fast.''

''No problem. Since you faxed us documentation that the Kostner firm has the legal authority to handle all business decisions for the flower shop, we are glad to be of assistance.''

Ray took out his pen and waited for the name and address of the person who had charged an order for a dozen roses yesterday afternoon. He scribbled it down and thanked the woman before slamming the cover shut on the phone. Everything he needed to know in two little words. Nasty words that blew his and Cappan's theories into shrapnel.

Now all he had to do was tell Jodie she'd been right all along. Statistics lied. Her survivor instincts had not. The card used to order the flowers had belonged to Max Roling. Ray shoved his knotted fists deep into the pockets of his trousers.

Jodie going to New York to face a killer. Like hell she was. He'd stay with her twenty-four hours a day if that's what it took to keep her in Natchitoches until the man was caught. Eat with her, work with her at his side, even sleep with her if he had to.

Sleep with Jodie Gahagen, and then walk away. He'd done it once. He'd sooner go hand-to-hand with a grizzly than try that again.

Chapter Five

Jodie stared at the walls of Ray's temporary Natchitoches office, the blood draining from her head, her mouth so dry she couldn't swallow. In her heart she'd always known the person who was stalking her had been the same man who'd plunged a knife deep into Max Roling's heart, twisting the blade until his life had spilled out on the street like used crankcase oil.

But somewhere inside her, she must have hoped otherwise. Why else would Ray's words be turning her stomach inside out?

"He's dead because of me." Strain tore at her voice, breaking the silence that hung in the air between them.

"He's dead because a lunatic took his life. This isn't your doing, Jodie." Ray paced the room, then stopped in front of her, rolling a chair closer and propping on the edge. He took her hands in his, holding them firmly, easing their cold shaking. "It's the work of a madman who has to be stopped."

"Right. Only no one stops him. I couldn't even get the police to seriously consider he was Max's murderer. They were so sure it was some punk kid, coming off a high and looking for a few bucks to start a new climb.''

"They'll listen now. You just sit tight. The fact that Max's credit card is tied in with the flowers will force them to listen. With this new bit of evidence, they'll have a lot more motivation for finding and stopping the man who's ruining your life. And when they try him for murder one, he can be locked behind bars for the rest of his natural life.''

Ray made it sound so easy. Sit tight and the police would handle everything. Trust justice. And put more people in danger, people she cared about more than life itself. "I can't do that," she told him, pulling away. "Especially not now."

She stood and walked to the window. Clouds were forming in the west, a new frontal system on the way, painting the old courthouse that stood across the street in shades of shadowy gray. The present building had been there since 1896, sturdy, unchanging, like the town. Perhaps its walls had seen murderers before. Perhaps the town had seen men as evil as the one who was either here now or on his way.

Perhaps not. All she knew was that she couldn't be the one that brought him to these streets. She couldn't be the cause of another death. Burning moisture gathered at the back of her eyelids. She tried to blink it away, but a tear escaped, sliding down her cheek. She whisked it away with the back of her hand, silently cursing it for exposing her weakness.

Ray eased behind her, so close she could hear his breathing, feel the warmth of it on the back of her neck. She kept her gaze riveted to a distant point outside the window. "I have to leave. It's the only way

I can make sure the boys are safe. And Grams. And even you, Ray, and anyone else who befriends me.''

"No."

There was no pleading in his voice. The word was a command, direct, final.

"I'm not doing this out of some death wish. I'm not looking forward to it, but I have no other choice. You're an intelligent man. Surely you can see that.''

His hands pressed into her shoulders, tugging and forcing her to turn and face him. She met his gaze, and the intensity in his dark eyes sent a new wave of chills skidding along her nerves.

"I'm not letting you leave, Jodie. Not as long as this killer's on the loose." His grip loosened, but his hands didn't leave her body. His thumbs moved along the veins in her neck, sweeping up to her earlobes and back down again, a slow hypnotizing rhythm.

"Why, Ray, why now? Why are you all of a sudden so concerned about my well-being? Nearly two years ago, you spent a week in my apartment. You danced with me on Broadway at two in the morning, shared hot pastrami sandwiches with me at daybreak, rode the carousel with me in Central Park. And then just walked away with a simple goodbye.''

"That was different.''

"Obviously." Different in a million ways. Then he had slept beside her in bed, made love to her until every muscle in her body had ached with delicious pain. And when the week was over, he had said his goodbyes hurriedly, as if their time together had been a careless holiday he was ready to put behind him.

"You never even returned my calls. So what in the world makes you think you can just stroll back into my life now and give orders?''

She was shaking inside, but somehow she forced the outside to play the game, to hang tough when she was dragging her heartbreak out for public display. "Why now?" she insisted again.

"Because..." He backed her to the wall, his hands on her shoulders. His body was so close the front of his white dress shirt brushed against the smooth cotton of her blouse.

"Because, I...I can't stop myself."

She didn't get the chance to argue. Before she could open her mouth, his lips were pressed against hers. She pushed her hands into his chest, hard, afraid of the feelings that wrestled with her feeble hold on control. Control lost. The world spun around her, and instead of pushing, her hands and arms wrapped around him, pulling him closer.

His kiss deepened, his body pressing into hers, rocking her against the wall. Passion dipped inside her, exciting parts of her body she'd never known existed until the week she'd spent with him in New York. Now it was as if he'd never left. As if the nightmare of the stalker didn't exist.

She parted her kiss-swollen lips, and the play of his tongue tangling with hers left her weak and struggling for air. But still she couldn't pull her mouth away, couldn't bear to have his arms not around her, his fingers not digging into the flesh of her back. Tiny moans gurgled inside her, and she arched her body, pressing her hips against his, reveling in the hardness that she had brought to life.

The intercom on the desk buzzed. She barely heard it. It buzzed again, persistently, and Ray managed to pull away, grabbing the receiver. His "What's up?" was hoarse, strained with the passion that had to be tearing at him the way it was her. The receiver bobbled between his cheek and shoulder while he straightened his tie and rubbed at the wrinkles in his shirt.

"Put him through."

Jodie's pulse slowly returned to somewhere near normal. Ray was obviously talking to someone with the NYPD, giving them the facts about the credit card. The rest of the conversation made no sense at all.

"What was that all about?" she asked when he'd hung up the phone.

He tossed the legal pad he'd been scribbling on across the desk. "The kiss or the phone call?"

"Both. You can start with the phone call. The kiss we'll discuss later."

His gaze raked across her. "The investigation into the stalker has officially escalated to a homicide case. And, they believe your stalker is still in New York City."

"Why would they believe that? They have no idea who he is."

"A watch engraved with Max Roling's initials turned up in a pawnshop this morning. His sister identified it. She'd given it to him last Christmas."

"Oh, poor Janie. They were so close. Neither of them had married yet, and they spent lots of weekends together. They both loved the city. They were from a little town in Illinois." She was rambling. She couldn't help it.

"Concentrate on the positive, Jodie. If the man is in New York, then he's not here."

"*Ifs* are not reliable."

"They're as reliable as anything else we have to go on. And that means, you, the boys, your grandmother, all of you are perfectly safe. In fact, until this thing is wrapped up, this is the best place for you.''

''And if the police are wrong? If the man is here in Natchitoches? If he frightened Gloria Bigger into her heart attack?''

''Then we'll know soon enough. Gloria's condition is listed as stable. If someone was in her shop last night, she'll be able to describe him. But the evidence points to the fact that your stalker's in New York. If he is, he can't hurt you or the boys.''

''I can't take that chance.''

''You have to, for all the reasons you mentioned before. You have two babies who depend on you for everything. They need you alive.''

Two babies who needed her. Ray was right. No matter how badly she wanted the lunacy to end, she couldn't willingly put her life in danger. Not if there was any other way to stop the madness.

''What if you and the police are wrong, if the man is already here, watching and waiting?''

''Then you'll still be safe. Ben will be with you and Grams and the boys during the day. I'll be there at night.''

''It sounds too simple, too easy.''

''Not simple, just safe. So forget this nonsense about leaving town.''

Jodie closed her eyes, determined to think with reason. Everyone had advice, but they didn't know this man, not the way she did. He was the terror she woke with in the morning and climbed into bed with at night.

Still, if she could stay here with the boys and know they were safe, know Grams was safe... ''I can't promise you anything, Ray, except that I'll think about it and that I won't act foolishly.''

''That's a start.'' He slipped a finger under her chin and tilted it upward. ''Just hang in there, Jodie, and give the wheels of justice a little time.''

''You never answered my question, Ray. Why are you so concerned about what happens to me?''

He slid a finger down her nose and across her mouth, then slowly traced the lines of her bottom lip. ''I think I did answer the question a minute ago, for both of us. It's just that the answer has flaws.''

''Flaws or limitations?''

''Both.''

Flaws and limitations, the story of her life. She didn't even want to imagine what kind of limitations could go with a kiss so powerful, they had both been left as weak and disoriented as midday drunks.

''We'll talk about it tonight,'' he said, moving back to his desk. ''Right now I have an appointment with a fee-paying client. One of Dad's regulars. He keeps the firm on retainer just so he can have instant attention.''

''I can take a cab back to Grams's.''

''No cabs. No strangers. I've already arranged for Dale to drive you home. He's the student worker from the university. Six-four and built like a wrestler. You'll be in good hands.'' Stretching across the desk, he punched the intercom button and asked his dad's secretary to find Dale.

Jodie slung her handbag over her shoulder. ''I'll see you tonight,'' she said. He only nodded, his head already bent over a manila folder of typed forms.

She opened the door and went to wait for Dale. The outer office was chilly, a forecast of the cold front that was dropping the outside temperature by the minute. Still, a flicker of heat ran through Jodie's blood. Flaws and limitations or not, the kiss had proved one thing.

She had not imagined the passion she and Ray had shared in New York. And it was still alive, not just inside her but burning in him as well, easily raised to four-alarm status.

When all of this was over, if it ever was, she wanted one more chance with Ray Kostner, not as her bodyguard, but as her lover. One chance to see if what she felt was love or just a young girl's fantasy that didn't know when to die.

And one more chance to see if he had what it took to be a husband and father. Either the flaws would win or she would.

THE EARLY AFTERNOON showers ended, leaving cooler temperatures and earth that squished instead of crunched beneath Jodie's rubber boots. She trudged along, tugging the wagon carrying Blake, Blair and a conglomeration of stuffed animals and plastic toys behind her. Fortunately, Grams's lot was large, nearly an acre, a yard size unheard of in New York. It gave Jodie and the boys room to roam without leaving the protection of home.

Especially with this, she thought, patting the walkie-talkie attached to a belt loop at her waist. One for her, one for Grams and one for Ben. Instant communication. Another of Ray's ideas. Another ploy to convince her to stay in Natchitoches.

Ray was determined that she was not going to leave. His reasoning was still a mystery to her. It would have made sense if he'd believed her when she'd told him the boys were his. Surely any decent man would feel obliged to protect the mother of his sons.

But he believed what he chose to believe. Mr. No Commitment turned macho protector from a stalker he kept insisting was thousands of miles away. His actions did not match his claims. If he'd really believed there was no danger, he'd be sleeping in his own bed at night, not camped out in Grams's guest room.

She stopped and pointed out a scurrying squirrel to the boys. Blake clapped his hands, and Blair tried to crawl out of the wagon. If he could see it, he wanted it. The simple logic of childhood. She could use a little simple logic herself these days.

"Jodie, is everything all right?"

She jumped, startled by the voice.

"I'm fine, Ben. Where are you?"

"Down by the boathouse, cleaning up some gardening tools. I just thought I'd check on you."

"We're fine."

"Then over and out."

Checking and playing with his new toy. He and Grams both were acting like troopers. Actually, more like children playing espionage. And, if Ray's scenario held true, it would stay that way. No one would get hurt.

She shuddered and looked around, a sense of uneasiness shrouding the peace of the garden. It wasn't fair. A man too cowardly to identify himself had drawn her and her family into his circle of fear, robbed her of her right to live without terror.

And she was not the first woman to face this kind of nightmare. It happened far too often, according to

Cappan and the literature she'd read on the subject. But usually the woman knew who was watching and following her, threatening her privacy and often her life. Somehow, Jodie was sure knowing would be easier. It was impossible to fight an identity without form.

She'd spent all of the boys' afternoon nap time sitting on the back porch, following Ray's orders. Searching hidden crevices of memory, she'd conjured up everyone she'd come in contact with in New York in the past year. If there was even the most remote chance they might be the stalker, she'd listed their name, as detailed a description as she could come up with and anything else she knew about them.

Tomorrow Ray would fax the names to Detective Cappan. He could check the ones she'd added since she'd given him the original suspect list and see if any one of them had a record. Ray would also fax the descriptions to his friend André in New Orleans. Ray wanted the drawings of possible suspects shown to everyone in the apartment building where she had lived. If someone had seen one of the men hanging around, either coming or going, they would have something to go on.

Anything would be miles ahead of where they were now.

Her list of possible suspects had grown. A few of her past clients, a couple of neighbors, an intern she'd fired for making unwanted advances to her secretary, a guy who worked at the deli by the office. Once she'd started, the list had grown, broadened to people she hadn't considered before.

The basic similarities were that they were all male. They all flirted, a little. They all looked at her in that

way men do when they want you to know they like
what they see. And none of them seemed nearly as
sick as the man who had sent the bizarre notes.

Bits and pieces from the notes he'd left stabbed
their way into her mind, impervious to the miles that
hopefully separated her from the man who knew more
about her than any lover she'd ever known. Descriptions of the way she looked after her shower, her wet
hair dripping onto the tattered blue robe. Sensual details about the fragrance she wore, the way she shook
her hair under the dryer, the way she applied creams
to her face and body.

She stopped beneath a tree, her chest closing tight,
stealing her breath. If she ever saw this man, surely
she would recognize him. Evil that strong had to leave
its mark, must surely haunt the eyes.

The police disagreed with her, telling her it could
be anyone. More than likely, he would blend into a
crowd, one of the masses. But she couldn't buy it.
She'd felt him, not his touch, but his aura. It had been
cold, dark, frightening.

The way it had been last night at the flower shop.
She shivered and tugged her sweater tighter. Maybe
the feeling wasn't reliable after all. It was almost as
if *he* were here now, behind a bush, on the other side
of the fence, maybe in the boathouse. But he wasn't.
The watch he'd stolen from Roling had hit the pawnshop today.

Which meant *he* had to be in New York and she
was freaking out again. She started walking, slowly,
still deep in thought. Blake put up a howl. She
stopped and bent to kiss his pudgy little cheek. "So,
you like speed, do you?"

He waved his hands at her and managed to throw

his bear over the high sides of the wagon. She picked him up and brushed a giant magnolia leaf from his tummy. The bear hairs were a little damp from his overboard experience, but fortunately he'd missed the mud.

"So, you want to play rough." She tickled Blake's stomach with the head of the soft bear, and he erupted in giggles. "And I guess you want action, too," she said, pulling Blair in on the fun. After a minute of play, she renewed the walk, heading down to the river, this time at a pace that kept the boys happy.

"Two babies and a pretty lady surrounded by the glories of nature. A Kodak moment."

Jodie's heart slammed into her chest like a runaway train. She spun around and stared in the direction the voice had come from, her fingers tightening around the walkie-talkie. "What do you want?" she asked, staring into a smiling face that peeked over the wooden fence.

"I'm sorry. I didn't mean to startle you. I just heard laughter and had to check it out. I'm glad I did. A pretty woman is always a refreshing sight." He stuck a hand over the fence, extended for her to shake. "My name's Greg Johnson."

She studied his eyes. They were brown, deep-set and huddled under thin blond brows, but no more evil than any other eyes she'd ever seen. Still, she ignored his outstretched hand and kept her distance. "What are you doing in the Mayans's backyard?"

"Getting a little fresh air. Admiring the view. I'm Miss Selda's new tenant. She gives me the run of the place, yard included, so I'm not trespassing, if that's why you're looking at me like I might be a gypsy out to kidnap you."

"I wasn't aware Miss Selda had a new tenant," she said, still watching his eyes.

"She does now. I moved in two days ago. She had a note posted on the bulletin board at the drugstore. I saw it, called her, and, as they say, the rest is history."

Jodie let her gaze move past the eyes. The man was slightly older than her, thirty-five or so. His ears were too big, his nose a little pointed, but the grin that spread over his face more than made up for the minor flaws. In her prestalker life, she would have instantly warmed up to him. Today, it was only frigid caution that ran through her blood. She searched her brain for a snatch of memory, something to let her know if she'd seen this man before.

"What are you doing in Natchitoches?" she asked, bending to pull Blair's cap down over his ears.

"Taking pictures. I was just thinking, you and the boys, down by the river, maybe in the motorboat. That would make a great shot for your Christmas cards."

"No." The word flew from her mouth.

"Okay, just a thought. I wasn't going to charge you."

"It's not that." She started to explain, but thought better of it. She studied his face again, memorizing the shape of his nose, the cut of his sun-bleached hair, the way his brows hung low. If nothing else, doing the descriptions for Ray had taught her that she was not nearly observant enough. This time she would be.

"Are they the kind of pictures you usually take, family photographs?" She fished for more facts.

"No. I'm a freelancer, which means I shoot anything someone will buy. I'm on my own for this assignment, though. A friend of mine and I are doing a book on Cane River plantations. Hopefully we can get an editor to bite on it.''

"Where are you from?" She tried to sound casual.

"Everywhere. Nowhere. I was homeless before it got all the press. This town a while, and then I move on. That way my photos don't have time to get stale.''

The wind picked up, whistling through the trees, like a woman moaning, or crying for help. Blair tried to stand up, impatient to be moving again. She resettled him in the wagon, handing him a stuffed raccoon Grams had sent him for his first birthday.

"Where was your last assignment?"

"Up north. They've already had their first snowstorm. I was glad to relocate. What about you?" he asked, his gaze raking across her.

Blair started to cry as if on cue. "I have to be going," she said. "My sons are getting hungry." She turned the wagon and started back toward the house.

"I hope to see you again, soon. After all, we're neighbors now."

"I don't have time to visit much."

"Yeah. I'll bet. Babies are a lot of work even when they don't come in pairs." He walked his side of the fence, keeping up with her. "Anyway, I'm glad we met. I was watching you this afternoon.''

"Why were you watching me?" Suspicion gnawed at her control.

"I can see your back porch from my room. The first time I'd looked out it was still raining. When I looked again, all I could see was your red hair, shining in the sun. I said to myself then, you should have been a hair model.''

"Thank you."

"It's not from a bottle, is it?"

"What?"

"The red. Your hair."

"No. Why do you ask?" She was walking faster now, but he was matching her stride, her on one side of the fence, him on the other. A wall of wood between them, instant communication on her hip, Ben somewhere nearby, so why was her heart beating like the drums in a hard rock recording?

"I like natural stuff," he answered. "You know, women who don't try to gussy up too much, fool men into thinking they're something they're not. Funny, but fake comes through in a photograph easier than it does in real life. Maybe because everything stops in a picture, suspended in time, forever. The image is still there even when the people are gone."

A door slammed, and Jodie looked to the house. Ray was there on the porch, watching her. She looked back to Greg Johnson, but the fence line was deserted. Her visitor had disappeared as quickly as he'd materialized.

Ray walked toward her, his unbuttoned suit jacket swinging with the rhythm of his gait, his tie already loosened and pulled away from his neck. Tall, familiar and confident. She took a deep and thankful breath. He had never looked better in his life.

HE YANKED THE TAB on the can of cola and took a long swig, letting the liquid roll down his throat. The last taste of powdery pills washed down with the cola. The medicine controlled the impulses that drove him, buried them beneath a thin layer of sanity. At least it was supposed to. But sometimes the feelings hit too hard, like a boxer delivering the killer blow. When that happened, the pills were useless.

He'd been on the verge of that yesterday, and it had made him make a costly mistake. He shouldn't have used Max Roling's credit card. Cops didn't worry about one woman with an admirer who didn't quite play by the rules. Murder was different.

But the impulses had taken over, and he had picked up the phone and ordered the flowers. The mistake had left him no alternative but to go to the florist shop last night. Destroy the order form with the card number and name so no one would be the wiser. And he'd done just that, though the fool woman had complicated matters, walking in seconds before he'd have been out the door.

He would have killed her to keep her quiet, if he hadn't been sure she was going to die anyway. A nice, natural heart attack, just like the others. Only this time, he wouldn't have had to waste his precious resources.

But the old broad was tough. Still, he was sure she couldn't have gotten a good look at him in the dark. At least, he was almost sure.

He took another long drag on the soda. Whiskey would have been better, but the pills didn't mix well with alcohol, and he had to stay focused, especially now.

Lay low. Just a man doing his job. He'd fooled everybody for years, and he would do it again. It was easy when he stayed focused, when he was the one in control. Amazingly easy.

He finished the drink and crushed the can between his fingers.

Jodie was a good girl, not like the others. Only a man was sleeping in her house. *If he ever found out the two of them had been together...*

Then it would be all over. For both of them. Even if the man wasn't defiling Jodie, it would be over soon, one way or another. It was time for him to make his move.

Chapter Six

Three days had passed since the arrival of the yellow roses. The cops had no news, police checks into the background of Selda's tenant had turned up zero and Gloria Bigger remembered nothing. Everything was back to the way it had been a few weeks ago except now Jodie was in Natchitoches instead of New York, waiting for the next horror to drop into her life.

"You're playing instead of eating," she said, picking up the spoon herself and coaxing Blair to open his mouth. Instead, his hand flew into the offering, sending the tiny green peas scattering across his tray.

Ray picked that opportune time to stroll into the kitchen. "Say, aren't you supposed to put the food in their mouths?"

"Very funny."

Not to be outdone, Blake put his lips together and blew, demonstrating a new noise he'd perfected in the last couple of days. Drool bubbled from his mouth and rolled down his chin as he banged his hands on the tray of his high chair.

"That's telling him, Blake," she said, pushing a slice of cooked carrot in front of him. "Now, open up and try this." He closed his lips tight.

"Can't say I blame you, Blake. I'd hold out for pizza." Ray walked to the kitchen counter and poured himself a cup of coffee. "Do you want a cup?" he asked, lifting his in Jodie's direction.

"No, I have my hands full right now. And after this it's bath time."

"It's a good thing. Either that or you'll need to hose them down." He dropped into the chair closest to hers. "How did you learn to do this mothering stuff? Do babies come with some secret set of instructions for parents only?"

"Trial and error." She gave up on the carrots and went back to the peas and baby food chicken. "Mostly error. Although, fortunately, there are lots of good books on raising children."

"You must have read them all when you found out you were getting double trouble."

She kept working, suddenly aware that Ray was watching her every movement. He was asking questions, but she was sure he didn't want truthful answers. "I panicked at first, but the idea grew on me."

"You do a good job. I've known women who couldn't handle one, and you take care of two like it was fun and games."

"It is fun. It's also lots of work."

"And no pay."

"Wrong." Blair stuck his finger out, reaching for her face, his own brand of intimacy. He touched her lips and she kissed his sticky fingertips. "I've never had this kind of reward from anything else I've ever done."

"Then, I'd say those are two very lucky kids."

"I'm the fortunate one, Ray. I can't imagine life without them." And he was the unlucky one. Except he had everything he'd ever said he wanted. He'd left Natchitoches behind and made it big in a city where the lights never dimmed and the party never stopped.

He talked a good story, but here he was back in town, helping his father out in an emergency and risking his life to protect hers. That reeked of responsibility. Maybe she'd misjudged him. Maybe he'd misjudged himself.

"You look worried. You're not thinking about Selda's new tenant again, are you?" he asked, scooting his chair out of the line of fire of a pea that shot from Blair's spoon.

"No. I was thinking that I could use some help bathing the boys. What are you doing for the next half hour?"

His face screwed into perplexed wrinkles, and his fingers circled the near empty mug nervously. He tilted his mug high, drinking the last drops of the coffee as if it had some power to save him from her impossible request. When he set it back on the table, the clacking of pottery on wood filled the room.

"Okay," he said, his eyes narrowed. "I'm game. But remember, I'm a novice at this."

Jodie felt tight fingers of anxiety circling her heart. What had she been thinking? Surely not that exposure to parenting would change Ray Kostner.

"Everyone's a novice the first time." She wiped a layer of sticky dinner remains from Blair's face. "And only the tough survive."

"You make this sound like some kind of test."

"Do I?" she asked.

"Yeah." Ray got up from his chair and walked over to stand beside her, the cocky half smile he'd perfected to irresistible levels, splitting his lips. He took Blair from her arms, his hands brushing her breasts in the process, an innocent touch that took her breath away.

"Why would I give you a test?" she asked, her voice catching on the question.

"I don't know. Maybe because you know I can't resist a challenge. Maybe you just want to see if I'm the coward around babies I told you I am." He turned his back before she had a chance to think of a worthy response.

She followed him up the stairs to the bathroom, a wriggling Blake tucked under her arms. Bath time with Ray Kostner. She had to be losing her mind. To him this was a new game, one you could leave behind when something more exciting came along. And she'd be left to deal with more painful memories.

Minutes later, the boys were naked and fastened into bath safety seats that kept them from climbing and falling in the slippery water. One child she might have handled without the seats. Two left her seriously shorthanded.

"Hey, this isn't so bad." Ray scooted a toy boat across the water, making putt-putt noises as the boys laughed and splashed.

Jodie soaped a soft baby cloth and handed it to him. "Then you're ready to advance to the actual cleaning stage."

Ray took the soapy cloth. "What do I do with this?"

"You scrub. Just pretend Blair's your Porsche and you're taking off a little road dust."

"You mean I have to treat this splash machine like he's gold?"

This time *she* splashed *him*. "He's a lot more valuable than that mass of metal and chrome you drive."

Ray flicked a stream of water in her direction. "Your mother's vicious," he teased, dabbing Blair's stomach with the soapy cloth. "But I'll pay her back later."

"I'm really worried. A man who can't handle bathing a small boy is no match for me."

"What do you mean, can't handle the job? We're doing just fine. Tell her, big boy."

"I don't know about the Porsche, but dabbing gently at a few exposed parts doesn't get it with little boys." She demonstrated the correct process, wiping Blake's face, getting the ears and under both chins while he tugged at the cloth and tried to wriggle out of her grasp. "You have to leave no spot untouched."

"No spot untouched, uh?" Ray's voice fell to a husky drawl.

His gaze raked across her, from the tip of her disheveled hair, down her water-splattered blouse to settle on her jeaned bottom that stuck out behind her as she knelt on the bath rug. Awareness sizzled inside her, and she wrung the cloth in her hands into a tight wad.

"Maybe we should try the bath routine again later, when the boys are in bed. I'll soap, you rinse."

Desire rose up inside her, sweet and choking. She pulled away. It was crazy to think like this. She had too much at stake here to let Ray take control of her feelings, building fires when he had no intention of staying around long enough to keep them burning.

If she let him, this would be New York all over again. Fun and games, only then it had been *sans* babies. They had laughed and played and made love in every corner of her tiny apartment. When the week was over, he had walked away without a backward glance. And she had been left with new life inside her, growing just beneath her breaking heart.

Blair splashed his hands across the surface of the water, and a spray of soap bubbles flew up and landed on the front of Jodie's blouse. Ray ran his fingers across the bubbles, scraping off a fluffy pile and flipping them back into the tub. The circle of dampness left by the dissolving bubbles gave her away. Her right nipple was hard and erect pushing at the lacy fabric of her bra and blouse.

He dabbed at the pinkish outline, massaging with the corner of a hand towel he'd dipped into the tub. The bathwater was only comfortably warm, but invisible steam rose between. Ray leaned closer, his eyes smoky with desire, his lips inches from hers.

When they touched, her breath rushed from her body, leaving her too weak, too dizzy to think. A shower of splashing water from Blake's hands hit her just in time. She lunged past Ray and grabbed a towel.

"They're clean enough," she said, her voice low and shaky.

"Too bad. I was just beginning to enjoy this."

"Good." Bending low to extract Blake from his seat, she lifted his dripping body and handed him to Ray. "If you like bath time, you'll love slipping these wriggling arms and legs into pajamas."

"*Undressing* was always my speciality."

Heat climbed her body and flushed her face as new images tangoed through her mind. A trail of clothes, hastily shed, leading to any surface big enough for two naked bodies. The sofa, the floor, the shower. Her mind reeled as she rescued Blair from the tub and started down the hall, Ray and Blake a step behind.

"Humpty Dumpty sat on a wall." Ray's boisterous rhyming echoed down the hall.

"Why, Ray, I didn't know they taught nursery rhymes in law school," she quipped, doing a poor imitation of a mother without worries.

"Oh, yeah. It's basic first-year trial procedure. Did Humpty really topple on his own, or was the wall's poor construction the reason for the fall?"

"And what was the verdict?"

"The jury's still out."

"I can identify with that."

Ray caught up with her as she reached the door. One arm around a wriggling Blair, he used the other to grab her elbow and pull her to a stop. "The jury is in on your case. The man is as good as caught, and he will be tried and convicted."

"You sound so sure." He was, of course, but he didn't know the way this man could move in and out of a building, an apartment, a bedroom without being seen. He didn't know the cold aura of terror this man carried as a shield.

"I am sure." His fingers trailed down her arm. "I've made mistakes before. This time I won't."

Mistakes, flaws, limitations. Easy excuses that got him off the hook, let him walk away from responsibility, let him pick and choose when and how much to risk.

She watched Blake climb Ray's chest, his red head bobbing up and over his father's shoulder, a father he and his brother might never get the chance to love.

And that might be Ray's biggest mistake of all.

Her heart constricted. The last thing she wanted for

her boys was a father who'd turn his back on them, taint their lives with rejection, poison their self-confidence with denial.

She hugged Blair to her, her lips burying in the whisper soft baby hair. She loved her boys so much she had to protect them at all costs from any source of danger or heartbreak. That was the only fact she was sure of.

That and the knowledge that she couldn't let Ray tear the heart from her again.

JODIE PULLED A light yellow sweater over her head and smoothed it over the top of her brown flannel skirt. The temperature was hovering in the high fifties, and in Natchitoches that constituted sweater weather. Cotton, of course. Wool was about as useful to Louisianians as steak to a vegetarian.

Bending at the waist, Jodie let her hair fall free, fluffing it with her hands and then straightened to a standing position. Loose curls bounced around her shoulders, falling into casual disarray, wild, the way Ray liked it. A quick stroke of blush and a swipe of bronze lipstick finished her grooming routine.

Turning sideways, she checked her profile in the full-length oval mirror that swung from a frame of cherry. Not bad for the mother of twins, she acknowledged, running her fingers along the smooth lines of her stomach. She was five pounds less than her pre-pregnancy size.

Too bad her petite figure had only worked against her. Another trait the stalker found appealing. It was spelled out in one of his notes, in red, and in words that still sent icy shivers through her.

She hugged her arms about her. A week ago, she'd

just begun to relax, to believe that moving to Natchitoches had been the solution she searched for.

But now she was walking the tightrope again. The only difference was that this time she was never alone. Ben was nearby during the day and well into the night, under orders from Ray not to leave until he arrived.

Which was getting later and later. She might have enlisted his aid in bathing the boys once, but, as always, Ray had his own priorities, and they obviously didn't include baby-sitting.

The last two nights he'd arrived at Grams's house after the boys were asleep, and he'd dressed and disappeared in the mornings without stopping in the kitchen for more than a fast cup of coffee.

Jodie suspected he'd have preferred to have had that in his dad's law offices if he'd been sure Grams wouldn't have followed him down there to make sure he drank one of hers. She was upset enough he wouldn't binge on bacon and eggs and other artery-choking breakfasts.

Ray Kostner, man of the hour, ready to play. Ready to boss and protect. Her guess was his hour was up and he was sorry he'd ever jumped into the macho male protector role. Maybe he'd tell her that this afternoon after they visited the hospital.

Finally, Gloria's doctors had agreed to let their recovering patient have visitors outside the immediate family and the police. Detective Butch Deaton had spoken with Gloria once. He'd left her bed convinced Gloria had been alone in the shop when her heart had dived into a state of massive shutdown.

He'd delivered the message to Jodie in person, staying for dinner at Grams's invitation, assuring them both that he was watching the house even though the evidence pointed to the stalker's being in New York.

Jodie wished she shared his certainty. But if he was wrong, if the stalker had been at the florist shop that night, then his face might be embedded somewhere in Gloria Bigger's subconscious. All they had to do was pull the description out of her, and she could put a face to the formless monster.

A last glance in the mirror, and Jodie decided to tie her hair back from her face. Ray liked it flying loose, and she had no desire to ignite desire. She'd make sure he knew she was with him only because he had insisted on bullying his way back into her life, not to set a husband trap.

She slid open the top drawer of the dresser. The usually neat stack of scarves were fluffed instead of folded, as if someone had tossed them and let them parachute into place. Ice water coursed her veins.

Trembling, she clutched the top edge of the dresser for support. She was overreacting. The stalker couldn't have been here in her bedroom. They had been home every day. But even as she whispered the denial, she knew her words were a lie.

She ran her fingers beneath the scarves, searching until they encountered the prickly edge of the scrap of paper she knew she'd find. She pulled it out, her heart racing, blood rushing to her head in dizzying spurts.

This time the note was a Valentine, homemade from red construction paper and a thin parchment doily. The words were written in red ink. She forced her gaze to fasten on them, shimmying as they were between her shaking fingers.

Roses are red
My heart is blue
Don't run away again
Or you'll pay the price, too

Pay the price, too. Like Roling. Her insides churned sickeningly. A man who killed for no reason except some sickness that festered in his mind, and he had been here, in this room. Steps away from her sons. Steps away from Grams.

But the killer wanted her.

The hinges on the door creaked behind Jodie, and she spun around. Ben stood in the shadow of the door, watching her. He stepped inside and closed the door behind him.

Jodie stuffed the note in the front pocket of her slacks. "You frightened me, Ben." She struggled to steady her voice. "Is something the matter?"

"Yea, ma'am. I need to talk to you."

His gaze darted about the room, and he fingered a baseball cap, bending the soiled bill, the muscles in his arms strained as if it were a task worthy of his strength. Her heart beat erratically.

"Has something happened? Did you see someone?"

"Oh, no ma'am. It's nothing like that. It's just, well, it's my son, Grady."

"Grady?" She tried to focus on Ben's words instead of the fear that twisted inside her. "Is he sick again?"

"No. It's not that. But he's here."

"In the house?" Her mind skittered crazily over every frightening possibility.

"No, of course not. In Natchitoches."

"You mean he's back for a visit?"

"No. He's packed up and left New York. Moved back in my place. Says he got fired and couldn't afford to pay his half of the rent up in Brooklyn. I think his roommate kicked him out, though he wouldn't admit it. He always defends those so-called friends of his."

She shook her head. "But he didn't live in Brooklyn. He lived in Pittsburgh."

"Not for six months or more. Didn't Miss Emily tell you?"

"No, she must have forgotten. Are you saying that you were in New York all the time you were out of town?"

"Yes ma'am. I thought you knew."

"Why didn't you call me, Ben? Why didn't you visit me?"

"I don't cotton to those subways much." He stared at the carpet. "Besides, you didn't ask me to."

"I didn't know you were in town. When did Grady arrive in Natchitoches?" she asked, her mind whirling with frightening suspicions.

"A few days ago. He needs a job."

She knew what Ben was after, but the last thing she wanted was his son hanging around the house. There was little chance he was the stalker, but she couldn't take even little chances. "Maybe he can find employment in town," she suggested, trying to sound positive.

"Yes, ma'am. Maybe so."

"With the Festival of Lights preparations in full swing and the Christmas tourists about to invade, I'm sure there are several local businesses that can use some extra personnel."

He looked at her doubtfully, and shrugged his shoulders.

"Any other time, Ben. But things are not going well." She reached in her pocket and wrapped her fingers around the note. Her flesh crawled and her hands grew clammy. The madman had held this same note in his hands. Maybe minutes ago.

"What is it, Miss Jodie? You look like a ghost's walking over your grave."

"The stalker. He was here, Ben, in this room."

"He couldn't have been. I was here all the time, Miss Jodie. I had the walkie-talkie on every second."

"I'm not blaming you, Ben," she said quickly. "It's no one's fault. It's always like this. He moves silently, invisibly, like a phantom."

"What do you want me to do, Miss Jodie?"

"I need you to stay here in the house with Grams and the boys while I go to the hospital to see Gloria Bigger. I wouldn't go now, but it's necessary."

"I won't leave them for a second."

"I don't know what we'd do without you, Ben."

"With all Miss Emily's done for me over the years, I'm just glad to be on the doing end for a change. Besides, I like you a whole bunch, Miss Jodie. You know that."

He studied his shoes. "I was wondering, Miss Jodie, do you think I could bunk in the boathouse for a while? That way I'd be here on the premises all the time, and Mr. Kostner could just come and go like he wanted. He wouldn't have to come around at all when he was working late."

Unexpected disappointment settled in her stomach, cold and hard. It was so like Ray to weasel out of a responsibility she'd never asked him to take on. "Is this Ray's idea?'' Her words came out rougher than she intended, more like an accusation.

"No, ma'am. I haven't even talked to him about this. I know he's helping out around here now, but I don't see as where I live is any of his business.''

A little resentment leaked from his tone. It took Jodie by surprise. It was out of character for Ben, at least out of the character he showed around her. Maybe Ben ran a lot deeper than the easygoing surface he displayed when she was around.

"I haven't talked to Miss Emily, either.'' He shuffled his feet and twisted the cap in his hand. "Not yet, anyway. I thought I'd ask you first. Truth is I was thinking about moving in the boathouse anyway, before I knew you were moving back home. That was if Miss Emily didn't object. She needs someone to keep an eye on her, what with her memory coming and going like fireflies on a starry night.''

"And she's very lucky to have you looking out for her. It's fine with me if you move in. I'm sure it would be fine with Grams, too. But what about your son? He might not be too happy about your running off and leaving him.''

"Not that boy. He don't care a good two cents about my company. It's the freebies he's here for. I don't fool myself. Not anymore. He don't have no more use for me than his momma did.''

"In that case, we'd love having you. If you need anything, we can raid the attic. There's enough furniture up there to fill a couple of plantation homes.''

"I don't need a thing. Those old bunk beds that used to be in your room are out there. A TV, too. And Miss Emily put a microwave out there last winter so's I could warm my lunch and make me some of that instant hot chocolate when my old bones got chilled. And if I get a notion to do more than open a can or two, why that old range your grandpa used to fry fish on still works. They don't make 'em like that any more.''

"Then it sounds like you're all set."

The purr of Ray's engine drifted through the open window. "I have to go now, Ben. Just watch the boys and Grams until I get back. And if anything happens, anything at all, call Butch Deaton at once." She scribbled down a couple of phone numbers. "The top one's his office, the bottom one's his beeper."

"Did you tell him the stalker's been here?"

"No, but I will. I'll call from Ray's car phone."

"Take care, Miss Jodie. A woman like you, so pretty and sweet. You can't trust a man. Not any man."

"I'll take care, Ben. But I do trust some men. I trust you."

She gave him a quick hug and walked to the boys' room. Before she left the house, she needed a second alone with them. She was the one the stalker wanted, and there was no reason to believe he'd hurt her children. Still, even the thought of his evil invading their lives filled her heart with overwhelming dread.

She couldn't sit back and wait any longer. The note beneath the scarves had robbed her of that choice.

Chapter Seven

Jodie climbed into the passenger seat of Ray's car without waiting for him to play gentleman. He slid under the wheel and started the motor.

"You look upset," he said, backing out of the driveway and into the street.

"I had a visitor today."

"Who was that?"

"The stalker."

He turned to face her, deep grooves forming in his forehead. "What happened?"

She told him the story of finding the note. He let her talk uninterrupted, the muscles in his arms straining the fabric of his shirt, the veins in his neck and face popping out like the lines on a road map. A car pulled in front of him, and he slammed on the brakes, a string of curses flying from his lips. She was sure the car had not provoked his fury.

"How did he get inside the house without being seen or heard?"

"If I knew that I could stop him." She reached for the cellular phone. "I have to call Butch Deaton. I'm supposed to tell him at the first sign of the stalker."

Ray listened while she shared the story again, but

this time he reached over and wrapped his hand around hers.

"Tell him to get someone out there on the double. Check every door and window for forced entry. And comb every inch of your bedroom for fingerprints."

She repeated his directions into the phone.

"Who's coaching you, Jodie? It wouldn't be Ray Kostner, would it?"

"Ray and I are on the way to the hospital to talk to Gloria Bigger."

"I've already talked to her. She doesn't remember anything about that night."

"I know, Butch. But I'll feel better if I talk to her myself."

"I understand. I know how tough this is on you. We'll find the man, Jodie. I'll have a crime scene team at your house in minutes."

"I appreciate that."

"I'll get back with you later today. And don't worry about a thing. The NYPD might not have caught him, but we will."

She finished the conversation and hung up the phone as Ray swerved into the hospital parking lot.

The harsh odors of disinfectants blended with the sweet smells of gladioli and daisies as Jodie and Ray stepped into the hospital room. Sunlight peeked through half-open blinds, creating lined patterns of shadows on the bleached white bedsheets and the chrome of the side railings.

"Company. It's about time." Gloria greeted them from an almost upright position, propped as she was on three pillows. Her face was a pasty hue, her eyes encircled by gray layers of puckered skin.

Jodie stopped, knowing she shouldn't stare, but unable to look away. She'd run into Gloria at the check-out counter of Wal-Mart a couple of weeks ago. That image haunted her now. Then Gloria had been the picture of health, a chubby middle-aged matron full of gossip and glowing comments about the twins.

"How are you?" Jodie asked, stepping closer and taking Gloria's hand.

"Too puny to be half as ornery as I like, but I'm getting there."

A smile wrapped around Jodie's heart. The woman might be weak, but the zest for living was still there.

"You were never ornery," Ray said, flashing a smile and his charm. "Belligerent at times, but never ornery. You managed to control me in Sunday School for a couple of years if I remember correctly."

Gloria scooted up higher in the bed, her thin lips breaking into a smile. "That's an attorney for you. Always changing your words to say the same thing in a different way, just so no one knows what they're talking about. His dad's the same way."

The three of them chatted for a few minutes, the way people do who've known each other's families for all their lives but have never been close, touching the surface of safe topics. Today, the talk was mostly about doctors and their fading bedside manners and about the growing size of injection needles.

It was ten minutes into the visit before Ray managed to steer the conversation into focus. "Did anything unusual happen at the shop the night you had your coronary?"

"You mean besides nearly dying?"

"That was bad enough, I know, but did something happen to frighten you before the attack?"

"To tell you the truth, I don't remember much of

anything that happened that night. I know I was going there to meet the two of you, something about a ticket you wanted me to check. Did you find it?''

"No, but that's okay." Jodie scooted to the front edge of the uncomfortable chair. "We think someone might have been in the shop that night when you got there. Do you remember seeing anyone?"

A dark shadow robbed the light from Gloria's eyes. Shivering she hugged her arms across her chest.

Jodie felt the same chill that inundated Gloria, but this time the cold was heated with hope. "Don't be afraid, Gloria. Just tell us if someone was there."

"I'm not afraid. Never have been. But this medicine. It makes you dream, you know, strange things. A man stealing your breath away, an ambulance that never reaches the hospital. The weirdest images pop into my head, but I can't give them credence."

"What kind of images?" Jodie's pulse was racing now, and she had to keep Gloria talking.

"Last night I could have sworn someone slipped into my room, and told me he had to kill me. I woke up screaming."

"You mean someone tried to kill you here, in your hospital room?"

"No, honey. It's the medicine. Dr. Creighton says it makes people imagine all kinds of things."

"But what about at the flower shop? You weren't taking medicine or having nightmares then. Was someone there?" Desperation clawed at Jodie's insides. "Did you see someone in your shop?"

"No. I don't even remember seeing you and Ray, but I'm sure glad you showed up when you did."

Ray walked over to stand behind Jodie. He massaged her shoulders, but the tight coils of pressure didn't loosen. She couldn't walk away again empty-handed.

"I'm trying to find someone Gloria." She struggled to keep her voice calm. "I think he's the one who ordered the bouquet of flowers from you, the yellow roses you delivered to me at Grams's house. I think he might have even broken into your shop."

"Why would he do a thing like that? I sent the flowers just like he said. Well, now that's not exactly true. He wanted red roses, but I was fresh out. But the yellow ones were nice, and I even found a card with a heart on it. He was bound and determined the card have a heart on it somewhere."

"Did he say why?"

"No. He had a nice voice, though, real friendly like. I think he likes you."

Jodie rubbed a stabbing pain in her right temple. It was time to try a new tack. "What did the man in your dream look like, the one who tried to strangle your breath away?" She was clutching for any shred of hope now, but she couldn't leave without trying everything. It was possible the fear she wasn't ready to face consciously was manifesting itself in her dream.

"I don't know. Nightmares, they're more a feeling than a movie, at least mine are. A bunch of shadowy images that make you wake up shaking."

"But was he tall? What color was his hair?"

Gloria shook her head, and squinted her eyes half shut. "I don't know. Officer Deaton asked me the same thing. I told him I don't remember a thing, but I promised to call him immediately if I do."

"Then we have the bases covered." Ray tightened his grip on Jodie's shoulders. "We'll go now, Miss

Gloria, and let you get some rest, hopefully the non-nightmare kind.''

"I've had enough rest. That's all they let you do in this place.''

"For good reason, so you'll get well fast. Your doctor already warned us not to wear you out.'' Ray took Jodie's hand and led her to the door. She managed a proper goodbye and kept a semblance of calm until the door shut behind them.

"He was there,'' she said, when they were out of Gloria's earshot. "I could see it in Gloria's eyes when we first asked if she'd seen someone in her shop that night.''

"All I saw was confusion.''

"No. He was there. For some reason, she's blocked it from her mind. Or maybe the medicine has.''

"We'll find him, Jodie. I faxed the names of your possible suspects to Cappan and your descriptions to the artist in New Orleans. He wants to talk to you about a couple of them. We can call him from my office.''

She rubbed a spot between her temples, fighting the beginning of a headache that threatened to be a zinger.

Ray dropped an arm around her shoulders. "Are you okay?''

"I'm disappointed.'' She leaned for a second, needing the support of his strength.

"A description from Gloria would have been nice. But, don't worry, baby, it'll be over soon.''

Baby. An arm around her shoulder. All the right actions, from the wrong kind of man. "You don't have to do any of this, Ray. I've told you before. It's not your battle.''

"You're wrong. I do have to do it.''

"Why?"

"You need me."

She pulled away. "I never told you that."

"I know. You're too stubborn." He took her hand and tugged her along at a snail's pace. "Right now you're even doing a good *imitation* of a mule."

"Just take me home, Ray. You can pick up your things and move back into your own home. You can go on with your life."

"My life right now is protecting you. And I'm taking you back to my office. We have a killer to catch."

"WHAT ABOUT THIS MAN?"

Kostner was grilling, falling into his lawyer routine, and he could tell Jodie was rebelling. Her responses were growing so sharp, he could feel the prick. But he had to get to the bottom of this for both their sakes. She was in danger of losing her life.

He was in danger of ruining his, of making a colossal mistake, by falling for Jodie Gahagen so hard he'd never be able to walk away. He'd escaped by the skin of his teeth before. Yet the second he was near her, his well-rehearsed inhibitions flew out the window.

He tapped the eraser end of his pencil on the description she'd labeled number five. Dark hair cut short, medium build, in his early twenties. Nice-looking. He asked his question again, rephrasing it slightly. "What's your contact been with this man?"

"We've been over his description before. We've been over all the descriptions before, several times." She uncrossed her right leg and crossed her left, this time swinging her foot toward him.

"We talked about him, but you didn't say much.

All I have in my notes about this guy is a two-sentence description and the fact that he works at a deli by your office.''

"It *was* my office. Past tense. And you don't have any more about him because that's all there is. He flirts with me when I buy fresh fruit. Innocent flirting. He does the same with every female. You told me to list every possible suspect. I did.''

"You overlooked one.''

"The mayor of New York City? We don't run in the same circles.''

"So how about your sons' father? You must have run in the same circles with him, a least for a while.''

She stopped swinging her leg. Her brows drew together, and her eyes shot daggers. Just like earlier, the mere mention of the boys' father put her on edge. There was a story there, but Ray wasn't sure he wanted to hear it.

Either the man was a complete jerk, and Jodie had found out in time not to marry him or he was the biggest fool in the world. He'd walked away from one of the best catches of all time. Gorgeous, smart, good sense of humor, at least most of the time. And so sexy she could heat a room to boiling point in thirty seconds flat.

Ray let out a heated breath. Maybe the boys' father was only runner-up to the biggest fool in the world. Still, it wasn't as if Ray had walked away without reason. He was just smart enough to know he didn't fill the bill as husband or father material. He couldn't be counted on when the going got rough. He'd proved it one time too many.

His dad's secretary buzzed in from the outer office. He switched the speaker on.

"You told me I could have the afternoon off for my grandson's birthday party. I'll be leaving in about five minutes. Do you need anything before I go?"

"Not that I can think of, Barbara." At least not anything she knew how to do. A one-man law office with no paralegals. One secretary, one part-time student research assistant. Life in the dark ages. "Enjoy yourself."

"I will."

The interruption over, he zeroed in again. "Back to the subject of the boys' father. Ex-lovers are at the head of the suspect heap when you're trying to identify a mystery stalker, Jodie. You know that."

"The boys' father is not a suspect."

"Were you in love with him?" God, where did that question come from? Not only was it irrelevant, it was none of his business. And Jodie would mince no words in telling him so. She'd probably march out the door as well.

"Yes."

The answer caught him off guard, pounding him squarely in the gut with the force of a boxer's punch. Her gaze was fixed on him, her eyes smoky, but not with anger. He wished it had been. Anger, hate, anything but the dark, hazy passion he saw swimming in their depths.

The same look she'd given him time and again during his week in New York City, always after they were quiet and spent, his love still inside her, his arms still wrapped around the curves of her seductive body.

Today the look was for someone else. Someone who had come into her life within weeks after he'd left. While he was in New Orleans trying to get her out of his mind, some other guy was...

Tension crawled Ray's spine, tightening every nerve and muscle into painful knots. And he had asked for this kind of misery.

"I think we've covered enough for one day." He yanked open the top drawer of his desk and slammed the legal pad he'd been making notes on inside. "I'll drive you home and then come back here and try to finish up before midnight." He stood up and grabbed his suit coat from the back of his chair. "Trying to keep my career afloat while taking care of Dad's is a major effort."

"Sit back down, Ray. Now it's my turn to talk."

He didn't sit. It wasn't his style to be equal with a sparring partner, and from the tone of Jodie's voice, a big-time confrontation was brewing. Instead he leaned against the front edge of his desk, his suit jacket hooked on a thumb swung over his shoulder, his gaze locked with hers.

"There's absolutely no reason for you to continue to stay at Grams's house," she continued, her shoulders straight as a lamppost, and just as unyielding. "Not only are the police going to watch the house now that they know the stalker is a murderer, but Ben is moving into the boathouse."

"When did this develop?"

"This afternoon, right before you picked me up."

"Does my being there bother you that much, Jodie?"

"How could it? I never see you. Since I asked you to help with the boys the other night, you've managed to stay away until we're all fast asleep. I don't blame you. You never know about these single mothers and the traps they lay to get a husband."

"Is that what you think?" His hands gripped the

edge of the desk. "That I've been staying away because I didn't want to be with you?"

"What else was there for me to think?"

What else? The truth. That the more he saw her, the more he wanted her. That every nerve in his body, and a few parts that didn't classify as nerves grew hard just thinking about her in the next room, dressed in some clingy little nightie, her body stretched across a crisp white sheet, her hair falling like fire over shoulders as soft as fresh cream.

He left his desk and walked over to the office door, turning the lock.

"What are you doing?"

"Come here, and I'll show you. I don't want there to be any more confusion about why I don't come back to Miss Emily's at night until I'm so tired I can't think."

She stood up, but she didn't come closer. She didn't get the chance. Ray crossed the room in a split second, dropping his jacket on a chair as he went. His arms wrapped around her, pulling her close while his mouth sought her lips. The taste of her rocketed through him, bringing him alive deep in his soul.

Her lips parted beneath his, warm, loving, the Jodie he remembered from a hundred sleepless nights. Nights when hours of New Orleans revelry had dimmed his wit but not his memories. Nights when every sound, every smell, every female voice reminded him of Jodie Gahagen and one week in New York City.

The memories merged with the present. His hands skimmed her back, his fingers digging into the threads of the soft sweater. Her body was supple, soft and yielding, but her mouth was hot and demanding. Her tongue pushed its way between his lips, seeking out his own and the dark recesses of his mouth.

Breathless, he pulled his mouth away, but not his body. "This is why I stayed away, Jodie. Why I can't see you except in public places." He buried his face in her hair. "Because I can't be around you without wanting you like this."

She swallowed his words with her mouth. "Want me, Ray. Want me like this. I'm tired of fear and running. Tired of men who sneak through closed doors and hide behind notes and gifts." She trembled against him. "I need to be held, to be loved, like this."

He drowned in her kiss, and all he could think about was wanting more. His hands slipped under her sweater. The first touch of his fingers to her heated skin sent shock waves coursing through him. He worked at the clasp of her bra until it let her breasts fall loose, soft mounds of flesh resting against him. His thumbs circled the nipples, pink and perfect and berry hard.

It was the wrong place, the wrong time, but he was powerless to stop himself. He worked his lips down her neck, and then touched them to her breasts. She moaned, soft gurgling cries that tore at him, releasing new waves of desire so primal he had to take his hands off of her or take her right there. He backed her against the wall, his body against hers, his hands pushing into the painted wood above her shoulders.

Jodie came up for air only to tear at the buttons on his shirt, pulling them loose and pushing the fabric aside until she could rake his bare chest with her fingertips. Each touch was like flames licking at his self control. If they'd been anywhere else but his office…

"I want you, Ray. Now. This minute." Her words were more demand than pleadings.

"In a law office?" Doubts shook from his lips.

"The door's locked."

True. And the way he felt right now he could take her on Front Street with the whole town looking on. He lifted her in his arms and carried her to the desk, setting her down on the edge. With one free arm, he swept his hand across the polished surface, raking papers and folders into a pile at one end, more than a few falling to the carpet.

His fingers fumbled with the buttons of her blouse, hers with his zipper. Somewhere deep in his mind, he knew he was breaking the rules he'd set, forgetting the boundaries. But somewhere else, somewhere much closer to his heart, he was following dictates that couldn't be ignored.

Moments later, Jodie's cries filled the room, and he exploded inside her.

His strength returned slowly. Finally, he moved, stretching to an upright position and yanking his trousers into place. It was then he heard the sound, slight, like muffled movement in the outer office. Tilting his head, he listened, but there was nothing more.

Overactive nerves, he guessed, as Jodie stirred beside him, the smoky look he remembered so well dancing in her eyes. And this time it was all for him.

Chapter Eight

"You should have seen the man. He was a sight. Out in my backyard on his all fours shooting a picture of a regular old armadillo like he was on some African safari."

"That's some tenant you got yourself this time, Selda. Next thing you know he's liable to stick that camera in the wrong animal's face. He'll be coming in smelling like a polecat and you'll have to fumigate the whole upstairs."

Jodie only half listened to the two women's conversation and laughter. Selda and Grams had been neighbors ever since Selda had married, over thirty years ago. They'd hugged and cried through the deaths of both husbands, bonding the way only women who've celebrated and suffered together can.

Selda was twenty years younger than Grams, spry as a fox before the hunt, and she kept a keen eye out for her neighbor. There wasn't much they didn't know about each other, but every time they got together, they still gossiped and giggled like a couple of teenage girls.

Jodie smiled in spite of herself. In a world of constant change, it was nice to know some things never varied. Emily and Selda definitely fit into the latter category.

"Did you meet him yet, Jodie? Jodie?"

"I'm sorry, Selda, did you say something to me?"

"My word, child, your mind must be a thousand miles away. I was just asking if you'd met my new tenant yet. He's a nice-looking guy. A Yankee, but you're used to those northern men, you might like him."

"I met him a few days ago." Jodie looked up from her position on the sitting room floor. One twin was climbing over her, the other was pulling apart a string of colored plastic links. "But don't get any matchmaking ideas," she added.

"Well, of course not. I wouldn't think of it. Would you, Emily?"

"I don't know. He'd have to be a sight better than having a lawyer in the family. I keep telling her don't get mixed up with the likes of Ray Kostner. Too handsome for his own good."

Reverse psychology. Jodie wasn't fooled for a minute. Grams smiled like a Cheshire cat the minute Ray appeared, and she'd like nothing better than seeing her granddaughter married to the man. If she knew what Jodie had done a couple of afternoons ago in the Kostner law office...

No, she'd never believe it.

Jodie stretched her legs, and the gentle ache in her thighs reminded her of something else that never changed. The way she felt about Ray Kostner.

Not that she needed a reminder. The man who'd eaten, drunk, slept, laughed and loved in her apartment for a week two years ago was alive and well, and had crept back into her life. And either he was as crazy about her as she was about him or he did the best imitation she'd ever witnessed.

But no matter how he felt about her, it didn't alter facts. When he finished helping her and his dad out of their respective jams, he'd walk away again just like he had before.

Marriage, commitment, family life, they simply weren't part of his future. Neither were two of life's most wonderful blessings. She reached down and picked up Blake, hugging his lively body to her before letting him wriggle out of her clutches.

Her babies needed a father, a willing father, one who loved them unconditionally. The way love had surrounded her growing up, constant and reinforcing, a buffer for all of life's blows. And when the small plane had gone down robbing her of her parents, her grandmother had stepped in, opening her arms so wide, Jodie had become lost in their comfort. So lost, she was able to find herself again, secure in knowing that was what her parents would have wanted.

She leaned back on her elbows and watched the boys, one of them half crawling, half scooting across the carpet, the other tasting a plastic link to see if it could measure up to ice cream. Both totally adorable.

Her stomach churned, the familiar tension-induced indigestion that didn't respond to antacids. She'd tried to tell Ray about his sons when she'd learned she was pregnant. He'd refused to return her phone calls, breaking her heart in the process. She'd tried again when they were born, and again the night the stalker had laid his murderous hands on Blake.

When she'd finally found the courage to tell him outright that he was the father of her sons, he'd refused to believe her, preferring to think she'd lie than to believe he had fathered two magnificent boys.

The pain stabbed at her again, a dull knife pricking at an old wound. When Ray was with her, holding her in his arms, she saw only what she wanted to see, only what her heart would let her see. And that was the greatest tragedy of all, that she could love so completely a man who could only play at love.

But life wasn't a steak you could order prepared to your taste. She didn't want a stalker either, but nonetheless a madman was wrecking her life. Grams didn't want to lose her memory and her vitality, but the years were still taking their toll.

She and Grams were measuring up when they had to. Maybe, underneath the facade of money and glory, Ray had enough strength to do what was right, too.

"Jodie, honey, would you mind giving that pot of vegetable soup on the burner a stir? And add a little salt and pepper to it. I haven't put the seasonings in yet. Selda and I'll keep an eye on the boys."

This time Jodie heard the request. "I'll be happy to," she said, standing up and starting for the door. She padded down the carpeted hall in her stockinged feet.

The aroma hit her as she lifted the lid of the big stew pot, mouthwatering odors that took her back to being ten and ravenous, visiting Grams's house for summer vacation, running in from playing ball or jumping rope. Corn, okra, green beans, carrots, all picked in the summer from the vegetable patch Ben tended behind the house and frozen or canned by Selda and Grams.

She took a soupspoon and ran it across the top, scooping up a sampling of the bubbling liquid and blowing across it to keep it from burning her mouth. It was always better to taste Grams's concoctions before adding seasonings. Sometimes she forgot salt and pepper altogether, sometimes she gave it a double dose.

The hot juices washed over her tongue, a medley of flavors. And seasoned just right.

The doorbell jangled loudly, and Jodie jumped nearly from her skin, dropping the lid back onto the pot with an unmelodic clang. Grams hadn't mentioned expecting company. Her fingers stroked the walkie-talkie at her waist, caution running along every nerve. Better to be safe than sorry."

"Ben, are you there?" The seconds of silence seemed like minutes.

"I'm here, Miss Jodie. Do you need me?"

"No. Someone's at the door, but I'm sure it's nothing to worry about. I just wanted to make sure this thing works."

"It's working just fine. I'm out at the boathouse washing up, but if you need me, just give a holler."

"I will. Thanks, Ben."

"No trouble, Miss Jodie. Nothing I do for you is a mite of trouble."

Jodie headed for the door, but Grams beat her to it. She was already ushering in Butch Deaton, making a fuss over him the way she did anyone who stopped by, her southern hospitality in top form.

"Well, of course you're not inconveniencing us. You just come right on in. Selda and I were just having a cup of tea. Could I get you one?"

"No, ma'am. I just stopped in to talk to Jodie for a few..."

He'd spotted her coming down the hall before he finished his sentence.

"Anything new?" she asked, not daring to hope for much.

"A few developments. Can we talk in private?"

"I'll stay here and help Emily with the boys. You talk as long as you need to," Selda offered without waiting to be asked.

Jodie thanked her and led Butch out to the back porch, although she wasn't sure how private it was. Selda's tenant might be perched at his upstairs window doing his voyeurism routine. But unless Butch planned on yelling, he wouldn't be able to hear their conversation.

"We don't have a match back on the prints taken from the dresser," Butch said as the screen door closed behind them. "But they were all small, probably yours or Grams's."

"So we're nowhere."

"Pretty much. I talked to Cappan this afternoon. It seems like he's been doing a lot of conversing with Ray Kostner." A frown pulled at his lips, and his eyebrows bunched.

"Ray said they've talked. I'm sure Cappan will tell you the same things he tells him."

"I don't know why he's telling Kostner anything. He's a lawyer, not an officer of the law. He doesn't have a damn bit of authority. Pardon my French, Jodie, but it makes me madder than hell. The man's not even a local lawyer. He's just here on a little vacation, helping his dad out in an emergency."

She put her hand up to silence his tirade. "Look, Butch, if you have a fight with Cappan or Kostner, take it up with them. I have enough problems."

"I'm sorry, Jodie. You're right. But you know how Kostner is. Ever since he substituted for me and took you to your senior prom, he acts like he owns you. I'm tired of his trying to hog the ball."

"Well, I guess you'll just have to take it away from him and run with it yourself," she said, her patience so thin she considered breaking all of Grams's hospitality rules and throwing him out. "To tell you the truth, Butch, I don't care who runs with it. I just don't want it dropped. I have too much at stake. Do you understand?"

"Of course, I understand. I'm the detective in charge here. But I don't want Kostner messing things up."

"They're already *messed* up." She bit her tongue. Jumping down Butch's throat wouldn't help matters. Still, at times like this, she longed for the anonymity she'd had in New York. A world where she hadn't dated the cop in charge of the investigation. A town where she'd never slept with the lawyer who'd decided to name himself as her public defender and bodyguard.

"Let's start over, Butch. Hello, it's good to see you. Now, is there anything else I need to know?"

"I'm afraid so. I hate to be the one to have to tell you."

Right. That's why he'd rushed right over. "Just tell me, Butch. I can take it."

"They picked up the man who hocked the watch. A young good-looking actor wanna-be who lives in the area around the pawnshop. Problem is, he's not our guy."

"But he had Max's watch."

"He told them he was walking home near daybreak

and just happened on the body. According to him, your friend Max was already dead. He couldn't do anything to help him, so he gave in to temptation. Grabbed a plastic bag from the corner trash bin and helped himself to the watch and a ring. He still had the ring when the police apprehended him.''

''What makes them think he's telling the truth?''

''He passed the lie detector test.''

''That can't be one hundred percent reliable.'' Frustration drained her spirits until she felt as if she'd been washed and wrung into twisted knots. ''How can they be sure he's not the man who's been stalking me, that he's not the one who killed Max?''

''You're not his type.''

''I'm a woman.''

''Bingo.''

She dropped into a chair, too limp to stand. Her best hope had just collapsed at her feet. Butch hooked a chair with one foot and dragged it next to hers. He sat down, too close, invading her space.

''He's not off the hook yet, but chances are slim he's the man. Cappan's not giving up, though. They're still watching the area around the apartment you moved out of. I don't know how they'd notice anybody new there, though. The place is crawling with strangers, some a lot stranger than others.''

She nudged the toe of her shoe against a splinter that had split away from the porch floorboards. ''How do you know about the area around my apartment?''

''You really know how to deflate a guy. I was there, last summer. I'd hoped you'd remember.''

She blew a rush of hot air out of her mouth. Goofed again. ''Sorry, Butch. I do remember. We went to dinner at Sardi's.''

"Yeah. All my life I'd heard of that place. You wore a black dress, with little cutouts at the waist, and a neckline that cut clear down to here." He reached over and ran a finger from her neck to the swell of her breasts.

The movement came from nowhere, and she jumped up tipping her chair over backward. It clattered across the porch, bouncing off a small table.

"I'm sorry. I just got carried away, talking with my hands, you know. I didn't mean to frighten you."

"You didn't frighten me. You touched me. Inappropriately. Don't let it happen again. Not if you want to continue to be friends."

"At one time we were a lot more than friends."

"We *dated*. In high school. And even then everything below the neck was off-limits. Just so we both know the rules. Touch now is relegated to handshakes. That's the way I conduct business."

"I'd like to do more than work together, Jodie. I've always liked you. You know that. If I hadn't upset you by getting in that fight and breaking my nose the day before your prom, we might have kept dating after you graduated from high school. You might have been the one I married instead of that two-timing hussy I got hung up with."

This absolutely could not be happening. She had known Butch ever since she moved to Natchitoches. They had dated a few times during high school. If they'd even kissed, she didn't remember it. Now he was acting as if they'd been partners in some torrid fling. They obviously shared a different set of memories.

"Look, Butch, let's just forget today happened."

"I'm sorry. I was out of line. How about letting

me take you to dinner, to make up for it. Hands to myself. I promise.'' His lips split in an easy smile.

"Not now, Butch. I'm terrible company. I will be until the stalker is stopped.''

He picked up the chair she'd sent careening across the porch and set it upright. "I understand. You just be careful. And it's none of my business, but I'd watch out for Ray Kostner if I were you.''

The screech of the side gate sliding on its hinges caught them by surprise. Jodie swung around in time to see Ray rounding the side of the house. She wondered if he ever used front doors.

He walked up and put a possessive arm around her waist. "Why should she watch out for me, Butch?''

Jodie stepped back, watching the interplay of fiery emotion that crackled between the two men. For a minute she thought they might come to blows. The idea of grown men fighting over her would have been hilarious if the situation weren't so serious.

Butch backed down first, the muscles in his face and arms relaxing, the fake smile finding his lips again. "She should watch out for you because you're a big-city boy now. We hometown folks always keep our women home and our money in our pockets when you guys come around.''

"Good idea. Only Jodie's not your woman. The truth is, you don't have anything I want, Butch, so you can quit worrying.''

"I'm not worried, Kostner. Count on it. And I can handle my own business. So, unless you're planning on running for chief of police, I expect you to leave the criminal investigating up to me. After I catch the criminals, you can go to court and try to get them off. That is what you do, isn't it, put the killers back on the street so they can harass innocent people like Jodie?''

"I like to think of my clients as innocent until proven guilty. And if I take their case, I believe they're innocent.''

"Good. You don't interfere with my investigation, and I won't try your case.''

"Fair enough.''

This time, Ray gave a few inches. Jodie excused herself while the two men shook hands and hopefully agreed to disagree more amiably. She had babies to feed and bathe, bedtime stories to read, and lullabies to sing.

BEN PACED the narrow boathouse, glaring at his son, not trying to hide the anger that was twisting his gut into ragged steel. "I told you not to come out to Miss Emily's house.''

"Why not? I'm family, and this is where you're shacking up now.''

"I'm staying here to keep an eye on things.''

"To keep an eye on Miss Jodie. I could handle that job for you. But then that was always a task you enjoyed taking care of yourself.''

"Don't smart mouth me, Grady. I don't know why you came back home in the first place. You never liked it here. You only make trouble. Butch Deaton told you last time he wasn't cutting you any more slack.''

"I missed you, Dad. Besides, I don't need any of Butch's slack. My nose is clean. I just came back to Natchitoches to escape the New York winter. They're brutal, not like the mint julep season down here. The only ice you get is in your drink glass.''

Grady pushed back the shabby curtains and stared out the window. Ben watched him, knowing he hadn't stopped by just to visit, but not sure what he wanted. He never knew with Grady. He'd thought the time he'd spent with him in Brooklyn might have drawn them closer. Instead it had only pushed them further apart.

Grady had asked him to come, to stay with him while he recovered from stomach surgery. Medical complications had drawn the intended week into eight. Way too long to suit Ben. Grady took pain pills by the handful and drank way too much. Still, he was his son, and all the family he had left.

"Look, son, I'll give you a few dollars if you need it. But I want you to get out of here. I can't afford any trouble with Miss Emily or with Jodie. They've taken care of me, and I'm going to take care of them."

"I don't need your money. Not tonight. I've got a friend waiting for me in the car out front, and he's got plenty of money. Zackery Lambkin, you remember him. You met him in New York, another one of my friends you didn't like. Creepy, I think that's how you described him."

"He's trouble, that's what he is. And he's a long way from home."

"Nah. He's originally from Shreveport. Disney has it right. It's a small, small world. He wanted to know where my dad worked, so I thought I'd show him. He's impressed."

"Where are you going when you leave here?"

"Out."

"No trouble, Grady. You know what happened last time you got mixed up with those buddies of yours."

"I spent a night in jail. No big deal. Not when my dad's got friends like Miss Emily and Parker Kostner." He sauntered to the mini fridge and yanked open the door. "Do you have any beer around here?"

"No, just a couple of soft drinks."

"Soft drinks. You're a good man, Dad. Too bad Mom didn't see it that way."

Grady grabbed a cola and left, slamming the door behind him and not bothering to say goodbye. Ben didn't take offense, not at his son's lack of manners. He was used to that. Everything he'd tried to teach his son had backfired, and Grady had picked up the exact opposite traits. Evidently his mother had been the better teacher.

Ben walked out of the boathouse. The night was still, but his joints ached. That meant either rain or trouble, and there wasn't a cloud in the sky.

JODIE FLICKED the switch on the tape recorder by the bed, filling the darkness with a recorded lullaby. Bending over, she tucked Blair in for the night, smoothing the light blanket over his backside. "Sweet dreams, darling," she whispered, kissing his cheek lightly.

Moving to Blake's bed, she repeated the routine. So precious, in his blue jammies, his thumb stuck between his lips, a thin red curl flipping about his ear. Two years ago, she'd been a career woman, thoughts of babies and diapers floating in the back of her subconscious only as a distant dream.

Now they were the only things in her life that really mattered.

She padded down the narrow hallway. The house was whisper quiet, and dark shadows climbed the walls of the narrow hall. From nowhere, the taste of fear pooled on her taste buds, and the smell of it choked her lungs. She stopped walking and leaned against the wall, her heart racing as an unexpected shot of adrenaline fueled her body.

The fear was unfounded. She was safe. Grams was safe. Her boys were safe. Butch had a patrol car passing the house at regular intervals, ready to answer a 911 call in seconds. She sucked in a ragged breath and listened.

An old English shepherd's song seeped from under the crack of the boys' door and wafted down the hallway. The sound of light snoring came from Grams's room. And any minute Ray would be returning from his visit with his parents.

Hands steady, she turned the knob on her bedroom door and slipped inside. A wisp of wind caught the gingham curtain, unfurling it like a sheet hanging out to dry. Funny, she didn't remember leaving the window open. Perhaps the cleaning girl had.

Her finger fondled the walkie-talkie. One call and Ben would rush to her side. He'd walk every inch of the house with her, put her fears to rest. But there was no reason to call him. It was just her nerves playing tricks on her.

The room was neat as a pin, nothing bothered, nothing out of place. But the stalker had never left a mess. He'd only rearranged things, moved her intimate belongings around, touched them, stretched them into bizarre shapes.

Her fingers trembled as she cracked open the dresser drawer. Her hand brushed the silky softness of her scarves. They were folded exactly as she had left them. One more drawer. The stalker's favorite.

Her breath caught and held as she eased it open, but the panties and bras were in their places. No one had been here.

Shivering, she hugged her arms across her chest and walked over to close the windows. They were French, the kind that swung out and let in plenty of fresh air. Once in high school, she'd climbed through in the middle of the night, stretching onto an overhanging branch of the pecan tree.

The tree was still there, but trimmed so that the nearest branch was much farther from the house. She got on her knees in the window seat and leaned out. If someone really wanted to, he might be able to climb the tree and swing in through an open window.

She shook her head. No one had, and from now on she'd make sure the window stayed locked tight. She closed the shutters and stepped out of her shoes, unzipping her skirt and letting it slide to the floor. She needed a shower, hot, sudsy. Enough to warm her inside and wash away the stench of fear.

Wriggling out of the rest of her clothes, she pulled back the shower curtain.

And the horror hit home again.

Chapter Nine

Ray pulled into the driveway in front of the Gahagen house and skidded his car to a stop. It had been a long night, most of it spent haggling with his dad over minute details of a case he could have handled in his sleep. In New Orleans, he might be a legend, but at the office of Parker Kostner, he was still the son who never quite made the grade. Bygones were never bygones.

If Jodie hadn't needed him, Ray would have packed his bags and headed back to New Orleans in a New York second. New York. Just the words piled on another layer of fatigue.

Two years ago New York had been just another city in North America, one he could well do without. But a week in the city, in a tiny apartment that could have fit into the bedroom of his own spacious living quarters in New Orleans, and his satisfying lifestyle had been turned into so much muck.

All of a sudden the man who had everything he thought he wanted or needed had realized how much he was missing. Now fate had hurled him and Jodie back together in a game of wits with a madman. He banged one fist on the steering wheel. Life just wasn't fair.

This afternoon's escapade in his temporary office might be his biggest mistake yet. Making love to Jodie was like an addict's fix. It satisfied for a short time, only to whet the desire for more and more and more. Even now... He pushed the thought aside. What he needed was sleep.

Grabbing his briefcase, he stepped into the cool night air. He sucked in a huge gulp, hoping it would clear his mind. It didn't. Once thoughts of Jodie invaded his brain, neither mind nor body was easily put to rest.

He glanced at her window and then at his watch. Half past midnight, and her light was still on. His pace quickened, the fatigue that had been weighing him down growing lighter with the seductive prospect of seeing her again.

Fumbling for the newest key on his chain, he fitted it in the hole and turned it, opening the door and stepping into the foyer. The house was quiet. He tiptoed up the stairs, trying unsuccessfully to avoid the creaks of a house that should have finished settling half a century ago.

He stopped at the guest room first, depositing his briefcase and suit jacket and pouring two fingers of whiskey from the crystal decanter Miss Emily had set out for him as soon as she realized he was a semipermanent guest.

She'd made a production of the amenity, placing the decanter and shot glasses on a silver tray atop the mahogany secretary that she'd proudly pointed out dated to Civil War days. She saw him as a prospective grandson-in-law. Ray could all but see the designing wheels turning through her nearly translucent skin.

Of course, that was only because she didn't know the real Ray Kostner. Perhaps she should talk to the judge, ask him why he gave up the career he loved when it was in full swing.

Ray downed the drink in a single swig and poured another. He should just drop into bed like he'd planned before he'd noticed the light in Jodie's window. Jodie, forbidden fruit, delectable and luscious, so damned tempting his mouth watered at the thought of her. He slipped out of his shoes and loosened his tie before dropping all pretense of giving up the chance to see her tonight.

A minute later, he tapped lightly on her door.

"Come in, Ray."

"How did you know it was me?" he said pushing the door open and stepping inside.

"I heard you drive up."

Jodie's voice was low, strained, and her skin had turned shades of ghostly white. "What's wrong?" he asked the question, but he knew the answer. It was written in the fear that glazed her eyes and pulled her lips into thin, trembling lines, the same way it had the night the bouquet of roses had been delivered.

"You heard from him again, didn't you?"

"A present." She motioned toward an opened package that sat beside her on the bed. "I found it in the bathroom, behind the shower curtain."

"That worthless piece of trash." He walked over to the bed and picked up the box. It rested in a nest of red, shimmery paper, a shiny red bow as topping. Cradling it in his hand, he lifted the lid.

The soft tinkling sounds of music escaped, the serenade to accompany a pair of lovers who twirled round and round inside a glass gazebo.

"A music box?"

"Right, one that plays 'New York, New York.' A perfectly harmless reminder that no matter how many police are watching, he can walk into my house at will."

"Where did you find it?"

"It was in my bathtub. So thoughtful of him to go to the trouble to hide a present in the spot where he knows I strip to nothing, where he knows I won't even be able to shower now without fearing he's just a step away."

She stood, her hands knotted into fists, her eyes the deep emerald of a tossing sea. "And if that wasn't enough, he left his calling card."

"A red heart."

"Yes, with another message."

She walked to the dresser and opened the top drawer, taking out a folded construction paper heart. He took it from her and unfolded it.

The message was printed in black crayon.

"Save yourself." He read it again, this time to himself.

"I don't know what this lunatic wants from me. I don't have a clue who he is. Which means I'm exactly where I was when this whole thing started. Except now I've given up my job and traveled from one end of the country to the other to escape him."

"You're not where you were." He took her hand in his. She was rigid, torn with frustration. "Butch has turned this into a full-scale investigation."

"And in spite of that, the man walked into my

house and deposited a wrapped package in my bathtub.''

Ray felt the tightening in his jaw, the urge to bury a fist into something, anything. But he had to fake a calm he didn't feel.

He could all but see Jodie on the next plane to New York, walking the streets like a vigilante patrol. Setting herself up to be the next victim. He wasn't about to let that happen. So he had better start talking.

"My guess is the man will be identified and arrested within the week."

"And my guess is Mars will collide with Venus, and the New Orleans Saints will win the Super Bowl."

Ray switched tactics. "I know you're upset, Jodie, anyone would be under the circumstances. That's why this is not the time to make rash decisions."

"It's past time. I will not play games with a madman under Grams's roof. I have to protect her. I have to protect Blake and Blair. If anything happened to them…'' Her voice dissolved into a shaky whisper.

"Nothing will happen to them. Ben's here. I'm here. Cops are watching the house."

"That's not good enough. Not anymore. I have a plan, Ray, but I'll need your help. Don't panic, it doesn't involve baby-sitting, and I won't be going to New York, at least not yet."

"So, why am I not relieved?"

"I want the stalker to contact me."

"He just did."

"No, I mean I want a face-to-face confrontation. No strike and disappear. I can't deal with a phantom."

"How do you propose to arrange this meeting?"

"Don't laugh. I've given this a lot of thought. I'm

going to take out an ad in the personal column. A note to my stalker that I'd like to meet him, thank him in person for all the gifts. I'll have it framed inside a heart.''

''What makes you think he reads the personals?''

''He writes. Maybe he reads. Do you have any better ideas?''

''The police...''

''The police have taken weeks to find out the man killed Max. Even if I fail miserably, I can't do much worse.'' She walked over to the dresser and picked up a notepad. ''This is what I have in mind,'' she said, pointing at a lengthy list scribbled in longhand.

Ray read silently, detail by detail, the knots in his stomach pulling tighter with every word. Her plan was dangerous at best, deadly at worst. She wouldn't listen to reason, not in the mind-set she was in now. Which meant he had to make a few plans of his own.

''You can't talk me out of this, Ray, so don't even try,'' she announced, when he'd finished reading her bizarre scheme to use herself as bait to trap a murderer.

''Okay.''

Surprise drew her brows into auburn arches.

''You are a very brave woman.'' He kissed the tip of her nose. ''And I'm sure you will not put the mother of your sons into unnecessary danger.'' A new tactic, probably also useless.

''I'm not trying to be a hero. I just need my life back. I have to know my babies are safe.''

This time the pain inside her broke through her determination, shattering her voice into shaky cries. He held her in his arms rocking her to him, absorbing the sobs that shook her body. He eased her down, placing her head on the pillow, his arms still locked around her.

He held her like that, her hair across his shoulder, the warmth of her breath against his skin until she was fast asleep.

JODIE TWISTED beneath the sheet, curling her knees up to her waist. Slowly, she opened her eyes, rubbing until the moonlit bedroom took form. The last thing she remembered was Ray holding her while torrents of tears finally broke loose.

The room was empty now. Flexing her feet, she pulled them over the side of the bed. Her mouth was so dry she could barely swallow. Sliding into her slippers, she went to the bathroom and filled a paper cup with water from the tap, drinking it down in thirst-quenching gulps.

The baby monitor was quiet. She checked it, overly cautious, just to make sure it was turned on. It was. The boys were obviously sleeping soundly. Still, she felt the need to see them. As she'd done so many nights lately, she grabbed a quilt from the top of the bed and threw it over her shoulders, padding down the hallway to sit in the rocker and watch them sleep. It was far more effective than tranquilizers or aspirin to calm her ragged nerves.

She pushed into their room. The rocking chair swayed, and her heart plunged to her toes before the shadowy form took shape. She leaned against the door frame, her heart still racing. "What are you doing in here?"

"Watching my sons sleep." Ray's words sank in slowly, like feet in quicksand.

"What did you say?"

"I'm watching my sons sleep."

Alarms went off in her head, shaking her from the dregs of sleep into full wakefulness. Ray stood, his frame catching the moonlight that peeked through the window and casting a shadow that engulfed her. Slowly, almost silently, he walked to Blair's crib and towered over the sleeping child.

"He's perfect. They both are. Innocent and trusting. They deserve so much. Instead they got a father who denied them." Ray reached into the crib and touched the back of his fingers to Blair's cheek.

Jodie's heart constricted. Father and son. Picture-perfect. Except for the tension that filled the air, suffocating, burning, a stifling blanket of fear and confusion.

Blair squirmed in his bed, waking to the noise of voices invading his dreams.

"This isn't the place to talk, Ray." She turned and walked out, his footsteps following behind her. She considered the kitchen and coffee, buying time to think, but Ray caught up with her and took her arm, leading her into her bedroom.

The moment of truth had come, but there were no feelings of exhilaration, just a dull throbbing in her temples and a duller ache in her heart.

Ray closed the door and leaned against it, his dark eyes glazed and unreadable.

Jodie struggled for calm. "What makes you suddenly think the boys are yours?"

"Not think, Jodie. I know they're mine. What I don't know is why you didn't tell me when you first found out you were pregnant."

"I called you. You didn't return my calls."

"You never indicated there was a problem. You

merely said you missed me and wanted to hear my voice.''

She met his accusing stare. ''Believe me, one part of me longed to tell you the truth from the very beginning. But the other part of me, the sensible part, knew you meant what you said. You wanted no part of commitment. So I did what I thought was best for my sons. I want Blake and Blair to know unconditional love, not rejection.''

He stepped closer, his breath hot on her flesh. ''Jodie Gahagen, the perfect mother. It was too bad you were seduced by a man who was never worthy of you.''

''Not seduced, Ray. I made love to a man I loved. Together we created two individuals, so precious I can't bear to think of life without them.''

''So you went through the pregnancy and the birth all alone. You were always a fighter.'' He turned his back on her and paced the room before finally stopping to stare out the window.

Jodie stepped behind him. ''You didn't answer my question, Ray. Why are you suddenly so sure Blair and Blake are your sons?''

He turned, wrapping his fingers about the flesh of her upper arms, his gaze meeting hers. ''Because you're too strong to be reduced to lies even in the face of death.''

''It took you a long time to figure that out.''

''Too damned long.'' His voice grew hoarse. ''Or maybe I knew it all along. Maybe I'm just not as strong as you are, Jodie. Maybe I ran from the truth the way I've run from a lot of things in my life.''

''But now you have it all figured out?''

"No. Not at all. I'm still not sure how it happened. We were careful. We used protection."

"Nothing is one hundred percent except abstinence. We pushed the odds that week."

"You know I never meant for this to happen." Ray walked to the dressing table and picked up a silver-framed picture of Jodie and the boys outside her New York apartment. The images couldn't have been clear in the muted glow of moonlight, but he studied the snapshot as if he were memorizing every line.

Finally he returned it to its spot of honor. "I should have been there." The self-accusation in his voice surprised her.

"Why? You told me all along you didn't want any commitments. You were honest."

"I told you I wasn't husband material. I'm still not."

"Then I guess you don't have any problems. You're not a husband."

His eyes raked over her and he crossed the room, stopping inches away, looking for all the world like a man who had no desire to run away. One hand under her chin, he tilted it upward until their gaze locked. "You're a remarkable woman. Knowing all you did about me, you still chose to have my babies."

"I didn't choose anything. I missed my period and went to the doctor. He confirmed what the drugstore test indicated. I was pregnant." She backed away.

"You had a choice. A choice that might have been better for you, for your career, for your lifestyle. People make it every day. But you chose to give our sons life. And I didn't even have the courage to return your phone calls."

"You didn't know."

"I'm not sure I could have handled things differently if I had. That's the scary part." He walked away from her. Dropping to the window seat, he patted the spot beside him. "Sit by me," he whispered.

She hesitated, then gave in to her own need to be close to him. She could convince herself of anything in the bright light of day, almost believe she didn't care at all if he chose to have to nothing to do with her or their sons. But this was the middle of the night, and her needs lay naked and exposed.

"It's so hard to accept that I'm a father," he whispered, reaching for her hand.

"Is that why you chose not to believe me when I told you they were yours?"

"No. That was pure fear. I've let down everyone who ever needed me, everyone who ever mattered to me. I couldn't handle knowing I was doing it again." He knotted his hands into fists and then stretched them out again in repetitive motions.

"But I think I always knew they were my sons, at least at some level. When I first found out you had given birth to twins, I tried to picture you with another man, making love the way we made love."

She swallowed a surge of pain. "And did you get comfort from those thoughts?"

"The same kind of comfort I'd get from a rattlesnake bite." His hands knotted into fists again.

"I'm a simple woman, Ray, not nearly so complicated as you. If you want me to understand you, you'll have to spell things out for me, make your feelings crystal clear."

"My feelings? They change by the minute. Elated? Confused? Nervous? Petrified?"

"That runs the gamut. Throw in morning sickness

and the awkwardness of carrying around a twenty-pound stomach and you pretty much have the same symptoms I had during the pregnancy.'' She wasn't being vindictive, just honest.

His muscles were taut, a man geared for a fight, but it was his own demons he was battling. The skirmish was far from over, and she had no idea who'd come out the winner. Still, she needed a few questions answered, now while Ray was dealing with the truth and with his own feelings of inadequacy.

"Why didn't you return my calls, Ray? We'd been acquaintances forever and good friends since the night of my senior prom. Earlier, if you count the kiss on the cheek at my fourteenth birthday party as a sign of friendship.''

"Do you still remember that?'' he asked, his eyebrows raised in surprise.

"Of course, I didn't wash my face for days. You were my first case of serious puppy love.''

"Before you found out I was really a dog.''

"I've never thought that. I just thought you had a twisted sense of values. Money and fame at any cost, and get as far away from family as you could. That's why I avoided contact in Baton Rouge when I was in college and you were in law school at LSU. No matter how I felt about you, I knew it wouldn't work.''

"You were wise for your years.''

"I thought so at the time. But you seemed so different that week in New York. You were fun, romantic, thoughtful. The new Ray Kostner. I had high hopes for you.''

"And *you* were a sex-crazed goddess.'' He trailed a finger down her arm.

"I was not sex-crazed. Intimately uninhibited, maybe. And I don't remember your complaining."

"You *were* sex-crazed, and I loved it. But you made me *feel* and that scared the wits out of me."

"You find me so tempting, you avoid me. I'm missing something here."

He leaned against the side of the window, watching her. "It's pretty simple. When I'm with you, I forget who and what I am, start thinking that we're right together, start thinking I could be the husband and father you'd expect me to be. The truth is, it's not going to happen."

"Men have careers and families all the time, and do both well. Look at your dad."

His mood changed instantly. Tension stormed between them, so heavy she could feel the weight of it crushing against her chest.

"Sure," he said. "Parker Kostner. The Judge. Everything to everybody. Well, to almost everybody."

She shuddered, chilled by the bitterness that dripped from every word. "Is there trouble between you and your father?"

"Trouble? How could there be? The Judge is the perfect father. Too bad he got royally shortchanged on sons."

A shiver skidded her spine. This was a scene from a bad movie, the story of someone else's life. Not Ray Kostner's. He had it all. "You're obviously upset about something, but you're not making sense. Your dad is proud of you. He's always been."

"Is that what the world sees? Good. He'd like that." Ray gestured a sign of surrender. "Can we just drop this, Jodie? I'm not here to blackball my father. He is what he is. I am what I am."

"And what is it that you think you are?"

"A tough lawyer who's damn good at what I do, because I do what I'm good at. I don't cut the mustard as a son, and I don't have a chance of making it as a husband or a father. So, it looks like you and the boys drew a bad deal, the same as my dad. The truth is I can't be counted on." He stood up and paced the room.

This was incredulous. Ray was calling on the most feeble excuses she'd ever heard. If he tried this in court, the prosecuting attorney would bury him. "Let me see if I have this straight. Just because you don't think your dad appreciates you, you're willing to give up the chance to have a family of your own."

"Drop it, Jodie. This isn't about an argument. It's about me and what I am and am not capable of."

"Don't talk in riddles, not to me. I've been through too much these past few months. If you prefer a life void of commitments, I can buy that. I have no intention of trapping you. But if you think you can walk out of my life with some cock-and-bull story about caring about me too much to hurt me, about not having what it takes to be a father when you've never even tried, you have another thing coming."

"Don't read anything into a few nice deeds, Jodie. It's the week in New York that's the lie, a pretense that I was someone else. I'll do right by you and the boys. You'll never want for anything, but I can't become someone I'm not."

"So why are you here, Ray, pushing your way back into my life, making demands, risking your life to protect mine?"

"To trap a stalker. I'm not the man to hang your hopes on, but that doesn't mean I'll let some murderous lunatic threaten you and walk the streets to do it again. I told you I won't stop until this man is behind bars.''

''But just don't depend on you to be there when I need you, right?''

''Right.''

He started to walk away. She grabbed both of his arms and stopped him. Rising to the tips of her toes, she placed her lips on his. The kiss was wet and sweet, and so exciting she felt it tumble along every nerve ending.

''And don't expect me to be here all warm and eager waiting for you when you decide you need me too much to walk away,'' she said, pushing him toward the door.

He looked at her for long painful seconds before he disappeared down the hallway.

Jodie watched him go. The man might be a brilliant attorney, but he didn't have a clue when it came to his own virtues. When this was over, she'd gladly hang her hopes and her dreams on him. That is, if she was still alive to do so.

JODIE SPENT the next morning perfecting the ad. It would start its run on the Saturday before Thanksgiving, three days away. The details were fine-tuned, ready to run like a well-geared car.

The ad was simple: ''To my secret admirer, The flowers were beautiful, the music box was delightful. I'm saving myself, for you.''

The rest was in small print. If he wanted to meet her in private, he was to call her. The telephone company was connecting the line today. Grams had bought the explanation that the line was for business purposes, although Jodie had no idea what she thought her business was.

The only activity she'd involved herself with that remotely resembled employment was the journal she was keeping on the life of the stalked. Hopefully, she'd live to see her experiences published in an article that would help other women in the same predicament.

Even if the stalker saw the ad, he might not call. The man was smart, and this smelled of a trap. But the man was also mentally off balance, and she saw his attempts as a sick way of reaching out to her. This might be the type of opening he was looking for to reveal himself.

The danger would be minimal. All the calls would be taped. In essence, she was bugging herself. If he called, she would meet him. It was up to the police to figure out how they would keep her safe and make the arrest. That was the one weakness of her plan, the one element she couldn't control.

Ray was furious. Butch claimed she was crazy. But it was not their lives that were being split into a thousand splintered parts.

She was meeting with Butch this afternoon to set up the finer points of their strategy.

JODIE SAT IN Butch Deaton's cramped office, listening to one side of a long-winded phone conversation. The woman on the other end of the line was obviously complaining about her neighbor's barking dog.

Bored and restless, Jodie's gaze took in the room. A spiderweb in the far corner of the ceiling, a shamrock-shaped stain on the carpet, a silver-framed photograph of a young blond woman with smiling eyes and heavy makeup on the top of a chipped file cabinet.

Finally, Butch dropped the receiver into the cradle and looked her way. "Sorry to keep you waiting," he said, rummaging through the clutter on his desk to recover a manila file folder.

"You said something important had come up and for me to rush right over. What is it?"

"The nurse at the hospital called. Apparently Gloria Bigger's memory is returning. She asked to speak to you."

"Then why did the nurse call you?"

"Because this is police business, Jodie. No one wants to see you hurt, least of all me."

"When did the nurse call?"

"This morning, about ten."

"And we're waiting until two in the afternoon to talk to her?"

"I had things to take care of. Besides, we've waited days for this description. A few hours won't change anything."

"Can we go now?"

"Absolutely. You can ride with me if you don't mind a squad car."

"As long as we leave the flashing blues turned off."

"I thought you were in a hurry."

"The hospital is only five minutes away. The barking dog has already taken twenty."

"It's a small town. We keep our taxpayers happy when we can. Besides, Gloria's not going anywhere."

Ten minutes later they pushed through the door of

Gloria's hospital room. The sheets were pulled up over an empty bed. The nurse stopped in the door, sympathy written all over her face as she told them the patient had died a little over an hour ago.

Chapter Ten

The drive back to the police station was cloaked in silence. The nurse had said Gloria Bigger died from a heart attack. It had come on suddenly, and it had been massive. The only good thing was she hadn't lived long enough to suffer much.

This time even Jodie couldn't blame the stalker.

Butch led her back into his office. "We can talk about your plans later, Jodie. I know Gloria's death has you upset. I'm a little shaky myself."

"I'd rather get this over with, Butch." She tapped the cover of a spiral-bound notebook. "My plans are outlined in here. They're pretty much the same as when we talked on the phone."

"Mind if I have a look before we talk?"

She stood and walked over, opening the notebook and placing it in front of him. "Like I told you, the ad starts Saturday. I plan to meet the stalker if he calls. I'd like for you or one of your officers to tail me."

"If the man's got any brain cells at all, he won't fall for this. He's wanted for murder."

"He doesn't know that. He broke into the florist shop and stole the incriminating record."

"In a state of panic. I'm sure after he calmed down

he realized how easy it would be to trace the credit card information from the company.''

"So we know he makes mistakes." She took her seat again. "I think he'll come, Butch. I can't explain it, but I feel this man is desperate and he's calling out to me. What's the point of following me, of leaving me notes and gifts, of letting me know he's obsessed with me if he thinks it's going nowhere?"

"Oh, he'll come to you, Jodie. But it will be when you least expect it, when he can't stand keeping his identity a secret another second."

"Maybe he's to that point now."

"I hope not. I plan to stop him before he reaches that stage. I could do it more effectively if you'd let me handle the investigation without interference."

"I appreciate your concern, Butch, but I have to do this."

"Then it's my job to protect you. You're a citizen, misguided, but still a citizen. Besides, you and I go back a long way."

"This is not about friendship, Butch. I need your help as a police officer."

"And you'll have it. One hundred percent, but that doesn't mean I like it."

"But you do think you can protect me?"

"In theory it should be easy. In reality, anything can happen."

"What do you think of my choice of meeting places?"

"The old Coxlin place. Great choice. For the stalker. It's isolated, large and rambling and in ruins, surrounded by acres of woods."

"Which means there's also hiding places for you or one of your officers. I could wear a wired microphone, maybe even get a taped confession that he murdered Max.''

''You read too many detective books. Even if the man reads the ad and falls for the trap, this type of setup doesn't come with guarantees.''

''I trust you.''

''You could be making a fatal mistake.''

''Let's hope it's the stalker who makes the mistake.''

''And I definitely wouldn't count on that.'' He closed her notebook and scooted it to the back of his desk. ''I'll take a ride out to the Coxlin place later and see what I think. Do you want to go with me?'' Pushing his chair back, he stood up, raking his hair back with his hands.

''Yes. What about tomorrow? That way we can decide exactly how to handle the situation, where your man will be hiding and how I can signal him.''

''I'd like to talk you out of this, Jodie.''

''I wish it wasn't necessary. But the man has to be stopped before he loses all control and someone else ends up dead, the way Max did.''

He walked her to the door. ''I just don't want that someone to be you.''

''Neither do I, Butch. Neither do I.''

JODIE LEFT the police station at half past three. Gloria Bigger was on her mind as she pulled to a stop at the traffic light on Front Street. Tears moistened her eyes. Another death. There was no way of knowing if her stalker was behind it. But somehow, she was sure he was.

On impulse, Jodie pulled into the semicircle of parking that followed the paths and grassy areas along the river—the peaceful oasis in the middle of the oldest part of town.

The sun peeked over the tops of oak and cottonwood trees, shaking a tail of glimmery gold over the river. A fishing boat motored past, the man at the bow tipping his hat to a tall, slender woman who was being walked by a prancing Pomeranian on a jeweled leash. Two preschoolers played chase around the circular pavilion that was already strung with bright colored lights for the upcoming festival.

Life as usual. For everyone but her. Opening the car door, she slid from beneath the wheel, and stepped out. She grabbed her handbag in lieu of locking the door. The fall nip in the air made a cup of coffee at The Bakery seem too good to pass up.

She was sorry for the decision the minute she walked through the door. Sara Kostner was at the counter, paying for a bag of pastries. Not that she had anything against Sara, but today was not the time she wanted to make small talk with Ray's mother. Not the time to pile on guilt either, but seeing Sara did just that.

In the end, Ray might be willing to walk away from his sons, but Jodie doubted Sara would be as easily deterred from knowing her grandsons. Another complication, another knot in the spidery web that had entangled Jodie's life with Ray's. Sara turned, and a smile curved her lips and lit up her face.

"Jodie Gahagen, what a nice surprise." She picked up her bag of pastries and hurried in Jodie's direction.

"Hello, Sara." She extended her hand. Sara ignored it and went for a hug.

"We've been so worried about you. Ray said you had some lunatic bothering you in New York and that's why you came down here to stay for a while. Have they caught the man yet?''

''Not that I know of.'' Funny, she hadn't even considered that Ray had told his parents about her situation, but then he had to come up with some explanation for sleeping over every night. Left to her own conclusions, Sara would have been hard-pressed not to expect the worst. And a loose woman would not meet with Sara Kostner's approval.

''Then it's a good thing you came back home. I know your grandmother would love it if you decided to stay permanently. We feel the same about Ray, but he won't even talk about moving back.''

''His work is in New Orleans.''

''It could be here. Parker would love for him to take over the firm.'' The smile vanished from her face. ''Not that he'd ever ask him. And not that Ray would consider it if he did.''

''No, your son seems to like his life as it is.''

''But I don't have a clue why. Working day and night. Living alone. It's time he settled down and had a family.''

Jodie remained silent. The responses that flitted through her head were much better left unsaid.

''I'd love to stay and chat a bit,'' Sara said, glancing at her watch. ''But I don't like to leave Parker long. He's mending nicely, but I worry about him. He complains when I fuss over him, but I can't help it.''

''Perhaps I can stop by one day for a visit.''

''Parker would be delighted. And bring the boys. We'd love to see them. I live for the day Ray decides on one woman and gives me some grandchildren.''

Jodie nodded past the lump that had settled in her throat without warning. Denial cast a long shadow.

She said a quick goodbye and watched Sara walk out the door. A minute later Jodie followed behind her. Her taste for coffee was lost. Now the only craving she had was to go home and hug her boys.

The parking area was nearly empty by the time she returned to her car. A pickup truck parked near the water, a blue Ford parked under the biggest oak.

She fished the car keys from her pocket and slid into the driver's seat, turning the key in the ignition. The silence was ominous, an instant dread that ground in her stomach. She turned the key again. No reassuring hum. Not even an angry growl or sputter.

This had happened once before, right before she left New York. The car had been working fine when she'd parked it. When she'd returned, the engine hadn't started. A chill stole her breath. She lowered the window and sucked in a gulp of air.

This was Natchitoches, not New York City. She was surrounded by family friends, business owners who knew her grandmother, who had gone to school with her dad, who knew her name and where she lived. Today she'd go home to Grams and the boys.

That day she'd gone home to a gift, a pair of gloves to warm her hands after being stranded in the dark, in a cold car whose engine wouldn't respond.

The message had been clear. The stalker had been watching and then had beaten her to her apartment to put the gift in place.

She fit her trembling hands around the key again and gave it one last try. The engine didn't respond. She stepped out of the car. She'd find a phone booth and call Selda.

"Hello, neighbor. Having car trouble?"

The voice startled her, triggering a rush of adrenaline. She spun around and stared at the man who'd come up behind her. Recognition was instant. Selda's new tenant was staring at her, a smile splitting his face, his eyes laughing.

"The engine won't start."

"I'll take a look at it if you like. If we can't start it, I can give you a ride."

"Is that your blue car?"

"That's it. I was taking some pictures of the old courthouse but the workers on the other side of the river caught my eye. This Festival of Lights must be some display."

"I thought you were in town to photograph plantation homes."

"I am. But lucky for you I stopped off in town before heading home. Why don't you pop the hood and let me take a look?"

"It was running fine earlier," she said, opening the door and releasing the hood catch.

"Does this happen often?"

"No. Only once before."

"What was the matter with it then?"

"I don't remember," she lied, not sure why she felt the need.

He rolled up his sleeves and propped the hood on the safety rod before his head disappeared inside. "Here's your problem."

She walked around the car and peeped under the hood. Wires, valves, belts and thingamabobs. A greasy puzzle with no cheat sheet. If the whole thing had been installed backward, she wouldn't have known. "I don't see a problem."

"This little wire's your culprit. It's supposed to be connected right here."

He demonstrated, fitting the wire into place and tightening the connector on the battery. That was the one part she could identify. She'd had to have it replaced once. New York winters ate batteries like monkeys ate bananas. That's what her mechanic had said when explaining why she should purchase the most expensive one he had.

"Now try it," Greg said, pulling a white handkerchief from his pocket and adding a little more grease to the black stain that was already there.

She did. This time it hummed beautifully. "You saved the day, Mr. Johnson, isn't it?"

"My pleasure. And the name's Greg, especially when a beautiful redhead is asking."

"Then, thank you, Greg. But I'm curious," she said, "what would have made the wire disconnect?"

"A bad bounce in the road. Maybe nothing. Sometimes they just work loose. Or maybe fate just wanted us to meet again."

"I doubt that. Fate hasn't been on my side lately."

"Then maybe it's my fate, and you just got caught up in the undertow."

"Well, for whatever reason, I appreciate the assistance. If I can ever return the favor—"

"You can," he answered, too quickly.

She eyed him warily.

"You could have dinner with me tonight. Tell me if I'm jumping to conclusions or out of line in inviting you, but I don't see a ring on your finger."

"Well, it's a long story," she joked, realizing she was beginning to feel at ease with the lanky photographer with the easy smile. She wasn't entirely sure that was good, but he did seem harmless.

"Then will you have dinner with me?"

"Why? All you know about me is that I have two sons and a car that dies at inopportune times."

"I know a lot about you."

"How would you?" The wariness intensified as quickly as it had faded.

"My landlady loves to talk. Besides, like I told you, I have a good view of your back porch from my window. That seems to be one of your favorite resting spots."

"When do you work if you're always watching me?"

"When the light is right. So, are we on for dinner? I promise not to bore you with stories of the big shots that got away."

"I'm afraid not. My life is in a state of flux right now. And, to be perfectly honest, there is someone else."

Jodie sensed a change in her rescuer. Not in the smile. It never left his face. It was the eyes that changed, grew darker, more intense.

"I'm disappointed."

"Don't be," she said. "In my present situation, I would be lousy company. And if the situation changes, you never know, I just may take you up on your offer."

"Then you better hurry, or you might miss your chance."

"It won't be the first time."

"Or hopefully the last." He tipped his hat and walked away.

A strange man, she decided, friendly, but a little quirky. *Everyone you know is a suspect.* Ray's words echoed in her brain. She tried to picture Greg Johnson sneaking into her house or plunging a knife in Max

Roling. The thoughts made her blood run cold, but they didn't ring true.

Shifting into reverse, she backed out of her parking place and headed home. Hopefully not to another gift.

RAY KOSTNER STRETCHED, his mouth opening into a killer yawn. Keeping up with his own business long distance and running his dad's office had turned into a lot more work than he'd anticipated. But that was not what was dragging him down.

It was the past, attacking him without mercy, digging into dark crevices of his brain and pulling out memories he'd thought were buried too deep to be unearthed. Another reason Natchitoches was no good for him.

"You're a disappointment, son. You've gone too far this time. I have no choice but to step down as judge."

Words from the past tore at his strength, reducing him from the man he'd become to the boy he'd been. He'd never been good enough to please his dad, so he'd gone the other way. Pushed the limits until they'd broken, and his father's life had come crashing down around them.

But he wasn't that rebellious kid anymore. He'd matured, made it to the top in a dog-eat-dog world. He'd just handled and won one of the highest profile criminal cases to hit Louisiana in many a year. But, back in Natchitoches, he was still Parker Kostner's son.

It shouldn't matter, but it did. The truth was he'd exchange all his *Times Picayune* headlines for one acknowledgment from his dad that he'd been wrong about him. Maybe then he'd believe it himself. Maybe then he'd believe he could handle the role of husband

and father without letting everyone who mattered down again.

Strange, but he could see himself in Natchitoches now, working in this very office, going home to Jodie and the boys at night. At a decent hour so he could help bathe them and tell them bedtime stories.

Or maybe his dad was right, had always been right. Maybe he thrived on controversy, gave in to cheap thrills, went for the pleasure of the moment, let people down. Maybe Jodie and his sons would be better off without him.

When this was over, he'd have to make decisions. Right now, the only thing of importance was keeping Jodie safe. He'd talked to Cappan again, and though hundreds of miles apart, they'd reached the same decision.

A stalker who traveled across the country to torment a woman he'd never been involved with was a dangerous psychopath operating on a short fuse. And the next explosion could be at any minute.

That's why Cappan needed Jodie to return to New York. He had to question her further, in person. And she needed to look at mug shots of multiple sex offenders.

Jodie Gahagen, the girl he'd taken to the senior prom, young and innocent, vivacious and witty and one terrific kisser. She'd changed. Now she was one hell of a woman and a fantastic mother. And still a terrific kisser.

Picking up the office phone, he punched in her number. He needed to hear her voice, tell her he was on the way back to her house. Miss Emily answered on the second ring.

"Is Jodie there?"

"No, she's out."

"Where did she go?"

"Let's see. I think she said she was going over to Selda's. No, that wasn't it. I don't remember, but she'll be back."

Leaving Emily and the boys at night didn't sound like Jodie. Apprehension pitted in his stomach. "Do you have the walkie-talkie?"

"It's right here somewhere. Here it is, hanging on my hip."

"Give her a call."

"What do you want me to tell her?"

"Just call her. I want to know where she is."

"Oh, I don't have to do that. I remember now. She was going down to the boathouse to talk to Ben."

"You're sure?"

"Well, of course I'm sure. Now what was it you wanted me to tell her?"

"Nothing, Miss Emily. I'll see her in a few minutes."

He said a quick goodbye and slammed the receiver into the cradle. In two seconds he was heading out the door.

Chapter Eleven

Jodie trod the worn path to the boathouse. The sky was cloudless, the stars so bright she felt she could reach out and touch them for luck. But, as always, the peace and beauty were flawed by the nagging worries that forever preyed in her mind.

She pulled the flannel cape across her chest. The boathouse was in sight, and a beam of light from the unshuttered window told her Ben was still awake. She'd felt bad about cutting him off so quickly the other day. Tonight seemed the perfect time to let him know she appreciated all he was doing for them.

Voices rumbled through the air. She wasn't close enough to make out all of the words, but the tone was unmistakable. Ben was arguing with someone. Her first urge was to turn around and march back to the solace of the house. She didn't give in. Under present circumstances what she didn't know could definitely hurt her.

The voices became more distinct which each step. When she knocked on the door, the loud quarrel quieted instantly.

"Who's there?"

"It's Jodie, Ben."

He jerked the door open. "Is something the matter, Miss Jodie?"

"No, I just walked down to chat for a while. Did I come at a bad time?"

"No. Come on in."

Her gaze swept the room. Grady stood in the corner, taller than she remembered, and muscular like his dad. His hair was cut short, stylish and he was dressed casually in trendy, khaki pants and a collarless shirt.

"Hello, Jodie. Long time, no see."

"It's been a while. You've changed. I almost didn't recognize you."

"Changed for the better, I hope. I'd know you anywhere. Still the prettiest girl in town, just like my dad always says."

A blush heated her cheeks. "Thanks to both of you. If I'm interrupting something, I can come back later."

"An argument," Grady answered honestly, "but it can wait."

"We don't want to bother you with our family squabbles," Ben interjected. "Have a seat, and I'll get you a soda."

"Thanks." She sat on the only decent chair in the place. This was no way for Ben to live, cramped in a spot originally built for housing fishing supplies. Grady propped against the long table where her grandfather had skinned and filleted his catch. Ben dropped to the sagging bed.

She was glad she'd made this visit. At least she could provide a decent mattress for him. She'd see to it first thing tomorrow. Grams would have done it already had she realized the condition of this one.

"You're really going the extra mile, Ben, staying

out here when you could be at your own place, sleeping in your own bed.''

"But then he'd have to put up with me, or else kick me out. He's loath to do either of those things.''

Ben shot his son a look that couldn't be misinterpreted. Grady ignored it and kept talking.

"That's why I have to find a job and get a place of my own. What about around here? The boathouse could use a coat of paint, the gazebo needs power washing, and the fence between here and Miss Selda's needs to be repaired. There's a break down by the water's edge big enough for a grown man to climb through.''

"You certainly seem to know a lot about the place.''

"I gave it a once-over the other afternoon when I was out here to see my dad. I'm thorough. And I work cheap.''

If he worked free, she still wouldn't have wanted him around the place. She hadn't liked him as a teenager when he'd come out in the summer and helped his dad cut grass and weed the garden. He hadn't had much to do with her, but he had hung around when she was outside, appearing from nowhere and scaring the wits out of her more than once.

Now it was his reputation that caused her not to want him around. Troublemaker and loafer, though she had to admit he didn't look the part.

"I could use a little help," Ben said, from his spot near the door. "It's my own fault, but I did let things get ahead of me when I was out of town.''

His comment surprised her. She was sure she'd interrupted a heated argument, yet Ben was encouraging her to hire Grady, to make it necessary for them to spend more time together.

She could turn Grady down without hesitation, but it was a lot more difficult to say no to Ben, especially with him living here in one ill-equipped room in order keep her, Grams and the boys safe. He could have stayed in the house, of course. Grams had offered use of one of the guest rooms but he'd refused to even consider it.

Grady leaned against the door frame, studying her reluctance. "Of course, if you don't want me around…"

"That's not it. Look, we'll give it a try. See if it works out."

The smile that crossed his lips seemed genuine, but the taunting look in his eyes made her regret her hasty decision.

Everyone's a suspect. The familiar phrase hammered in her head, tightened the muscles in her throat so that she could barely swallow the soda Ben had given her. How much longer could she go on like this, wary of everyone she ran into, even people she'd known all her life?

One sign of trouble and Grady would be out of here. She couldn't take chances. And she'd make sure Butch had Grady's name on the list of suspects he was checking out.

Eager to leave, she downed a few more swallows of the canned drink and excused herself. The wind had picked up. It wasn't gusty, but strong enough to sway the branches and tease a few of the last leaf holdouts from their stronghold.

Lost in unpleasant thoughts, she walked to the edge of the water.

"A nice night for a walk."

She turned at the voice, her heart racing the way it always did when Ray appeared. "Is that what brought you here?"

"No, I came looking for you." He stepped behind her and wound his arms around her waist, burying his lips in her neck. Tiny shivers of delight feathered her skin. Suddenly she didn't want to go back to the house, didn't want to talk about stalkers or police reports.

"Let's take the boat out, Ray."

"What brought that on?"

"You. The moonlight. The need to feel normal again."

"I'm game. I'm not dressed for it, but I'm game."

"If your shoes get wet, they'll dry. If your clothes get dirty, have them cleaned."

"You have answers for everything."

"That's the problem. I don't have answers, and I'm so tired of searching for them. For a few minutes I'd like to be uninhibited, unafraid, the way I used to be. The way we were when you visited me in New York."

"I'm not sure I have the energy to be the way we were then," he teased.

"Not that. I want to laugh, to act silly, to have fun."

"But not to make love?"

"If it happens."

Ray ran his fingers through her hair, silky curls that tangled his fingers. Leaning closer, he touched his lips to hers and then drew away, sucking in a shaky breath. The taste, the feel, the flowery fragrance. All Jodie. All devastating.

''If I stay with you another minute, it will happen.''

''But first the boat ride.''

''Won't you mind leaving Grams and the boys alone?''

''Not tonight. Butch talked the chief into assigning a man to watch the house. He's pulling the first shift.''

''Then a boat ride it is.''

Minutes later he was guiding the small fishing craft down the Cane River, the hum of the motor breaking the silence, the wind in their faces easing but never dissolving the burdens of dealing daily with a killer.

''I feel like the big bad wolf out with Little Red Riding Hood the way that cape's flowing behind you.''

''It's russet, not red.''

''Moonlight's deceiving.''

''Life's deceiving.''

He didn't have an argument for that. They rode in silence for fifteen minutes, and for the first time in days, Ray could almost feel his muscles letting go of the tension. He slowed the motor and guided the boat to a small wooden dock that jutted into the river.

''Where are we?''

''A fishing camp. It belongs to a friend of mine, but they don't use it much anymore. It's quiet. We can talk, and laugh and act silly with no one to hear us.''

''Don't make fun of me. You have to admit the boat ride was a good idea.''

''Great.'' He killed the motor and stepped out, tying the boat to a post. Jodie joined him on the dock. They walked together, hand in hand, up a grassy hill toward a rustic cabin. An owl hooted, the only sound in their world of isolation.

Jodie stopped and stared up at him, moonlight shimmering in her eyes. "Too bad the world can't always be this peaceful."

"It can. It will be again." He held her close and she cuddled against him, soft where he was hard, curves where he was planes and angles. The ache inside him swelled to strangling proportions. "We just have to keep you safe long enough to see it."

"We're supposed to be laughing and acting silly," she said.

"And making love. But first I have to bring up something serious."

"You are the big, bad wolf," she groaned.

"I talked to Cappan today."

"Can't this wait until tomorrow?"

"No, tomorrow you'll be packing for a trip to New York. The two of us will be leaving the day after that."

"I'm busy, Ray. You know that. I'm still working out the plans for my project. It's Tuesday now. The ad runs Saturday. I have to see Butch again."

"If the trip's successful, you won't have to go through with your plan. Cappan has some ideas."

"I talked to Cappan when I was in New York. Many times. His ideas were useless."

"This time will be different. He has mug shots of everyone in the New York area who's been convicted on multiple sexual offenses in the last decade. He needs you to see if one of them looks familiar. By the time we get there, he'll also have a computer printout of every stalker case that even remotely resembles yours."

"Cappan's been busy."

"He's pulled out all the stops. Even gone so far as

pulling up past serial killer data to see if your guy could be a copycat.''

''Too bad he wasn't that cooperative before I gave up my job and moved to Natchitoches.'' She pulled away and walked to a worn hammock that swung between two pines.

''But I was just a woman complaining about some man sending her gifts and breaking into her house without taking anything. We had to wait until the NYPD were convinced the guy had committed a murder before they got serious.''

''Cappan's serious now. And so am I.''

''Plane reservations to New York are not always easy to come by on short notice.''

''We have reservations. We have a direct flight out of Shreveport at eight o'clock Thursday morning. We meet with Cappan right after lunch.''

''Why did you wait until now to tell me?''

''Cappan didn't let me know until this afternoon that he could provide everything I asked.''

''So this was all your idea?''

''It would have come to this eventually. I just pushed the buttons a little sooner.''

''I have the boys, Ray. I can't just up and leave.''

He dropped beside her in the hammock. ''I've already talked to Selda. She'll stay with your grandmother until we get back. And you said Butch already has cops watching your house.''

''Butch took credit, but that was your doing, too, wasn't it?''

''I talked to the chief of police. He owed my dad a favor.''

''So everything is set.''

''You can say no.''

"And miss the chance to get a real lead? Not on your life. I just wished these actions had come sooner, while Max was still alive. While Gloria Bigger was still alive, even though no one but me is convinced the stalker frightened her into the initial heart attack."

"I know." He traced the lines of her face, trailing a finger down her forehead, over her nose and to her lips. "I wish a lot of things were different."

She tipped her head toward him. "Kiss me, Ray. Make me forget for a few minutes that the world is cursed with people who destroy other people's lives."

He pressed his lips against hers, and she melted into him, warm and willing. The kiss fed his hunger but didn't begin to satisfy the needs that raged inside him.

"Do you want to go back now?" he asked, "while I can still pull myself away from you and walk back to the boat?"

She wrapped herself around him and pulled him down into the roped folds of the oversize hammock. And that was all the answer he needed.

THE HOUSE WAS DARK and locked up tight when they returned. Ray fiddled with the key until the back door opened.

Jodie flicked on the light. Her hair was tangled and wild from wind blowing across the water and from making love in a swaying hammock. Her blouse was wrinkled and buttoned crooked, with one side hanging down inches past the other.

She'd never looked more sexy. Ray fought back urges that should have been well satisfied from heaven in the hammock.

"Are you hungry?" she asked, opening the refrigerator and peeking inside.

"Famished."

"How about a BLT on toast?"

"With cheese?"

"Melted and gooey."

"You talked me into it."

Ray peeled the slices of bacon apart and placed them into the frying pan while Jodie sliced a large tomato and a hunk of cheddar cheese.

"We make a good team," she said, slipping a sliver of cheese between his lips.

He let the comment ride. No matter how good things seemed at this minute, he couldn't make promises, not about teams or partnerships or anything that spoke of permanence. Not until he was sure he could make it work. Until he was dead certain he would not fall short again.

His temporary silence did not daunt Jodie. She kept up her cheery chatter while they finished making the sandwiches and then devoured them.

Ray wasn't fooled for a minute. The party atmosphere only covered the surface, like a thin layer of gold over dull, imitation metals. Hopefully their trip to New York would lead to an arrest that could change everything, give her back her life.

And take her back to New York, away from him.

The phone jangled loudly, interrupting his thoughts.

"You answer it, Ray. I hate phone calls this time of night. They're never good news." She picked up the kitchen extension and handed it to him.

"Hello."

The caller was Butch Deaton. "I saw lights on. I thought I'd check and make sure everything's all right."

"Everything's fine. Jodie and I were just grabbing a snack."

"It's a little late for eating, isn't it?"

"Not if you're hungry."

"Tell Jodie I called. If she needs me tonight, I'll be practically within yelling distance."

"I'll let her know."

Ray hung up the phone. "Your Officer Unfriendly seems to be interested in getting more friendly these days, at least with you."

"I know. He has some crazy idea the two of us might have ended up together if he hadn't broken our date for the senior prom."

"Your senior prom." Ray stepped closer. "I remember it well. I had just graduated from LSU. My mom asked me to do a favor for her."

"Take me to the prom?"

"Yeah. It cost her twenty bucks. I needed gasoline to drive to New Orleans that weekend."

"You mean you were paid to date me?" She wadded a napkin and threw it at him.

"Cold, hard cash."

"If I'd known that I would have never let you kiss me good-night."

"Yes, you would have. You initiated the kiss."

"I certainly did not."

He reached over and wrapped an arm around her waist, pulling her to him. "You did. Looking up at me with those big green eyes, tossing that mane of gorgeous wild hair. The same way you're doing now."

And then his lips were on hers. And he was lost in her again. He lifted her like he might have done Blake or Blair and carried her up the stairs.

He couldn't fight his feelings for her any longer. Not sleeping under the same roof. But when this was over, when the stalker was caught, then he'd have to deal in reality.

The reality that he was not the man she thought he was. The reality was that if he didn't walk away, he would hurt her and the boys, let them down the way he had let down everyone in his life who had ever mattered.

And no matter what leaving did to him, it wouldn't be as bad as watching the love she had for him turn to bitter resentment. It wouldn't be as bad as ruining Jodie's and his sons' lives.

JODIE ROLLED OUT another round of pie dough, flexing her wrists, and laying on the muscle power. Physical activity was great for releasing tension, and after this morning's meeting with Butch, she had more than her share. He'd argued every point, but finally they'd managed to agree on enough of them that everything was set in case the killer really did answer her ad.

"How many more of these rounds do you need?" she asked, turning and spilling a little more flour down the front of her apron in the process.

Selda stopped beside her. "You're just getting started, honey. We're making a hundred meat pies."

"A hundred! Who's going to eat them?"

"A hundred tourists. These are for the church booth. Last year we made enough money the first weekend of the festival to take the golden agers to Branson for five days."

"We're going back next spring," Grams added. "Selda's got a thing for Mel Tillis."

"You should talk. You were drooling over John Davidson."

"I was not. That was my false teeth slipping." Their laughter filled the kitchen.

Selda slammed another package of meat on the table and peeled off a layer of butcher paper. "Do you think this ground beef's too lean, Emily?"

"Way too lean, but the pork's a little fatty. Cooked together we should have enough meat drippings to give the pies a decent flavor."

"I don't believe anyone mentioned we were making a hundred pies when you enlisted my help," Jodie complained good-naturedly.

"You didn't ask." Grams and Selda exchanged sly smiles.

"I've been had."

Blair agreed with her, bouncing a rattling set of plastic keys off the tray of his high chair.

"Did you bring the sage?" Grams asked from her position on her all fours. She was rummaging in the bottom cabinet for her biggest mixing bowl.

"You told me you were going to get the sage and some cayenne pepper."

"The pepper's on the counter. Did you buy sage at the store, Jodie?"

"It wasn't on my list."

"Well, we'll just have to stop cooking and go get some. You can't make Natchitoches Meat Pies if you don't have all the right spices," Selda said.

"I don't know how I forgot to put it on the list."

"No reason to fret," Selda said, wiping her hands on the tail of her apron. "It won't take but a minute to run up to Brookshires."

"I'll tell you what," Jodie said, fitting her fifth circle of pie dough onto a slice of waxed paper. "The boys and I will go to the store and get the sage and anything else you need. They're ready for a break."

"You are such a sweetie," Selda purred. "You're lucky to have her around, Emily."

"That's the truth. I plan to keep her here, too, even if I have to go out and find her a husband to do it."

"The way that Kostner boy's hanging around, I'd say he's sweet enough on her to swing for a diamond."

"Hmmph! That fellow's not her type. The man will talk your ears off, and he's a little too thin," Grams snorted, never tiring of her own version of the matchmaking game.

"Well, a man that handsome could slip his shoes under my bed any night," Selda replied. "Of course, I'd have to double up on my heart pills."

The two women erupted in giggles again.

Jodie unstrapped the safety catches on the boys' high chairs and sat the twins on the floor. Blair crawled toward the table leg and started pulling up. Blake headed for a spot of spilled flour.

She grabbed them both, balancing one on each hip. "I'll be back in a few minutes. Are you sure sage is all you need?"

"That's it." Emily followed her to the door. "Be careful," she said.

"I will. The store will be full of people this time of day." Jodie bent down and kissed her grandmother's cheek. No matter how hard Grams tried to present a calm front, the fear was there, just under the surface of carefree chatter, hiding beneath the thin veil of daily routine. And Jodie had brought the trouble down on all of them. She wasn't sure how, but she had to have done something to cause the stalker to pick her out of all the women in New York City.

The drive to Brookshires was uneventful. She parked near the exit and pulled the double stroller from the trunk before unbuckling the twins' car seats. No use to bother with a cart for one item.

"Mommy's going to make this quick. A can of ground sage and then home again, home again, clickety clack." The phrase was accompanied with one of her silliest faces. Blair giggled; Blake stuck a pudgy hand into her face. He was the doubter. It took a lot more than a silly face to convince him being buckled into a stroller was going to be fun.

Wednesdays were obviously a good day for shopping. Fewer people than usual walked the aisles, most with half-filled baskets, and there were no long checkout lines. Jodie walked straight to the spice aisle. She pushed the stroller to the side while she searched for the sage.

"Jodie Gahagen!" The greeting was a high-pitched squeal.

She turned to find a statuesque blond standing behind her, a wide smile showing off a row of perfect white teeth.

"Mary Lou Skelton!" Jodie fell into a bear hug. "It's been years."

"Nine. Tommy and I got married the summer after high school graduation and moved to Little Rock. You were the smart one, going to LSU. I was so envious."

"You were never envious of anyone. How's Tommy?"

"Still sweet as ever. What about you? Did you get married, or are you one of those career women?"

"I'm...unattached now." That covered it better

than the choices Mary Lou provided. "How's your family?"

"Daddy retired, just last month. He and Mom are moving up to Hot Springs Village so they can be close to us and the kids. We have two boys and a girl. Do you believe it?"

"I have twins myself." She turned back to her sons. "Oh, my God, my boys."

"What's the matter?"

"Blake and Blair! They're gone." Terror slammed into her, knocking the breath from her lungs. For a second, her body was frozen in fear. The next second adrenaline shot through her in energizing bursts.

She rounded the corner of the aisle. They were there, sitting calmly, each with a sucker, one end clutched in their pudgy hands, the other stuck in their mouths.

She bent down beside them, relief coursing through her in relentless waves. "Where did these come from?" She pulled the candy from their mouths and they wailed in protest. The suckers were red, heart-shaped. She clutched a shelf filled with canned vegetables for support. *He* had been here. In the one split second she had turned her back, he had pushed the boys around the corner and given them the suckers.

She wanted to cry, to scream, to beat her fists against the stacks of cans and send them clattering to the floor.

"Why are you so upset, Jodie? I mean it's just a sucker. They didn't choke or anything."

"It's not the candy. Someone moved them. While we were talking, someone pushed their stroller around the corner."

"Why would they?"

"To drive me crazy. To let me know he was here, watching me. To let me know I can't stop him." Her voice was shaking. So was she, but she couldn't control herself.

Mary Lou backed away, the look on her face proof that she didn't think the drive to crazy would have to be very far. "Maybe you just walked away from them without thinking, you know, while you were looking at groceries."

Jodie struggled for a calming breath. She had to pull herself together for the boys' sake. "No, it's a long story, Mary Lou. But, the boys are fine. That's all that matters."

"Are you sure you don't want me to call someone?"

Like a psychiatrist. Reading Mary Lou's mind was not a challenge. "There's no reason to call anyone." No reason at all. The police hadn't been able to stop him. And in spite of all of his efforts, neither had Ray.

"If you're sure you're all right?" Mary Lou took another step backward, obviously eager to be on her way.

"I'm sure." She waved Mary Lou off and bent again to hug her boys and wipe the tears from their eyes.

"No more candy," she said, giving each tummy a gentle tickle. "We're going home. Mommy will keep you safe."

Her heart was pounding as she paid for the sage and walked to the car. But still she stole furtive glances in every direction. There was a man loading his groceries in the car, a mother trying to keep up with the preschooler who skipped in front of her, a pregnant lady pushing a cart of groceries. Not one person who could possibly be a suspect.

Mommy will keep you safe. The promise echoed in her head as she started the car and drove back to Grams's house. She would keep that promise or die trying.

Chapter Twelve

Jodie rubbed her burning eyes. She'd spent hours staring at countless mug shots that had gotten her the same place every other step in this dance with the devil had. Nowhere.

"Just a few more, Jodie," Ray urged, giving her shoulders a quick massage.

"It's a waste of time. None of these people look familiar. And none of the people I named or described had a record. Cappan even checked out the guy who sells roasted nuts at the corner by my old apartment. He's squeaky clean, at least in this sense."

She vacated the chair next to Ray's, standing and stretching her neck back as far as it would go without making it hurt more than it already did. Every muscle in her body ached, not only from the activities of the afternoon, but from three months of strain, from tension that woke with her in the morning and slept with her at night.

Cappan walked to the open door and peered in. "Any luck?"

"Nothing but dead ends." She walked over and retrieved her raincoat from the back of a chair, folding it over her arm. "I feel like I've looked at snapshots of every psycho in the state of New York except the one tormenting me.''

''Who isn't in New York at the time.''

''No, the man did what you said he wouldn't, followed me from one end of the country to another.''

''Maybe he'd already done that.''

''I don't follow you.''

''We've been looking for someone who lives, or at least lived, around this area. We could be way off base. Your stalker might be someone from your past, someone from Louisiana who followed you here, or at least came up here looking for you.'' Cappan propped a hip on the door frame.

''That's impossible. I've lived up here five years, ever since I graduated from LSU.''

''What brought you here?''

''I wasn't running from an ex-husband or lover, if that's what you're suggesting. I didn't have one. I came up here with a group of five friends, all women, all of us wanting a taste of big-city life. I'm the only one who lasted.''

''But say someone, like Ray here, was so obsessed with you that he couldn't get you out of his mind.'' Cappan twirled a yellow pencil around his fingers, his gaze moving from first one then to the other of them. ''He comes up here to see you and wham!'' Cappan popped a fist into his palm to emphasize his point. ''The man becomes a full-blown basket case, out of his head crazy for you. He doesn't want to live here, so he tries to frighten you into returning to Louisiana.''

''That's absurd.''

''Not really.'' Ray leaned closer, nodding his head in agreement. ''Actually, I'd already thought of that, only I can't imagine anyone going so far as to kill a man just to get you to return home. But if the person were from Natchitoches originally or Baton Rouge or anywhere else around there, it would explain how he knew where to find you."

"On the other hand," Cappan said, "in five years you must have broken a few hearts in New York. Your sons' father, for example."

"I told you he isn't a suspect," Jodie answered. "We can leave him out of this."

"Under the circumstances, I can't do that."

"I'm the father, Cappan." Ray glared across the table.

"Sorry, I didn't know. Miss Gahagen refused to divulge that information before she left New York."

"Now you know. So let's get back to finding the killer before he loses it and strikes again. The way I see it, all we really know is that the stalker is obviously obsessed with Jodie."

"And crazy enough to kill because of it."

"But like I told you on the phone," Ray said, "I'm worried about the stalker's reference to 'the others.' In my mind that strengthens the possibility that this man doesn't know Jodie. A serial killer who chooses his victims at random."

"I've been thinking along those same lines. Only not necessarily at random. Maybe the man has criteria. The color of her hair, her southern accent, the way she walks."

"You sound like you might have found something." Ray drew his body to full attention, the muscles in his arms straining against his long-sleeved shirt.

"No, unfortunately. The Serial Killer Task Force

has checked the pattern of Jodie's stalker with every open case we have. Only one is close. A couple of women down in the Village, not too far from where Miss Gahagen lived. They complained to neighbors and the police that they were being watched and that someone had been in their houses, going through their things when they weren't home. They turned up dead, about a year apart.''

''When was that?'' Ray asked, picking up a yellow legal pad.

''In the late eighties. No arrests were ever made. But the pattern was different. There were no notes, no gifts, no contact at all.''

''And there's been nothing since then?''

''Not around here. Not that matches the intensity Jodie's dealt with, except, of course when the women knew the suspect. Jilted boyfriends and husbands. That sort of thing.''

Cappan tapped the eraser end of the pencil against his chin. ''I have heard of something similar recently, but I don't give the tale much credence. The man stalked women he was in love with without letting them know who he was. Eventually, he killed them. He had a foolproof plan that kept the police from catching him. That's all I remember about it.''

''Can't you track it down in the police computer or through the FBI?''

''I tried. Couldn't find a thing. That's what makes me think it might have been a made-up scenario. If it was fact, it didn't happen anywhere around here. I can guarantee that.''

''How much danger do you think Jodie is in?'' Ray asked, ''Based on past stalker cases that you can verify.''

"A fair amount. I'd say right now you're in more." He pointed his pencil toward Ray. "The man's killed at least once before. According to Jodie, he stabbed Max Roling to death just because he saw him hugging her. You said you're living in her house. I'd say that makes you a prime target."

"And our sons?"

"The way I see it, the risk goes way down there. The man is obsessed with Jodie. He's probably trying to get up the courage to make a bigger move, let her know who he is, maybe abduct her. If he fails, he may lose control and become violent with her, but I don't think he'd touch the kids. The fact that she's a mother may even be a part of what attracts him to her."

"But he has touched them." Jodie insisted. "He moved Blake from one crib to another when we were still in New York. This week he gave both of them suckers."

"He's touched them. He hasn't hurt them. He had the opportunity to if that was what he wanted. But nothing is certain with a nut like this." Cappan walked over and stopped in front of her chair. "Promise me something, Ms. Gahagen."

"What?"

"This man is dangerous. Let the police handle this case. Promise you won't do anything foolish, that you won't go through with the personal ad scheme."

"How do you know about that? I didn't mention it to you."

"Ray mentioned it on the phone. I agree with him that it's suicide to play games with a sicko. So for all your sakes, give up playing undercover cop."

"I'm afraid I can't make that promise."

Jodie only half listened to the next few minutes of

discussion. They were only rehashing anyway, a confirmation that the trip to New York was a waste of time, energy and money. The money, of course, had been Ray's. He seemed to have an endless supply.

By the time they left the office, even the cold November rain was a welcome change from the bombardment of disappointments and foreshadowings of doom the day had brought.

Afternoon traffic was snarled beyond belief, and after five minutes of sitting in one spot, serenaded by blasting car horns, Ray and Jodie gave up the dry taxi in favor of walking the remaining eight blocks back to the hotel.

They shrugged into rain gear and took off at a steady pace, water dancing about their feet as it pooled in the cracks and splashed from the onslaught of an army of homebound workers. A million people, all in a hurry to get somewhere else.

And here in the masses, a killer had picked Jodie out and attached his life to hers. Why? Ray had asked himself that question a hundred times before. If they knew that they might begin to find answers to the question of who.

He took Jodie's arm, guiding her around a major puddle. "We can duck in somewhere for a drink if you like."

"No, thanks. I'd just like to get back to the hotel and into something dry. And I want to call Grams, just to make sure everything's all right."

"How can it not be? Selda's staying over to help with Blair and Blake, and I hired enough off-duty cops to provide round-the-clock protection inside the house."

"I appreciate that."

"They're my sons, too. Besides, I knew you'd never leave them to make this trip if I didn't, not after the lollipop episode at Brookshires."

"I still wish we could have flown back tonight."

"The late flight was booked solid. Besides, the boys are fine, Grams is fine, and you need a night to be wined and dined in style. The stress level in your life is off the charts."

Conversation stopped as they rounded the corner and hurried toward the door of the Waldorf. Ray's thoughts continued. He had more than wining and dining in mind. Hopefully he'd also be able to drill some sense into Jodie. Isolated meetings with someone who could well be a serial killer. The possibility was driving him out of his mind.

But then everything about Jodie Gahagen was driving him out of his mind. Without Jodie his life had been planned, predictable, prosperous. He hadn't had to deal with personal shortcomings. Hadn't had to look inside himself and see the man who lived beneath the trappings of success.

At thirty-one he'd already made a name for himself as a leading defense attorney in Louisiana. After his last case, his stock had climbed even higher. Big-bucks clients from all over the U.S. would be ringing his phone. They'd already started. The work was piling up, and his partners were yelling for his return.

Everything he'd ever thought he'd wanted was falling into his hands.

What Jodie had to offer was marriage, commitment, children. All of the things he'd been sure he never wanted. Even more sure he could never handle.

He could still walk away when this was over. Send a check every month, have the boys visit during the

Christmas holidays, a couple of weeks in the summer. Jodie would never cling or beg. She'd be the perfect mother. He'd be the louse of a father.

Nobody would be surprised, least of all dear old grandpa Parker. He'd predicted it years ago.

"You let me down, son. You let your mother down. You let everyone down who loves you. You always do."

Ray pushed the hotel door open, the weight of the past and the worries of the present balanced precariously on his shoulders.

Jodie needed dry clothes. He needed a stiff drink.

"This is the perfect nightcap." Jodie snuggled beside Ray in the carriage, the hoofs of the horses providing the sound effects, Central Park providing the scenery.

The rain had stopped while they were at dinner, and when they'd exited the restaurant, the air sported a fresh, just-washed feel, too tempting to forsake for the hotel room. Hand in hand, they'd walked down Fifth Avenue.

Jodie had pointed out the sights and Ray had admired them appropriately. Saint Patrick's Cathedral had been his favorite, but he was also duly impressed with a few gems in the window of Tiffany's.

"No wonder you love this city," he said, tucking the blanket around her. "You must miss it terribly."

"I do." She paused, taking a reading on her own feelings. "And I don't."

"I can see how you wouldn't miss some things, like the traffic and lack of sunlight. But you must miss nights like this."

"I didn't have a lot of nights like this. Usually it

was work all day, pick up the boys, go home and spend precious little time with them.''

"Sounds tough.''

"Oh, no. I'm not complaining. I loved my life, at least I did until it was stolen from me. But being with Grams these past few weeks has made me face the fact that she's getting older.''

"She's a remarkable woman, feisty as a mother lion.''

"Nothing gets by her.'' Jodie laughed and snuggled closer. "I'm thankful she and the boys have had a chance to get to know each other. I guess I'm not sure I want to leave her again. Or even return to a job that takes so much of my time and energy from Blair and Blake.''

"Family.'' Ray ran his fingers through her hair, his fingers entangling in the curls. "You fit in yours so well.''

"You seem to fit in yours just as well.''

"Appearances. They're like a good witness. They say the right things, leave the rest unsaid. The jury has to dig beneath the surface to find the truth.''

"Like the powerful undercurrent between you and your dad?''

"See, you'd make a good juror.''

"Not really. I do better when someone just tells me the truth.''

"The truth has two versions.''

"I'd like to hear yours.''

"I doubt it, but you deserve to know, especially since it affects you as well now. But not right this minute.'' He pulled her close and buried his face in her hair. "A carriage ride through Central Park is no time to pull skeletons out and rattle their bones.''

"No, it's the time for romance." She caught his lips with hers, nibbling and feathering his mouth with kisses until she felt his muscles relax. Her fingers walked the front of his shirt, down to his belt, and lower still.

"No way, lady." He took her hands in his and pulled them out from under the blanket. "First a desk in a law office and then a hammock," he whispered, his tongue caressing her ear. "But not in a carriage."

"Of course not. I'd never dream of such a thing."

"Yeah, sure, says the insatiable sex goddess."

She poked him in the ribs. "You'll be begging when we get back to the hotel."

"Darn right, I will. Unless you beat me to it."

She snuggled closer, burrowing under his arm and close to his heart and wished the night would never end.

JODIE BRUSHED HER TEETH and washed away the evening's makeup before slipping out of her dress and into a teal teddie with scallops that rode the curves of her breasts. The lacy scrap of satin was a far cry from the oversize nightshirts or simple cotton gowns she usually slept in.

She'd slipped it into her luggage at the last minute, then taken it out, then tucked it back under her underwear and zipped the case shut. Ray had shown up to pick her up just as she was unzipping the suitcase to remove it again. Now she was glad she'd brought it along.

She was in love with Ray Kostner. If she'd ever had any doubts, they had disappeared over the last few days. He was always there, putting her first, never making light of her fears, but doing everything in his power to protect her and the boys.

All the signs were there that he loved her as much as she loved him. Everything except a verbal declaration. He admitted the boys were his, although until he'd mentioned it to Cappan today, it had been their secret. And there had not been a word about what would happen between them when he returned to New Orleans.

Life for her and Ray existed only in the here and now. The future was hazy, a smoky cloud that cast a tint of gray over even their best moments. That was the part of the relationship that worried her, the indication that even if she outsmarted the stalker, their love story was not guaranteed a happy ending.

If she was reading all the signs wrong, if he didn't love her, she could accept that. It would tear the heart right out of her, but she would live with it. If he wanted nothing to do with his sons, she'd grant him that, too. Not so much for him, but for them.

Her position had never waffled. Blake and Blair would be surrounded by love and protected from the type of rejection that could whittle away their self-confidence and destroy their spirit. She'd seen it happen to some of her friends. She wouldn't let it happen to her sons.

Their future as a family lay in Ray's hands. She would fight to the death in a battle she could win, but she would never settle for crumbs. If he wanted to be a father, she expected him to be there for them, dependable, nurturing and loving. If he wanted her, it would be all or nothing. Marriage, commitment and passion ever after.

With steady hands, she raked back the mass of tangled curls that fell over her forehead and dotted a splash of flowery fragrance behind each ear. Satisfied that she looked as good as she could on a minimum of maintenance, she slipped her blue terry robe over everything.

First the terry robe and talk. Then the teal nightie and...whatever the night brought.

RAY STOOD AT the window, staring out at the New York skyline. He wondered how many women out there were suffering the way Jodie had been, alone in a city of teeming millions, stalked by a man who took his pleasure from torment.

Jodie stepped into the room, and his heart took the familiar lurch. He had so little of value to offer to a woman like Jodie, but he would give her what he could. He'd protect her from a killer, with his life if it came to that. Too bad he hadn't protected her from getting involved with himself.

"You look devastating," he said.

"If old terry robes turn you on, you are easy."

"*You* turn me on. In or out of the robe. Preferably out." He tugged at the tie that circled her waist, pulling her toward him.

"I love it when you talk dirty to me."

"Who said anything about talking?"

"Actually, you did." She pulled away. "Earlier tonight, in the carriage."

Ray felt his gut twist painfully. "That talk can wait. It will spoil a perfect night."

"I'd like to hear it."

"Hearing it won't change anything."

"It will help me know you better."

His hands fisted at his side. "It will do that all right,

let you know just what kind of man fathered your sons. That will make your day.''

"It's night, not day and too late to worry. You've already made several of my days and nights. Besides, you should know what I'm made of by now. I can handle disappointments.''

"Then maybe I am the man for you. I can dish them out. But then you know what I'm made of by now, too. You were pregnant with my sons. I ignored your phone calls. You were being followed by a madman, I was in New Orleans defending one of our illustrious senators.''

"You were doing your job.'' She took his arm and led him to the love seat. ''And you didn't know about your sons then.''

"You can make excuses all you want, Jodie. But you'll get tired of them eventually. There will finally be one disappointment too many. Ask my dad.''

"No. I'm asking you. What happened between you and Parker?''

Ray got up from the love seat and walked to the stocked bar in the corner of the room. ''Can I get you something?''

"No, I'm fine.'' Her voice was soft, reassuring. He wondered if it would be that way after she heard the disgusting truths.

He took out a small bottle of whiskey and poured a shot into a glass, swishing the amber liquid around, buying time. Pulling the memories from the dark crevices of his mind was taking its toll.

"I don't know how well you knew me during my high school years.''

"I knew about you. You were Mr. Cool, the town bad boy.''

"That was me, all right. Charm the girls, skip class, get kicked off the football team when we were headed for state. The team lost the championship game miserably, and my friends hated me for the loss."

"All of that was a long time ago. Surely you aren't still concerned about what happened when you were a teenager."

"No. It just establishes the pattern my life has taken. My dad wanted a perfect son. I heard it for as long as I can remember. 'You are the son of a judge. People expect you to be better than the others. *I* expect you to be better.'"

He tilted his head back and took a long swig of the whiskey, feeling the burn and wishing it were more harsh. Physical pain was a comfort compared to baring his soul.

"That must have been hard on you."

There it was again, the cool voice of reason, spewing from the mouth of a sexy redhead who had been through hell herself. She never ceased to amaze him.

"It was too hard. So I took the path of least resistance. I went the opposite direction, looking for things that would shock, things that would make the citizens' of Natchitoches tongues wag, things that would make my dad lash out at me for being the disappointing son I was."

"But you went to college and turned your life around."

"I went away to college and got Sylvia Stevens pregnant."

"Sylvia Stevens?" Jodie's voice rose an octave or two. Now he had her attention.

"The one and only. Sweet, hometown girl who raced from one beauty title to another. We made love one night after a fraternity party. A month later she showed up at my door and told me she was pregnant with my child.''

''Did you love her? Did she love you?''

''No, to both questions. I told her I doubted the baby was mine.''

Memories grappled with his self-control, tension turning his stomach into a war zone. He ground his right fist into his left palm, his mouth set so tight he could feel his teeth grinding together.

''She was scared to death, sure her mom was going to go ballistic when she found out her daughter would have to drop out of the Miss Louisiana Pageant. Apparently, the contests were as much for her mom as they were for her. Sylvia begged me to run off with her and get married.''

''What did you do?''

''I demanded proof the baby was mine. I should have been supportive. But, true to form I handled everything all wrong.''

''What happened?''

''Sylvia took an overdose of sleeping pills. She didn't die, but she came close.''

Jodie sat quietly, her gaze penetrating, unreadable.

''Have you heard enough?'' he asked.

''Not until I've heard it all. What happened to the baby?''

''Turns out there wasn't one. It was a missed diagnosis on the doctor's part. But complications resulting from the overdose forced her to withdraw from the Miss Louisiana Pageant. Her chance at becoming Miss America was lost, and once again I was guilty of spoiling someone's dreams. And no one hated me more than I hated myself.''

"You weren't to blame. How could you even think that? You had no way of knowing she'd react so dangerously when you asked for proof of parentage. You couldn't have been more than eighteen at the time."

Ray poured himself another drink. "Neither Sylvia nor her mother saw it exactly the way you do. And like all tragedies, there's an epilogue."

"She can't still blame you."

"No. Blame wasn't good enough. Sylvia went to my dad and asked for money to start her life over. A lot of money in exchange for keeping quiet about the fact that his son had caused her such pain. She failed to mention to him that although we had made love, there never was a baby. He thought she had lost it when she took the sleeping pills."

"That's blatantly dishonest. Surely he didn't give her money without asking you."

"Of course. He would have given her twice that amount to keep her from blabbing the story to his friends. Natchitoches is a small town. They don't forgive too easily, at least that has always been my dad's theory. Not when it's The Judge's son who's involved."

"Then all of you were wrong."

"No, I was wrong. I've regretted my mistakes every minute of every day since I ruined my dad's and Sylvia's lives, but regrets don't change anything."

"People were disappointed, Ray. Their lives weren't ruined."

He met Jodie's gaze. Her eyes burned with concern and a depth of understanding that touched his soul. It was as if her compassion released the doors he'd closed on his past and let him explore the disillusionment in a new light.

"My dad and Sylvia wouldn't agree with you. I committed a mistake that made it possible for Sylvia to believe she was pregnant. I let her leave in a state of fury. And, at least in my dad's eyes, I led him into blackmail, caused him to break the law he'd spent his adult life interpreting."

"But you were only a freshman in college. You panicked and understandably so. Maybe you didn't handle the situation with great empathy, but asking for proof of parentage was sensible. You can't be blamed for the overdose and certainly not for your dad giving in to blackmail threats."

"Why not? I caused everything else bad that happened in my parents' lives. My parents never forgave me and neither did Sylvia and her family. Apparently the houseful of trophies she'd won meant nothing without the Miss America crown."

"Even if she'd made it that far, she had only a chance of winning. Your dad is not still paying Sylvia money, is he?"

"No. He stopped after the second payment. That's when some reporter found out that hard-hitting Judge Parker, the man who had no empathy for anyone found guilty of unlawful behavior, was paying a young girl to keep quiet."

"How would a reporter find out?"

"From Sylvia. My dad quit paying. She followed through on her threat to make us suffer for her pain and disappointment. And she had copies of the checks to back up her story."

"The killing cycle of deceit."

"The only solution in my dad's mind was to step

down from the judgeship. He hung up his robes and slipped into a depression that lasted for two years. Being a judge was his life, his symbol that he was what a man should be, better than the best. I took that away from him and nothing I can do now will change that.''

Jodie walked over and wrapped her arms about him. The pain in his gut intensified. ''I always let the people down who depend on me. If you were smart, you'd be running out the door now,'' he whispered.

''I'm not running anywhere.'' She hugged him close, the warmth of her melting the ice that coursed his veins.

''You'll be sorry. You can't count on me. Ask my dad.''

''I don't have to ask anyone. I can see for myself who you are—a troubled boy who matured into a wonderful man.'' A tear trickled down her cheek. He whisked it away with his fingertips.

''Don't you see,'' she continued, the love in her eyes so tangible, he felt he could hold it in his hands. ''In spite of all the conflict between you and your dad, he called, and you put your own career on hold to come running. You moved into my house the second you realized I was in danger, and you've barely left my side since. You've put your own life on the line to keep me and our sons safe.''

She stretched on tiptoes and touched her lips to his. ''I love you, Ray Kostner. I think I have since the first time you gave me a careless peck on the cheek on my fourteenth birthday.''

''You beat me.'' He kissed her moist eyes and the tip of her nose. ''It was the night of your senior prom that did me in. The last kiss, at your front door. I fell so hard my head was still ringing from the blow years later, when I finally looked you up in New York.''

''We saw each other several times when I first got to LSU,'' she said, her mouth inches from his. ''You showed me the ropes, the impressive law student helping out the freshman coed. I never once guessed you cared about me.''

''I didn't have the right. I still don't.''

''I do. I claim the right to love you.''

While he watched, she slipped out of the terry robe and let it slide it to the carpet. ''I want you, Ray, all of you. Tonight and forever.''

''I can't promise anything.''

''I didn't ask for promises. I said I love you. Unconditionally. The way you are.''

Emotions exploded inside him. Whether he deserved it or not, Jodie was here, knowing the truth and still loving him. For now, that was all that mattered. He picked her up and carried her to the bed, laying her atop the cool sheets, watching her hair spread like a halo of fire over the pillows.

She pulled him down beside her, running her fingers across his chest, catching the matted dark hairs around her fingers.

''The nightie is exquisite,'' he whispered, responding to her touch with the primal cravings she always aroused. ''But it has to go.''

''You first.''

She ran her finger down his torso, loosening the tie at the waist of his pajamas and scooting them down past his hips. He shed them quickly and then started on her, untying the lacy ribbon, releasing her breasts.

He buried his mouth in one, caressing, sucking, kneading the nipple with his lips and tongue until it stood at rock-hard attention. Only then did he start the exotic journey down the smooth flesh of her belly, his hands sliding over her hips.

Tiny moans escaped her lips, driving him on.

He teased and taunted every soft curve, his fingers and lips seeking the places that gave her the most pleasure. His efforts were rewarded with streams of liquid fire.

"Please, Ray," she begged. "I need you now."

He raised over her and she spread her legs, curling them around him, her body thrusting toward him. He slipped inside her, pushing, throbbing with the need to satisfy her before he lost all control.

She came in an explosion of passion, so intense it sucked her breath away, so perfect he soared with her to the heights before collapsing almost lifeless into the afterglow of fulfillment.

He rolled over, still inside her, her body moist and warm next to his. He didn't know if he was right for her, couldn't believe that joy like this was his for the taking. He only knew that life had never felt so wonderful before.

He closed his eyes and pretended Saturday and her possible date with a killer was only a nightmare that would be gone when he opened them again.

Chapter Thirteen

The sun had just poked its head above the horizon Saturday morning when Jodie crept from the bed, careful not to wake Ray. They had both lain awake until the wee hours this morning, making love, talking about what the day might bring and then holding each other until they fell asleep.

Ray and Butch both saw only the danger in the personal ad. Jodie saw more. It was a chance to draw the stalker out of the shadows and into the light. And if the stalker actually read the ad and called, Butch would be the real undercover cop, following her in secret, watching her from a safe distance, stepping in if the stalker presented any danger. Arresting him when they had the evidence to make murder charges stick.

She had to go through with this. She had everything to gain. She had nothing to lose.

Except her life.

If all went as planned she would be face-to-face with the man who had broken into her apartment, run his hands over her intimate apparel, released his evil all around her like a poisonous gas, deadly yet invisible.

She hugged her arms about her chest and fought the apprehension that rode her nerves like a river of ice.

Ray roused, stretching, one foot escaping the covers. "What time is it?"

"It's early. I woke up and couldn't get back to sleep. I'll go downstairs and start the coffee." She bent over and kissed the top of his head.

"Are you all right?"

"Of course, I'm all right. And don't go around asking me that all day. If you do, Grams will know something is up. As it is, she doesn't suspect a thing."

"You underestimate the lady. She can't remember past her last step, but she's as shrewd as they come at figuring out what you don't want her to know."

"Tell me about it. That's why we have to be extra careful. No one knows about the ad but you, me, Cappan and the local police. We have to make sure it stays that way if this plan has a chance of working."

"Just us and every man, woman and child who reads the personal ads."

"But all they have is a phone number," she assured him.

"Phone numbers can easily be matched to addresses."

"Go back to sleep," she whispered. Sliding into her slippers, she tiptoed down the stairs and into the foyer. Unlatching the dead bolt, she opened the door and scanned the area. No newspaper, and there probably wouldn't be one for another hour. But at some houses in Natchitoches and in the surrounding areas, the paper would have already been delivered, the weekend supplement with the personal ads folded neatly inside.

Seconds later, she had the coffee brewing and a couple of pieces of wheat bread in the toaster. The sun was pouring in the window now, painting the kitchen floor and walls in blinding beams.

Pulling out a tray, Jodie loaded it with two coffee cups, spoons, sugar, cream, toast plates and a crystal bowl of preserves. Not a full breakfast, but a bite. She'd be surprised if either she or Ray managed to get it down.

When the coffee was ready, she filled a silver pitcher and added it to the tray. The trappings of a holiday for lovers to counteract the ominous cloud that hung over them. Careful not to spill the coffee, she ascended the steep staircase to her bedroom.

"What is this?" she said, pushing through the door. Ray was lying in the middle of the bed and Blake was climbing over him, trying to grasp and pull one of his dad's ears.

"He was awake, rooting around like a hungry armadillo, so I went and got him before he woke Blair. He was wet. I changed him."

Ray held Blake up so Jodie could admire his handiwork. "We didn't bother putting the pajama bottoms back on. He said he needed more freedom to kick."

"Oh, he did, did he?"

"Yeah. It sounded like, 'gibber ga ga gaboo,' but I understood him."

"You are a man of many talents." She sat the tray on the table.

The phone rang, shattering the moment. They both grew silent, listening as the newly installed second line completed its first and second rings. Before it started its third, Jodie picked up the receiver.

"Hello." The word was almost lost, stuck in her throat behind a strangling lump.

"Are you the lady who put the ad in the personal column?" The voice was low and husky, and she could hear deep breathing through the line.

"Yes." She had to push the word out of her clogged throat.

"What do you look like? Are you pretty with long blond hair and big breasts? If you are, I'd like to meet you. Anytime, anywhere. I'd like to…"

Violent shivers shook Jodie's body while the raspy voice on the line told her in painstakingly filthy detail what he'd like to do to her.

Shaking, she slammed the receiver into the cradle.

"It wasn't him," she said. "It was an obscene caller who didn't even know what I look like."

"The kind of low-life pervert that ad of yours is bound to appeal to. Give it up, Jodie, now, while you still can."

She ran a finger down his cheek. "I'd like nothing better. You must know that. But I can't go on living in constant fear for myself and everybody I love."

The red lights on the baby monitor lit up like a Christmas tree, and loud howls blasted forth from the box.

"Looks like your brother's awake, Blake." For once, the howls were a welcome relief. Jodie's nerves were too shot to argue with Ray.

He wrapped an arm around her shoulder. "I didn't mean to get upset with you, Jodie. But when I saw the look on your face while that man poured out his filth, I wanted to climb through the phone and plant a fist upside his head."

"Let's just drop it, Ray. If it takes hearing a few

bad words to find Max's killer and stop the assault on my life, I can handle it.'' With that she was out of the door, hoping she was telling the truth. Caller number one still had her quaking.

THERE WERE A couple of more calls on Saturday morning. The second rivaled the first for indecent proposals. The third was a soft-spoken man who claimed he was looking for a lasting relationship with a good woman.

By the time the boys were down for their afternoon nap, Jodie had stuck the cordless phone in her pocket and retreated to the back porch for a cup of tea. Ray was in the study, typing on his laptop.

She settled in the wooden rocker, letting her heavy eyelids close and her mind wander. Male voices shook her to attention just before sleep claimed her.

Grady and Butch walked up from the back of the property, talking and laughing like old friends. It had been less than an hour since Butch had called for late-breaking information on the success of the ad.

Now he was here, obviously checking on everything for himself. Somehow she was sure the visit was due to a request by Ray. The no-ties man was doing an excellent imitation of a worried husband and father. Had she not been walking on eggshells herself, she could have appreciated the attention a lot more.

"He's been hanging around the boathouse, asking me a bunch of questions," Grady said, his voice carrying from the walk to the porch.

"I want you to keep a close eye on him for me. I don't trust the man as far as I can spit."

"Who is it that you don't trust, Butch?" she asked as he neared the porch.

"Selda's tenant."

"I thought you already checked him out."

"I did. Record's clean, but I've had a man tailing him the past couple of days. He hasn't been near a plantation. Close as we can tell, he's just hanging around town, taking a bunch of pictures of everything and everybody and asking a lot of questions about things that shouldn't concern him." He propped a foot on the bottom step. "How friendly has he been with you?"

"We've talked. Nothing out of line. In fact, he started my car one day when it had stalled in town."

"You didn't mention that to me."

"It had nothing to do with you. He wasn't threatening, just helpful." She stared up at the window to his room. The blinds were closed tight. "He did ask me if I'd have dinner with him sometime."

Butch's eyebrows shot up like question marks.

"It was nothing, Butch, really. I mean he took no for an answer without getting upset. I think he's just lonely. At first I was a little suspicious, but he seems so...so normal."

"Depends on how normal you think voyeurism is. Grady tells me he sees him in his window all the time watching you when you're in the yard or on the porch with the boys."

All of a sudden the air felt heavy and humid, a suffocating blanket that choked her breath away.

"Stay away from him, Jodie."

"Believe me, I will. Unless the stalker calls—" She broke off in midsentence. Grady was still in the yard but he watched her like a fox eyeing a chicken nest. One mistake and he'd pick it up, know something was up, figure out that she and Butch were laying a trap. And the more people who knew, the more chance the all-knowing stalker would find out as well.

Everybody's a suspect. The words settled in her stomach like bitter broth.

Butch climbed the steps and sauntered over to the rocker, his voice low, meant only for her ears. "I'll be running errands this afternoon, but I'll have my beeper on every minute." His eyes and voice issued a warning. "Call me, at once, if anything changes."

"I will."

Butch lingered another second, and she sensed his own nerves were as rattled as hers. One more person she was pulling into danger. She attempted a smile. He tipped his hat and shuffled back down the steps and over to the gate where Grady waited, a foot propped on the wooden post.

They talked a few minutes more, about fishing, the upcoming festival and the problems it created for the local police. Finally Butch glanced her way, tipped his cap again and swung open the gate.

A yellow jacket flew from the creaking wood and into his face. He slapped wildly, flinging his arms, hitting himself on the tip of his crooked nose, backing up so fast he all but fell on his behind.

Grady roared in laughter. "You're not afraid of a little old bee, are you, Officer Deaton?"

Butch shut him up with a look. But Grady was still grinning when Butch marched through the gate. He walked to the edge of the porch.

"I've been meaning to thank you for the job," Grady said, resting his elbows on the planks that extended past the porch railing.

"No need to. The coat of paint on the boathouse spruced it up nicely. You've earned your pay, such as it is. I'm sure you could earn more in town with all the preparations for next weekend.''

"The big weekend. Thousands of tourists in town. Not a good time to be checking for strangers, is it?''

"I wouldn't know. That's not my job.''

"No, I guess not. You've got bumbling Officer Deaton for that. And, my dad, of course. He pictures himself some big hero, stepping in and catching the crackpot who's been bothering you.''

"Just what do you know about my *crackpot?*''

"Just what my dad volunteered when I came to work here. Some nut's following you around, sending you flowers and stuff. I'd hate to be the man if my dad does catch him. He'll leave here in little pieces.''

"Gentle Ben. He doesn't have a violent bone in his body.''

"Not unless you rile him.''

The conversation rolled like thunder in Jodie's head, striking holes in her solution. Grady knew too much about her and the stalker situation. Perhaps the whole town did. Which gave the stalker the advantage and significantly reduced the odds that the trap would work.

Mumbling an excuse, she left Grady standing and went back inside, creeping into the room where Ray was working. Tucking her feet under her, she curled up in an upholstered reading chair to watch him. As always, his presence eased her fear and doubts and strengthened her resolve.

This time when her eyes closed, they stayed that way until the boys woke up from their naps, demanding her attention.

THE UNBEARABLE TENSION that had hovered over the weekend still pounded in Kostner's head on Monday

morning as he drove to the office. Five more calls
came in on the second phone line. One had been
Butch. The others had been strangers whose conversations had convinced Jodie they were not the man of
her nightmares, though judging from her reactions,
some certainly had the potential for being dangerous
in their own rights. Her ad had played into their hands
nicely, providing a phone number for immediate grat-
ification.

Ray massaged his right temple, wishing he'd started
the day with a couple of painkillers. Now he'd have
to wait until he got to the office and hit the supply in
his desk drawer. Only it wasn't his desk drawer today.
He'd be moving to the smaller office. Parker was returning to take over his throne.

Ray pulled the car to a stop in front of his dad's
house. No need to get out. Parker was at the door, hat
on his head, briefcase in one hand, his cane in the
other. Punctuality was important. One of his top five
sermons.

Ray was always late. This morning was no excep-
tion.

"You said you'd be here ten minutes ago," his dad
said, scrunching into the front seat, tapping the globe
of his watch before buckling in.

"Good morning, Dad," Ray offered. "It's nice to
see you, too."

"Well, of course, son. It would have been nicer ten
minutes ago. I'm probably sweating in this dadburned
overcoat your mother insisted I wear. She thinks I'm
going to freeze in forty degree weather."

No use to point out to him that he could have put
the coat on after he arrived to pick him up. They both

grew silent, and Ray turned on the radio to ease the tension. Parker beat an impatient rhythm with his cane, tapping it against the floorboard.

Ray slowed automatically. Old habits of rebellion died hard. But this time he refused to slide back into the games he'd always played. The accelerator responded instantly to the pressure of his foot, returning the car to its previous speed as his mind went back to Jodie.

If she called, he'd be out of the office like Superman to the rescue. She was not keeping a date with a madman without him, not even if every policeman in the parish were there to watch over her. He had pressured until she promised she would not leave the house without alerting him.

"What do you think about Carl Baker?" Parker asked, bringing up the case Ray had been summoned from New Orleans to handle.

"I think he's innocent. Don't you?"

"That's why I took the case. Do you think we can convince a jury of that?"

"Unless the prosecutor digs up a witness that proves we're wrong. Shreveport murders are a little out of your ballpark, aren't they?"

"A little. Carl's dad's a friend of mine. Besides, it's only an hour's drive to Shreveport, less now that I-49 is finished. The world is shrinking. There's plenty of work in this area for a good defense attorney."

"Too much for you right now, according to your doctors."

"If I listened to them, I'd be an invalid."

"A six-week rehabilitation period after a bypass is not considered excessive for a man your age."

"See, you've been listening to your mother. Age

doesn't mean a thing. I've been doing my job in this town ever since I passed the bar exam.''

Ray didn't respond. He didn't want to spend the morning arguing, and his father had a way of construing all of his comments as negative. Slowing, he pulled over to the curb and stopped in front of the law office. ''Why don't you get out here and open up? I'll park the car in the back.''

Parker did, opening the door and getting to his feet a lot more slowly than he had before the surgery. Every movement he made these days was slower than usual. And no matter the friction that met every contact between them, it hurt Ray to see his father weak and struggling.

Ray parked the car and took the back steps to the second-floor office. He usually ran them, hungry for the exercise he missed. In New Orleans, he started each day with an hour workout at the gym, ending with a stint in the steam room and a hot shower.

Today he walked, using the time to work out how he was going to tell his father that Carl Baker had asked him to take over as lead attorney. The case was challenging, but the last thing Ray wanted to do was throw another curve at a man who liked his pitches straight and down the middle. And in his control.

Ray pushed through the door and into the outer office. The room smelled of disinfectant and lemons, the handiwork of the cleaning crew. When Barbara showed up at nine, it would also smell of strong coffee.

A tormented groan rumbled from his dad's office. Ray felt the air sucked out of him. In three steps he was across the room, busting through the door.

His dad lay on the floor, his eyes rolled back in his

head, a straight-backed chair laying across him. Blood dripped from his head and pooled on the carpet.

"A man...in the dark...waiting." Parker closed his eyes and fell silent.

Adrenaline shot through Ray, refueling a body that shock had temporarily drained and rendered useless. He lunged for the phone with one hand and his dad's wrist with the other, checking the pulse as he punched in 911.

Working on automatic, he gave the information to the operator and turned his attention to his father. The bleeding was from a flesh wound, a gash across the top of his eye where the chair had apparently made contact. A knot as big as a baseball had popped up on his forehead, just under the cut. The pulse was weak, the breathing an unsteady rasp that rumbled from his chest.

The next five minutes passed in a murky blur of empty reassurances that didn't lighten when the ambulance arrived and the paramedics lifted Parker onto the stretcher.

"Hold on, Mr. Kostner. We've got you now. We're starting the oxygen and heading out of here."

His dad's hand fell from the stretcher and Ray grabbed it, holding on to it. Every fiber of his body twisted in silent rage as the truth slammed into his brain. Jodie's stalker had struck again.

The attack had been meant for him.

He stooped over to pick up his dad's cane. It was then he noticed the fish fillet knife just under the corner of his desk and bloody footsteps leading to the door of the adjoining office, the one he had taken over.

"DO YOU THINK this bird is big enough?" Selda asked, stuffing the turkey with corn bread dressing.

"Unless we're feeding the whole block," Jodie said reassuringly, balancing Blake on one hip so that he could see the Thanksgiving action.

Blair was under the table, looking for the plastic stacking donut that had rolled from his grasp. Already, he hated to be held, wriggling back to freedom as soon as she picked him up.

"It's just us," Selda said, "and Greg's joining us, too. Working in a strange town is no way to spend the holidays."

"What about Ben?" Jodie asked.

"He said he wasn't comfortable at a fancy family dinner, not that this is. But I'm packing a plate for him and one for his son."

"And Eloise Grimes," Grams added, from the far corner of the counter where she was peeling and cubing sweet potatoes. "Her son and his family run off to Lafayette for the holidays every year and just forget she's around. I'm picking her up from the nursing home and bringing her here."

As always, Selda and Grams shared their Thanksgiving bounty with as many as they could and loved every minute of it. Jodie decided her sons could learn a lot from these two selfless women.

"What about the Kostner boy?" Grams asked as if it were an afterthought. "Is he going to come sniffing around when the work's all done?"

Selda called her bluff. "If he didn't, you'd be the disappointed one."

"Ba ga ma um." Blake gave his answer.

"Which means Ray will be here any minute," Jodie translated. "He's at the hospital in Shreveport this morning, visiting with his dad."

"How's Parker doing?" Selda asked.

"Improving steadily. His heart withstood the blood loss without any apparent harm. He still has a bump and nasty bruise on his head, though."

"Do they have any idea who attacked him?" Selda looked up from her turkey to watch Jodie's face as she answered.

"No. Just a robbery attempt," she answered, following police orders to keep suspicions under wraps. "Apparently, Parker surprised him, and the thief reacted violently."

"I hope they get him. This has always been such a peaceful town. It breaks my heart to see things like this happen."

The telephone in Jodie's apron pocket jangled. For a second, she almost picked it up and answered, but the chill of reality twisted inside her, stopping her.

"It's my business line, I need to take this call where it's quiet," she whispered, trying and failing to keep her voice calm. "Watch Blair for me." She didn't wait for a reply. As soon as she'd stepped into the hall, she punched the button and put the receiver to her ear.

"Hello."

"Hello, Jodie."

Her heart slammed against the wall of her chest.

"Who is this?"

"A friend."

Her heart was racing now, her nerves on edge, her will battling the paralyzing effect of suffocating fear. "Are you the friend who sends me flowers and gifts?"

"I'm the friend who watches over you." The voice was muffled, disguised in some way, impossible to identify even if she'd heard it before.

"I tried to keep you a good girl. But you didn't want to be good, did you?"

She could hear his breathing, heavy with the evil inside him. She hugged Blake so tightly he squealed in protest. Dropping to the couch, she let him wriggle from her lap to the floor.

"I do want to be good. I'm trying to save myself for you. But it's hard when you never let me see you."

"Does the man who sleeps in your house sleep in your bed, Jodie?"

"No. He has his own room."

"You're lying to me. He's been with you. Even in his law office, you let him make love to you. The smell of him is all over you. You are not a good girl, Jodie Gahagen."

Oh, God. This man was sicker than she thought. He had to be stopped now, before he killed again.

"But I want to be good. You could help me. If I could see you, maybe then you could save me."

"Or maybe this is a trick."

"It's not a trick. I just want to meet you, face-to-face. There's a house on the outskirts of town. It's deserted. No one will see us meet there."

"If the police follow you, I'll know it. No matter how clever they are, they are not as clever as I am. You should know that by now."

"I do. I know that better than anyone."

"I won't hurt you, Jodie, not if you're by yourself. But if you lie to me, I can't promise anything. I go crazy sometimes."

"Like when you killed Max Roling?"

"Don't make me do something like that again. Come alone, Jodie. Do you understand?"

"Yes."

She gave him the directions, slowly, her mind in such turmoil she could barely think, her voice so shaky, the words were a muttered garble.

"When shall I meet you?" she asked.

"Now." The disconnecting click of the phone signaled he was through talking.

She reached down and picked up Blake, hugging him close, kissing the top of his head. She'd do the same with Blair. Hold him close. Her sons would give her the courage to do what she had to do to stop a madman.

She punched in Butch's beeper number, putting in her number when the recorded voice gave the instructions. She would tell Butch, but not Ray. He was probably on his way home from Shreveport by now, but she didn't want him to show up at the Coxlin place.

She had to believe she would return safely. But this way, if something should happen to her, Blake and Blair wouldn't be left alone. They would still have a father.

And Ray would not be sucked into her chasm of madness and death.

Chapter Fourteen

Jodie left Highway 119, pulling onto a gravel roadbed that wound through oaks, dogwood and pine on its journey to the old Coxlin place. She was not alone. Rabbits, squirrels, even a doe scurried out of her way, as if sensing she was bringing evil into their hideaway.

The road ended at the house. She killed her engine, lowering the car window and listening. All was quiet, and there was not another car in sight. But Butch should be inside the house by now, hidden in the dark caverns of the attic, waiting for her and the stalker.

Sliding from the car, she stepped off the road, onto what used to be a path to the house. Her feet sank into knee-high grass. Cautiously, she made her way to the old wooden steps leading to the half-rotted front porch.

She slipped her hand to her neck, caressing the small locket Butch had provided, the one that held the tiny microphone that would record the stalker's every word. Take his own testimony and use it to prove his guilt. That was part of the plan she and Butch had worked out down to the last precise detail.

Ray had never approved of the plan. He had refused

to listen to reason even though both she and Butch had insisted that an extra person made the setup all the more risky and far less likely to succeed.

Today it would be her, Butch and a madman. Shaking, she gulped in a huge helping of air and took the first step. The rough wood groaned at her weight, and a shudder ran through her. Was Max's killer waiting just inside the door watching her, hidden in dark shadows? The way he had done so many times before.

There was only one way to find out. Nerves riding the edge of control, she crossed the wide porch and pushed through the heavy door before her resolve had time to weaken.

A spiderweb tangled in her hair and eyes. She brushed it away. Silence met her ears. She waited for long seconds and then walked deeper into the interior of a house that had withstood tornadoes and floods only to see its past grandeur dissolve into rot.

She'd been here only twice before. One Halloween on a dare when she was a freshman in high school. The second time had been with Butch Deaton a few days ago.

Today it seemed far more ominous. Dark, crumbling walls, rusted chandeliers that hung at precarious angles, dank, musky odors that choked her breath away. A tomb would be more welcoming.

Bad analogy, she decided, forcing herself to take a deep steadying breath of the stale air. Maybe the stalker wasn't coming. Or maybe he'd beaten her here, parked his car behind dense clusters of trees and undergrowth. Maybe he was waiting for her to find him. More moves in his bizarre game of terror.

"Is anybody here?" Her voice crawled the walls

and the rafters, delving into depths of blackness and echoing back like a high-pitched wail.

Even that was welcome relief from the maddening silence. The squeak of the door was not. She jerked around.

"Butch?"

"Who were you expecting?"

"The stalker." Disappointment rushed her senses and sharpened her tone. "You promised you'd stay hidden until the stalker showed up."

"But there's no one here but you and me, Jodie."

"He's coming. He has to be. We had this all worked out, Butch."

"You are so eager to meet the stalker." He stepped closer and snaked an arm around her shoulders, tangling his fingers in her hair. "Are you sure you're ready for him, Jodie? Alone and helpless, the way you are now. Out here where no one can hear your screams?"

His tone grew dark, and icy fingers of fear crawled her skin. But he was frightening her on purpose, trying to dissuade her from doing this again.

She pulled away from him. "I'm not alone, Butch. You're here. But we may as well leave now. Even if the stalker was going to show, he won't with you out in the open. I told you he made me promise not to bring anyone."

"And did you do as he asked, or is Ray with you, hidden in the woods, waiting to rush to your rescue if I don't do the job?"

"I'm alone."

"Perhaps the man who wants you for himself is here with us right now, thinking of how it would feel to crush you against him."

"Cut out the fright tactics, Butch. They won't work with me. I've lived with fear too intimately and far too long to break now."

He reached a hand toward her, then stopped and whirled toward the door as it squeaked open again. This time it was Ray who marched in.

"What in the devil is going on here?"

"Your girlfriend threw a party," Butch answered. "Only the guest of honor didn't show." His voice returned to normal, the Gothic tone discarded like old chewing gum.

Ray unhooked his beeper and threw it in her direction. She caught it one-handed.

"Test it, Jodie. It works fine. So, why didn't it go off before you drove out here? You were not supposed to go through with this unless I was here."

"Just settle down, Ray. I can explain everything."

"Good. I just covered thirty miles in about twenty minutes, panicking every second about what I'd find when I got here. This better be one hell of an explanation."

She didn't have one he'd buy, and she was too frustrated to lie. "Did you ever stop to think that I might know what I'm doing, that I didn't need you to come tearing out here like a macho knight on a quest to save the ignorant maiden?" Without looking back, she marched out of the house and dropped behind the wheel of her car, slamming the door behind her. She left both men standing in a cloud of dust as she spun out.

A few minutes ago she'd been alone, drowning in fear. But at least then there had been a chance that the nightmare she'd been living with for over three months might come to an end. Now there was nothing except the fierce guilt that gripped her heart like ribbons of steel.

Max was dead because of her. Gloria was dead because of her, although no one but Jodie believed the stalker had been in her shop that night. And Parker Kostner was in a hospital, lucky to be alive. Like Russian roulette, the next victim would fall to the luck of the twirl.

Grams, Ray, herself. Even Blair or Blake, totally innocent, totally dependent on her. How had she let this evil creep into their world? She gunned the engine, frustration churning inside her like black coffee left to boil on an open burner.

The stalker had outsmarted them again.

THE PERSONAL AD hot line stayed silent the rest of Thanksgiving Day, giving Jodie time to cool down and all of them time to enjoy a dinner laden with calories and taste and blessed with laughter.

As always, life had gone on. The boys had still entertained with toddler antics, Grams had still told fascinating stories, Selda had still made them laugh. And Ray had glared at her over the top of the turkey, too upset with her to give an inch.

Now dusk was starting to fall on another day. Friday evening and no further attempts at contact by the stalker. Impatience twisted inside Jodie. A dozen times or more, she had checked the phone to make sure it still had a dial tone. But the problems were not with the instrument. They lay with the stalker.

Either he had smelled a trap from the start or he had been frightened off by Butch and Ray. But Jodie hadn't given up. The phone was with her now, tucked into the pocket of her green windbreaker. It rested silently while she pushed the boys in baby swings Ray had attached to a low-hanging branch of the centuries-old oak tree.

Grams was inside dozing; Ray was on the porch, spread across the wicker settee, the work he'd brought home from the office moving from one pile to another and back again as he scrutinized page after page. So much for taking the day after Thanksgiving as a holiday.

"That must be pretty interesting fare," she called out. "What are you working on?"

"I'm reviewing cases involving serial killers."

The familiar chill played hopscotch on her nerve endings. "I'm sorry I asked."

"Me, too. And sorrier that I don't have some earth-shattering discoveries to share with you."

"The boys are tired of swinging. I think I'll load them in the wagon and walk down to the river. Do you want to come?"

"I'd love to, but I want to finish this."

"All work and no play..."

"He who finishes his work by sunlight, reaps rewards when the moon shines."

"Who said that?"

"A wise and handsome sage who has plans for playing with you in the moonlight."

A pleasurable warmth spread to her cheeks. Yesterday he had remained a stoic chunk of ice. Finally, he was thawing. She'd assured him she would not meet the stalker again without keeping him fully informed.

"Grams is right," she said, pushing a wind-tossed lock of hair from her eyes. "You do have a twisted lawyer's mind."

"The better to seduce you with, my dear."

She picked up the rubber ball Blair had dropped a minute ago and threw it at him. It missed by a foot.

"And we can only hope you're never elected president. The first pitch of the season might wind up in the stands."

The boys squealed with delight when she piled them into the old wooden wagon. Minutes later, she was moving at a steady clip, down the path that led to the boathouse and the river. Halfway there, she stopped, intrigued by a rendition of an old Elvis Presley song punctuated by rhythmic swishing.

She peeked over a holly hedge. The serenade was courtesy of Grady and an oversize radio. The swishing noise came from a machete. Muscles bulged as a shirtless Grady swung the sharp blade expertly, rhythmically. The machete sliced through a cluster of overgrown berry bushes, leaving the butchered branches to fall where they might.

Blake protested the fact that the wagon was no longer moving with a couple of squeals. Grady looked up and caught her staring. Perspiration dripped from his forehead to be absorbed by the dirty headband that rode the top of his eyebrows.

"Hello, boss lady," he said.

"Jodie will do fine."

"Sorry. Guess my manners aren't good enough for Jodie Gahagen. But you know me, just the son of the white trash gardener trying to get by."

"Ben has never been trash."

"No? You'd never know that by his living arrangements in that old boathouse." He put one hand over his eyes to shade them from the sun. The other still clutched the machete. "Anyway I'm glad you happened along. I appreciate the employment, but this will be my last day to work for you. Next week I'll be heading back to New York.''

''I thought Ben said you were living here now.''

''I thought I might. It's not working out the way I'd hoped. Natchitoches is just a little too quiet for me. Besides, by next week I'll have taken care of the business I came for.''

His gaze raked over her, lingering too long on certain areas. Feelings of uneasiness prickled her skin. ''What business might that be?''

''Personal. A woman I wanted to see one last time, to find out if we could make a go of it.''

''Could you?''

''No. She's interested in someone else. A bad choice on her part.''

Blair fussed and pulled at her skirt. This time she ignored his pleas for attention. ''Do you have a job in New York?''

''No, but I'll find something. Of course, I won't be able to live in the Village like you did. I'll move back to the real low-rent district, share my place with a few rats and roaches.''

''How do you know where I lived?''

''My dad treated me to dinner one night. Afterward we walked down to the Village and looked up your place. I suggested we stop in and surprise you. My dad refused. He doesn't go where he's not invited.''

''Jodie!'' The piercing yell of her name stopped the conversation cold. Selda was jogging down the path, her short legs going faster than Jodie had ever seen her move.

''Come quick, Jodie. You have to see this.'' Her breathing was hard and fast.

"Has something happened to Grams? To Ray?"

"No. Just come, Jodie. To my house, upstairs to Greg's room. I think I've found your stalker."

They stopped just long enough to pick up Ray who had disappeared inside for another stack of files. This time Jodie was thankful he was nearby. Selda was not making a lot of sense.

"I don't usually go into rooms I've rented out, not without good reason," Selda explained, leading Jodie and Ray, each holding a child, up the stairs to the second level of her rambling house.

"Why did you go into the room this time?" Ray asked.

"I didn't. I mean the door was ajar. I knocked, and it opened on its own."

"And you found evidence that Greg is the stalker?" The doubt in Ray's voice did nothing to dissuade Selda.

"Just wait. I'm not saying anything. You have to see it for yourself."

Ray reached the door first, but Jodie squeezed past him, stepping inside only to stop cold, her feet nailed to the spot. Greg's bed was neatly made, the white chenille bedspread papered with photographs. Color and black-and-white. All sizes. At least two dozen different poses.

All of Jodie.

"How did he get these?"

"No sweat there." Ray waved his hand toward an assortment of telescopic lenses that lined the top of a walnut armoire. "The question is, why?"

Jodie picked up the pictures, one by one, vertigo gnawing away at her equilibrium. There were shots of her alone. Reading in the back porch rocker, shelling pecans on the back steps, her skirt pulled up to cradle the lapful of nuts. And an enlargement, a color shot of her drying her hair in the sun, her head down, the wet strands shimmering like liquid fire.

The next picture she touched was of her holding Blake and Blair. She shuddered, her breath balled up inside her, struggling for release. He'd said she and the boys would make a great family scene. He'd proved it, over and over.

Picture-perfect images of her playing with the boys on the back porch, pulling them in the wagon, picnicking on a blanket by the river.

She hugged Blair to her, felt his tiny heart beating against her chest. She buried her lips in his wispy red curls, then reached a hand to Blake. Her fingers traced the lines of his baby smooth face, his feathery eyelashes, his perfect nose, his sweet pink lips.

More precious than life, their innocence captured in the camera eye of a killer. Fury took over now, replacing the fear she had lived with for months. This man had taken so much from her, leaving cold, hard emotions in their place.

"Call Butch Deaton, Selda."

Ray slipped an arm around her, but it didn't soothe her. Nothing would ever soothe her until she knew Greg Johnson would never again walk the streets to prey on innocent people.

JODIE DROPPED to the porch swing. The boys were fast asleep and Grams had retired early as well. It had been an eventful day. But tonight, for the first time in months, she would sleep knowing the living nightmare was finally over.

Greg had returned to his apartment at Selda's to

find Butch and two other officers waiting for him. According to Butch he was still protesting his innocence loud and long, demanding to see a lawyer. Nonetheless he was behind bars for now, the snapshots confiscated as evidence in the case against him.

And Butch had assured her no judge in the parish would grant parole. Not unless God himself intervened with a miracle. Jodie wasn't worried. She was sure God had not taken league with the devil.

She sipped from the mug of hot chocolate at her fingertips, savoring the warmth as it slid down her throat. All the pieces were falling into place. All but one, and he was standing at the edge of the porch, staring into the darkness.

"I have to go back to New Orleans, Jodie."

The words shattered her newfound peace.

"When?"

"Tomorrow. I'll visit my dad in the hospital and then take a flight from the airport in Shreveport."

"You'll miss the festival."

"I know. At least you and the boys will be able to enjoy it without worry."

She walked over and stood beside him. "We'd enjoy it a lot more if you were there with us."

The muscles in his arms tightened, and his hands gripped the porch railing. "Maybe, for a while."

"No games, Ray. Not after all that's gone between us. Just say what you're thinking." Now she was the one straining for control.

He turned, finally meeting her gaze. "I'm not the man for you, Jodie."

"You're the man I want, the man I love." Moisture burned at the back of her eyes. She fought to keep it at bay.

"No. I'm the man you think you want. But I'd never be able to live up to your level of perfection. The more you and the boys wanted from me, the less I'd be able to give. I'd disappoint you time and time again, until resentment would be the only emotion we'd feel for each other."

He turned away again. She moved in front of him, standing on tiptoe, forcing him to look her in the eye. "Do you love me, Ray?"

"Love has nothing to do with this."

"Do you love me? Because if you can look me in the eye and tell me you don't, then I won't say another word. But if you do, then give us a chance."

"A chance to fail?"

"Maybe. Or maybe for more happiness than you ever dreamed possible."

He shook his head. "I can't, Jodie. I can't do this to you or to my sons. I'll send you money, all the money you need. You can stay here in Natchitoches or go back to New York, but you won't have to work unless you want to. You can be a full-time mother to our sons. I'll visit them when I can."

"No."

"It's the best choice for everybody." His voice was heavy with the pain of finality.

Pain gripped her heart, but she held her head high. "I don't want your money, Ray. I don't want visits once a year to dredge up old heartaches. My sons don't need a father who rejects them." She called on every ounce of strength she possessed and forced her ultimatum through clenched teeth. "Either you commit to being a full-time husband and father or you are out of our lives forever."

"Go ahead, push me, Jodie. It's when I buckle. It's

time you saw me at my worst. That way you can walk away without looking back.''

''I'm not the one walking away, Ray. You will be. All or nothing. It's your call.''

He turned away from her and slammed a fist into the porch post. The tears she'd tried so hard to fight broke loose as the only man she'd ever loved took the steps two at a time and disappeared through the back gate.

HE SAT AT an old table in the basement of the house he had grown up in. The house was falling to pieces around him, the way his mother had in the year before her death. The men had quit coming then, quit knocking on her door at all hours to disappear into her bedroom. The laughter and moans of pleasure had stopped. So had the sickening odors of defilement.

It didn't matter anymore. It was time for him to leave Natchitoches and the memories far behind. Maybe if he was out of this house, the urges would die like his mother had or just go away one day and never return the way his wife had deserted him.

But the urges hadn't died yet. Tonight they were stronger than ever. Tonight the basement was filled with Jodie Gahagen. He'd taken out some of the mementos he'd stolen from her apartment in New York and placed them on the table.

A pair of silky panties, a tube of lipstick and one almost empty bottle of body lotion. Items so insignificant to her she'd never missed them. Items that fed him, driving him to do what he had to do.

Painstakingly, he twisted the cap from a glass vial of the liquid that would end Jodie's life. Four vials, saved up from legitimate prescriptions that were meant to save his life.

Jodie could have saved herself. Instead, she'd flaunted her body in front of Ray Kostner, intoxicating him with her sensual ways, making love to him in the law office, even inside her grandmother's house.

Nice women didn't do that.

His hand shook the way it did when the images of the past merged with those of the present. His mother. His wife. The young blonde in Bossier City, the petite brunette in Ruston. All women who flaunted their bodies in front of unworthy men.

Now Jodie had to die. Saturday night. It would be the high point of the Festival of Lights.

And just like the others, no one would know she had been murdered. He was too smart for all of them.

Chapter Fifteen

Ray was up at sunrise for the drive to Shreveport. The night had been long and sleepless, leaving plenty of time to think of Jodie's ultimatum. To know he would never again wake up to the feel of Jodie cuddled against him. Her hair feathering his shoulders, her face seductive even in sleep, her body warm, waiting to be wakened by the touch of his lips on hers.

To know he would never see his sons grow up, watch them ride their first two-wheeler, play their first game of baseball, catch their first fish. It was like saying he was ready to have his heart ripped from his body while he watched.

He had rights as a father. Jodie knew that as well as he did. She also knew he would never pursue them if it went against her wishes. She wanted a husband to share her life with, a dependable father for her boys.

It was no more than either she or his sons deserved. The question was the same as always: Was he man enough for the task? Or would he fail like he had so many times before when push came to shove?

The drive to Shreveport took an hour. It seemed like ten. The only consolation was that his dad had improved to the point that he was leaving the hospital today.

Ray would go back to New Orleans knowing Parker had recovered enough to take over his own cases, even handle Carl Baker's defense. And Jodie was safe. Mission accomplished.

Yesterday's events replayed in his mind, the way they had done dozens of times throughout the night and early morning, like a CD that never stopped. Only the CD seemed warped, and the distortions played havoc with the meaning. Ray's fingers tightened on the steering wheel.

Greg Johnson was the type of man Ray would have taken as a client, a man being railroaded by a hungry cop and a frightened woman, the case against him built solely on circumstantial evidence. The snapshots they'd found in his room proved he'd taken pictures of Jodie without her permission. Nothing else.

If the pictures Ray had seen had been the only evidence, he would have attributed them to infatuation. And infatuation with a vivacious, beautiful woman did not make you a criminal. Infatuation with Jodie Gahagen only proved you were human.

But a police search of Greg's room had turned up many more photographs, some showing Jodie in various states of undress, obviously taken without her permission. Shots snapped in New York, inside her apartment, around her office, shopping in the city, playing with the boys in Central Park.

An ironclad case against Greg Johnson. So, why couldn't he accept their good fortune and let it go?

He swerved onto the exit ramp near the hospital, making a few turns and pulling into the covered parking lot. His dad was apparently up and talking. Like his old self, Mom had said.

Parker had requested that Ray stop by this morning. He had a few things he wanted to discuss, but Ray had a few things to say, too. He was a father himself now. It changed the way he looked at his own father, especially when he had come so close to losing his dad in an attack meant for him.

This time he hoped he had the courage to tell his dad what he'd never been able to before. A few minutes later Ray strode into the quiet of the hospital and through the door of room 619.

"Hello, son." Parker's voice was weak but steady. "I was hoping you'd stop by before you flew to New Orleans."

"Mom said you wanted to talk to me."

"I do."

Ray pulled up a chair. "You're looking good."

"I look like a tomato vine in a Louisiana drought."

Ray smiled. His dad's statement was far more accurate than his own.

"But I'm alive. And that's what matters."

"You're right. Look, Dad. I know my apologies don't mean much to you, but I'm sorry about what happened."

"It wasn't your fault. If the swine hadn't attacked me, it would have been you."

Finally, a tragedy his father didn't think was his fault. For a second, Ray was tempted to leave it at that. Conscience forced him to take a deep breath and plow ahead.

"It *was* my fault. The attacker wasn't a chance burglar. I think he was waiting in the office to stab me with a knife we found under your desk. Apparently it slipped out of his hand when he hammered you with the chair. He must have heard me coming and ran before he could find it.''

''Why would someone want to kill you?''

''It's a long story. I'll tell it to you some day when you're feeling a lot better.''

''Did you catch the attacker?''

''Not then. But he's in jail now. At least the police think they have the right man.''

''You don't?''

Ray hesitated. ''The evidence looks convincing.''

''Good. But that's not why I wanted to see you. I've had time to think while I was in here, about a lot of things. Looking death in the eye makes you do that.''

Ray's sentiments exactly. ''I've given—''

''Wait. I want to finish what I have to say. Then you can respond or not.''

Ray leaned back in the chair, his body tightening into the familiar coils his father's lectures always generated. ''I'm listening.''

''I've made some mistakes in my life, costly ones. You and your mother have been the ones to pay.''

Now Parker had his serious attention. This lecture was significantly skewed, the starting point miles off center from the thousands he'd heard before.

''I wanted everything to be perfect, the opposite of what I grew up with. It's no excuse, but I grew up in hell.'' Parker's voice grew weaker, and his eyes took on a vacant stare, as if all of him had turned inward.

''My father drank too much,'' he continued, staring at his hands. ''My mother was sick, what they would call manic-depressive now. Then I only knew she was sweet and loving one minute, screaming uncontrollably at me the next.''

Ray studied the pain in his dad's face, surprised at the power of memories that had lived inside him for so long. ''I always thought your parents had died when you were young.''

''No, but by the time Sara and I met and married they had died. My dad wrapped his pickup truck around a tree. My mom died of an overdose of tranquilizers a few months later. End of story. At least it should have been.''

Parker stretched to pour himself a glass of water. Ray started to help, but his dad waved him off, fiercely independent as always. Lifting the glass to his lips, he took a long, slow drink before continuing.

''Not a pretty story but it's life. I'm not telling it to you to make excuses, just to help me explain, and hopefully to help you understand why I turned into such a lousy father. I had spent my youth ashamed of my parents, embarrassed by our lives. I was determined to leave that all behind me.''

''But I didn't let you.''

''I didn't let myself. I pushed you when I should have been clapping you on the back, criticized when I should have been hugging.'' His fingers tangled in the top sheet. ''Turned against you when you needed support.''

Ray tried to think of something to say. No words came. Only a dryness in his throat and a stinging at the back of his eyelids.

''I knew I was pushing too hard, but I couldn't stop myself. You and your mom were the best things that had ever happened to me, yet I couldn't do the one thing she wanted most of all. Give you the support you deserved.''

Parker pulled himself up and sat on the side of the bed, his thin legs and bare feet dangling from beneath the wrinkled hospital gown.

''I know it's years too late to make up for what we lost. But it's not too late to tell you that I'm damn proud of you, Ray, and always have been.'' His eyes misted. ''And not too late to ask you to forgive me.''

''I guess I'd have to ask for the same forgiveness. I cost you the judgeship.''

''Did you believe that all these years?''

''Of course, you stepped down rather than face public shame and embarrassment for what I had done.''

''No, I stepped down because I wasn't fit to sit in judgment of anyone. I succumbed to blackmail to protect my good name. I told myself that it was for you, but in my heart I knew it was for me. That's why I had to learn again to live with myself.''

''I don't know what to say.''

''You don't have to say anything. I wouldn't have blamed you a bit if you'd never spoken to me again after I accused you of ruining your mother's and my life. But you were a better man than I ever was. Every time I've ever needed you, you were there. Just the way you are now.''

''It looks like a day of confessions. I need to tell you something I should have said a long time ago.''

Parker stiffened as if preparing for a blow. ''Go ahead. I probably deserve whatever you have to say.''

''It has nothing to do with deserving. It's unconditional. I learned that from a very special lady.'' He got up and stepped to the bed, wrapping his arms about his dad's stooped shoulders.

"I love you, Dad." The words were barely a whisper, but they were out and that was all that mattered.

Sara stepped into the room at that minute, and her gaze darted from her husband to her son, confusion spelled out in the lines of her face and the pull of her lips.

"Are you all right, Parker?" Her voice carried a ring of alarm.

"I'm fine. I was just telling my son that I love him. Now if the both of you would get out of here, I could get some rest."

Neither of them missed the quick swipe of a finger across his eyes. Ray gave his dad's hand a squeeze and backed toward the door, stopping only to give his mom a goodbye peck on the cheek.

"I'm out of here. Take care, Dad. You, too, Mom."

Sara was still staring at them as if they were aliens who'd landed from out of space and taken over her husband's and son's bodies. She wasn't far from wrong, Ray decided, opting for the steps instead of the elevator and taking them two at a time.

JODIE LIFTED BLAIR over the side of the crib rails and handed him his stuffed raccoon, his favorite out of his current menagerie. "You take a good nap, young man. When you wake up you'll be going to your very first Festival of Lights celebration."

Tonight she and the boys would go to the party at Selda's daughter's house. The house downtown, with grassy grounds backing up to the Cane River. From the comfort of Lydia's huge yard, they would have prime seats for the night's events.

They would watch the millions of Christmas lights burst forth in color at the same instant, filling the sky with their glow. Lydia's guests would marvel as shimmering reflections danced over the surface of the river. The boys would delight as the music from dozens of marching bands wafted on the night air. And, finally, the crowning glory. The heavens would blaze with a dazzling fireworks display.

And tonight she and her sons would do it without the risk of danger. They would also do it without Ray Kostner.

"Grams, did I have any phone calls?"

"Phone calls? I don't think so. Well, yes, Selda called to see if you wanted to ride with her to the party."

"I know. I talked to her. I told her I'd take my car in case the boys get fussy and I need to bring them home early. Why don't you go ahead and ride with her so she won't have to go alone? We'll meet you there."

"You can't wait too late, now. The first weekend is the worst. There'll be thousands of people rushing around, all trying to get the best spot on the parade route."

"But we won't be in that crowd. We're watching the lighting display and fireworks from Lydia's backyard."

"You still better get there early. Once that traffic backs up, it doesn't budge. The whole town is deadlocked until after the fireworks. Even then it moves like molasses. One night Selda and I just gave up and spent the night at Lydia's house. So you can forget any idea of leaving early."

"I'll still take my car. I need to stop at the store

for diapers, but we'll leave here as soon as the boys wake up from their nap.''

''What about that Kostner boy? Is he going to be tagging after you again?''

''No. He's back in New Orleans.'' Her heart twisted painfully in her chest. But she refused to give in to gloom. Not when the stalker had been stopped. ''Besides, I think it's you he's tagging after, the way you wait on him hand and foot. Could be, it's you he's sweet on.''

A tinge of pink lightened Grams's cheeks. ''Don't be teasing me like that, Jodie Gahagen.'' She pushed her wire glasses up a little higher on the bridge of her narrow nose. ''Only guy I ever let get close enough to get sweet on me was your grandpa, God rest his soul.''

Jodie gave her a warm hug. ''My grandpa was a very lucky man.''

RAY EYED THE speedometer and cursed the traffic. Both lanes of the interstate were lined with cars, trucks, vans and a fair share of motorbikes, all heading for opening night of the Festival of Lights. And none of them getting there very fast.

The plane he was supposed to be on was probably touching down at the New Orleans airport about now. He'd driven all the way to the airport and then turned around.

Intuition, the sense of survival, too many years of defending men against criminal charges. Probably a little of all of the above. At any rate, in spite of the evidence Butch had collected, he was not convinced Greg Johnson was actually Jodie's stalker.

Which meant he wasn't certain Jodie was safe. Until he was, he could never return to New Orleans. He'd spent the first part of the afternoon talking with an FBI agent. Another wasted effort. North Louisiana had more than its share of murders every year, but there was no record of the type of serial killer he was looking for.

Traffic slowed again, and Ray's speed dropped to a crawling forty miles an hour on a new interstate system meant to go seventy. Three-thirty.

Reaching for the cellular phone, he punched in the Gahagen number. Six rings later he was about to hang up when Miss Emily said hello.

"Is Jodie there?"

"She's upstairs getting ready for the big party at Lydia's. If you were half smart, you'd be here going with her."

"You give good advice. Tell her to wait for me at the house. I may be late, but I'll be there to pick up her and the boys."

The conversation dissolved in a fit of static, and Ray could barely make out Grams's promise to deliver the message. That done, he called his dad's office to retrieve his messages. He had to have something to fill his time while he watched the bumper of the car in front of him crawl down the highway.

The first call was a hang up, the second a woman wanting an appointment. The third was Cappan. Call at once. He even left his home number.

Ray made a mental note of it and then punched it in. Cappan answered immediately.

"Hello, Cappan. Ray Kostner. I got your message. What's up?"

"A couple of things. I'm glad you got my message before you left town. I looked up Greg Johnson like you asked. He doesn't have a record but he has an illustrious background.''

''Yeah. What's the story?''

''It appears he's a very aggressive photographer. Once he was arrested for tailing some city councilman in New Orleans. When the story broke that the guy was on the take, your guy Greg was there with a full supply of pictures of the man's rich lifestyle.''

''Anything else?''

''Pretty similar. Only this time it was some big-name football player. He tended to like wild parties. Greg managed to crash them and wound up with the full story in pictures.''

''Sounds like a real charmer.''

''He has some legitimate credits, too. Some of them very impressive. Apparently he makes pictures talk.''

''So, if he expected that a story about a serial killer and his beautiful victim was about to break, he might be snapping pictures like crazy.''

''That's what I was thinking, only that wouldn't explain the snapshots of Jodie in New York.''

''The ones he claims he didn't take.''

''But the police found them in his apartment.''

The static started up again. Ray waited until it cleared. ''You put some legwork into this. I owe you one.''

''You don't owe me. I'd hate to see anything happen to Miss Gahagen. She's some woman, but I guess you know that.''

''Yeah. I definitely do.''

''Oh, and one more thing. Remember that story I told you about, the one about the psycho who stalked his victims and then killed them?''

''The one who was too smart to get caught?''

"That's the one. I kept asking around. It seems the fellow telling the story was one of the police officers from Louisiana, up here training with our community policing program."

Static rumbled like thunder over the wires. Ray gritted his teeth and swallowed a curse. "Keep talking. I'm still here."

"Well, one of our guys, a fellow named Lando, was out with a bunch of the trainees after a session. They started drinking. He said this guy told a bizarre tale about some man following women, sending them gifts and flowers. He claimed he was only trying to keep them pure. When he caught them with another man, he killed them."

"Where was this?"

"The man didn't say. According to the story, the killer was supposed to be too smart to get caught. But he must have slipped up somewhere if the cop knew about him."

"What was the name of the man who told the stories?"

"Lando doesn't remember. The only thing he knows for sure is he was with the bunch from Louisiana. They've been up here a half dozen times or more during the past few months. The training's finished now, though."

"Did Lando give you a description of him?"

"Tall, a little overweight, brown hair. Said his nose was a little crooked like it had been broken before. So if this killer was so smart he never left a clue, how do you think they caught him?"

Ray beat a fist against the steering wheel. "He made the oldest mistake in the book, Cappan. He couldn't resist telling someone what he'd gotten away with.''

The phone connection faltered again, the static now overtaking the line. Ray hung up the phone. He'd heard enough. Now he just needed to get to Natchitoches. He glanced at the speedometer and cursed the snail's pace he was traveling.

He punched in Jodie's number again. This time the phone rang a dozen times but there was no answer. Apparently she hadn't gotten his message to wait on him or else ignored it. Good.

She would be much safer at a party surrounded by friends. He dialed Lydia's number. A busy signal droned in his ear. He'd try it again in the next few minutes. He needed to warn Jodie that her stalker was still on the loose.

A stalker whom Jodie would trust with her life.

"THESE PECAN PRALINES all but melt in your mouth, Selda. I'd love to have the recipe.''

"It's easy as making candy.'' She laughed at her own joke. So did everyone else within hearing distance.

Jodie leaned back on the quilt she'd spread in the yard. Blake and Blair were right beside her, in their double stroller munching on slices of banana. Lydia's school-age youngsters had served as entertainment committee, pushing them around the yard and pointing out each design in the spectacular light display.

The first weekend in December had arrived and the weather was perfect. Light sweaters were the uniform of the evening and there wasn't a cloud in the sky. Lydia's guests had feasted on home-cooked specialities, brought to the party in stuffed picnic baskets and casserole dishes.

Fried chicken, smoked hams, potato salad, baked beans, yams, fall squash and even a pot of chicken and dumplings. All washed down with pitchers of iced tea and pots of strong coffee and followed by banana pudding and chocolate cake. And of course, Selda's pecan pralines.

The leftovers would have fed another group of the same size. Home cooking and plenty of it. It was the way of the south. Even Butch had shown up a few minutes ago, leaving his duties long enough to stop by for a bite of food. Hyped as he was, he'd only eaten a bite or two. It was Natchitoches's big night. The local police surely had their hands full.

But things were quieting at Lydia's. Everyone had gathered into clusters of friends and families, waiting for the fireworks to start. The only thing missing was Ray. Jodie's heart settled like lead in her chest.

"Jodie, telephone," Lydia called from the distance, just as she started to put the boys on the quilt beside her. "You'll have to take it in the house. No telling where the cordless phone ended up with this bunch of people. I think it's been off the hook half the evening. My husband said he tried to get us for hours."

"Can you keep an eye on the boys, Grams?"

"We'll watch them, Miss Jodie," Selda's grandkids chimed in before she had a chance to answer.

"And I'll help them," Selda assured.

Jodie hurried to the phone, her traitorous heart racing. Maybe it was Ray, calling to say he missed her already, as much as she missed him. Calling to say he didn't want to live without her.

"Hello."

Her greeting was met with silence.

"Hello. Ray, is it you? Hello."

Nothing. The caller hadn't hung up. There was no dial tone. She waited, then tried again. "If someone is there, say something."

Apprehension crawled her skin. She counted to ten, forcing her breathing to steady and her pulse to slow. The stalker was in jail. She was safe. She couldn't let the past torment her this way.

Finally, she pasted a smile on her face and walked outside, down the back steps, over the grassy yard that sloped toward the river.

The first fireworks of the night took to the sky, crashing above her in fiery splendor. Reds and greens and touches of gold. She made her way through the guests, all with their heads back, their gazes glued to the sky.

Finally she saw Grams. Selda was right behind her. So were Lydia's two children.

"Where are the boys?"

Another crash, another spray of colorful stars in the sky.

"Where are the boys?" Her voice rose with the panic that twisted inside her.

"They were right here a minute ago." Selda jumped up from her quilt and ran over to Jodie.

Jodie's gaze swept the area, cold fear strangling her breath from her body, clawing at her insides, tearing through her mind in waves of horror.

The stroller was down the hill, at the edge of the river. For a second her legs were watery worthless limbs, too numb to move. Then she ran, her feet flying, her lungs burning.

She fell to the ground beside the stroller, tears

stinging her eyelids. The boys sat calmly, still buckled into place. She picked up one and then the other, holding them to her chest, rocking them in her arms.

Selda and Grams stopped beside her, panting from the fastest they'd walked in years. "Is everything all right?"

"Yes, the boys are fine."

"I guess one of the kids around here gave them a ride while I was staring at the fireworks. I'm sorry, Jodie. I should have been watching closer."

"It's okay. No harm done."

The two women started back up the hill. Jodie bent down to fit Blake back into his seat. Something was stuck to the back of the stroller. She hadn't noticed it in her initial excitement over finding the boys, but it was there, shining in the glow of the fireworks that were building to a crescendo in the sky over their heads.

A note.

No. It just couldn't be. Her brain screamed the denial, but even as she lifted the note closer to her eyes, she knew the nightmare had returned. Shaking, she read the words inside the red heart.

I'll be waiting for you at the Coxlin place. Come alone.

MORE THAN AN HOUR had passed by the time Jodie maneuvered through the traffic and reached the drive that ran from the highway down to the old Coxlin place. She slowed, driving through dark shadows and whispering pines to her rendezvous with a killer.

Somewhere in the blackness that surrounded her Butch Deaton's car should already be parked. He had responded to her call to his beeper number immediately, trying to persuade her not to come here tonight and then finally agreeing to carry through on their previous plan. He had called her back on her car phone just minutes ago, assuring her the plan was in place.

The house was in front of her now, the steep pitch of the roof silhouetted against the moon, like it had been that Halloween night so long ago. Haunted, her friends had said. That night they had been wrong. Tonight they would have been right. Haunted by a madman.

She pulled the car to a stop. No sign of anyone, but that didn't mean the killer wasn't inside waiting for her to enter. Trembling, she opened the car door and stepped onto the soft earth. She forced her lungs to breathe, forced one foot in front of the other as she crossed the overgrown path that led to the house.

The bottom step creaked at her weight, and her heart slammed against her chest. He was here, like he said. The door was open, and a figure stood just inside, his large frame backlit by a flickering glow.

As she watched he stepped back into the shadows.

She gulped in a ragged breath and took the last few steps to the open door.

"Come in, Jodie. I've been waiting for you."

Chapter Sixteen

"Butch." A quick surge of relief crashed into a shudder of disappointment. "Why are you in here?"

"I came to meet you, Jodie, the way you wanted me to."

The dark tone of his voice drew gooseflesh to her skin. She looked past him. Logs in the fireplace were beginning to blaze and flickering light from a dozen candles danced along the shadowed walls and crept into the far recesses of the room.

Evil accosted her senses. Thick and tangible, dark and choking. "He's somewhere near, Butch. I can feel him." Her voice was a raspy whisper.

"Very near."

"You have to hide quickly. If he sees you he'll run like he did before."

"Not this time." He stepped closer, out of the shadows and into full candlelight.

"Come upstairs with me, Jodie." He extended a hand.

But something was wrong, dreadfully wrong. Butch's dark eyes were glazed over, his voice a hoarse slur.

"You've been drinking, Butch."

"No, Jodie. I'm perfectly sober. Completely in control."

She backed toward the door.

"I asked you to come upstairs with me, Jodie."

"No. You're drunk. I'm getting out of here."

He grabbed her arm and twisted it behind her. Pain shot through her in mind-numbing stabs. She struggled to break away. His arm flew up, and the blow struck her across the side of the head.

"Don't fight me, Jodie. Just do what I say so I don't have to hurt you again. I don't like to hurt people, not even bad girls like you. I'm a gentleman."

She stared at him, her brain slowly absorbing the unflinching truth. "You, Butch. You're the stalker, the man who murdered Max."

"Does that surprise you? It shouldn't. I've always liked you, Jodie. Even in high school, you were the prettiest girl in the class. Thin and lithe, your skin smooth as silk. And you always smelled so clean and wholesome. You were a good girl then." His finger traced a shaky line from her forehead to her lips and then slid down her neck to the rise of her breasts.

"Why are you doing this?"

"You made me do it." He shoved her toward the stairs. "That's why I have a surprise waiting upstairs for you."

"Don't do this, Butch," she pleaded, her voice scratching against the dryness of her throat. "I'm a good girl. I saved myself for you, just like you said."

"No. I thought you were different, but you're like the others." His voice rose, the accusing tone of a mother scolding a child. "You were with Ray Kostner. You let him touch you. His smell is all over you, defiling you."

He shoved her again, pushing her up the rickety

stairs. She tried to think. This was not the Butch she knew. His mind had slipped into a black chasm, his body following its dictates as if in a trance. Somehow she had to get to the man beneath the veil of insanity.

"I'm your friend, Butch. I can help you."

"You were never my friend. You used me. That was all. Even in high school you thought you were too good for me. You let me take you out, but it was Ray you let kiss you on the lips. You broke a date with me so that you could go to the prom with him."

"That's not true, Butch. You broke the date. You'd been in a fight. Your nose had been broken. It was swollen and bruised."

"It doesn't matter. One kiss from Ray Kostner and you dumped me. You're like the other women. I should have known it last year when I visited you in New York. You flaunted your body in front of me, a hussy in a little black dress that was made to drive men wild."

"It was just a dinner dress, Butch. People dress up more in New York."

"Don't beg now, Jodie. It's too late. You knew I wanted you, but you pushed me out the door. But I couldn't quit thinking about you. I wanted you so badly. That's why I looked you up again. All alone with your babies. I wanted to save you. You wouldn't heed my warnings."

"No." Her voice wavered. She bit her lip hard, determined not to give in to tears or weakness. But how could she reason with a madman?

One by one, he forced her up the stairs, his mouth at her ear. "You only want a man for one thing. You and the others. All beautiful, all bad. That's why you have to die the same way they did."

"What others?"

"The other women like you. Flaunting themselves like cheap whores. But they didn't want a decent man. They pushed me away just like you did. So I watched them and waited, until the time was right."

"And did you send them gifts, too, and write them notes?"

"A few, not as many as I did you. You were special. I gave you chance after chance, but you kept going to Ray instead of me. I tried to stop you. I told you that you were making a mistake. You wouldn't listen."

They reached the top of the steps. He took her arm and pulled her down the narrow hallway.

"Where are you taking me?"

"You'll see." He stopped at a half-open door that hung precariously from broken hinges. "Close your eyes, Jodie. That way you can enjoy the surprise."

His rough hand swept over her face, covering her eyes for her when she didn't do it on her own. A final shove and she was inside. He dropped his hand, brushing it across the front of her body.

"All for you, Jodie."

She gasped and stumbled backward. The room was filled with red roses, their fragrance gaggingly sweet. Nausea welled up inside her.

"For your funeral."

Her funeral. The thought melted the shock that was destroying her will. Her gaze spanned the room, searching for anything that might serve as a weapon. Reason was out of the question. She had to fight for her life.

And she damn well would. Blake and Blair depended on her. She would not let a madman take her away from them. She would not let a murderer win.

"If you kill me, you will go to jail. Ray will not rest until you do."

"But Ray won't know I killed you. You made it so easy for me, Jodie. The personal ad, the place, the timing."

She stiffened. A minute ago, she'd almost felt sorry for Butch, felt as if some demon had taken over his body. But he knew exactly what he was doing, had orchestrated this whole encounter with the skill of an artist.

Butch was not possessed. The evil was all his own. She knew now he was capable of anything.

"Why did you kill Gloria Bigger? You did kill her, didn't you?"

"So you finally figured that out. I killed her because I had to. She saw me that night when I went to the florist shop. I made a mistake. A bad mistake. I should never have used Max Roling's credit card in Natchitoches. But I did it without thinking. The training in New York was over, and I was so desperate to contact you, to let you know I was on my way back to you."

"So you went to the florist shop that night to steal her copy of the ticket. But all it took was one phone call from Ray to find who had sent the flowers."

"I didn't count on Ray. I thought you would call the police. I would have handled everything myself. That's why I didn't send you anything in Natchitoches until I was on my way back from the final training session. I had to be sure no one else was assigned to your case."

"You planned everything so well." She took a step closer to a glass container of roses. A second is all it would take to lift it over her head and bring it smashing down on his. But she'd have to find a way to divert his attention elsewhere. She needed to keep him talking while she thought of a foolproof plan.

"You even attacked Parker Kostner without getting caught."

"I didn't mean to hurt *him*. It was his son I meant to kill."

"Then why did you hurt him?"

"It happened so fast. I was waiting in the dark. When the door opened, I swung the chair. I didn't kill him. He didn't deserve to die."

"You didn't kill him because you heard Ray coming. And you had lost the knife."

"You're wrong. I didn't even realize I had dropped the knife until after I'd left the building. I never kill without reason."

"You are a very smart gentleman," she said, inching still closer to the heavy crystal container.

"Very, very smart. That's why no one will ever catch me. I walk into hospitals, apartment buildings, even business offices without anyone objecting. Just a policeman doing his duty. No use to kick doors down like they do in the movies. We have tools that open doors faster than you can with a key."

"So that's how you got inside my New York apartment?"

"Of course. Your neighbors saw me and smiled. So nice to have a policeman checking on you and keeping you safe from your stalker."

He laughed, low and mocking, and the sound echoed through the cold room, chilling her to the bone. "Even your grandmother was cooperative, inviting me in for tea and leaving me alone to pay visits to your bedroom. The bedroom where you entertained Ray Kostner."

"Greg Johnson didn't take the pictures of me, did he, Butch? You took the pictures."

"He took the ones that were on his bed. The others were mine. I watched you from an empty apartment just across from yours. Watched you through a lens that magnified every curve of your body. Watched you rub lotion into your skin, smooth, sensuous strokes up and down your legs, between your thighs. You did it to torment me."

"No." She eased backward, slowly. "You know I'm a good girl, Butch. And it's late. I need to go home now and check on my sons. You need to go home, too. You're a *policeman*."

She stressed the word, praying to get through to the man who had sworn to protect.

"Policemen protect the world from women like you. I'm doing my job." He grabbed her arm and pulled her toward him.

"Policemen don't kill."

"Of course, they do. They kill the people who deserve it. That's why we have guns. But we've talked enough, Jodie. Now I have my last gift for you."

One arm wrapped around her, his fingers digging into her shoulder. With the other hand he reached into his pocket and fished out a plastic bag. His gaze remained fastened on her as he slipped a syringe from the wrinkled plastic. "Just a shot, Jodie, quick and simple. Your heart will speed up, faster and faster until it bursts from the pressure. Then it will all be over."

"You won't get away with this."

"Ah, but I will. I always do. Time and time again. The autopsy will show a heart attack. You came here and found this roomful of flowers and it frightened you so badly you went into cardiac arrest.

"Some people will even wonder if you put the flowers here yourself. You thought someone was stalking you, and you let it drive you crazy."

Jodie trembled. Her last chances were slipping away. A few more moments and the needle in his hand would be plunged into her flesh. If she was going to die anyway, she would go down fighting.

In one jerking movement, she lowered her head and buried her teeth into the hand that dug into her shoulder. Butch yelped in pain, but his grip tightened. She struggled, heaving her body toward the vase.

She never reached it. Instead his hand wrapped around her throat. She gasped, fighting for air as life ebbed away. Finally, she collapsed against him. Only then did he release his hand on her throat and push her onto the floor.

A noise rumbled in her head, like a door slamming shut. Butch stiffened. Balancing the needle on his leg, he reached into the holster at his side and hoisted his revolver.

"Jodie!" The voice boomed through the house.

Ray. But it couldn't be. He was in New Orleans, running away from her, from his sons.

He called her name again, and then she heard his footsteps on the stairs. The gun in Butch's hand was pointed toward the door.

She forced air into her burning lungs and screamed. "He has a gun! Don't come up here!"

She felt Butch's hand before she saw it, slamming her against the wall. And then she felt the needle, piercing the skin, stinging. She fought to push it away. Strength surged inside her, an explosion in her chest.

She jerked her knee, hard, landing a blow into Butch's crotch just as a fireplace log came flying through the open door. Butch fell backward, firing the gun as he did. Bullets sprayed the room, ricocheting like marbles.

But she was free. With one hand she jerked the needle from her arm, hurling it towards Butch as he reloaded. It missed its mark, crashing against the wall. The glass splintered and the remaining drug seeped onto the floor.

Her chest was caving in from pressure now, but she forced her body to move. Grabbing the vase, she lifted it high above her head and brought it down with killing force.

Water and shards of broken glass sprayed the room as Butch sank to the floor. She fell on top of him, pounding her fists into his chest.

"How could you kill Max? How could you kill Gloria? How could you? How could you?"

Tears fell like rain from her eyes, and her heart beat so fast she thought it would burst from her chest, but she couldn't stop.

Her heart was still racing when Ray gathered her in his arms and held her close. It was still racing when he rocked her to him, his voice so shaky that for a minute she thought one of the bullets had found its target.

It was still racing when he wiped the tears from her eyes and placed a long, warm kiss on her lips.

It was then that she noticed they were not alone. Two policemen stood in the door, guns drawn, staring at them.

"Did you shoot him?"

"No, I didn't have to," Ray answered. "Jodie knocked him out cold."

"Looks like your suspicions were right," the other officer said, his gaze taking in the sight of vases of roses and half-burned candles.

"Looks like it." Ray led Jodie past the body and the officer who was leaning over it. "Now, it's in your hands. I'm getting the bravest little mother in the parish out of here."

JODIE SAT on the back porch, leafing through the information from the advertising firm where she had worked in New York. One of her clients had a debut product he wanted to introduce to the world of consumers. He'd liked her work in the past and he'd asked for her specifically this time, even if it meant conducting business via electronic means.

It was the perfect opportunity. She could be here with Grams and work her schedule around Blake and Blair. Surround herself with their love while she worked through a heartache that might never heal.

Ray had walked out of her life, the same way he had done before. Completely. No thanks for the memories. Not even a proper farewell between him and his sons.

He'd stayed with her all night after the fateful meeting that led to Butch's arrest. He'd taken her to the hospital and then held her while the epinephrine Butch had injected into her veins ran its course. Cradled her body against his while her heart rate had slowed to normal.

The next afternoon, he'd left for New Orleans to take care of an emergency he said he had to deal with personally. He'd promised to call.

That had been seven long nights ago.

At first she'd taken him at his word, the same way she'd done when he walked out of her apartment two years ago in New York City.

Once again she'd jumped at every ring of the phone, run to the window whenever a car stopped outside, waited up every night for some word. Only this time she didn't phone him. He knew what she wanted. He knew she loved him. It was his call.

If he chose to have no part of her and their sons, she'd swallow the pain, cry her tears in the loneliness of night, heal the jagged edges of her broken heart with love for her boys.

She'd be mother and father to them, surround them with so much love they'd never miss having a father. And she wouldn't miss him, either.

A tear stung at the back of her eye. She fought but couldn't stop it from escaping to roll down her cheek. One day she wouldn't miss Ray Kostner. Maybe, if she lived long enough, but who lived to be a thousand?

Grams opened the back door and joined her on the back porch. Selda followed a step behind, a plate of cookies warm from the oven in hand.

"I hope we're not interrupting anything," Selda said.

"Not a thing."

"Good. Greg filled me in on some details, especially the ones concerning how Butch tried to frame him. I thought he'd leave town as soon as he got out of jail, but he's still here and he's still snapping pictures. Now I'd like to hear the rest of the story, if you feel like talking about it. Like how Ray Kostner ended up at the Coxlin place at just the right time."

"Apparently he changed his mind about flying to New Orleans that day," Jodie said, retelling the story she'd already shared several times with Grams. "He talked to the detective from the NYPD while he was driving back to Natchitoches for the Festival of Lights. That's when he got the idea that Butch was my stalker. Another call, this one to the local chief of police convinced him his hunch was right. Butch was one of the officers who had been in New York this summer for some special training."

"Then Ray Kostner went right straight to Butch's house," Grams added. "He lives on an acre or so just north of Highway 6, so he could get there even with the parades going on and traffic blocked all over town."

"But obviously Butch wasn't there. I saw him at Lydia's not long before that," Selda said.

"No, but Ray took a page from Butch's handbook," Jodie said. "He let himself in. There were a number of prescription drugs in the house, enough to ride an emotional roller-coaster wave for days. Evidently, Butch kept his problems a secret around Natchitoches. He saw doctors in Shreveport, Alexandria and even Longview, Texas, to get the drugs that either kept him sane or drove him crazy. The jury is still out on that."

"I didn't know it was that easy to get drugs."

"I don't think it is, Selda, at least not around here where people know him. But he had found ways. Apparently he's had psychological problems ever since high school. They escalated when his mother died and again when his wife ran off with another man. That was the year he killed the first woman."

"And he confessed all of this?"

"No. Most of it the local police have discovered since his arrest. He has admitted to killing six people in all, though."

"Most of them with medicine from the insect bite kits Ray found in his house," Grams added, her memory doing an amazing job of remembering the details.

"I'm still not sure how the insect bite kits fit in with all of this." Selda passed the plate of cookies around and took one herself, biting into it and wiping away the crumbs that fell into her lap.

"The kits contain small amounts of epinephrine. That's the medical term for adrenaline in drug form. Butch took the medication from several kits, until he had enough in the syringe to cause a heart attack."

"You are lucky to be alive."

"I am. I wouldn't be if Ray hadn't shown up when he did."

"Ray?" Grams scratched her head. "Did I tell you he called yesterday while you and the boys were at the park?"

Her heart did a flip-flop. "No. What did he say?"

"That he'd be picking you up this afternoon at three. Said he had something to show you."

"Probably a ring," Selda mused. "That boy's so sweet on you, he lights up like one of those Christmas light displays every time you walk into the room."

Warmth spread through Jodie like wildfire. Ray had called. He was coming back to her. She glanced at her watch. Five before three. She ran trembling fingers through her hair, a useless attempt to tame it.

Punctual for the first time Jodie could remember, he rounded the corner of the porch at precisely three o'clock, as always opting for the back door. He hugged Grams and Selda and stopped beside her. She was already on her feet, but he pulled her into his arms, holding her extra tight and kissing her full on the mouth. Not overly passionate, not in front of company, but enough to know that she sure had been kissed.

"Did you miss me?" he asked, his lips curled in a devastating smile.

"Have you been gone?"

He faked a wince of pain and turned to Grams and

Selda. "May I steal my woman away? I promise to have her back in an hour."

My woman. The words danced inside her. "I can't leave now. The boys are asleep."

"We'll watch them," Selda said, winking at Ray. "Even if you're gone more than an hour."

Ray led her to the Porsche, opening the door for her, bending to kiss her again.

"Where are we going?"

"It's a surprise."

"I don't like surprises."

"You'll like this one. At least I hope you do."

He drove a few blocks east and then cut back toward the river, turning down a street shaded by towering oaks. It was an older section of town, with big houses, neatly groomed with wraparound porches and charming gables.

He pulled up and parked in the winding drive of one that sported a new coat of paint.

"Who lives here?" Jodie asked, lowering the car window.

"That's what I want to talk to you about. I'm not good at this, Jodie. I've never done it before. But I think beneath that magnolia tree would be a good spot."

He climbed from under the steering wheel and darted around the car and to her door. Hand in hand he led her to a spongy carpet of damp leaves.

"Jodie Gahagen." His voice was husky with emotion. "I love you. I want to spend the rest of my life with you and with our sons."

Tears filled her eyes.

"You don't have to answer this second."

"Yes."

"I know my track record isn't too good."

"Yes, Ray."

"But I'll work on improving it."

She put her finger over his lips. "I said, yes, Ray. I'll marry you."

He swept her into his arms, twirling her around and around until they were both drunk with movement and love. Leaning against the tree for support, he fished in his pocket. "It's here somewhere." A second later he came up with a jewelry box. He lifted the lid and pulled out a ring, a band of gold with one twinkling diamond in the center. Holding her hand, he slipped the ring on her finger.

"It's beautiful."

"Is that why you're crying?"

"I'm not crying."

He took a handkerchief from his pocket and dabbed at the tears running down her cheeks. "One more thing," he said, swinging his hand in the direction of the house. "What do you think?"

"About what?"

"The house. It has a perfect tree in the backyard for hanging swings, and there's lots of room for sandboxes and playing catch. I could put a basketball goal over the garage. When the boys are older, I mean."

Jodie put a hand to her temples to stop the whirling in her brain. "You're going too fast."

"I know. You said all or nothing. I want it all. I've already put a down payment on the house, but I can get out of it if you don't like it."

"But your job is in New Orleans."

"Not anymore. I gave notice today. I'm going into practice with my dad. Maybe not forever, but for now. I'd like to get to know him while I still can. I'd like our sons to know their grandparents and their Grams."

"You don't have to do this, Ray. I love you. I'd live with you in New Orleans. As long as we love each other, any place we live will be home."

"I know. And I may want to move back to New Orleans some day, but, for now, I'd like to be here in Natchitoches. I want to have time to spend watching my sons grow. Maybe a daughter or two as well. I want to be a real husband and father. I wouldn't be able to do that in the demanding position I just left."

"I love you," she said, her voice catching on the words that sprang from her heart.

He leaned close, touching his lips to hers. He kissed her long and hard, their breaths mingling, the passion inside her bubbling like champagne.

"Now, would you like to look at the house?"

"Yes." She left him behind, running up the walk.

"Wait, I have to carry you over the threshold."

He did, kissing her again in the process.

"I already love it," she said. "Where's the bedroom?"

"Since when did you ever need a bedroom?"

She stuck out her tongue and took off at a run, taking the steps two at a time. He caught up with her at the top of the landing, wrapping his arms around her.

They dissolved in a flurry of laughter and a wellspring of love. It was a long time later before they continued the tour and finally made it to the bedroom of a house they'd already christened with their love.

WHEN THE BOUGH BREAKS

Susan Kearney

Prologue

"I've been a bad girl," Maritza confided to her sister, Lisa McCalliff from her deathbed.

"Oh, please." Out of respect for Maritza's dire condition, Lisa refrained from rolling her eyes. "You haven't been listening to Mark's propaganda again, have you?"

Mark didn't deserve a sweetheart like Maritza for a wife. Lisa had never liked her brother-in-law, and she had never been more disgusted with him than at this moment after he'd just stalked out of the room, angry with Maritza as if it was her fault she was about to die and leave him. But Lisa couldn't fault the man for his joy over his new son. Through the window, she watched the big ex-commando cradle the infant in his arms, his face full of pride.

When he jarred the baby a little too roughly, she winced and returned her attention to her sister. The labor had lasted too long and had left her weak and frail-looking.

Lisa smoothed back damp hair from her sister's forehead. "You're a great wife."

"But not so loyal."

"Oh, come on. You defend Mark even when you know he's wrong."

"And I'll never be a good mother."

"Of course you will."

Maritza eyed her calmly and bravely. "Sis, the doctor was square with me. I'm not going to live long enough to raise my son. Let's not waste our last minutes together lying about the mess I've made of my life. I need your help."

"You got it." Lisa squeezed her sister's hand and tried to hold back tears. Apparently the doctor had told Maritza about the internal hemorrhaging, the bleeding they couldn't stop.

"I don't trust Mark to raise my son."

What? Lisa totally agreed with the assessment, but had never expected to hear her sister voice it. Mark might have enough charm to fool casual acquaintances, but they both knew all too well that Maritza's husband was controlling and short-tempered—especially when he'd been drinking. "What are you saying?"

"My son wasn't born early."

"He wasn't?"

"I fudged the dates so Mark would think he's the father."

Oh…my…God! Her sister's news stunned and shocked and actually pleased her. Not that Lisa believed adultery was a good thing. She didn't. But Maritza had been in such a difficult situation. Mark wasn't the worst of husbands, but he came close. He drank too much, verbally abused his wife, had tried to disrupt her career and generally made her life sheer hell. Lisa feared the day the verbal abuse would explode into violence. She'd begged Maritza to leave the man, but her sister had been determined to stick to her wedding vows. Yet somehow saintly Maritza had summoned up the courage to find a little happiness outside of her miserable marriage, and Lisa couldn't fault her for it.

"I'm glad that bastard isn't your son's father."

"His real father is Brody Adams."

"Brody Adams?" The name sounded familiar.

"The man who owns the land in Colorado where we wanted to dig," Maritza reminded her.

"You met him?"

"When he refused the university permission for our team to excavate on his land, I decided to talk to him."

"And you slept with him?" Lisa couldn't hold back her astonishment.

Maritza was a dedicated archaeologist, a valued member of Lisa's team, but she'd never thought her sister would do anything so impulsive. While Lisa had always been too busy studying to take much notice of the opposite sex, her sister, even though she was somewhat prim, had always made time for friends and social activities.

"It wasn't like that. I went to Colorado and met Brody at a party while Mark was out West investigating that divorce case for his PI firm. Brody was kind to me. Big and strong and so gentle. He was the handsomest man there and had his pick of the women, yet he danced with lots of older ones, especially the widows who'd come alone. Later we talked and I never got around to asking him for permission to dig on his land. He was so caring and I had a few drinks. One thing led to another…"

"You needn't explain." Lisa didn't know whether

to laugh or cry. She'd never have expected her do-it-by-the-book sister to contact the Colorado rancher, never mind sleep with him.

"I want you to understand, sis. Brody doesn't know I'm connected to the university. He doesn't know I'm married. I didn't even tell him my last name. I heard he looked for me the next morning, but I'd already panicked and fled. And he never knew about my pregnancy, either. His address is in my purse."

"I'll get it." Lisa kept her voice steady, but her hands shook. That her sister had kept these secrets shocked her so much that she wondered if she'd ever really known her sister at all—and now it was too late.

"It was easier to let Mark believe the child was his." Maritza shuddered. "Mark has a mean streak when he drinks."

And he always drinks. "I know."

When Mark drank, he blamed everyone else for his shortcomings and failures. According to him, he'd been dishonorably discharged from the army because his sergeant had been jealous of the way his wife looked at Mark, but Lisa suspected his drinking had been the real issue.

"Promise me that you'll take my son to his real father."

Lisa stuffed the precious paper with Brody Adams's name, address and phone number into her bra. "Consider it done."

"And watch out for Mark. He can be meaner than a rattlesnake."

"Don't you worry about him." Mark might be mean, but he always screwed up.

"You'll like Brody Adams, sis."

"Uh-huh."

Maritza's skin had paled to a translucent white. Her hand grew cold, but she smiled, lost in her memories. "I wish I'd met Brody first."

"If he doesn't want your son, I'll raise the little guy myself," Lisa promised, wondering how she would keep that promise.

Maritza shook her head. "An archaeological dig is no place for a child. That's why I gave up fieldwork to do theoretical research."

Lisa thought of the dirt, the sharp digging tools, the often uncooperative weather. Hell, she had no idea how to take care of a baby in a clean and baby-proofed two-bedroom, two-bath house with a white picket fence—and Maritza knew it. "I'll manage somehow."

"Really?"

She forced a smile. "You know me. I'll check out a few library books. Do some research on child rearing. I'm good at research."

"I know. But I imagine a family man like Brody will want his child." Her sister's voice grew weaker. "I hope my son gets your height, not mine."

Lisa stood just shy of six feet tall and possessed red hair that matched her temper, but she lacked people skills, which her sister had in spades. "And you got the big heart." Which was why it had been so easy for Mark to take advantage of her sister. Maritza had once told Lisa that Mark had been abused by his father and knew no other way to behave.

Sad. But Maritza had made his problems her problems and had paid the price with her unhappiness.

"My son's getting a good heart from both sides of the family. His father is special."

Lisa bit her tongue. Now was not the time to argue over Maritza's judgment in men—especially a man she'd known for one night.

Lisa watched the nurse take the baby from Mark and place him back in the crib. "He's beautiful," she said, blinking back tears. "Do you have a name picked out?"

Maritza grabbed her wrist. "Let his real daddy name him."

"You're sure?"

"Yes." Her grasp weakened. Her eyelids kept fluttering closed.

"What about the birth certificate?"

"I told the nurse it could wait."

"All right." Naming the baby could wait.

"Tell Brody to...love...our son...for both of us."

"I will." Lisa forced words past the lump of grief in her throat. "And the baby will have me, too. I promise."

But her sister didn't hear her. She was gone.

Chapter One

Three weeks later

Lisa was out of options. And desperate.

Mark hadn't believed her when she'd told him the baby wasn't his.

Social Services hadn't believed her when she told them that when Mark drank, he often forgot to feed the baby and change his diapers. The one time they'd made a surprise visit, Mark had been sober, charming and cunning. The baby had been immaculately clean, the house spotless. She wouldn't have been surprised if he'd paid someone at Social Services to give him advance warning of the inspection.

A lawyer told her she had no chance of winning custody. Apparently the law didn't care about the biological father. The law considered the father to be the man married to the mother at the time of the baby's birth.

Which left her with no legal options.

But no damn way would she renege on her promise to her sister. The sisters hadn't been connected just by blood. They were friends and partners.

Lisa would do whatever was necessary to ensure her nephew's safety.

Now, she would break and enter, snatch the baby and run from New Mexico to Arizona to Colorado— a circuitous route to hide her trail and prevent Mark and the cops from following her. During the past two weeks, she'd sold her condo, closed her bank account and left no forwarding address. And every minute she'd taken to set her plan in motion, she'd wondered if the baby was clean or hungry or cold. She'd told no one of her intentions, not even the university, which would fire her as soon as Mark filed formal kidnapping charges. Nor had she said anything to the members of her archaeological team, who would wonder and worry about her disappearance, but she hadn't wanted to place her colleagues in awkward positions if they were questioned by the police or the FBI.

Mark lived in a cheap track house on the outskirts of town. Lisa had never understood why he and Maritza hadn't bought a more upscale home. While Mark's PI firm didn't make much profit, Maritza earned decent money. But the total lack of security at the subdivision would work in Lisa's favor.

Earlier in the day she had sent over a case of beer to Mark's home, with a note from some supposedly distant relative. She was betting that by now, five hours later, Mark would be drunk and passed out on the sofa. As she sat in her parked car in front of his house, she estimated from the sounds of the screaming infant that Mark had to be virtually comatose.

It was time to fulfill her promise to Maritza. She would rescue her sister's baby.

Except she knew nothing about children. She'd spent her childhood playing mostly by herself and reading books. Her idea of fun had been trying to put a chicken carcass back together, not playing tag or skipping rope. As an adult, she hadn't had contact with children. She didn't know how to hold a baby or feed one, but how hard could it be? Even primitive cavewomen took care of their babies. Surely her instincts and common sense would be better than Mark's neglect.

But was kidnapping him the right thing to do?

Yes.

After she'd told Mark point-blank that the baby wasn't his, he'd warned her never to come near him or the child again. As Lisa climbed up the crooked block steps, she noticed the front door cracked open.

From the stoop, she could see down the hallway and into the kitchen where Mark sat at the kitchen table, his head slumped on one shoulder, his eyes closed. Lisa didn't hesitate. She scooted inside.

Her heart slamming into her ribs, she went straight to the back bedroom where Brody Jr., which was how she'd come to think of him, was screaming. The room reeked and she desperately wanted to give the baby a bath. But there was no time. She cleaned his bottom with damp wipes, winced at the rash, then changed his diaper. Finally she placed the bottle of formula she had ready into his mouth and wrapped him in a blanket.

The silence, except for the baby's hungry gulps, urged her feet to move faster. At least she didn't have to worry about tripping over anything. Mark was fanatically neat, a trait he'd picked up in the military. When he was sober, he kept the place and the baby immaculate—unfortunately he drank every weekend.

Since Maritza's death, his drinking appeared to have increased in frequency.

Ten more steps and she'd be out the door. Another sixty seconds and she'd have the baby safely ensconced in his car seat. Soon, they'd be free. Lisa's heart tripped in anticipation. On shaking legs, she carried the baby past the sleeping man and out the door.

So far, so good.

The bottle slipped out of the baby's mouth, and he shrieked in protest.

"Easy, little guy," she whispered. At the sound of her voice the baby's cry decreased to a puzzled whimper, almost as if no one had ever spoken to him before. That thought made her more determined.

She propped the bottle back up, but opening the car door with one hand while she held the baby and bottle with the other proved to be a real juggling act. How did mothers manage? Desperation made her careless. She placed the baby into the car seat, but again the bottle dropped from his hungry mouth, this time rolling across the floor of the car.

He wailed loudly. No need to worry about his set of lungs. However, a neighbor in the lot across the road turned on a light. A dog barked.

She had to get out of here.

Fumbling, she found the straps. "Shh. Don't cry. You'll have regular meals from now on, I promise."

This time, her words did nothing to calm the five-week-old baby. He screamed even louder. She tried the pacifier. He spit it out.

"Can't blame you, fellah. You want those calories."

She eyed the bottle and tried not to think about germs. After wiping the nipple clean with her sleeve, she placed it back it his mouth, praying a few bacteria would boost his immune system, instead of making him sick.

Oh, God. Were those police lights in the distance? She'd hoped to be in another state by the time Mark sobered up enough to notify the police.

Had a neighbor reported her stealing the baby? How ironic that she'd walked right past Mark but might be caught by a nosy neighbor. But then, that was how most criminals got caught—by forgetting to cover a detail.

She could spend the rest of her life in jail.

Maybe she should put the baby back in his crib. She still had time. She hadn't gone anywhere yet. Unless they caught her with the baby in her car, they couldn't charge her.

But this might be the best opportunity she ever had. If she failed now, Mark would be forever wary. He could move, change his identity. She might never see the baby again.

Okay. She took several deep steadying breaths and started the car. Had she forgotten anything?

Just her seat belt. She snapped it on and jerked the car into gear.

Easy.

No speeding.

No calling attention to herself.

She could do this.

As she drove out of the subdivision, her pulse beating a tattoo in her throat, the police car passed her going the other way. Perhaps the cops were there on another matter. They might not even know about her and the baby.

Steady.

Just drive.

After she pulled out onto the highway, she checked the rearview mirror. She could see the headlights of numerous trucks and cars, but no flashing blue and red lights. Behind her the baby sucked contently on the bottle.

Had she made a clean getaway?

MARK GILMORE OPENED his bleary eyes at about five in the morning. He'd always been an early riser, even after a late-night card game. He straightened his neck and groaned at the headache that felt as if a troop of soldiers were stomping between his ears. Not bothering to remove his clothes, he staggered to the shower, ignoring the nasty taste in his mouth, just turned the water on hot and stepped under the spray.

For once, at least, the kid wasn't crying. It figured that the one time he'd gotten a decent night's sleep, he'd done so in a chair, leaving him one hell of a crick in his neck.

Damn Maritza for dying, leaving him with all the work. Not that she'd been that great at housework or cooking. How could she tend to his household when she was always thinking about her dumb archaeological theories?

But a man had to do what a man had to do—even if it meant working all day, giving up his poker night with the boys and taking care of his son, instead. Yeah, he'd handle it. As his daddy used to say, family was all a man had to keep him going when times got bad.

Mark finally found the energy to take off his sopping clothes. He left them in the shower stall, wrapped a towel around his hips and popped several aspirin into his mouth, chewed and swallowed. They left a distressing taste, so he walked into the kitchen to make coffee.

There was no coffee. Maritza had forgotten again, no doubt daydreaming about the Anasazi and their basket weaving, instead of keeping her mind focused where it belonged—on her family.

No, Maritza was gone. How could he keep forgetting?

But what did he expect with so many details to recall? He had to do everything now. Buy the coffee. Even feed the baby. Mark mixed a bottle of formula, heated it in the microwave, puzzled by the extra bottle still in the microwave. While he waited, he popped the top of a beer. Best way to cure a hangover was to have a hair of the dog that had bitten him.

He padded down to the baby's room, the bottle in one hand, the beer in the other, feeling close to human. At the sight of the empty crib, he stared.

What the hell?

Had he gotten so drunk last night that he'd forgotten to put the baby in the crib? Mark took a swallow of beer.

Think.

He'd come home from work, paid the sitter and found a lovely case of beer on the front stoop. Vaguely he recalled the baby crying and fixing a bottle around ten. So that was why the extra bottle was still in his microwave. He hadn't fed the baby last night. However little Mark *had* been in his crib.

And then his brain kicked into PI mode. He'd been set up. The beer hadn't come from a distant relative. There were no distant relatives—just Maritza and Lisa. His bitch of a sister-in-law had convinced Maritza that a woman shouldn't give up a career for her husband and should keep her maiden name for professional reasons.

Professional, my ass.

Lisa had always hated him. She must have sent him that beer and he'd taken the bait. She'd probably waltzed in last night and kidnapped the kid. No one else would have taken the baby.

Lisa had lied to him about the baby's paternity, lied to Social Services about his being an unfit father, lied all along, trying to take the child. She probably coveted his son because she couldn't make one of her own—and that was because no man would want her. When her lies hadn't worked with Social Services, she'd kidnapped his son. To make sure, he picked up the phone and dialed her number. Disconnected.

She'd likely left town. The facts fit, but in case he'd miscalculated, he'd swing over to her place to see if she was still around. But he already knew she'd be gone.

Mark slammed his fist into a wall.

Damn her to perdition!

How dare she take his son? How dare she come between father and child?

He crushed the empty beer can, tossed it at the trash. Already full, the trash can toppled, spilling the empties across the floor. In a black rage, Mark kicked a stray can, sliced open his toe. Then he swore, picked up the phone and dialed 911.

"Do you have an emergency to report?"

Mark slammed down the phone. He couldn't go to the cops—not unless he wanted to become a laughingstock in this town. After all, he was a private investigator. Once he could concentrate on business, instead of doing the child-rearing chores of the wife who'd died on him, he'd be plenty successful. If it came out on the news that his sister-in-law had made a fool of him by taking his son and that he'd had to ask the cops for help to find them, his reputation would suffer and business would go down the tubes.

Mark popped open the last beer and ignored his bleeding toe. He'd go after the bitch himself. And when he found her, he'd make her pay. Make her pay not only for taking his son, but for all those nasty things she'd said to Maritza about him. Make her pay for the lie she'd told about little Mark. That baby was his. The only family he had left. And no interfering woman was going to take away his son. After all, family was everything.

It was just a matter of time until he hunted her down and found them. He certainly had time to finish his beer.

One week later

LISA OPENED HER EYES. Today was Tuesday so she must be in Phoenix. Seven stops in seven days. She'd done lots of driving, lots of motel hopping. Sometimes she'd deliberately left misleading clues. She'd told one hotel clerk she and the baby were taking the next flight south to Mexico. She'd told a restaurant waitress she was heading for Montreal, and she'd mentioned to a bellhop that she was going to the Big Apple to start a career on the stage. Mark might be a screwup, but he had sly street smarts, which made her wary and careful.

She kept flicking the radio from station to station like a news junky, waiting for the kidnapping to be announced. But she heard nothing. She hoped that Mark simply didn't care that she'd taken the baby. But her sister had been married to Mark for three long years, and Lisa knew the man had a stubborn streak. Despite his appetite for alcohol, she'd seen him give up drinking for months at a time. He'd likely been dishonorably discharged from the military because of his drinking, not because he hadn't been a good commando. She wasn't sure what kind of training he'd had, but she never doubted that he was dangerous.

However, she had to put Mark out of her mind and focus on taking care of Maritza's baby. Too bad all her schooling hadn't included one course in child care. Lisa knew how the Inuit and Hopi and Navajos cared for their infants, but she wasn't sure how often BJ needed to be fed, how much he should sleep. And meanwhile she prayed his real father wouldn't be another man she couldn't trust.

When it came to caring for baby BJ, she followed a natural rhythm. She let the baby sleep when he was tired, and when he awoke, she bathed, diapered and fed him. Soon, they'd established a routine of sorts. Luckily for her, he was a happy baby. He didn't mind the long car rides, sleeping while she drove. BJ had already enriched her life a thousandfold. When he stared at her with those big blue eyes, wrapped his tiny fingers around her thumb, she couldn't have refused him anything. Certainly not a chance for a real father and home, a shot at a good life.

Tomorrow she would start driving toward Colorado and Brody Adams's ranch. She had no real hope that the man would want his son, but she'd promised her sister that she would bring the baby to him. She hadn't, however, promised to leave him.

Maritza had believed that Brody would want his son. Lisa didn't have that kind of faith. Not many single men would appreciate a stranger showing up on their doorstep and handing them a child. Children were big responsibilities. They needed feeding and cleaning and teaching and holding and loving. A tall order for any parent who'd deliberately brought a child into the world, never mind for a bachelor taken by complete surprise after a one-night stand.

If she didn't approve of Brody Adams, Lisa planned to keep the baby. She knew of husband-and-wife teams that brought children along with them on archaeological digs. Yeah, for a summer, maybe. Not full-time. Perhaps she could find a nanny, but she wasn't sure she could afford one. And she'd always have the worry of hiding out from Mark.

One thing at a time. So far there had been no reports of the kidnapping on the news. Maybe Mark had changed his mind about wanting the baby. So her primary goal was getting to know Brody Adams before making any permanent decisions. She'd figure out how to meet him during the long drive north.

AFTER PUTTING IN a fifteen-hour day of ranching, Brody Adams had gone into town and picked up the mail. Now he was looking forward to getting home, parking his pickup truck, taking a hot shower, eating a grilled steak and then catching the news.

But no matter how tired, dirty and hungry he might be, when he saw a car backed into a ravine at an angle that indicated the driver was likely good and stuck, he stopped. Folks out here still helped one another.

And mountains often blocked the cell phones that city people relied on to call for help.

Since Brody recognized his neighbors, their cars and trucks on sight, even if he hadn't spotted the Arizona plates, he would have known the driver wasn't a local. He parked his truck, took out a powerful flashlight and an emergency medical kit. Last year a man driving way too fast for local conditions had hit a patch of black ice and skidded off a cliff. Brody and a foreman had pulled the man out of his car and a chopper had airlifted him to a Denver hospital. He'd been lucky to survive with a few broken bones.

This situation didn't appear as dire. The light of a campfire flickered behind the car. And the rear tires in the ditch looked as if the driver had backed up just a little too far and tilted over.

He shone his light into the car. Empty.

"Hello? Anyone here?"

That was when he heard the click of a gun. "Don't move another step, mister." The voice was low, sure—and female. "And keep your hands where I can see them."

Brody froze. He'd seen all kinds of people in trouble, and by far the worst were the ones who were out of their element and scared. Fear led to bad decision-making. But from the sound of that husky voice, she didn't sound as much scared as wary. He couldn't blame her for drawing a gun on him; he just hoped she had the sense not to shoot. A woman out here alone needed to protect herself, so he put the flashlight and emergency kit down and raised his hands slowly.

"I'm not moving."

"Ah, a sensible man. You have a name?"

"Brody. Brody Adams. This is my land you're on," he added.

"I thought the road was public."

"It was until you turned off the highway about seven miles back."

"You own seven miles of land?"

"Yes." Actually he owned about two hundred square miles of land. But no matter how sexy she sounded, he wasn't into bragging, not with her holding a gun on him. "I saw the car and thought you might need a tow out of the ditch."

"We're fine."

"We?"

"The baby and me."

"Can I lower my hands now?"

"Sure. But please don't make any sudden moves."

She was polite. And when she stepped out of the darkness into the light from his flashlight, which still rested on the ground, he saw booted feet, long slim legs encased in jeans that tapered upward to slender hips. Her middle seemed to bulge.

Then she stepped closer and he realized she was wearing a baby sling, as his sister-in-law had with his nephew. There was nothing wrong with this woman's proportions, especially if a man liked leggy, six-foot-tall models. In the darkness he couldn't make out her features, but from her tone, he estimated her age to be about the same as his.

"You got a name?"

"Lisa Madison."

"Hi, Lisa. I'm going to reach into my back pocket and hand you my ID, okay?"

"Why?" She sounded puzzled.

"My ID has my address. It'll prove I live here."

"And that makes you...?"

"A solid citizen."

"Never mind." She eased the safety back onto the gun and stuffed it into her front pocket. "Sorry to pull out the weapon, it's just that before you stopped I thought I heard... Anyway I believe you."

"What happened before I stopped?" He couldn't imagine any of his men threatening a woman, and if they had, he'd fire them on the spot. Out here folks didn't prey on women in trouble.

"Well, I heard rustling in the bushes, the two-legged kind. Then the trucker stopped and probably meant no harm, but I didn't like his looks and told him to be on his way. He didn't take kindly to my suggestion until I pulled out my gun."

"What kind of truck was he driving?"

"Diesel fuel."

He'd look into it tomorrow. He bought enough fuel to supply a small town. If the gas company couldn't send out a reliable driver, he could switch to another supplier. "So are you stuck?"

"Actually the baby and I were just camping out here."

At first he thought she was being sarcastic. Then he realized she was serious.

"I didn't know this was your land. But since we're trespassing, it's only fair that we should share our campfire. Would you care for some coffee, Mr. Adams?"

"Sure, and call me Brody."

He'd come across many fishermen and hunters on his land, but in all his thirty years of living here, he'd never come across a woman and baby camping on their own.

He accepted the hot coffee, which smelled delicious, and noted the carefully made campfire, ringed with rocks to prevent an accidental fire. She'd rigged a tent hammock between two trees, and she'd picked a brand known for weathering thunderstorms and freezing temperatures. She might not be from around these parts, but she was no tenderfoot. So why wasn't she camping in a state park? Why hadn't she known that she was on private property?

Brody sipped his coffee and tried not to stare at Lisa. In the firelight he could make out her huge round eyes of a color he had yet to determine, a wide mouth that had yet to smile and long red shimmering hair that made a man want to run his hands through it. She stood up straight, comfortable with her height, which almost matched his, and shrugged out of the baby carrier, her movements practiced and competent.

Brody had a half-dozen assorted nieces and nephews, so when he saw how young the baby was, he almost choked on his coffee. What woman took an infant camping in the wild? And where was her husband?

"Cute kid," was all he said.

"Would you do me a favor and hold him for a second?"

"Sure."

He adored babies and he'd had lots of practice. But he also knew that new mothers tended to be very protective of their infants. Sheesh, his sister-in-law wouldn't let him hold little Jilly unless he'd first washed his hands and was sitting in an armchair. Yet this woman casually turned over her kid to a stranger as if the baby was no more important than a sack of feed.

"How old is he?"

"Five weeks and two days. When he was born he was bald, but then all that dark hair started coming in." She sounded as proud as any new mama. While she carefully watched him to make sure he held the baby properly, she busied herself placing a grill over the fire and laying out two steaks, all without asking if he was hungry. As the flames licked the meat, enticing his nostrils, he smelled a setup—but for the life of him, he couldn't figure out what she was up to. Women came on to him all the time, but not by asking him to hold their babies.

"Where's his daddy?"

Lisa shrugged.

"Does the little guy have a name?"

"BJ." She placed potatoes wrapped in foil in the hot rocks around the fire. "We're on a quest for his father."

Chapter Two

"At least I'm off the hook," Brody said. "Because I assure you, we haven't met. I'd remember."

"Don't worry, I'm not planning to slap a paternity suit on you." Lisa chuckled to put him at ease. She had no intention of informing him yet that he was the baby's father. She might have spent more time in a library than on dates, but even she knew that she'd bungle things for sure by bringing up that subject too soon. "If we'd ever...well, I would have remembered, too." She looked him up and down, letting him see the gleam of appreciation in her eyes, hoping she was doing this right and massaging his ego with a bit of flirting.

Brody had surprised her several times already. He hadn't bristled when she'd pulled the gun. He hadn't asked a bunch of personal questions that weren't his business. And he'd come prepared with the medical kit to help. But she wasn't about to trust Maritza's judgment about the man—not yet. Appearances could be so deceiving. Look at Mark. He'd even fooled Lisa in the beginning with his charm and good looks, but he wielded that charm to hide his true nature.

And Lisa had become way too attached to little BJ

to consider turning the baby over to his father until she'd gotten to know Brody Adams a lot better. But she had to admit he was kind. What Maritza had failed to mention was the sexy tilt of his Stetson hat, the steel in his tone that contrasted nicely with his fine manners and the way he sat back and assessed a situation before jumping right in to fix things. Most men would already have looked at her car, made a sarcastic comment about woman drivers and bragged about how they'd have her right out of there in a jiffy. Brody Adams seemed more sophisticated than the average cowboy.

Yet, from his booted leather feet, to his straight-legged jeans, to his plaid shirt, he was all cowboy. His face was tanned from spending hours in the sun, and she liked the way the corners of his eyes crinkled with laugh lines. More importantly, his large hands held BJ with an ease that made her realize he had experience with babies.

Oh, God. He could even be married with a few kids of his own.

She couldn't imagine disrupting an entire family because of her sister's one-night stand. For the first time she considered how telling this man the truth could unsettle his life.

"You have any kids?" she asked.

"Nope."

He could have been lying, but he hadn't hesitated. She glanced at his hand, but didn't see a wedding ring. He'd caught her looking and responded with a glint of mischief in his eyes. "I'm not married, either."

She didn't feel the least bit repentant, although she murmured the polite words. "Sorry for prying." If she'd had a little more experience with men, she might have better social skills, but as usual she'd just have to rely on her intelligence to carry her through the awkward situation. "You looked so comfortable holding little BJ that I figured you must have a few of your own. His bottle is right there in that bag. Would you mind feeding him?"

"No problem. My brothers both have children." He spoke like an indulgent uncle, but she sensed a sharp mind behind his folksy attitude. Brody had large hands with long tapered fingers. She imagined that those hands were as capable at reining in a stallion or lassoing a stray cow as they were at holding little BJ. And when he reached for the bottle and the pulse in his neck throbbed under the flickering firelight, she suspected he was aware of much more than he'd let on.

So her instincts about him were right on target. There likely were a few parts to her story that he didn't believe, but she didn't know exactly where she'd slipped up. She hadn't lied except at first when she'd claimed she hadn't known this was his land. She'd mostly just skirted the truth, but he'd picked up on the absence of details like a good reporter. She wasn't accustomed to interviewing fathers to see if they were fit. Give her a pottery shard to identify and categorize, and she was a whiz. She flipped the steaks, let him continue to feed the baby, noting that he periodically stopped to burp him.

He probably knew more than she did about kids, but that didn't mean he wanted a son. And no way would she come right out and ask. She'd learned a long time ago not to ask questions where she wouldn't believe the answer—no matter what it was. She needed to know what was in his heart. And to know his heart, she needed to spend time with him.

She gazed into the fire and realized that no matter how carefully she'd thought through her actions, there were complications she hadn't anticipated. Like her outright attraction to Brody. She'd been hoping for someone decent—not a hunk who could have ridden beside Brad Pitt in a western and drawn his share of sighs from the women in the audience.

Brody cleared his throat. "It's time to flip the steaks again."

"Thanks." She expertly used the tongs, slathered sauce on the meat and then turned the potatoes. "I tend to daydream wherever I stare into a fire."

"You do that often?"

"Hmm?" He'd caught her off guard. Most men would have asked what she was thinking about. Brody had a way of asking sideways questions, coming from a different angle that kept taking her by surprise and reminding her of the keen mind under that hat.

"You stare into flames a lot?" He rephrased his question as he expertly tipped the last of BJ's formula so that no air flowed to the nipple.

"I like the outdoors."

If he noted her evasive answer, he didn't say anything. BJ had finally finished his bottle. Brody held him up against his shoulder, gently patting his back and rocking him to elicit one final burp.

She wanted to go over and take the baby from him. And she didn't know why. She'd deliberately handed BJ to his father to see how well Brody would cope with the baby. She'd expected him to fail, and when he didn't, disappointment coursed through her. She wasn't sure why. Instead of searching for an answer she didn't want to face—for example, that she might be getting more attached to the baby than she'd planned—she shoved another branch into the fire. "Is he asleep?"

"Almost."

She pointed to her right. "Would you mind putting him in the hammock for me?"

"Sure."

Brody didn't question their sleeping arrangements. His long legs quickly took him and the baby to the edge of the circle cast by the firelight, but she was keenly aware of his every move. Once the baby was zipped into the hanging hammock, he couldn't fall out. And the gentle night breeze should rock him right to sleep.

Without the baby between them, the darkness and the welcoming firelight seemed more intimate. Although she had her plan all worked out, she kept delaying. So she fussed with the food, and when Brody returned to the fire and accepted the plate with his steak and potato, she deliberately avoided touching him, avoided meeting his gaze.

He eyed with interest the handful of bean sprouts she'd added. "Salad?"

"Best I could do under the circumstances."

"Thanks." He settled next to her, folding his lean body into a compact space, and dug into his food. It was a tribute to either her cooking or his hunger that he didn't say another word until his plate was empty. "That sure hit the spot."

"Glad you enjoyed it."

He set his plate aside, stretched out his legs and eyed her. "Now are you going to tell me what's going on?"

There was no point in delaying any longer. Her mama had always told her never to ask a man hard questions on an empty stomach. So she'd fed him, even arranging to do so on neutral territory. But although the food and fire may have relaxed him, it didn't mean he'd agree to her request.

"Look, I lied earlier when I said I didn't know this was your land. I came here to meet you."

He raised an eyebrow. "So you planned all this?" He indicated the food and the fire and the hammock.

"Yes."

"You planned the car that looks stuck, but isn't?"

"Yes."

"The food?"

"Yes."

"The camping?"

"Yes."

"Why not just knock on the front door?"

"I figured you wouldn't let me inside long enough to hear me out."

"How did you know I'd be coming by tonight?"

"I've done my research. I know you regularly go into town every Thursday to pick up the mail. There's only one road in and out so…"

He chuckled and shook his head. "Lady, you sure are one piece of work. I can't wait to hear your reason—which I assume depends on whether I passed all your little tests."

He was even brighter than she'd estimated. And she so enjoyed intelligent men, especially ones who looked as good as this one. Come to think of it, she wasn't sure she'd ever seen such intelligence packaged quite so…muscularly. He didn't have the kind of bulk of a man who lifted weights, but the lean hard body of an outdoorsman who did strenuous physical work every day.

Yum.

"You passed with an A plus."

"So?"

"I'm an archaeologist from Southwestern University. My team has been studying the Anasazi—"

"Hold on." He held up a work-callused hand. "I received a letter from some lawyer who represents Southwestern University. They wanted to dig up my land—"

"I wouldn't call archaeology digging up—"

"—and I refused. So you've come here to change my mind, have you?"

He was quick.

If she and Maritza had looked anything alike, he might have put everything together by now. Luckily she resembled her father, who was tall, and Maritza, their five-foot-one mother. Lisa's complexion was fair, her eyes green, her hair red, and Maritza had olive skin, brown eyes and dark hair. From Lisa's appearance, he'd never guess the two women were siblings. Since Maritza had told Lisa that she hadn't mentioned she was an archaeologist or worked for the university, he shouldn't be able to draw any connection between them.

Lisa looked him straight in the eye. "I thought if we met in person, I could convince you we'd only be a minor pain in the ass."

"As opposed to a major one?"

Hmm. This might be more difficult than she'd anticipated. However, she had to change his mind for two reasons. She wanted to get to know him better to evaluate his daddy qualities, and she really would like to explore his land for traces of the Anasazi. She kept her voice low and reasonable, ignoring the simmering tension that had risen between them.

"My team is made up of professionals. You'll know we're here, but we'll try to stay out of your way."

"You'll try?"

"And if we make a major find, the value of your land will skyrocket."

He shook his head, a black lock of hair falling onto his forehead. "I inherited this land from my father, who inherited it from his father, who inherited it from his father. I fully intend to someday pass these acres on to my own family. So if the land is worth a few more dollars per acre, it means nothing to me."

"Aren't you interested in advancing social science?"

"Not particularly."

"Have you ever been to Mesa Verde, Brody?"

"Can't say that I have."

Somehow she wasn't surprised that the man lived within an hour's drive of one of the greatest archaeological sites in his state and hadn't had the inclination to visit. At least he hadn't said no to her request outright. She still had a chance to change his mind.

"A few thousand years ago the Anasazi—the name means "ancestral enemies" in Navajo—built a city of dwellings into the sides of a cliff." As always when she spoke about archaeology and the old ones, her voice expressed an enthusiasm she couldn't suppress. "The Anasazi civilization expanded through some of the harshest deserts and survived for centuries in one of the most hostile environments on earth. And then they disappeared."

"So did lots of other civilizations."

"I'd like to find out why. And I believe those answers may be buried on your land."

LISA'S VOICE MESMERIZED Brody as she spoke about the Anasazi. While Brody had no interest in a bunch of old bones and broken pottery shards, he was most intrigued by Lisa Madison. Besides her enchanting voice, he liked the way her eyes banked with fire when she spoke about her work. And her well-thought-out campaign to talk to him intrigued him. Most women with a body like hers and a face to match would have gone the seductive route, or they would have used their woman-alone status to win sympathy. She'd done neither, approaching him in a way so unique that he wanted to know her better—which might be exactly what she'd intended.

For a few minutes he'd actually hoped she was flirting with him, but that was wishful thinking on his part. Usually he knew when a woman wanted his attention. He wasn't so good at reading minds, but around these parts, women often spoke plainly enough even for a man more accustomed to cows than socializing to get the message.

"What's that?" Lisa interrupted his thoughts, her head cocked to one side.

If he hadn't been thinking so hard, he would have noticed the rumble from the ground sooner, a sound he recognized immediately now that she'd called his attention to it. "Stampede."

She leaped to her feet. "Are we in danger?"

"The cattle shouldn't be anywhere near this close to the road, but we aren't taking any chances."

"Agreed."

"Grab the baby. We're getting out of here."

The thundering roar intensified, a clear indication the cattle were running their way.

Lisa sprinted for the hammock and the baby, which were in the direction opposite to the elevated road and safety. They had just moments to act. He took a few seconds to kick dirt onto the fire, then slung her backpack over his shoulder and picked up the baby carrier.

Lisa grabbed BJ and bolted for the road. Brody tossed her pack and the baby carrier up the ten-foot-high embankment, then grabbed her arm. With the baby to hold and her sneakers slipping in the slick grass on the steep incline, she kept sliding backward.

"Let me take him," he said, his steps more secure as he dug the pointy toe of each boot into the dirt to secure a toehold.

She didn't hesitate, giving him BJ. "Go. I'll be right behind you."

The pounding of five-hundred-pound terrified animals made the ground shift and tremble like an earthquake. The hooves trampled everything in their path, sending up clouds of dust and making breathing difficult.

Brody gasped in air and spat out dirt as he used every muscle in his thighs and calves to strain upward.

The animals had drawn so close he could smell their fear in the thick night air. He struggled up the incline with the baby, knowing they hadn't much time, but refusing to look behind him and waste a precious second. He used his free hand to gain purchase in the thick grasses, and finally he reached the top, swung the baby, then himself, over onto the shoulder of the road. The cattle charged straight toward them. He picked up the infant and saw that Lisa wasn't even close to reaching the top.

"Hurry up."

"Go! Go! Get BJ to safety."

Damn it. He didn't want to leave her, but those cattle could still stampede right up this embankment.

Brody sprinted for his truck, yanked open the door and placed the baby on the floor so he couldn't accidently roll off the seat. He yanked open an emergency kit and pulled out a flare, knowing he was too late, with the herd just yards from the spot where he'd abandoned Lisa to the horrible fate of being stomped to death.

He heard the sound of gunshots.

Smart woman. Could she turn the herd with gunfire? Or were the animals too close?

He rammed the cartridge into the flare and fired it, hoping that together their actions would turn the herd. In the flare's bursting red light, he watched the cattle jam up against the bottom of the embankment, the animals at the front flattened by those from behind.

When he saw her arm clear the top, he ran back to grab her hand and help her roll to safety. She scrambled to her feet, and together they raced to the truck.

"BJ's on the floor!" he shouted.

He opened the door, dived over the passenger seat, scrambled behind the wheel and started the engine. Lisa plunged in after him. With one arm, he helped her onto the seat while she scooped up the baby.

"Hold on." As the herd cleared the embankment, he gunned the engine and she pulled the door closed.

Then he drove fast, skidding and sliding over a road never meant for speed. Eventually they outdistanced the tiring herd.

Slowly his pulse rate settled and his thoughts turned from surviving the stampede to the woman and baby beside him. Lisa cradled the infant, who hadn't once cried or let out a peep of complaint.

As Brody realized that the baby's silence might not be normal, the hairs on his neck stood on end. Had he shaken the baby during their mad flight? Somehow cut off his air supply?

"Is he okay?"

"He's sleeping."

"You're sure he's breathing?"

"Yes." She might have been shaking on the seat beside him, but her voice remained strong and calm. "And I can feel his little heart beating beneath my hand." She drew a seat belt over her lap. "Thanks for your help. If we'd been alone out there, we might not have made it."

"No problem." She was recovering fast after one helluva scare, and he appreciated that he hadn't had to deal with a hysterical woman. She'd kept her cool out there. If she hadn't thought to fire her gun, she might not have survived at all.

Brody picked up his radio microphone and clicked it three times, then waited for a reply. "I'm taking you to my ranch. In the morning we'll go back and see about your car."

She breathed in deeply and let the air out slowly. "You think there's anything left?"

"Hard to say. Sometimes the animals will stomp on anything in their path. I've seen them flatten a truck. Then again, sometimes they swerve and avoid objects. I'd like to know what started that stampede."

"What do you mean?"

"Well, cattle aren't brilliant animals, but they usually have a reason for panicking. Lightning can set them off.''

''But there wasn't a storm in sight.''

''A wolf or coyote could do it. Tomorrow we'll look for tracks, but the herd could have stampeded over any tracks.''

''Can a person start a stampede?''

''Sure, why?''

''Before you showed up, I thought I heard someone skulking around my car. It was probably nothing.''

''You keep anything valuable in it?''

''Just my notes.''

He frowned at her. ''Why don't you tell me more about the Anasazi relics? Are they valuable?''

Chapter Three

Lisa didn't get a chance to answer Brody's question because a voice came over his radio and interrupted their conversation. The voice sounded so similar to Brody's in accent and tone that she would have thought he was on the other end of the signal if he hadn't been sitting right next to her.

"What's wrong?" the strong male voice asked.

Brody clicked the microphone and spoke into it. "We had a stampede about seven miles from the main highway, just east of our road."

"How many head?"

"At least five hundred. It's petered off by now, but I want you to send out two men. Make one of them Evan. He's our best tracker. Tell him I'd like to know what set off those cows."

"You okay?"

"I'm fine and I've got company. Picked her up during the stampede." Brody held up the microphone to her. "Say hello to Ken, my ugly brother."

"Hi, Ken. I'm Lisa Madison."

"Howdy, ma'am." He chuckled. "Leave it to my brother to pick up a woman during a stampede."

Brody took back the microphone. "Don't be telling Mom and worrying her over nothing."

"Too late."

A woman's voice came over the radio. "I heard that, Brody. You sure you're okay?"

"I'm fine. And what are you doing working this late?"

"Paperwork. And don't change the subject."

His mother's voice had a no-nonsense ring to it, but the love came through between every word. For a moment Lisa was jealous. Obviously his family cared about one another a great deal. And the easy teasing between brothers reminded her that she and Maritza had been that close. She blinked back tears.

She wasn't all alone in the world, though. She had BJ—but maybe not for long. She reminded herself once again not to get too attached to him. The little tyke slept peacefully in her arms. She couldn't stop herself from breathing in the scent of baby lotion, gently patting his soft skin and thanking her lucky stars that no one had been hurt.

They could have died. And it would have been her fault. If Brody hadn't been there to carry the baby up that incline, neither she nor the baby would have survived. She'd had no business taking an infant camping—any real mom would have known that. BJ should be in a safe apartment or house, not rattling around in a car in the middle of nowhere.

Brody tapped her on the shoulder. "That okay?"

"Huh?" She hadn't been listening to his conversation with his family.

"Everyone's up at the ranch house. Mom isn't going to be happy until she hugs me and then counts all my fingers and toes."

"Whatever you want to do."

"I'd like to tell them why you're here. Is that okay?"

"Sure."

He glanced sideways at her for a second. "You don't understand. Their reaction will be volatile at best, hostile at worst."

After what she'd just survived, she could only summon up a smidgen of alarm. After all, she wasn't here to win a popularity contest, just to find out if Brody would be a good father for BJ. And maybe do a little digging for Anasazi ruins on the side.

She frowned at him. "Why would your family be hostile when they don't even know me?"

"Because almost every stranger that shows up these days wants our land or our water."

"But they aren't for sale. And I'm not asking you to sell, so what's the problem?"

He made his voice sound sympathetic. "I guess it's hard for someone who hasn't grown up here to understand. We don't cotton to outsiders coming to a place we've owned for generations and telling us how to run our business."

She didn't really get what he was saying. "I would never presume to tell you how to raise your cattle."

"Oh, really?" He gave her a challenging look.

"Really."

"Okay." He grinned his charming grin and she tried to concentrate on his words, rather than how that grin made her belly curl with heat. "Suppose my cattle are grazing on the site you want to dig up. You'd want me to move them, right?"

She sighed and refrained from rolling her eyes at the night sky, where the stars loomed so much larger and brighter than in the city. "Is that really such a big deal when you own the land as far as the eye can see?"

"I suppose you think I'm unreasonable," he teased.

"Cautious."

How could she think him unreasonable when she suspected he was pulling her leg? She couldn't be annoyed with a man who'd just saved her life, could she?

"You're direct and diplomatic," he said. "I hope you have more where that came from, because we're almost there."

He drove along the side of a curve that followed the edge of a mountain, and then she stared in surprise. She didn't know what she'd expected. But what she saw clearly, with all the exterior lights on, was a three-story two-columned house with a huge front porch and balconies on the upper floors. It was perched on the mountainside and overlooked a valley.

A white picket fence separated the yard of stately oaks and pines from the fields. Colorful wonderful-smelling flowers greeted her senses. "That's your house?"

"It's Mom's. Although she'd love for all of us to move in, we like our privacy. I live in a place about a mile farther down the road, and it's nowhere near this fancy. My brothers and their wives have their own homes nearby." He grinned and parked beside a sweeping staircase that reminded her of the old Southern mansions she'd seen along the Mississippi River. "But if we don't stop in, Mom won't be a happy woman, and I avoid provoking her when at all possible."

He spoke about his mother with love and respect,

even though he was complaining at the same time. She liked that about him, liked the way he cared about his mother's feelings, liked the way he admitted that he cared.

After turning off the engine, he walked around to open her door for her. She thought of her dirty jeans, her bare feet and her messy hair. She looked at that immaculately tended house with colorful geraniums in the window boxes and shook her head. "Maybe I should wait here."

"Best to get it over with now."

"It?"

"Mom loves to give the third degree to pretty women who show up with her sons," he teased. "First thing Mom will want to know is if you're single."

"I am. But we aren't on a date," she protested. She wrapped the sleeping baby's blanket around him to stave off the cool night air and cradled him over her shoulder. Past experience told her that jostling wouldn't disturb him.

"Think she's going to believe that?"

"It's the truth."

"Yeah, well, she'll take one look at us and think we've been rolling around in the dirt."

"We have been rolling around in the dirt," she said, "just not the way—"

"Brody. I'll think no such thing." His mother moved down the well-lit front steps. She was a tall woman, though not as tall as Lisa. The resemblance stopped there. His mother's gray hair was immaculately coiffed, her makeup perfect, her skin tanned and lined. She wore designer clothes and shoes that matched, but she didn't hesitate to throw her arms around her dirty son and hug him.

Then she suddenly pushed back. "Sorry, I'm forgetting my manners. I'm Mia Adams."

Lisa wiped her free hand on her jeans, then held it out. "Lisa Madison."

Mia Adams's handshake was firm, her nails perfectly manicured, her scent expensive. But it was her level assessment that impressed Lisa straight off and made her glad again that she'd done her homework before approaching the Adams clan. Here was a strong woman, the matriarch and backbone of this family, a woman who'd lost her husband to a heart attack more than a decade ago. She could have sold the land, but she'd chosen to stay near her children and her grandchildren. Lisa respected that choice.

Two men strode down the steps, one of them balancing a six- or seven-year-old girl on his shoulders. She could immediately tell the men were brothers by their dark hair and similar facial features, especially their dark-gray eyes. Brody was a few inches taller, but all of them were lean and handsome.

Brody introduced them. "Meet Ken, Riley and Samantha."

"Sammy," the little girl insisted. "Are you and Uncle Brody going out?"

Riley snorted, probably to cover up a chuckle. "What did your mother tell you about asking impertinent questions?"

Sammy shrugged. "Grandma says there's no such thing as a bad question."

Riley glared at Mia. "You told her that?"

"Mm. She's using my own words against me again." Mia defended herself, but clearly she was a doting grandma, none too upset by her granddaughter's forthright question.

Little BJ picked that moment to awaken. "This is BJ," Lisa introduced him, taking him off her shoulder and cradling him so the others could see his face.

"He's...an infant?" Mia looked from the baby to her son to Lisa, then back at the baby.

"Five weeks," Lisa said.

BJ surveyed the group before screaming in protest. She rocked him gently, knowing it would do no good. "He's hungry. And the baby formula—"

"—is back at the camp where our cows stampeded." Brody was obviously thinking out loud.

"Camp?" Mia asked.

Sammy tugged her father's hair. "I want to go camping. And we don't need another baby."

"Sorry," Riley apologized over BJ's cries. "My wife just had a baby and Sammy isn't used to—"

"Our baby cries all the time," Sammy complained.

Brody spoke to his mother. "You have any formula in the house?"

"Of course." Mia took Lisa's arm and guided her inside. "In fact, I have a nursery outfitted so when my grandchildren come to visit, they can be comfortable. I'd invite you to stay—"

"Mom, she's not staying here," Brody interjected with a finality that surprised Lisa. She'd gotten the feeling that Mia usually had her own way.

"I wasn't going to invite her. Not with Keely upstairs with the chicken pox." Mia spoke to Lisa. "I've already had the chicken pox and her mother hasn't. I'm nursing my granddaughter back to health or I'd invite you to stay here."

"I understand," Lisa said, wondering if she should even be bringing BJ into the house.

As if reading her mind, Brody informed her. "Keely's stayed upstairs the entire time. We won't go up there. However, Mom—" he turned to Mia "—I want a man guarding this house until we figure out what's up."

"Is that really necessary?" Mia ushered them through a grand foyer with marble floors and Western paintings on the walls. Then they passed through a living room with Southwestern decor of turquoise and peach into a functional kitchen with warm honey-colored wood and cream tiles. High ceilings and hanging baskets filled with herbs created a homey air, suggesting that the kitchen was the heart of this home.

"Until I know what or who started that stampede, I'm not taking any chances with your safety."

"What do you mean?" Ken asked.

Riley and Samantha had followed them inside. Brody signaled his brother with a look that the ensuing conversation might not be suitable for the child.

Riley leaned over and kissed his mother on the cheek. "It's time for Sammy to go to bed."

Sammy shook her head. "No, it's not. Daddy just doesn't want me to hear about the stampede."

"Samantha!" Her father grabbed her dangling ankle and squeezed gently. "That's enough. Tell everyone good-night, sweetheart."

"Night. Night."

After Riley and Sammy left, Mia retrieved a bottle of formula and popped it into the microwave. BJ stopped fussing, entertained by the plants hanging from the ceiling.

Brody finally answered his mother's question.

"Mom, a half hour before the stampede, Lisa thought she heard someone skulking around." He held up a hand to stop her from saying anything. "It could have been a wild animal, but then, it's odd that the stampede headed directly at us."

The microwave beeped and Mia took out the bottle, screwed on a nipple and handed it to Lisa. "I hope it's okay."

"Thanks. BJ eats often, but he's not fussy." Lisa urged the nipple into his mouth and the baby sucked hungrily.

Just then a radio in the kitchen crackled to life. "Evan to base."

Lisa recalled the tracker Brody had asked to look over the ground for evidence. Brody picked up the speaker. "Brody here. Find anything?"

"I can't be sure, but the wire fencing appears to have been cut."

"Tracks?"

"Sorry, boss. The grounds've been trampled to a pulp. Come sunrise, I'll examine the perimeter. Maybe I'll pick up something."

"Thanks, Evan."

Mia frowned at Brody. "You're thinking the stampede was deliberately started? Why?"

"I don't really know. Lisa was going to tell me more about the value of Anasazi artifacts when we were interrupted."

At the confusion on Mia's and Ken's faces, Lisa spoke up. "I'm an archaeologist from Southwestern University. I was hoping to look for an Anasazi site on your ranch." Lisa knew that by telling them her real career background, she'd increased the possibility that they would discover her identity. Yet she believed the risk was low—especially since there was still no publicity about the kidnapping. She hoped Mark had forgotten about BJ and that she could stay on the ranch long enough to evaluate Brody.

Ken rubbed his chin. "What does archaelogy have to do with the stampede?"

Brody shrugged his broad shoulders. "We don't know if it's connected at all. For all we know, that developer who's after our water rights did the dirty deed."

"Maybe she's working with him," Ken suggested.

"Yeah, right." Lisa snorted, too dirty, tired and upset to hide her sarcasm. "I placed myself and my baby in front of a stampede to help a developer grab your water rights? I don't think so."

"Sorry. I'm not thinking clearly," Ken apologized, sounding genuinely sorry. "You didn't need my accusation on top of what you've already been through. It's been a long day. I think I'll turn in."

"Me, too." Mia wiped down the counter with a sponge. "Lisa, help yourself to more formula and any of the baby paraphernalia in the downstairs nursery."

Lisa burped the baby and realized that no one had said one word of protest about her work or the possibility of a dig on the ranch. Perhaps that would come later. Except for Ken's one insult, the family had been gracious toward her. "Thank you."

After she'd collected a cradle, extra baby clothes, diapers, formula and a few other items, Brody escorted her back to the car. She didn't question his decision that she should accompany him to his home. She had no vehicle to take her back to town, and she had to think of BJ's comfort first.

Once they reached his A-frame house, they both

got caught up in chores. Brody had two German shepherds that needed attention, along with three cats and a giant tank of saltwater fish. She could hear him feeding the animals as she changed BJ and settled him into a cradle in Brody's spare bedroom, where she would be staying.

She hadn't seen much of his home, but the huge stone fireplace that halved one entire wall of two-story glass overlooking the valley, combined with a comfy-looking leather sofa and colorful throw rugs, reminded her of the man who lived here. Brody might run one of the largest ranches north of Texas, but he was unpretentious, open and friendly—a family man without a wife and kids. Despite the earlier sparks between them, she almost felt comfortable sharing his home.

His footsteps on the wood floors as he moved from room to room reassured her as much as the balmy scent of the pine floating through the screened windows. He brought her a robe and a long soft shirt that smelled of him, then offered to toss her clothes into the washer. Life had taken some odd turns in the past few weeks. She'd never lived with a man, and now here she was sharing the night with someone she hadn't known this morning, worried about his seeing her underwear. Yet less than two hours ago, they'd been running for their lives.

THE NEXT MORNING Lisa awoke to the scent of frying bacon, perking coffee and toast. It took a few minutes to push past her normal morning fogginess. Waking every two or three hours during the night to feed a baby tended to make one groggy. She'd tried not to disturb Brody, but she'd heard him up and around once or twice, although he'd never come downstairs, leaving her a privacy she appreciated.

Sometime during the night, she'd removed her clothes from the washer and popped them into the dryer. After the last feeding she'd retrieved them, pleased to have clean undies, jeans and a shirt. The sneakers she'd kicked off were back at the camp, so after she changed BJ's diaper she padded barefoot into the kitchen.

"Good morning."

Brody poured her a cup of coffee and gestured for her to help herself to the baby formula stacked by the microwave. He'd washed the bottles BJ had used through the night, a chore she'd left until morning since she hadn't wanted to make any more noise then she had to.

"Hope we didn't keep you up last night."

"No problem."

She sipped the coffee, careful to keep the hot liquid well away from the baby. She noted that Brody hadn't said whether or not they'd disturbed him, and she suspected they had. "Coffee's good."

"Hope you like bacon, eggs and toast."

He wore straight-legged jeans, a soft blue-plaid shirt and was also barefoot, his boots on a mat by the door. For a bachelor, he kept his home immaculate, but she noted the touches that made the house a home. Pictures of his family. A bleached cow skull with horns hanging on the wall. Trophies on a shelf next to the TV.

"I don't usually eat breakfast, but I'm starved."

"The mountain air has a way of pushing the hunger buttons." He fixed her a plate. "There's orange juice in the fridge."

"This is great."

"I've already had breakfast," he said. "Why don't you let me feed the baby again so you can eat while the food's still hot?"

"Thanks." She handed BJ to him, surprised he'd made the offer, until she recalled that he'd already fed BJ yesterday while she'd cooked the steaks. "I should warn you, it takes me about an hour to wake up, even with caffeine."

He grinned at her words, then the grin faded. "I thought we'd go back to your car this morning and see what's left."

She bit into a crisp slice of bacon. "You don't sound optimistic. I can just imagine trying to explain to the car-leasing company that my vehicle got crushed by a stampede."

"They'll have no choice but to believe you after they see the car."

"Either that or my insurance will skyrocket because after telling them that story, they'll think I've been drinking."

Brody crossed his ankle over his other knee, propped the baby in his lap and fed him with an ease that kept surprising her. "You lease a car?"

She was barely awake enough to remember those sideways questions of his that would throw her if she didn't take care. She sipped her coffee and thought before answering.

"Leasing's more convenient than owning. My work can take me away from home for months at a time. A mechanic told me that engines don't like to sit idle for that long."

Brody nodded as if in agreement, then changed the subject. His voice was casual, yet she got the distinct impression that he'd been thinking about what to ask her for a while. "You never got around to telling me what's so valuable about your notes."

She didn't need to be awake to talk about her work. "The last site I researched suggested the Anasazi built trails that followed astronomical alignments from Chaco, which is the hub of a mysterious network of far-reaching roads. One of those trails goes directly to Mesa Verde. I believe another one passes right through your ranch."

He raised an eyebrow. "So if your notes are stolen, you won't be able to dig?"

She chuckled. "Don't sound so hopeful. I've memorized the coordinates."

"So who else would think your notes valuable?"

"My handwriting is so bad that I doubt anyone could even read them except..." She'd been about to say Maritza. Sheesh. Now wouldn't *that* have blown her identity.

"Except?" he prodded.

"A former partner of mine."

"Maybe this partner..."

Lisa shook her head, the food clogging her throat. "My partner died."

"I'm sorry." Brody picked up the baby and burped him. He waited for her to pull herself together, then asked gently, "You okay?"

No. "Yeah." But she pushed away her plate and had the sudden need to hold BJ. "I'll take him now. Thanks."

She wondered if Maritza's death would always hit her like this. Sneak up when she wasn't expecting it and overwhelm her with grief. When she saw the look of pity in Brody's eyes, she was almost positive that he assumed the partner who had died was the baby's father—not a woman. She could be wrong. But she saw no need to enlighten him. Not yet, anyway.

Twenty minutes later they'd returned to her campsite in Brody's pickup. BJ had fallen asleep in the car seat she'd borrowed from Mia, and they rolled down the windows and left him inside to sleep.

Brody parked near the remains of her vehicle. The car was totaled, as she'd expected. Oddly, the sneakers she'd kicked off had survived intact. Dirty but intact.

Brody retrieved them for her and she put them on, then followed him to where he surveyed her car, which lay on its side in a ditch. ''I brought cutting tools, but with the windows smashed, we can just reach inside. What was in here?''

''My notes were in my suitcase.''

''In the trunk?''

''No, the back seat.''

''Not here.''

''Maybe when the car flipped over, it got thrown out.''

They walked around the car in ever widening circles but found nothing. No tracks. No papers. No sign of her luggage.

Brody found a few trampled pieces of bright blue and red plastic. ''Does this look familiar?''

''Looks like pieces from BJ's toys.''

She stared at the broken plastic in his hand, realizing once more that they'd barely escaped death, and shivered. The warm spring day didn't warrant the slick cold fear that shimmied down her spine.

Had the cows tipped over the car? Could one of them have caught a horn on the strap of her suitcase and toted the bag miles away? Or had the stampede been a deliberate effort to kill them and someone had searched the car afterward?

She'd always believed that someday Mark would find her, but not this soon. And even if he had somehow discovered her whereabouts, he wouldn't have endangered the baby—not unless he'd become unhinged.

Lost in her thoughts, she walked toward Brody. A gun fired.

Oh, God. For a split second she froze.

Chapter Four

Brody reacted instinctively to the gunshot. He dived toward Lisa, tackling her, trying to break her fall as they toppled to the ground. They rolled down the ditch and he ended up lying on top of her.

Lisa squirmed beneath him as he tried to shield her with his body. For a tall thin woman, she cushioned him in all the right places. And despite the danger he couldn't ignore the scent of her freshly shampooed locks, especially with his nose buried in her hair.

"Stay still," he ordered.

In typical female fashion, she did the opposite and attempted to shove him away. "Get off of me."

"Not yet." He pinned her to the ground. "Not until we figure out if someone's shooting at us."

Still trying to shove him away, she demanded in a fierce whisper, "I've got to get to BJ."

"Give me a minute." Brody took off his hat, raised it over the ridge. When nothing happened, he slowly stood.

Lisa didn't wait for his permission to go. She scrambled to her feet, sprinted to his truck, her long red hair flying behind her like a banner in the sunlight. He followed her at a slower pace, his thoughts racing.

On a ranch this size the gunshot could mean anything from one of his men shooting a rattlesnake to a call for help. But these days the men used the radio whenever possible. While three gunshots in the air was the centuries-old signal calling for aid, one gunshot seemed ominous, especially since it had sounded so close to where the stampede had occurred.

Lisa turned to him, her eyes filled with relief and something else that looked a lot like suspicion. But what did she have to be suspicious of unless there were things she wasn't telling him? Like what had really been in her stolen notebook?

Then she glanced at the baby, and he wondered if his imagination was working overtime. Her face softened. Her voice trembled. "BJ's fine. He didn't even wake up."

"Good." Brody flicked on the radio and spoke into the mike. "Brody here. I heard a shot fired by the entry road. Anyone know where it came from?"

"This is Evan. I'm on the north ridge. You'd better get up here, boss."

Brody motioned for Lisa to get back in the truck. Although he'd explored many parts of the ranch, he wasn't familiar with every mountain and gully. But he knew the area Evan was describing, because the ridge could be seen from the valley. "What's happening?"

"We had us a trespasser."

Brody started the engine and headed toward the ridge. "A hunter?"

"I don't think so. He left behind a pick and a shovel."

Occasionally someone got it into their heads that they might find gold in the creek beds during the spring runoff. But they usually tried to remain hidden and didn't go drawing attention to themselves by firing weapons.

"Who fired that shot?" Brody asked.

"That would have been me, boss. I ordered the man to freeze and he took off. I fired a warning shot in the hopes he would stop, but he kept running into the woods. I'm tracking him now."

"Stay in touch."

"Will do. In the meantime, you should take a look at what he was digging."

"Why?"

"Isn't the woman with you interested in old baskets?"

Brody glanced at Lisa, who appeared as baffled by the conversation as he felt. "She's an archaeologist."

"She might want to have a look, then."

Brody turned off the radio and concentrated on his driving. "I can take this old mining trail partway up to the ridge. After that we'll have to walk."

"You think someone stole my notes and started digging on your land?" Lisa asked. Her tone was composed but underneath he caught a thread of stress.

"Sounds like it." He took the right fork and changed into four-wheel drive. "Tell me how you usually work."

"What do you mean?"

"What happens after the university's lawyers get you permission to dig?"

"If we have funding in place, we gather a team. Before we go, we do lots of research."

"Then what?"

"We stake out an area into a grid."

"If you found anything valuable on my land, does the university own the object?"

"That depends on the agreement between the landowner, the fund-raiser and the university."

"What about private collectors?" he asked.

"What about them?" She hung on tight to the dash as the truck bucked over a bump.

"Do they buy objects on the black market?"

"I have no idea."

He couldn't tell if he'd insulted her or if she was hiding information from him. She had definitely avoided his eyes the few times he'd glanced her way. As the road steepened he had to concentrate on his driving, but his mind kept turning over puzzle pieces that didn't fit.

"What did you hope to find on my land?" he asked.

"A previously undiscovered Anasazi site."

"That's it?"

"It would be a fantastic opportunity. Our research at Chaco led me to believe that we might find the Anasazi equivalent of Mecca—a sacred place where the Anasazi made a pilgrimage to prove their faith."

"Did their religion include the use of valuable objects? Gold and silver icons, perhaps? Or emerald scepters?"

She shook her head. "That's unlikely."

His tires skidded at the steep pitch of the trail and he chose a lesser angle, slid to a halt in a cloud of dust, then parked. "We'll have to walk from here."

BRODY REMOVED A GUN from his glove compartment and shoved the weapon into the waistband of his jeans. With a trespasser running around the mountain, he'd prefer to have a weapon if needed, especially after that stampede last night.

Lisa placed the baby in a sling and packed formula and spare diapers into her backpack. "Which way?"

Brody eyed her load. "I can carry—"

"Thanks."

She shrugged out of the sling and handed him the baby. He'd expected her to give him the backpack. This woman puzzled him. When the shooting had started, she'd been concerned enough over BJ's safety to risk getting shot to reach him, but now, she handed him over as if the child was simply spare baggage. But maybe she figured the baby was safer with him, considering the steep climb and uneven footing.

The hike to the ridge was not a straight one. Several times he stopped and turned to give her a hand, but she never required his help. He could see eagerness on her face. Clearly she loved what she did, and Brody realized that if the trespasser had uncovered ruins, as Evan had suggested over the radio, it would be even more difficult to refuse her permission to dig than before.

Brody had to be out of his mind for even considering allowing her to stay. He had enough on his hands running this ranch without inviting outsiders in to disrupt the spring branding. And yet, he liked Lisa Madison. Although she seemed oblivious to any sexual tension between them, he figured she was just better at hiding her reactions than other women. Because occasionally he caught her watching him—when she thought he wasn't looking—and she had this speculative expression in her eyes that resembled desire.

Brody really didn't have time for her kind of distraction. He knew better than to start a relationship with a career woman. Riley had made that mistake when he'd chosen his first wife, who'd been a reporter. She'd found life on the ranch dull compared to her big-city job in Denver, and a divorce had followed the wedding only six months later. His brother had chosen better the second time, picking a local girl who could ride and rope as well as any man.

Nope, career women and ranching just didn't work. Still, Brody couldn't seem to help falling into step beside Lisa and taking her hand. She jerked at his touch, but that didn't prevent him from lacing his fingers through hers.

"Just a few hundred more yards," he told her.

She didn't tug her hand away, but she didn't exactly squeeze his fingers, either. "I've visited Canyon de Chelly, Hovenweep, Montezuma Castle, Pecos and Bandelier, but I've been waiting a long time to explore a virgin site."

Great. She probably hadn't even noticed that they were holding hands. Clearly her mind was on her work. He could almost feel excitement radiating from her, and she increased her pace in her eagerness to reach the ridge.

They strode over blue Halgaito shale, past pine trees in a deep draw and zigzagged upward over ledges where wispy grasses barely clung to the rocky side of the cliff. Sagebrush grew between cracks in the sandstone wall.

At the next switchback, she stopped on the edge of rimrock to take her bearings. "The Anasazi liked to build their dwellings on the edges of cliffs like this one. In summer the cliff walls would shade them from the sun and in winter would block the cold winds."

"How long ago are we talking about?" he asked,

more to listen to her melodious voice than out of real interest.

"They inhabited the whole of the Colorado plateau in the 1300s." She strode forward again into a sharp bend, and then halted with a gasp, her head tilted back, her eyes bright with excitement as she stared at the cliff face.

He saw vivid red paintings that were protected from sun, wind and snow by an overhang of sandstone. Amazing. All this time his family had owned this land and he'd never known those paintings were there.

Her voice was hushed in wonder. "These images are similar to the pictographs on the inner walls of the third-story of the Cliff Palace."

"What do they mean?"

"They represent the Anasazi awareness of an arcane astronomical phenomenon called lunar standstill. This area could very well mark their holiest site."

She didn't seem to notice when BJ started to fuss. Brody took the baby out of the sling, mixed him some formula and sat on a rock to feed him. Meanwhile Lisa stood studying the wall paintings, her pencil moving over the sketch pad she'd taken out of her backpack.

Brody changed BJ's diaper, placed the infant back in the sling and rejoined Lisa, who was so wrapped up in her work that she appeared to barely notice him. "We should go."

"In a minute."

He waited a minute and glanced over her shoulder. She'd captured the essence of the pictographs and was now busy shadowing in details.

"Those pictures have been here for centuries. They aren't going anywhere."

"You're right." She sighed and shoved the sketch pad into her backpack. "Thanks for feeding BJ."

"I didn't think you'd noticed."

She grinned at him, this time reaching out and taking his hand. "You'd be surprised what I notice."

"Like what?" he asked, pleased more than he could say that she'd made the gesture. Her hand seemed small within his. Soft. And precious.

"You'd make a great dad. Not many bachelors have your fathering skills."

"I like kids. I also like women and I'd like to have a family someday."

"I'm surprised some country girl hasn't made you the right offer."

"Perhaps I'm not looking for a country girl," he said, wondering why he said it. Perhaps he didn't like her pegging him so easily, or perhaps he just wanted to see how she would respond. Or perhaps he wanted what he couldn't have.

She eyed him out of the corner of her eye. "What a crock."

"Excuse me?"

"I'm not buying that."

She'd met him only yesterday. How dare she presume to know him better than he knew himself. How dare she practically call him a liar. How dare she be so right. "You don't know me very well."

"You forget I'm an archaeologist. It's my job to extrapolate from just a few details."

"Like what?"

"Let's see. You work eighteen-hour days, right?"

"So?" She'd captured his interest now.

"So you need someone to take care of the homestead while you do your thing."

She sounded so sure that she knew exactly what he wanted, and he was irritated that his brothers would have agreed with her. Just because he loved the ranch and his work didn't mean he had to choose a country girl for a wife, did it?

"This ranch requires running like any big business."

Her voice dripped sarcasm. "Do you think CEOs have time for families, either?" She peered at him. "You have issues, you know."

"I do?" Damn her. How had they gotten on such a personal topic? She had no right to psychoanalyze him. He'd always enjoyed intelligent independent women and the fact that they wouldn't fit into ranch life made them safe to go after.

"Do you realize the moment I took your hand, you decided that maybe something could happen between us? But it can't."

Oh, really? He liked nothing more than a good challenge. And he knew better than to ask her why nothing could happen between them. No point in letting her think about the negatives. "Are you always this blunt?"

"Yeah. A bad habit of mine. I have no right to criticize. I'm not good with people."

"How come?"

"I've spent more time with books and artifacts than with dates. If I offended you, then I'm sorry. But you pushed one of my hot buttons."

"We were holding hands, not planning a marriage."

"I know. It's just that my sister married a man who didn't like her career."

Ah, so this was more about her sister's husband

than about him. "Your brother-in-law didn't like your sister's working so much?"

"He didn't like her working at all. And when she did, he still expected home-cooked meals, an immaculate house and..."

"And?"

"His needs satisfied—even when she was exhausted. Before she married she was this bright vibrant woman who put herself through college and earned her doctorate. She marries and suddenly her husband wants to do her thinking for her—except he didn't have half her brains."

He winced at the raw pain in her tone, suspecting there was more ugliness to the story that she wasn't telling him. "I'm sorry. Do you think your sister will get divorced?"

Pain filled her eyes. "I don't want to talk about my sister."

He'd hit a nerve. He was beginning to see that Lisa had a lot of prickly areas. So why didn't he walk away and leave her with her baby and her ruins? Instead, he yearned to take her into his arms and comfort her.

A strained silence fell between them. After a few minutes she regained some of her composure. "I probably owe you another apology."

"What for?"

"I'm...not sure."

He chuckled and then he did take her into his arms. Well, he hugged her as much as a man with a baby in a sling across his chest could without squashing the baby. She smelled wonderful as she leaned over little BJ, her lips frosted with coral lipstick just an inch from his.

He didn't know if he came to her or she came to

him or if their lips met halfway. She tasted like sunshine, warm and fresh and light as air. He wanted to gather her closer, run his fingers along her spine and feel her flesh against his, but with the baby between them, he couldn't.

Yet, her kiss teased and tantalized and tempted him to think of more than kissing her. Desire surged, hard and fast. If she could cause his head to spin with just one kiss, what could she accomplish if they made love?

Whoa. He was jumping way ahead of himself.

Sure he found her stunning, but he also realized that the contradictions in her behavior had him on edge. One minute she and he seemed *sympatico,* but the next she could be glaring at him with disapproval. However, no little spat could prevent him from enjoying her kiss. Not when his blood sang and his ears roared and all the blood in his body went south.

If the baby hadn't been between them, if a trespasser hadn't been roaming on the ridge, he might have tried for more than a kiss. In fact, it took all his willpower just to enjoy what she was willing to give him at the moment. She might have claimed that she wasn't too experienced around men, but she kissed him until his breath came in deep rasps.

When she pulled back, her eyes were questioning his with confusion. He grinned. "If that's the way you apologize, we should argue more often."

"Are you making fun of me?"

"I was saying that I wouldn't mind if you kissed me again."

It was her turn to laugh, and the sound stirred him like a pleasant wind chime in a gentle breeze. One he wouldn't tire of hearing anytime soon. Her tone was pure and exotic, yet mellow.

"I have better things to do than kiss you again, Brody," she teased.

His name on her lips warmed him straight down to his bones. "Are you saying that some old ruins are more interesting than me?"

She groaned. "Have I insulted you again?"

"If I said yes, would you kiss me again?" he countered.

She grinned, taking his hand and tugging him farther up the incline. "I'll have to owe you one."

He looked forward to that. Especially since his lips still hungered for another taste of her. Their first kiss had been all too brief, and yet somehow she'd touched his emotions with just the lightest caress of her mouth.

He didn't begin to understand her but he did want to know her better. He wanted to know how her mind worked. He wanted to know what turned her on. And he realized that he would never know unless he allowed her to stay on the ranch and explore her ruins.

Up on this ridge, far out of the way of his cattle, how much trouble could she and her team be?

LISA HAD NEVER felt quite this flustered before. First she'd opened her mouth and stuck her foot it, insulting the man whose permission she needed to dig. Then she mentioned her sister when she'd had no intention of doing so and then she'd kissed him.

Talk about sending mixed signals.

She wasn't here to start a relationship with the man, but to evaluate him to see if he'd be a good father to BJ. She'd had no business taking his hand, teasing him, encouraging him. And yet…she couldn't seem to stop herself. That kiss had simply knocked her for a loop and made her think of running her hands over his chest, unbuttoning his denim shirt and... What was wrong with her? She wished she could blame the thin mountain air for her acting like an irresponsible teenager.

Or maybe discovering those amazing pictographs had unbalanced her libido. Every archaeologist dreamed of making a major discovery, and right now she sensed she was on the verge of doing so. Excitement mixed with sadness that Maritza couldn't be here with her to make the moment perfect.

She didn't know what she was about to find, but Evan had mentioned baskets. And after the stunning pictographs, she suspected that this site might have been the holy one for which she'd been searching.

When she saw the cliff dwellings that had been hidden for possibly centuries, all personal thoughts had flown right out of her head. The Anasazi built their homes beneath arching sandstone overhangs. And this site probably hadn't been found until now because it was set back into the mountain, taking advantage of a deep natural cave, but she recognized the same style of construction.

Even from here she could see into one room with a broken wall where ceramic pots lay strewn in the dust. On the floor lay a heavy stone ax.

Brody stopped beside her and she appreciated that he didn't speak, giving her the opportunity to take in the magnificent find. While the site might not be anywhere near as large as others she'd visited and studied, this one was her first official find. She wanted to skip and dance, and she sensed Maritza's beaming presence.

She turned to Brody, who had just checked BJ's hat to make sure his face was shaded from the sun. "Thanks for bringing me up here."

"I had no idea—" he gestured to the cliff dwellings "—that those paintings were there. Over the years we've found arrowheads but figured they were Navajo." He frowned at a very modern shovel lying on the ground. This must have been where Evan found the trespasser digging. "You think he stole anything?"

She walked closer, careful where she placed her feet. "It looks like he broke into a grave. I see pieces of skeletons and skulls."

"So did he pick the grave site by accident? Or did he know what he was doing?"

She glanced from him to the shovel. "You think an archaeologist would have... But why?"

"You tell me. What's significant about this site?"

"I don't know."

"Boss?" Evan's voice squawked over Brody's walkie-talkie.

"Yes?"

"He got away. Took off on a dirt bike and has probably hit town by now. I've circled around for more tracks, but don't see anything."

"Thanks, Evan. Pass the word to the foreman that anyone on a dirt bike is to be approached with caution. I'll phone the sheriff when I get back."

Brody turned to her. "Now that you've found this place, how long will it take you to study it?"

Hope leaped into her breast. "If my team joins me? A few weeks. I don't think the site's that large, and we shouldn't get in your way."

"What about if whoever was trespassing comes back? Will you post guards?"

She shook her head. Gathering her team had one major drawback—Mark might be able to trace her through her co-workers. However, the team members knew how to keep a secret, and they were loyal to her and Maritza. If she asked them not to reveal her location, they wouldn't.

"Once my team arrives, guards shouldn't be necessary. And they can be here within a few days."

"What about the baby? You can't keep him up here at night when it's cold."

"I don't suppose…"

He eyed her with a warm smile. "You can stay at my place. Under one condition."

"What's that?"

"You have to tell me what you find up here."

"Agreed." She held out her hand and he shook it. "You don't drive a very hard bargain. You could have asked for more."

"A man doesn't always like to ask…"

Suddenly she realized they were no longer talking about the site. He was referring to that kiss. She knew it. And the heated look in his eyes disturbed her—not because he was interested, but because she couldn't stop her answering rush of desire.

Chapter Five

Three days later

Brody surveyed the site and saw that Lisa had accomplished an amazing amount of work in a short period of time. Two days ago, her entire team had arrived on his ranch with everything from simple brushes and shovels to complex radio-carbon-dating and calibration equipment. Yesterday they'd formed grids with string over the site, and today they were diligently recording every find with both words and photographs.

While Brody's interest in archaeology hadn't increased, he kept taking time from ranch work and finding excuses to visit the site. Okay, to visit Lisa. Although she'd accepted his invitation to stay in his home, she left before daylight and returned long after dark in a new rental car she'd leased in town.

She took the baby with her and he seemed to be thriving. Yet every time Brody visited she found an excuse to hand the child to him.

Brody glanced down at the infant and grinned. BJ had big blue eyes that followed his every move. The baby slept often, his temperament was wonderful and he ate every chance he got. Brody could have sworn the little fellow had gained a pound or two since he'd been here. But he found it odd that BJ's mom worried as much about her discovery as she did about the baby. Not that she ever neglected BJ. He was clean and well fed. She'd taken care to prevent his tender skin from sunburn. His physical needs were seen to.

Yet Brody had the distinct impression that she wanted him to spend time with her child. Him and only him. He'd noticed that she didn't hand the baby to members of her team. Maybe that was because all of them were busy.

He was busy, too. With the spring branding well under way, they'd culled the herd. He kept only the best cattle for breeding purposes and moved the cows he intended to sell to greener pastures for fattening.

Although Evan kept searching for clues to the stampede, the tracker had found nothing. And since Lisa's team had moved onto the site, she'd reported no further problems.

So he had plenty of work but too much time to think about Lisa.

Ever since their kiss, he kept wondering if he'd dreamed the entire incident. During the past few days, they'd barely exchanged good-mornings, never mind another kiss. If he didn't ride up to the dig, he might not see her at all.

She'd been as good as her word about keeping out of his way. Only, he no longer wanted her out of his way.

He was pleasantly surprised, therefore, when Lisa joined him on a prominent ridge set away from the site where he'd fed the baby. She offered him a sandwich and a glass of lemonade. "Hungry?"

"Yes. Thanks." He would have accepted just to have her company, but he hadn't eaten since dawn and his stomach rumbled.

She spread out a blanket to sit on, took BJ and placed him in a crank-up baby swing she'd borrowed from his mother. "BJ loves the motion and the top keeps him shaded. He'd rather sleep in that swing than in his cradle."

Brody swallowed a bite of sandwich and took a seat on the blanket beside her. Although she seemed content to watch her team work from this ledge, he suspected that she itched to return to work. Too bad. He'd been patient and now he wanted some of her time.

"I bet BJ would enjoy a horseback ride," he said. "I brought a gentle mare. Why don't you put him in the sling and we can explore?"

She frowned at him. "BJ's too young to take on a horse."

He washed down the sandwich with tart lemonade. "My dad had us in the saddle before we could walk."

"And I shouldn't leave."

"You mean you don't want to leave."

She patted him on the shoulder. "Don't take it personally."

Yesterday he'd asked her to go to lunch with him in town and she'd said no. Now she didn't have time for a short horseback ride. He remembered how touchy she was about a man compromising a woman at work and reminded himself to tread carefully.

He raised an eyebrow. "How else can I take your constant rejections of my company?"

"Poor Brody." She grinned at him. "I feel so sorry for you."

"Don't archaeologists have to research the surrounding terrain?"

"You're always doing that."

"What?"

"Coming at problems from a new angle."

"Mmm." He finished his sandwich.

"You want me to ride with you, but you know I have to work. You know exactly how I feel about a man taking a woman away from her responsibilities, so you try to tie the ride to work."

"Is that a yes or a no?"

"Did Mia ever tell you that you're stubborn?"

"Frequently. By the way, Mom says that the chicken pox quarantine is over. If you need a babysitter, she's able."

"That's kind of her."

"Don't kid yourself. She's hoping to give you and me some alone time." His mother thought it high time he settled down and created more grandchildren for her to spoil.

She frowned at him. "What did you tell her?"

"I didn't have to say anything. She spied a smudge of lipstick by my mouth."

"Oops."

"Mom likes you."

"I like her, too. Tell her I appreciate the offer."

"You can tell her yourself. She's invited us to dinner tomorrow night."

She eyed him with both exasperation and interest. "Did you put her up to it?"

"Maybe."

"I don't know what to do with you. I have work."

"It's not going anywhere."

"My team has a budget. We only have funds for—"

"Hold up." He sniffed the air and turned around, searching the sky.

"What?" She looked back and forth into the woods for anything suspicious, but he was looking upward.

"There's a fire!"

FINDING LISA HADN'T BEEN as easy as Mark had expected, but her stealing his child had given him plenty of incentive. After learning his quarry had sold her house, closed her bank account and left no forwarding address, most PIs would have run out of options. Neither her friends nor her university archaeological team had known her whereabouts, either—or they just weren't talking.

But he had his connections and ways of finding people. He was a damn good PI. It wasn't his fault he couldn't get enough work. And instead of taking the cases that did come in, he was chasing his sister-in-law and his son. However, he had every intention of making her pay.

Yet Lisa had covered her trail so well that she'd left him with only dead ends—until he'd recalled what Lisa had said to convince him that the baby wasn't his. She'd said that Maritza had met someone else. He'd thought hard and long. Checked his phone bill. Asked his neighbors and Maritza's coworkers questions.

Someone had mentioned that while he'd been working a case in California, Maritza had gone to Colorado. It hadn't been hard to find out her schedule. The university secretary had been happy to tell him where she'd stayed. And the hotel clerk remembered Maritza.

From there it was just a matter of time until he learned about a wealthy sponsor who'd thrown a party. He'd gotten a list of attendees. Spoken to a few people who recalled seeing Maritza and Brody Adams together.

So he'd put two and two together and had come to the Adams ranch. And he'd found just what he was searching for. Lisa, his son and the man who may have cuckolded him all together in a tidy package.

Mark had sat down with a beer and done some heavy thinking. He wanted his son. But he also wanted revenge on the woman who'd stolen him. And he didn't mind getting even with the rich cowboy, either.

He still didn't want to inform the police about her kidnapping the baby, since it would hurt his career. But perhaps there was another way to destroy her reputation and set the police on her trail. Mark didn't have the experience to pull off what he had in mind, but he knew the right man for the job—and luckily he owed Mark a favor.

LISA SCRAMBLED to her feet and picked up the blanket. "Is there anything my team can do to help?"

Brody didn't answer. He was already on his radio. "Brody to base."

"Come in, son."

"Mom, we've got a fire near the north ridge. Have the men gather by the road. Call town and tell them to send the Forest Service."

"Which way is the wind blowing?" Mia's voice was calm and clear.

"Fire's coming in our direction. I'm going to lead the archaeological team due east to Mirror Lake."

"Roger that. Be careful."

"Always. Love you, Mom."

"I love you, too. Base out."

In just the minute he'd taken to speak to his mom, the sky had darkened with smoke. Lisa saw no sign of flames, but this high up the land was dry, the pines, oaks and underlying brush still thick enough for the fire to rage out of control.

Lisa didn't have to call her people. They'd smelled the smoke, dropped their tools and gathered round.

Her assistant, Kevin Gant, had already instructed people to gather their equipment. At six foot six, Kevin, thin and bald, stood out in the group of scientists. He checked off gear in his notebook and directed people to place the most valuable machines inside the baked walls of the ruins where they had the best chance of surviving a fire.

Penny Lundmark, her chief cataloger, carefully placed an Anasazi basket and pottery shards in a pit dug in the ground, where they'd be safe. One of the men took a shovel and began to throw dirt over the items to protect them.

"There's no time for that!" Brody yelled. "Grab a water bottle and prepare to move out."

Lisa removed BJ from the swing, placed him in his sling and strapped it to her chest. She stuffed diapers and extra formula into her backpack and grabbed her notebook. Meanwhile her team stored equipment, packed away supplies and straightened the camp in just minutes.

"We haven't much time." Brody slung her pack onto his back and spoke to the others. "Hurry, people.

Take plenty of water, hats and sunglasses. Blankets, if you have them. Let's move.''

She glanced from her team to Brody, who looked ten times more confident than she felt. His broad shoulders were squared, his jaw set, but she didn't understand the suppressed anger she saw in his eyes and didn't have time to question him—not with lives at stake.

''We aren't heading down to the cars?'' she asked.

''That's the direction the fire is coming from. We have to move away at a perpendicular angle. Walking is tough and some of your team members aren't in the best of shape.''

Her chief researcher, Marty Dilowitz, was over sixty and had had a heart attack last year. Penny Lundmark was the fittest of the group, a triathlete. But Joanna Bessener, who was in charge of landscape and soil analysis, was going to make this her last dig before having a baby in four months. Neither the pregnant Joanna nor Marty would be able to travel very far or fast.

Concern must have shown on her face. Brody squeezed her shoulder. ''We'll be fine. But we need to get moving.''

Again the group gathered around them. Brody put Kevin in the rear. ''It's your job to help the stragglers.''

Kevin nodded. ''We won't leave anyone behind.''

''I'll take the lead.'' Brody headed along a ridge in a direction Lisa hadn't been before. She couldn't help wondering what they would have done if he hadn't been here. None of them had explored any area besides the immediate canyon where the Anasazi had built their homes.

Brody set a quick pace and she glanced over her shoulder, sure that Joanna and Marty would have trouble keeping up. She was correct and thought about asking Brody to slow down—until she glanced upward. Sparks gusted from the thick black smoke swallowing the sky.

Although their air was still clear to breathe, they couldn't count on remaining ahead of the fire unless they hurried. Brody headed at right angles to the flames, but she worried about the fire flanking them.

She increased her pace to catch up with him. "Where are we going?"

"There's a mountain lake about two miles away."

"All of us can't make—"

"We have no choice." He pointed to an animal path. "Can you keep going?"

"Yeah."

"I'm dropping back to help the stragglers. Don't slow down."

The air at this altitude was thinner than at home, and her lungs burned from the fast pace. But she didn't dare stop. Every time she thought about slowing, she glanced behind her and saw that the smoke was gaining on them. Right beside her, Penny was having no trouble, but then, she was in great physical shape.

For the second time in less than a week Lisa found herself running for her life. First the stampede, now the fire. While both incidents could be accidents, she didn't believe it. The sky had been clear until the smoke blew in, and lightning hadn't started this fire. For it to have occurred upwind of their site so that the fire burned in their direction couldn't be accidental. She suspected she'd just stumbled across the reason for Brody's banked anger. He'd known right off that the fire had likely been set. And since it was so close to the archaeological site, the arsonist might have a grudge against her team.

Still, rival archaeologists might be jealous of their find, but a scientist wouldn't start a forest fire because of it. Nor would he start a stampede. Could Mark have found her? But if so, he would have made an attempt to take back BJ.

Perhaps the incidents had nothing to do with her. Brody had his own enemies, those developers who'd wanted his water rights, for example. However, it seemed odd that the tracker had chased a trespasser from the site three days ago and now they had to contend with a fire.

The trail's steepness caused her calves to burn. She was in decent shape, but no exercise fanatic like Penny. Hiking uphill with the baby strapped to her chest had her breathing in great gulps of air. If she felt this weary, some of her team members must be close to exhaustion.

Brody hurried back to her as she reached a fork in the trail. "Go left."

"How's everyone keeping up?"

"I don't like the color of Marty's skin. Joanna is tired but looks okay."

She peered back anxiously over her shoulder. "How long until those flames catch up with us?"

"Just keep going and watch your step."

He'd evaded answering her question, which served to increase her fear. She'd cleared the peak and the terrain sloped downward now, which relieved the burning in her calves. But small pebbles and loose dirt made the path treacherous. With the baby strapped to her, she couldn't afford to stumble and risk hurting him.

She picked her way down the slope and noted that Penny seemed to be having as much trouble as she was. When the trail flattened a bit, Lisa looked upward. Very little blue sky remained. Instead, billows of black smoke loomed overhead, blocking the sun and the clouds for miles.

Even worse, she couldn't see Kevin's tall body bringing up the rear, which meant that part of the group had yet to reach the peak she'd recently left behind. And from a quarter mile below the top, the red, orange and yellow flames looked close enough to lick up the back side of the mountain.

Oh, God.

She was responsible for her team and hadn't even realized she was placing them in danger. Hadn't realized how spread out they'd all become. And she felt torn between her obligation to keep going with the baby and her responsibility for her team.

Penny pressed on ahead, leaving Brody and Lisa alone. When no one else cleared the ridge, Lisa bit her lower lip in consternation. "Perhaps I should go back to—"

"No." Brody's reaction was immediate. "If anyone goes back, it'll be me. But let's give them another minute."

A minute could be a long time. "How much timber will you lose?"

"It'll grow back." His eyes narrowed as he peered at the ridge, then he unclipped the radio from his belt. "Brody to base camp."

They heard just static.

"Brody to base camp." He tried again, then re-clipped the radio to his belt.

"Maybe no one's there?"

Brody shook his head. "Mom mans that radio during a crisis. She won't leave until she knows that everyone's safe. The mountains might be blocking the signal."

"Might be?"

"I served two years in the military in communications. That static almost sounded as if someone's jammed the frequency."

"You don't sound sure."

"I'm not," he admitted without hesitation. She liked that about him—Brody didn't put on airs. He was a man clearly comfortable in his own skin, and when he didn't know something, he had no problem admitting it.

She shifted from foot to foot in impatience. Knowing that good people, her friends and associates, were scrambling for their lives had her adrenaline racing.

She had to distract herself. "You think the fire was deliberately set, don't you."

"We may never know."

"But what do you think?" she pressed.

Before Brody answered, Kevin's head cleared the ridge, and he waved them to go onward. Relief surged through her because the entire group had reached the peak and now headed downward. She started walking again.

Brody took her arm and urged her along. "We should be making better time going downhill."

The urgency in his voice startled her. He obviously knew something she didn't. The flames behind them didn't appear any higher or closer.

"What's wrong?"

"Keep walking, but listen."

She did as he asked, picking her way around a rabbit hole and almost tripping over a downed branch. Even distracted by her journey, she could hear the strange rush of air. Almost like a bear's pain-filled roar.

At the noise, her neck prickled. "What is that?"

"The fire's sucking in oxygen to feed the flames."

"You've been caught in one of these forest fires before?"

"Not here. I've helped out other ranchers during a few firestorms. Once, we fought the flames for weeks. Finally Mother Nature sent in a huge rainstorm and doused it for us."

"Are there any cattle in danger?"

"Not unless the wind shifts." He tugged her arm. "Come on. If you have enough spare air to talk, you could be putting it to better use getting on down the mountain."

She knew she should save her breath. But conversation distracted her from the danger roaring up behind them with the ferocity of a cyclone.

"How far to the lake?" They were still heading downhill. She should be able to see the water or Penny, but she couldn't. Her only view between the trees was more trees and the occasional deer or Dali sheep leaping ahead of them.

"Around the next bend."

He made it sound as if the next bend was a few yards away, but a good ten minutes later, with no sight of Mirror Lake, she began to wonder if he'd gotten them lost. Until she rounded one last copse of trees and almost fell into the water.

She knew immediately how the lake had gotten its name. About a mile across and twice as long, the lake reflected the rocks and trees along its banks as clearly as a mirror. She wanted to climb over the rocks and dip her hands into the water, but BJ took that moment to awake and let out a scream.

Penny frowned at the baby but said nothing. Lisa dropped to her knees, took BJ out of the sling and found the problem. "Just a wet diaper. Do I have time to change him?"

"Sure." Brody handed her the backpack he'd toted for them. "I'll head back to help the others."

Penny explored the nearby shore while Lisa changed BJ, but the baby didn't settle down. He shouldn't be hungry yet, but she mixed him a bottle and tried to feed him, anyway. He turned his head away, his tiny lips clamped shut against the nipple.

Now what?

Huge tears rained down BJ's cheeks. She checked his clothing to make sure nothing was too tight, then rocked him against her shoulder. She felt his forehead. A little warm perhaps, but he wasn't burning with fever, either. Now would not be a good time to come down with an ear infection.

He'd been a healthy baby and his crying spurts hadn't lasted long—until now. Perhaps her fear had somehow communicated itself to him. Poor little guy. He was not much more than a month old and had already survived his mother's death and a stampede, and now he had to make it through a forest fire.

"Quite the exciting life you live, BJ." At her words he turned his head and looked at her.

"If that's my signal to keep talking, I can do that. Gosh, little guy, those cries are loud enough to scare away the bears.'' She looked around warily. ''But even if there are bears, they won't mess with us. They'll be too busy running from the fire.''

If she kept BJ, she would have to improve her storytelling skills. While right now her voice soothed him, her words weren't suitable for a child, not unless she intended to scare him right back into crying again.

However, a moment later, she had to fight from crying herself, when from behind her she heard a heart-stopping scream.

Chapter Six

Brody reached the stragglers just as the pregnant Joanna stumbled. He read the fear for her unborn child in her eyes and hurled himself forward, catching her by the shoulders. Both of them toppled, but he broke her fall. They slid down the steep trail together, but she screamed the entire time, making his ears ring and increasing his concern. Until they stopped sliding, he had no way of discerning if she'd broken any bones or injured her baby.

Finally they stopped and in a panic, she tried to scramble to her feet. He closed his arms around her and held her still. "Steady. You don't want to fall again."

"Let me go. The fire's coming."

"Are you hurt?" he asked, concerned by her pallor and the terror in her eyes.

Joanna raised her voice in a shrill shout. "We almost burn alive, then we slide down a goddamn mountain and you want to know if I'm hurt? Every bone in my body hurts."

Lisa raced toward them. She must have left the baby with Penny because she didn't have him with her. "Joanna, are you okay?"

Joanna ran her hands over her rounded stomach. "I think so."

"You're not having any contractions, are you?"

Brody realized that Lisa had left the safety of the lake and run back toward the fire to try to help the other woman. And now that she realized the other woman was fine, she helped her to her feet, coddling her with no apparent concern for the approaching flames.

He waved Kevin and the others on toward the lake, then rose to his feet and ushered the women down the hill. Joanna had burst into tears, sobbing in fright, while Lisa patiently tried to console and reassure her friend and co-worker.

Meanwhile, Brody tried his radio again. And again he got nothing but the jammed signal. Saving these folks would be his responsibility. Without radio contact, he couldn't call the sheriff's office to ask for their helicopter to extract them by air. Nor could one of his brothers bring in horses to carry them out.

At least Lisa and Kevin were keeping their cool. He wasn't too pleased that earlier Penny had pushed on, but now she was helping Lisa with the baby. Brody glanced ahead at the only part of the sky that hadn't been swallowed by the gray smoke, hoping for rain. But the sun shone brightly there, mocking his puny efforts to keep these people alive.

Mirror Lake could keep them from burning to death. But they couldn't stay near the banks because when the fire swept through, burning trees along the shoreline would topple into the water. Unfortunately the mountain lake was shallow only for a short distance from the shore. In addition, the water would be icy-cold. If they stayed in it too long, they could suffer from hypothermia and drown as easily as they could burn onshore.

With the fire bearing down on them, Brody estimated they had only minutes to prepare. He rejoined the group and assessed them. He had to take care of a pregnant woman, a senior citizen who could have a heart attack and an infant. "Can everyone swim?"

Penny handed BJ back to Lisa. "We can't survive long in that water."

"Don't you race in cold water like this all the time?" Joanna asked.

"We wear wet suits to prevent hypothermia," Penny said.

Penny was only trying to share her knowledge, but he'd prefer she didn't frighten the others. Brody refrained from frowning at her. "We need to find branches, a log, anything we can float on. Keeping our heads out of the water will be a good start."

Lisa stared at him as if just realizing the problem of swimming in icy water with an infant. "How far out can we wade before the water is over our heads?"

"About ten feet."

"We have to find a way to keep BJ dry." There was that contradiction again. Her fierce protection of BJ just didn't fit with the way she was always handing the baby to him to care for.

He nodded. "Agreed. Everyone spread out and look for logs and branches we can use to float on—except for Marty and Joanna. You two save your strength."

"Let me take the baby." Joanna held out her arms. "I can watch him for you while I rest."

"Thanks." Lisa handed BJ to the woman, but Brody could sense her reluctance to be separated from the infant. Still, they needed every pair of free hands to gather wood.

Lisa and Brody headed off together. "What exactly are we looking for?" she asked. "The baby can't swim and he'll freeze to death in that icy water in minutes."

Brody squeezed her hand, trying to sound more confident than he felt. "He'll be fine. We need to find some dead branches that will float him entirely out of the water. We can tie him to the sling. Luckily he's not very heavy."

Lisa surveyed the woods in frustration. "But there's no brush on the ground at this elevation."

Brody pointed. "There's a dead tree."

"But it's still standing and we don't have an ax."

He headed straight for the tree, an idea forming. He grabbed the lowest branch and swung himself up.

Lisa watched him, her head tilted back. "What are you doing?"

"Have to climb to where the branches are thinner. Maybe I can break off a section."

"Break it with what?"

Climbing and conversing at the same time was next to impossible. He saved his breath for climbing. When he reached a height of fifteen or twenty feet, he figured the dead branches might be thin enough to snap. He tried.

Nothing.

Watching from the ground with a combination of fear and awe in her tone, she said, "You're going to fall."

"That's the idea."

"What!"

He edged farther out on the branch, then used his

weight to tug. He got nothing for his efforts but scratches on his palms, which he ignored. From his high position he could see the flames clearing the peak but refrained from mentioning them. Fire traveled faster uphill, due to rising heat preparing the path. The flames would slow after reaching the peak but they still didn't have much time. He edged out farther, leaped for a thinner branch with lots of shoots, and tugged with all his weight. He dangled.

The branch cracked.

"Oh, my God." Lisa clapped a hand over her mouth.

He still hadn't broken the branch. He swung his legs. And heard another snapping sound. Then he was falling, the branches he held tangling with others and breaking his fall. He still smacked the ground hard, but his bent knees cushioned the impact and then he released the branch and rolled.

Tears in her eyes, Lisa hurried to him. "Are you hurt? Did you break any bones?"

"I'm fine."

"I don't know if that was the bravest or stupidest thing I've ever seen anyone do."

He grabbed the branch and dragged it toward the spot where they'd left the others. "*Stupidest* isn't a word."

"We're about to die and you want to correct my grammar?"

He dropped the branch, turned, grabbed her shoulders and kissed her. He didn't have time for a long kiss, but he wanted her to know that his feelings for her ran strong and deep. He communicated that by drawing her against his chest, demanding that she open her mouth, giving her no chance to say no. She might have been surprised, but she needed no coaxing, giving as much as she took and firing his senses.

When he finally pulled back, he grinned. "We aren't going to die. Not today."

"Okay."

"Okay what?"

"Okay, you've convinced me."

"Good." He grabbed one end of the limb he'd torn down and she took another. Together they dragged it toward the lake's bank. "How's your team going to feel about taking off their clothes?"

LISA CAST A SIDEWAYS GLANCE at Brody. He was not a man to suggest such a thing lightly. He appeared deadly serious.

"Why would we undress?" she asked.

They had rejoined the group and the others gathered around. Marty was floating over a good-size log and several smaller branches. Their efforts seemed pitifully feeble compared to the forces of nature pitted against them, but they'd had so little time. No tools. And only their ingenuity to keep them alive.

Brody spoke to the entire group. "The fire will slow after it reaches the peak, but the wind is bringing it our way. I suggest we all strip down to our underwear and spread our outer clothing over the rocks along the bank."

"Why?" Joanna asked.

"For two reasons." Brody kept his voice even and authoritative. As he spoke he removed his boots, shirt and jeans.

Lisa noted the lean muscles, the powerful shoulders and the flat stomach, but more important than his fit and oh-so-attractive body were his intelligence, strength and integrity. She couldn't think of a better man to be stuck with out here under these conditions. If he thought undressing could save them, she was all for it.

After he undressed, she handed him the baby and took his clothes. ''It's hard to swim with clothing. The heavy material will weigh us down. And also, if we leave our outer wear on the rocks, there's a good chance they'll be fine, and we can put on dry clothes again when we climb out of the lake.''

''And if they burn?'' Kevin asked.

Lisa set down Brody's clothes so she could undress. ''Then we'll have a cold trek back in our wet underwear. But unless we're extremely unlucky and a tree crashes on the clothes, they should be okay because there's little vegetation along the rocky banks.''

''Makes sense,'' Penny agreed. ''That water's going to be cold from winter snowmelt. We'll need dry clothes when we get out.''

Lisa didn't hesitate, stripping off her sweater and T-shirt, kicking off her shoes and shimmying out of her jeans. The cold air nipped at her bare flesh, and she tried not to think about how cold she'd be in that icy water. Tried not to think what would happen to BJ if his makeshift raft tipped over. One glance at the approaching flames convinced her she'd rather be wet and cold than on fire.

''I don't understand why we can't stay on the rocks,'' Marty complained.

''Brody already told you.'' Lisa walked out onto the bank and spread out her and Brody's clothes. Penny and Kevin had also undressed and joined her. ''You want to risk being under a falling burning branch?''

Marty scowled at the water. "I may take my chances. I'm not a good swimmer."

Brody took BJ and fashioned the sling around the limbs he'd climbed that tree to gather. He'd risked a terrible fall to save a child he didn't know was his, and she realized that if he'd known he was auditioning for the part of daddy, he couldn't have done a better job.

"Marty, you can hold on to the log," Brody coaxed. "But if you stay on the bank, the fire may suck all the oxygen out of the air. It's your decision but—" he jerked his thumb at the oncoming blaze "—you better decide quickly."

"Brody's right," Lisa said in an attempt to encourage her team.

Marty finally took off his clothes, but Lisa had her doubts about whether he'd get into the water. Brody must have had the same notion. He'd carried the branches with BJ to the water's edge and floated him. When Lisa joined him in the ankle-deep water, he leaned close and whispered. "Can you swim him out there?"

"I think so."

"Good, because Marty needs some help."

He turned to the assembled group, most of them already shivering. Behind them, the fire crackled, the flames leaping from tree to tree. She couldn't yet feel the heat, but the smoke burned her eyes, and her lungs ached with every breath. "Should we get in the water?"

"Not yet. We want to limit our exposure to the cold to the shortest amount of time possible." Brody's explanation made sense, and she hoped his timing was as good as his woodsman's knowledge. "When we go into the lake, everyone try to stay together. Drowning people don't have the breath to shout for help like in the movies, they just go under. If you see anyone's head go under, shout out to the group. Marty, Joanna, you both grab the log and hang on tight. Keep your heads above water. Are we set?''

The flames bore down on them. Waves of fire licked the trees, which burst into flames. Lisa squinted against the brightness and her eyes teared at the smoke. She prayed BJ's tiny lungs could filter enough oxygen for him to breathe.

''Now,'' Brody ordered. ''Let's go.''

They all moved farther from the shore. The wintery temperature of the lake stole her breath and numbed her flesh. She had difficulty pushing the floating branch with BJ out into the lake because, although her brain willed her arms and legs to move, her limbs refused to cooperate.

The others were having difficulty, too—except for Penny, who moved like a fish, although her lips turned blue just like everyone else's. Lisa heard gasps of surprise and several curses, but her team didn't panic and she was proud of them all.

She stubbed her toes on rocks several times, but could barely feel the injury due to numbness from the cold. When the water reached her waist, she started to shiver so hard walking was even more difficult.

Brody organized Penny and Kevin to help Joanna and Marty with the log. Then he joined her, steadying her and helping her push the baby out. Three yards and she had no more footing. Twenty feet and she was out of breath. Fifty feet and she couldn't take another stroke.

"Far enough," Brody shouted, but the wind sucked away his words.

"I need help." Joanna screamed. "Someone do something! Marty just went under."

"I've got him," Penny muttered.

Brody left Lisa's side and swam over. From ten feet away, Lisa could see their lips moving, but couldn't hear their voices. Somehow, though, Penny and Kevin and Brody draped Marty over the log and propped his face out of the water.

Lisa prayed Marty hadn't had another heart attack. The air was thin and hot. At least BJ seemed content. He slept in his makeshift rocker, well above the icy water.

She told herself she had to survive to take care of the baby. Keeping him safe would do no good if the rest of them drowned or died from hypothermia.

Then Brody was next to her again. "You okay?"

She tried to speak. "Y-y—" Gave up. And nodded. She no longer seemed to have control over her mouth and tongue. Shock. Cold. Numbness. Was this the way one eased from life into death? Gently. Without struggle.

Fight.

She tried to force her fingers tight around the branch, but had no idea if they reacted. She could no longer feel her fingers. Or her toes.

And then the fire swept over them, around them and moved on, leaving them in darkness, surrounded by the flames of burning trees along the lake's banks. Vaguely she heard Brody shouting at everyone to swim back to shore. Penny and Kevin kicked, pulling the log holding Joanna and Marty with them.

Lisa told her legs to move. *Kick, damn it.*

Her body no longer shivered. Horrified, she watched her own fingers release their hold on the branch. Before she could go under, Brody's arm crossed over her chest and he turned her onto her back. And then he must have dragged her and BJ to shore.

She didn't remember much of the swim. She knew only that Brody somehow towed her to shore and carried her onto the bank, where he set her down on a rock next to a blazing tree. Sometime during their ordeal the sun had set. She hadn't noticed exactly when, hadn't realized so much time had passed.

Like an iguana who instinctively searches for light and warmth, she edged so close to the fire that she could have blistered her skin. Fire should warm her, but the cold that froze straight to the bone wouldn't thaw. She could barely force out a question. "BJ?"

"I'll get him." Brody headed back to the bank, lifted the baby and his sling from the branch, walked back and set the sleeping baby down beside her.

"Th-th—" She wanted to say thanks, but couldn't. Brody seemed to understand and headed back to help someone else.

Lisa ached to pick up BJ. But she didn't want him to get wet and she didn't want to risk dropping him with fingers numb with cold. Penny staggered to the fire by herself and sat next to Lisa, her teeth chattering so hard she couldn't speak, either. Kevin and Brody helped Joanna to the fire, then half dragged, half-carried Marty over before they collapsed in exhaustion.

Lisa had been the first one to feel the fire's warmth and she was the first to recover. She found the strength to stand, turned around and let the fire warm her backside. She'd never been this cold and although her skin warmed up, it took a while for the heat from the burning tree to penetrate deeper and raise her core temperature. She had no idea how long they stayed by the fire, sharing the heat, none of them having the strength to speak.

She took it upon herself to leave the fire, go to the rocks and search for their clothes. And just as Brody had predicted, their clothes had made it through unscathed. They had dry shirts and slacks and shoes and socks to put on.

Lisa glanced at the members of the group, who sat with their backs to her facing the fire. Even if one of them happened to turn around, she doubted they could see her in the blackness. She stripped off her wet bra and panties, then put on her dry clothes. Her hair still dripped and she wrung out what she could, but at least her skin was dry from the fire. After dressing, she gathered the rest of the clothes and brought them over. Brody accepted his clothes with a nod of thanks.

Glad she was warm enough to speak again, Lisa didn't feel the least bit awkward telling everyone, "I took off my wet underwear before putting on these dry things." With survival at stake, modesty quickly went by the wayside.

Following her suggestion, one by one Penny, Kevin and Brody went off to change their clothes. Joanna didn't seem to have the strength to dress, so Lisa helped her.

The men dressed Marty. She was worried about him. He didn't seem to be recovering as quickly as the rest of them. His skin hadn't regained its normal ruddy color and he kept falling asleep.

Lisa picked up BJ and fastened the sling, taking

immense satisfaction in the tiny bundle of warmth against her chest. ''What do we do now?''

Brody slung an arm over her shoulder. ''We have a few choices.''

''Which are?'' Kevin asked.

Lisa watched Brody speak, wondering if they would have survived without his help and doubting it. He had taken charge of the group when his knowledge was the difference between their living and dying, but now that their situation was less critical, he seemed willing to share the decision-making.

Brody spoke quietly, his expression calm. ''We can stay together or split apart. We can walk out of here now or stay here for the night and leave tomorrow. Or we can just stay and wait for a rescue.''

''Is a rescue possible?'' Joanna asked.

''Very. Before we left I radioed base camp. Rescue personal know exactly where we are. They'll come as soon as safety permits.''

''When will that be?'' Penny looked up at the sky as if expecting a helicopter to land.

''Depends on the fire.''

''What do you suggest?'' Lisa asked, trusting him to make the best decision for them all.

''Marty and Joanna need to rest. The baby needs formula. And since I know the land the best, you and I should take the baby and walk out. Penny and Kevin should stay here with Marty and Joanna.''

''Sounds like a plan,'' Kevin said, and Penny nodded her agreement. Marty didn't respond and Joanna hugged her knees, brooding as she stared into the fire.

Brody gave a few last-minute instructions to Penny and Kevin, then he and Lisa started back the way they'd come. They had to pick their way past smoldering trees, but the little underbrush that was there had burned away, leaving them room to walk. The ground was hot but bearable to tread on. Luckily a stiff breeze whipped away most of the smoke; nevertheless, Lisa's eyes burned and teared and her lungs hurt. She tried not to think about the carcinogens entering her lungs and consoled herself with the fact that she was alive, and that studies had shown that the lungs of smokers who stopped smoking healed themselves.

Brody's hoarse voice sounded as raw as hers felt. "The best path out of here is straight back to the dig."

"I'm right behind you."

The path had narrowed, forcing them to walk single file. She concentrated on putting one foot in front of the other until BJ started to cry. "I need to change his diaper and give him the last of his formula."

"Okay."

Brody led her to a butte where the smoke wasn't as thick. Sand-covered mounds of earth and a lack of trees had prevented the fire from feasting here. He found a spot sheltered from the wind, and when she sat, the earth was still warm.

She fed the baby and changed him. BJ didn't go back to sleep but seemed content to stare out over the smoke and the remainder of the burning forest. The heat made her sleepy and she rested her head on Brody's shoulder, content for the moment just to be warm and alive and safe.

"You saved our lives back there. Thanks."

"No problem."

"Brody."

"Yeah?"

"Do you believe in fate?"

"You mean that our lives are preordained?"

"Yes."

"Do you?" he asked.

"I never did. I always thought we had free will, that the choices we make have a direct effect on our destiny."

"And now you don't?"

"It seems that over the last few weeks my life has changed in ways I could never have anticipated. As if some joker has taken away my old life and given me a new one."

"Having a child is a miraculous process."

She hadn't borne little BJ, but she was the only mother he knew. While he hadn't come from her body, caring for him had changed the way she looked at the world, just as Brody had suggested. But it seemed to her that fate hadn't just taken some unexpected twists, but that more than fate was stalking her. First BJ's birth, her sister's death, her decision to rescue BJ from Mark. Then the stampede, the fire and Brody turning out to be the perfect choice for little BJ's father. But she was running, running, running to a destination she'd never foreseen or expected.

"You rested enough to go on?"

"Yeah."

He helped her to her feet, keeping her hand tucked in his. She liked the contact, liked the feel of his strong fingers, the shared warmth, the intimacy of touching.

It hand't taken her long to rely on that strength, which she needed. But she told herself not to get too used to it. Her time here with Brody wouldn't be long.

With the return to the dig, all personal thoughts

ended. In the dying firelight the camp had an eerie look. Clearly something had disrupted the camp. Something that had nothing to do with the fire. "Someone's been here. Digging. Stealing."

anxiety. In the ringing stillness the room and quietly lie to. Clearly something has disrupted the camp. Something that had frightened in the very maddin. Someone's been here. Dhyana, darling.

Chapter Seven

"Brody to base camp."

"Is everyone okay, dear?" his mom answered, worry and relief in her tone. If he hadn't called in until tomorrow, she would have stayed by that radio.

Brody was glad the radio finally worked so that he could reassure her but also so that he could get help to the others. The thought of Joanna going into early labor and Marty's heart giving out weighed heavily on him. The sooner both of them received medical attention, the better.

"Yes, Mom. We're hanging in there. Tell the emergency workers that some of the archaeological team is still by Mirror Lake. They could use a lift out and some hot food. There's a pregnant woman who needs to be checked by paramedics and a man in his sixties who might need to see a cardiologist."

"I'll arrange it and a horse for you, as well. How are the baby and Lisa?"

"They're with me and both are fine, just tired. We could use some more baby formula, too."

"I'll send it with the horse."

"Thanks, Mom."

He hung up knowing that tears of relief were probably rolling down his mother's cheeks right now. Ranching was hard on a woman, and he knew how difficult waiting for news could be. Once his dad and brother had gotten stuck out on the range during a blizzard. They'd survived their ordeal, but although Mia had tried to hide her worry from ten-year-old Brody, he still recalled her sobs of relief when she finally got news of their safety.

Lisa frowned at the dig site. "This is a disaster."

The dig looked fine to Brody, so he turned to Lisa for answers. She'd remained amazingly calm and sensible throughout their ordeal, encouraging her people, watching over the baby and displaying a depth of character that fascinated him. She might be a sophisticated career woman, but she handled the outdoors like a pro. Now her green eyes narrowed to icy chips that warned him something she saw at the site had ignited her anger.

She fisted her hands on her hips and glared at the Anasazi dwellings. "We hauled the artifacts and our tools into that dwelling and buried the rest with dirt where the fire wouldn't reach them."

"Maybe the site just looks different in the dark."

"No." She looked around with irritation and pointed. "Someone dug up and stole the basket we found and scattered those pottery shards."

Although it was dark, nearby trees still smoldered and glowed eerily over the buildings. He could clearly see the shards where she'd pointed.

Like a warrior woman defending her home, Lisa started to advance, and he placed a hand on her shoulder to stop her. "Look, whoever raided the site is probably long gone, but let's be careful."

"Fine." She bent, scooped up a branch in her

hands, wielded it like a club and proceeded toward the dwelling where she'd indicated they'd stored their finds. As if sensing Lisa's determination to surprise whoever might be hiding inside, her baby didn't utter a peep.

However, no way was he allowing her to go inside first. Taking several long strides, he caught up with her and then forged ahead of her without bothering to argue. Clearly she thought of this site as her responsibility, and while he admired her courage, he wouldn't permit her to take that kind of risk.

Ducking into a doorway, he spun around, doing a fast check for any telltale movement. But nothing roused except thousand-year-old dust.

"Oh, no."

As she entered behind him and surveyed a ledge where someone had spiked a pick into a window, she gasped and dropped the club. "Theft is one thing, but why would anyone damage the site?"

He hadn't a clue, but a disturbing thought niggled at him. "Is anything missing besides the basket you already mentioned?"

"A few clay pots. A stone ax and arrowheads. A skull." She spoke about the artifacts as if they were as precious as rare diamonds.

"Anything valuable?"

Her shoulders squared with outrage and she lowered her voice in anger. "It's all valuable, irreplaceable and priceless. Those artifacts belong in a museum."

He refrained from releasing a pent-up breath all at once and let the air out slowly. "Let me rephrase the question. I'm not talking about the history behind the objects. I'm talking dollars and cents. How much are the stolen items worth to a collector?''

She shrugged. "That's what's so frustrating. No collector is going to pay much for them. And the way they were taken makes them worth even less.''

"Why?''

"Because a lot of the value comes from verifying the setting and the authenticity—neither of which can be done when an item is stolen from a site.''

He folded his arms across his chest. "Seems to me we're dealing with an amateur in more ways than one.''

She looked up from the trashed room to him, her finely arched brows narrowing, her gaze sharp. "What do you mean?''

"If the fire was set as a way to get you and your team out of here, it worked.''

"So theft was their motive?''

"Yes, but I doubt that whoever set the blaze intended for it to get so out of control. But it burned so fast and quickly they may have miscalculated.''

She bent, picked up a shovel and placed it out of the way in a corner. "How do you know that?''

"I'm guessing," he conceded. "But it's no coincidence that the first time this site has been left unguarded, someone stole your stuff. So it makes sense that whoever robbed the site set the fire.''

Her voice thickened. "The thief may have gotten caught in the fire, too.''

"It's possible that whoever stole your artifacts may have died in these woods." He stepped outside and tried the radio again to call Evan. "Brody to Evan.''

"Yes, boss.''

"Someone stole some items from the site. We think the thief may have also set the fire. Check for tracks."

"Fire's probably wiped them out, boss."

"Ten-four. Unless the thief got caught in the fire, too."

"I'll start a search immediately and keep you informed. Evan out."

He'd expected Lisa to follow him out of the dwelling, but he could hear metal hitting metal. He ducked back inside to find she'd set the baby down in order to stack tools in the corner. She now stood still, staring off into space.

He didn't tell her she might have destroyed forensic evidence such as fingerprints on the wooden handles of the tools. For important crimes Sheriff Lynch sent that kind of evidence to Denver. But Brody already knew without asking the budget-minded sheriff wouldn't consider wasting valuable department resources to attempt to recover a few arrowheads, a basket and some clay pots.

However, the burned timber was another matter. While Brody had no evidence to tie the two crimes together, in his gut he knew the same person had committed both. But right now, what concerned him more than catching the culprit was Lisa.

She wasn't crying, at least not on the outside, but from the way she was rocking and hugging herself and from the bleak expression in her eyes, he could tell she was very upset. Without stopping to think, he took her into his arms, cradled her against his chest and massaged her back.

"It's going to be okay."

"We could have died." She snuggled against him and he wrapped his arms more tightly around her.

"But we didn't."

"Maybe I should cancel the dig. Send everyone home."

"Maybe you should," he agreed.

"Damn you." She pulled back from his embrace, anger overtaking the sorrow. "You're supposed to argue. Not agree with me."

He grinned, not minding in the least that she'd caught on to his tactic—didn't mind as long as it worked. "So you don't want to leave?"

"Of course I don't want to leave. I've studied other archaeologists' sites, worked on the fringes. But this is the first time I've found a site and can head the entire investigative team."

"So don't go."

"Pottery shards aren't worth dying for."

He raised an eyebrow. "You're going to pack and give up? Run away after a few minor troubles?"

Her voice turned wry. "I'd hardly call a stampede, a fire and a theft minor."

"So what do you want to do?" He'd noticed that in her list of reasons to stay, she hadn't included wanting to be with him. He couldn't decide if that annoyed him or intrigued him. For a woman who came so easily into his arms, she sure had an independent streak. And he should never let himself forget that she put her work and the baby first.

Yet, in spite of himself, he kept forgetting that they couldn't possibly have a future together. He wouldn't give up the ranch. It was in his blood, what he did. And her career meant as much to her as ranching did to him. So why did he keep taking her into his arms? His reaction to her surprised him and threw him off-kilter. Protective instincts he hadn't known he had kept surging to the forefront. Combine those instincts with his urge to touch her and kiss her at every opportunity, and he wanted to convince her to stay. But she needed to make up her own mind. After all, it was her safety at stake.

"I suppose I could stretch the university's budget to supply a few guards."

"Now you're thinking. I know a few men who could use extra work."

"Thanks."

LISA HAD HEARD Brody making arrangements on the radio, but she figured they would walk to where they'd parked the vehicles and drive back to the ranch house from there. So when Brody's brother, Ken, and several ranch hands on horseback met up with them around the next bend, she was surprised.

Lisa's knowledge of horses came from television, but to her the snorting animals appeared nervous. Ken broke from the group, bringing up a spare horse without a saddle. "Mom said everyone's okay."

"Yeah. We left four people at Mirror Lake." Brody glanced at the spare horses. "I'm not sure any of the archaeological team can ride."

Ken handed the reins to Brody. "I brought my steadiest and gentlest mounts."

"Thanks."

"Why don't we just drive the car back?" Lisa asked, sensing she was missing something. Today had been exhausting. Escaping the fire, then the freezing water, then the long walk. Her precious site ransacked. Perhaps she wasn't thinking properly.

"Fire toasted the car. The gas tank exploded."

Lisa groaned. She'd totaled two cars in less than a

week. First in the stampede, now in the fire. She couldn't imagine that the leasing company would trust her with another vehicle.

One problem at a time.

She was torn from her thoughts when Ken started teasing his brother. "Mom figured with the baby, it'd be best to ride double."

"Oh, she did, did she?"

Ken chuckled. "Okay, so she's matchmaking again." From the sound of his tone, not only was Ken amused, he didn't mind acknowledging Brody's annoyance. So did that mean Brody didn't want to ride double with her? She restrained a sigh at the thought of rubbing against Brody, thigh to thigh, her butt to his crotch, for mile after mile.

Brody teased his brother right back. "I recall that the last time Mom did any matchmaking you got hitched."

"Best thing that ever happened to me."

For the first time, she liked Ken. For a man to so openly admit that his wife was the best thing that had happened to him was heartwarming. So was the way the brothers teased one another, a ritual that between the lines clearly said they were okay. Safe.

"Damn right," Brody said. "Now I don't have to go into town every Friday night and haul your ugly—"

BJ awoke with a hungry cry. Lisa took the baby out of the sling and felt his diaper. "He needs—"

"Sorry, ma'am—" Ken began.

"Lisa."

"I forgot. Mom sent formula and diapers and a spare set of clothes." He removed a pack tied to his saddle and handed it to Brody. "We've been waiting for the fires to die down and the wind to blow away some smoke before riding in.''

Brody nodded. ''The radio won't work on the other side of this peak, but call in on the way back.''

''Ten-four.'' Ken hesitated. ''Mom said not to bother you with business.''

''But?''

''We got a special-delivery letter from those developers. I left it on your desk.''

''Thanks.''

Ken and the ranch hands moved off, their horses' hooves clip-clopping on the burned earth. Lisa changed BJ's diaper, then fed him a bottle of formula. She tried hard not to look at how high the horse was off the ground, or think about how much damage a fall could do to the baby. Perhaps she should walk, but her legs were tired. She didn't know if she could go another mile, never mind several.

BJ sucked down the formula in his usual five minutes. She burped him twice. Brody had brought the horse over to a small knoll, from which he easily mounted.

She joined him and he must have read the trepidation on her face. He held out his hands for the baby. ''Why don't I carry him?''

''Good idea, since you have a better chance of staying on than I do.''

He lifted the baby smoothly and adjusted the straps to fit his broader shoulders. ''Don't tell me you've never ridden?''

''Does the merry-go-round at the state fair count?''

He fastened the sling to his chest and she realized her mistake. She'd thought she would be riding in front, but he clearly meant for her to sit behind him. At least she'd have him to hold on to.

"Take my hand." In her nervousness, she gave him the wrong one.

"Other hand," he instructed.

She switched. Even though she stood on top of the knoll, the horse's back still looked a long way up.

"Place your foot on top of my boot."

This time she used the correct foot and waited for his next instruction.

"On three, I'll boost you. All you need to do is throw your leg over his back. Ready?"

All she needed to do? Sheesh. Next he'd ask her to turn cartwheels. She'd never been athletic. In school she'd hated gym class, where she'd usually been the last kid picked for any team. "Maybe I should walk."

"On three. One. Two. Three."

He tugged her up with his hand and she used his foot to boost her upward. Suddenly she was settling her leg over the horse's back. When he released her hand, she clutched his waist.

"Don't look down," she mumbled.

"You always talk to yourself when you're nervous?"

"Yeah, but usually not out loud."

The horse began to walk, its muscles bunching and tilting her. She stiffened, pulled herself upright, and when she refrained from letting out a yelp, she was quite pleased with herself. With her feet dangling, her precarious movement and only Brody to hang on to, she held her breath, expecting to slide off at any moment.

"Relax."

"Easy for you to say."

"All you have to do is sit. While I appreciate the bear hug, if you keep it up, my ribs may crack."

"Sorry."

She loosened her hold—but not by much. And when the horse headed downhill, she slid right up against Brody, creating another unexpected problem. Her inner thighs rubbed against him. Worse, her breasts jiggled against his back. Her nipples immediately hardened and she tried to scoot back, fervently wishing she hadn't removed her bra back at the lake.

But she slid right up against him again. Not good. She'd thought her biggest concern would be falling off the horse, but she'd been wrong. Only two layers of thin material separated her flesh from his, and the constant friction was already making her fight not to squirm.

She gritted her teeth. "How long until we reach the ranch?"

"Maybe an hour. Why?"

"Just wondering," she muttered, eliciting a chuckle from him.

"Liar."

"I didn't anticipate—"

"How erotic riding double could be?" He chuckled. "Now you know why Mom instructed Ken to bring only one horse."

She groaned. "Your mother has a devious mind."

"Does it make you feel any better to know that my jeans are suddenly way too tight?"

She had no idea how to respond to his comment. On the one hand she liked the idea that he was turned on by her closeness, yet on the other, his admission made her even more aware of the fluttering in her tummy and the sudden breathlessness that came along with the knowledge she wanted this man.

Talk about complications. She had yet to tell him BJ was his son. That conversation would undoubtably be the equivalent of dumping a bucket of ice water on both their heads. She almost told him the truth, but just because she wanted an excuse to slam the brakes on her growing attraction to him didn't mean she should cut short the process of deciding whether he'd be a good father.

She bit her bottom lip. Hard. But pain didn't distract her from the fact that she found this man very desirable. She'd been charmed by the way he and his brother teased each other. She liked how he treated his mother with respect. She appreciated his broad shoulders and his tight buttocks snuggled right against her—

Stop it.

She'd never been a woman to catalog a man's body parts. So what if when Brody removed his shirt, his chest had been wide, tanned and muscular? So what if his shoulders were bigger than Texas? So what if his washboard abs were the kind that other men worked out for hours to get? Okay, the man had a great body. So what? She'd met lots of well-built jocks on the university campus, and they didn't affect her the way Brody did.

It was all she could do not to let her hands roam over him. Her fingers itched to slip under his shirt to touch his skin, but instead, she clenched her fingers around his belt loops.

And she couldn't help wondering if his jeans would have been just as tight if another woman had been clinging to him as she was. Was his reaction to *her?*

"What are you thinking?" he asked, his voice husky in the darkness that cloaked them in intimacy.

"Nothing."

He didn't allow her answer to stop the conversation. "What do you say to sharing the hot tub when we get back?"

She was going to be sore from the ride, and his suggestion appealed to her on several levels. Hot water. Him all to herself.

Bad idea.

She made up the first excuse that entered her mind. "I didn't bring a swimsuit."

"The back deck is private. There would only be me, you and the Rocky Mountains."

"Mmm."

He didn't press her for an answer, just let the natural friction of her body rubbing against his do the convincing for him. She didn't even realize when her hands stopping clutching his belt loops and began roving over his stomach as if they had a mind of their own.

No wonder he thought she'd share a hot tub with him. What was wrong with her? When other girls had been dating, she'd been working two jobs to put herself through school and studying. Her free time she'd usually spent with Maritza. So she wasn't all that experienced with men, her one previous affair had ended badly.

But even she knew that she had no business wanting a man with whom she had so little in common. Besides, she barely knew Brody. Except that he was brave and steadfast and reliable and kind and he kissed like the dream man straight out of her best fantasy.

That didn't make them compatible. He needed a woman to run the homestead, not an archaeologist who didn't know the first thing about cows or horses. She'd started out this ride hoping it would soon end, but as they approached Brody's house, they seemed to be moving too quickly. She needed to make a decision.

Fast.

Thoughts jumbled in her mind, pulling her one way, but her body was clearly tugging in the other direction, telling her to go for him. If their previous kisses were any indication, they would be good together, and yet, she had strong instincts of self-preservation. She didn't believe in having a fling. She wanted companionship and a chance for commitment, and if she'd learned one thing about people in her twenty-eight years, it was that men didn't change. Brody wanted a family that included a wife, kids and home-cooked meals. He deserved a woman who enjoyed cooking and cleaning and laundry, domestic skills she preferred to sluff off. Sure he sent out sexy signals but—

"We have company," he said.

"Huh?"

She'd been so deep in her thoughts she hadn't noted anything unusual. She leaned over to peer around his shoulder.

Two men stood smoking cigarettes on his front porch. She didn't recognize either of them, but Brody must have, because he'd stiffened at the sight of the visitors, then relaxed. Yet, since she was still leaning against him, she realized that a certain tension remained.

"Sheriff Lynch. Deputy Keegan. What brings you all the way out here at this time of night?"

The shorter, older man with gray hair flicked his cigarette aside, then ground out the butt with his heel. "Heard about the fire. And your recent stampede. We need to talk with you...in private."

Brody rode right up to the front porch and Lisa dismounted stiffly, her thoughts racing. Could the sheriff have investigated her? Her fake ID might hold up to lease a car, and she'd asked her associates here and at the university not to use or reveal her real last name or talk about her to anyone, but her faked identity wasn't designed to deceive a lawman with all kinds of resources at his disposal.

Don't panic.

The sheriff might be here for reasons that had absolutely nothing to do with her. He'd mentioned the stampede and the fire and might simply be here to investigate them.

Brody handed her the sleeping baby. As much as she would have liked to remain and listen to the conversation, she had no excuse to do so, and she turned toward the front door to leave the men alone.

"Stay a minute," Brody said. "Lisa Madison, meet Sheriff Lynch and Deputy Keegan. We might as well report the stolen artifacts now and save ourselves a trip into town tomorrow."

She'd almost forgotten the missing items. But with all that had happened today, she forgave herself. "Let me put the baby down, and I'll make a list."

The men didn't say a word until she'd shut the door behind her. She stopped on the other side and listened, but no sounds filtered through the thick walls. So she laid BJ in his borrowed cradle. The little guy had had quite the exciting day and didn't awaken, not even when she changed his diaper and placed him in clean clothes. Tomorrow morning she would bathe him.

Tucking the blanket over him, she noted that he seemed to have grown in just a few days. The cradle wouldn't fit him for much longer. Neither would his clothes. She'd have to make a trip into town soon to see to his needs.

With his tiny fingers closing into fists, he appeared so peaceful. She smoothed back a lock of hair, leaned down and kissed his brow. Her heart swelled with love for him, her last remaining tie to her sister. No matter how often she'd told herself not to get too attached, she knew that this precious bundle meant so much to her that leaving him might be the hardest thing she ever had to do.

Yet, for his sake, she would find the strength. She had to do right by him, and Brody had already proven that he possessed daddy-protective instincts. She hadn't missed his insistence on going first when entering the ruins, either. Yeah, he had great daddy and husband potential—just not for an archaeologist. Although she intended to stay long enough to make sure her initial impression didn't change, maybe it was time to tell Brody the truth to see how he reacted.

However, she wanted to wait until they were alone. When she exited the house with the list of stolen artifacts in her hand, the sheriff and deputy had left.

Brody held out his hand. "Walk me to the barn." He noted the list in her hand. "We can fax that to the sheriff in the morning. He promised to look into the theft but wasn't hopeful."

"Okay."

His tone sharpened. "There's another matter we need to discuss."

Uh-oh.

Chapter Eight

"Yes?" Lisa couldn't keep the tremble out of her voice and hoped he'd attribute her nervousness to the hard day they'd had and the lateness of the hour.

"Let me get the horse put up first."

Oh, great. Keep her on edge a little longer. She didn't trust herself to answer, so she just followed him to the barn.

Brody opened the double doors, and the scent of hay, animals and manure wafted into the night air. He led the horse to a stall, removed the bridle, then fed and watered the animal. He washed his hands at a sink and then escorted her back to the house.

She could no longer smell the smoke, but the balmy night air did nothing to calm her. She'd wanted to disclose her deception to Brody, not have a lawman do it. Had she waited too long to tell him the truth? She didn't know, but Brody didn't seem angry, just puzzled.

"The sheriff said a stranger in town was asking a lot of questions about me."

His statement threw her for a moment as relief washed over her, but she wasn't in the clear. Not yet. "What kind of questions?"

"About my schedule. What part of the ranch I work this time of year. When and where I go into town."

"Did the stranger have a name?"

"Lester Janson."

"You don't know the man?" she asked, her nerves settling as she realized that the sheriff hadn't questioned her identity. And neither the sheriff nor Brody seemed to think it likely that the stranger could have anything to do with her, or Brody would have already said so.

He shook his head. "The sheriff did a background check on the guy." He sounded reluctant to tell her more, or maybe he just didn't want to burden her with his problems.

But the scare made up her mind for her. It was time to come clean. She needed Brody to hear the truth from her own lips. But first she wanted to hear more about the stranger.

"And?" she prompted.

Puzzlement furrowed his brows. "There is no such person as Lester Janson. The social security number, Arizona address and phone number didn't check out."

Arizona? Her home state. All of her instincts fired on alert. However, Colorado and Arizona were neighbors. It could be a not-so-unusual coincidence that the stranger asking questions about Brody had a fake address in Arizona. Chances were he was from another state entirely and had used Arizona to throw off anyone checking.

She attempted to keep her voice calm. "Did the sheriff question him?"

"He tried. The guy's disappeared."

She stopped walking when they reached his front porch. "Why are you telling me this?"

His tone deepened and his lips lost some of their grim tightness. "Because I feel you need to be aware of the danger. I want you to stay here with me."

At his words her heart hammered. And guilt stabbed her. Here he'd been so honest with her and she'd lied to him right from the beginning. She couldn't do so any longer.

"I need to tell you—"

His mouth swooped down on hers and he nibbled her lips. "Can it wait?"

His persuasive kiss brought back all the pent-up sensations of the day. He smelled of soap, hay and leather. Her mouth craved his. Every inch of her yearned for more of his touch. She wanted to stay in his arms, allow the romance to blossom, enjoy the emotions flaring in her. With his arms wrapped around her, her chest pressed to his, her breasts ached and her nipples hardened, telling him of her need.

She jerked away. "No."

With his back to the porch light she couldn't read his eyes, but his tone remained tender, hopeful and husky with desire. "*No* you don't want to make love, or *no* it can't wait?"

"We need to talk."

He groaned and threaded a hand through his thick hair. "Do you have any idea how much I want you?"

She couldn't keep the need from her tone any more than she could disguise her pain at rejecting his oh-so-tempting offer. "You may not want me at all after you hear what I have to say."

He shrugged and said, "I'm willing to take my chances. Make love first and talk later?"

"I can't." She took his hand, again wondering if he wanted her for the right reasons. She wished she had more experience with men, but she supposed even lots of dating wouldn't have made her a mind reader. Brody himself might not even know if the attraction between them was more than sexual. "I have to straighten out the lies between us."

"Maybe we could discuss this in the hot tub?"

"I don't think so." She tugged him onto the front porch rocker. He placed an arm around her shoulders and she snuggled into the curve of his body, enjoying the closeness as much as the shared warmth.

"You should have been a suspense writer. I'm dying here. Tell me already."

"Does the name Maritza McCalliff ring any bells?"

He hesitated, probably from a reluctance to talk about another woman with her. "I met a woman named Maritza at a party and—"

"I don't need the details." She squeezed his hand. "Maritza was my married sister."

His lower jaw dropped. "Your sister?"

"Maritza never took her husband's name. I'm Lisa McCalliff, not Lisa Madison."

"Whoa. Slow down. You said Maritza *was* your sister?"

How like him to pick out the most salient point. "Maritza died about a month ago after giving birth to BJ."

She craned her neck to take in his expression, then wished she hadn't. His face had hardened into a mask and a muscle worked wildly in his jaw. She could almost hear him counting backward, and when he reached BJ's age plus the normal nine months of pregnancy, the arm around her shoulders stiffened. She gave him credit for not totally withdrawing from touching her.

His tone tightened. ''What exactly are you saying? You told me you were on a quest for the baby's father. I assumed you meant that he had left not knowing you were pregnant.''

''I misled you.''

''No sh—''

''Before Maritza died, she asked me to take the baby to his biological father. She didn't trust her husband, Mark. He has too many problems.''

''Just say it.''

''You're BJ's father.''

''You're sure?''

''Maritza was. You can have a DNA test done.''

He jerked to his feet, his voice gruff. ''You can bet your last dollar I'll be getting that test. I think I'll go inside now.''

Every line of his lean body was tense with anger. She considered allowing him to calm down, but she needed to tell him everything. Best to get it over and done with—even if her eyes burned with unshed tears at what she was doing to him. She'd just shattered the perfect world he'd created for himself.

''There's more.''

''More?'' His voice sounded tortured. Despite his wanting the DNA test, he believed the baby was his— she could read the anguish in his eyes and looked for just a smidgon of happiness at the idea of fatherhood. And saw none. Just grim shock.

He glared at her. ''What else?''

She twisted her hands in her lap and reminded herself that as difficult as this was for her, it was harder on him. ''Maritza never named the baby. I called him

BJ for Brody Jr.—'' he winced ''—but she wanted you to name your son.''

"How touching.'' His harsh sarcasm made her angry.

She rose to her feet and stood tall to look him in the eye. "Maritza died having your son. And it took both of you to make that baby. BJ's the best part of the story. Maybe you'd better sit back down for the rest.''

"What? You're about to hit me with a gazillion-dollar paternity suit?''

"Worse. I kidnapped the baby from Mark.''

"What!'' His eyes burned holes into her.

Her gut churned, but she fought against revealing her distress. She wished she could make this easier for both of them, but what was done was done. He had to know everything. She raised her chin, squared her shoulders and chased the trembling from her tone. "Mark's an alcoholic. He'd forget to change and feed the baby when he was drinking. I tried telling him the baby wasn't his, but he refused to believe me. I called Social Services, but he's a private investigator. I think he paid someone at the agency to warn him about the surprise visit. So I saw a lawyer and learned that the baby is legally Mark's because he was married to Maritza during her pregnancy and the baby's birth.''

"Let me get this straight. I'm harboring a kidnapper?''

"Yes.''

"BJ is my son?''

"Yes.''

"And I have no legal right to him?''

"I'm so sorry.''

He cursed. She didn't say a word, just allowed him

to absorb her news. Finally he turned and glowered at her.

"Is that it?"

"I'm afraid Mark might have found out where I was and followed me here."

"Why hasn't this kidnapping been in the news?"

"I'm not sure. I thought there would be a firestorm of publicity, but there's been nothing."

"This doesn't make sense. Why wouldn't Mark go straight to the authorities?"

"All I know is that he didn't. I'm guessing Mark either doesn't want his professional reputation hurt by the fact that he needs police help to find his baby, or…" She hesitated.

"Or what?"

She thought of the stampede. The fire. The stolen artifacts. "Or he wants revenge."

"Against you or me?"

"Probably both of us. He'd hate you for the time you spent with his wife, and hate me for taking the baby. I think the stranger asking questions about you in town might have been Mark."

"Maybe Mark decided he didn't want the baby."

"That's possible, but I don't think so."

"Why?"

"He's a control freak. Maritza escaped him by dying, which made him very angry."

"Maybe anger was his way of grieving."

"Maybe."

"But you don't think so?"

"He had a twisted way of looking at things. Remember how I told you that he didn't like her career? That part was all true. He was obsessive about her fixing his dinner and keeping the house clean. He resented every minute she spent at work. That she earned more money than he did made him feel worthless. I don't know if he was always warped like that, or if he came out of the service damaged. Everything was Mark's—Mark's car, Mark's house, Mark's baby.''

''Why didn't you tell me this before? Why all the lies?'' Brody's tightly controlled tone told her more than any shouting could have how deeply her news had affected him.

''I wasn't going to just hand BJ over to a stranger, not even to his biological father.''

Brody leaped to the right conclusion. ''That's why you kept handing me the baby. You were testing me.''

''If you don't want BJ, I'm prepared to keep him. In fact, I've gotten so attached to him, giving him up will be...hard.''

''Yeah, he's a great little guy. Worth all the trouble you've handed me.''

And that was when she knew without a doubt that he intended to keep his son. The problem was, she still couldn't be positive that he would make a good father. Mark had seemed like a good match for Maritza, but he hadn't revealed his true character until after they'd married. And that he'd fooled Lisa and Maritza so thoroughly made her wary of all men.

Brody's reaction to the news hadn't been encouraging—except for the statement that the baby was worth all the trouble that he'd brought with him. But then, she'd given the man quite a few shocks. She'd give him the benefit of the doubt—for now. She'd already kidnapped the baby once. If necessary she could do so again.

THE NEXT MORNING Lisa left BJ with Brody's mom, who was delighted to baby-sit her new grandson. Brody posted a guard outside the house to protect the baby, and she and he had taken his pickup truck into town. He dropped her off at the hospital to see Joanna and Marty. Joanna had been released, but the doctors wanted to keep Marty for another night to monitor his heart.

All her team members intended to return to the site and insisted that she continue to lead their group. Despite the danger, she wanted to stay, too. If Mark was behind the stampede and the fire, he could hunt her down and find her anywhere.

She strolled from the hospital down the city street. It was between the winter ski season and the summer tourist season, and almost every store had a red Sale sign in its window. For a small town, the variety of goods available surprised her. And the aromas from the restaurants enticed her, reminding her that she needed to eat.

She met up with Brody outside his attorney's office. The shock and anger of last night seemed to have evolved into a determination to solve all the problems in the most logical manner. First he'd spelled out her news to his family; next he'd talked to his lawyer.

"Any luck?" she asked, hoping his attorney would find a solution for the impossible situation she'd put him in.

Brody shook his head. "He suggests that we contact Mark and try to work out an arrangement outside the courts. Do you think there's any way we could change his mind about an adoption?"

"I don't know." Her stomach rumbled. "Mark is hardheaded."

"We'll know soon enough. We phoned him from my attorney's office and left a message on his answering machine."

She kept her negative thoughts to herself. No point in assuming the worst. She could be wrong. Maybe Mark hadn't called the cops on her because he really didn't want the baby back.

At the enticing scent of pizza wafting across the street and onto the sidewalk, her mouth began to water. "How about lunch? My treat."

Just then his cell phone rang. "Maybe my attorney got hold of Mark," he said hopefully, and then answered his phone. "Hello?"

Brody paused before he said, "Sheriff, let me put you on the speaker phone so Lisa can hear you." He pressed a button. "Okay, go ahead."

"I have a report from a Denver museum that someone tried to sell them some Anasazi artifacts this morning. The list includes a basket, arrowheads, an ax and pottery."

"Did the museum make the purchase?"

"Apparently they couldn't authenticate the objects. The museum still has them and the seller is waiting to hear from them. I thought you might want to follow up yourself, Brody. I'll have my secretary fax the museum director's name and phone number to your office."

"Thanks."

"Here's where you may luck out," the sheriff added. "The museum director has promised to stall the seller until you get to Denver. I suggest you contact him and fly out now."

"Thanks," Brody said. "Lisa and I will do that."

Details zipped through Lisa's mind. BJ. The archaeological dig. Spending a night away from BJ. Funny how her thoughts always circled back to the baby. "Will your mom be willing to watch BJ until we get back?"

He called Mia and she had no problem taking care of the baby. She also gave him the museum director's name and phone number that the sheriff had faxed. Brody wrote the information on his hand.

Lisa's stomach rumbled again and she checked her watch. It was after one o'clock. "Do we have time to eat before we leave?"

"We can eat a sandwich on the plane."

Brody escorted her back to the car and made yet another phone call. She expected him to phone the airlines, but he told someone to fuel an aircraft and then added technical jargon she couldn't follow. But it sounded as though he'd arranged for a private charter.

He drove straight to an airfield. On the way she had time to think. "You know," she said, "something about the theft isn't sitting right with me."

"What do you mean?"

"Stealing artifacts isn't like a smash-and-grab at a jewelry store where the item can be fenced at a pawnshop. The thief has to know where to find the items, what to take, then where to sell them."

"I wouldn't have a clue where to sell Anasazi artifacts."

"It's not exactly common knowledge, and yet the people who do have that knowledge wouldn't have taken something so common—or have turned around and tried to sell them to a museum."

"Now you have me confused. Are you saying the thief is or isn't knowledgeable about archaeology?"

"Both. That's why this doesn't make sense unless…"

"Unless what?"

"Unless the motive isn't money."

He frowned at her. "What else could it be?"

"Suppose someone wants to discredit me?"

"Huh?"

"My reputation is on the line. If I can't keep the site safe from theft, the university won't trust me in the future."

"So now you suspect one of your team members?"

She shook her head. "All of them were with us during the fire. They couldn't have stolen those artifacts."

"But they could have arranged for a stranger to steal them and sell them where they would be recovered. That would hurt your reputation and still keep the artifacts safe."

"Seems farfetched."

"But the facts fit. Tell me, if you couldn't continue as the boss, who would take over?"

"Normally Joanna, but with her pregnant, maybe Marty or Kevin, I'm not sure. We don't have a strict chain of command."

Could one of her team be working with a thief to discredit her? She recalled the missing notebook after the stampede and wondered if whoever had started that stampede had done so with the intention of stealing her notes.

"Then again, it might have been Mark," Brody suggested.

"Mark doesn't know or care anything about archaeology."

"You said that this might be someone with a little

knowledge. Surely your brother-in-law might have picked up a few things while he was married to your sister. Maybe enough to know how to discredit you.''

She could picture Mark stealing her notes and the artifacts, just for the sheer pleasure of destroying them. But try to sell them? She didn't think so. Perhaps they would find out when they arrived in Denver.

The hangar was tiny and the runway set in a valley between two mountains. She didn't like flying, and if she had to fly, she hated the little planes the airlines used for short hops. So when he parked beside a hangar next to a tiny two-seater aircraft, her stomach lurched.

''Come on.'' He took her hand and tugged her toward the plane. ''The fridge is stocked with cold drinks and sandwiches.''

''Where's the pilot?''

''You're holding his hand.''

Oh, God. His words froze her to the tarmac. ''You're a pilot?''

''Haven't crashed yet.''

She forgot all about food. Her stomach pitched and rolled and she was very glad she hadn't eaten breakfast or lunch. ''Don't even joke about it.''

He frowned at her, but when their eyes met, he must have seen real fear in her face. She didn't like to talk about one of the saddest times in her life or remind herself that with her sister gone, she and BJ were the last remaining members of her family.

Yet she owed him an explanation for her reluctance. ''My father was a pilot. He and my mother were flying from Phoenix to Denver for my grandfather's funeral when their plane went down. We couldn't find the bodies until spring.''

"I'm sorry."

"Could we check on a commercial flight?"

"Okay."

She appreciated that he didn't make fun of her fear and didn't attempt to talk her into getting into the tiny aircraft. The tightness in her throat eased, until she overheard his attempt to make travel arrangements. Apparently there wasn't a commercial plane flying out until the morning.

He clicked off his phone, and his voice turned sympathetic. "We could drive, but we won't get there today. What do you want to do?"

She looked at the plane and her feet froze. "How long is the flight?"

"Ninety minutes if the weather holds."

She glanced up at the clear sky and noted the dark clouds that hovered over the mountains to the east, where they were headed. Identifying the artifacts wasn't a life-or-death situation. She didn't have to put one foot inside that airplane. But if the seller returned to the museum and took the items back, she might never identify them.

Could she overcome her fear? Was identifying and retrieving the artifacts worth it? Her thoughts raced.

This was the first site she'd ever found, and someone had robbed it. Someone had set the forest on fire and endangered all of them. Could she really live with herself if she didn't have the guts to sit on a perfectly good airplane with a no doubt competent pilot and find out who'd done this?

She inhaled deeply. "Can I sit in the passenger seat before I make a decision?"

"Sure. I won't fire up the engines until you give me the go ahead."

"Thank you."

"For what?"

"Being so understanding."

"It's okay. I have a fear of spiders. Haven't been able to stand them ever since I was a kid."

Grateful for the conversation, she walked beside him to the plane. "I've never minded bugs, which is a blessing since I spend a good part of my life digging in the dirt."

He gave her a sheepish grin. "Grown men are not supposed to be afraid of spiders, and it's downright embarrassing. Even those harmless daddy longlegs give me the willies."

He opened the door and she craned her neck to peer inside the airplane. Her heart hammered against her ribs.

Okay, what's the worst that can happen? The plane cannot crash while it's still on the ground. It shouldn't bother her one iota to step inside the airplane, but she couldn't seem to bend her knee to take that step inside.

"Want me to distract you?"

"You think that's possible?"

A mischievous gleam entered his eyes. "I'll take that as a yes."

When he took her into his embrace, she thought he just meant to give her a comforting hug. However, there was nothing comforting about the kiss he planted on her lips.

Oh, my.

She'd thought her heart had been racing before, but now it was doing double time. Last night he'd been angry when she'd told him about her lies, and making love had been out of the question. She'd gone to bed wondering if she'd killed any chance for even a friendship between them. This morning he'd been aloof and she hadn't wanted to ask him how he felt about her. She'd sensed that he needed time to come to grips with all the surprises she'd hurled his way. So this kiss was her first real indication that he might forgive her.

While she didn't forget about the airplane ride, he'd certainly given her something else to think about. And as his hand slipped under her shirt and edged toward her breasts, she couldn't stop her reaction to his warm touch, and the iciness in her thawed. His distraction idea was a good one.

When he pulled back, she gasped for air. "Better?" he asked with a satisfied grin.

"Not all better."

"Then I'm going to kiss you again." He swept her up into his arms and carried her into the plane, tugging the door shut behind them. "I'm going to kiss the soft spot behind your ear and along your neck and jaw."

When he stood her back on her feet, he let her slide down against his hard chest. She hadn't made it to the passenger seat, but she was inside the airplane and feeling no ill effects. Just a little shakiness, and that could be the aftereffects of his kiss.

Looking directly into her eyes, he unfastened her bra and dropped his hands to her hips. He caressed her hips, then his hands spanned her waist and slowly stroked higher. He was going to touch her breasts.

Oh, God.

"Yes?" he asked.

"Yes."

She expected him to cover her breasts with his

palms, yearned for such a caress. But he didn't touch her there. Not yet.

Instead, he turned her around and eased her into the passenger seat. His hands came out from beneath her shirt and he placed them on her shoulders.

''How are you doing?''

Chapter Nine

Chapter Nine

Brody wished he could have enjoyed distracting her a little more, but he understood phobias too well not to sympathize with her plight. If he'd had to touch a spider, he didn't know if anything could distract him.

Her fingers gripped the seat so hard that her knuckles whitened. Her shallow breathing tugged at him, giving him the incentive to let her adjust to her surroundings—even though he yearned to be up and away.

He had dug deep and found more patience than he knew he had. Although she'd thrown one shocker after another at him since her arrival, he'd never felt more alive. He'd finally had time to digest her news and regain a bit of his equilibrium. He might not agree with every action she'd taken, especially her initial lying, but he understood why she'd done it. More importantly he now knew that she'd turned her life upside down, breaking the law and risking years in jail, for his son.

His son!

The thought still made him feel pride and joy and worry at how easily he could lose BJ. She'd kidnapped the baby to bring him to the ranch. So not only was Brody harboring a kidnapper, he was probably an accessory to the crime. There was no telling how many laws he'd broken. His attorney had suggested that he turn BJ and Lisa over to the authorities and pursue a legal adoption through the courts, but at the same time, he'd advised him that his chances of winning custody weren't good.

Their best bet was to find Mark and talk the man into letting Brody adopt the baby. He didn't intend to take no for an answer, and he clamped down hard on his emotions, unwilling to consider failure. Mark didn't answer his home or business phone. A neighbor claimed she hadn't seen him in a week. So Brody was eager to fly to Denver, hoping the thief might turn out to be Mark. Yet he was very aware that Lisa didn't think Mark could pull off this kind of scheme. Still, he had to follow every lead. Until BJ's custody was settled, his life would be in turmoil. So the sooner he settled the matter the better.

The fastest way to get to Denver was to fly—but he'd given his word to Lisa that he wouldn't start the engines until she was ready. She sat frozen in the seat beside him, her fingers still gripping the leather, likely leaving a permanent indentation.

In contrast to her still body, her voice shook. "If we go into the…" She licked her bottom lip nervously and tried again. "If we fly…if we start…can we still turn back if I can't handle…?"

"Yes. That's the great thing about your own aircraft. Although we'll file a flight plan, we can change our minds."

He didn't mention that once they reached the mountains and the stronger weather systems there, turning back might not be an option. While guilt stabbed him for not revealing everything, he didn't want to pile on more stress. His silence made him realize that even though he had the best of intentions, his desire to go after the thief, whom he hoped would turn out to be Maritza's husband, was great enough to keep information from Lisa. He was no saint, and realizing that made forgiving Lisa easier. It wasn't her fault that he and her sister had made a baby.

He and Maritza had hit it off that long-ago night. There had been something so vulnerable about her at the party. She'd been gentle, warm and flattered by his attention. Although Brody normally liked strong women, he couldn't resist her when she'd clung to him. That evening, conversation had led to flirting, then dancing, and finally to a romp in the hay. After her stealthy disappearance the next morning, he'd asked questions hoping to find her, but he figured if she'd wanted to pursue the relationship, she wouldn't have left while he was sleeping. For a day or two he'd expected a phone call, and when she hadn't gotten in touch with him, he'd left the pleasant memory behind.

They'd used protection that night, but apparently fate had intervened. If only she'd told him she'd gotten pregnant. But she hadn't. It was small consolation knowing that if she had lived, he could have spent an entire lifetime never knowing he'd fathered a child.

His son.

Letting Lisa keep the baby wasn't even an option. Brody wanted to watch his son grow into a toddler and learn to ride. He wanted to show him how to throw a baseball or—he grinned at the possibility of BJ taking after his mother—dig for fossils or arrowheads. He couldn't believe how strong his instinct was to protect that baby, and despite his angry words about a DNA test, he believed that BJ was his. He didn't know if any other child would have felt so right in his arms; he only knew he would never let him go back to a man who neglected him. Never.

''Let's go.'' She'd whispered the words, but they rang clearly through the cabin.

It was a measure of her love for his son that she'd broken the law to take him from Mark, and overcoming her fears now was another sign of love. She wanted BJ to be safe enough to make herself sick by flying. He couldn't help but wonder if she would really be able to leave BJ with him when the time came.

He performed a silent preflight check, then started the engines. After he spoke to the tower and received permission for takeoff, he wasted no time getting the plane into the air.

Once aloft, he spared a glance from his instrumentation. Lisa had closed her eyes. Her skin was pale and beads of sweat had broken out on her brow. But she hadn't asked him to land. Hadn't cried out even once as the plane left the airstrip and soared between the mountain peaks. Then again, she appeared almost catatonic. Maybe she was no longer capable of speech.

He tried to start an innocuous conversation that would require her to respond. ''When we arrive, how will you know whether the basket—''

''Does this plane have automatic pilot?''

''Yes.'' Apparently she didn't want to be distracted with archaeological details. ''Why?''

''Could you hold my hand?''

''Give me a few minutes.'' He refrained from mentioning that he had to first clear the mountains, not wanting to mention any detail that might escalate her fear.

He had to reach cruising altitude before turning on the autopilot. Usually when he flew, his heart lifted in happiness at the freedom. From here he could see the town, his ranch, a ribbon of highway, but the usual lightness that came with liftoff didn't happen. How could it with her sitting terrified beside him? Finally he placed the plane on autopilot and covered her hand with his. Her skin was cold and clammy.

He laced his fingers through hers. "Any better?"

"Don't ask me that."

"Okay." He didn't know what else to do for her. She didn't want to talk about work or how she was doing. And he was fresh out of ideas.

"Tell me about yourself," she suggested as if reading his mind.

"What do you want to know?" If he could keep her talking, part of her mind had to stay on the conversation and could focus less on her fear of flying.

"When you were a kid, what did you want to be when you grew up?"

"A rancher."

"What about as a teenager?"

"A rancher."

"I wanted to be an astronaut." She snorted at the irony. "Now I... You never wanted to be anything else?"

"I love working outdoors. There's a certain peace to be had working for yourself under a sunny sky or a starry night."

"What about when it rains and snows?"

"As long as I have a good horse, a warm coat and

a weatherproof slicker, matches and some grub, I appreciate every season.''

''Where do you take your vacations?''

''Since the ranch is my favorite place, I don't leave often.'' The plane struck an air pocket and dropped, before leveling out again. He saw her flinch. ''Want to hear a secret fantasy of mine?''

''Sure.''

''I like the ocean because it reminds me of the ranch.''

''How?''

''A sea of grass is similar to the Pacific. Both change colors with the clouds and sun. Both whip up in a storm.''

''What's the secret-fantasy part?''

Her hand grew a little warmer in his, but her eyes remained closed. He wondered if she was visualizing the scenarios he'd been describing and offered her more details to help her out. ''You're going to think I'm silly.''

''Would that be so terrible?''

''I'd like to vacation on a sailboat in the Caribbean. I imagine the gorgeous views, all that turquoise water and white sand beaches.''

''So why don't you go?''

''I don't know how to sail,'' he admitted, wondering if he sounded crazy to her. But then again, who cared? As long as he kept distracting her.

''Not knowing how to sail might be a problem. You'd have to know how to steer and navigate, or risk going aground on a coral reef.''

''I haven't told you the rest of the fantasy.''

''Oh?''

''I picture a beautiful redhead in a string bikini

lounging on the deck while I slather suntan oil over her long legs, her toned arms, her smooth back.''

''Are you partial to redheads?''

''I am now.''

Her startled green eyes opened. She ignored the sight of the mountains out the windshield and stared at him with an expression he couldn't read. ''You and I...we aren't right for one another.''

''Why not?''

''You like to fly airplanes.''

''Uh-huh. That convinces me.''

''You like to ride horses.''

''Mmm.''

''I'm not good at housekeeping.''

''Trust me, housekeeping isn't exactly what I have on my mind when I think of you.''

''Okay, I can see that you think we're the perfect pair. But I'm a kidnapper.''

''And I'm an accessory to a kidnapping.''

''Oh, God. I'm so sorry.'' Her eyes clouded with pain and her lower lip quivered. She'd gone from almost calm to sad in a second—which told him again how on edge she was.

Great, here he'd been telling her his fantasy to distract her from her fear of flying, and now he had her apologizing to him. *Way to go*. He felt lower than a skunk, especially since he knew better.

''You don't owe me any apologies. Want to hear the rest of the fantasy?'' He redirected the conversation.

''Sure.'' Her tone was tight.

He set about undoing the damage one careless comment had done. ''We anchor the sailboat in a deepwater harbor surrounded by a crescent beach with gentle lapping waves. The boat has one of those tents—''

''A bimini top?''

''For shade.'' He paused in the telling of his fantasy. How did she know about bimini tops or running aground on coral reefs? ''You're an Arizona woman who knows about boats?''

''Mm. I have all sorts of undiscovered talents.''

''I've always known you were holding out on me.'' He kept up the double entendres, his voice deliberately husky.

''I know how to sail. My college roommate lived in Santa Barbara. Her parents had a thirty-six-foot boat, and they invited Maritza and me to join them on a regular basis.''

''You know how to sail?'' he repeated in amazement.

''Yeah.''

''So you could kidnap me, sail me to some deserted Caribbean Island and take advantage of me?'' he teased.

''Is that your fantasy?'' She gazed at him, her eyes glittering with amusement.

''It is now.'' He wished he could think of a way to keep the enjoyment in her tone; it was so much better than the fear she'd almost banished. ''What about you?''

''What about me?''

''What's your secret fantasy?''

''A career woman should never admit—''

''I told you mine.''

''It's finding the right man.''

He wasn't sure he wanted his next question answered, but if he could distract her from the mountain pass they were flying through, he'd have to cope. "The right man? What will make him right?"

She shot him one of those I-know-exactly-what-you're-doing-but-I'll-let-you-get-away-with-it looks. "He'll have to be intelligent. Kind. Have a good sense of humor. And think of himself first."

"Excuse me? I didn't hear you right. You couldn't have said that you want him to think of himself first."

"Yes, that's exactly what I said. You see, I don't want the responsibility of making him content. I don't want to have to keep the house clean or cook or be at home 24/7 to keep him happy. I want him to be self-sufficient on his own. And to make oneself happy, one has to put oneself first, don't you think?"

"I've never thought about it." He glanced at her, puzzled and fascinated. "You didn't put yourself first when you went on the run with my son."

"But I did," she assured him. "I couldn't have been happy with myself if I went back on my promise to my sister, or if I left her child in such poor circumstances."

He wasn't sure exactly what that said about her character, but he had the urge to kiss her senseless. He wanted to wrap his arms around her and tell her that somehow he would keep her from going to jail, that somehow they would convince Mark to allow him to adopt the baby, but he wasn't a man who made false promises.

The plane hit another air pocket and she gasped. Her hold on the seat regained some of its former vigor, but she didn't close her eyes again. "How much longer?"

"We're past the halfway point. Air currents should settle down in the next ten minutes."

"Okay." There was pride and courage and fear in that one word. And thirty minutes later when he set down at a small airport outside Denver, it didn't take long for her to regain her natural coloring.

While he rented a car, she phoned the hospital to see how Marty was doing and was pleased to learn that his heartbeat had remained regular. Next she'd checked in with Mia, who was having fun getting to know her new grandson. And finally she phoned the museum director to tell him they were on the way to see the suspicious items.

Before they were in the rental car, she kissed Brody on the cheek. "Thanks for helping me get through that flight."

"If you like, we can drive back," he offered, not wanting her to have to dread the return.

"I don't want to think about that yet. I'm still enjoying your fantasy. Some time you'll have to tell me what happens on the deck after you slather all that suntan oil over your redhead's bare skin." Her eyes twinkled with mischief. "But right now, all I can think about is..."

"Yes?"

"Food."

FOR THE SAKE of saving time, they pulled into a drive-through fast-food place. They discovered they shared a love of French fries with salt and ketchup. She ordered a salad and he had a burger, which they consumed, along with large chocolate shakes. On the way to the museum, Lisa tried hard not to think about Brody's fantasy.

He'd probably made up the entire scenario to distract her from her fear or flying. He'd succeeded. Too well.

The idea of him smoothing oil over her skin on a rocking sailboat in the middle of the Caribbean had evoked powerful images that she couldn't easily dismiss, no matter how hard she tried. Nor could she deny the connection between them. Not just lust, though Lord knew, there was plenty of sizzle between them. But there was also a genuine friendship growing.

She'd seen him serious and caring and playful and romantic. And she liked everything—except that she'd finally met the right man and he was all wrong for her. He lived on a ranch. She had a career that she loved. He made it very clear he wanted sex, but she wanted love.

And the ugly thought kept niggling that he might be trying to sway her into letting him keep BJ.

She loved that little boy with all her heart. The only thing that made giving him to Brody tolerable was knowing BJ should be with the father who loved him. Sure, she could keep a baby clean and feed him, but could she keep him safe on a dig? And what happened when he needed playmates and schooling?

Leaving BJ would probably break her heart, but she didn't have to allow herself to fall in love with Brody and leave him, too, creating twice the pain. She could and would protect her heart from a double tragedy.

Knowing these basic truths, she should avoid Brody to protect herself from getting hurt. But she couldn't, not until BJ's future was settled.

BRODY HAD SEEN the items found at the dig before, but he couldn't tell an Aztec ax from an Anasazi one, never mind identify this particular Anasazi ax as the exact one that had been found on his land. As Lisa studied the items the museum director laid out, her eyes shone with enthusiasm. She held the basket with care and reverence, her lips pursed with her concentration. He was surprised to learn that he found her sexy when in career mode.

But after ten minutes in the crowded and stuffy storage room that lacked windows and smelled of must, he could no longer rein in his patience. "Well?"

Lisa spoke without hesitation. "These items came from our site."

"You are positive, Dr. McCalliff?" the museum director, Michael Newman, asked.

Doctor? Of course she had a doctorate. Brody had just never thought of her in that light before. While he knew she was intelligent, he wasn't thinking about her education. He was more likely to think about her beauty and enthusiasm for her work or her loyalty to BJ or how her kisses turned him on. Unfortunately, she hadn't studied all those years to give up her career to become a housewife. She'd made that abundantly clear. So why couldn't he keep front and center the idea that nothing permanent between them could work? His values hadn't changed. He wanted his ranch, his son and a family.

But damn it, he wanted Lisa, too.

She might have dumped the biggest problem of his life into his lap, but she'd also brought him a bundle of joy. A bundle he intended to keep.

"I'll have my team fax documentation to verify the accuracy of my evaluation. I'd appreciate if you could hold these items until the police arrive to take them into custody.''

"As you wish," Newman told her.

"And thank you for your vigilance. Without your co-operation we might never have recovered the items."

"Mr. Newman—" Brody inserted himself into the conversation "—when did the seller say he'd contact you again?"

"This afternoon. Why?"

Brody didn't answer the director's question. "He didn't leave you a phone number where he could be called?"

"No. I'll tell you the same thing I told that sheriff I spoke to this morning. The seller said he was from out of town and wanted to do a little sightseeing."

"What did the man look like?" Lisa asked.

Newman's eyes narrowed behind thick glasses. "I'm sorry. I've never been good with people's faces."

"Was he white, Asian, African-American?" Brody asked.

"White—but tanned."

"Hair color?" Brody prodded.

"Black."

"Height?"

"Hmm. Between five-nine and six feet."

"That could fit Mark's description," Lisa replied.

"Unfortunately it could probably fit twenty-five percent of the males in this country," Brody said, trying to keep the irritation from his tone. "What about his age?"

"Twenty-five to thirty-five."

Lisa bit her bottom lip. "I wish I'd thought to bring a photograph."

"You know this man?" Newman gave her a puzzled frown.

"It's possible he might be my ex-brother-in-law. We aren't sure."

"Does Mark have a Web site for his PI firm?" Brody asked.

Lisa had no trouble following his line of thought. "I should have remembered that his picture's on his Web site's front page."

Newman locked the storage room behind them and led them to his office. He went straight to his computer keyboard, typed for a minute, then looked up. "The name of his Web site?"

"Mark Gilmore dot com."

One moment later Mark's Web site, with his picture, appeared on the monitor. Brody studied the face carefully so he would recognize him on sight. Mark possessed dark brown eyes, a Roman nose and dark hair beginning to recede behind a wide forehead. He had a smile that inspired sincerity and confidence. His most distinguishable feature was his misshapen cauliflower ear.

"Is that the man who tried to sell you my artifacts?" Lisa asked the museum director.

He shrugged. "I wish I could be more helpful, but I'm just not sure. I'm not good with faces," he repeated. His phone rang and he picked it up. "Hello?" He paused. "Yes. That will be fine. See you then." He placed the receiver back in the cradle. "He's returning at five o'clock, right before closing." He picked up the phone again. "I'll notify the police."

"Just a moment, please." Brody's hand closed over Newman's. "Let's think this through."

"What's to think about? The man's a thief. We should call the authorities."

"Under normal circumstances I'd agree with you, but suppose he's only a henchman. We might need to follow him to his boss."

"Isn't that a matter for the police?" Newman asked.

"Not necessarily. The cops' job is to catch a thief and put him behind bars."

A secretary knocked on the door, then entered. "Mr. Newman, a shipment of gemstones has arrived and requires your signature."

"If you'll excuse me?" Newman left them alone.

Lisa leaned a hip against the museum director's desk and folded her arms over her chest. She waited to speak until the door shut and there was no chance of their being overheard.

"Tell me why you don't want to bring in the police."

He admired the way she was willing to hear him out and consider his opinion. "If it's Mark, I was hoping to bargain with him, and I can't do that if he's under arrest."

"I don't understand. What kind of bargain?"

"If he's arrested for theft, I'm pretty certain he'll lose his PI license. He won't want that."

"Go on."

"So if we do him a favor and fail to report his theft, maybe he'll agree to let me adopt BJ."

"You're assuming a lot. We don't know who stole those artifacts."

"True."

"And if it's not Mark?"

"Maybe the thief will lead us to him."

"That's a real long shot."

"What choice do we have?"

"Without the police here, this guy could also get away."

"Or lead us to someone else. It's a chance I'm willing to take for an opportunity to legally adopt BJ. Besides, the museum will return the artifacts after you prove that they're yours, right?"

"Probably."

"So the worst-case scenario is that it's not Mark and a thief gets away—although I don't intend to let that happen."

"I'm not sure Newman will agree."

"We'll think of something."

"I suppose I could offer him the first exhibit of artifacts from our site in exchange for his cooperation."

Brody grinned. "Now you're thinking." He grabbed her hand and squeezed. "Come on."

"Where are we going?"

"I want to check out the building and then set a trap for our thief."

Chapter Ten

Lisa didn't think Brody's plan was all that great. However, since she didn't have a better idea, she didn't protest. So a half hour before the seller of the artifacts, a man going by the name of Jared Coleman, was scheduled to meet with the museum director, she waited in the reception area for Jared to announce himself to Newman's secretary.

Right on time, Jared strode into the office smoking a cigarette. Lisa shook her head slightly to indicate to Brody, who waited down the hallway but still in sight, that this man wasn't her ex-brother-in law. Despite her doubt that the thief would turn out to be Mark, disappointment swept over her. She knew how badly Brody wanted to speak with Mark and settle BJ's future, but she'd always thought his idea that Mark was behind the theft farfetched. Maritza's husband had resented her work, so she never discussed it with him. And this type of theft and sale took some knowledge, which Lisa doubted Mark had.

Still, she initiated plan B, curious to learn if Jared worked alone. She turned the page of the magazine and waited for the secretary to send Jared to meet Newman. Jared didn't appear the least bit nervous. He slouched in a chair, flipped to the comic-strip section of a newspaper and buried his nose in it. She noticed that he appeared to be older and heavier than Mark. And he looked sleazy, which the suit with shiny patches at the elbows reinforced.

Jared never once looked up, not until the secretary told him to go on down the hall. And it took him a moment to refold the paper exactly along its former lines before rising.

Lisa stood before Jared did, smoothed her skirt, checked her watch and spoke to the secretary. "If you don't mind, I'll peek in on Mr. Newman and tell him I'll come back tomorrow. My baby-sitter has to be home at five-thirty, and if I'm late again, she'll quit."

"Ma'am, you cannot barge into Mr. Newman's office," the secretary said.

"It'll be okay. Just take a minute." By the time Lisa began walking, she had to hurry to catch up with Jared, who was two strides ahead of her and lighting a new cigarette from the stub of his last one. She shot a friendly smile at him. "I won't take any of your time with the director, really."

Her purpose there was simply to distract Jared from the cracked-open door of the storage room where Brody had just hidden himself. As they walked by, she made sure to remain on Jared's opposite side, giving Brody space to exit and bump into the man.

She had no clue what Brody planned after that and was worried. He'd told her to leave the details to him and to stand guard outside the door. *Yeah, right.* As if she wasn't going inside to hear exactly what was said. Those artifacts were stolen from her site and she was entitled to answers. If Brody thought for one moment she'd allow him to play cowboy while she took the role of helpless female, he didn't understand how she operated. Besides, she didn't quite trust the gleam in Brody's eyes as he moved in on Jared, grabbed the man around the neck from behind and practically yanked him off his feet into the storage area.

Jared issued one surprised yelp and dropped his burning cigarette. She crushed the cigarette beneath her heel and followed the men inside, surprised how easily Brody had removed Jared from the hallway. Somehow she'd expected a scuffle. But Brody had performed the maneuver like some kind of commando.

When Jared's face began to turn red as he gasped for air, the plan became all too real. She didn't like the horror in the man's eyes or the way his mouth gaped open like that of a dying fish as he tried to breathe.

The greasy fries she'd had for lunch rolled around in her stomach. Lisa swallowed hard and tried to remember that Brody had promised not to do permanent damage. She thoroughly disliked the use of violence, and while she understood that threats might make the man talk, she'd thought those threats would be verbal.

With a turbulent gut and a heavy heart, she shut the door behind them. He frowned at her for disregarding their plan, but his attention focused on the man he held immobile. With Jared off balance and tipped backward onto Brody's hip and Brody's stranglehold on his throat, the man couldn't fight.

Brody's threat came out cool and low. "I want answers, so I'm going to let you breathe, pal. If I don't like your response, then you get no oxygen. Deal?"

The man nodded and Brody loosened his neck hold

slightly. Jared wheezed. Finally he drew in air and his chest expanded.

"Did you steal the artifacts from my ranch?"

"Don't know nothin' about a ranch." Brody's arm began to tighten on the man's neck and Jared spoke quickly. "But I stole the artifacts."

"And set the forest fire?" Brody demanded.

"Hell, no. I almost got burned alive in that damn fire."

The man's voice was so indignant that Lisa believed him, but then again, she recalled his cigarettes and figured he might just be a superb liar.

"Who was there with you?" Brody asked.

"No one. I swear it."

"How'd you know about the site?" she asked.

"From notes I found in your car."

"You started that stampede?"

Beads of sweat broke out on Jared's forehead. His gaze went to Lisa as if he expected her help. She looked at him coldly. "I suggest you tell us what we want to know."

"I just wanted the notes and tried a different angle to get to the car. I didn't know cows would spook that easily."

"How'd you know about her notes?" Brody asked.

"I got a contact—"

Muscles in Brody's arm bulged as he applied the choke hold. "I want a name."

"I don't have one."

Jared's eyes seemed to protrude from his face, and again she had to force her face into a mask to refrain from wincing. The thief tried to yank Brody's arm from his neck, but his strength was no match for that of a man who roped cattle for a living. Jared's feet kicked feebly. Maybe thirty seconds passed, no more, but they were a long thirty seconds. And when Brody allowed him to breathe, he wheezed and gasped and choked with a noise that sickened her.

"Who told you about the artifacts?" Brody asked.

"Donald. Donald Van Dyke."

Finally a name, one she thought sounded familiar but couldn't quite place.

Brody continued his questioning. "What's he look like?"

"Don't know. He told me what to do and promised me a hefty commission."

"How much?" she asked, his words striking her wrong. The Anasazi artifacts weren't valuable enough to warrant this kind of attention.

When Jared named his payment, she frowned and all of a sudden the memory fragments clicked into place. "I've heard of Donald Van Dyke. He deals with private collectors on the black market. But why would he have sent you to sell them to a museum?"

"I just follow orders."

"Tell us how to find him," Brody demanded.

"All I've got is a phone number." Jared spilled the number and she called the police.

An hour later, after the police officers left with Jared in custody, Brody and Lisa were finally alone in the museum lobby. Both of them were disappointed that Jared didn't seem connected to Mark, but instead, to Van Dyke. She'd always thought Brody's theory was a long shot; nevertheless, she'd hoped he would be right.

At least she now knew it hadn't been Mark who started that stampede. Maybe he still didn't have a clue as to her whereabouts.

On their way out of the museum, Brody turned to her. "You were supposed to stay outside the room while I questioned Jared. Didn't you trust me not to hurt him?"

She shrugged off her resentment that he should take over. "If I hadn't followed you inside, we might not have as much information."

"What do you mean?"

"The museum would never have paid enough for those objects to cover Jared's fee."

"What are you saying?"

"Donald Van Dyke sells to private collectors. It's almost as if someone wanted Jared to get caught."

"Why?"

"We need to find Donald Van Dyke. Something's not right. I suspect someone may have hired Mr. Van Dyke for their own purposes."

"Could Mark have hired Van Dyke?"

"Possibly." She paused to compose her words. She wanted Brody to understand the kind of man they were dealing with. "Mark's crafty. With his PI contacts, he has the knowledge and the skills to hire others to pull this off. But I don't understand his motive."

Brody put an arm around her shoulders and drew her against his side. "My guess is revenge. He wants to discredit you. And if you're fired because he's framed you for stealing your own artifacts, no court in the world would give you custody of BJ."

She sighed. Such a scheme seemed too complicated for Mark, but she didn't have another theory. "So what do we do now?"

"We make a few phone calls to find out if any

neighbors have seen Mark at home or if anyone has seen him at work.''

"Okay."

"And I could use a shower and a decent meal.'' He pulled her closer against his side. "It's probably time to check into a hotel."

A hotel?

He'd said the words innocently enough, but suddenly she felt as though she had a decision to make. Although they'd shared his home, she and the baby had stayed in the downstairs bedroom. Now BJ wasn't here to help keep a distance between them. Neither was his family or her archaeological team.

Did Brody just want sex or did he have feelings for her? Feeling strangely vulnerable, yet excited by the prospect of being alone with him, she tried to sort out her conflicting emotions. And failed.

OVER DINNER in the hotel dining room, Brody and Lisa caught each other up on what they'd learned in their phone calls during the past few hours. Brody had checked them into a two-bedroom suite in an upscale hotel, and when Lisa hadn't protested, he figured he stood a chance of making love to her tonight. When he poured red wine into her glass and her eyes sparkled with a sizzling heat, he felt even more encouraged. Although he kept telling himself that if the evening didn't turn out as he hoped, he wouldn't be too disappointed, but he knew he would be.

He kept wondering what her flesh would taste like, imagined her long legs sliding against his on cool sheets, and had difficulty following her words. Her burnished auburn hair gleamed in the light from the restaurant fireplace. Shadows emphasized her high cheekbones. Then he focused on her lush lips and was finally able to concentrate.

The enthusiasm in her tone warmed his heart as she gave him news from home.

"Mia said BJ is fine. But another of your nephews has come down with the chicken pox."

"I never had them, so maybe BJ won't get them, either." He ate his food, barely tasting the artichoke hearts or delicious salad dressing. His mind wasn't on his taste buds or his stomach, but the gorgeous woman sitting opposite him. When had she come to mean so much to him? During the stampede? The fire? Or when she'd come clean with her story and told him how she risked jail to kidnap his son to protect him from neglect and possibly worse? Brody didn't know. All he knew was that he didn't want to do one wrong thing to turn her away from him.

He pushed aside the notion that he was attracted to her because she was the one he couldn't have. Not permanently.

"Maritza and I had the worst cases of chicken pox. We were six and seven years old and miserable." She smiled in bittersweet memory. "We took turns scratching each other. I still have a few dimples on my shoulder blade where I made her scratch too hard."

He'd love to find those dimples and survey them. In fact, if the opportunity arose, he'd take his time removing her clothing, one item at a time, exposing and exploring every curve and valley.

He supposed he should contribute more to the conversation, but it wasn't easy. He chewed a bit of pork and swallowed. "Mark's neighbors and co-workers have seen no sign of him. I've hired two PIs to watch his business and residence day and night and to phone if they spot him.''

Lisa sipped her wine and looked at him over the brim of her glass. ''It would be ironic if Mark has gone on an innocent vacation. Or drank himself into a stupor and holed up with some lady friend.''

''Did Mark fool around on Maritza?''

''I don't think so.'' She paused with a bit of sweet potato partway to her mouth.

''But?''

''He had his secrets.''

''What do you mean?''

''He'd sometimes disappear and refuse to say where he'd gone.'' She dabbed her mouth with a linen napkin, leaving a smudge of pink gloss. ''He always claimed he was on a case.''

''You didn't believe him?''

''Maritza did.''

''Sounds to me like there might be another woman,'' he said.

''Maybe. My sister would have been suspicious if her husband cheated regularly. Although Mark was out of town in Reno and Las Vegas often, he always left the number and room of the hotel where he stayed. That sound like a cheating husband to you?''

''The men in my family are loyal.'' He drilled her with a stare, liking the way she tried to hold his gaze but couldn't quite do it. She might be smart and well educated, but when it came to flirtation, she hadn't quite gotten the hang of it. He knew she hadn't been fishing for his views on the matter of loyalty. No doubt if she wanted to know something, she'd ask him outright. He liked her upfront attitude, even enjoyed the mixed signals she probably wasn't even aware she was sending him. One moment her eyes sparkled with enthusiasm, the next they became shuttered as she retreated into herself. "I don't have much experience with exactly how cheating men lie to their wives. However, the cities you mentioned, Reno and Vegas, are both known for gambling."

She cocked her head in thought. When a lock of hair swished over her chin, he gently brushed it back. The pulse in her throat fluttered a bit, telling him that his touch had affected her more than she wanted to reveal—especially since she kept the conversation right on track.

"A gambling problem would explain Mark's lack of money. I never understood why they didn't buy a decent house in a better neighborhood when my sister made a good salary. I always wondered if perhaps she kept her earnings a secret from him to bolster his ego."

"Seems to me, Mark should have been happy that his wife could contribute to the family income."

"He resented her earning more than he did."

"Oh." Brody didn't know what to think about her statement. The likelihood of meeting a woman who earned more than he did had never seemed great enough to warrant a lot of thought.

"Too many people tie their self-worth to money. I've never understood that. To me it's more important to do work that I love." She sipped her wine and cocked an eyebrow. "You're suddenly quiet."

"Out here we tie a man's worth to many things. Land. cattle. Family. Friends. I wouldn't resent a woman who had more friends than I have. I don't think I could hold it against her if she earned more than I do."

She grinned. "Easy for you to say, since the chances of that happening are about zilch."

"Oh, I don't know. If she bought me my sailboat and swept me away to the Caribbean..."

She swirled the wine in the bottom of her glass, her fingers curling seductively around the stem, and when she looked up, she changed the subject. "I did hear from an associate that Van Dyke operates out of an antique shop in Dallas."

Obvious reluctance to reveal this information filled her tone. He resisted drumming his fingers on the tabletop. "Why didn't you tell about me about tracing Van Dyke to Dallas right away?"

She took a deep breath and let it out slowly. He tried really hard to keep his gaze from her expanding chest, but the V-necked silk top hugged her curves. The necklace dangling between her breasts enticed him.

"I don't want to be away from BJ too long and I don't want to think about flying to Dallas," she admitted.

He placed a finger on her forearm, swirled it over her wrist in a circle, taking interest in her fast pulse, which might be caused by either the thought of flying or possibly going back to the room with him. He prayed for the latter, because she wouldn't be nervous unless she was considering making love to him.

His voice was husky. "I could give you something else to think about."

"Like what?" She arched a playful eyebrow, but didn't pull away from his not-so-innocent caress.

"Me," he said simply. "You could think about me in the same way I'm thinking about you."

"I already am, but I haven't yet made up my mind."

Damn, the woman could turn him on. She didn't play games. She didn't hide her emotions. All his blood suddenly went south, and he reminded himself that she hadn't said yes, either. Walking in suddenly tight jeans to escort her to their room would be painful, but when he considered the delights he might yet share with her, the trip would be well worth the suffering. If she said yes.

He shoved back from the dinner table and tossed his napkin onto his half-eaten meal. "Are we done here?"

"Oh, I don't know," she teased him. "Don't you want dessert?"

"What I want is you."

The waitress brought over a bill and he signed it, scribbling his signature and room number on the check. He took Lisa's arm and together they left the dining room.

"Brody, what exactly do you want from me?"

At the tremor in her voice, he stopped right in the middle of the lobby.

"I was hoping that we both wanted each other."

She bit her bottom lip. "I'm not sure that's enough."

"Maybe you're making this too complicated."

"And you're making it too simple," she countered.

"Am I?" He kissed her, gently, showing her with his actions how much he wanted her. And when she didn't pull back, didn't hesitate to match him move for move, he realized he had to slow down.

They pulled apart and he placed an arm around her shoulders. They crossed the lobby, heading toward the bronze mirrored elevators. He reminded himself again that the lady had not yet said yes to lovemaking. He could live with that. In fact, as long as he could kiss her again soon, he would be a very happy man.

LISA WASN'T SURE exactly when Brody convinced her to make love. Maybe it was the moment she realized that she'd lost the battle to guard her heart. She wished she could pinpoint the precise moment she'd fallen in love, but like an apple growing and ripening on a tree, her emotions just reached critical mass— and fell. Her feelings had grown during the fire when he'd so heroically saved their lives, and again when he'd forgiven her for lying to him, and again when he'd kissed her. She only knew that wanting him felt right in her heart, wrong in her head, but this might be her one shot to make love with Brody. She wasn't going to miss it.

She liked how he treated her. She liked how he made her feel about herself. Feminine. Desirable. And he did so without ignoring her intelligence. For now, that would be enough, and she'd let the future take care of itself.

"When did you first decide you wanted to make love?" she asked him on the way up to their suite in the elevator.

He kissed her brow. "Oh, no, you don't. I'm not answering a trick question."

She whispered into his mouth. "A trick question?"

"Mm. If I say that I wanted to make love to you from the moment we met, I'm shallow for being turned on by your terrific auburn hair and magnificent long legs. And if I say I only wanted you after I got to know you—because I adore how you use your mind—then I didn't appreciate your looks."

She chuckled at his explanation. "Clever man."

The elevator doors swished open, and they ambled down the hallway to the suite. He unlocked the door and the scent of fresh lilies surprised her, since they hadn't been there before. The lilies sat in a beautiful crystal vase, right on a shelf in the marble foyer.

She'd always loved flowers. His gesture might be mushy and sappy, but she couldn't help appreciating it. "When did you arrange—"

"I can't tell you all my secrets."

"Sure you can," she said, but as his head dipped toward hers to share a kiss, all thought focused on his mouth, the sensual line of his lips, the scent of wine on his breath, the angle of his jaw as he turned slightly to make their mouths mesh.

The urgency of his kiss inflamed the smoldering embers he'd kindled during dinner. She responded by winding her arms around his neck, threading her fingers into his hair and arching her back. His arms closed around her, and although they stood chest to chest, hips to hips, thigh to thigh, she resented the layers of clothing between them. She yearned to be flesh to flesh, to give him much more than her mouth. She wanted to love him, all of him.

"Let me go," she demanded, jerking back.

He raised an inquiring eyebrow. "Something wrong?"

"Oh, yeah," she teased, surprised at her boldness. "What?"

"You have on too many clothes." She couldn't believe she'd just said that, then stopped her self-censoring. She'd made up her mind to make love and she fully intended to do so and enjoy every minute, even if later she'd have to pay for it.

"Too many clothes? That can be rectified." With a happy grin he swept her into his arms.

She let out a tiny yelp of surprise, then settled her cheek against his chest and enjoyed the ride. A woman her height didn't often get carried, and the romantic notion made her warm from the top of her head to her dangling toes.

When he didn't head straight for the bedroom, she glanced at him. "Where are we going?"

"Close your eyes."

"Okay." She did what he asked and then he spun around until she lost all track of direction before he stalked off to who knew where. "You're just full of surprises this evening."

"You bring them out of me."

She heard a door open, felt cool air on her face. "Can I open my eyes?"

"Not yet."

He climbed a few stairs. She was thin, but tall, certainly no lightweight, yet he carried her with ease. His breathing remained steady and she snuggled into him, enjoying the aroma of his aftershave and the strength of his powerful arms.

She hadn't noticed any stairs in their suite. "Where are you taking me?"

"If I told you, it wouldn't be a surprise."

"Well, I hope it's someplace private."

"It is."

"Someplace where we can take off our clothes?"

He chuckled. "You sure do know how to tease."

"Thank you, sir. I'll take your words as a compliment." She fingered his shirt and unfastened the top two buttons. She smoothed her palms over his neck, his collarbone, his pectoral muscles. His flesh was warm as sun-baked honey, smooth to her touch. For a dark-haired man he had surprisingly little hair on his chest, just a light dusting, which she eagerly explored.

Her fingers found a whorl of hair and she tugged lightly.

"Ow."

"Let me kiss it and make it better."

She opened his shirt wider and licked the spot, found his nipple, bit down just hard enough for him to jerk. Then she licked him there, too.

"Woman, if you aren't careful, I'll drop you."

"Mmm. I'll take my chances." She went right back to teasing his nipple with her tongue as he carried her around a corner, then up more steps.

"Sorry you didn't take the elevator?" she asked.

"Are you kidding? I would have missed holding you in my arms."

He stopped walking and climbing.

"Can I open my eyes now?"

"Not yet, but I'm going to set you on your feet."

"Okay."

He guided her, then placed her hands on a railing. They were obviously outside. She could feel the breeze on her face and hear the sound of traffic far below. They must be on a balcony. Or the roof.

He moved up behind her and wrapped his arms around her. "Tilt back your head. Lean against me," he instructed.

"Now?"

"Now. Open your eyes."

Chapter Eleven

Lisa had seen stars before but never anything like this. They glittered like diamonds on a backdrop of lush black velvet. Mars had a reddish glow and Venus was almost as bright as the moon, although nowhere near as large. To the west, Orion's belt hung over the sky, and she could just make out the Big Dipper. She'd been partially right about their being outside. They were on the building's roof, but high walls had been built around the patio's edges to block out the city lights below them.

"Wow. This is some spot."

She stood in his arms for a long time, content to lean against him and study the fabulous view, content to push the doubts, the hesitations, the I-can't-believe-I'm-doing-this qualms aside. The high walls sheltered them from the cool night breeze, and when she finally stopped stargazing, she glimpsed patio loungers, potted palms with a hammock strung between two of them, a rooftop pool and several dining tables.

Brody planted a kiss behind her ear. "We have the place to ourselves until morning."

"This is wonderful, but how did you know that…"

"I didn't know. I wasn't taking you for granted,

not by any means, but I kept hoping.'' She wondered if he always knew the right thing to say. If he was always so smooth or if his mouth was as dry with tension as hers. ''And in case you're wondering,'' he continued, ''I've never been here before. Mom told me about this hotel, and I was saving the experience for the right moment.''

She noted he didn't say the right woman, but she was no longer so concerned whether he only felt lust. She intended to leave eventually, anyway, so what difference could it make? The attraction between them was real and right now. The reasons for it didn't matter.

He picked up a remote-control device and pressed buttons. The still pool suddenly frothed from underwater jets, the bubbling sound mixing with the rustle of palm fronds. ''How about a swim?''

She bent down and trailed her fingers through the water. ''It's even heated.''

She straightened and unfastened the top button of her blouse. He closed a hand over hers. ''I've been dreaming about doing that. Please don't deny me.''

''I won't deny you anything. Not tonight.''

At her words, he looked straight into her eyes. ''Tonight is for both of us. Whatever you want, you tell me, okay?''

Love for this man swelled and crested. He'd created the perfect setting, the perfect moment, and he'd made her feel like the perfect woman, special and cherished.

The evening possessed a magical quality that seemed to take over and encapsulate them in a private bubble. Her heart pounded so hard the blood roared in her ears. But she found standing before him while he slowly unfastened her blouse more sensuously exciting than she'd thought possible. She liked his attention on her, entirely focused, entirely fascinated.

"You're so beautiful. And your skin—" he caressed a tiny spot in the V of her open blouse with his thumb "—is exquisite."

She trembled beneath his touch. He couldn't possibly comprehend how much she wanted him to hurry up. "You dreamed of us...together?"

"Oh, yeah. And I always woke up too soon." His tone reminded her of mouthwatering crème brûlée or exotic sunsets over Machu Picchu and starved her for more of his touch. But he seemed quite content to go down her blouse button by button, barely parting the folds.

If he was going to take forever undressing her, she might as well get started on his shirt. Unlike him, she had little patience, practically ripping the buttons open in her haste. But after she removed his shirt, she took her time, enjoying the feel of her palms on his chest, breathing in his male scent. She brushed his dusting of chest hair, lingered over his nipples, wondered if he was ever going to slip her blouse off her shoulders.

Her entire body quivered in anticipation, but then he angled his mouth over hers, demanding what he wanted. A kiss hot enough to brand steel, one that seared to her toes as he took and took and took with his lips and tongue, needy and fierce, promising even more pleasure to come.

Sometime during their kiss, he expertly removed her bra. The cool air contrasted with his heat and she arched into him, releasing a soft moan. His arms closed around her and he lowered her to one of the loungers.

Then her hands busily tugged at his belt and zipper

and boxers. Damn. She'd forgotten his shoes and socks. No matter how much she tugged, his slacks weren't going to come off over those shoes. But she'd shoved the material over his ankles and couldn't reach his shoes.

At her groan of failure, he chuckled. In frustration she sat up and scooted to the foot of the lounger. "I've made a total mess of—"

He kicked shoes, socks, boxers and slacks off with ease and drew her back down. "You know, you're cute when you're in a hurry and frustrated."

Her hands slid below his waist to explore. "I'll show you frustrated."

"Easy."

Her hands closed around his sex, appreciating the taut hardness that told her he wanted her just as much as she wanted him. "Sorry, did I hurt you?"

He grabbed her wrists and tugged her away from him. "You feel too good."

"That's not possible."

"I'll take that as a challenge," he murmured low in her ear.

He drew her over him so that her back rested on his chest and she once again faced the night sky and the stars. She thought he would attempt to remove her slacks. Instead, he settled his hands on her waist and began to slide his palms up and down over her ribs, never quite touching her breasts.

She could feel his erection snuggled against her bottom and reached down to unsnap her slacks.

"Uh-uh. You agreed to let me do that."

"That was before I knew you intended to take all damn year," she complained.

"Such impatience." He chuckled and allowed the

tips of his fingers to brush the undersides of her breasts.

Her already erect nipples tightened to hardened points of need.

She grabbed his hands and placed them over her breasts, exactly where'd she wanted them for so long. "That's better."

"For such a reckless wench, you sure took a long time deciding you wanted me."

"Is that a complaint?" she asked, sighing as he used the pad of his fingertips to make tiny circular motions over her very sensitive nipples.

"An observation."

"So what else have you observed?" she asked, enjoying the contrast of the peaceful sky overhead and the riot of swirling joy, need, love and passion brewing within her.

"You've captivated me from the first moment we met." He plucked at her nipple, which made every nerve receptor tingle. "And now that all my fantasies are coming to fruition, the reality is even better."

"You do know how to flatter a woman. Especially since we've barely kissed."

"Barely?" He growled into her ear and took her words just the way she'd hoped—as an invitation. Only, from her position on her back he couldn't kiss her on the mouth. So instead, he blazed a trail of hot kisses down her ear and neck while his clever fingers continued to conjure magic over her breasts.

She turned her head to meet his mouth and their lips slanted, clashed, fused. Ah, she wanted this man, and as pure molten heat threaded to her core, she turned over in his arms, impatient with her slacks for separating them. She wanted the contact of his flesh against hers. She needed chest-to-chest, hip-to-hip, thigh-to-thigh contact, ached for his heartbeat to reverberate against hers.

But she'd promised him that he could undress her, so she simply captured his mouth with hers, arched her breasts against him and proceeded to rub against him like a cat. He groaned, wrapped his arms around her and wound his fingers into her hair.

When she came up for air, he finally unzipped her slacks, slipped his thumbs into her panties, and she wriggled free of her clothing. She knelt by his side ready to attack him, but made herself think practical thoughts.

"Do we have a condom?" she half asked, half demanded.

"I thought we were going for a swim," he countered with a lazy drawl that made her want to smack him upside the head. He acted as if he could wait forever. She couldn't, however, and she didn't know whether to be insulted or impressed.

"We can swim later," she suggested.

He reached for her and tugged her back on top of him. "I believe you offered me dessert."

She ended up straddling his stomach. "What are you talking about?"

He reached up and stroked her breasts. "Back at the restaurant, you asked me if I wanted dessert."

She could barely think with every nerve ending so taut. "You said you wanted me."

"Ah, so now I can have both—you and dessert." He lifted her hips and shifted under her, and then his warm breath blew on the heart of her femininity. "You said you wouldn't deny me..."

"Oh."

His tongue licked, stroked and caressed, delicately, persistently, tantalizingly. She reached down to hold on and his fingers laced with hers. "Oh, my. Yes."

"Right here?"

"Yes."

"You sure?"

"Yes."

"Positive?"

"Don't...stop...or..."

"Or what?"

"I'll...kill...you."

He chuckled, the combination of his warm breath and his talented tongue driving her over the edge into an orgasm so intense that it left her quivering. And then he eased back under her and somehow, while she was recovering, he'd donned protection.

Her head still spinning from pure pleasure, she brought him inside her. Her hips took over as she rode him under the glittering black sky. And later, much later, his fingers dipped between her thighs, and they came together again, explosively, lustfully, wondrously.

He held her against his chest and their heartbeats slowly recovered, but no matter what happened, no matter where her career took her, she would never forget this marvelous time together.

She kissed him. "Thank you."

"No. I'm the one who should be thanking you." He grinned at her. "Even if you did threaten to kill me."

"You're going to hold my words against me, aren't you?" She replied, very glad he couldn't see the heat rising on her face. Although she could get used to that kind of teasing from him, especially when it came after such delicious pleasure, she wasn't so accustomed to this kind of intimacy that she felt all that comfortable.

He rolled onto his side, stood and helped her to her feet. "How about that swim?"

She didn't yet understand how or why she'd felt easy and sure of herself while making love, but now shyness and uncertainty grabbed her. She felt oddly out of sync. As she lowered herself into the heated water, she appreciated the fact that he wasn't in a talkative mood. She needed to sort out her confusing mood shift.

She splashed water on her face, then ducked under the surface and flicked back her wet hair. Making love to him had overwhelmed her. Short-circuited her nervous system until all she could think was *wow!* Such a juvenile response, and now, what was wrong with her?

She should feel elated. She should be annoyed that the man was swimming laps, instead of cuddling with her, yet she didn't mind at all. She needed to settle her own thoughts. Match the cold and sketchy edginess in her gut to a rationale that made sense.

And then it hit her like a tidal wave.

He'd shown her how good it could be between them, and now she'd have to go on with her life, knowing what she was missing. Go to sleep over the next weeks, months and years, with the memory of this night to remind her of her loss. Grabbing on to happiness tonight would cost her dearly.

Falling in love with the man was the dumbest thing she'd ever done—like she'd had a choice. And they hadn't been just good together, oh, no. They'd been supernova, exploding spectacular.

She'd fallen in love once before, and then she'd walked away, regretful but positive she'd made the right decision. She'd loved her college sweetheart Aaron with all the passion of a first love. But when he'd chosen to become a cabdriver to thumb his nose at his parents, she'd decided he was simply too immature.

But this time when she left, she would be walking away from BJ, too.

When Brody popped up in the water in front of her, she was so deep in thought that it took her a moment to react to the wave of his hand in front of her face.

"Space to Lisa."

She blinked and refocused her thoughts. "Sorry."

"You okay?"

"Quite sated, thank you very much." She attempted to keep the conversation light. No way was she ready to discuss her thoughts. She didn't even want to think about leaving him, never mind saying the words out loud.

He saw right through her. "That's not what I meant."

"What did you mean?" she countered, tossing the conversational ball right back at him.

"You tell me."

She might not be good at hiding her thoughts, but she could be stubborn enough to avoid them. "Tell you what?"

"You had such a fierce expression in your eyes. What were you thinking about?"

"It's too dark to see my face."

"Darling, I could *hear* you think."

No matter how intuitive he might be at the moment, she remained firm and not the least bit inclined to let him in on her private thoughts. Distraction might work. "I never noticed that your ears were so big."

He chuckled, his laughter deep and rich. "That's because you were too busy noticing my big—"

"Nose?" she teased.

"My big—"

"Feet?"

He chuckled and ducked her under the water. She went down easily; in fact, she went low enough to grab his feet and pull him under with her. They both pushed off from the bottom and broke the surface, gasping for breath as they frolicked some more in the pool.

Later they made love again under the stars. And sometime in the early morning they returned to the suite where they slept in one bed, their bodies spooned together, awoke and made love yet again. A little later she opened her eyes to find the covers kicked off the bed, the pillows somewhere on the carpeting, but her head pillowed on his shoulder and his body keeping her warm.

The perfect night was almost over and she dreaded what came next. Closing her eyes, she drifted back to sleep.

THE CELL PHONE rang, pulling Brody out of a deep sleep. He opened his eyes, surprised to see broad daylight, checked his watch and couldn't recall the last time he'd slept until eleven. But then, he and Lisa hadn't slept much last night. They'd made love three times and each time had been better than the last. Now she cuddled beside him, so deeply asleep that she hadn't even flinched at the sound of the phone.

Brody fumbled for the phone on the nightstand,

and grabbed it before it could ring again. "Yeah?" he said.

"And good morning to you, too, dear." His mom's cheery voice ignored his grouchiness, yet she still managed to let him know exactly what she thought of his manners.

He tried and failed to make his voice less hoarse, less like he'd spent the night making love. "What's up?"

"You were going to call last night and give me the latest," she reminded him with a chuckle. "Did you finally try out that hotel with the rooftop I suggested?"

"Mom."

"You like her, don't you?"

He'd dated women for years and his mom had never before asked him that particular question. She must have sensed that Lisa was special.

"Can we change the subject?"

"Sure. You already told me what I wanted to know." She sounded smug.

He filled her in on the little they'd learned from Jared yesterday. "We're heading to Dallas."

"Fine. I've some shopping to do. I'm leaving the baby with Amanda, okay?" Brody's sister-in-law would take excellent care of the baby. No worries there. "I have two ranch hands standing guard at the house, one at the gate and several on yard detail. They have instructions not to let anyone inside."

"Thanks, Mom. BJ should be fine."

"Bye, darling. Love you."

"I love you, too, Mom." He hung up the phone and snuggled with Lisa. While he couldn't go back to sleep, he enjoyed the intimacy amd contentment that came with waking up beside her, knowing they would spend the day together. Whatever happened, he would never regret her coming into his life. She'd given him a precious gift last night. She'd given him herself, open and honest and lusty and giving. One fantastic package that had brought him one surprise after another.

He'd never expected his feelings to run so deep. The thought of this woman spending the rest of her life in jail for bringing BJ to him stabbed hard, made him anxious to fix the problem. But how? He was guarding BJ and hiring private investigators to keep watch for Mark. Except for following the lead to Van Dyke in Dallas—a long shot—what else could he do?

Perhaps they should just return to the ranch. File papers in court. If he was lucky, maybe Mark would never show up anywhere again to contest the adoption. Maybe his disappearance had nothing to do with the fire or the theft from Lisa's site. A private investigator must make a lot of enemies during his career. Perhaps an old client had come out of the woodwork.

And maybe snow wouldn't fall in the Rocky Mountains this winter.

No matter how cozy lying next to Lisa was, Brody's impatience wouldn't allow him to stay in bed for long. He got up and headed to the bathroom with his cell phone. If they were heading to Dallas today, he needed to check with the airlines. However much he hoped he could talk Lisa into another flight in his private plane, he wouldn't count on it. But just in case, he called the airport and ordered his plane refueled. Last, he ordered a full room-service breakfast—scrambled eggs with fresh orange juice, hot blueberry muffins and crisp bacon, coffee and fresh

fruit—then headed into the shower, trying to ignore
the ominous feeling in his gut.

MARK SET DOWN his binoculars on a rock. The fools
on the ranch had no idea he was up in the mountains
with a clear view of all they did. Or that he'd tapped
into their phones and could listen to every call.

Apparently from the conversation with dear old
mom, Lisa and Brody had hooked up last night. Mark
couldn't even imagine Ms. Hoity-Toity, the ice queen,
giving any man pleasure. Around him her tongue was
sharp enough to leave razor cuts. Her witchlike green
eyes reminded him of shards of glass that could slice
and dice as she looked down her nose at him with a
perpetual sneer of disapproval.

Camping out on the side of a mountain had several
advantages, like avoiding nosy town folk, but he sure
could use a shower and some hot food. He'd been
afraid a fire might cause some suspicious cowboy to
come investigate. So he'd been roughing it, and camping wasn't his idea of fun. Perhaps he should spend
a few hours in search of a more appealing site. In his
mind, no site was perfect unless it was a plush Vegas
hotel with a professional who knew how to please a
man after a night of poker.

Mark scratched a mosquito bite, annoyed that
Brody and Lisa were enjoying themselves and irritated that the rancher kept his son under constant
guard. Still, he doubted the ranch hands would react
like trained secret-service agents if Mark created an
emergency or a diversion that would allow him to take
back his son.

He even considered calling in the authorities, who
would simply go in legally, take the baby and arrest

the bitch for kidnapping. But first he wanted her to fail in the career she loved so much. The uppity female thought she could outsmart him, just because she held a doctorate. Well, Miss Doctorate was about to find out that she'd made a gigantic mistake when she'd gone up against him.

He'd already started down this road and couldn't turn back, if he reported her, he'd have to answer questions about why he'd waited so long to report the crime, and then he'd have to respond to questions of why he hadn't taken back the baby himself. No doubt, they'd question him about the fire, and while he couldn't be tied to the crime with evidence, his reputation would suffer. Business would evaporate.

Much better to stick to his plan of revenge and ultimate triumph. He killed another mosquito with the same satisfaction as knowing that Miss Know-It-All had a traitor in her midst. While he didn't understand why anyone would bother stealing those artifacts when they were worth so little, he recognized that Lisa felt quite differently about them. Good.

She'd be upset. The woman hated failure and he intended to take her down a few pegs—publicly.

Just wait until she learned what he had in store for her.

Chapter Twelve

The flight to Dallas in Brody's plane didn't bother Lisa as much this time, and she felt confident she might eventually conquer her flying phobia. During the smooth flight, her stomach hadn't done any flip-flops. She'd been proud that she hadn't needed to clutch the seat except during takeoff and landing. Perhaps having found the courage to follow her heart and make love to Brody last night had made her a braver soul. Still, once the plane had landed, her shoulders ached from the tension of holding herself stiff for hours.

As Brody taxied the aircraft to a complete stop under a sunny Dallas sky, she released her seat belt with a measure of relief. She anticipated the sun on her face, breathing in summery Texas air and stretching her cramped leg muscles.

But the moment Brody unlatched the door, she heard a police siren heading in their direction. She climbed from the plane, her stomach reknotting.

Relax.

From the air she'd noted that the private airport ran alongside a highway. The cops were probably after a speeder. Or on the way to a car accident.

So what were two police cars doing barreling down the tarmac? Straight at them.

Oh, God. Mark must have finally reported the kidnapping.

Her knees shook and the blood seemed to drain from her head. She thought she might faint.

Beside her, Brody took her hand and squeezed. "Take it easy."

Two police officers exited their respective vehicles and approached cautiously. A tall, skinny cop with a tanned face and a nervous tic by his eye and an overweight policewoman with blond hair in need of a root job approached.

"I'm Officer Robins and this is Officer Diaz. Ma'am, are you Lisa McCalliff?"

"Yes."

"You're under arrest."

Lisa gasped and her knees practically buckled. It was one thing to contemplate this moment, but the reality was much worse than she'd imagined. She'd failed to protect BJ. All her efforts had been for nothing.

I'm so sorry, little guy. Sorry, Maritza. Sorry, Brody, for the mess I've made of your life.

The police had found her and they would find BJ, who would be sent back to Mark. She'd failed big time. Her best hadn't been good enough. Mark had outsmarted her.

Until now she'd always thought of the police as honorable men and women on the right side of morality. But not now.

She was going to jail.

So long, sunshine. So long, career. So long, Brody and BJ.

They were going to lock her away.

"Turn around and place your hands behind your back."

She might never again be free to enjoy her life. To carry on her work, to enjoy the people she loved. She'd never again hold little BJ in her arms or kiss Brody good-night. She'd no longer have the luxury of feeling torn between her career and the man she loved.

The police officer read Lisa her rights. Brody stepped back and she couldn't bear to look at him. He appeared calm, but then, she was nearly hysterical, so by comparison anyone would look calm.

"Why are you arresting her?" Brody asked.

"Sorry, sir."

"What are the charges?" he asked again.

"Sorry, sir. By law we don't have to tell you that."

At the police officer's response, Brody's eyes narrowed.

Cold metal clicked over her wrists, and all too quickly the officer was ducking her head and helping her into the back seat of the car. She didn't understand why the police had arrested her and not Brody, but was glad that his future hadn't been annihilated along with hers.

And she was fiercely glad that they'd made love last night, that she hadn't wasted the opportunity. Once they locked her up, her memories might be all she had to keep her sane.

Brody spoke quickly. "Don't say a word, Lisa. I'll get you the best attorney in Dallas and pay the bail."

She nodded, although she didn't think murderers or kidnappers got bail, but she didn't speak. Humiliation washed over her, but then the size of her failure drowned that out, and her failure would take others with her. Poor little BJ.

Leaning back, she closed her eyes. She had no idea how long the ride to the police station took.

She drew deep into her own thoughts, her own world and she stayed there while they fingerprinted and photographed and processed her. She didn't need the cops to tell her why she'd been arrested; she'd known since she'd taken BJ from Mark that this moment might arrive. And since the police officers hadn't questioned her, they needn't have read her her rights or even told her why she'd been arrested. She'd seen a character on *NYPD Blue* once in a similar sort of mess, but she'd never thought she'd find herself in a holding cell, waiting for an arraignment to appear before a judge.

Brody would do his best to attain a top-notch attorney, but she didn't expect to get off on a legal technicality. She was guilty and without a shred of evidence to back up her claim that Mark had neglected BJ—not that evidence would matter, anyway. She'd broken all kinds of state and federal laws, and no doubt the FBI had a case file on her.

Processed and uncuffed, she sat in a holding cell on a concrete bench behind a locked and barred door, and dropped her face into her hands. The worst part, the absolute worst part was that once the authorities sorted out the mess, BJ would go back to Mark. She could forgive herself almost anything, but not her failure to protect her innocent nephew.

"Lady, you want your one phone call?" a police officer asked her.

She shook her head.

"Suit yourself."

Lisa knew no one in Dallas and besides, Brody would do his best for her. Still, despair settled over her like a chilling mist. Drawing her legs to her chest, she held her knees and rocked back and forth. She'd seen bad times in her life, but never had she lost all hope.

Such deep helplessness frightened her because she saw no way out. Literally or figuratively. Her cell consisted of a seatless toilet in plain view of the police officer guarding the cell, a concrete bed where she could lie down and a sink. Overheard fluorescent lights chased away every shadow. There was no one to talk to, nothing to read. No television set. All she could do was sit and rock or pace the floor of the eight-by-ten foot space, alone with her thoughts and her failure.

She'd promised Maritza to take BJ to his father, but her planning should have been better. Maybe she should have taken the baby out of the country and sent Brody a message to meet his son overseas. Maybe she should have—

Stop it.

Being cooped up in this cell was bad enough. She didn't have to torture herself with should-have and could-have recriminations.

But what else did she have to think about? The minutes ticked by so slowly she wanted to scream from the boredom. The years ahead suddenly seemed endless.

Another few hours which seemed like months, passed. The police officer finally unlocked her door. "The judge is ready for you now."

Lisa forced herself to her feet. She expected to be transferred by police car to a courtroom, but instead, she was led to a room with a television monitor. On the monitor, she could see a courtroom with a judge, Brody and an attorney. The bailiff read a case number. The attorney argued with a DA. They mentioned stealing money, not a baby. She never once heard the word kidnapping.

As much as she wanted to ask questions, she had enough sense to remain silent. If the authorities didn't know about the kidnapping, then maybe her arrest had something to do with the stolen artifacts. Had she been framed for stealing from her site? It was the only other thing she could think of that made any sense at all.

Bail was set.

She was getting out of here.

Yes.

She didn't understand the charges, had no idea how Brody had succeeded, but her heart lifted with renewed hope. If they were releasing her, then maybe her situation wasn't as serious as she'd believed.

Another hour later she flew down the hall straight into Brody's arms. She wanted to believe that the nightmare was over, but feared it was just beginning. As much as she would have liked to stand there and let him hold her, she needed to know what was going on.

She looked into his eyes and knew he was as upset as she. "I don't understand. They arrested me for stealing?"

"Not here."

He ushered her into an air-conditioned car. After sitting on concrete, the leather seat seemed the height of luxury.

Brody slid behind the wheel. "You were arrested for embezzlement."

"What!"

"The funds from the university for the archaeological dig have been transferred to your personal bank account and then were withdrawn."

"But I didn't—"

"Did Maritza have access to those accounts?"

"Yes."

"Well, maybe Mark forged a few signatures."

"Why?" She took a moment to digest his news. She hadn't been arrested for kidnapping or theft of the artifacts, but embezzlement. The news came out of left field. Nothing made sense to her, and after the horrible hours in that cell, she didn't trust herself to think clearly. "Why would Mark set me up for embezzlement?"

"Revenge. I suspect your reputation may never be the same."

That no longer seemed so important, not when measured against kidnapping charges. Hopefully, if Mark had forged her signature, the truth could eventually come to light and she could prove her innocence. Her major concern was still BJ.

"Or maybe Mark needed the money he took from your account," Brody suggested. "Or he wanted to delay us until Van Dyke could disappear. I hired another PI to check on Van Dyke. He's gone. Left the city."

Brody's cell phone rang. He pulled the car into a parking lot, then answered. "Hello."

His face paled and he hit the speaker button.

"SOMEONE JUST TRIED to sneak into the house to steal BJ." Mia's voice sounded tearful.

Brody repeated the news to Lisa. He reacted on autopilot, outwardly calm, but racked by gripping fear for his child, anger that he couldn't go to the law, and sympathy for Lisa, who had already been through so much. However, he didn't even consider keeping the news from her. She loved the baby as much as he did.

"Don't worry, BJ's safe," his mom told him. "I shouldn't have gone into town to shop, and I'm heading back to the ranch now. I won't let the baby out of my sight again."

"And the intruder?" Brody asked, his heart pumping too hard. Adrenaline had kicked in the moment he'd heard that BJ was in danger, and now he had no one to chase, no one to fight.

"He got away."

"How?"

"Out the window. He must have gassed the two men outside the baby's room, because when Ken found them, they were so groggy he couldn't wake them. Luckily your brother heard the dog barking and came running. Otherwise…"

Brody owed Ken big time and made a note to thank his brother. "When did this happen?"

"Just after it got dark. After Ken came running, the intruder went out the window."

"The second-story window?"

"He slid down a rope and had a motorcycle stashed alongside the house. He headed straight for the hills. By the time the hands could saddle the horses and follow, they'd lost him. Evan and Riley are following the bike tracks in the dark, but whoever he is, he knows how to hide a trail."

"Can we fly back tonight?" Lisa asked Brody.

"Sure. I'm instrument-rated, but are you okay with flying in the dark?"

"Yes."

She sounded very sure that she could handle herself, and he ended his mother's call and made arrangements at the airport for the plane's refueling. He knew BJ would be safe. If he knew his mother, she would place even more guards around BJ. They would be fine. But his gut churned with the need to return home.

"Does Mark ride a motorcycle?"

"I don't know." She threaded her hand through her hair, realized it was a mess and started to braid it. "He never spoke much about his past to me. Since Maritza knew I didn't like him, we didn't discuss him that much."

"What kind of physical shape is he in?"

She finished the braid and clipped the tail with some gadget from her purse. With her hair pulled back from her face, she looked younger, more vulnerable. But her keen mind was focused on their problem.

"Mark might drink too much, but he sweats off the beer in the gym. He keeps a set of weights in his garage and uses them regularly. And he jogs a few miles a day."

"So he could climb into Mom's house through a second-story window?"

"Easily."

She'd already told him her ex-brother-in-law was a streetwise PI. With his commando training and his athletic abilities, he sounded like a regular James Bond. Great. And Mark had surprised them in Dallas, timing her arrest to take place while he attempted to take the baby back in Colorado. Obviously, to pull this off, he'd somehow been watching their every move. The man was operating at high efficiency, seemingly a few steps ahead of them—except that BJ was safe in his crib. Mark had failed to take the baby.

But Brody had no doubt he'd try again.

Brody concentrated on his driving, but his thoughts disturbed him. "I wish I knew how Mark knows what we're doing almost before we do it."

"Is it possible he tapped your cell phone?" she asked.

"I doubt it. But I've been in constant communication with the ranch." Suddenly the pieces clicked into place. The communications that had been jammed on the mountain. Now Mark's uncanny timing. He had access to high-tech equipment, and if he didn't care about breaking laws, he could have heard every word Brody and Mia had exchanged.

Brody stepped on the gas, heading straight for the airport. Coming to Dallas had been a waste of time, and he regretted every moment it would take to fly home. But now that he knew how Mark was getting his information, it was time to set a trap.

"Can I borrow your cell phone?" Lisa asked.

He handed it to her without much curiosity. She probably wanted to check in with her team.

"Eric, it's Lisa McCalliff."

But then, no one on her team had the name of Eric.

"Sorry to bother you at this time of night. I just want you to know that I will personally replace the funds. Somehow I'll find a way to pay back the university, but—"

She paused and stiffened. Whatever the man was saying to her couldn't have been pleasant. Her tone sharpened. "Eric, give me credit for a little sense. If

I was going to steal from my site, which I didn't, I wouldn't try to sell such simple artifacts to a museum where I'd likely get caught, now would I? And I believe that my signature was forged. When the bank inspects those checks, I expect you to eat those words.''

And then she ended the call.

''Problem?''

''Eric not only thinks I stole those funds, he accused me of stealing the artifacts, too.''

''Doesn't he know that you were with the team at the time, running from the fire?''

''He thinks I hired Jared Coleman to resell the artifacts—as if I would be so stupid. Let's see. First I spend years getting my doctorate, I finally get my first dig and then I throw it all away for money?''

Her tone was angry and he much preferred this to the defeat he'd seen in her face when the police had arrested her. She lifted her chin and the fight in her tone made his nerves settle. ''Eric is insecure, so anyone's success makes him nervous. He especially resents that women are in the field, competing for opportunities and recognition with men.''

''Is there much of that on college campuses these days?''

''You'd be surprised.''

BACK AT THE RANCH, Brody insisted on speaking outdoors on the back porch, with the television turned up high inside. His rationale made sense to Lisa. If Mark had bugged the phones, he could have also bugged the house. Tomorrow a specialist would come in and search Mia's house, as well as Brody's, for listening devices, but meanwhile, they took precautions.

The cool Colorado night air with the aroma of fresh pine and sweet grass welcomed her. Just this afternoon when she'd been in that jail cell, she'd never expected to appreciate the mountains and valleys like this again. She'd never thought she'd have more precious time with Brody—although she couldn't think about what was going on between them, not with BJ at risk.

She wouldn't be at peace until they figured out a solution. Brody had his plans, but she wondered if she should stay here with BJ or attempt to take the baby and leave the country. But here, at least, she had help. And she'd hear Brody out before making up her mind.

Brody plugged a radio into a socket and turned up the volume.

"Mom, can you watch BJ for another night?" Brody asked in a whisper, then signaled her to whisper, too. Apparently he feared the bugs inside the house could pick up their conversation, or feared there might be more bugs out here, too.

"Of course," Mia agreed. "Whatever I can do to help." But her shoulders sagged with stress, and the dark circles under her eyes gave away that she hadn't been sleeping well.

Lisa's arrival with BJ had placed the entire family under enormous pressure. There was no telling who had broken which laws. By taking care of the kidnapped baby, Mia may also have become a criminal. Yet clearly the woman would do anything to help her son and grandson.

"Thank you," Lisa whispered. She hugged Mia. Although she wasn't quite sure what Brody had planned, she was ready to help if she could. "I didn't mean to cause so many problems."

"You aren't the problem. It's Mark. I wish we could ask the authorities for help."

"I have a plan, ladies." Brody paced on the porch, his long legs eating up the distance in a few strides before he spun around and headed back to the women. He spoke for their ears alone.

Mia grabbed his forearm, her eyes intense, but she kept her voice down. "What do you want to do?"

"You and I are going to pretend to have a fight."

"A fight?"

"You'll insist on keeping BJ here. I'll tell you that I'm taking the baby home, that Lisa and I can protect him by ourselves."

Mia frowned. "But you just asked me to watch him."

"Exactly. BJ *will* stay here. We'll wrap up a doll and pretend to take him. You'll dismiss the guards but give them a note to stay here, remain on the job and hide. Let them know the place may be bugged. For good measure, after we leave, you call Ken on the phone and tell him about our fight."

"Then what?" Lisa asked, realizing he was setting a trap without putting BJ at risk, a plan of which she approved.

Brody folded his arms over his chest. "I'll expect Mark to make a move on the doll. My house will appear unprotected, but I'll post guards around the perimeter and in the barn. When he shows up, we'll grab him."

"Then what?" Lisa asked.

Brody's face hardened. "Then he and I will talk and come to an understanding."

"Suppose he doesn't agree?" Lisa asked, concerned by this plan, but admitting it had some merit.

She liked that Brody intended to talk. He didn't sound violent, just very determined.

Brody's voice might have been a mere whisper, but it was laced with steel. "Let's deal with one problem at a time."

Lisa knew Brody well enough to realize there was more to his plan, but that he didn't want to share. So as they all trudged back inside the house to begin their mock fight, she didn't insist on details. She didn't want to have a *real* argument in front of his mother and risk the bugs picking it up. Nevertheless, she intended to learn from Brody about how he intended to deal with Mark. She didn't like being left in the dark.

Fifteen minutes after the fake argument, she and Brody were in his pickup truck, with Lisa holding the doll as if it was a real baby. Brody turned up the radio, and she snuggled against him on the seat so they could have a conversation.

"So how do you plan on convincing Mark to give up custody of BJ?" she asked, prepared to plague him until he told her, but he spoke freely.

"I think Mark likes to gamble and party."

She looked up at him in surprise. "So?"

"Think about it. He takes off for Reno and Vegas, gambling cities. How many gamblers do you know that don't like money?"

She thought aloud. "I always wondered what Maritza did with her money. They could have afforded a better home and a decent car."

"And he embezzled that money from the university. All along we've thought he wanted revenge. But it seems to me the man might be amenable to a financial arrangement."

"I don't know. Maybe that will work if you can

prove to him that he's not the biological father.'' She hoped Brody was correct, but he was thinking logically. Could Mark be as reasonable?

She no longer had any doubts that Brody would be a good father. And a great husband. However, she still didn't believe she was the right woman. She wasn't even sure she *wanted* to be the right woman.

Between her career goals and watching Maritza's terrible marriage, Lisa had never let down her guard around men. She suspected that in the past, she hadn't trusted herself enough, hadn't wanted to be that vulnerable.

Yet Brody made her feel secure. Around him, she trusted her feelings. Maybe because he always seemed so steady, so rock solid. Maybe because he handled responsibility and love with equal ease. He certainly loved his mother and his son. And he openly displayed that affection, leaving no doubt in her mind that he and BJ belonged together.

Brody interrupted her thoughts. ''After you took the baby, Mark should have gone immediately to the police. He didn't. A parent who genuinely loved his child would care more about the child than his business reputation. He'd want the child back at any cost.''

''You're speculating. However, your theory does seem to fit with what I know about Mark.'' She rested her head in the hollow on his shoulder. ''So what do you plan to offer Mark to give up custody?''

''Whatever it takes.''

Chapter Thirteen

Lisa had hated saying goodbye to BJ again so soon after being reunited, but she understood the need to keep him protected. And she really required a decent night's sleep. She and Brody had barely slept at the hotel last night, and today had been exhausting, flying from Denver to Dallas, being arrested, then the late-night flight back to Colorado. She'd barely kept her eyes open during the drive back to Brody's house, but she was determined to shower and wash off the stench of the jail cell before going to bed.

But the moment they walked onto the front porch, Brody's cell phone rang, the sound shrill in the quiet mountain air, causing her gut to clench. No one ever called this late at night with good news.

Maybe it was a wrong number.

Yeah, right. And maybe the sun wouldn't rise in the morning.

Brody flipped open the phone, pressing the speaker option so she could hear. "Hello."

"Brody, Mom's been taken." Ken's voice had an edge of panic, and Lisa held her breath, waiting to hear the rest, sensing worse news to come.

"What do you mean, taken?" Brody kept his voice even, but the hand that held the cell phone shook.

"Mom went to put out the dogs before bringing them in for the night. The dogs came back. She didn't."

Oh, no. Lisa had brought the Adams family nothing but trouble since the day she'd arrived. A stampede. A fire. Now their mother, who was so gracious and welcoming and kind, had been taken from her home.

"You check the barn?"

"She's not there and every horse is accounted for. She didn't up and go for a ride or a walk, but we checked the back pasture, anyway. And the garage. Her car is still here, too. And you know how she always takes her cell phone with her when she leaves? Well, it's still here, right next to her purse on the shelf by the front door."

"What about BJ?" Brody asked, then took Lisa's hand and they headed for the truck. No verbal communication was needed between them. Obviously they needed to go back to Mia's home. Brody continued his conversation in a level tone, but held her hand so tightly it almost hurt.

He must be going through hell. First the shock of fatherhood, followed by the attempt to take his son, and now his mother was missing. What else could go wrong?

Although she didn't believe that negative thoughts caused bad luck, she wished she hadn't thought of that question. Jerking open the truck door, she tossed in the doll, then slid into her seat, grabbed her seat belt and had barely snapped it in place before Brody floored the truck.

How far would Mark go to get what he wanted?

He had a temper, especially when he drank, but the worst he'd ever done was throw a book across the room, and that hadn't been at Maritza but at the wall.

Through the phone's speaker, Ken sounded edgy and on the verge of panic. "I've got three men guarding BJ, and the other hands out searching for Mom." Another phone rang in the background. "Hold on a sec."

All traces of Lisa's former sleepiness had vanished with the first ring of the phone. The wait for Ken to come back on the line seemed interminable, especially with Brody driving way too fast down the road, his tires spewing clouds of dust behind them.

Finally Ken spoke to them again. "Evan's found motorcycle tracks and Mom's slipper by the rose-bushes under the hummingbird feeder."

"It's almost as if he wanted us to know that he has her." Brody swore at the news or a pothole, she wasn't sure which. "We're on the way over right now."

"Should I call the sheriff?"

Brody's phone beeped, signaling another call coming in. "Hold on."

Driving one-handed, he pressed flash to switch callers.

"Call the authorities and she's dead."

At the sound of Mark's voice and the motorcycle's engine coming in loud and clear over the speaker phone, fear spiked down Lisa's spine. "That's Mark," she told Brody in a whisper loud enough for Brody to hear but hopefully too soft for Mark. All along she'd suspected Mark was behind their problems, but until now she hadn't known for sure. His call confirmed her worst fears, that he would somehow get BJ and that nothing she or Brody did would stop him.

Brody acknowledged her identification with a nod. "What do you want?" he asked Mark, speaking with much more confidence than she felt. Of course, he *was* driving the truck like a maniac, swerving around ruts, his headlights occasionally catching a squirrel or rabbit scurrying over the road.

"I want my son."

"Don't give him the baby," Mia shouted, her voice firm and fearless.

Damn. Mark had Mia. He must have gone for the baby and failed, so he'd taken the first available hostage.

Lisa and Brody heard a short struggle, and Lisa couldn't imagine how Brody kept himself under tight control, especially when Mia screamed.

"Mark must have hurt her." Lisa heard the agony in Brody's voice. She wished she could do something to help.

Mark cursed. "Your old lady's a tough old broad, but she's now down for the count."

"Is she still alive?" Brody's tone snapped with authority, but he swerved onto the shoulder and jerked the steering wheel hard to regain control of the truck.

"Of course she's still alive. Injured maybe. Bleeding a little, but then, head wounds tend to do that."

Brody didn't say a word.

"Not to worry." Mark chuckled. "Without her, I have no bargaining chip."

"I want to talk to her."

"She's not able to speak right now. Maybe later. Now as I was saying—"

Brody disconnected the phone.

"What are you doing?" Lisa gasped.

"I need time to think. How can Mom be unconscious and still ride the motorcycle? Something doesn't seem right to me."

Lisa never would have thought of that or had the nerve to hang up on the man. "Maybe Mark only wants us to think he's on the bike?"

"I'm beginning to think that he's using misdirection to keep us off balance. Maybe he's deliberately left tracks to lead us in the wrong direction."

The phone rang.

Brody didn't answer.

"Aren't you going to—"

"Let the bastard wait."

She refrained from saying that Mark had Mia. Brody didn't need her reminding him of the obvious. On the second ring she bit her lip to keep from saying a word. She couldn't stand it. Her fingers itched to hit the talk button, but she didn't.

Brody let the phone ring three times before he finally answered.

Mark's voice rose in fury. "I want my son or you'll never see your mother alive again. See you tomorrow. Oh, and if you bring in the authorities—"

The line went dead.

Brody swerved around a corner, tires squealing. She held on to the door and braced a foot against the dash. "Brody, slow down. Getting us killed won't help your mother."

"You're right." He eased off the gas pedal but not by much. "Mark believes I can't rescue Mom until he tells us where she is. Maybe we can use that."

She frowned at him, horrified at the choice he had to make between saving his mother or keeping his son. However, if he said the wrong thing now and even suggested giving BJ to Mark, she and BJ could still disappear.

"Your mother is a very brave woman."

"She'd give up her life for any of her children or grandchildren without a second thought, but that's not going to happen."

She swallowed the fear in her throat. "You'll give Mark what he wants?"

"He'll never get my son, but maybe if I show up with a large amount of cash and the promise of a DNA test to prove BJ is mine, it will satisfy him enough to release Mom."

She was about to ask more questions when Brody dialed his phone.

"You aren't calling the authorities, are you?"

"My attorney. I want the custody papers drawn up legally."

He spoke into his phone, not even apologizing for the late hour. She understood his need to do something. Anything. But even if they had the papers and cash right now, they had no idea where Mark had taken Mia or if he'd agree to Brody's terms.

She waited until Brody hung up the phone, then asked, "What time does the bank open?"

"It doesn't matter. The bank president is a personal friend. He'll bring me whatever I need, whenever I need it."

Brody made that phone call, too, arranging for the money. The bank president promised to personally deliver the funds to the ranch within the hour. Lisa had never thought much about wealth and money. As long as she lived decently and could pay her bills, she was happy. To her, wealth had always meant enough endowments to the university to fund a dig. But personal wealth like Brody's had a multitude of advantages.

When they drove up, every light in Mia's house appeared to be on. She and Brody met up with his brothers in the front driveway. The men all shared the same worried expressions. While Ken had regained control of his earlier rage, from the way he kept grinding his teeth, the effort cost him.

Brody brought his brothers up to speed, repeating his conversation with Mark and his arrangements with his attorney and the bank president. His brothers had nothing to add regarding the search for their mother. The ranch hands had followed the motorcycle tracks to a creek, where they'd lost the trail. So now the brothers and Lisa drank hot coffee and waited.

She appreciated that no one blamed her for putting Mia in danger. Nevertheless, guilt sickened her. Mia was somewhere out there, hurt, and Lisa desperately wanted to do something to help, but handing BJ to Mark wasn't an option.

Within the slowest hour that had ever ticked by, Evan called on his radio to report that he was following the creek upstream, looking for the place where the bike had left the water; another hand was doing the same downstream. Lisa prayed they would find a clue to lead them to Mia, but she recalled Brody's comment about how unlikely it was that Mia was on Mark's bike, and she wondered what her ex-brother-in law was up to.

An hour later Brody had met with his attorney and then signed for a duffel bag stuffed with the cash they hoped Mark would accept, instead of the baby. It was about two hours before dawn when Brody pulled her aside from his brothers for a private conversation.

His voice was deep and commanding. "I'm going after Mark now."

"But you don't know where he is."

All night Brody had kept his composure, but she'd seen the strain in his shoulders, the shadows in his eyes and the grim determination in the set of his mouth. She didn't like that he intended to go into danger without consulting his brothers or that he clearly intended to leave her behind.

"We finally got a break. After that fire, the ranchers and developers around here have been nervous. A fellow pilot called me about a campfire he saw on my land during an overhead flight. Mark wants us to believe that he went north or south. He can't head into town without drawing attention to himself, since he's a stranger and everyone knows everyone's business, so that leaves one direction and a big fat cave to hide in. And that's where the pilot saw smoke."

A cave? Maybe. Maybe not. She sighed in frustration. "He could be anywhere."

"True. But he thinks like a commando. When he leaves clues behind, he's misdirecting us to do what he wants us to do. So I started thinking what I would do if I were in his position. He's outnumbered. Doesn't want my hands to find him by chance. And he needs to set up a meeting with us tomorrow. So he can't be that far away."

She'd go along with Brody's scenario as long as it was hypothetical. "Go on."

"Mark would need a place where he could watch the ranch and your site to monitor our comings and goings. He'd also need telephone wires to tap into our conversations."

She shoved a lock of hair behind her ear. "There aren't phone wires anywhere near the dig site."

"There are if I go north a few miles." There it was again. Quite baldly, he'd stated his intention to go alone. With his jaw set in a rigid line and his shoulders squared, he was a man whose mind was set. "There's an old copper mine out that way. And a large cave."

Normally the idea of a cave would have excited her. Ancient peoples often took advantage of the gifts Mother Nature gave them. Why build a shelter to protect one's family from the elements when a perfectly good cave was there for the taking? Caves didn't just shelter people, they helped preserve their remains, their art and their tools. But now was not the time for archaeology.

Mark could also use the cave to his advantage. In a cave he could build a fire and remain out of sight. Most of the smoke would dissipate before rising out the roof, and they'd probably caught a break that the pilot had spotted smoke. A cave would give Mark a place to hide Mia that the hands wouldn't discover during their normal duties. Yet, she didn't want Brody to jump to conclusions and head out on his own.

"If you head to the cave and discover that Mark's not there, you may miss his call." As she'd learned during the fire, cell phones in the mountains weren't reliable.

"I should be able to ride there and back within a few hours."

She shoved the discomfort of sitting on a horse for that long from her mind. "I'm coming with you."

"You'll slow me down."

She didn't dare say that there was no rush. Not with

Mark holding Mia captive. Every minute might be critical, but Brody would not do his mother any good if he got himself killed.

She threw up her hands in disgust, then let them fall on Brody's shoulders. "You show up without me pretending to hold a baby, and Mark will probably shoot you on sight. To give you a shot at negotiation, we need to appear as if we're bringing him what he wants."

"You don't get it. I intend to take him by surprise."

"How?"

"There's a side entrance to the cave. I'm hoping he won't know about—"

"Trust me. Mark will have his ass and his escape route covered." Brody's story didn't quite ring true. He was lying to her about something; she just hadn't figured out what, and her fear escalated. "And why aren't you bringing your brothers?"

"I am."

She folded her arms over her chest, scowled at him and just waited.

"Okay, I lied. I thought if I told you my brothers were staying, you'd agree to stay, too."

She unfolded her arms and placed them around his waist, hesitating just for a moment when she slid her hand past the gun he'd tucked into his pants. "You need me."

"I don't want to risk—"

"It's my life. My decision."

"I need to focus on saving my mother. If I'm worried about you, I'll be distracted."

"Oh, pul-lease. Saddle me a nice gentle horse and let's go."

BRODY RODE UP the trail with his brothers, a few ranch hands and Lisa. Rather than argue with her, he'd told her that if she couldn't keep up on horseback, she'd have to go back to the ranch. He'd expected her to quit as soon as they started up onto the steeper ground, yet she'd clung to her saddle defiantly. Under other circumstances, he would have smiled.

She didn't belong out here. She bounced in her saddle like a greenhorn, so that instead of moving with the animal, every step jarred her. Tomorrow she'd be stiff and sore, but he was more concerned about whether she could stay on the horse if anyone fired a gun, or if her horse shied at a rabbit. Ken had chosen the most steady mount in their stable for her, but any horse could buck or step into a hole or…

He kept glancing over his shoulder, hoping she would fall behind and he could send a hand to escort her home. But she kept up with a dogged determination, by sheer willpower.

And he loved her for it.

He loved her.

That's why he was so worried about her. That's why he'd tried to insist she stay behind. That's why his stomach had been in knots from the moment she was arrested until the moment the judge had set bail. That's why he couldn't resist her even though he knew her career would take her from him.

He loved her.

Hell of a time to realize his feelings, as he was leading her into a dangerous situation. He had to be nuts to allow her to come, and if anything happened to her, he wouldn't forgive himself. Although she'd decided on her own to accompany him on this journey up the steep mountain slope, he hadn't had to lend her a horse. Even now it was dangerous, probably not as dangerous as facing Mark. He could increase the pace so that she couldn't possibly keep up.

But that would be a betrayal of her courage, and he couldn't do that no matter how concerned he was about her safety. He was in love and that meant he had to give her the freedom to make her own choices—even if it meant she was harmed, even if it meant she left him for her work.

He loved her. He loved her smiles and her intelligence and most of all, her courage. So he kept the pace to one she could manage and his trepidations to himself. When he came to a fork in the trail, he sent Riley and another man to the right with a wave of his hand.

They paused while he gave final instructions. "Cover the back entrance to the cave. If Mark tries to leave with a hostage, do what you must to stop him."

"Got it. But what if he sneaks out alone?" Riley asked.

"Hold him until I get there. I want to talk to him. Make a deal. Are we clear?"

"Yeah, boss. But suppose he doesn't want to stay around to talk?" the hand asked.

"Detain him if you can. I don't want any heroes. Or anyone to get hurt."

At his words Lisa nodded. "Mark doesn't fight fair, and I suspect he knows every dirty trick, so be careful."

The hand tipped his hat to her. "Ma'am."

Riley and the hand departed, and after Brody's party reached a pass close to the mountain's peak, he sent Ken and the remaining hand on their way, leaving him alone with Lisa. "Thanks for warning them."

"No problem." The trail widened and she drew up next to him, slightly out of breath from her exertions. "Why didn't we bring more help?"

"I'd like my conversation with Mark to be private."

"Why?"

"Our transaction may not be legal."

She cocked her head to one side. "What do you mean?"

"Some people might say we are buying a baby."

"Oh."

"I don't care, as long as Mark signs the papers. If I handle this right, I'm hoping no one will ever know about the money. We need to hurry. I want to arrive before dawn." He urged his horse into a slow canter across the flat plateau.

A hundred things could go wrong. Mark might not be where they thought he was, and they might have to ride back to the ranch and wait for Mark's phone call before heading out in a completely different direction. Or the man might shoot them on sight.

I'm coming, Mom. Hang in there.

He knew his mother would remain calm and do whatever she could to defuse the situation. However, Mark might have gagged her. Or she could still be unconscious. He refused to consider that she might not be alive. Mark wouldn't be stupid enough to kill anyone before he got the baby. A smart man wouldn't resort to violence at all.

Yet, Lisa's warning to his men remained with him. He reminded himself that Mark didn't play by the rules. And that he might be drunk when they arrived. Belligerent. Unreasonable.

However, so far, the man had planned brilliantly. Brody slowed as the trail began a steep descent. "Lean back to help your mount," he instructed Lisa.

"Oh, God," she muttered under her breath as the horse slid on its hind legs.

Now was not the time for her to change her mind. She needed distraction and information.

"There's another reason I think Mark has chosen the cave as the place to make his stand."

"What?"

"We used to camp here as kids."

She frowned at him. "I'm not following you."

"This area is the one place on the ranch where I'm...uncomfortable," he admitted.

"What do you mean?"

Although voices could carry in the night air, they were still far enough away from the cave's main entrance for him to speak without fear of being overheard. And now that they were past the steep descent, the ground had flattened again. To one side was the area that had gone up in flames. Behind them was the valley where they grazed cattle. And before them were mountains, where the snows from the spring run-offs widened the creeks into small, cascading rivers. Last time he'd been here as a kid, it had been summer.

"When we were kids, Mom and my father loved to get away from the ranch."

"What happened to him?" she asked.

"He died of a heart attack."

"I'm sorry."

"Back then my folks would pack a few horses and the whole family would come here for a week or two.

My brothers and I played in the woods, in the creeks and in the caves.''

"How extensive is this cave?"

"From the front, it appears to be only about fifty feet deep and about as wide. My parents didn't know about several back doors or the small pool deeper inside. And we didn't tell them. It was our fort. Our special playground. Every summer when we returned, we'd explore deeper into the cave's winding passages.''

"How old were you and your brothers then?"

"Ten. Twelve. Old enough to think we were invincible.''

"You never got lost?"

"Nah. We equipped ourselves with flashlights and spare batteries. And we unrolled string through the passages so we could always find our way back even if the flashlights went out. We were careful.''

"So why don't you like to come here anymore? And how would Mark know that?"

"Probably from my medical records. These days everything can be found online.''

"Mark isn't great on a computer, but he does have a buddy he hires to dig up information for him. Maybe that's who helped him frame me for embezzlement.''

With edgy determination, he led her back to his story. "The last time I was here, I fell into a hole and couldn't get out. Ken stayed with me while Riley raced back to get Dad. They didn't return for two hours.''

He tried to keep his voice level, but she must have picked up something that conveyed how horrible his ordeal had been, because she prodded, "And?"

"The hole was filled with spiders. Millions of them."

She shuddered, but her voice was soft with understanding. "So that's why you hate them."

"The spiders didn't bite. But they crawled over me for hours. By the time Dad got me out, well, I don't remember him getting me out. I just remember being in that pit and waking up in the hospital."

"You don't have to go into that cave."

"Yes. I do." He turned to her and she reached over to squeeze his hand. "Just thought you should know that the last time I was here, Dad carried me out in a semicatatonic state."

Chapter Fourteen

The cave loomed out of the side of the mountain, and after Brody's story, ominous feelings about entering filled Lisa with trepidation. When she smelled smoke, a sign of Mark's presence, her pulse skipped and skidded.

Brody had been right.

"He's here all right," she whispered. They slid off the horses and secured their reins to a tree branch a good distance from the cave.

They approached stealthily on foot.

Lisa had expected darkness, but after they rounded a bend in the path, she could see the fire burning deep inside the cave. But no Mark.

"Try not to look into the flames," Brody told her, "so you'll keep your night vision."

"Now what?" she asked. She could see no way to approach in secret. But if they could sneak inside, maybe they could take Mark by surprise, since he wouldn't be expecting them to have discovered his hideout.

"There's a side entrance about a hundred yards to the left," Brody said. He took her hand and led her straight to a narrow opening in the rocks. He set the duffel bag with cash in front of it. "We'll have to crawl on our bellies, but it's wider once we go through the opening."

"Okay."

He pressed a penlight into her hand. "Don't turn it on unless absolutely necessary. I don't want to warn him of our presence."

She nodded and her fingers closed around the tiny light like a lifeline. "What about the doll?"

"Push it in front of you."

Fortunately Lisa wasn't claustrophobic. The opening wasn't large enough to enter on hands and knees. She followed Mark's example and lay on the ground, then used her forearms and elbows to pull herself through.

He'd said the passageway would widen, and it did, but not by much. She wriggled on her belly and kept shoving the doll into the bottom of Brody's boots for reassurance. She could only imagine what devils he battled in the darkness, unable to see if he might be crawling into any spiders. But he shoved the ransom money in front of him and kept a steady pace.

The cave smelled dry, the air surprisingly fresh, almost as if air currents moved freely through the cavern system. It seemed as though they'd crawled for at least ten minutes when Brody's hands clasped her waist and helped her to stand.

She'd never been in such blackness, and she clutched the penlight and doll more tightly. Brody was the only one who knew the way out. In the darkness she couldn't see him, even though he stood right next to her. And if for any reason he lost it, she could be stuck here.

However, his brothers would come for her. She

would be fine. Her concern was for Brody. "You okay?"

"I could use a distraction."

Without hesitation she reached for him, tugged his head to hers and found his mouth. His arms around her tightened and she didn't mind at all. His kiss started out as desperate, determined, but then the magic that always seemed to spark between them gentled him. The tension in his shoulders eased and finally he drew back.

"Thanks. This way." He took her hand, and they walked up over a smooth surface, then down again. She allowed her hand to trail along the wall and ignored the edges of rock that bit into her flesh. She would not complain. She'd asked to come here; she needed to be a help, not a hindrance.

The sound of water cascading into a pool, then voices echoing through the chamber, made her realize they were nearing their destination. A glow of light to the side of their passageway made it easier going, but Brody had slowed their pace. Then he stopped.

She squeezed his hand. "Mia's alive," she whispered. "Can you make out what she's saying?"

"He's got her in the spider pit."

"You don't know that."

"He just said so."

Oh, God. Brody's hearing must be better than hers. Either that or his mind was making up things.

"You deal with Mark. I'll free your mother."

"Thanks. I'm okay," he whispered, his tone low but fierce.

When they rounded the corner, they found Mark leaning against the wall, his back to his motorcycle and a shotgun across his knees. Mia was sitting in the pit, her hands and feet tied. The pit was dark and too deep for Mia to climb out, even if her hands and feet had been free.

At their entrance, Mark aimed the shotgun at Brody's chest as if he'd expected them. *Damn. Damn. Damn.* They'd hoped to take him by surprise, but Brody appeared collected and calm, as if he was facing an employee, instead of an irate kidnapper with a gun pointed at his chest.

Mark took one look at the doll in Lisa's arms and sneered, "Where's my son?"

"Safe," Brody answered. He unzipped the duffel and held open the two sides so that Mark could see a sliver of cash. "I brought you something I'm hoping is more to your liking."

"I came for my son," Mark insisted, and he cocked the gun.

Sweat beaded on her forehead, and Brody ignored Mark's hostile action. He lifted one duffel handle and opened the bag temptingly wider. "Here's enough money for you to retire. Sign the custody papers and you walk out of here a rich man."

While the men traded words, she edged toward the pit. Mark rubbed his chin, but kept his gaze on Brody and didn't seem to notice her until he snapped, "Just what in hell do you think you're doing?"

"Mark, I'm untying Mia. I know how smart you are. You don't want to spoil the enjoyment of being a rich man by having the authorities after you for murder."

"Don't tell me what I want." Mark ordered, aiming the gun at her. "And don't take another step."

She saw the empty beer cans stacked by the wall. How much had he drunk tonight? His words weren't slurred. He could be cold sober. But drunk or sober, he was dangerous as long as he had that gun.

Brody unzipped a side pocket of the bag.

"Hey." Mark aimed the gun back at Brody. "Move real slow."

Brody did as he asked and removed the documents. "Sign the papers."

"Why should I?"

"You have one million reasons." Brody nudged the bag and let the firelight reflect on the pile of money. "And why would you want to raise my kid?"

Mark licked his lips. Lisa edged closer to Mia but kept her gaze on Brody, taking her cue from him. She had to give him credit. He didn't sound desperate but reasonable. He had the sense not to challenge Mark, yet he negotiated from an inner strength that was inherent to his character.

And Brody may have sensed the other man weakening. "Sign over custody to me. We have two witnesses. It's legal. I don't want any trouble. The money's in cash. Untraceable."

Mark hesitated.

"Lots of people know we're here." Brody spoke softly and Lisa sat on the edge of the pit. "You shoot us, and Riley and Ken will go for the sheriff." While Brody continued to speak, she lowered herself until she dropped into the hole beside Mia. Mark must have seen her, but he paid no attention.

Omigod. There were spiders down here. But they didn't bite. Lisa brushed them off and started to untie Mia's hands as Brody said convincingly, "You don't want my baby, Mark. Sign the papers. Take the money and have a good life."

"WHY NOT?" Mark chuckled, glorying in his moment of triumph. "Hand them to me."

Brody handed him a thick legal document opened to a signature page and a pen. Mark didn't bother reading. He signed and smiled as little Miss Hoity-Toity let out a gasp from the pit. Apparently she didn't like spiders. Too damn bad. The spiders were nothing compared to the little surprise he had planned for all of them.

Contemptuously Mark tossed the document back at Brody's feet. The man was a fool. Didn't he understand that he, Mark, intended to have it all? The money, his baby and revenge? He wished he had another beer to help him celebrate the victory.

But as euphoria swept over him, he realized he didn't need booze. With a million in cash he could party, find a real woman who would appreciate him. He would have it all. Oh, yeah. Because this sap, Brody, mommy dearest and his own ex-sister-in-law were about to die. Slowly. And if Brody thought to outsmart him by escaping out the side entrance, he'd learn differently since the entrance was set to blow.

Mark grabbed the duffel, then ordered Brody, "Get in that pit with your wife and mother."

"Mark, no!" Lisa shouted. "You've won. Just go."

"Don't want to see your lover reduced to a zombie by a few little old spiders?" Mark taunted. He fired a warning shot over Brody's head.

Brody scooped up the papers, jumped into the pit and let out a yelp of pain. He must have landed awkwardly.

Mark leaned over the edge, pleased by Brody's injury. "You all have fun climbing out now."

Then he walked toward his motorcycle and swung the heavy duffel bag across the handle bars. A man like him could go far with one million dollars. So long, Colorado. Hello, Las Vegas.

He gunned the motorcycle, adrenaline pumping. He'd won. He would go get his son and no one would stop him. He roared out of the cave on his bike. And then he detonated the dynamite charges that would make the cave-in seem like an act of nature and bury his victims beneath so much rock that the pit would become their coffin. He roared with laughter as the dirt and rocks tumbled down. No one would be coming after him.

Elated, he gunned the motorbike, taking the dirt path at full speed, racing across the plateau with the wind in his hair and a grin on his face. He was invincible!

The ditch in front of him wouldn't slow him. Nothing and nobody would ever stop him from doing what he wanted again. He gunned the bike and jumped.

THE EXPLOSION BLASTED Lisa's eardrums. Dirt and rocks tumbled and she ducked, clinging to Mia whose hands and ankles she'd managed to untie just before the ceiling came down. Dust filled her mouth and she tried to ignore the spiders crawling over her, wished the cave-in hadn't extinguished the fire.

Had they survived the blast only to be buried alive? Too late she knew why Mark had signed those custody papers without an argument. He'd figured dead people couldn't claim a baby. But they weren't dead yet.

She couldn't worry about that bastard right now.

She slapped a spider from her neck and felt around in her pocket for the penlight. It was gone.

Don't panic. Don't panic. Don't panic.

''Mia? Brody?'' she called out, her terror rising when neither of them responded. But perhaps their ears had yet to recover from the blast. She forced herself to feel around the pit.

And found a shoulder. A thin shoulder. And shook it gently. ''Mia? Mia, wake up.''

The woman didn't answer, but her hand grabbed Lisa's and squeezed. Maybe Mia was too injured to talk.

In the inky dark, Lisa felt for the woman's face and brushed away spiders.

Mia groaned. ''Thanks. My hands are still numb from being tied.''

''Can you stand?'' Lisa tugged her hand.

Mia groaned but stood. ''Brody? Where's Brody?''

''He jumped into the pit right before the blast.'' She kept the news to herself that Brody may have injured his foot in the fall. ''I found you first.'' Lisa shuddered at the prospect of stumbling around in the pit, stepping on Brody's broken ankle, but she had to find him.

And the spiders…

They're harmless. Harmless. They don't bite. She repeated those words in her head like a mantra. At least the dust had started to settle and it made breathing easier. The air wasn't stuffy, which gave her hope that every access hadn't been closed. Finally she bumped into Brody.

''Mia, I've found him.'' Lisa shook him, praying for some kind of response. ''Brody? You okay?''

When he didn't answer, Mia let out a whimper.

Lisa felt around in Brody's pocket for his flashlight. "Don't fall apart on me, Mia. I'm barely hanging in here. I've found Brody's flashlight."

"Turn it on," Mia told her.

"But if he sees these spiders…"

"They leave in the light."

At Mia's words, she flicked on the light and she and Mia spent the next few minutes brushing the spiders from an unconscious Brody. Lisa tried to assess his injuries. "His head is bleeding, but his breathing's regular. I think the blast or the fall may have knocked him out. And his ankle is broken. Let's sit him up."

The two women yanked and shoved Brody until he was propped in a sitting position.

"Now what?" Lisa asked, hoping Mia had a brilliant idea. Meanwhile she shone the light around their prison. She didn't like their options. The women couldn't lift an unconscious Brody out of the pit. Maybe she or Mia could boost the other woman out, but they only had one light between them. The person who got out of the pit would need the light to explore the cave to seek an exit. But without a light in the pit, the spiders would return.

She shone the light on a cave-in of rocks that were piled next to the pit. "If one of us could climb out, shove those rocks into the pit, maybe we could walk on top of the rocks and pull Brody out."

"You go for it. I'll boost you up." Mia laced her fingers together and cupped her hands.

Lisa positioned the lit flashlight very carefully on the rim of the pit where it couldn't fall. Then she placed her foot in Mia's cupped hands. "On three. One. Two. Three."

Mia hefted. Lisa planted her hands on the edge of

the pit—which promptly crumbled beneath her hands. Both women tumbled backward. Lisa landed hard on her butt.

Mia stood, dusted off her hands. "You okay?"

"Yeah. At least I didn't land on my head." Lisa looked up. "There's nothing to hold on to and the edge crumbled."

"This time we try the narrow end. After I boost up your foot, place your other foot on my shoulder. When you make it over the rim, go on your belly," Mia suggested.

"Sounds like a plan." Lisa didn't want to waste time and scrambled back to her feet. Their air could run out, and those flashlight batteries would only last for so long.

The women assumed their positions in the corner. "One," Mia counted. "Two. Three."

Mia boosted. Lisa jumped, tried to place her other foot on Mia's shoulder. Missed. Again they fell. Harder this time. Lisa landed on her side. Pain shot along her rib. She ignored it as Mia helped her up.

"Again?"

Lisa nodded. "Let me catch my breath."

"You know, I believe we skipped a step."

"What do you mean?"

"I loved the circus," Mia told her. "Every time they came to Denver, I took the boys. If I remember correctly, I'll boost, then you plant a foot on my thigh and reach for my hand. Then you step on my shoulder. And then lunge for the wall, because I don't know how long I can hold you."

"Got it." Lisa had no idea if Mia's plan would work, but since she didn't have a better idea, she was up for another attempt.

"Ready?" Mia asked. "One. Two. Three."

Mia boosted. Lisa jumped and planted a boot on Mia's thigh. "Go. Go." Mia urged her up. And somehow her foot ended up on the woman's shoulder.

Lisa lunged, scrambled and rolled. Below her she could hear Mia saying, "Yes. Yes. Good job."

Lisa picked up the flashlight, careful not to lean too close to the crumbling edge. Then she shone it around what had previously been a large chamber. Much of the ceiling had caved in and she didn't see a way out, but refrained from saying so.

One thing at a time.

She hurried to the rocks. "Mia, get on the far side of the pit with Brody. I don't want to risk having any of these rocks fall on you."

Mia moved. Lisa set about the task of shoving heavy rocks down into the pit. She couldn't always stand upright, and sweat poured into her eyes. It would take more rocks than she could push to fill the pit, but she saw no other options.

"Stop and rest," Mia ordered.

Lisa sank to her knees, panting, ribs aching.

"Let me rearrange these rocks. Pile them up in the corner." Mia heaved and swore. But she never stopped. "I could probably climb out now, but it'll take both of us down here to lift Brody out."

Lisa shook her head. The walls of the pit were vertical. "Let me do a little digging. Move back." She used her legs to kick dirt down onto the rocks. And in doing so, she created a slope in the corner that gave them a better chance of tugging Brody out of the pit.

Again she carefully set the flashlight on the rim where her descent wouldn't disturb it. Finally Lisa slid back down into the hole. Mia grabbed the custody papers that lay beside him and then each women held Brody under a shoulder. They staggered with him to the rocks, half-carrying, half-dragging him. They barely made three steps.

"This isn't working." Lisa hadn't realized how difficult it was to lift two hundred plus pounds up over their heads.

Brody moaned. Then one leg went rigid under him and he supported most of his weight.

"Welcome back, Brody, darling," Mia told him in a voice that a mother might use on a child. "You've been hurt. Keep your eyes closed and do exactly what I say."

He didn't listen.

Brody's eyes popped wide open. He shuddered. The two women looked at each other. Then Lisa did the only thing she could think of to draw his attention away from his surroundings. She dragged down his head and thrust her tongue into his mouth. She intended to shock him, draw his attention from the pit until he steadied. She couldn't imagine what he was going through, but it had to be bad. The man had been knocked out and had awakened to find himself in his worst nightmare.

He hadn't eased himself into the pit, as she had done with the airplane by taking a step at a time. She didn't know how badly he was hurt or if he was reliving the past. She tried to make him think of something else. Fast. So she used her lips and her tongue, urging him to respond.

He kissed her, then pulled back. "I'm okay. Did Mark get away?"

"Yeah. Then he set off an explosion and trapped us in here. Can you walk?" she asked, thinking it best to keep him talking and moving, but he sounded stronger with every word he uttered. Mia gave her a thumbs-up.

"My ankle's broken. And we have to get out of here. Fast."

"Don't worry. The spiders are afraid of the light."

"It's not the spiders I'm worried about. Mark's going after BJ. That's why he set the blast."

He wasn't worried about the spiders but his son. And if she ever needed proof that he was terrific father material, he'd just given it to her. Especially when she looked down and saw his foot horribly cocked and swollen. Hurt, buried alive and facing a terrible childhood fear, he was worried about BJ. She marveled at his strength.

"Lean on us," she suggested. "Use our shoulders like crutches."

Slowly the three of them inched up the pile of rocks. Brody groaned in pain, but he never even suggested they stop to rest. Partway to the top, Lisa stopped, removed his hand from her shoulder and placed it on the wall to steady him before she climbed ahead. Then reaching back, she tugged on his hands. Mia pushed from below and then all three of them were finally together, on the ground and out of the pit. Progress.

"Where are the custody papers?" Brody asked.

Mia gestured at the papers tucked in the waistband of her slacks. "Right here."

"Well done," Brody murmured.

"We need to find a way out of here," Lisa said. "Any ideas?"

Brody took the penlight and searched the area. "Try to the right of that red-colored pile of sand."

Lisa followed the light and saw tiny eddies of spinning dust that had to be caused by moving air. She hurried toward the spot and began to dig. Four hours later, after breaking several nails and sweating buckets, she wondered why she'd ever liked to dig in the dirt.

Mia had helped her dig, and so had Brody. He'd insisted on doing his share, even though he couldn't put any weight on his ankle. She wanted to tell him to rest, that he was injured. But she took one look at the fierce determination on his face and kept silent. Worry for BJ drove him.

Finally she saw daylight and heard voices. She stuck her head out the opening and yelled, "Help. Over here."

Ken came running. "You okay?"

"Brody's got a broken ankle. Mia and I are fine. Is BJ safe?"

"The baby's fine," Ken told her, and she shouted the news to Mia and Brody, then squirmed back inside, leading Ken to the others. Brody held out an arm to her, and she snuggled into its curve, careful not to bump his ankle.

Ken helped his mother out of the cave first. "I'll be back in a minute to help you with Brody."

Lisa and Brody were left alone. "I wouldn't have made it without you," Brody told her.

"Sure you would—"

He tilted her chin up so their lips touched. "I love you."

Lisa could have sworn she heard Mia mutter, "It's about damn time." Apparently their voices carried farther than they'd realized. But she didn't want to spoil the moment by grinning. Instead, she settled her lips on Brody's. "Love you, too."

After a moment he pulled back. "I want us to stay together. Marry me?"

Her eyes brimmed with tears. "I can't do that to you. I'm a kidnapper and might spend the rest of my life—"

"With my brother." Ken had returned. "Mark's dead. He tried to jump his bike over a crevice and didn't make it. Maybe he forgot to compensate for the weight of the duffel bag filled with money. Riley recovered the body and the cash. He's on the way down with his load." Ken grinned at them. "So since Mark never told the law about you taking the baby, you're in the clear to become my sister-in-law."

Mark dead? She was in the clear? Her emotions turned from surprise to relief to wonder. Her life could actually be going right again. "There's still the embezzlement charge."

Brody kissed her. "We'll beat it. Together."

He'd asked her to marry him and she wondered if he was delirious. She placed a hand on his forehead, but he didn't feel feverish.

"Well?" Brody prodded.

"Well what?"

"Are you going to marry me or not?"

"Not."

"You don't love me?"

"I didn't say that."

"You don't love BJ?"

"You know better."

"Then what's the matter?"

"I'm an archaeologist."

He grinned at the hole she'd dug to get them out.

"I can appreciate a wife with skills. Besides, if I can be a rancher and a husband, you can be an archaeologist and a wife."

"But my work—"

"I'd rather have you some of the time than none of the time. We'll work it out."

"Okay."

"Is that a yes?"

She chuckled and snuggled against him. "Yes. Yes. Yes."

Epilogue

One year later

Brody held his giggling son in front of him in the saddle while Lisa rode with their baby daughter. The last year had brought changes to his life, all of them good. Who'd have thought that Mark's blast would have exposed an Anasazi site? Lisa now had a lifetime of research to do right here on the ranch and was building a reputation as a respected archaeologist in her field. Between taking care of their children, her team and the ruins, she had more than enough to keep her busy and happy.

Mark's forged checks hadn't held up under the scrutiny of experts, and she'd been cleared of all charges. However, after the ugliness with the head of her department, she'd chosen to sever her ties with the university—especially after the police discovered that Joanna Bessener, the pregnant team member, had hired Van Dyke to steal and resell the artifacts. Apparently the woman had wanted to discredit Lisa and usurp her position. An investigation had revealed that Joanna had a history of emotional instability. Lisa let the university sort out the mess. Now, she funded her research with private endowments and government grants.

And during the time his broken ankle had taken to heal, Brody had learned how to delegate. On a ranch this size he needn't supervise every foreman. He'd hired more men, which left him time for his family and for visiting the archaeological site and, more importantly, his wife.

Lisa guided her mount with a skilled hand. She might have started slowly, but she'd taken to riding with enthusiasm. "Look, BJ, see the pretty butterflies?"

Brody turned his horse so his son could see the bright orange-and-black butterflies settling on wild flowers of blue and gold. He hoped that wherever Maritza was she would know their son was safe, loved and happy. While the boy would never need the money his mother had set aside in a trust fund for college, he would always know the woman who'd borne him had done so out of love.

BJ clapped his hands. "Pretty."

Brody kissed the top of his head. "I've finally decided on this little guy's name."

Lisa grinned. "Maybe I should clap, too. It's about time."

He grinned at her over BJ's head. "It's a tough decision."

"You've had an entire year." She sighed. "Well, tell me already. What's his name going to be?"

"BJ."

She rolled her eyes heavenward. "And what, pray tell, do those letters stand for?"

He knew she'd called him BJ for Brody Jr., but

having two Brodys in one family was confusing. "What about Brad Jason, after my father?"

"Sounds like a plan."

At the hot glance he sent her, her breath hissed in. They'd brought along a blanket and when the kids took their afternoon nap, he intended to shower her with kisses in the sunlight. She'd brought him so much happiness. A son. A daughter. And herself. He could no longer imagine life without her.

He raised an eyebrow. "Is that really what you've been thinking about? A name for our son?"

"Actually I was thinking about you," she admitted.

"About my new haircut?" he teased, realizing that very soon they'd have to stop this kind of banter in front of the kids. But for today, he would enjoy himself.

"I wasn't thinking about your new haircut."

"Then you must be thinking about my new boots."

"Not exactly."

"My charming grin?"

"I was thinking about your daddy capabilities," she teased right back.

"My daddy capabilities?"

"You think you could get these two kids to nap while I bathe in the waterfall?"

"I think I could handle that. Did you bring a swimsuit?"

"Nope." Her eyes twinkled. "Think you can handle that?"

He tipped his hat and chuckled. "With pleasure, ma'am. With pleasure."

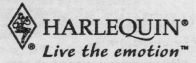

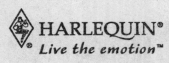 

HARLEQUIN®
Live the emotion™

Harlequin Books and Konica present
The Double Exposure Campaign!

Expose yourself to Intrigue. Collect original
proofs of purchase from the back pages of:

UNDER WRAPS 0-373-83595-7
GUARDED SECRETS 0-373-83593-0
WHISPERS IN THE NIGHT 0-373-83596-5
KEEPING WATCH 0-373-83594-9

and receive free Konica disposable cameras,
each valued at over $5.99 U.S.!

Just complete the order form and send it, along with your proofs of
purchase from two (2), three (3) or four (4) of the featured books above,
to: Harlequin Intrigue National Consumer Promotion, P.O. Box 9047,
Buffalo, NY 14269-9047, or P.O. Box 613, Fort Erie, Ontario L2A 5X3.

Have you enclosed your proofs of purchase?

Remember—the more you buy, the more you save! You must send two (2) original proofs
of purchase to receive one camera, three (3) original proofs of purchase to receive two
cameras and four (4) original proofs of purchase to receive all three cameras.

Visit us at www.eHarlequin.com

CARLA NEGGERS

THE
MIST

QM-626

MIRA®

Recycling programs for this product may not exist in your area.

ISBN-13: 978-0-7783-2773-8

THE MIST

For questions and comments about the quality of this book please contact us at Customer_eCare@Harlequin.ca.

www.MIRABooks.com

Printed in U.S.A.

To Jim and Maureen,
and to Todd and Martha.
Family!

Chapter 1

Lizzie Rush tensed at her table by the fire, watching out of the corner of her eye as a tall, fair-haired man entered the small village pub, shutting the door firmly against the gale-force wind and steady rain that had been lashing the southwest Irish coast for hours. The man wore an expensive trench coat unbuttoned over a dark brown sweater neatly draped across a flat abdomen, dark brown trousers and leather shoes that, although suited to walking the isolated hills of the remote Beara Peninsula, looked to be free of mud and manure.

The half-dozen local fishermen and farmers Lizzie had seen arrive over the past hour had hung up wet, worn jackets and scraped off their shoes and wellies or shed them and set them by the door. The men were gathered now over pints of Guinness and mugs of coffee at rickety tables by the front window. They paid no attention to the newcomer, nor did the brown-and-white springer spaniel flopped on the stone hearth close to the peat fire. The dog belonged to the barman and presumably was accustomed to the comings and goings at the pub.

Lizzie drank the last of her strong coffee. The past day had been a whirlwind. A last-minute overnight flight from Boston to Dublin. A few hours to check in to her family's small hotel in Dublin and try to talk herself into abandoning her trip to the Beara Peninsula. No luck there. Then it was back to the airport for a short flight west across Ireland to the tiny Kerry County airport and, finally, the drive here, to this quiet village on Kenmare Bay, in the rain and wind.

She set down her mug and turned a page in the beautifully illustrated book of Irish folktales she was reading while enjoying coffee and warm blackberry crumble by the fire. As tempting as it was, she knew she couldn't give in to the lure of the cozy, romantic atmosphere of the pub and let down her guard. As the newcomer walked over to the bar, she reminded herself he could have a weapon— a gun, a knife—concealed under his trench coat or tucked next to an ankle.

Or he could be an ordinary, if well-dressed, tourist getting out of the gale.

The barman, a wiry, sandy-haired Irishman named Eddie O'Shea, filled a pint from the tap. He'd been eyeing Lizzie with a mix of suspicion and curiosity since she'd shed her own dripping jacket and hung it on a wooden peg by the door, but he gave the newcomer a warmer reception.

"Ah," he said with a smile and a little hoot of surprise and recognition, "if it isn't Lord Will himself."

Lord Will.

Lizzie forced herself to calmly turn another page in her book.

"Hello, Eddie," the newcomer said in an upper-class British accent.

Eddie set the pint on a tray on the gleaming, polished five-foot stretch of wood in front of him and sighed. "You wouldn't be in Ireland for a bit of golf, would you?"

"Not today, I'm afraid."

Lizzie stared at a lush watercolor of a quaint Irish farm, grazing sheep and trooping fairies. Of all the things she'd anticipated could go wrong on this trip, having William Arthur Davenport turn up in the same Irish village, the same Irish pub she was in, wasn't one of them.

She let her gaze settle on the details of the captivating watercolor—the pink-and-lavender sunrise above the green hills, the purple thistle along a country lane, the mischievous smiles of the fairies. The book was the work of Keira Sullivan, a Boston-based illustrator and folklorist with deep Irish roots. Lizzie had yet to meet Keira, but she knew Simon Cahill, the FBI agent with whom Keira was romantically involved.

Simon, Lizzie reminded herself, was the reason she was in Ireland. She'd heard he was here with Keira on the Beara Peninsula while she painted and researched an old Irish story. As much as Lizzie hated to disturb the new lovers, she felt she had no choice. She had to act now, before Norman Estabrook could make good on his threat to kill Simon and his boss, FBI director John March.

Norman would kill Lizzie, too, if he discovered the role she'd played in the FBI investigation into his illegal activities over the past year, culminating in his arrest two months ago on suspicion of money laundering and providing material support to transnational drug traffickers. He was a thrill-seeking billionaire with a long reach. There was no doubt in her mind that he would never go to trial, much less end up in prison. For Norman Estabrook, death was preferable to confinement. He was under arrest now—he'd given up his passport, posted a huge bond and agreed to stay on his Montana ranch under electronic surveillance. But it wouldn't last. There was talk he was about to cut a deal with federal prosecutors and walk.

And when that happened, Lizzie thought, he'd come after the people he believed had betrayed him. Simon Cahill, John March—and their anonymous source.

Her.

When she'd finally decided to come to Ireland and talk to Simon face-to-face, Lizzie had created a cover story that would explain her presence on the Beara Peninsula without giving herself away. If not the truth, it wasn't an outright lie, either.

She simply hadn't counted on Simon's handsome, dangerous British friend turning up in Ireland, too. She had no desire to pop onto Will Davenport's radar.

Lizzie decided she wouldn't mind being a tiny fairy right now. Or a shape-shifter. Then she could turn herself into an ant.

An ant could disappear into a crack in the floor and not be noticed by the man at the bar.

She'd done her research. Will Davenport was the younger son of a British peer, the marquess of something—she couldn't remember his exact title. Peter, Will's older brother, managed the family's five-hundred-year-old estate in the north of England, and Arabella, his younger sister, designed wedding dresses in London. At thirty-five, Will was the wealthy owner of various properties in England and Scotland, with offices in an ivy-covered London brownstone.

That wasn't all he did. Two years ago—supposedly—he had abruptly abandoned his career as an officer with the Special Air Service—the SAS—to make his fortune. Lizzie, however, strongly suspected he had merely shifted from the SAS to the SIS, the British Secret Intelligence Service, popularly known as MI6.

She did know her spies.

Surreptitiously she tucked a few strands of black

hair back under her red bandanna. She hadn't tried to disguise herself so much as make it less easy for anyone to describe her later on. "Oh, yes, I saw a woman at the pub. She had on a red bandanna and hiking clothes."

If things went wrong for her in Ireland, which they seemed about to do, that wasn't much for anyone, including the FBI, the Irish Garda and MI6, to go on.

Lizzie picked up her fork and scooped up the last of her warm crumble, fat blackberries oozing out from under the simple crust of sugar, flour and butter. She sat with her back to the wall, facing out into the pub. "It's hard for someone to stab you in the back if you've got it to the wall," her father had explained on her thirteenth birthday. "At least you'll have a chance to defend yourself if someone tries to stab you in the heart. You can see the attack coming."

Harlan Rush didn't look at life through rose-colored glasses, and he'd taught Lizzie, his only child, to do the same.

She wanted rose-colored glasses. She wanted, even for a few minutes, to be someone who could settle into a quaint Irish pub on a windy, rainy afternoon without considering that a killer could walk through the door, looking for her.

Across the pub, in their thick West Cork accents, the local men kidded and argued. Alone at her table, alone in their country, Lizzie was struck by their ease with each other—one that spoke of a lifetime together. She was on her own, and, by choice, had been for much of the past year, at least when it came to her dealings with Norman Estabrook and the FBI.

"I was hoping Keira would be here," Will Davenport said, with just the slightest edge of concern in his voice.

Just Keira? Why not Simon, too?

Lizzie settled back in her chair and reached down to pat the dog, his fur warm from the fire.

Something was wrong.

Eddie set another frothy-topped pint on the bar. "Keira's gone to Allihies for the day to research that old story. The one about the three brothers and the stone angel. It got her in trouble once. It hasn't again, has it?"

"I stopped in Allihies before driving up here," Davenport said. "She wasn't there, but I haven't come because of the story."

"The grandfather of the woman who told it to Keira heard the story in the Allihies copper mines. The last of them shut down years ago. Keira planned to visit the museum that's opened in the old Cornish church there." The Irishman lifted the pints onto a tray and gave Davenport a pointed look. "The mansion the British owners built for themselves has been turned into a luxury hotel."

The Brit didn't rise to the bait. "Things change."

"That they do, and sometimes for the better. Other times, not."

"Did Keira say when she'd return?"

"You'd think she'd be back by now, with the gale. That story of hers has drawn curious tourists all summer." As he walked out from behind the bar with the tray, Eddie glanced toward Lizzie. "They're all wanting to find the stone angel themselves."

"Assuming it exists," Davenport said.

The Irishman shrugged, noncommittal, and carried the beers to his fellow villagers. Lizzie was aware that both he and Will Davenport had played a critical role in uncovering the identity of a serial killer who'd become obsessed with Keira's story. She and Simon had, from all Lizzie had heard, encountered true evil. That was two months ago, when Simon was supposed to be laying low ahead of Norman's arrest.

While Eddie delivered the drinks, Davenport walked over to the fire, his gaze settling on Lizzie. She was used to being around men. She worked as director of concierge services and excursions for her family's fifteen highly individual boutique hotels, and she'd grown up with her four male Rush cousins, who now ranged in age from twenty-two to thirty-four. They were all striking in appearance, but, even so, she felt herself getting hot under the Brit's scrutiny. He had the bearing and edgy good looks that could spark even the most independent woman to fantasize about having her own prince charming come to her rescue.

Lizzie quashed that thought. No Prince Charming for her. Not now, not ever.

He nodded to her book, still open at the mesmerizing illustration of the farm. "Is that the Ireland you've come here to find?" His eyes, Lizzie saw, were a rich hazel, with flecks of blue, green and gold that changed with the light. "Fairies, thatched roofs and pretty gardens?"

Lizzie smiled. "Maybe it's the Ireland I have found."

"Do you believe in the wee folk?"

"I'm keeping an open mind. Keira Sullivan's quite the artist, isn't she? I overheard you and the barman. I gather you know her."

"We met earlier this summer. Did you just purchase her book?"

"Yes. I bought it in Kenmare this afternoon." That wasn't true. Keira's young cousin in Boston, Fiona O'Reilly, a harp student, had given it to her, but that, Lizzie decided, was something Will Davenport didn't need to know. "I heard about the story that brought Keira here. Three brothers tussle with fairies over an ancient

Celtic stone angel. The brothers believe the angel will bring them good fortune in one form or another, and the fairies believe it's one of their own turned to stone."

Davenport studied her with half-closed eyes.

"It's a wonderful story," Lizzie added.

"So it is." His tone gave away nothing.

Lizzie pushed her empty plate to the center of the table. She wanted more coffee, but she'd already drunk two cups and figured they'd give her enough of a caffeine jolt to counteract any jetlag. She was accustomed to changing time zones but had slept only fitfully on her flight from Boston.

She turned the book over to the full-color, back-cover photograph of Keira Sullivan in a dark green velvet dress. She had pretty cornflower-blue eyes, and her long blond hair was decorated with fresh flowers. "Keira could pass for a fairy princess herself, don't you think?"

"She could, indeed."

Lizzie doubted she'd ever pass for a fairy princess, even if she wore velvet and sprinkled flowers in her hair.

Not that she was bad looking, but her eyes, a light green, seemed to have perpetual dark circles under them lately. She'd had a rough few days.

A rough year, really.

"Do you know Keira?" Davenport asked.

"No, we've never met."

"But you're familiar with the story—"

"It was in all the papers," Lizzie said, not letting him finish. "Yes."

He was clearly suspicious now, but she didn't care. His presence and Simon's absence were unexpected and called for a revision of her plan. Whatever she might have ended up telling Simon, she had no intention of telling his friend Lord Davenport anything. She needed more information about what was going on, where Simon was, where Keira was.

"What brings you to the Beara Peninsula?" Davenport asked.

"I'm hiking the Beara Way." She wasn't, and she didn't like to lie, but it was easier—and possibly safer for all concerned—than telling the truth. "Not start to finish. It's almost two hundred kilometers. I don't have that much time to spare."

"You're on your own?"

She gave him a bright smile. "Now, that's a bold question to ask a woman having coffee and crumble by herself."

His eyes darkened slightly. "I trust you've a room for the night. The weather's terrible." He gestured back toward the bar where Eddie had returned with his empty tray. "Perhaps Eddie could direct you to a local B and B."

"It's decent of you to be concerned." Lizzie doubted concern for her had anything to do with his motive. She'd sparked his interest by having Keira's book out, by being there alone by the fire. If she was staying nearby, he wanted to keep an eye on her. "I have a tent. I can always camp somewhere."

She saw the beginnings of a smile. He had a straight mouth, a strong jaw, a hint of a wave to his dark blond hair. As good-looking and expensively dressed as he was, he wasn't in any way pretty or soft.

"I wouldn't have taken you for a woman who likes to sleep in a tent," he said, with the barest hint of humor.

In fact, she thought, he was right. It would take more than a suspicious British spy to get her to sleep in a tent in any weather. Not that she hadn't, or couldn't, or wouldn't if she needed to—but she'd have to have good reason. Wind, rain, rocks, uneven ground, no indoor plumbing. She wasn't fussy, but she did like the basics.

She got to her feet. Her walking shoes, which she'd bought before leaving Dublin that morning and scuffed up to make them look less new, had toes shaped like a duck's bill. They were ugly but comfortable and, supposedly, indestructible.

"The gale's dying down already." She tried her smile again on Davenport, but it had no visible effect. "I haven't heard the windows rattle in the last ten minutes."

"You're American. Where are you from?"

"Las Vegas." Arguably true, given her lifestyle. There was a Rush hotel in Las Vegas, and she'd spent a great deal of time there.

"Is this your first trip to Ireland?"

"No, but it's my first visit to the Beara Peninsula." Lizzie turned the book of folktales to the front-cover illustration of a lush, magical-looking glen with fairies frolicking in the green. "Keira Sullivan has a talent for painting places that people can believe, want to believe, are real. Do *you* believe in fairies, Lord Will?"

"It's just Will. I allow Eddie his fun. What's your name?"

She didn't want to get into names. "I should go," she said, slipping the book into her backpack and leaving enough euros on the table to cover her tab.

Will said nothing as she hoisted her pack onto one shoulder. The dog looked up at her with his big brown eyes, and she leaned over to him and whispered, *"Slán a fhágáil ag duine."* Which, if she remembered correctly, was Irish for some kind of goodbye. She liked to think it was a phrase her Irish-born mother would have taught her if she'd lived.

The local men watched her from their tables, Eddie O'Shea from behind the bar, all of them accustomed, she thought, to the routines of their lives. Farm, sea, village, church, family. They'd all come up in the talk Lizzie had overheard. Her own life had few such routines, and she doubted Will Davenport's did, either.

She grabbed her jacket off the peg by the door and pulled it on, zipping it up as the men at the tables roared with laughter at a story one was telling. Why not stay and sit by the fire for the evening and never mind why she'd come to Ireland and this tiny, out-of-the-way village?

But that, of course, was impossible.

She headed outside. The wind and rain had eased, leaving behind a fine, persistent mist. She dug out her cell phone and saw she had two text messages from her cousin Jeremiah, the third-born of her Rush cousins. He worked at the Whitcomb, her family's hotel in Boston. He was tawny-haired, blue-eyed and good-looking and claimed, as his brothers did, that Lizzie had them wrapped around her little finger.

An exaggeration.

Jeremiah never used text shorthand. His first message read:

Cahill and March in Boston.
No Keira.

Lizzie read the message again to make sure she hadn't made a mistake. Simon Cahill, a special agent with the FBI, and John March, the director of the FBI, were in Boston? Why?

She'd run into Simon a half dozen times over the past year. He was a handsome, broad-shouldered bruiser of a man, a black-haired, green-eyed natural charmer who had persuaded Norman Estabrook that he was an ex-FBI agent with an ax to grind against March, his former boss.

Such, however, was not the case.

Had Simon already been on his way to Boston when

she'd left for Ireland last night? Lizzie almost laughed out loud. Talk about ironic. She'd come to Ireland to convince Simon to do all he could to keep Norman in custody and not to fall for his line about having stumbled into a network of violent criminals. He had meant every word of his threat against Simon and Director March. It wasn't just about vengeance, either. Norman was no longer willing to sit on the sidelines. He was itching to do something dramatic and violent himself.

Lizzie returned her phone to her jacket pocket and shivered in the chilly early evening air.

If Keira Sullivan hadn't gone to Boston with Simon, where was she now?

And why was Will Davenport here and so serious?

Lizzie smelled pipe smoke and noticed an old man in traditional farmer's clothes seated on the front bench of a wooden picnic table by the pub door. His face was deeply lined, his eyebrows bushy above steady eyes that were a clear, even fierce, blue. He held up his pipe, smoke curling into the mist. "You'll be wanting to go to the stone circle."

She eased her pack off her shoulder. "For what?"

"For what you're looking for, dearie."

"How do you know what I'm looking for?"

He pointed his pipe up the quiet street. "There. It's down the lane and up the hill. You'll find your way." His eyes, gleaming with intensity, fixed on her. "You always do, don't you, dearie?"

Steadying herself against a sudden gust of wind that blew up from the harbor at her back, Lizzie peered past the rows of brightly painted houses—fuchsia, blue, yellow, red, mustard, all a welcome antidote to the gray weather. She loved the unique light, the special feel of being back in Ireland.

But find her way to what?

When she turned to ask, the old man was gone.

Eddie O'Shea's springer spaniel wandered out of the pub and trotted up the village street in the direction the old man had pointed.

There was no one else about. A basket of flowers hung from a lamppost, swinging in the breeze, and Lizzie could identify with its drooping and dripping pink geraniums, purple petunias and sprays of lavender.

The dog paused and looked back at her, his tail wagging.

Lizzie could no longer smell the old farmer's pipe smoke in the damp air. If she'd been drinking Guinness instead of coffee she'd have been sure she conjured him up. As it was…she had no idea.

"All right," she called to the spaniel. "I'll follow you."

Chapter 2

Beara Peninsula, Southwest Ireland
5:50 p.m., IST
August 25

Will Davenport stabbed the toe of his shoe into the wet gravel in front of the small, traditional stone cottage where Keira was staying while Simon was in Boston. The cottage was situated on a narrow lane cut along an ancient wall that ran parallel to the bay and the mountains. A steady wind blew dark clouds across the rugged, barren hills that swept up from the harbor to the spine of the peninsula.

He had resisted the temptations of Eddie O'Shea's pub—a pint, a fire, camaraderie—and returned to his car, finding his way here. Rambling pink roses scented the damp, cool air as the remains of the storm pushed east across Ireland. To the north, across Kenmare Bay, he could see the jagged outlines of the McGillicuddy Reeks of the Iveragh Peninsula, another finger of land that jutted into the Atlantic.

Keira's car was parked in the drive by the roses, and a light glowed in the cottage kitchen, but she hadn't come to the door when he'd knocked.

Was she having a bath, perhaps?

She had arrived in Ireland in June to paint and look into the Beara Peninsula origins of the folktale she'd heard in a South Boston kitchen. The *Slieve Mikish*—the Mikish Mountains—at the tip of the peninsula held rich veins of copper that had drawn settlers to the region thousands of years ago. Will had driven along Bantry Bay on the southern side of the peninsula, the weather deteriorating the closer he came to the Atlantic and Allihies. He'd talked to Simon briefly and had hoped to find Keira poking around among the skeletal remains of the long-abandoned Industrial Age mines scattered across the remote, starkly beautiful landscape. When he hadn't found her, he'd headed to the pub on Kenmare Bay, discovering not his friend's new love but a hiker with striking light green eyes and one of Keira's books.

Pushing back a nagging sense of worry, Will checked his BlackBerry and saw he had a message from Josie Goodwin, his assistant in London, who had arranged for his flight into Cork and the car that had awaited him.

Josie's words were straight to the point:

Estabrook free 9 AM MDT.

With a grimace at the unpleasant, if not unexpected, news, Will dialed Josie's number.

"I was about to call you," she said without preamble when she picked up. "I have more. Apparently Estabrook couldn't wait to get off his ranch and left in his private plane immediately after signing his plea agreement. I gather he's never been one to sit still. He must be stir-crazy after two months."

"Did he go alone?"

"Yes."

"Then he kept his promise to provide authorities with all he knows about his drug-trafficking friends?"

"The Americans must be satisfied or they wouldn't have let him go free."

"Josie, the man threatened to kill Simon and Director March."

"He insists he was speaking metaphorically."

Someone who didn't know Josie well could miss her wry tone, but she and Will had worked together for the past three years. He didn't miss it. "Metaphorically," he said. "I'll have to remember that one."

"Ireland is a long way from Montana, Will. Estabrook has no history of violence, nor is he suspected of having been involved with his associates' violent crimes. Not that participating in the spread of the poison of illegal drugs isn't a kind of violence."

"I'm at Keira's cottage now," Will said. "Her car is here, but she's not. She must have gone for a walk."

"From what Simon's told me, she does love to walk. They're a remarkable pair, aren't they, Will? True love is a rare thing, but they've found it."

This time, Will heard wistfulness in Josie's voice. She was the thirty-eight-year-old single mother of a teenage son and a woman who had faced more than her share of heartbreak. She was also a capable, resourceful member of the British Secret Intelligence Service, and Will trusted her without hesitation. She understood, as he did, that their lives and work ran more smoothly, more easily, unencumbered by romantic entanglements. She'd learned her lesson the hard way through personal experience. He'd learned his by example.

Matters, he thought, for another day.

"Have you talked to Simon?" he asked.

"Briefly. He appreciates that you're in Ireland and Keira's not alone. He'd never have left her if he'd known Estabrook would be released. He and March had hoped they could keep him in custody."

Will resisted any comment on the FBI director. He and March had a history, not a good one. "A woman was at the pub just now, reading one of Keira's books. A hiker. Small, slim, light green eyes, black hair. American. Do you recognize the description?"

"Long hair, short hair?"

"I don't know. Long, I think. I only saw a few strands. The rest was under a red bandanna."

"Ah."

Will sighed. "She said she's from Las Vegas and is here hiking the Beara Way."

"Alone?"

"As far as I could tell, yes."

"Seems a lovely thing to do," Josie said. "But you don't believe her, do you, Will?"

He didn't hesitate. "No."

"You wouldn't be drawn to an Irish village where an ancient, magical stone angel was reportedly discovered in a ruin?"

"Josie…"

"I've jotted down the description and will see what I can learn. One never knows. Good luck finding Keira. Simon trusts you completely."

"I owe him, Josie."

"Yes, you do."

Will stared down through the gray mist and fog down toward the harbor, remembering back two years to a tragic, violent eighteen hours in Afghanistan that ended with Simon Cahill saving his life. It was a debt they both understood could never be repaid—and yet Will kept trying. But it wasn't why he'd come to Ireland. He had come, simply, as a friend.

"Will," Josie added crisply, "Simon knows you're not some fop who spends all his time fishing and golfing. He's aware by now that you weren't in Afghanistan to catch butterflies."

She disconnected before Will could respond.

He shoved his BlackBerry into his coat pocket, but part of him was still back in Afghanistan, alone, dehydrated, bruised and bloodied, determined to stay alive for one reason: he owed the truth to the memory and the service of the two SAS soldiers—his friends—who had died at his side hours earlier on that long, violent night. At great risk to himself, with only an ax, a rope and his own brute strength at his disposal, Simon had come upon the bombed-out cave and freed Will. Together they then dug out the bodies of David Mears and Philip Billings, who had died because Will had trusted the wrong man.

Another friend.

Myles Fletcher.

Will made himself silently say the name of the man— the British military officer and intelligence agent—who had compromised their highly classified mission, only to be captured and dragged off by the very enemy fighters he had embraced as allies.

After reuniting Will with his SAS colleagues, Simon had returned to his own classified mission on behalf of the FBI. He had never asked for an explanation of Will's presence in the cave—or thanks for saving his life.

After two years, Myles Fletcher's remains had yet to be recovered. Presumably his terrorist allies had turned on him and killed him after he'd served his purpose. There wasn't a shred of evidence that he was still alive, but Will wouldn't be satisfied until he had definitive proof.

The FBI had been onto a drug-trafficking and terrorism connection that had evaporated due to Will's failed mission. John March considered Will ultimately responsible for Myles's treachery.

Simon didn't blame Will for anything, but Will had discovered in their two years of friendship that little fazed Simon Cahill.

Except being on one side of the Atlantic while the woman he loved was on the other.

Will buttoned his coat and locked the memories back into their own tight compartment as he walked out to the lane in search of Keira.

Chapter 3

Beara Peninsula, Southwest Ireland
6:20 p.m., IST
August 25

Lizzie pulled off her bandanna, relishing the feel of the cool wind and mist in her hair. Eddie's dog had led her onto a narrow country lane that followed a stone wall between bay and mountains. She tried to enjoy her walk past rain-soaked roses, holly and wildflowers, fragrant on the wet summer evening. She smiled at lambs settling in for the night and stood for a moment in front of an old, abandoned stone cottage, a reminder of the long-ago famine and subsequent decades of mass emigration that had hit West Cork hard.

Up ahead, the spaniel paused and looked back, tail wagging. Lizzie laughed, dismissing any notion that he was trying to lead her somewhere or was connected to her strange encounter with the old farmer.

Too little sleep. Too many Irish fairy stories.

She came to a cheerful yellow-painted bungalow. A red-haired woman stood at the kitchen sink while a man, handsome and smiling, brought a stack of dishes to the counter and young children colored at a table behind them.

Feeling an unexpected tug of emotion, Lizzie continued along the lane. If nothing else, the cool air and brisk walk were helping to clear her head so that she could figure out what to do now that Simon Cahill was in Boston.

She could hear the intermittent bleating of sheep, out to pasture as far up into the rock-strewn hills as she could see. Pale gray fog and mist swirled over the highest of the peaks, settling into rocky dips and crevices. Given her cover story, she'd stuffed her backpack with hiking gear, dry clothes, flashlight, trail food, even a tent. All she had to do now was get herself onto the Beara Way and keep going. Hike for real. She could leave her car in the village and follow the mix of roads, lanes and trails up the peninsula to Kenmare, or down to Allihies and Dursey Island.

How many times had she debated walking away from Norman Estabrook and all she knew about him? She'd met him when he'd been a guest at her family's Dublin hotel sixteen months ago. He was a brilliant, successful hedge-fund manager who had the resources to indulge his every whim, and as an adrenaline junkie, he had many whims. He was known as much for his death-defying adventures as his immense fortune. He wasn't reckless. Whether he was planning to circumnavigate the globe in a hot-air balloon, jump out of an airplane at high-altitude, or head off on a hike in extreme conditions, he would prepare for anything that could go wrong.

At first, Lizzie had believed he was hanging out with major drug traffickers because he was naïve, but she'd learned otherwise. She now suspected that, all along, Norman had calculated that if he were caught, prosecutors would want his friends in the drug cartels more than they wanted him, the financial genius who'd helped them with their money. He was rarely impulsive, and he knew how to leverage himself and manage risk.

Lizzie had been at his ranch in Montana in late June when he'd realized federal agents were about to arrest him. He was a portly, bland-looking forty-year-old man who'd never married, and never would marry. Shocked and livid, he'd turned to her. "I've been betrayed."

He'd meant Simon Cahill, not her. Norman had hired Simon the previous summer to help him plan and execute his high-risk adventures. He'd known Simon had just left the FBI and therefore might not be willing to look the other way if he discovered his client was involved in illegal activities, especially with major drug traffickers.

Turned out there was nothing "ex" FBI about Simon.

In those tense hours before his arrest, Norman hadn't looked at himself and acknowledged he'd at least been unwise to cozy up to criminals. Instead, he'd railed against those who had wronged *him*. Other than a few members of his household staff, Lizzie had been the only one with him. He had never had a serious romantic relationship that she knew of—and certainly not with her. The people in his life—family, friends, staff, colleagues—were planets circling his sun.

The rules just didn't apply to Norman Estabrook. He'd gone to Harvard on scholarship, started working at a respected, established hedge fund right after graduating, then launched his own fund at twenty-seven. By forty, he was worth several billion dollars and able to take a less active role in his funds.

Lizzie had paced with him in front of the tall windows overlooking his sprawling ranch and the big western sky and tried to talk him into calling his attorneys and cooperating with authorities. But if she'd learned anything about Norman in the past year, it was that he did what he wanted to do. Most people about to be handcuffed and read their rights wouldn't get on the phone and threaten an FBI agent and his boss, but Norman, as he'd often pointed out, wasn't most people.

She'd watched his hatred and determination mount as he'd confronted the reality that Simon—the man he'd entrusted with his life—was actually an undercover federal agent.

That John March had won.

Retreating from the magnificent view, he had picked up the phone.

"Don't, Norman," Lizzie had said.

She wasn't even sure he'd heard her. Spittle at the corners of his mouth, his eyes gleaming with rage, he'd called Simon in Boston and delivered his threat.

"You're dead. Dead, dead, dead. First I kill John March. Then I kill you."

Lizzie remembered staring out at the aspens, so green against the clear blue sky, and thinking she, too, would be dead, dead, dead if Norman figured out that for the better part of a year she'd been passing information about him anonymously to the FBI. Until his arrest, she hadn't known if the FBI was taking her information seriously and had Norman's activities under investigation. She certainly hadn't known they had an undercover agent in position.

They didn't know about her, either. *No one* did.

Even with FBI agents spilling onto Norman's ranch—even when they'd interviewed her—Lizzie had kept quiet about her role. When she decided to head to Ireland, she'd taken steps to maintain her secret. Hence, the backpack, walking shoes and tale about hiking the Beara Way. Let Simon think she was stopping in on him and Keira while she was in the area. Get him talking about Norman, their mutual ex-friend, and her belief that he already had people in position to help him when he'd called Simon from his ranch that day. That he was serious and had at least the beginnings of a plan in place, and the FBI should get it out of him. For the past two months, she'd expected "conspiracy to commit murder" to be added to the list of charges against him. The FBI had his threat against its director and one of its agents on tape. Surely they'd be investigating whether he could carry it out.

Maybe they were, but here she was, her jacket flapping in the stubborn Irish wind and Simon Cahill and John March across the Atlantic in Boston. Lizzie hoped they were consulting on how to keep Norman in custody.

She came to a track that wound up into the hills and noticed fresh paw prints in the soft, wet dirt. Assuming they belonged to the springer spaniel, she followed them up the steep track. She'd go a little ways, then head back to her car. She couldn't fly to Boston tonight. She could go back to Dublin or find a local bed-and-breakfast. She needed sleep, food and information on Norman in Montana and Simon and March in Boston.

The dirt track curved and leveled off briefly at a hand-painted Beware of Bull sign nailed to a gate post. Lizzie paused and gazed out across the open pasture, where the distinctive silhouette of a prehistoric stone circle was outlined against the dark clouds.

Eddie's dog leaped from behind a large boulder, startling her. "There you are," she called to him, laughing at her reaction. "Hold on. I'm coming."

Not waiting this time, the dog pivoted and bounded up past scrubby junipers and over clumps of gray rocks toward the circle.

He obviously knew he had her.

Lizzie climbed over the barbed-wire fence and dropped onto the wet grass on the other side, dodging a sodden cow patty. Carefully avoiding more cow manure, she made her way across the rough, uneven ground of the pasture. In a sudden blur, the dog streaked back toward the fence and the dirt track, deserting her. She shrugged and decided to continue on to the stone circle, one of more than a hundred of the megalithic monuments in West Cork and south Kerry alone. As she came closer, she jumped from one rock to another, skirting a patch of mud. She entered the circle between two of the tall, gray boulders that had occupied their spots for thousands of years.

A breeze whistled softly up from the bay.

Lizzie counted eight heavy standing stones of different heights that formed the outer edge of the circle. A ninth had toppled over, and there was a spot for a missing tenth stone. A low, flat-topped slab that looked as if it had been turned on its side—the axis stone—made a total of eleven.

Below her, past green, rolling fields, the harbor was gray and churning with the last of the storm. She stood very still, absorbing the atmosphere. She had never been to a place so eerie, so strangely quiet. The ancients had chosen an alluring location for their stone circle, whatever its original purpose.

"I can understand how people see fairies here," she whispered to herself.

A shuffling sound drew her attention, and she turned just as a fat, brown cow edged slowly along the thick junipers outside the circle.

She felt uneasy, nervous even, and didn't know why.

A presence, she decided.

Another cow? The dog?

Was the old farmer out there in the shadows and fog? She remembered his strange words.

"You'll be wanting to go to the stone circle."

"For what?"

"For what you're looking for, dearie."

Lizzie noticed a movement in a small cluster of trees

and took a shallow breath, listening, squinting toward
the hills as she eased her pack off her shoulder.

Something—someone—was out there.

She wasn't alone.

Chapter 4

Beara Peninsula, Southwest Ireland
7:10 p.m., IST
August 25

As she eased back between the two tall boulders, Lizzie felt her right foot sink deep into a low spot. She ignored the shock of water and mud oozing into her socks and placed a palm on one of the cool, wet stones.

The wind gusted and howled over the exposed hills and rocks, bringing with it a fresh rush of rain.

She shivered. Maybe that was all it was—a last gasp from the storm.

She heard a sound behind her and turned sharply. Across from her, a slender woman entered the ancient circle, her long, blond hair whipping in the wind. She wore an oversize Irish fisherman's sweater that hung almost to her knees and, Lizzie suspected, belonged to Simon Cahill, because this had to be Keira Sullivan.

She slowed as she approached the low axis stone.

"It's okay—I'm a friend," Lizzie said quickly, not wanting to startle her. Maybe *friend* was a stretch, but she could explain later. "I know Simon. Simon Cahill. You're Keira, aren't you?"

The other woman's eyes narrowed, her skin pale in the soft gray light. "I walked up here from my cottage. I came across the pasture—I've been restless. I was down at the old copper mines today and tried to blame the ghosts there, and the gale." She frowned without any obvious fear or panic. "What was that?"

Lizzie had heard it, too—rustling sounds toward the cluster of trees on the hillside. It wasn't the storm. Someone else was out there.

"It's not ghosts or the gale," she said, letting her backpack slip farther down her arm, ready to drop it and run, use it as a weapon—a shield. "We have to go."

Black clouds surged down the mountains. Rain, hissing and cold, pelted Lizzie's jacket and her bare head, soaked Keira's hair and wool sweater. But Keira didn't seem to notice the suddenly worsening conditions. "Who do you think is out there?"

"I don't know." Lizzie noticed the cow break into a run away from the trees. "We should hurry."

Keira pointed in the same direction. "There."

Lizzie had no time to answer. A man—compact, wearing a black ski cap—burst out into the open and charged through the gap in the circle.

"He's after you," Lizzie said. "Run, Keira. Run!"

"I can't leave you—"

"I can fight. Go. Please."

The man lunged for Keira, but she darted away from him, diving behind one of the standing stones.

He swore and pivoted after her. He had an assault knife in his right hand. Lizzie leaped into his path and swung her backpack hard against the knife blade, using her own momentum to add force to the blow. With a grunt of surprise, he lost his balance and stumbled backward over a protruding rock. Before he could regain his footing, she hit his knife again with her pack, following up with a sharp, low side kick to his left knee.

He yelped in pain and dropped the knife. Lizzie knew she had to press her advantage and quickly got in another low kick, scraping her foot down his shin. She stomped on his instep, not thinking, relying on her instincts and training. She'd practiced these moves a thousand times.

The attacker went down onto his back, writhing in the mud, manure and wet grass. Lizzie snatched up his knife before he could get to it and dropped onto her knees, putting the blade to his throat as he rolled onto his side and tried to get up.

"Keep your hands where I can see them," she said, "and don't move."

He complied immediately, his breathing shallow, as if he were afraid she'd cut him with the knife if he gulped or panted. One side of his face was pressed into the mud.

Lizzie turned the edge of the blade so that he could feel it against the thin skin over his carotid artery. "Do as I say or you're dead. Do you understand?"

"Aye. I understand."

He spoke with an Irish accent. A local hire, maybe. He could be faking the accent. Lizzie could manage a decent Irish brogue herself, and she was born in Boston. He was in his early to mid-thirties, with a jagged scar along his outer jaw that looked as if he'd earned it in a previous knife fight gone bad.

"You've broken my damn knee," he said.

"I doubt that."

Despite his pain, he spoke without fear, as if he knew it was only a matter of time before he'd get his knife back and complete his assignment.

Kill Keira Sullivan.

Lizzie had never killed anyone herself and hoped she

never had to, but she knew how to do it. Her father had seen to that.

"I'll check him for more weapons," Keira said.

Lizzie nodded, breathing hard.

Keira knelt in the muck and patted the man down from head to toe with a steadiness and efficiency that didn't surprise Lizzie. Keira's uncle was a homicide detective in Boston, and Keira herself had stood up to a killer in June.

She produced another assault knife in her search but no other weapons.

Lizzie controlled her reaction even as her thoughts raced. Norman wasn't waiting. He was acting now. Had he specified what he wanted done to the woman Simon loved? How he wanted her killed?

Undoubtedly, Lizzie thought. Norman would relish such details and control.

Was he going after Simon in Boston? John March? Who else?

She maintained her grip on the knife. "The man who hired you isn't just after Keira. Who's next?"

He hardly breathed. "I don't know anything."

"My friend, you need to be straight with me." She paused before asking again, "Who's next?"

He tried to swallow against the sharp edge of the knife. "It doesn't matter. You're too late. I can't stop what's going to happen. Neither can you."

"That's not what I asked."

He carefully spat bits of grass and dirt from his mouth. "Go to hell. I'll not answer a single question you put to me."

He was calling her bluff. Lizzie didn't know if she should cut him—if it would do any good in getting him to talk.

She heard a dog growl just outside the stone circle, a low, fierce sound that wasn't from Eddie's springer spaniel.

With her would-be attacker's spare knife in one hand, Keira stood back as a large black dog bounded into the circle and onto the prostrate axis stone next to her, directly in the Irishman's line of sight. He nervously eyed the hound. A knife to the throat didn't impress him, but a snarling black dog appearing out of nowhere obviously did.

Keira addressed the thug calmly. "Tell this woman what she wants to know. It'll ease the dog. He senses the danger you pose to us."

The man licked his lips. "I don't like dogs."

"Then answer me," Lizzie said. "Who's next?"

He hesitated a half beat. "The daughter of the FBI director."

"Abigail," Keira breathed, her blue eyes steady but filled with fear as she looked at Lizzie. "Abigail Browning. She's a homicide detective in Boston."

Lizzie knew all about Abigail Browning, John March's widowed daughter, but kept her attention focused on the Irishman. "What's the plan?" The rain had subsided to a misting drizzle, but she could feel mud and water soaking into her hiking pants. "Tell me."

"I can't. I'll be killed."

The dog gave a menacing growl and leaned forward on the ancient stone, lowering his head as if at any moment he might pounce on the man below.

"There's a bomb," the Irishman whispered, shutting his eyes, then quickly opening them again. He obviously didn't dare lose sight of the black dog.

"Where?" Lizzie asked.

"Back porch."

"It's a triple-decker. Whose back porch?"

Keira gasped, but Lizzie couldn't take the time to explain how she knew that Abigail Browning lived on the first-floor of a Jamaica Plain triple-decker she co-owned with two other Boston Police Department detectives, including Bob O'Reilly, Keira's uncle.

Their attacker didn't answer.

"Tell me now," Lizzie said.

The dog bared his teeth, thick white drool dripping from the sides of his mouth, and the Irishman responded with a visceral shudder.

Definitely not a dog lover.

He bit his lower lip. "First floor. Browning's place."

"When?" Lizzie asked.

He turned his gaze from the dog and fixed his eyes on her. "Now."

She stifled a jolt of panic. He wasn't lying. Between the thought of the dog ripping out his intestines and her cutting his throat, he wasn't willing to risk a lie. Her father had told her at around age fourteen there was nothing like the fear of bleeding out to motivate a man.

"We need to call Boston," Keira said.

Lizzie nodded in agreement, but her heart jumped when she saw a tall man crossing the pasture toward the stone circle.

Will Davenport.

Keira saw him, too, and cried out to him as he entered the circle. "Will! There's a bomb—I have to warn Abigail."

He sized up the situation with a quick glance. "All right. I'll call." He spoke with complete control. "Tell me the number."

"I don't have Abigail's number memorized. It's at the cottage."

"What about your uncle?"

She nodded. "It's easier if I dial." He passed her his BlackBerry. Keira had tears in her eyes, but her hands didn't shake as she hit buttons. "If they're all there…if Abigail's on her porch…" She continued to dial.

Will crouched next to Lizzie and placed his hand over hers on the knife. His hand was steady, warm. His eyes, the flecks of gold gleaming, leveled on hers. "Let me take care of him. You help Keira."

Lizzie didn't budge. "How do I know you're not going to take the knife and kill us both?"

"Because I don't need the knife."

There was that. Lizzie loosened her grip on the handle. "I have bungee cords in my pack. We can use them to handcuff him."

"It would seem you think of everything," Will said as she eased her hand out from under his and he held the knife at the Irishman's throat.

Rainwater streamed from Keira's hair down her face as she spoke to her uncle in Boston. "Bob. Thank God…"

She faltered, and Lizzie stood up. "The people in danger are your family and friends. Please. Let me do this." She put out a hand, and Keira gave her the phone. Lizzie forcefully addressed Keira's uncle on the other end. "Listen to me. Take cover. Take cover *now.*"

"Who the hell is this?" O'Reilly demanded.

"A bomb's about to go off on Abigail's back porch."

He was already yelling. "Take cover, take cover! Scoop, Abigail, Fiona!"

The phone crackled.

Lizzie heard a loud booming sound.

An explosion.

"Lieutenant!"

The connection went dead.

Chapter 5

Boston, Massachusetts
2:37 p.m., EDT
August 25

Two almost simultaneous explosions shook the triple-decker and knocked Bob O'Reilly off his feet. He landed on his left side, more or less in a sprawl, his cell phone clutched in his hand. He'd banged the hell out of his elbow but otherwise was all right.

He rolled onto one knee and jumped up, his ears ringing, his heart racing. He yanked open his back door and ran out onto the open porch of his top-floor apartment.

He could hear glass cracking, metal popping and what he swore was the hiss of flames.

"Fiona!" he yelled. "Scoop!"

Scoop Wisdom, another detective, had the second-floor apartment, but he and Fiona were picking tomatoes in Scoop's garden in the postage-stamp of a backyard.

Fiona was the eldest of Bob's three daughters.

Had they heard him yell for them to take cover?

"Dad! Daddy!"

Fiona.

She was screaming, but it meant she could talk.

His baby was alive.

Bob gripped the railing and leaned over, trying to see through the black smoke billowing up from below. "Hang on, Fi." He sounded as if he were being strangled. "I'm coming."

"Scoop. *Scoop!*" She was shrieking now. "Oh, my God!" Her next words were unintelligible.

Bob tried not to react to her panic and fear. He saw flames now, licking up the support posts of the two porches under him.

He'd never make it down the back steps. He'd burn up.

He retreated into his kitchen and grabbed the small fire extinguisher by the stove, a Christmas present from Jayne, his youngest, who'd printed off a checklist of what to do to prepare for a disaster—power outages, floods, earthquakes, hurricanes.

Bombs going off.

Keira was in Ireland. How had she known about a bomb on Abigail's porch?

Who was the other woman with her?

Bob forced his thoughts back and tucked the fire extinguisher under his arm as he ran through his living room and out into the main hall.

There was no smoke in the stairwell. That was one good thing.

Was another bomb ready to go off?

Using his thumb, he hit 911 on his cell phone as he charged down the two flights of stairs. The dispatcher came on, and he identified himself as an off-duty police officer and gave his address, stated the nature of the emergency.

An explosion. A fire. Possible injuries.

"I think an off-duty officer is hurt," Bob said. "Detective Sergeant Cyrus 'Scoop' Wisdom. He's out back with my daughter, Fiona O'Reilly, age nineteen."

"Where are you?"

"First floor. Inside. I'm checking on a second off-duty officer, Abigail Browning."

The interior door to the apartment she shared with her fiancé, Owen Garrison, and the main door into the building were both ajar, which Bob took as a positive sign that she'd gotten out. He burst outside and ran down the front steps, expecting to find Abigail out on the sidewalk. Owen had left earlier. Bob had heard them laughing down on the street.

Her car was there, but she wasn't.

He said to the dispatcher, "She could have gone out back to help Scoop and Fi. That's where the fire is."

"You need to find a safe place and stay there."

"I'm a police officer. I know what I need to do. Stay on with me. I'll let you know what I find out."

"Lieutenant, you need to wait for help."

"I am the help."

"There could be another explosion. If there's a gas grill, the propane tank—"

"That's it," Bob said. "The second blast must have been the propane tank to Abigail's grill."

"Then you understand the need to stay where you are."

True, but Bob yanked open the unlatched gate to the narrow passage between his triple-decker and the one next door. Smoke blackened the still, late-summer air and burned his nostrils. He coughed, tasting fire.

"Daddy! Help me!"

Fiona was sobbing now as she cried out for him. She hadn't called him Daddy since she was ten. She was due to start her sophomore year as a classical harp major at Boston University, and now she'd been caught in a bomb going off at her father's house.

She deserved better.

Bob shoved his phone into his pants pocket and shouted to her. "Keep talking to me, kid. Where are you?"

He felt the wall of heat before he saw the orange and red flames engulfing Abigail's porch, a duplicate of his except neater—and now mostly obliterated by the blast. One structural beam was gone, another was burning, flames working their way up to Scoop's second-floor porch as if the devil himself were spewing them.

Anyone out back when the bomb had gone off and sent shrapnel flying everywhere would be in serious trouble, but Bob saw only flames, charred wood, debris.

He didn't see Abigail fighting her way through the fire, or Scoop or Fiona in the thick smoke blackening the small yard.

"Fiona, where are you?"

His throat was raw, burning, tight with fear. The fire extinguisher would be useless against the main fire, but he held on to it in case of smaller fires or secondary explosions. He pulled his polo shirt over his mouth and nose and pushed through the smoke, past the outdoor table where they all spent as much time as possible during Boston's too-short summer. The concussive wave from the explosion had knocked over the cheap plastic chairs, but the two Adirondack chairs had stayed put.

"Fiona! Scoop! Abigail! Someone talk to me."

"Here." Fiona's voice, slightly less hysterical now. "We're behind the compost bin. I can't move."

"Why can't you move?"

"Scoop…"

Bob jumped over a tidy row of green beans into Scoop's vegetable garden, his pride and joy. He'd kept them in salads all summer and shared whatever was ripe—first the peas and spinach, then the beans and summer squash. Now he was unloading tomatoes on his housemates. He'd been talking about freezing and canning some of next summer's harvest.

Next summer.

He'd be there. He had to be. Scoop wasn't meant to die this way.

Not in front of Fiona.

A moan, a sob came from behind the compost bin on the other side of the garden. Bob thrashed through tomato and cauliflower plants. Scoop had made the bin himself out of chicken wire and wood slats. He'd bought a book on composting. Now, at summer's end, the bin was full of what he referred to as "organic matter."

And earthworms. He'd ordered them from a catalog and told Bob not to tell Fiona because she was into the romance of composting and didn't need to know about the worms. He'd explained what they did to help speed the process of turning garbage into dirt. Bob's eyes had glazed over while he'd listened.

He stepped over a cauliflower plant, letting his shirt drop from his mouth as he saw Scoop's foot peeking out from the edge of the compost bin, toe down inside his beat-up running shoe.

No movement.

"Daddy. I can't…Dad…" Just out of sight behind the bin, Fiona was hyperventilating. "Scoop can't be dead!"

"He's not dead."

Bob blurted the words without knowing if they were true, something he tried never to do. But they had to be. Scoop was all muscle. He was a boxer, a wrestler, a top-notch cop.

Steeling himself for what he might see, Bob took a quick breath, sucking in smoke, and stepped behind the compost bin.

Scoop was sprawled facedown on Fiona's lap. She'd

wriggled partway out from under him and was half sitting, pinned between him and the bin. Her thin, bare arms were wrapped around him, smeared with blood and blackened bits of shrapnel.

Bob could see that most of the blood wasn't hers.

She looked up at him with those wide, blue eyes he'd first noticed when she was a tot. Tears streamed down her pale cheeks, creating little rivers of blood and soot.

"Fi," he said, forcing himself not to choke up. "You okay? You hurt?"

"Just a little shaken up. I—Dad." She gulped in a breath, shivering uncontrollably, teeth chattering, lips a purplish-blue and bleeding from where she'd bitten down on them. "Scoop. He saved me. He saved my life."

Shrapnel from the bomb or something on Abigail's porch—a propane tank, a grill, a bucket, the railing—had ripped into Scoop, cutting his back, his arms, his legs. His shirt was shredded, the white fabric soaked in blood. A hunk of metal stuck out of the back of his neck, just below his hairline. Several other pieces were embedded in the meat of his upper left arm.

A single jagged piece of metal was stuck in his leg below the hem of his khaki shorts.

Bob knelt on one knee and checked Scoop's wrist for a pulse, getting one almost immediately. "He's alive, Fi."

She tightened her grip on him, blood seeping between her fingers. "What happened?"

"There was an explosion. Firefighters and paramedics are on the way. Just don't move, okay?" Bob tried to give her a reassuring smile. "Don't move."

Scoop moaned and shifted position, maybe a quarter inch.

Bob said, "Don't you move, either, Scoop."

Most of the blood seemed to be from superficial cuts,

and the blast could have just knocked the wind out of him, but Bob wasn't taking any chances. With his shaved head and thick muscles, Scoop was a ferocious-looking cop even bloodied and sinking into shock. If he wasn't feeling pain now, he would soon.

Bob hesitated, but he knew he had to ask. "Before the blast—did you see Abigail?"

Fiona paled even more. "The phone rang. She…"

"Easy, Fi. Just take it slow." But Bob could feel his own urgency mounting, dread crawling over him, sucking the breath out of him. He had to concentrate to keep it out of his expression, his voice. "Okay?"

"She went to answer the phone."

"When?"

"Just before the explosion." Fiona squeezed her eyes shut, fresh tears leaking out the corners and joining up with the rest of the mess on her cheeks. "Not long before. I can't remember. Minutes?" She opened her eyes, sniffled. "I…*Dad.* I'm going to be sick."

Bob shook his head. "Nah. You're not going to puke on Scoop."

Had he misinterpreted the partially open doors? What if Abigail hadn't been fleeing the fire but, instead, someone had gone in after her?

Why?

What was he missing?

He placed his palm on his daughter's cheek, noted with a jolt how cold it was. "Help will be here soon." He spoke softly, trying to stay calm, to be assertive and clear without scaring her more. "We can't move Scoop. It's too dangerous."

"I'll stay with him."

Bob nodded. "Okay. The fire won't get here. Do what you can to keep Scoop still, so he doesn't dislodge a piece of shrapnel and make the bleeding worse. You be still, too. You could be hurt and not feel it."

"I'm not hurt, Dad, and I know first aid."

He lowered his hand from her cheek. She'd always been stubborn—and strong. "Hang in there, kid. I won't let anything happen to you." But hadn't he already?

Her lower lip trembled. "You're going to find Abigail, aren't you?"

Abigail. He pushed back his fear and nodded. "Yeah."

"It's okay, Dad." Fiona gave him a ragged smile. "You can count on me."

His heart nearly broke. He hated to leave her, but she and Scoop would be better off staying put than having him try to get them out to the street.

And he had to find Abigail.

Bob leaned his fire extinguisher next to the compost bin and pulled his cell phone out of his pocket. "I don't know what all you heard," he said to the dispatcher, "but you can talk to my daughter."

Fiona's fingers closed around the phone. They were callused from endless hours of harp practice. She should be practicing now, but here she was, the victim of some dirtbag.

He couldn't think about that now. "The 911 dispatcher is on the line. He'll help you. Do what he says."

She nodded.

Bob looked back toward the house. Scoop's porch was on fire now, too. The triple-decker was a hundred years old. Bob had seen others like it burn. Firefighters would have to get there fast if they stood a chance of saving it.

Didn't matter to him one way or the other.

He ran back through Scoop's vegetables and across the yard. The heat was brutal. Sweat poured down his face and soaked his armpits and chest, plastered his undershorts to his behind. Gunk burned in his eyes.

He could hear sirens blaring maybe a block away, but he couldn't wait. When he reached the street, he took the front steps two at a time.

Black smoke drifted out from Abigail's apartment.

Pulling his shirt back up over his face, he dived into her living room, but he didn't see her passed out on the floor.

No sign of her in the dining room, either.

The smoke was thick, dangerous. The fire was close.

He took another couple of steps, but he couldn't get to the kitchen or the bedroom in back, closer to the fire.

He was coughing up soot. He felt his knees crumbling under him but stiffened and made sure he didn't collapse. He was fifty and in decent shape. It wasn't exertion that had him out of breath as much as emotion, but he locked the fear into its own dark compartment and focused on what had to be done.

Get Scoop and Fiona out of the backyard and to the E.R.

Find Abigail.

Find the bastards who'd set off a bomb on her porch.

No question the fire wasn't an accident. Keira and the other woman in Ireland had been right that it was a bomb.

Two hulking firefighters materialized on either side of him and got him by the arms and led him back outside. He shook them off when they reached the sidewalk. "An off-duty police officer is out back with my daughter. He's hurt bad. She isn't." His eyes felt seared as he pointed toward the gate. "They're behind the compost bin. Scoop. Fiona. Those are their names."

The firefighters took off without a word. More firefighters poured off trucks, heading inside and out back. Paramedics arrived. Two police cruisers. Bob looked back at the triple-decker. He and Scoop and Abigail had just put on new siding. A new roof.

Tom Yarborough, Abigail's partner, a straight-backed

son of a bitch if there ever was one, got out of an unmarked car and approached the house. Bob forced himself to think. The FBI, ATF, bomb squad, arson squad—the damn world would be on this one.

Neighbors drifted out of houses up and down the street to check out the commotion, see if they could help. Find out if the fire would spread and if they should get out of there. Yarborough, already taking charge, addressed two uniformed officers. "Keep them back." He looked at Bob. "You okay?"

"I'm fine." Bob spat and filled him in on Scoop and Fiona. "Firefighters are back there now."

"How'd the fire start?" Yarborough asked.

"Bomb on Abigail's back porch."

Yarborough had no visible reaction. "Where is she?"

"Missing."

"What about Owen?"

Bob shook his head. "He wasn't here."

"Is he a potential target? What—"

"Hell," Bob interrupted. "I have to warn him. Give me your cell phone."

Yarborough flipped him an expensive-looking phone that Bob immediately smudged with soot, sweat and blood. *Scoop's blood.*

"Bob," Yarborough said. "Lieutenant, I can dial—"

"I don't know his number. You'd think…" He opened up the phone and stared at it. "I should have all Abigail and Owen's numbers memorized. They have enough of them. Cell, here, Beacon Street, Texas, Maine. The way they live. Their luck. I should know their numbers."

"Owen's cell phone is in my address book."

Bob squinted at him. "In what?"

"Let me, Bob," Yarborough said. He took the phone, hit a couple of buttons, handed it back to Bob. "It's dialing."

Owen picked up on the first ring. "Hey, Tom."

"It's Bob." A thousand bad calls he'd made in his nearly thirty years as a cop, and he could feel his damn voice crack. "Where are you?"

"Beacon Street." A wariness, a hint of fear, had come into Owen's voice. "What's going on? Where's Abigail?"

"Are you safe?"

"Talk to me, Bob. What's happened?"

"I don't know. I'm at the house. She's not here. There's been a fire." No point getting into the details. "Listen to me. I'm sending Yarborough over there. He'll check things out. Right now, you need to get everyone out of the building."

"The fire was set," Owen said.

"It was a bomb, Owen. Move now. Abigail's one of our own. We'll find her." But Owen was ex-military and one of the world's foremost experts in search-and-rescue. He was head of Fast Rescue, a renowned rapid response organization. He'd think he could find her, too. "You know this is different. It's not what you do—"

"I'll be in touch."

He disconnected.

Bob didn't bother trying him again. Owen wouldn't answer. He'd get everyone out of the Federal Period house on Beacon Street owned by his family and used as the offices for their charitable foundation. Then he'd go after Abigail.

"I'll get over there," Yarborough said.

"There could be bombs at Fast Rescue headquarters in Austin and their field academy on Mount Desert Island. If people are there—"

Yarborough gave a curt nod and ran back to his car.

A self-starter. That was one good thing about him.

Bob noticed his hands were steady as he hit more buttons

on Yarborough's phone to see if Abigail's cell number popped up. It did, and he hit another button to dial it.

One ring and he was put through to her voice mail.

He waited impatiently for the tone, then said, "It's Bob. Call me."

A young uniformed officer, a thin rookie with close-cropped blond hair, approached him with obvious concern. "Sir, you need to take it easy. Maybe you should sit down."

"Maybe?"

He grimaced and rephrased, "You should."

"That's better. No maybes. Now go do something. I have to get back to my daughter. Keep the firefighters from tackling me to the ground."

"Sir, I think you should get off your feet."

"You think? Are you arguing with me?"

The kid turned green. He'd need to get some spine if he was going to make it in the BPD. "No, sir, I'm not arguing with you. I'm telling you to stay back and let the firefighters do their job."

Bob stared at the kid and felt nerves or craziness or something well up in him. He broke into a barking laugh, then covered it with a cough. He bent over, hawking up a giant black gob and spitting it on the sidewalk. When he stood up straight, he had the awful sensation that he was about to cry. Then he'd have to retire and buy a house next to his folks in Florida, because he'd be finished.

The rookie was looking worried. "Lieutenant?"

Bob went very still and pointed to a dark, still-moist substance on the curb about a yard up from where he'd spit. "There. Check that out. Looks like blood, doesn't it?"

"I'll cordon off the area," the rookie said with a sharp breath.

Bob bent over to get a closer look at the spot. It had to

be blood. "Abigail didn't just step out for a walk," he said half to himself.

"I don't think so, either, sir."

He stood up straight. "What do you think, rookie?"

The cop flushed but held his ground. "Everything suggests that Detective Browning has been kidnapped."

"Yeah." Bob wiped the back of his hand across his face, the weight of what had just happened hitting him. The stark, stinking reality of it. "I think so, too."

A line of shiny black SUVs rolled onto the residential street.

"The feds," the rookie cop said. "How did they get here so fast?"

"Abigail's father is in town."

"The FBI director? Just what we need."

The SUVs stopped well back of the fire trucks. Bob realized he didn't have enough of a head start to outrun the FBI.

Nowhere to go, either.

"The spot," Bob said to the rookie.

The kid jumped into action and bolted for his cruiser, shouting to his partner, a woman who looked just as young, just as inexperienced.

Down the street, Simon Cahill leaped out of the back of the middle SUV. He was a man who could dance an Irish jig and was in love with Bob's niece, Keira, but right now what Bob saw coming at him was pure FBI special agent.

The SUV started moving, but stopped again. This time, John March got out. His iron-gray hair and dark gray suit were still perfect despite the heat and the awful scene in front of him. March had been a hotshot young detective when Bob was a rookie. Now he had about a million G-men behind him, but his eyes, as black as his daughter's, were filled with pain.

Bob understood.

March hadn't jumped out of the SUV because he was the head of the FBI, but because he was Abigail's father.

Simon got to the sidewalk first. "Bob," he said, "what's going on?"

Bob's mouth was dry, his eyes and throat burning. He looked up at the hazy sky and collected himself as March joined. There was just no way out of it, and Bob told Simon and March about the blast. "We're looking for Abigail now." He kept his tone as coplike as he could. "Firefighters are still checking her apartment, but I was in there and didn't find her. Her front door and the main front door were both standing open right after the blast."

"Her car's here," March said.

"We're cordoning off the area, checking vehicles. If she was shaken up in the blast, she could have wandered into someone's backyard."

Simon stepped out of the way of more firefighters. "What about Owen?"

Bob's head throbbed. "He's on Beacon Street. Yarborough's heading there now. What are you two doing here?"

Simon answered, his voice steady. "Abigail called about an hour ago and asked us to meet her. She didn't say why."

Bob didn't know why, either, but he had an idea. Earlier that summer, she'd learned that her father had a tight, almost father-son relationship with Simon Cahill that had started twenty years ago after the execution-style murder of Simon's father, a DEA agent. She'd been trying to wrap her head around that one for weeks and could have asked them both over to talk about it.

And just before they arrive, a bomb goes off?

There was also Norman Estabrook's threat against Simon and her father, and the serial killer Simon and Keira had taken into custody in June, as well as dozens of other ugly cases Abigail had been involved in. Before Bob could follow up, the rookie cop came back up to him, white-faced now. "Lieutenant…I just…"

The kid was standing next to March, who said quietly, "Easy, Officer. Just say what you have to say."

The rookie didn't meet the FBI director's eyes, as if he thought he might go up in a puff of smoke if he did. "I just spoke to Detective Yarborough. Owen Garrison wanted to come over here and headed to his car after evacuating the Garrison house. He checked it first, and…"

"And what?" Bob asked. "He found a bomb?"

The rookie nodded. "Yes, sir. The bomb squad's on the way, but Mr. Garrison has already disarmed the device himself."

"Himself," Bob said, sighing.

Simon and March didn't speak, but they were well aware, as Bob was, that Owen would know how to disarm a wide variety of bombs. The one in his car opened up a second crime scene.

How many more bombs would they find? Who'd planted them? How? When?

Why?

It was going to be a long day. Right now, Bob just wanted to see Scoop and his daughter, but he had to get one more bit of black news over with.

He turned to Simon. "Keira called from Ireland."

The color drained from Simon's face. "Why, Bob?"

"She and another woman called to warn me there was a bomb on Abigail's back porch."

Chapter 6

Lizzie had used the bungee cords in her pack to tie the Irishman's wrists behind his back. He was sullen now as they headed back to the village, she on his right, Will on his left. Keira walked quietly behind them. The black dog skulked in the shadows above the ancient wall along the lane.

"Keep up," Lizzie said to the Irishman, "or we'll leave you to the dog."

He turned his gaze to her, his eyes flat. "I'll keep up."

When they reached the village, the dog bounded off suddenly, disappearing into the hills.

Lizzie glanced back at Keira, her hair hanging in wet tangles. She'd tried calling her uncle in Boston again but was unable to get through to him. "There's still hope," Lizzie said. "Don't give up."

Keira smiled faintly. "You're an optimist."

"Most days."

"Most days I am, too."

But she obviously knew, as Lizzie did, that hope and

optimism wouldn't dictate whether Bob O'Reilly and whoever else was at the triple-decker in Boston had survived the blast. It would depend on luck, skill, training and timing.

Unless fairies showed up. For all Lizzie knew, they'd had a hand in what had just happened up at the stone circle. She and Keira had dealt with the Irishman and kept him from killing them, but the mysterious black dog had persuaded him to tell them about the bomb.

It was all very strange.

There was no question in Lizzie's mind that Norman Estabrook was responsible for the attack on Keira Sullivan and the bomb in Boston. He'd gone after Simon's new love and John March's daughter.

And it was just the beginning.

Eddie O'Shea and two other small, wiry men, all in wool caps, materialized out of the shadows and jumped lightly off the stone wall onto the lane. Lizzie had had no idea they were there. The barman fell in next to her. "My brothers, Aidan and Patrick," Eddie said by way of introduction as the other two men dropped back to Keira.

Will greeted the brothers with a nod. He'd said little since the connection to Keira's uncle in Boston went dead. He was a man, Lizzie thought, of supreme self-control. He'd briefly questioned the Irishman, who insisted he'd come to the Beara Peninsula alone and had no partners waiting in the village. Lizzie believed him, if only because of his deep, palpable fear of the black hound.

Aidan pulled off his jacket and draped it over Keira's shoulders, and she managed a smile, thanking him. When they came to the pub, Eddie's dog was at the door to greet them.

The pub was empty, the local farmers and fishermen

gone home for the night. The springer spaniel collapsed lazily in front of the fire.

Will shoved their would-be killer onto a chair at the table Lizzie had vacated earlier. His ski cap had come off in his scuffle with her. He had sparse, dark hair and blue eyes, and she saw now, in the light and relative safety of the pub, that he was muscular and fit. She realized she'd done well to best him.

She also realized Will would have had no trouble if he'd arrived in the stone circle a bit sooner. Lizzie reminded herself not to be fooled into thinking his expensive clothes and aristocratic background meant he couldn't fight as well as any other SAS officer and spy.

"I'll ring the guards," Patrick, the youngest O'Shea, said.

"Patrick and I'll watch for them," Aidan, the eldest, added, and the two brothers headed down a short hall to the back of the pub.

Keira shrugged off Aidan's coat and hung it on a peg, then joined Lizzie and the dog by the fire, all of them muddy and wet. The pub was toasty warm, but Lizzie had to fight to keep herself from shivering. She slipped the thug's spare assault knife into her jacket pocket and held her hands toward the flames, spreading out her fingers. She noticed bloody scrapes on her knuckles and wrists, but she couldn't remember any pain and felt none now.

"I'll have Patrick and Aidan fetch some ice and bandages," Eddie said.

"Thank you, but there's no need, really." She gave him a quick smile. "What I'd truly love is a sip of brandy."

He nodded, but gave his bound fellow Irishman a hard glare. "Move a muscle, and I'll have a knife to your throat before your next breath."

The thug glowered but said nothing.

Eddie went behind his bar and got down three glasses

and placed them on a tray. Keeping an eye on his customers, he uncapped a bottle of brandy and splashed some into each glass.

Keira took a breath, containing her emotion. "Why are you here?" she asked Will. "Have you talked to Simon?"

"Earlier. Not in the past few hours. I spoke to Josie at your cottage and again on my way to the stone circle." He studied her carefully, obviously debating how much to tell her about what he knew. "Norman Estabrook's no longer in U.S. federal custody."

Lizzie concentrated on the flames. She knew Will would be watching for her reaction.

Keira stayed steady. "Simon was right, then. Estabrook cut a deal with prosecutors in exchange for his cooperation."

"They can re-file charges at any time if he doesn't hold up his end," Will said, then added, "There's more, I'm afraid. He left his Montana ranch this morning on a solo flight in his private plane."

"Then no one really knows where he is." Water dripped from the ends of Keira's hair, mingling with the dog's muddy prints on the warm hearth. "Will, Norman Estabrook threatened to kill both Simon and John March."

"I know, Keira. He has no history of violence, and apparently he and his attorneys were able to persuade prosecutors that he spoke in the heat of the moment."

"I don't believe that," Keira said.

Neither did Lizzie, but she was staying quiet.

Will glanced at the bound Irishman, then at Lizzie, then shifted back to Keira, his expression giving away nothing of what he was thinking. "Is there anything I can do for you?"

"I'm fine, thanks to—" Keira turned to Lizzie with a look of embarrassment. "You just saved my life and I don't even know your name."

After what had happened at the stone circle and in Boston, with a possible British spy with them in the pub, Lizzie was even more determined not to get into names. Simon would recognize her, but he wasn't here—and the attack on Keira and the bomb in Boston changed everything.

She needed a new plan.

She moved away from the fire, out of Will's immediate line of sight. He was handy in a fight, but she had to get her bearings before she dared giving up her anonymity.

Eddie brought the tray of brandy over to the fire and handed a glass each to her, Keira and Will. For a split second, Lizzie thought the barman's suspicion of her had eased, but as he stood back with his empty tray, he tilted his head and frowned at her.

Still didn't trust her.

He turned to Will. "I told Patrick and Aidan I'd wager our black-haired stranger here knew how to knock together a head or two." He sniffed at the bungee-corded thug. "I see I was right."

Keira warmed her hands over the peat fire. "I wasn't much help." She glanced at Lizzie. "You certainly do know how to handle yourself in a fight."

"Adrenaline," she said.

"It was more than adrenaline."

"I've taken a few self-defense classes." Starting with her father when she was two. "Luck helps. I had surprise on my side. Our friend here had size, strength and experience."

"And two knives," Keira said.

"If he'd managed one good punch, he'd have knocked me clear across the bay to the Ring of Kerry."

Keira smiled, but Will didn't react at all to Lizzie's attempt at lightheartedness. The glow of the fire reflected in his eyes, deepening the gold flecks. His control was not, she knew, to be mistaken for nonchalance. He was a very capable, dangerous man on high alert.

"Why didn't you run when you had the chance?" Keira asked.

"Story of my life," Lizzie said with a smile.

Will sipped his brandy. "You fought with real skill."

"A maniac coming at you with a knife'll do that."

Keira pushed up the sleeves of her oversize sweater, the hem of her skirt soaked and muddy. She was clearly worried about her family and friends in Boston—about Simon—but she had a kind of inner serenity that Lizzie admired. Serenity wasn't her long suit.

She took one small sip of her brandy and set the glass on the table. As tempted as she was, she wasn't about to settle in for the evening with a bottle of brandy and a chat with the Irish police, who would arrive soon.

She moved in front of the man who'd attacked her. He was outnumbered and unlikely to kick her. Nonetheless, she knew how to fight from a bound, seated position and, assuming he did, too, stayed clear of his feet. "You didn't decide to attack Keira on your own, out of the blue," she said. "Who hired you?"

He turned his head from her. Even if he didn't respond, his body language would be instructive and perhaps give her—and Will Davenport—answers. Will undoubtedly had far more experience with interrogations than she did, but her father had taught her basic techniques.

"You didn't sneak off to the stone circle on a whim," Lizzie said. "Who sent you?"

The Irishman shifted back to her, cockier and less fearful now that the black dog had gone on his way. "D'you have someone in mind?" he asked sarcastically.

An unexpected coolness eased up Lizzie's spine and made her catch her breath as she remembered a night in

Las Vegas in June, in the last days before the FBI arrived at Norman's Montana ranch with a warrant for his arrest.

"I do." She spoke in a near whisper. She'd come to believe Norman wanted to bloody his own hands, but now she realized he'd also wanted the drama of this multipronged attack. He'd needed help to pull it off. "I do have someone in mind. He's British. Maybe forty, with medium brown hair, gray eyes. About your height. Noticeably fit."

"How would I remember him?"

She put her palms on her thighs and leaned forward, eye to eye with him. "He's dangerous and charming and very focused. You'd remember."

"No one I know," the Irishman said.

Lizzie had no idea whether or not he was telling the truth, but she was aware of Will studying her, assessing her in steely silence. Her description of his countryman had clearly struck a nerve.

Maybe he was the one she should be questioning.

She tried not to let him distract her. "Why attack Keira with a knife? Why not shoot her? Why not poison her blackberry crumble?"

"Because of the serial killer," Keira said suddenly, quietly from the fire. "That's why, isn't it?"

The Irishman averted his eyes, giving his answer.

Lizzie saw now what he'd planned. "A copycat killing. You wanted to throw the guards off your trail by making it look as if someone was imitating the serial killer who was here earlier this summer."

He breathed in through his nostrils. "I've hurt no one."

"Not for lack of trying, my friend." She ran a fingertip along the rim of her glass on the table. "Eddie and his brothers would recognize you if you were a local. Where are you from? Dublin? Cork? Limerick?"

He didn't react to any of the cities she named.

Will stepped forward and unzipped the Irishman's right jacket pocket. "Let's have a look," he said, withdrawing a battered leather wallet. He opened it up and slid out a bank card with his thumb. "Michael James Murphy. Is that your real name? I expect it is. You thought you had an easy job tonight, didn't you, Mr. Murphy?"

"I tried to save her. That one," Murphy said, nodding toward Keira, his tone slightly less sullen. "I saw this black-haired witch meant to do her harm. It's lucky I happened on when I did."

Lizzie rolled her eyes. "Such a liar."

He glared at her. "You can fool them, maybe, but you don't fool me. I'll explain myself to the guards."

"Great. You do that. In the meantime, you're alone out here on the Irish coast with all of us."

He smirked at her, unimpressed.

Keira turned from the fire, her cheeks red now from the heat, a stark contrast to the rest of her deathly pale face. "He must have been watching for me on the lane and saw me walk up to the stone circle." She drank more of her brandy, holding the glass with both hands. "I thought the rain had stopped for good and a walk would ease my restlessness. I was missing Simon. Afraid for him."

Keira's love for a man Lizzie had kept at arm's length for the past year felt as natural and honest as the Irish night.

Michael Murphy—or whatever his name was—snorted at Lizzie. "You almost broke my poor knee. It hurts like the devil."

She was unrepentant. "What did you expect me to do when you came after me with your knife?"

"I was scared out of my wits, trying to save Keira. Untie me. I've done nothing to deserve being trussed up like a Christmas turkey."

"Nothing?" Lizzie raised her eyebrows, almost amused at his brazenness. "That's rich, my friend."

She took her brandy glass to the bar and set it on the smooth wood, resisting a sudden surge of loneliness. She had friends. Family. Why was she doing this on her own? She glanced at Will, his quiet control as he dialed his BlackBerry more unnerving than if he'd been in a frenzy. He would be focused on first things first. He'd see to Keira's safety.

Then he'd deal with Lizzie.

Her trip to Ireland wasn't going at all as she'd hoped it would. Instead of disrupting Norman's plans for violent revenge, she'd landed in the middle of their execution. She could no longer pretend she'd just stopped by the little Irish village to see Simon Cahill while she was walking the Beara Way. Simon and his friend Lord Davenport had only to put their heads together and, with their resources inside and outside of government, they'd figure out who she was. In the meantime, she had room to maneuver.

Will held his BlackBerry out to Keira. "It's Simon. He and Director March weren't present when the bomb went off. Your uncle and cousin are unhurt." He hesitated for a fraction of a second. "Detective Wisdom is seriously injured."

"What about Abigail?"

"She wasn't in the blast."

Keira took the phone. "Simon," she said in a raw whisper, "I'm fine. I love you."

Lizzie's throat tightened as Keira spoke to the man she loved. She'd found her soulmate, and Simon had found his.

Every instinct Lizzie had told her she had to get out of there now or she wouldn't be able to leave. She didn't want to end up under the thumb of Irish law enforcement.

They'd call the FBI and the Boston police, and then where would she be?

In cuffs herself as a material witness, or even a suspect.

If Scoop Wisdom was able to talk, he'd tell the FBI and his BPD colleagues about the black-haired woman he'd caught lingering in front of the triple-decker yesterday afternoon. He'd walked out from the backyard with a colander of green beans that, somehow, made him look more intimidating.

"Can I help you?" he'd asked her.

Hesitating, debating with herself, Lizzie had opted not to tell him the truth. "No. Sorry. I'm just catching my breath." She'd smiled. "Shin splints."

He hadn't bothered hiding his skepticism, but he hadn't stopped her as she'd gone on her way, boarding her flight to Ireland that evening. She'd decided to talk to Simon Cahill instead of John March's detective daughter, Abigail, or her detective friends.

And now, twenty-four hours later, a bomb had exploded on Abigail's back porch, severely injuring Detective Wisdom.

Lizzie reached for her backpack on the hearth. Had she screwed up by not talking to him yesterday? If she had, would he and his detective housemates have found the bomb?

Her father would tell her not to look back with regret but to learn and to help her figure out what she needed to do next.

She felt the sting of her cuts and scrapes now. "Norman isn't flying off to a resort to celebrate his freedom," she said, addressing Simon's British friend. "He'll be furious that his plan didn't work. He'll try again."

Will eased closer to her, his eyes changeable and intense in the heat of the fire. He was taking in everything, studying her, seeing, she was sure, more than she wanted to reveal. An image came, unbidden, unwanted, of them together in a pretty Irish inn, with no worries beyond which book to read or which bath salts to choose.

"You obviously know Estabrook," he said quietly. "Are you a friend?"

"Norman doesn't have real friends."

"He's very wealthy. Some people are drawn to wealth."

"Yes. Some people are." Lizzie saw clearly now what she needed to do. If she was to be of any help now that Norman was acting on his intentions, she had to remain anonymous for as long as possible. She couldn't explain her association with him and his entourage of wealthy investors, adventurers, staff, hangers-on and drug traffickers. "I imagine by now most everyone knows Norman Estabrook's not your basic mild-mannered billionaire adventurer. If you'll excuse me—"

"You've had an ordeal tonight." Will brushed a fingertip across her hand, just above her split knuckles. "You're hurt."

She gave a dismissive shrug. "Nothing a nice hot bath and a lot more brandy won't cure." She lifted her pack onto her shoulder, feeling her jetlag, too. "Please don't stop me. I'm no good to anyone sitting in a garda interview room."

His eyes stayed on her. "I'll find out who you are."

"You could take my backpack from me and find out now, but you won't. We're both in a foreign country." She tilted her head back and challenged him with a cool smile. "You don't want to get into a tussle with me just as the guards arrive and risk getting yourself arrested. You and Keira have enough to explain as it is."

The change in his expression was subtle, but something about it instantly had her conjuring images of fighting him, sparring with him, blocking, counterattacking. Going all out, no-holds-barred.

It was sexy, the idea of getting physical with her very own James Bond.

Further proof, Lizzie decided, of the deleterious effects of jetlag, adrenaline, a knife fight in an Irish stone circle and two sips of brandy on an otherwise perfectly normal brain.

It was time to go.

She lifted Murphy's assault knife out of her pocket and handed it to Eddie O'Shea. "Thank you for the brandy and for your help tonight. Your brothers, too."

He took the knife, his suspicion, if anything, even more acute now. "Just here walking the Beara Way, you say."

But the barman didn't stop her, either, as she headed back out into the quiet, pretty village.

She heard a dog barking in the distance and, high up in the hills, the bleating of sheep. The wind had died to a gentle breeze, and the rain had stopped, the air cool, scented with roses and lavender.

The picnic table was empty. There was no old farmer with a pipe and strange talk.

Lizzie walked past the brightly painted houses and the lampposts with their hanging flower baskets to her little rented car.

No one followed her.

She got behind the wheel but warned herself not to let down her guard just yet, even for a few seconds. As she started the engine, she felt the ache in her muscles from the bruises she'd incurred doing battle in the Beara hills, and she acknowledged a desire to go back to the pub and believe she had allies there, people she could trust.

Instead she pulled out onto the street and found her way back to the main road, the sky slowly darkening over Kenmare Bay.

She wondered how long she had before the Irish

Garda, the Boston police, the FBI and one handsome British spy came after her.

Probably not long.

Chapter 7

A phone call...

Abigail Browning remembered teasing Scoop and Fiona from her back porch about tomatoes. She'd been laughing when she'd gone inside to answer the phone.

She was between the two men who'd grabbed her off the street a few minutes later and was walking with them now on what felt like a marina dock. They'd thrown a smelly car blanket over her head and shoved guns in her ribs. They were pure, brazen, hired thugs who obviously would prefer to shoot her and dump her body—or not to have kidnapped her in the first place.

They'd have just let her burn up in the fire.

She smelled saltwater and the fishiness of low tide. The sounds of boats in front of her and traffic behind her suggested a marina in busy Boston Harbor.

She suppressed her anger and fear and concentrated on what was in her control right now, at this moment.

She could listen, assess, stay alert.

Conserve her energy and try to survive.

"You should take the blanket off my head. It'll draw attention."

"Anyone asks, we'll say you're seasick, and the bright light makes it worse," the man on her right side said in a South Boston accent. "You go along with us."

"How? Turn green on command?"

He inhaled sharply, telling her he didn't like her answer. Didn't like her.

She'd debated staying out on the porch and not answering the phone. Owen would call her on her cell phone. Tom Yarborough, her partner, would page her or try her cell first. But her father and Simon were on their way, and they would call her home phone if something came up.

It was hot outside, and Abigail had figured she'd scoot into the kitchen, take the call and fill a pitcher of iced tea and bring it out.

Her front doorbell had rung as she'd answered her phone.

Or was she imagining that part?

No. She was sure.

The voice on the other end of the line had been very clear and precise. It hadn't been the man with the South Boston accent. Probably the driver of the van waiting in the street. "In five seconds," he'd said, "a bomb will go off on your back porch. Five…four…"

By three, Abigail was in the living room.

At zero, as promised, came the explosion, thrusting her to the floor and sucking the wind out of her. She'd crawled to her feet, her ears ringing as she'd pulled open her front door.

Scoop…Fiona…Bob…she remembered thinking she had to get to them.

She'd run into the main entry and opened that door. As she'd leaped down the steps, two men swooped in on her in a coordinated maneuver and dragged her to the van.

Disoriented from the blast, she'd clawed one of them—the one with the Southie accent—enough to draw blood, but she'd been unable to do more to defend herself.

They stuffed her in the back of the van, dived in with her and sped off, a third man at the wheel.

Three armed men against her. Not good odds. When they finally came to a stop, the driver had muttered something about going on ahead to get things ready and left Abigail with the two men in the back of the van.

"Careful," the man to her left said now. "We don't want to lose you to the sharks, do we?"

"Sharks," she said through the blanket. "Funny."

Half lifting, half shoving her, they got her onto what was obviously a boat. A decent size one, too. They forced her down narrow steps before pulling the blanket off her head and taking her into a small, dark stateroom, where they pushed her onto a metal chair.

Working quickly, they blindfolded her with some kind of scarf, tying it so tightly, it pulled even her short hair enough that her eyes teared up. Using what felt like rope, they tied her hands and ankles to the chair back and legs.

Abigail knew she had to control panic and claustrophobia before they could get started and spiral, taking on a life of their own. She breathed in through her mouth to the count of eight. She held her breath for eight. She exhaled through her nose for eight.

Finally she said, "I hope you didn't bleed on me."

Her sarcasm was met with a backhand smack to the left side of her face, striking her cheekbone. The pain was immediate and searing, but she bit it back.

"Ouch," she said without inflection.

"It'll be a pleasure to kill you when the time comes," the man with the Southie accent said.

She did her breathing exercise again.

In for eight. Hold for eight. Out for eight.

"Estabrook and his Brit friend can deal with her," the man added "This whole business stinks. I'm going up for a drink."

"They'll be here in a few hours," the second man said.

"Then they can have a drink with me."

Abigail heard a door shut, the click of a lock turning. She listened, but heard no one breathing nearby, no footsteps.

She was alone.

Estabrook.

So. Norman Estabrook was free. He was the reason Abigail's father and Simon were in Boston. The reason, ultimately, that she'd called them that morning and asked to talk to them.

Had Estabrook just tried to carry out his threat to kill the men he claimed had betrayed him?

Abigail did three more sets of her breathing exercises and pictured Owen on his deck at his summer house on Mount Desert Island, smiling at her. He was rugged, hard-edged, a sexy mix of Boston and Texas, a search-and-rescue expert and a man of action who wouldn't take to having his fiancée kidnapped.

But what if he'd been targeted, too?

And Simon and her father. What about them? Had the men who'd grabbed her known they were en route to see her?

Did they know why?

She stopped the thoughts in their tracks. Even if she was alone, there could be a surveillance camera in the room. She didn't need to spool up if she were being watched for signs of distress.

In for eight. Hold. Out for eight.

The boat got underway. The marine patrol would be on the lookout for her. She hoped her captors made a mistake—that they'd already made one and the yacht was under watch now, SWAT planning her rescue.

Owen...

Abigail saw him coming to her on a moonlit Maine night and felt him making love to her, imagined every touch, every murmur of his love and passion. She heard the waves crashing on the rocks outside their window and the cries of the seagulls in the distance.

He was with her.

Whatever happened, Owen was with her.

Chapter 8

Beara Peninsula, Southwest Ireland
9:10 p.m., IST
August 25

Farther up the peninsula, Lizzie turned off the main road onto a sparsely populated lane that crawled over the twilit hills and would take her to the market village of Kenmare at the head of the bay. It wasn't a shortcut, but she hoped she'd be less likely to run into the *An Garda Síochána*—the Guardians of the Peace.

In other words, the police.

Once in Kenmare, she would go on to the small Kerry County airport and fly to Dublin.

At least she had the start of a new plan.

She pulled over to the side of the road—it wasn't much more than a sheep track—and got out, welcoming the brisk wind in her face. The physical effects of her first real fight with an opponent determined to kill her and the thought of what had happened in Boston had left her drained.

And encountering Will Davenport had left her thoroughly rattled.

She looked out across the hills that plunged sharply to the bay, its water gray under the clearing, darkening sky. She walked along a barbed-wire fence. She hadn't passed another car since leaving the main road. The only evidence of other people were the lights of a solitary farmhouse far down on the steep hillside.

A trio of fat sheep meandered across the rock-strewn pasture toward her. Even in the dark, she could see the splotches of blue paint on their white wool that served as brands. She could put aside her distaste for camping and pitch her tent right here among the rocks and sheep and forget everything she had on her mind, including the good-looking Brit who, she suspected, would have her name before the clock struck midnight Irish Summer Time.

Will Davenport could become a very big problem. As she watched the sheep nudge closer to the fence, she wondered how Will knew the Brit she'd run into in Las Vegas. Because she was sure he did…

Yes. He definitely could become a problem.

She'd arrived in Las Vegas in late June after a few days on her own at her house in Maine and a quick stop in Boston to make an appearance at the family hotels' main offices. Her uncle, Bradley, her father's younger brother, ran the company and had been losing patience with her erratic schedule. He'd even begun making noises about finding another role for her. She was very good at getting a lot accomplished in a short time and had managed to placate him. Traveling from one Rush hotel to another had allowed her the flexibility to dip in and out of Norman's world as well as to breathe new life into her ideas about the concierge services and excursions the hotels offered. Her uncle, however, liked to see her at meetings and behind a desk once in a while. Since his older brother lived in Las Vegas, Bradley hadn't objected to Lizzie's heading there. He'd given up seeing her father at meetings or behind a desk a long time ago.

She'd enjoyed being back in the hot, dry, sunny,

vibrant town her father called home, but Norman had arrived unexpectedly that same morning for a high-stakes poker game. Lizzie hadn't been able to bring herself to smile at him. Still unaware of Simon's undercover mission at that point, she'd been trying to figure out what else she could do to fire up the FBI to go after Norman. But none of his drug-cartel friends had been with him, and she'd made an effort to relax.

During a break in the game, a man with close-cropped brown hair had approached Norman and spoke to him briefly out of Lizzie's earshot. Whatever they discussed, it had seemed important. She'd retreated to the hotel bar, and ten minutes later, the Brit joined her. She did her best to look bored as she simultaneously nursed a bottle of water and a martini.

He'd eased onto the stool next to her. Unlike Norman, he'd struck her as being very fit. "More of that water in your bag, love?"

"Sure." She'd reached into her tote bag and handed him a bottle. It was Vegas. She knew to stay hydrated. "I'm Lizzie Rush. Who're you?"

He'd taken the water and uncapped it. "You should behave, love." He'd winked at her, and she'd noticed he had gray eyes. "Sorry, I can't stay. I'm in a rush. No pun intended."

He'd left, chuckling to himself, and later that night, Lizzie had reluctantly flown to Montana with Norman. Simon had been scheduled to join them after visiting his friend Will Davenport in London. He and Norman were to work on plans for future high-risk adventures.

Three days later, Norman was under arrest.

Lizzie had provided the FBI with a description of the mysterious Brit in Las Vegas, anonymously, over the Internet, a trick she'd actually taught her father.

As far as she knew, nothing had come of it.

She'd asked her father about him before she'd left for Montana. "Who's the Brit?"

"No one I know."

He could have been telling the truth.

Or not.

And now here she was in Ireland with sheep nuzzling up to her. She got a disposable cell phone out of her jacket pocket and dialed her father's cell phone. "It's me, Dad. Are you in Las Vegas?"

"Losing at poker. How are you, Lizzie?"

She could hear the worry in his voice but sidestepped his question. "Do you remember the Brit who stopped to talk to Norman Estabrook in June?"

"Who?"

"You heard me. I asked you about him that night, and you said you didn't know him. I'm wondering if you've run into him since, or maybe done a little digging."

"I'm losing at five-card stud, sweetheart. Just dying here. Where are you?"

She pictured him at his poker table at the hotel, at just under two hundred rooms their largest. Harlan Rush was a tawny-haired, square-jawed man in his late fifties. He was handsome and rich, and he'd swept her Irish mother off her feet thirty-one years ago after she'd stayed at the Whitcomb Hotel in Boston on business. She had been in Irish tourism development.

Supposedly.

Lizzie didn't want to tell her father where she was. "Let's just say I'm jetlagged."

He sighed. "You're in Ireland. I told you not to go there. Years ago. I told you."

"Ireland isn't the problem."

"It's bad luck for us."

"I love it. Cousin Justin is doing great at the Dublin hotel, which, I might add, is a huge success. Maybe Ireland was bad luck for you and my mother."

"I remember you reaching for her as a baby. 'Mama' was your first word. She was gone, and it was still your first word."

"Don't, Dad."

"You're in trouble. I can hear it in your voice."

She looked up at the sky. There'd be stars tonight. She could stay here and watch them come out. "I think the Brit we saw in Las Vegas might know another Brit, Will Davenport, who is friends with Simon Cahill."

"Cahill? The FBI agent?" Her father groaned. "Lizzie."

"And I think Will is from your world," she said.

"*Will,* he is now? How well do you know him?"

"We just met over brandy in an Irish pub."

"You only drink brandy when you're in trouble."

"Not only," she said with a smile, hoping it relaxed her voice, "but it's the best time."

"Go back to Maine and watch the cormorants."

"Dad—"

"That bastard friend of yours, Estabrook, was turned loose this morning. He's not your problem. You understand that, don't you?"

"Sure. So, nothing on my Brit in June?"

He hesitated just a fraction of a second. "No name. No nothing. Forget him, Lizzie. If he and Lord Davenport are friends, forget him, too."

"I said his name was Will. I didn't say 'Lord.'"

"What, he *is* a lord? I was being sarcastic."

True or not, her father wasn't telling her everything, not because he was a liar, but because he never told her or anyone else all he knew about anything. He could have researched Simon Cahill's friends as easily as she had—before or after Norman's arrest. Her father had never particularly liked her hanging out with Norman and his entourage.

"Will *is* from your world, isn't he?"

"Just because I taught you a few things doesn't mean you should be jumping to conclusions about what I used to do for a living."

"Is that a yes or a no?"

"You're an amateur with the skills and the instincts of a pro, Lizzie, but you're still an amateur. You don't have anyone behind you. You stand alone."

"I have you."

"Lizzie." He took in a breath. "If you need me, I'll be there for you. You know that."

"I do, Dad."

"Your aunt Henrietta is in Paris buying linens."

"I adore Aunt Henrietta, but do you know what it's like to shop with her?"

"I do. Pure hell. Paris is closer to Ireland than Maine. Pop over and help her. Get drunk on expensive brandy. Have some fun, Lizzie." He hesitated before continuing. "The Davenports are a fine British family. A bunch of good-looking devils, too. If you have cause to drink brandy, having a sip or two with a Davenport isn't a bad thing."

That was all the endorsement she needed. "Thanks. You can go back to your poker game. You're not bluffing on a pair of threes, are you?"

"I wish. Stay safe, my girl."

"I love you, Dad."

After she hung up, Lizzie smiled as more sheep joined her trio and crowded along the fence, the wind blowing their long, woolly coats. Because of her father, she could defend herself in a fistfight, spot a tail, disarm a rudimentary bomb. "The first step, Lizzie," he'd told her, "is knowing the bomb is there."

She returned to her car and dug a change of clothes out of her pack, just as prosaic as the ones she had on, but clean, and put them on right there at the side of the road, in front of the sheep. She kicked off her mud-and-manure-encrusted shoes and tossed them in the trunk in exchange for a pair of pricey little flats she'd picked up at Brown Thomas in Dublin. Her father had hated and avoided Dublin for as long as she could remember. It was where Shauna Morrigan Rush, his wife, Lizzie's mother, had died.

An accident, according to Irish authorities and John March, the young Boston detective who'd looked into her death, later to join the FBI and become its director.

Lizzie shut the car trunk, questions coming at her all at once.

"Resist speculating," her father had told her time and time again. "Discipline your mind. Focus on what you can do."

Easier said than done when knives, bombs, FBI agents and spies were involved, but she would do her best.

A horned sheep baaed at her, and she baaed back.

"There," she said with a laugh. "I could just stay here and talk to the sheep."

She remembered having formal tea with her grandmother, Edna Whitcomb Rush, a stern but kind woman who had never expected to help her older son raise a daughter. She'd tried to explain why Lizzie's father had to be away for long periods. "He's a scout for new locations and ideas for our hotels."

Ha. A scout.

Harlan Rush was a spy, and he'd taught his daughter everything he knew.

Lizzie abandoned the sheep and climbed back into her

car, started the engine and continued along the dark, isolated road. She glanced in her rearview mirror.

Still no sign of the garda or Will Davenport on her tail. At least not yet.

Chapter 9

Simon ran his fingertips over a colored pencil sketch Keira had done of the ancient Celtic stone angel she still swore she'd seen on the hearth of a ruin in the southwest Irish hills.

There'd been a black dog that night, too.

She and that village were quite the combo.

She'd given the sketch to Fiona O'Reilly, who'd taped it onto the far wall of the chandeliered drawing room where she and her friends often gathered to play Irish music, courtesy of Owen Garrison, whose family had owned the elegant Beacon Hill house for more than a century. The sparsely furnished first-floor room was used for meetings and functions. The offices of the Dorothy Garrison Foundation, established in memory of Owen's sister, were on the second floor. Owen was just eleven and Dorothy Garrison just fourteen when she'd drowned near their family summer home off the coast of Maine. Their distraught parents had relocated from Boston to Austin, Texas. After a stint in the army, Owen founded Fast

Rescue, a highly respected nongovernmental organization that provided rapid response to disasters, natural or manmade, anywhere in the world.

Simon, a search-and-rescue expert himself, had volunteered for Fast Rescue eighteen months ago after he and Owen had become friends through John March. Owen knew March because of their ties to Maine, where Owen had discovered the body of March's son-in-law, Christopher Browning, an FBI agent murdered four days into his Mount Desert Island honeymoon. Last summer—seven years later—his widow and Owen had fallen for each other and finally uncovered the identity of Chris's killer.

At the same time, Simon had begun working a deep undercover assignment for the FBI, insinuating himself into Norman Estabrook's world of high stakes adventure, finance and criminal activity. A year later, just before Norman's arrest in late June, Simon had met Keira Sullivan…and a few hours ago, because of him, she'd almost been killed for a second time that summer.

A second simple sketch depicted a Dublin windowbox at Christmas. The box was filled with pinecones, evergreen boughs and baubles and draped with sparkling gold ribbon. As always, Keira had captured more than just a scene…a mood, a wish, a dream.

Simon's own mood was dark. His sole commitment was to finding and stopping Norman. It wasn't a wish or a dream—it was his damn job.

The small foundation staff had been sent home, but the bomb squad had gone through the building and given the all clear. Law enforcement was still everywhere, especially in the alley where Owen had discovered the bomb in his parked car. Bob O'Reilly had been by, in a focused and formidable rage at the day's events. Two bombs in his city. A friend and fellow police officer in stable but critical condition. Another friend and officer missing. A daughter traumatized.

A niece attacked in Ireland.

Keira.

But she was unhurt and in the care of the Irish police. The overriding priority now was the safe return of Abigail Browning. Every available law enforcement resource was deployed in the search for her.

BPD officers and FBI agents were posted at the Garrison house, hovering in the foyer. Simon had first laid eyes on Keira there in June, just days before she'd discovered her stone angel in an Irish ruin. He could see her standing in the doorway that night with her fairy-princess blue eyes and long, flaxen hair. Maybe it had been love at first sight. Maybe it hadn't, but love her he did. He'd joined her in Ireland in early August. While Keira sketched and painted, Simon did what he could to aid the ongoing investigation into Estabrook and his drug-trafficking friends.

He walked across the bare wood floor to the middle of the drawing room, where Owen was silently staring up at an unlit chandelier as if somehow it could offer him hope, if not answers. Simon recognized his friend's stillness and pensiveness as his way of containing his emotions—the gut-wrenching fear they all had for Abigail.

"I'd trade places with her in a heartbeat," Owen said, his gaze still on the chandelier.

"She knows. She'll latch onto your feelings for her and use them to give her strength. You've seen it before with people in tough situations."

Before coming to Boston in June—before meeting Keira—Simon had joined Owen and Fast Rescue in responding to a major earthquake in Armenia. They'd pulled dozens of children from the rubble of their collapsed

school. Many were seriously injured. Some came out unscathed. More hadn't survived. Owen had never flinched from doing, getting others to do, what had to be done.

How many children had said they knew that someone
would come, that they wouldn't be left there alone? How
many had drawn strength from thoughts of their mothers
and fathers—of the people who loved them—as they'd
waited for help?

Owen was impatient and action-oriented by nature,
and his reserve now was an indication of just how deeply
worried he was. "Bob says the blood on the sidewalk
isn't hers."

Simon nodded. A haemostatic test had confirmed it
was human blood—but it wasn't Abigail's type. "I'm
guessing that means she was in good enough shape to
fight back when she was grabbed."

"I hope so. What's the update on Scoop?"

"He's stitched up and sedated. A hunk of shrapnel that
hit the base of his skull is causing problems, but doctors
are more optimistic than they were at first."

Owen shut his eyes briefly. He knew how to stay
focused in a crisis given his years in the military and his
experience responding to horrific disasters all over the
world. Earthquakes, tsunamis, mudslides, floods. Terrorist attacks. But this was personal.

"I don't want to be here standing under a chandelier."
He shifted to look at Simon, the strain showing now in
his angular face. "I hate feeling helpless."

Simon tried to smile. "A man who just disarmed a car
bomb isn't helpless. It's been a while, hasn't it?"

"Not long enough."

"Amen to that."

"It was a simple device."

"Still would have blown you to Kingdom Come."

Owen remained tense, serious. "Thanks to Keira, I had warning. The bomb at the triple-decker was exploded by remote control. The one in my car was designed to go off when the key in the ignition was turned. There was enough C4 to blow up the entire car and kill anyone inside or in close proximity."

"No one had to watch for you to get in," Simon said.

Owen looked back up at the chandelier. "Why kill me and kidnap Abigail?"

"That's a good question."

"Tom Yarborough interviewed me himself—I told him everything I could think of. I left Abigail in bed early this morning and headed out to my car. I didn't see anyone on the street there or here who didn't belong. I parked in the alley where I always park and got to work."

"Fast Rescue work?"

He nodded. "We're moving the headquarters to Boston."

"Since when?"

"We made the decision in early August. I haven't told Abigail." His voice caught, almost imperceptibly. "I was keeping it as a surprise. The move will help cut down on travel. We're…" He let his voice trail off. "It doesn't matter now."

"It does matter. Ab will be thrilled, but she'll also slice you to ribbons for keeping secrets."

Owen's smile didn't reach his eyes. "I would argue there's a difference between a surprise and a secret."

"Go ahead. Argue that when Ab's back."

"You know she hates being called Ab, which, of course, is why you do it." He turned to Simon with a faint, grim smile. "The chandelier needs dusting."

"I'm sorry about all this, Owen."

"It's not your fault. Don't even go there. Any word on Estabrook?"

"Still no sign of him or his plane. There's a search underway, but he flew into remote country. It could be days, weeks or even months before we find him. We might never find him."

"Especially if he doesn't want to be found."

Simon understood where Owen was headed. "Norman gave up damning details on some very violent people who can't be happy with him. Today's festivities could be their work. They could be responsible for the bombs, the attack on Keira. They could have lured Norman up in his plane, or he knew they were after him and decided to disappear. He could be a target, too."

"Is that what you believe, Simon?"

He didn't hesitate. "No, but we have to keep an open mind."

"Law enforcement has to consider every angle," Owen said. "I don't."

"It's also possible that Norman will return from his flight by nightfall and what happened here and in Ireland is the work of someone involved with one of Abigail's cases, old or new—or one of Scoop's or Bob's. It could have something to do with you or her father. Belief only gets us so far," Simon added. "We can't jump the gun and miss the real bad guys because of wrong assumptions."

"But it's Estabrook," Owen said.

Simon was silent a moment, then nodded.

"He obviously had help. Pulling off three simultaneous attacks within hours of his release means he must have had at least the barebones of a plan in place, probably before he was arrested. What's the purpose, Simon? What does he want?" Owen broke off, shook his head. "You should get out of here. Go to Ireland and be with Keira."

There wasn't anywhere in the world Simon would

rather be right now than with Keira. He thought of her in the stone circle above her cottage, a killer coming at her with a knife, and couldn't push back a wave of regret. "If I'd gone fishing with Will Davenport in Scotland in June instead of coming here to Boston, none of you would be in the middle of this mess. Keira would be safe."

"Or dead," John March said bluntly, entering the room. More FBI agents crowded into the foyer but kept a reasonable distance. "That serial killer was already interested in her Irish story and would have had free rein if you hadn't been in her life. Who's to say what would have happened? And Keira's safe now."

But Abigail, his daughter, wasn't. Genuinely shaken, Simon wished he could melt into the cracks in the floor. "I have no right when you and Owen…" He didn't finish his thought.

"You have every right," March said. "Estabrook's gone after the people closest to us. He doesn't want them."

Simon nodded. "I know. He wants us."

"And he doesn't just want us dead. I could handle straightforward revenge, but he wants us to suffer first." March looked at his future son-in-law. "Owen, I don't know what to say."

"I want to go after her, John."

"No. It's too risky. We don't know enough. Work with us. Maybe you saw something, or Abigail said something…" March stopped abruptly, his expression tight, controlled, a reminder that he'd worked in law enforcement for almost forty years. "Abigail wouldn't want you to go solo, either."

"Then let me go to Montana and help look for this bastard. I can find his plane. I have search-and-rescue teams ready to go."

March sighed. "Someone—undoubtedly the man you

want to fly to Montana and find—tried to kill you today. You do know that, don't you?"

"I was warned in time. I found the bomb. I'm alive." Owen walked over to the tall windows that looked out on Beacon Street and across to Boston Common. "I'm not dwelling on what might have happened."

"Crews are searching for Estabrook now."

Owen glanced back at March. "Not my crews."

Neither Simon nor March responded.

Simon joined his friend at the windows. Pedestrians passed by on the street—tourists, students, state workers, business people. "I've been trying to understand Norman's thinking for a year. He faces death to feel alive." Simon hesitated, then said, looking back at March, "He thwarts authority to feel alive."

"Why me, Simon?" March asked quietly.

It was Owen who answered. "He sees you as an equal. Equals are rare in his universe. Everyone else is a lesser mortal to him, but you…" He shrugged. "You're the head of the most powerful law enforcement agency in the world."

The FBI director, who'd been a surrogate father to Simon since his own father had died twenty years ago, joined them at the windows. As March stared outside, Simon could feel the older man's pain, his fear for his daughter. His emotion was almost unbearable to witness.

"I'm not wealthy," March said finally. "I don't go on high-risk adventures. I'm just a cop. That's it. Whether I'm on a beat here in Boston or in an office in Washington, I'm still just a cop doing a job."

Simon shook his head. "Not in Norman's eyes. You're a challenge. He wants you as an enemy. Going up against you and the entire FBI is another way for him to face death."

Owen turned from the windows. "He'd rather die in action than wither away in a prison cell."

"That works for me," March said. "My wife's under protection in Washington. You two should be, too. Turn yourselves over to agents. Let us see to your safety."

"I'll work with the FBI and help in any way I can," Owen said stiffly, "but I'll see to my own safety."

Simon's eyebrows went up. "You're kidding, John, right? I spent a year with Norman and his drug-trafficking pals without a net. *Now* you're worried?"

"Simon..."

"Forget it. I'm working this investigation now that Keira's in safe hands."

He didn't go into more detail. Will Davenport was in Ireland, and he and March had a history, not a good one. Simon didn't know the specifics but suspected their animosity went back to Afghanistan and how and why Will had ended up trapped in a cave with two of his men dead, a third dragged off by enemy fighters. Simon had been there himself on assignment for the FBI. He suspected his reasons for being near the cave were at least marginally related to Will's reasons, but the Brits had clammed up after the tragic loss of three of their own—or at least had clammed up to him. Maybe not to March.

Simon saw that March was scrutinizing him with an expression that was more cop than friend or father figure, and he knew his comment had sparked the FBI director's interest.

Time to make his exit.

He clapped a hand on Owen's shoulder, nodded to March and left without saying anything else. What more was there to say? He headed into the foyer and down the front steps onto the wide sidewalk. A half-dozen fellow FBI agents and BPD officers watched him, and he wondered if they had orders to make sure he didn't go off on his own.

Too bad if they did.

The air was warm, even hot, in the fading afternoon. He thought of Will's description of the woman who'd intercepted the man sent to attack Keira in Ireland. "Long, straight black hair and light green eyes," Will had said. "She's small, but very fast and self-assured. I saw her tackle Murphy from a distance. She had him on the ground, his own knife to his throat, before I'd cleared the fence. Who do you suppose she is, Simon?"

He'd said he had no idea, which was true.

Now, he wasn't so sure. A woman did come to mind, but it made no sense at all.

Lizzie Rush, kicking ass in an Irish stone circle?

She was one of the many high-end members of Norman's entourage who'd claimed to be shocked by his illegal activities.

The FBI agent who'd interviewed Lizzie after Norman's arrest had described her to Simon. "Clueless. A little annoyed. Very eager to get back to her reprobate daddy in Las Vegas."

The last time Simon had run into her, she was wearing a slim, expensive black dress with a bottle of water and a martini at her elbow as she'd amused herself at a cocktail party at Norman's Cabo San Lucas estate. Afterward, she, Norman and Simon had discussed preliminary plans for a Costa Rican adventure. She obviously knew her business, if not what her financial-genius friend was up to.

So what was she doing in the same Irish village as Keira?

"I'd have managed on my own somehow," Keira had said, not with bravado but a calm certainty that Simon had learned over the past two months not to doubt. "But I was glad to have help."

Regardless of who'd saved whom, someone had sent a killer after her.

Simon crossed Beacon Street and took the steep, stone stairs down to Boston Common. A breeze stirred through the tall trees, and he glanced back at the Garrison house to see if anyone had followed him.

Not yet, but his fellow law enforcement officers were still watching him. In their place, he'd be doing the same.

He dialed a London number on his cell phone. "Moneypenny," he said when Josie Goodwin, Will's assistant, answered. "Dare I ask where you are?"

"Special Agent Cahill," Josie said. "I suspected I might hear from you tonight."

"I have a name for you."

"I'm ready."

"Lizzie Rush. If she's our black-haired mystery woman, you can have Will tell her to back off and mind her own business."

"Perhaps she knows more than you realize."

"Then she can call me and tell me. She's bored, rich and very pretty, Josie. She can't interfere—" But he stopped abruptly. He'd been thinking about Lizzie Rush ever since he'd spoken to Will and Keira, when and where he'd seen her, her relationship with Norman. What if she *did* know more than he'd realized? He sighed. "Hell, Josie."

"Indeed, Simon," she said. "Suppose this woman has been a quiet player right from the start? Is it possible Director March had an anonymous source funnel him information?"

It wasn't just possible. He did have one. A dozen times over the past year, March himself had handed Simon critical pieces of information—photographs, names, account numbers—that could only have been obtained by someone close to Norman Estabrook. March never confirmed or denied the existence of a source and instructed Simon not to speculate. Just take the information and do his job.

Of course, Simon had speculated, especially in the weeks since Norman's arrest. Various names came to mind—accountants, bookkeepers, hedge-fund staffers, household help…

But Lizzie Rush?

"Leave her to Will," Josie said.

Simon heard something in her voice. "Moneypenny," he said, "you wouldn't be holding back on me, would you?"

"Why, Simon, what a thing to say."

She disconnected in mock horror.

Which told Simon she *was* holding back. Josie Goodwin was a force unto herself, but she would only go so far with Simon, friend of her boss or no friend. Will was a lone wolf who lived a dangerous life and tried to protect those around him from that life.

It wasn't always possible, Simon thought as he dialed Owen's cell number. "March still breathing down your neck?"

"Right here."

"I'll help you get to Montana."

Owen was silent a moment. "Thank you."

"Like you aren't already plotting how to get there on your own. At least my way will keep you from getting arrested." But Simon couldn't maintain his normal good cheer. "I've done search missions with you, Owen. If anyone can find Norman's plane, it's you."

"I'm ready to leave now."

Simon managed a smile. "I thought you might be."

Seeing how his Boston residence had just been totaled by fire, smoke and water damage, Owen had nothing to pack. He could always stop at a Wal-Mart on his way to Montana.

As he shut his phone, Simon looked east toward Boston Harbor, squinting as if it would help him see past the tall buildings and the Atlantic and connect with Keira in Ireland. He concentrated on his love for her. Will wouldn't leave her until he was satisfied that the garda, her fairies and the O'Shea brothers would keep her safe.

Keira had objected, but she also understood.

This one wasn't her fight.

Chapter 10

Keira stood at the pine table in her cottage on the lane below the stone circle, shoving art supplies—paints, pencils, brushes, sketch pads—into a wooden case. "The woman who helped me tonight knew what to ask. She knew names. Bob, Scoop, Abigail. Simon. Owen." Keira paused, raising her eyes to Will. "She knew everything. Who is she?"

"I don't know," Will said, shrugging on his coat.

Garda detectives had inspected Keira's cottage for explosive devices and were waiting outside to take her to a safe place. Will had arrived in the stone circle too late to be of any real use. Simon would hate himself for not being there. But it didn't matter, did it? Their mysterious black-haired woman had dispatched Murphy and questioned him like a professional, then boldly went on her way ahead of the guards' arrival.

They were looking for her now.

But she'd been right: Will could have stopped her. Why hadn't he?

He already knew the answer. He hadn't stopped her for the same reason he hadn't interrupted her when she'd asked Michael Murphy about the Brit she'd believed had sent him to kill Keira.

"He's dangerous and charming and very focused."

Keira paused a moment in her packing. "You're going to find out who she is, though, aren't you?"

"Yes."

"You didn't stop her from leaving."

"No, I didn't."

Keira's cornflower-blue eyes leveled on him, but she said nothing further as she flipped through a stack of small sketch pads, choosing two to take with her.

The scent of the rambling pink roses out front sweetened the breeze that floated through the open windows, gentler now that the gale had died down. Keira's hair was tangled, her clothes and shoes muddy from her ordeal in the stone circle. The Irish detectives had told her she could shower later at the safe house where they were taking her.

Keira had made it plain she didn't want to go anywhere except to Simon and her family and friends in Boston. She could refuse protection, but she didn't. Garda teams had kicked into immediate action upon their arrival in the village, taking away Michael Murphy, cordoning off the stone circle and searching the pub, Keira's cottage and the boat she and Simon had shared for much of the past month for explosive devices and hidden thugs.

"Bombs, Will," she said suddenly, reaching for a nub of an eraser. "I keep thinking about Scoop. He's a great guy. He adopted two stray cats—the firefighters got them out safely." She dropped the eraser into her box and wiped the back of her hand across tear-stained cheeks. "He's in critical but stable condition. Will…"

He touched her slender shoulder. "Keira, I'm sorry. I know how difficult this is for you."

"Scoop's strong. He'll pull through." She picked up the brush she'd dropped. "He has to. And Abigail. I can't—if I think about her, where she could be, what she's going through, I'll fall apart, and that won't help anyone."

Will had learned from Simon that his newfound love had moved from city to city for years, at home everywhere and nowhere. Finally she'd returned to Boston to be near her mother, who had withdrawn from the world to live as a religious ascetic in a cabin she'd built herself in the woods of southern New Hampshire. Keira had developed a closer relationship with her uncle, Bob O'Reilly, and younger cousins in Boston, and she, Abigail Browning and Scoop Wisdom had become friends.

Then Simon Cahill had entered her life.

"It's not Simon's fault." Keira again fastened her gaze on Will. "He's a target just like the rest of us."

"What has Simon told you about Norman Estabrook?"

"We haven't talked about him that much. He's petulant, vindictive and brilliant. He courts danger to feel alive." She reached for more art supplies as she continued. "He trusted Simon with his life."

"It wasn't misplaced trust," Will said. "Simon never did anything to deliberately endanger Estabrook."

"From what I gather, he's obsessive about safety measures and backup plans. Whatever happened today—whatever went wrong or right—he'll have various courses of action from which to choose."

"That won't make him easier to find."

She nodded grimly. "Simon and I have only just found each other. I can hear him singing Irish songs now. He and my uncle have beautiful voices. I can't sing a note. My mother, either. A few months ago, she was living a quiet, solitary life of prayer in the woods, and now she's back in the city with all this…" Keira snapped her art case shut. "I wouldn't blame her if she gives up on us and goes back to her cabin."

"Your mother's safe, Keira," Will said. "The Boston police and the FBI won't let any harm come to her."

He read her expression, saw that she was as stubborn and independent as Simon had promised she was, and also as brave. Wherever the garda tucked her for her own safety, she'd do what she could to help the investigation. She wasn't one to sit back.

There was a light knock on the kitchen door, and an officer poked his head in. "Two minutes, and we have to go."

Keira took a breath. "I don't even know what I've packed, but I suppose I can always ask someone to make a supply run for me if it comes to that." She raised her eyes again to Will. "You'll have to come meet the gang one day. We're supposed to do Christmas in Ireland this year. My uncle, my cousins, my mother and me."

"It'll be cold, dark and wet."

She smiled. "I hope so. I promised to take my cousin Fiona to pubs to hear Irish music. She has her own Irish band. I want to talk to her, see her—Scoop saved her today. Simon didn't say so outright, but there must have been a lot of blood." Keira sniffled back more tears, as much from anger and frustration as worry and grief. "I don't want to run and hide, Will."

"That's not what you're doing."

"Isn't it?"

She didn't wait for an answer and retreated to the cottage's sole bedroom, emerging in less than a minute with a brocade satchel, her hair brushed and pulled back into a ponytail. She was lovely, creative and unexpectedly pragmatic. Will wouldn't be surprised if the garda had found a safe house in the village. She seemed protected there.

"I'll do whatever I need to do," she said quietly. "You know that, don't you?"

"And Simon knows." Will smiled at her. "You and your fairy prince will soon be reunited."

Keira took his hand, squeezing it as she leaned forward and kissed him on the cheek. "Whatever debt you think you owe Simon, he says you don't owe him anything. You never did."

"This isn't about debts owed, Keira."

"No. I suppose it isn't." Her eyes steadied on him with just a hint of a spark. "If you end up in Boston, beware of sneaking around under the noses of the police there. You've never met my uncle, but he'll be on a tear after what's happened."

"He's Boston Irish, isn't he?"

"Yes."

Will winked at her. "Then I don't need to meet him."

She let go of his hand and whispered, "Be safe."

He left before the guards could change their mind and take him into custody for additional questioning. He'd parked on the lane, his car spotted with bits of pink rose petals flung there in the wind and rain, a tangible reminder, somehow, of Keira's ordeal.

As he drove toward the village, he looked up at the wild hills silhouetted against the dark Irish night. He hated to leave Keira, but she would be safe here.

And he had a job to do.

A light shone in the window of the pub, and the door was unlocked. Will found Eddie O'Shea behind his bar, cleaning up for the night. The guards had gone, their investigative work completed, at least for now.

When he saw Will, Eddie said, "A bomb sweep is a fine way to scare off paying customers. Will you be wanting a drink, Lord Will?"

"Coffee, please, if you have it."

"I've water still hot in the kettle." He set a coffee press on the bar and scooped in fresh grounds. "Next time, ring me when you feel an urge to come to Ireland. I'll be on my toes for trouble."

"The trouble started before I arrived."

"True enough. It was the same earlier this summer with Keira and her stone angel and that other bloody killer." The barman shuddered. "I've pictures that'll never leave my head from those terrible days."

"I wish it could have been otherwise, Eddie."

"As do I." He poured water over the grounds, replaced the top on the press and set it in front of Will to steep. He got out a mug and a pitcher of cream, his movements automatic, routine. "The guards talked to our friend Michael Murphy. It's his real name. He's too dim-witted to make one up. He's a known thug in Limerick."

"Good at his work?"

"Not good enough...fortunately for Keira and her black-haired friend." O'Shea pushed the coffee paraphernalia in front of Will and looked thoughtfully at him. "The guards wish we'd stopped her from leaving the scene."

Will knew they did. "You saw her for yourself—her torn knuckles, her muddy clothes, the way she handled Mr. Murphy. Would you have wanted to take her on?"

"She wasn't too quick to give up his knife."

And she'd disarmed him, weaponless herself. Murphy hadn't expected her, and even when he saw her, he'd obviously discounted her as a threat, especially a lethal one. He was strong and capable, a veteran fighter, but she'd had his face in the mud and manure before he'd had a chance to land a single blow.

Eddie showed not the slightest edge of fatigue despite the night's events. "I expect the guards will have to sort through layers of tawdry criminals to get to whoever hired Murphy. Man, woman or animal."

"I expect so," Will agreed, pouring his coffee. It was very hot and very strong, and suddenly he hoped he'd have reason to sit here one evening, chatting with the amiable Irish barman over matters that didn't involve violence.

"You don't know where the guards have taken Keira, I suppose?" Eddie asked.

Will shook his head. "I'm sorry, no."

"I'd be wasting air asking them. As long as she's safe." He nodded to the coffee. "What else can I get you? I've a bit of blackberry crumble left. There's soup, but Patrick made it, and it's not fit for the pigs."

"No food. Thanks."

"You're gloomy."

He was, and he knew why. The evening had launched him back two years, to the cave in Afghanistan and the deaths of men who'd trusted him.

For their sakes, he had to focus on the task at hand.

He drank some of his coffee and addressed the barman. "Did you see Michael Murphy in the village earlier today?" He paused. "Before today?"

Eddie emptied the stainless-steel kettle into a small sink. "I don't remember seeing him before tonight. I told the guards as much."

"He could have a partner. I understand that strangers come in here on a regular basis—particularly this time of year, particularly this summer with the publicity over Keira's stone angel. Did anyone strike you as not belonging? Someone who wasn't a typical tourist, perhaps?"

Will set his mug on the bar and kept his gaze on the Irishman. "Think, my friend. Who stood out to you in recent days?"

Eddie took the still-hot coffee press and dumped the grounds, then rinsed the glass container in the sink and set it to drain. Finally he said, "A Brit like the one our black-haired friend described was here a week ago, maybe more."

Will got very still. "Tell me about him."

"He had soup and left."

"Were Keira and Simon here?"

Eddie shook his head. "Not yet. They arrived from the north five days ago on the boat you loaned them. This man was here before then."

"Did he ask about them?"

"No. I'd recall if he did. Given his manner, I'd wager he was a military man. He had a self-control that reminded me of you, Lord Will." Eddie slopped an overly wet cloth onto the bar. "Not that I know about military men."

Will kept his hands steady even as his heartbeat quickened. So much for self-control. He envisioned Myles, arms crossed on his chest as he lay on his back and gazed up at the starlit Afghan sky and said, quite sincerely, he was as comfortable sleeping there, on the rocks in the open, as he'd have been at Buckingham Palace. In the eight years Will had known and trusted him, Myles Fletcher had never shown a hint of a grasping nature. He'd never shown himself to be a man who could betray his country—his mates.

"What else can you remember?" Will asked, keeping his tone even. "The smallest detail could be significant."

"He paid with euros and sat alone, kept to himself. He asked for water—no coffee or alcohol. When he left, he walked down to the harbor, then down the lane. Aidan, Patrick and I took turns following him. He knew it and didn't care."

"Did he stay overnight in the village?"

"I don't know where he stayed. We lost him eventually. He brought up Keira's story about the stone angel when he was in here, but only for a moment, and he wasn't the first nor the last. It's been happening all summer."

"What did you tell him?"

A spark of mischief flared in the Irishman's eyes. "I told him to find a rainbow and follow it to a pot of gold."

Will smiled in spite of his tension. Eddie O'Shea enjoyed keeping his pub, but he wasn't one to suffer fools or intruders gladly. And he liked Keira and Simon. But who didn't?

Eddie continued mopping the bar with his wet cloth. "Did we do the right thing after all, Will, in letting our black-haired woman go?"

"You're worried about her," Will said.

"What if she's in over her head and a danger to herself? To others? We could have stopped her, Lord Will." The barman stood back and dropped the cleaning cloth into the sink, then got a dry one and soaked up the excess water on the gleaming bar. "Not without a fight, I'll wager, one I'm not sure we'd have won. She knows how to put her foot to the right spot on a man, I'll say that. I could see it when she came in here." He motioned toward the pegs by the front door. "The way she took off her jacket and hung it… Never mind the rest."

"From what I witnessed," Will said, "I'd guess she's received training."

"Of your sort?"

He let Eddie's question slide unanswered.

"Is that why you let her go?" Eddie's eyes shone with

both amusement and suspicion. "A strapping Brit like yourself, worrying a tiny woman would best you."

"She'd just bested an armed, hired killer."

"Ah. You wouldn't stand a chance, would you?"

Will pictured her at the fire with Keira's book of folktales and smiled. "I didn't say that." He passed a business card that Josie had made up for him in London across the bar. "Call me anytime. For any reason."

"And the same, Lord Will. You call me anytime. I'll do whatever I can to help." Eddie took Will's empty mug and set it in the sink. "Who's the Brit you're thinking I saw?"

Will knew he couldn't answer. A lie, the truth—neither was acceptable, and so he said nothing.

Eddie seemed to understand the line his question had crossed. "If I see him again?"

"If you see him again," Will said carefully, "treat him like a shopkeeper who's here on holiday."

"Or he'll kill me in my sleep?"

Josie Goodwin answered from the door. "It won't matter if you're asleep," she said as she unzipped her coat, its style more suited to London than a quiet Irish village. She walked over to the bar, steady if visibly shaken. "I came as soon as I could. I'll be of more use here than in London should Keira need a hand, and perhaps I can persuade our garda friends to share information. I miss the city already. It's bloody dark out there."

A strongly built, attractive woman in her late thirties, she was as pale as Will had ever seen her. He'd been aware of her presence in the door, but he didn't know how much she'd overheard. He started to introduce her to Eddie, but the Irishman put up a hand to stop him. "I'll leave you two to your chat. I can see I won't be wanting to hear what you have to say."

As he retreated, Will felt Josie's emotions, checked,

under control but there. "Josie," he said, "we don't know—"

She cut him off neatly. "Let me just say my piece and get it done. You should go back to London, Will. Leave this mess to the Americans and the Irish to sort out."

"You've more on our mystery woman?"

"Her name is Lizzie Rush." Josie eased onto the tall bar stool next to Will. "She's one of the hotelier Rushes. She's in charge of their concierge and excursion services and leads quite an adventurous life."

"What's her connection to Simon?"

"She was with Norman Estabrook in Montana the day he was arrested. The FBI questioned her but didn't detain her."

"Are she and Estabrook romantically involved?"

"No. Absolutely not, according to what little I have managed to learn. He liked having attractive, successful people around him. She was one of them."

"Does she have a connection to John March?"

Josie sighed. "I'm still digging."

"March would use anyone to get what he wants."

"He's a suffering father right now, Will."

"I know. The man's in an impossible position."

"He often is." Obviously restless, she jumped down from the stool and went around to the other side of the bar, where she helped herself to a glass and a bottle of Midleton Rare Whiskey. "You can't let your dislike of Director March interfere with your judgment."

"It's mutual dislike, but also impersonal on a certain level since we've never met face-to-face. I'm convinced he's known more about Myles than he's ever been willing to tell us. He doesn't believe I can be fully trusted." Which was more than Will had ever admitted to Josie about his attitude toward the current FBI director and was all he planned to say. "Is Lizzie Rush a rich woman meddling in affairs of no concern to her because she's bored and has a zest for adventure, or does she have her own quarrel with Norman Estabrook?"

"She could also be on his side in a peculiar way," Josie said as she splashed whiskey into her glass, adding without sympathy, "If she's sticking her nose where it doesn't belong, she could get it cut off."

"Instead of fleeing, she stopped Keira from being killed."

"Which by itself means nothing, Will. You know that. What you saw tonight could have been staged, cooked up by her and Murphy to mislead us. This woman could have her own agenda and not give a damn about Keira, Estabrook, Simon or anyone else."

There was no one on the planet more clear-eyed or more unlikely to let emotion cloud her judgment than Josie Goodwin. Will recognized how much he'd come to rely on her not just for her efficiency, but as a sounding board. "I suppose theoretically she could have her own plans that could get mucked up if Keira and the people in Boston were killed."

"What about Abigail Browning?" Josie asked, taking a swallow of her whiskey even before she set down the bottle. She choked a little and gave her chest a pound with her fist. "Sorry. I haven't had a drop of alcohol in months. I was crying over my sorrows too many nights and…" She waved a hand. "Never mind. Perhaps our Lizzie Rush, regardless of why she was here, can help find Detective Browning."

Will narrowed his eyes. "You've more information?"

"Not much. I spoke to Simon." She got a pained look. "It's not good. There are no witnesses or substantial leads, and so far, there have been no calls for ransom."

"But no body, either, I gather."

"Correct. No body." Josie made a face as she swallowed more of her Midleton's. "You know I don't care for whiskey, don't you?"

Will smiled. "Yes, Josie, I know."

She coughed, took a smaller swallow this time. Her eyes, a dark blue, were hard and unforgiving, a contrast to the vulnerability her pale skin suggested.

A woman of contrasts, Josie Goodwin.

"You're a wealth of information, as always," Will said. "What would I do without you?"

"Live a lovely life in Scotland, I've no doubt." She returned the whiskey bottle to its place in Eddie's lineup. "Do you believe Miss Rush could help us find Myles Fletcher, that bloody traitor?"

"Josie…"

"It's a serious, professional question, Will."

"We've no reliable evidence that he's alive."

Josie polished off her whiskey, giving a final shudder of distaste as she turned back to him. "The barman's description, Will. It fits."

"It fits other British men, too, I'm sure. It isn't definitive by itself."

Josie gave him a long, cool look as she rinsed her glass. "You're trying to spare me."

He attempted a smile. "You? Never."

"All right, then. We'll do this your way. There's no good answer here, is there? Either Myles Fletcher was a traitor killed two years ago, or he survived and is now a cold-blooded mercenary."

Myles Fletcher was a name Will knew Josie didn't want to utter and certainly wasn't one he wanted to hear. "I should have worked harder to find him."

"We all did everything possible. Everything, Will."

"What if he's not—"

"Don't." Her voice was hoarse, her eyes dark and intense. "Don't, Will. Please."

He acceded to her wish with a reluctant nod and didn't continue.

"If Estabrook has hired Myles or allied himself with him in any way, it means he has someone on his payroll who can help him realize any violent impulses he has." Josie fell silent a moment. "I hope that's not the case."

"I do, too."

She didn't look at Will. "If Myles is alive, I hope he's lost his memory and has opened a tea shop in Liverpool. If not…" She glanced up, her cheeks less pale now. "I had the chance to smother him to death."

"Josie."

"All right, then. On we go. I'll investigate possible connections between Myles and Lizzie Rush, between him and her family." Josie hesitated, then said, "Perhaps she's in love with him. Myles does have a way with women."

"From her questioning of Michael Murphy, I would say Lizzie doesn't know him at all—"

"Which could be what she wants you to think." Josie came around to the other side of the bar. "I needn't remind you that Myles is a capable, ruthless killer. If he's alive, Will, don't think you can reason with him."

"Josie, I'm sorry his name's come up."

But she wasn't finished. "If you see him, put a bullet in his head. Find a way to do it. He's a predator. He hovers in the bush, waiting for the right moment, the right prey. Then he springs. I know, Simon. I was his prey once."

"He manipulated both of us, in different ways," Will said softly. "We owe his service, what he once was, an open mind."

Josie zipped up her coat, her eyes bitter now as well as hard. "Myles knows how to make people see what they want to see in him." She went on briskly, before Will could respond. "Interestingly the Rush family doesn't own a hotel in the U.K. They do, however, own what I understand is a charming hotel in Dublin."

"And how is this relevant?" Will asked.

"Because I reserved a room for you there for tonight. It should be quite lovely. You can see for yourself and let me know. They're expecting you for a very late arrival."

"Do you believe that's where Lizzie went, or do you know?"

"An educated guess, and either way, it's a good place to start. You *are* going after her, aren't you?"

Will thought of Lizzie Rush's green eyes, black-lashed and bold, yet, he was sure, hiding secrets, fears. But didn't everyone?

"Yes," he said, "I'm going after her."

"Excellent. I approve." At last, a glint of humor. "Give my best to Simon when you see him. And Keira?" Josie asked, more subdued, speaking as if she knew the woman Simon Cahill had fallen for earlier that summer, although the two of them had yet to meet. "She's all right?"

Will nodded. "Impatient to be with Simon."

"Ah, yes. One can imagine. Well," she added, "you should leave. Dublin's over three hundred kilometers, but you'll manage. You're accustomed to odd hours, long days—" she gave him a wicked smile "—and longer nights."

Will sighed and gave no comment.

"In any event," Josie said, "you've much to keep you wide-awake and on your toes."

"I see that plans have been made and announced, and I have only to comply."

"Finally he sees the light."

But their cheerfulness was momentary. "What about you, Josie?" Will asked her.

"I've booked a room at a five-star hotel in Kenmare, but perhaps I would be wise not to make the drive over these dark roads after gulping whiskey. Imagine the international row if I'm picked up by the Irish authorities. Much better to work with them discreetly."

Eddie O'Shea wandered back in behind his bar, nothing in his demeanor indicating he'd eavesdropped. "My brother Aidan has a room at his farm down the lane," he said to Josie. "You'd be welcome to stay."

Josie smiled, looking genuinely delighted. "A night on an Irish farm. A perfect ending to a difficult day."

Chapter 11

Boston, Massachusetts
6:25 p.m., EDT
August 25

The late afternoon sun beat down on the sidewalk in front of the triple-decker where Bob had lived for the past three years. There was no shade and no breeze. Sweat trickled down his temples and stuck his shirt to the small of his back. The firefighters had put out the fire and torn up and hosed down what they needed to, creating a big mess but saving the building, at least structurally. Abigail's and Scoop's back porches were cinders. Her apartment would have to be gutted to the studs. Hard to say yet about the other two places. They'd have to get the insurance people out here.

At least no one found any other bombs.

Ever since the ambulance had left with Scoop, bloodied, in rough shape, Bob had made it clear he was in charge of the investigation. He'd gotten through the major briefing with city, state and federal law enforcement personnel held on the street outside the crime scene tape. He had detectives canvassing the neighborhood for witnesses, processing the scene, putting together rudimentary timelines.

The working theory had dirtbag, or dirtbags, slipping into the backyard of the triple-decker and placing an explosive device under the small gas grill on Abigail's first-floor porch. Since she and Owen rarely used the grill and, given their busy lives, spent little time sitting out on the porch, the bomb could have been there for a few days, a few hours. It had been detonated by a remote-controlled switching device.

The bomb in Owen's car had to have been placed there after he'd arrived on Beacon Hill. Otherwise he'd have blown up when he turned the key leaving Abigail's apartment that morning.

According to Fiona, Bob's warning had given Scoop a split second to grab her and dive behind the compost bin.

Saved by dirt and kitchen scraps.

Only Scoop.

They'd all done the drills. What happens if police officers are targeted by a series of bombs?

This, Bob thought. This is what happens.

He was satisfied that people were doing what they were supposed to, except the idiot who'd thought it would be okay to tell his ex-wife, the mother of their three daughters, where to find him.

Tight-lipped and drawn, Theresa O'Reilly glared at him under the hot sun. "Never again." She pointed a blunt-nailed finger at him in that way she had. "Do you understand me? *Never* again."

Bob let her anger bounce off him. Getting into it with her never worked. "Fiona doesn't want to go home with you and the girls."

"I don't care what she wants. She's not going back to her apartment."

"Whoa. I'm with you, Ter."

Without consulting either parent, their eldest daughter

had decided to sublet an apartment for the summer with three of her musician friends. The bomb squad had been through their place in Brighton but hadn't found anything. They'd also checked the South Boston water-front apartment where his sister, Eileen, Keira's mother, was house-sitting after giving up her crazy life in the woods. She'd left Bob a message on his cell phone saying she was praying for everyone's safety. That was good. He'd surprised himself by saying a prayer himself.

For Abigail, he thought. For her safe return.

Theresa's eyes filled with tears. "I'm sorry." She was shaking, her teeth chattering. "It's awful. This whole thing."

Bob felt terrible. "Yeah. I know. I'm sorry, too."

She was chief of operations at a high-tech firm in suburban Lexington. They'd met when he was a patrol officer and she was an office temp with big dreams. They'd stuck together until Jayne, their youngest, was four. That was seven years ago. He'd tried marriage again two years later, for about three seconds. Theresa hadn't remarried, but she had a boyfriend. Another executive. She'd sworn off cops after Bob.

He couldn't stand his ex-wife's fear. "Dyeing your hair these days, Ter?"

"Go to hell. And don't call me 'Ter.' It's Theresa."

"Okay. It's Theresa."

She sighed, dropping her arms to her sides. Her hair was a honey-blond—total dye job, he was sure—and she had lines at the corners of her eyes and around her mouth, but she looked good. The years hadn't been so kind to him. He needed to take off a few pounds, and there were brown spots on his arms and face that hadn't been there before. He was a redhead. His doctor was always on him about sunscreen.

Yeah. How about burning his face off in a fire? What would sunscreen do for that?

"Bob?"

"I'm tuned in, Ter. Just waiting for your next shot."

She shook her head at him. "Bastard." She touched his arm, briefly. "Are you all right?"

"Never better."

He glanced at the black FBI SUV where BPD detectives were reinterviewing Fiona. She'd had a break and sat in the air-conditioning for a while, had something to eat and drink. Now she was slumped against the SUV and back at it.

Enough already.

"Wait here," Bob told his ex-wife. "I'll spring Fi as soon as I can. It'll be a few minutes."

"I'm not going anywhere."

He knew she was true to her word. For all the ways they irritated each other, she was a devoted mother. His legs felt wobbly as he headed for the SUV. Adrenaline dump. Nothing a couple of shots of Jameson's wouldn't cure. They'd help the guilt, too. Theresa had wanted him to go to night school and become a lawyer like John March. All those years ago, begging him. She'd never liked police work. She'd never gotten used to the anxiety or believed the statistics. "You carry a gun to work, Bob," she'd told him. "What more do I need to know?"

No answer to a question like that. What more *did* Theresa need to know?

He saw Tom Yarborough make his way over to her. Yarborough had been a rock since the explosion, professional, focused, but not unemotional. He and Abigail had worked together for eight months and were always butting heads. Bob had straightened out a few disagreements between them, but they both were top-notch homicide detectives who respected each other. Abigail was just easier to get along with.

Theresa was dabbing a tissue at her eyes now. Bob couldn't take tears and turned his attention to his daughter.

Fiona had gone through her ordeal first with him, in the initial hysteria as the paramedics were working on Scoop, and then in more detail, with more control, with Yarborough and Lucas Jones. Lucas was Abigail's former partner. He'd been promoted to lieutenant last fall and moved over to narcotics. Since Norman Estabrook was in cahoots with drug traffickers, Lucas said he should be in on the investigation. He was still with Fiona as she slumped against the side of the SUV. He'd left a picnic with his young family in Roxbury to head to the scene. He was built like a sparkplug and relished being a professional more than a tough guy. But he could be both.

"How you holding up, kid?" Bob asked his daughter.

She gnawed on her lower lip. "Okay."

"She's wrung out," Lucas said, "but she's doing great."

If Bob had to pick someone to interview his daughter, it'd be Lucas. The guy was a peach as well as one of BPD's finest detectives. But Bob didn't want Fiona talking to cops. He wanted her back with her friends, playing Irish drinking songs.

Down the street, Simon Cahill arrived and showed his FBI credentials to a uniformed BPD officer. He had two FBI suits with him who'd obviously been assigned to keep him alive, but he split off from them and walked over to the SUV. He looked cool, unfazed by the action around him, but that, Bob had learned, was Simon. Even so, he wasn't the affable man who'd danced and sung to Irish tunes with Keira in the triple-decker's backyard two months ago. A yard that was now charred, wet, bloody and filled with crime scene investigators.

"Bob…" Simon took a moment to clear his throat. "I'm sorry."

"For what? Did you set the bombs?"

"I should have seen this through before I got involved with Keira. Estabrook was already obsessed with John March, but—"

"Stop. You know regrets won't help now."

"You're right." He blew out a breath, recovering his composure. "I'd like to take Fiona through what happened."

Lucas heard him and stepped away from her, protective. "You can see my notes."

Simon ignored him, his eyes on Bob.

Bob sighed. "One fed talks to her. You. That's it."

"I'll see to it."

"And I stay," Bob added.

Lucas didn't look happy, but he moved off without argument. Simon opened up the back door to the SUV, reached inside and got out a bottle of water. He flipped open the top, shut the door and handed the water to Fiona. She mumbled her thanks.

"Feeling okay?" Simon asked.

She nodded. The paramedics had checked her over, but, except for a few cuts, scrapes and bruises, she was fine. She'd cleaned up as best she could, and Bob had bullied his way upstairs to his place and fetched her a fresh shirt. It didn't smell that bad of smoke and it was in better shape than the shirt she'd worn over there that morning, now soaked in Scoop's blood.

Staring at the sidewalk, sipping her water, Fiona said that she was picking tomatoes with Scoop and humming Irish tunes, and next thing, he flung her behind the compost pile and there was smoke and fire and debris—and blood.

"Did you see anyone before the blast?" Simon asked.

She shook her head.

"What time did you arrive?"

"Around two. I wanted to talk to my dad about our Christmas trip to Ireland. You know Keira's going with us, right? Our grandmother was born in Ireland, and my dad and her mom are of Irish descent on both sides."

Simon smiled gently. "I'm familiar with your Irish family roots."

"I had some information I printed off the Internet about where to have tea in Dublin on Christmas Eve. Doesn't that sound like fun, having tea in Ireland on Christmas Eve?"

Bob worked harder on his gum. He'd already been through two packs. Simon wouldn't care about tea in Dublin or anywhere else, but he said, "I can see your dad at high tea, can't you?"

"He'll love it."

"Probably will. So, you got your print-outs together and headed to your dad's place. Where were you?"

"The Garrison house on Beacon Street. I was practicing harp."

"Any of your friends there?"

"No, I was alone. Well, except for Owen, but he was upstairs at the foundation offices. He was there when I arrived at ten." She'd obviously already gone through the timeline. "Mostly I just practiced."

"Did you take the T over here," Simon said, "or did you drive?"

"The T. Then I walked. It was a beautiful day. *Is.*" She sucked in a breath and took a gulp of water. "I feel sick."

Simon ignored her. Bob would have, too. "Where'd you get on the T?"

"Downtown Crossing. The Orange Line."

"Anyone get on with you?"

"I think so. I didn't pay attention. No one stuck out to me."

"Anyone get off the T with you?"

"No, and no one followed me. I always check. It's habit." Her eyes lifted to her father. "My dad taught me to notice things."

Simon didn't even glance sideways at Bob, just stayed focused on Fiona. "So, you're walking toward your dad's place…"

"I didn't notice anything unusual then, either. Cars, people. When I got here, I went out back. I didn't knock or ring the doorbell or anything."

"Your dad was expecting you?"

She nodded. "I'd called him on my cell phone when I got off the T. I went out back and yelled up to let him know I was here."

"Gate to the backyard was unlocked?"

"Yes. I just walked right in. I told Dad I'd pick tomatoes and bring them up to him. Scoop had plenty. *Has* plenty." She shot an angry look at Simon and then Bob as if she expected them to argue with her, but it didn't last. She continued, less combative. "The firefighters and paramedics stomped on the tomatoes getting to us, but I think some of them are still okay. Scoop will be back in his garden soon."

"All right." Simon leaned against the SUV, not looking hot, tense or remotely exhausted, despite the guilt and tension he had to be experiencing. "You're in the backyard. You give your dad a shout. Was he outside?"

Fiona shook her head. "He came onto his back porch when he heard me. He said hi, then went back inside."

"And Scoop was in the garden?"

"That's right."

"Did he invite you to join him, or did you invite yourself?"

"I invited myself. I love tomatoes."

"So you join him. Then what?"

She drank more water before she answered. "Abigail said hello."

"Where was she, do you remember?"

"Her porch. I thought at first she was in her kitchen, but I…" Fiona's hands trembled visibly. This was where her story took a turn from picking tomatoes in the summer sun to hell. "I was wrong. She was on her porch."

"What exactly did she say?" Simon asked.

Fiona thought a moment. "She said, 'Hey, Fiona, don't let Scoop pawn off wormy tomatoes on you.'"

Simon smiled. "Scoop have anything to say about that?"

"He held up a gorgeous, round, red tomato and said, 'See that, Browning? You can't buy tomatoes that pretty.'"

"And she said?"

Fiona's lower lip trembled in a way that reminded Bob of her as a baby. "Nothing. Not that I heard." She scrunched up her face, concentrating. "A phone rang. I didn't think of it until now. That must have been—that's why she went inside."

"To answer the phone," Simon said.

"Then Dad yelled, and Scoop grabbed me."

"So first the phone, then your dad, then Scoop."

"Yes."

"Then what?"

"Scoop hurled me behind the compost bin."

"Did he say anything?" Simon asked.

"Not a word. He knocked the breath out of me. I had just enough time to notice I couldn't breathe when the bomb exploded. I had no idea what was going on. Then Scoop…" She was taking rapid, shallow breaths now, off in her own world of memory, fear. "Everything felt like it happened at once. The explosion, the concussion—it felt like the air was being sucked out of me, the whole backyard. Scoop grunted and then—there was so much blood."

"It was pieces of the grill and the propane tank that hit him," Bob interjected. "Scoop's injuries had nothing to do with saving you. If he'd jumped behind the compost bin by himself, he still—"

"If I'd protected him instead of him protecting me, he'd be fine," Fiona said stubbornly, adamant. "Just like I am now."

Before Bob could respond, Simon stood up from the SUV. "That's not the way it works. You're a nineteen-year-old college student. Scoop's a cop. He did what he's trained to do."

"He's a hero," she said.

Bob didn't speak. He couldn't now. He'd lose it, and that wouldn't help his daughter.

And it wouldn't help Abigail.

Fiona handed Simon her water bottle, her hands steadier. "I didn't see anyone on the street or at the houses next door. I didn't hear anyone. Nothing. Not even a dog barking or a television. It was all background noise to me. White noise. I remember humming 'Irish Rover' as I came into the yard."

Bob had heard her, his sweet daughter humming one of her Irish tunes. He hadn't remembered until now.

She smiled suddenly at Simon. "You and my dad both can sing. You should sing with my ensemble sometime."

Fiona always said "ensemble," Bob thought, never band.

Simon winked at her. "We can dance an Irish jig, too."

"That's right, yes! I had no idea until this summer. Dad kept his talents bottled up inside him for years." She turned to Bob, strands of blond hair stuck to her pallid cheeks. "Because of Deirdre McCarthy and what happened to her."

Bob grimaced at the mention of the girl who'd lived on his street when he was growing up and was brutally murdered at nineteen, changing his life forever. He said, "Deirdre had the voice of an angel. Mine's nothing in comparison."

"I keep thinking about her," Fiona said. "I never knew her. She died—she was murdered—long before I was born, but it's like her spirit's been a part of our lives and I didn't even know it."

Bob didn't want her thinking about Deirdre, but what could he do? By not talking about Deirdre McCarthy for thirty years, he'd kept the tragedy and horror of her death out of his daughters' minds, out of their consciousness, and yet her long-ago murder had inspired the devil-obsessed serial killer who'd come after Keira in June.

Would his daughters and niece have been more prepared if they'd known about Deirdre, if he hadn't tried to protect them?

He jerked himself back to the matter at hand.

Simon opened the back door of the SUV and tossed in the empty water bottle, then shut the door again, hard— just, Bob knew, to break some of the tension and refocus Fiona. He returned to his position against the SUV. "You said earlier you heard Abigail scream after the explosion."

"I know that's what I told you." Fiona stared again at her hands. "But I didn't hear her scream. I thought I did, but I didn't. I don't know what I heard. Everything really didn't happen all at once. It was the phone ringing and then Dad yelling and then Scoop grabbing me and *then* the explosion. In that order. It was all so fast. I know people say that, but it was."

"You've done well to break it down for us," Simon said.

But she looked up at her father. "Did you see something, Dad? How did you know to warn us?"

He hadn't told her about the call from Ireland. About Keira. The other woman on the line. He hadn't told Lucas Jones or Tom Yarborough, either. They hadn't asked him the question Fiona had just asked. They weren't being patient or negligent. They were just taking things in order.

Simon knew, but he said nothing.

"Dad," Fiona said, "if you warned us, someone must have warned *you,* right? Who?"

"You and your dad can talk in a bit," Simon said. "Let's go back to your practicing this morning at the Garrison house. Did you notice anyone there—"

"Who could have planted the bomb in Owen's car? I don't know. I don't think so." She was clearly fading, getting impatient, frazzled. "I can't…I don't know."

"I have just a few more questions, okay? We'll go through them without your dad."

Bob didn't protest. He kissed his daughter on the head and started back toward Theresa, but the ATF and FBI and state detectives and the whole damn lot pounced and dragged him down the street for another briefing.

The ATF guy, who was Bob's age, was pontificating. "It was C4," he said. "It's ideal for this kind of bomb. Just a quarter pound will destroy a propane tank and the surrounding structure."

The BPD bomb squad guy agreed. The fire department's arson squad guy threw in his opinion.

Bob chewed a fresh piece of gum. "The bombs didn't place themselves under Abigail's grill or in Owen's car, and she didn't just evaporate." He worked the gum harder. "Someone grabbed her and stuffed her into some kind of vehicle and got her out of here. Under my damn nose."

No one said anything.

He continued, all eyes on him. "The phone call got her inside off the porch. These bastards didn't want to kill her.

Scoop, Fiona—didn't matter if they died. Me. Who cares? The blast could have thrown Abigail off her feet. Stunned her, knocked her out. Whatever, the bad guys were ready and hauled her out to a waiting vehicle." Bob nodded to the spot on the sidewalk on the other side of the crime scene tape where he'd noticed the blood earlier. "She got a piece of one of them."

He paused, but still no one spoke. He knew what they were thinking. With one colleague in serious condition and another missing, he was slipping into posttraumatic stress syndrome.

He could feel his pulse tripping along. "I was focused on the blast. The diversion worked. I didn't see a thing. The vehicle—nothing."

"How'd they get to her porch and plant the bomb?" the ATF guy asked.

Bob wanted to strangle him. "Gee. I guess I probably let them in and showed them Abigail's grill and said, Hey, there's a good spot. No one'll notice a bomb there."

"Any telephone repairs, cable repairs, electricians, carpenters—"

"I gave my statement. Scoop'd give his, except he's unconscious. And Abigail's not here, in case you haven't noticed."

The ATF guy winced. "Sorry, Lieutenant."

The arson investigator said, "Anything we can do for you, Bob? For your family?"

Bob had a half-dozen retorts ready, none of them nice, but he saw the earnest look on the guy's face. Everyone wanted to help. Everyone felt lousy for him.

He had to get out of there.

He found refuge in the passenger seat of his heap of a car and scraped gunk off his cell phone, then dialed Eddie

O'Shea at his little village pub on the southwest Irish coast. Bob had already talked to Keira and an Irish detective about the attack on her. Now he wanted to talk to the bartender. They'd met earlier in August, when Bob had ventured to the land of his ancestors for the first time. He went with his sister in the days after she'd finally given up on her solitary life in the woods and rejoined civilization, such as it was. Keira had already fallen for Simon.

Bob hoped Simon would be on the trip to Ireland at Christmas with Keira, his daughters and his sister. They could sneak off for a beer or two. Christmas seemed far away now. Out of reach and impossible.

O'Shea answered after a couple of rings.

"Irish cops still there?" Bob asked.

"They've gone. They searched my pub for bombs, Bobby."

O'Shea insisted on calling him Bobby. Drove him nuts. "Find any?"

"Just Patrick's cooking."

It was a valiant attempt at humor. Eddie O'Shea had lived a quiet life before June when Keira had wandered into his pretty village on Kenmare Bay. "Trust no one," Bob said. "The guards. Your Irish fairies. No one, O'Shea. Do you hear me?"

"Are you well, Bobby?"

"Burned off my eyebrows."

"Simon?"

"A man with a mission." Bob felt his throat constrict. He'd developed a liking for Simon Cahill, and no question Simon believed he'd brought Norman Estabrook down on them all. Bob wasn't so sure. It was like Estabrook was a deadly virus lying dormant in their lives, just waiting for a chance to spread and do its damage. "I want to hear about this Irishman who tried to kill my niece."

"He knew about the bomb."

"The one in my house. There was another one in a car."

"Ah. He didn't mention that one. He's a hired man."

"Why did he tell Keira?"

"He didn't. He told that black-haired firebrand."

Keira had described her to Bob. "Any word on who she is?"

"Not that anyone's told me. She knows what she's doing, Bobby, I'll say that."

"But she's not law enforcement?"

"Ah, Bobby…I don't want to think about who she might be."

"Like what? A spy?" Bob's head pounded. "Never mind. You're a bartender. You love conspiracies. Was she alone?"

"Yes. She said she was walking the Beara Way, but she knew about Norman Estabrook, the billionaire Yank—"

"I know who he is."

"That's not a surprise." Eddie hesitated, then said in a near whisper, "Lord Will was here, Bobby."

"Simon's friend?"

"We can trust him. I'm sure of it. And Keira. She'll be safe here, Bobby. She has more spine than most."

"That she does." Bob didn't want to hang up. He hated the idea of Keira being across the ocean, alone, worried about Simon, targeted by a killer. She'd always been like another daughter to him. "Crazy artist. Tell her to cool her heels and paint pictures of Irish fairies and thistle, and I'll be in touch when I can."

Bob disconnected and got out of the car. The ATF guy came over. "Who were you talking to just now, Lieutenant?"

His open suspicion and arrogance went up one side of Bob and down the other, and he decided he just wasn't doing anymore right now. "A bartender in Ireland," he said. "I asked him for his recipe for rhubarb crumble."

Bob headed back to his ex-wife and his daughter before the ATF guy could rip his head off.

Chapter 12

Off the coast of Massachusetts
7:45 p.m., EDT
August 25

Abigail rode out another wave of nausea, forcing herself not to give in to seasickness. What would Owen say? He'd never been seasick in his life. Thinking about him gave her strength. He'd tell her to sleep while she could. Bob, Scoop, Yarborough, Lucas—her father. They'd all tell her the same thing. Simon would, too, but she didn't know him as well as the others.

Although some days she wondered if she knew her father at all.

She squeezed her eyes shut and fought back tears. They would only make her blindfold wet and worsen her discomfort. She ached, and she itched, and she wanted to fight these bastards but couldn't. They'd taken turns checking on her, providing a sip of water, threatening her if she tried to escape.

Two men whose voices she didn't recognize were arguing on the other side of the door. One man was clearly American—petulant, arrogant. The other was British— fearless, angry.

"You promised you'd be there for me," the American said.

The Brit snorted. "Not like this, you bloody fool."

"*Don't* talk to me that way."

"I'll talk to you any way I choose. I agreed to do a job, and you went behind my back and hired these utter morons to indulge your petty desire for vengeance."

"There's nothing petty about anything I do. I don't care what your credentials are, you're a mercenary who works for me. You're to do as I say."

"I will, but in my professional judgment—"

"You've made your opinion clear," the American said, less irritated. "Let's go forward from where we are now and not worry about the past. Agreed?"

A moment's hesitation. "Agreed."

The door creaked, opening abruptly. Abigail straightened as best she could. Her shoulders and thighs were painfully stiff, and her fingers and toes, despite her efforts to wiggle them, had gone numb.

She heard footsteps circling her chair. "My, my. You have had a difficult day, haven't you?" It was the American, smug, yet also, underneath, clearly agitated. "I have, too. I had a long, hard journey from Montana."

Norman Estabrook.

Abigail forced herself not to react.

"The risks I've taken today and the aggravation I've experienced are worth it, Detective Browning, just to see you here, at my mercy." He was in front of her now. "Your daddy and your friends in law enforcement have no idea where you are or where I am. None whatsoever."

"Enjoy your role as kidnapper in chief while you can, Norman." Abigail hated the raspiness of her voice, but at least it was strong. "It's not going to last. You screwed up today, didn't you? Everything didn't go as planned, did it?"

She felt his breath hot against her face. "I have you. I have Abigail March Browning, John March's daughter. Tell me, Detective. Don't you think your father needs his own personal devil to fight?"

"We can call and ask him."

"He needs me. He needs an enemy who is his equal. You learned about good and evil this summer, didn't you? The serial killer who came after your friend Keira was fascinated with the devil. You investigated him. He understood that God needs Lucifer."

Abigail suppressed a shiver of fear. She'd learned more about the nature of evil in June than she'd ever wanted to know. In her eight years as a detective, she had never come across such flat-out evil—the conscious, deliberate choice to commit vile acts of gratuitous violence on innocent people.

"I don't know about God and Lucifer," she said. "My father's an ordinary human being. So are you."

"There's nothing ordinary about me. Prosecutors and even my lawyers made the mistake of thinking I was like other men. I have resources and connections the FBI can't touch."

"You won't when you're in prison."

Estabrook gave a low chuckle. "Your father must be in torment right now, knowing that I have you and he's responsible. Knowing he had me, and he let me go."

"It wasn't his idea. He objected to your deal. He's not all powerful."

"He didn't believe I was capable of violence. He wanted my friends more than he did me. Imagine the possibilities going forward, Detective. I challenge the most powerful law enforcement officer in the world every day for the rest of his life, until he finally dies a bitter, broken old man."

"You're just not that special," Abigail said.

This time, Estabrook's laugh wasn't right in her ear, and she realized he must have stood up straight. His voice was congenial when he spoke. "At first I just wanted John March dead. Now, I want him to suffer. I want him to suffer and suffer and suffer." Estabrook was silent a moment, then added, "There are others I want to kill with my own hands."

Abigail concentrated on her breathing before fear could take hold, as her captor obviously hoped it would.

In for eight. Hold for eight. Out for eight.

She heard a door click shut but continued with her breathing exercise. She did three sets before she stopped and focused again on her surroundings.

"You have relentless friends." It was the man with the British accent, speaking softly, close to her. "They're looking for you now."

"Estabrook's gone?" she asked, calmer now.

"For the moment."

She swallowed, her mouth and throat dry from lack of water—and from tension, from fighting panic, nausea and claustrophobia. "It'll go better for you if you set me free now, before my friends find me."

"I take your point."

He sounded pragmatic, neither relishing nor concerned about the prospect of going up against various arms of the law enforcement community.

"What time is it?" she asked.

"Around eight o'clock. Are you injured?"

"I'm fine. Let me go before—"

"You're in a tough spot, Detective. I suggest you not waste your energy arguing for something that can't happen."

"Then tell me about my friends who were home when your bomb went off. Scoop, Bob, Fiona." She used their first names to humanize them, to make them real to this man. "What's their condition? Are they all right?"

"There were no deaths, and Detective O'Reilly and his daughter are uninjured."

She steeled herself against any emotion. "Scoop?"

"Detective Wisdom was cut by flying shrapnel. He'll survive, but he'll have a rough go for a while."

"Owen," Abigail whispered. "What about him?"

"A handy sort, your man Owen."

She sank into her chair, her arms aching from being tied behind her back. How could she have brought this down on her friends? "You have baggage," Bob had told her when she was a rookie determined to make detective, a grief-stricken widow who had quit law school and wanted to help other people get answers. He hadn't minced words. "Husband an FBI agent killed on your honeymoon in an unsolved homicide. Daddy set to become the next FBI director. I should send you packing back to law school."

At first, Bob had considered Owen more baggage, with his wealthy family, his constant travel with Fast Rescue. These were distractions as far as Bob was concerned, reasons she couldn't dedicate herself to the job, reasons she didn't fit in with the department and never would. But she had proved herself.

She heard footsteps as the Brit approached her in her chair. "All of you are remarkably lucky," he said.

"That's what I feel right now. Lucky. Did you try to kill Owen, or did you mean to kidnap him, too?"

"Kill."

Her stomach lurched, but she refused to throw up. "Another bomb." She kept her tone unemotional, professional. "Where? His family's house on Beacon Street?"

"His car."

"Bastards."

"He was warned in time. So, love," the Brit said, closer to her now, "how do you suppose that happened?"

Abigail wriggled in her chair to distract him from any hint in her expression that she had even the remotest theory.

"You're meant to respond," he said mildly.

"I have no idea how it happened. I was stuffed in the back of a van. But your plan hasn't worked the way it was meant to, has it?"

"Did I say it was my plan?"

She realized he was in front of her, perhaps a few inches away, and she warned herself not to be misled by his quiet, almost wry tone. This was a disciplined, controlled and very dangerous man.

"What do you want with me?" she asked.

"Nothing at the moment, love. You and your friends are formidable foes. Your dad as well."

"That's the fun of it for Norman, isn't it? You're a pro. You know he's taking unnecessary risks for his own amusement."

"Perhaps in our own way, love, we all do."

Abigail tried to relax her jaw muscles and ease the tension in her neck and shoulders. "I've heard a small boat pull up to this one several times. What did you do, fly Estabrook into a private airport, then bring him here?"

"That doesn't matter now, does it?"

"That's true. You can walk away. Help me. Let me go back home and plan my wedding."

The Brit gave a short laugh. "And what would I get by walking away? Hold still, love. I'm going to cut the ropes on your wrists and ankles."

"What's your name? What should I call you?"

"Fletcher."

"First name or last name?"

"Either."

It might be real, or it might not. "You're British?"

"Long live the Queen."

He had a sense of humor, anyway.

"Wrists first," he said. "You'll feel the knife. Don't panic, although I can see you're not the type."

He slid the cool blade of a knife between Abigail's skin and the rope. He was too efficient—too professional—to indulge in unnecessary cruelty. If he decided to kill her, he'd be quick about it, at least.

"Easy, love," he said as she felt the bonds give way. "Go slow. You'll be stiff. You've been in the same position for a while. I'm freeing your ankles next."

As she eased her arms over the back of the chair and onto her lap, Abigail winced at the flush of pain and barely noticed him tackling the ropes on her ankles. She slowly pushed one foot forward, biting back tears. Blood rushed into her toes and fingers, and, against her will, she moaned out loud. He untied her blindfold, carefully peeling it from her eyes. She blinked a few times, unkinked her arms and legs, and finally focused on her surroundings. There was a light on now, and she could see a pool table in the middle of the stateroom, next to her chair, and a low sectional sofa on the length of an interior wall.

Her captor leaned back against the pool table, giving her a moment. He was a clean-shaved, exceptionally fit-looking white male, approximately forty years old, skimming six feet, with close-cropped, medium brown hair and gray eyes. No visible scars or tattoos or other distinguishing features. Not that any were needed for Abigail to remember him.

He smiled. "Take a good look, love. You'll want to describe me accurately to your sketch artists." He gestured to the left side of her face. "The men hit you?"

She resisted a wisecrack. "The one with the South Boston accent did."

"He's a bit of a hothead. Care to take a moment while I'm here and freshen up?"

She nodded. "Yes."

He stood up from the pool table and gently took her by the elbow. "On your feet, then."

He started to help her up, but she shook him off and rose on her own. She was stiff and sore, but steady. He led her to a door in the back of the stateroom, next to a wet bar.

"Knock when you've finished. You have two minutes."

"I can't—"

"You can, love."

He opened the door and shut it softly behind her when she went in, leaving her in the pitch-dark. She banged up against something—a sink, she thought—and righted herself, feeling on the wall for a light switch. She found one and flipped it on. She saw she was in a small, tidy head equipped with a shower, sink and toilet. There were dispensers of liquid soap and hand cream, a basket of potpourri, a stack of neatly folded hand towels. Touches of comfort and elegance for the prisoner.

Abigail locked the door and turned on the water in the sink while she did her business.

She washed up with soap and water as best she could, skipped the hand cream and buried her face in a fluffy, expensive white towel, indulging in a few seconds of self-pity and fatigue. But there was no time. She dropped the towel on the floor and stuck her mouth under the faucet and drank as much water as she dared. She didn't want to be sick, but she couldn't count on when she'd be allowed to drink again. Or eat. She was starving.

Finally she inspected herself for injuries that adrenaline and the numbness from sitting in one position for so long could have kept her from feeling. Her wrists and ankles were rope-burned but not bleeding. She had bruises here and there from struggling to get free on the ride to the marina, but nothing she needed to worry about.

"Thirty seconds," Fletcher said from the other side of the door.

She looked in the mirror at the swelling on her cheek. She'd have a shiner.

When she unlocked the door, Fletcher took her by the elbow and led her back to her chair. "I won't tie you up again," he said, sitting her down, "but not because I trust you not to attempt escape. Because I know you won't succeed."

"Where are you taking me?"

"For a little boat ride." He straightened, looked at her without expression. "Do you play pool?"

"Not really."

"Your chance to practice, then, love."

"Why did you stay with me if you weren't going to tie me back up?"

"I wanted to be here in case you passed out once you got on your feet." He nodded to the wet bar. "There's ice, food and drink. Help yourself."

"Thank you."

He left without another word.

Chapter 13

Dublin, Ireland
1:05 a.m., IST
August 26

Lizzie welcomed the lights and activity of Dublin late at night. Her cab dropped her in front of her family's boutique hotel, located on a side street off St. Stephen's Square. Two uniformed bellmen, one of them her twenty-two-year-old cousin Justin, greeted her at the brass-trimmed main door with a bow that always made her feel like a princess, which she decidedly was not, especially tonight. She was too stiff, too scraped and felt too hunted to be anything but what she was—a woman who needed a hot bath and a friendly face. Although the flight from Kerry to Dublin was less than an hour, she finally felt her fatigue, dragging down her spirits, making her even more aware of her isolation—of what she'd done.

Fresh out of college, Justin was the youngest of the Rush brothers, working in Dublin for at least the next six months. His sensitive mouth and dreamy navy-blue eyes were from his mother, but his tawny-hair and square jaw were all Rush.

He eyed Lizzie's backpack, her walking shoes tied to

the strap by their laces. She'd brushed the mud and dung off them as best she could, but he wasn't impressed. "Those shoes, Lizzie. Do you want me to toss them?"

He hadn't had Rush frugality drilled into him by their Whitcomb-Rush grandmother the way she had. "You don't think they can be salvaged?"

He peered at them. "What did you do, tramp through a pasture? They're filthy inside and out, and, no, I don't think they can be salvaged." He shifted his gaze to her. "Where have you been?"

"A stone circle in West Cork."

"In a gale?"

"The best time."

She smiled and started up the half-dozen steps to the lobby, but he grabbed her muddy pack from her. "Excuse me, ma'am, but carrying luggage, even luggage that smells like a barn, is my job."

"You're not supposed to comment on whether a guest's luggage is old, ripped, cheap—"

"Covered in sheep manure?"

"I think it's cow manure."

"Terrific," he said without enthusiasm.

When they reached the lobby, quiet and softly lit this late, Lizzie felt herself start to relax. She was back on familiar ground and just wanted to sink into one of the comfortable chairs angled in front of the fireplace.

Justin was staring at her bloodied knuckles now. "What did you do, get into a brawl in your stone circle?"

"I discovered that Beware of Bull signs are posted for a reason."

Technically it wasn't a lie. Her cousin looked skeptical, but there was no need to involve him or anyone at the hotel in her problems, or to give them any information that the garda or the FBI might decide they wanted.

She retrieved her room key from the front desk and turned to Justin. "I'll take my bag upstairs myself. If anyone asks about me, say I'm in Las Vegas. No. Not Vegas. My father's there. Rome. Tell them I'm in Rome."

"How is Uncle Harlan?"

"Losing at poker last I spoke with him."

"He wouldn't know what to do with a winning hand," Justin said. "I can have your shoes cleaned overnight. Try, anyway."

"Thanks, Justin, but I'll hang on to them." Lizzie pushed a hand through her hair, still tangled from the wind and her fight with Michael Murphy. "Do you happen to know if a Brit named Will Davenport is scheduled for a late check-in?"

"Lizzie…"

She could see from her cousin's expression she'd guessed right. Justin would be on top of all guest arrivals. "When he gets here, call me, okay? He's British. Tall, blond."

"We're talking about Lord Davenport, right?"

"You know him?"

"We've never met. His younger sister's a wedding dress designer in London. Lady Arabella Davenport."

"How do you know these things?"

He grinned. "I'm the bellman. I know everything. Lady Davenport designed the dresses for a wedding here this summer. Mum was visiting then, and you know how she is."

Lizzie did, indeed. Her aunt loved anything connected with fabrics and design, especially if it involved hotels or weddings. Preferably both. "She put you through an analysis of every stitch?"

Justin gave a long-suffering nod. "It would help if you'd hang out with her once in a while and let her talk to you about these things."

"I adore Aunt Henrietta, but talking wedding dresses—"

"Better than taking on an Irish bull."

Lizzie pictured Arabella Davenport's older brother walking into the quiet pub before her fight in the stone circle. Whatever his sister's talents, Lizzie was certain that his didn't involve weddings. As controlled and polite as he'd been, he'd clearly arrived in the little village on Kenmare Bay prepared to do battle. But she suspected he arrived everywhere prepared to do battle.

She shook off the image. "I'm wiped out, Justin. I'll see you in the morning."

She got two steps before her cousin spoke again. "Did Lord Davenport have a role in muddying your shoes?"

She glanced back at him. Perhaps because he was the youngest, or so much his mother's son, Justin had a tendency to see more than most people in a similar position would see. "It's a long story."

"With you, Lizzie, it always is." He sighed. "I'll call when your Brit gets here."

Should her circumstances call for a quick exit, Lizzie's one-bedroom suite was conveniently located on the second floor near the stairs. She brought her backpack into the bathroom and set it on the tile floor, where any crusts of dried mud and manure that fell off would do the least damage. As she stripped to her skin, she fought back images of whipping her pack against Michael Murphy's assault knife…of the drooling, snarling black dog…of the swirling fog and mist.

Instinct and training had taken over the moment she'd realized she wasn't alone in the stone circle, but now, in the familiar surroundings of her favorite hotel, she could finally let down her guard—at least until Lord Davenport arrived. But she and Keira Sullivan had come close to being killed a few hours ago. Would Will have arrived in time to save them if she'd failed?

A moot question, Lizzie told herself as she pulled on a cuddly hotel robe and tied it tightly around her waist.

She went into the beautifully appointed living room of the suite and ordered a full Irish breakfast from room service. Her blackberry crumble was long gone, and she was starving. But she resisted ordering brandy, or a martini.

She sank onto the sofa and grabbed a deck of cards off the coffee table, an antique she and her aunt had bought two years ago at an estate sale in County Clare. Each of the hotel's thirty-seven rooms was individually decorated, as much as possible, with furnishings and objets d'art from Ireland.

Against her father's objections, Lizzie had spent eighteen months working at their Dublin hotel, loving every minute. She and her aunt had crawled through countless Irish galleries, choosing Irish paintings, pottery, sculpture, glasswork, throws and whatever else caught their fancy. Lizzie recognized a copper vase they'd found at a gallery in Kenmare. It was fashioned by a contemporary Irish metalworker but reminded her of the old mines where Keira's story of the stone angel had originated.

Lizzie moved the copper vase and a stack of books on Ireland aside, creating space on the table, and dealt the cards into four piles of thirteen each for a game of bridge. She sorted the hands and counted up the points, then silently bid each one as if she didn't know what was in the others. She produced an offense and defense and played the game. Flipping one card after another, keeping track of aces and kings and trump cards, scooping up winners and losers. The process anchored her mind while allowing it the freedom to roam.

She had to have her thoughts in order before she made the call she knew she had to make.

The offense won. She dealt another hand.

Her breakfast was delivered by a longtime employee of the hotel, an older woman who didn't ask why Lizzie was having breakfast at such an hour. She set the tray on the coffee table, and when she left, Lizzie debated eating her meal, taking her bath and going to bed. She could postpone her call and tell Justin to never mind and not to let her know after all when Will Davenport arrived.

Instead she buttered a chunk of brown bread and took a bite as she got out her disposable cell phone and dialed a number she'd received in a terse e-mail last summer. She'd called it only twice before, preferring to stick to e-mail whenever possible.

It was just after 9:00 p.m. on the U.S. East Coast, but John March picked up after the first ring. "Where are you?"

"Ireland." No reason not to tell him that much. "Norman didn't go on a joy ride this morning. He didn't crash into a mountain or run into mechanical problems and make an emergency landing somewhere. You know that, don't you?"

"Yes."

"I'm sorry about what happened today. I wish I'd known sooner. Are Scoop Wisdom and your daughter—"

"You're the one who needs to do the talking."

Lizzie's heart jumped painfully. "The bomb was a diversion, wasn't it?" Her father had taught her about bombs, diversionary tactics. "Norman had your daughter kidnapped, didn't he?"

"Talk."

She picked up her fork. If she let John March intimidate her now, she'd be of no help to him or anyone else— especially Abigail Browning. "I'm debating whether to try black pudding," she said, poking it on her plate. "What do you think?"

"It's made with pig's blood. Tastes like sausage."

She could hear anguish in his voice. "White pudding?"

"No pig's blood. Suet, oatmeal. This and that."

"Doesn't sound very appetizing. I guess some things I just don't want to know."

"That's true for any of us."

Under the strength and determination that had characterized the FBI director in her dealings with him, Lizzie now heard the terror of a father for his missing daughter.

"Are you still in Boston?" she asked.

"Yes."

"Simon?"

"He's still here, too."

Lizzie stared at the warm brown bread, butter, eggs, bacon, grilled tomatoes—the black and white pudding—on her simple white china plate, all a reminder of normalcy. She'd led a relatively normal life of family, work, travel and the occasional romance and adventure before she'd let her curiosity—her sense of duty—ask questions and see things others might ignore. Once she'd found herself in a room of violent drug traffickers, what was she supposed to have done? She'd started by e-mailing names and surreptitious photos to John March.

But hadn't she been looking for an excuse to contact the detective who'd looked into her mother's death thirty years ago?

It didn't matter. Instead of dropping out of Norman's circle of friends as she otherwise would have, Lizzie had dived in and hung on for the next year.

"Norman will never look at himself and understand he was arrested because he did wrong." She spoke calmly, despite her own fatigue and fear. "He'll blame you and Simon. And me, if he ever finds out what I've done."

March didn't soften. "You're the woman who saved Keira Sullivan and warned Bob O'Reilly about the bomb."

"I'm not sure Keira needed my help. An Irish gale, an ancient stone circle, a black dog out of nowhere. Spooky." Not to mention an aristocratic British spy. Lizzie stabbed her fork into the black pudding and cut off a small piece. "For all the time I've spent in Ireland, I've never tried black or white pudding. I suppose you have Michael Murphy's file on your desk by now?"

"The Irish authorities are cooperating in the investigation."

An oblique response. "He's Norman's doing."

"No one's leaping to any conclusions."

"I am," Lizzie said.

"Estabrook has no reason to take this risk."

"Did he have any reason to circumnavigate the world in a hot-air balloon?"

"That's an adventure."

"You're articulating a professional point of view. I understand that, but you don't believe it. You know as well as I do that Norman is responsible for what happened today. Yesterday here in Ireland, actually. It's after midnight." She eyed the bit of pudding on the end of her fork. "Maybe you have to grow up eating black pudding to appreciate it."

"You're exhausted. I can hear it in your voice."

"Maybe a full Irish breakfast will help. I've been banged up before, but I was in my first real fight for my life tonight." She felt herself sinking deeper into the soft cushions of the sofa. "For someone else's life, too."

"You won," March said.

"I could have killed Murphy. I had his own knife at his throat."

"Did you want to kill him?"

Lizzie let her mind drift back to the moment in the stone circle when she'd first became aware of the shadows by the cluster of trees. "No. I didn't want to kill him."

"Why are you in Ireland?"

"I was reading about Irish fairies and decided—"

"You wanted to talk to Simon," March said.

"It doesn't matter now. I was almost too late to help Keira. I *was* too late to warn your daughter."

"Bob O'Reilly's daughter and Scoop Wisdom are alive because of you."

Lizzie felt no satisfaction at March's statement. "Norman has virtually limitless resources."

"The U.S. federal government can match them."

"He could be anywhere by now. Trust me. He has a plan. He's not anyone's victim. He's compulsive, and he's a thrill seeker. Be sure your profilers understand what that really means. Be sure you understand. I didn't see it myself at first, but Norman is a dangerous, violent man."

She heard March take in a sharp breath. "You let me believe you're a professional. You're not, are you?"

She didn't answer.

"I want to know who you are," he said.

"You'll find out on your own soon enough. Please listen to me, Director March. You can't tell a soul about me or what I've done. You can't come after me. You'll be risking my life and my ability to help find your daughter if you do."

"I can have an agent meet you tonight, wherever you are. Let me help you. I don't want you to endanger yourself or this investigation by taking unnecessary risks."

"There is one thing." Lizzie hesitated, wondering if she was going too far—if she'd gone too far already. But she didn't stop herself. "I have a tall, handsome, patrician Brit on my tail. Will Davenport. He and Simon are friends. He came to Ireland to see about Keira. Can I trust him?"

"Even if you can, would you? Do you trust anyone?"

It wasn't a question she wanted to answer tonight. "Norman doesn't know I've been helping you. I want to keep it that way." She tried a bite of the black pudding. "You didn't steer me wrong. Black pudding tastes like sausage."

She shut her phone before he could respond.

Would March figure out who she was and have her hotel stormed by armed agents at sunrise? He could make it happen, even in Ireland.

But he wouldn't. John March was a hard man who often faced only bad choices, and right now, she was safe and his daughter wasn't. And he'd made his choice. He would let his anonymous source have room to maneuver and give her a chance to find Norman Estabrook—and save her own skin as well as his daughter's.

Lizzie ate a few more bites of her meal before she gave up and headed for the bathroom, turning on the water in the tub as hot as she could stand. She added a scoop of lavender bath salts and, as they melted, shed her robe and dipped slowly into the steaming water. The heat eased the ache and stiffness in her muscles and the scent of lavender soothed her soul. Images washed over her—Simon and Norman in Montana going over plans for a Patagonia hike…the enigmatic Brit winking at her in Las Vegas… Scoop Wisdom walking out to the street with his colander of beans… Keira Sullivan and the black dog in the stone circle.

Will Davenport eyeing her over his brandy.

Lowering herself deeper into the tub, an image came to her of John March at her family's hotel in Boston last August. It was the anniversary of her mother's death, and he was drinking Irish whiskey alone at a table in the pub named in her honor. Lizzie had been in Boston, making one of her strategic appearances at the hotel offices, and had stopped at the Whitcomb.

She hadn't approached the FBI director and former Boston detective and doubted he'd been aware of her presence. Now she couldn't help but wonder where they'd all be if she'd identified herself as the anonymous source who'd been supplying him information on Norman Estabrook and his drug-trafficking friends.

But she hadn't.

She got out of the tub, dried off with a giant towel and slipped back into her robe. She returned to the living room and, no longer in the mood for a chat, set her tray in the hall and called down for its removal. When she sat back on the sofa, she managed to deal another hand of bridge, but she didn't sort the cards and instead curled up under a throw made of soft Irish wool and gave in to her fatigue.

When the telephone rang, she bolted upright, instantly awake. She glanced at the clock as she answered. It was almost 4:00 a.m.

"He's here," Justin said. "What should I do now?"

"Send him up."

"Lizzie? Are you sure?"

"I'm sure."

"All right, I won't tell anyone."

She felt a surge of heat. "It's not like *that*." But she couldn't tell him the truth. "I'll explain one day, Justin, I promise."

"I imagine it'll be a tale."

"Let Davenport think he's checking into his own room and I'll take it from there."

"You lead a complicated life," her cousin said.

As Lizzie hung up, her bathrobe fell open, the cool night air hitting her exposed skin.

This won't do, she thought. She'd come to Ireland to talk to an FBI agent about a man she was convinced would commit murder, not to greet a British lord in nothing but a hotel bathrobe.

Best to jump into some clothes before Will Davenport got to the door.

Chapter 14

Dublin, Ireland
3:47 a.m., IST
August 26

By the time she heard a key card slide into the slot in the door, Lizzie had on a long knit skirt and a T-shirt. She was still barefoot, but at least she wasn't naked under her bathrobe. She unchained the door and opened it. Will had his trench coat slung over one arm and a scarred leather bag in his hand, which at least meant she didn't have to worry about Justin turning up.

"I had a feeling you were good," she said.

Will gave her the slightest smile. "And I had a feeling you were on the other side of this door."

"We Rushes like to keep an eye on spies in our hotels."

"You're imaginative. May I assume I'm invited in?"

"You may."

Lizzie stood back, and he walked past her and set his bag on the floor next to the coffee table. As she shut the door, she noticed him glance at the scattered cards on the table. She ran a hand through her hair, remembered she hadn't combed it since her bath and wondered what had gotten into her, arranging for an MI6 agent to share her room.

She scooped up the cards. "Playing bridge by myself helps me think. My method of creative problem solving."

"What problems were you trying to solve tonight?"

"You. What to do when you showed up."

The soft light from a brass floor lamp created shadows that darkened his eyes and made them even more difficult to read. "And your answer was to have me sent up here to your room?"

"No, I'd already figured that one out. I knew I didn't want you wandering around on your own and eliciting secrets about me from the staff." Not to mention her cousin.

"You worked here yourself prior to becoming director of concierge services for all your family's hotels."

"Ah. You've been busy."

"I have an able assistant."

"I loved working here. I learned a lot. Ireland offers an incredible variety of opportunities—great restaurants, rich history, natural beauty."

"So it does."

"Most of what the staff could tell you about me is innocuous enough. I can speak a bit of Irish and have a fondness for Irish butter and fresh Irish seafood, especially mussels, and I love to walk." She tidied up the deck, using both hands, which, she noticed, were trembling slightly. An annoyance, but she blamed her interrupted sleep, not the man across from her. "But I decided I didn't want anyone telling you about my Grafton Street shopping sprees."

As far as she could tell, Will didn't respond to her attempt at humor or even notice it. "Has Norman Estabrook been to this hotel?"

"I met him here, actually. A year ago this past April." She set the cards back on the table. Interrogation time. "He hired Simon Cahill as a consultant a few months later."

Will laid his coat over the back of a chair. He looked every inch the British lord turned SAS officer and spy as his gaze held hers. "Perhaps you should tell me who you are."

"You're here. Obviously you already know."

"Lizzie Rush, hotelier and—what else?"

"I haven't had time for much else lately."

"Why did you come to Dublin tonight?"

"Would you believe I got tired of walking the Beara Way and had a hankering for nice sheets?"

His outright smile caught her off guard. "No."

"It's my favorite of our hotels. It opened twenty years ago—over my father's objections. He's not much on Ireland, but my aunt and uncle fell in love with Dublin. I was ten years old, and I wanted to come here so bad."

"Your father wouldn't allow it?"

"I never told him how much I wanted it." She spun over to a chest and pulled open a drawer. "My feet are cold," she said, grabbing a pair of wool socks. "I arrived in Dublin this morning and checked in here before I went off on my adventure. I always stay in this room. Cute, isn't it?"

"It's lovely." He obviously didn't care one way or the other about her suite. "Did your father visit you during your posting here?"

"No, he did not," she said, dropping onto a chair and slipping on her socks. It was an intimate thing to do in front of a man she'd known for mere hours, but cold feet were cold feet. "My father and I get along, in case you're wondering. We just have different views on Ireland."

"Lizzie…"

His sudden intensity mixed with the softness of his voice shot her up from her chair. This was *not* one of her Rush cousins. "I'm talking too much. You must be hell in an interrogation. You're so smooth and—" She stopped herself. How many of his interrogation subjects would be affected by the concern in his voice, the drape of his sweater on his broad shoulders? "Never mind. I dozed off, and now I'm in one of those crazy half-awake, half-asleep states."

"You're not accustomed to the intensity of the fighting you did earlier tonight, and you're jetlagged. Why did you fly from Boston?"

"I didn't say I did."

The slight smile again. "As I said, I have an able assistant."

"Does that mean I really do have MI6 on my case?"

"You have a flare for dramatics as well as an active imagination."

"It's been that kind of year. Our main offices are in Boston. I spent a lot of time there growing up." She didn't go into more detail. "How's Keira?"

"She's safe in garda hands."

"That's good. I assume you wouldn't be here otherwise. I wish I could have met her under better circumstances. What happened in the stone circle was…" Lizzie tried to find the right word and realized she couldn't. "It was different."

"Where did you learn defense tactics?"

She gave him a knowing smile. "I read the SAS handbook on self-defense."

"You've been doing research of your own, I see."

"You're not denying you're a British SAS officer?"

"Did Simon tell you about my background?"

He had her there. She'd given herself away. "I knew you and Simon were friends, and I'm a curious type—which is how I ended up in a knife fight in the Irish hills. What about you?"

"I was looking for Keira. Were you drawn to Estabrook because of his adventures? I gather you're something of a daredevil yourself."

"I wasn't drawn to Norman at all. I just hung out with him and his friends on and off. Long weekends, vacations, when he was at one of our hotels."

"You came a long way to find Simon."

This time, she was ready for the dodging and darting of his questions. "I came a long way to hike the Beara Way. I'd heard Keira's story about the stone angel and thought I might run into her and Simon."

With a glimmer of a smile, Will moved close to her, just inches from her, and before she could catch her breath, he touched his fingertips to her hair. "You're an adept fighter but not a particularly adept liar."

"Not tonight, maybe. Ordinarily I'm a very adept liar."

"You were concerned Estabrook would go free, and you arranged a cover story that would allow you to talk to Simon without his thinking you'd come to Ireland specifically for that reason."

"Norman's legal situation was added impetus for me to choose the Beara Peninsula for my hike." She licked her lips, dry now, sensitive. "I've wanted to walk the Beara Way for some time."

"You didn't last long, did you?"

"A gale and a knife attack took all the fun out of my adventure."

"You also started in the very village where you'd expected to find Simon. Do you always hike alone?"

Lizzie decided she was in over her head with this man and broke for the closet. She yanked open the door. "Call downstairs for whatever you need," she said, standing on her tiptoes to reach up to the shelf. "Help yourself to the tub. The lavender bath salts here are my favorite. My aunt Henrietta and I picked them out together. I soaked for thirty minutes earlier tonight. Almost fell asleep and drowned myself." But as she glanced back at him with a breezy smile, she realized she now had him picturing her in the tub.

Definitely in over her head.

She pulled a fluffy duvet and pillow down from the shelf. "You can have the bedroom. I'll take the sofa. That way," she said, carrying the bedding to the sofa, "I can hear you if you try to sneak out."

"Lizzie."

She unfurled the duvet. "If I'm wrong about you, I can defend myself. I don't care if you're SAS, MI6 or a bored British aristocrat."

Will slipped an arm over her shoulders and turned her gently to him, surprising her. "You're exactly what you seem to be, aren't you?"

"And that would be?"

"A hotelier who's more comfortable picking out bath salts and hiking the Beara Way than defending herself and a perfect stranger from a killer."

"Maybe I'm comfortable with picking out bath salts *and* taking on killers."

"I should have followed you from the pub. I could have spared you…" He seemed to shake off any regret. "Lizzie, you're not a professional. Whatever you're up to, you don't have to go about it alone."

He *was* good, she decided. Under the expensive clothes and polished manners, the upper-class bearing, were the quiet competence and self-assurance of a man who knew what he was doing—who, in fact, had real training and experience.

But Lizzie had held tight to her secrets for a long time. Once she let go of them, they wouldn't just be hers anymore. She'd be giving up the security they'd provided her for over a year. She'd be forced to trust whomever she confided in.

It was a big step. Too big.

"What I'm up to right now," she said lightly, "is falling asleep on my feet."

Will responded by easing his arm down her back to her hips, as if helping her to stay upright. "You're trying to keep yourself from telling me the truth."

No kidding. "What I've told you is the truth."

"It isn't everything."

"A two-way street, I'm afraid." She suddenly realized she still smelled of lavender and wondered if he noticed. "You're an attractive and dangerous man, Will Davenport, and you're wearing a very soft, warm sweater. That's a near-irresistible combination for a sleepy woman."

He kissed her forehead, so close now she could feel the warmth of his sweater. "Then I'll be noble and resist for both of us," he said, a slight roughness to his voice that suggested resisting wasn't that easy for him.

Lizzie's throat tightened, and part of her wanted just to sink into his arms and let him protect her, keep her safe. How much longer could she carry on alone? Norman had crossed a threshold in the past twenty-four hours. People had nearly died. A woman was missing. *He* was missing. But he still trusted her, Lizzie thought, and that gave her a certain leverage with him, perhaps the only leverage anyone had. If she let anyone—the director of the FBI, Simon, this Prince Charming of a stranger with her now—interfere, she risked losing the one advantage she had in helping to find Abigail Browning.

And, possibly, in staying safe herself.

Will touched a thumb to her upper cheekbone. "You've dark circles under your lovely eyes. You're exhausted."

He let his thumb drift down to the corner of her mouth before his hand fell back to his side. "Good night, Lizzie."

"Why did you come here?" she asked, a little hoarse.

He winked at her. "The lure of a beautiful, mysterious woman."

"You're a very charming liar, Lord Davenport."

"Sweet dreams," he said.

He picked up his bag and ducked into the bedroom, shutting the door softly behind him.

Lizzie blew out a breath.

A *very* attractive, dangerous man.

She stretched out on the sofa in her skirt and T-shirt and pulled the duvet and her wool throw up to her chin.

Morning couldn't come soon enough.

Lizzie had left her robe on the bathroom floor.

Will picked it up and hung it on a hook on the back of the door, noting that the soft terry cloth was still damp from her bath.

A perilous observation, that one. He abandoned it before it could take hold and spawn images that would make for an even longer night ahead.

"Too late," he muttered, picturing small, green-eyed Lizzie Rush settling into her bath.

The bathroom smelled of lavender and, very faintly, of dried mud. He saw the rucksack she'd had with her on the Beara in a corner behind the door and immediately seized on the distraction. If he was too "noble" to take advantage of her fatigue and her own desire for distraction, he was perfectly at peace with having a look in her rucksack.

He got onto one knee and unzipped the main compartment. It was packed with supplies anyone would take on a multiday hike. The garda had her bungee cords. After seeing how quickly she'd thought of them and the skill with which she'd used them on Michael Murphy, Will wouldn't be surprised to discover she'd packed them with tying up a prisoner in mind. He continued his search but found no weapons or any other items that would immediately undermine her story of how she'd happened upon Keira Sullivan and the man sent to kill her.

Feeling no guilt whatsoever at having invaded her privacy, Will showered and returned to the bedroom. It was small and tastefully decorated in neutral colors, but he found himself unable to relax. He stared at the closed door to the living room and debated going out there to argue sleeping arrangements.

He could also go out there and demand Lizzie tell him about the Brit she'd described to Michael Murphy and whom Eddie O'Shea in turn had described to Will.

If it *was* Myles…

Now, when Lizzie was about to fall asleep and would just be letting down her guard, was the perfect time to confront her. Why had she asked about that particular man? What did he have to do with Norman Estabrook and her relationship with the American billionaire? But not only had Will seen the dark circles under Lizzie's eyes and the tremor in her hands, he had to acknowledge an attraction to her that was both dangerous and compelling.

And perfectly natural, he thought with a small smile.

She needed sleep and time to recover from her ordeal, and he needed a few hours to chase back the ghosts and remember why he was here, now, in Lizzie Rush's suite in Dublin. His physical reaction to her only complicated matters.

He could have easily carried her in here and made love to her.

He could hear David Mears and Philip Billings teasing him about his love life. "You're a lone wolf, Will," David had said; he had been a stocky, hard-drinking man with a wicked sense of humor. "Heaven pity the poor woman who falls for you."

Philip, a formidable ladies' man but who had lately fallen for one of Arabella's friends back in London, had hooted in agreement. "And heaven pity you when you meet your match, because such a woman won't be like any you have in mind. She'll knock you on your arse, and we'll be there, Mears and me, saying we told you so."

Will pulled back the duvet on his bed and climbed in. The sheets, too, smelled of lavender.

Chapter 15

Off the coast of Massachusetts
1 a.m., EDT
August 26

Abigail had just started to play pool when Estabrook and the Brit—Fletcher—entered her stateroom. She'd slept fitfully before giving up, deciding she preferred to stay awake and alert. Estabrook wore a porkpie hat and yachting attire that might make a casual passerby less likely to recognize him, but he'd had his face plastered in the media for weeks while people speculated why a self-made billionaire would take up with ruthless criminals. Abigail had made a point of memorizing his face after he'd threatened to kill Simon and her father.

Fletcher calmly grasped the pool cue in her hands. She relinquished it without a struggle. "I'm not very good, anyway—at pool. You're right in thinking I could do some damage with the cue."

He said nothing as he set the cue aside.

Estabrook smirked at her. "I see your black eye's blossomed, Detective. Have you slept?"

She decided to answer. "A little."

"As much as I relish your father's suffering, I regret seeing you suffer. You're in pain, and you're frightened."

Abigail wanted to kill him. "You should let me go. Release me and give up the people who actually set the bombs. It wasn't you. You were in Montana."

Of course, since he'd hired the men who'd carried out the attacks, he was ultimately responsible. There'd be no deal. He hadn't beamed himself east. There'd be a trail, and her colleagues in law enforcement would pick it up and follow it to her. She trusted them. In the meantime, she had to stay alive and do what she could to throw Estabrook off balance and keep him there.

He thrived on risk and wouldn't rattle easily.

"Don't play me for a fool, Detective. May I call you Abigail?" He smiled, having fun with her.

"Sure. Why not?"

"Have a seat," he said.

She shrugged and started for the sectional on the wall.

"Not there." Estabrook smiled nastily and pointed to the metal chair his men had tied her to earlier. "There."

Abigail made herself keep her eyes on him. "Suit yourself."

Fletcher stood back, quiet, observant, and she passed him and sat down, stretching out her legs and crossing her ankles. During her hours alone, she'd done yoga to loosen up after having sat in one position for so long. "If you give yourself up," she said, addressing Estabrook, "I'll tell my friends you're not the one who smacked me in the face."

"Do you think I care?"

"You will when they catch up with you."

He leaned against the pool table and put his hands on either side of him, gripping the edge as he gazed down at her. "Your father put Simon up to betraying my trust and friendship, but they've failed. Here I am, a free man."

Abigail yawned. "Bugs you, doesn't it, that the feds used you to get to bigger fish? You're not happy being a little fish. You knew exactly what you were doing when you hooked up with drug traffickers, but it never occurred to you they were a bigger deal than you were."

Estabrook smiled, as if he was reading her mind and drawing strength from her fear.

Let him. She'd have her chance. "So what happened today?" She kept her voice matter-of-fact. "Your guys screwed up. Did they not know my father and Simon were in Boston?"

"I hired professionals," he said, an edge in his voice. "I gave them free rein to make decisions based on their best judgment. I operate that way in everything I do. Micromanaging is a sign of weakness."

"They were on their way to see me—Dad and Simon." She said "Dad" deliberately and saw Estabrook's reaction, the gleam of fury in his eyes, the thinning of his mouth. She didn't let herself react to his hatred. "If your guys had better intel and had just waited a few minutes…" She sighed. "But, no. They pulled the trigger on their bomb and grabbed me."

Estabrook breathed in through his nose. "I wish I could have been there when Simon and your father arrived to smoke, fire and blood."

"Your guy's blood. He dripped on the sidewalk."

Fletcher remained impassive, but she could see she'd gotten to Estabrook. He stood up from the pool table, his hat crooked on his head. "You're not half as clever as you think you are, Detective."

She ignored him. "I was home all morning, and Scoop went down to his garden early. He's trying to stay ahead of the harvest. I figure your guys planted the bomb sometime before this morning. Overnight? Yesterday? I guess it could have been anytime. There were two explosions. The second was my gas grill, right? Haven't used it in weeks."

"All moot now, my dear," Norman said.

"True, but I have to think about something besides my testimony at your trial. Your guys could have hit the trigger anytime, but they didn't. Why wait?"

"Synchronicity."

"Ah. You wanted to time everything with your release."

"Why were you meeting Simon and your father?"

"To discuss you," she said coolly.

Estabrook seemed to like her answer. He moved in front of her and leaned in close, his eyes puffy, bloodshot under the broad rim of his hat. "You bear a strong resemblance to your father. I see him in the shape of your mouth, your nose. It can't have been easy growing up with such a man. Do you blame him for your husband's death?"

"No."

"Christopher Browning was an FBI special agent. Your father wasn't director then, but he was very powerful. He's kept secrets from you, hasn't he?"

"Everyone has secrets. You, for instance. Your secret? You know you don't measure up. You've known since you were a scared little boy." Abigail swallowed, felt a twinge of nausea. She'd never done well being cooped up, never mind on a boat. "You're still that scared little kid inside. It's nothing to hide from. Let me go and stop this before you can't turn back. Before someone ends up really hurt."

She could see he'd tuned her out. He stood up straight and reached for a pool cue, a fresh one, not the one she'd used. "Until this summer, you had no idea your father was a surrogate father to Simon." Estabrook turned to her knowingly. "Did you, Detective?"

"No, I did not."

"Brendan Cahill and your father were friends. He was a DEA agent in Colombia. He was murdered when Simon was fourteen."

"I imagine you're real familiar with the DEA and FBI."

His grip on the pool cue tightened visibly. "Your father saw to Simon for twenty years, and you had no idea. So many secrets, Detective. So many secrets your father has."

"My father stayed in contact with a boy who'd lost his own father and tried to help out when he could. It wasn't a secret. I just didn't know about it. Simon's a great guy and a fine FBI agent. A lot of your criminal colleagues are being rounded up and arrested thanks to him—and you and your cooperation with the feds." Abigail gestured to her plush surroundings. "Is that what this is about? Are you getting away from them? Trying to convince whoever's left among your drug-cartel friends that you're dead? Are you afraid they'll come after you?"

Estabrook laid the cue on the pool table. "You shouldn't deliberately try my patience, Detective."

His tone—cool, remote—turned her stomach. He was, she thought, a man eager to commit violence. Keeping her own tone conversational, she changed the subject. "Where are we going? Do you own property on the New England coast? Are we heading to some place in particular—a friend's house maybe? Or are we just sailing in circles?"

He picked up the eight ball and cupped it in his fleshy palm. "What's a friend, Detective?"

There was a sudden sadness about him that Abigail wasn't about to fall for. She knew it had nothing to do with real fellow feeling but only with his narcissistic view of himself and his place in the world.

He set the ball back on the table and shifted to Fletcher. "You know what I want," he said, and abruptly left the stateroom.

Fletcher waited a few seconds after the door shut before he walked over to Abigail. "You can stand up if you'd like." He nodded back toward the pool table. "Go ahead and return to your game."

"Not afraid I'm going to shove a pool cue up your—"

"No," he said with an unexpected smile, "I'm not, and not because you're not capable of doing so but because you know you need me."

"And why do I need you, Mr. Fletcher?"

His gray eyes settled on her. "Because I can get you out of here alive." He took her by the hand and helped her to her feet. "Simon Cahill and your father had help from someone else with close ties to Mr. Estabrook."

"I wouldn't know." Abigail removed Estabrook's cue from the table, returned it to the rack and got hers. She kept her voice even. "They're FBI. I'm BPD. Two different things."

"Mr. Estabrook wants the identity of this person."

"What difference does it make now?"

"I get paid more if I deliver whoever it is to him." Fletcher gathered up the scattered balls and racked them. "You know, Abigail, or you know more than you realize."

She picked up the white cue ball. A name came to her. She pushed it back down deep. But it was there.

Lizzie Rush.

Lizzie was wealthy, elegant and attractive and would fit in with Estabrook's friends and hangers-on, but her family was connected to Boston and she had a personal interest in Abigail's father.

In fact, Lizzie Rush was the main reason Abigail had asked Simon and her father to meet her that morning, before the bomb went off.

She set the ball on the table and lined up her pool cue, even as regret washed over her. She hadn't told Owen about her questions, her suspicions. She could rationalize her silence: she didn't know enough; she was acting as a police officer and not just out of personal curiosity.

The truth was, she'd learned to keep secrets at her father's knee.

Her father, who would be terrified for her now, was one of the best men she'd ever known. His secrets arose out of his sense of duty and commitment. They were a product of who he was—a man who could be trusted, who didn't speak out of turn and often faced tough choices.

Fletcher lifted the rack from the triangle of balls and stood back. Abigail shot the cue ball across the table. It smashed into the racked balls and sent them spinning everywhere. Three solid-colored balls went into pockets. Pure luck. She had no idea what she was doing.

"You were right," Fletcher said with a smile, "you're not very good."

She almost laughed as she lined up another shot. "You're connecting dots that can't be connected," she said. "I can't help you. I've been busy with my own job."

"Who can help me, then, love?"

Her stomach lurched.

Fiona.

Abigail tapped a solid red ball into a corner pocket and forced Bob's daughter out of her mind. Her name, her image, everything about her. But she could see Fiona just last night, playing a small harp with her Irish band at Morrigan's Pub at the Whitcomb, the Rush hotel in Boston.

"This isn't a good idea, Fiona."

"Why not?"

"I can't explain. Who do you know here? Who have you met?"

"No one, really."

Fiona had blushed, and Abigail had noticed a young, cute, male Rush standing in the door and wondered if she'd overreacted and Fiona wasn't about to stumble into one of John March's labyrinths. As much as Abigail loved her father, she was well aware that he had left a complex trail behind him in his near sixty years on the planet.

Fiona knew every Irish bar in town that offered live music, and Morrigan's would be one of the better paying and more prestigious. She could have found it on her own, but she hadn't. She'd found it because *her* father knew Abigail, who was head over heels in love with Owen Garrison. And Owen's family, with its strong ties to Beacon Hill, often stayed at the Whitcomb and put up friends there.

Abigail's father had known the Garrisons even before she'd met Chris Browning, who had grown up just down the rockbound shore from their summer home on Mount Desert Island. But her father's relationship with the Garrisons had nothing to do with her concerns about Fiona O'Reilly playing Irish music at Morrigan's.

Her concerns had everything to do with the woman in whose honor the bar had been named—Shauna Morrigan, Lizzie Rush's mother.

Even to think about any of them now, with Fletcher watching her, Abigail knew, was dangerous.

As she leaned forward, lining up another shot, she felt the strain of the last hours in her lower back. She was dehydrated and knew she needed to drink more water, but the thought nauseated her. "You'll have to speak up," she said. "My ears are still ringing from you bastards blowing up my apartment and smacking me in the face."

"We have time."

She concentrated on taking her shot, but she was too late. Fletcher had already seen that she'd lied.

"Enjoy your game," he said quietly, and left.

Chapter 16

Dublin, Ireland
7:23 a.m., IST
August 26

The bedroom door was still shut when Lizzie awoke, the early morning sun finding its way through the sides of the room-darkening window shade. She slipped into comfortable slim black pants, a black top and her new flats and dabbed on just enough makeup to convince people she'd slept okay.

Making as little noise as possible, she went out into the hall and took the stairs down to the lobby. She smiled at the woman at the front desk, who was new, and headed for the hotel's small street-level restaurant, its tables covered in Irish lace. Lizzie chose one on the back wall that had a view of the door out to the lobby. She ordered coffee and scones and chatted a moment with her waiter, a college student from Lithuania. Last night on the Beara Peninsula suddenly seemed surreal, and she half expected her cousin to wander in and act as if she'd just arrived from Boston and none of it had happened. Her fight in the stone circle, the bomb, Abigail Browning, Norman's disappearance…the fair-haired Brit asleep in her suite.

Lizzie could blame her delusions on jetlag and go shopping.

But as she spread her scone with butter and raspberry jam, her handsome suitemate, dressed in another deliciously soft-looking sweater, joined her at her table.

Without waiting for an invitation, he sat across from her. "My sister loves Dublin. I'll have to ask her if she's stayed here."

"She's a wedding dress designer in London. Arabella. It's a pretty name. You have an older brother, too. Peter. He manages the family farm, that being a five-hundred-year-old estate in the north of England."

"All of which," Will said, marginally impressed, "you could find on the Internet."

"In fact, I did."

She'd also done a bit of spying on the Davenports herself when she was in London in early July, but she chose to keep that fact to herself. Will had sparked her interest after she'd learned Simon wasn't ex-FBI after all and remembered the two men were friends.

Will's pot of tea and a steaming scone arrived. For a man who had slept only a few hours, he looked remarkably alert. And serious, Lizzie thought.

He poured his tea. "You're playing a very dangerous game, Lizzie. It's time to stop."

She reached for more jam. She'd combed her hair and pinned it back, but she suspected there were still knots in it. It'd been a long night on the sofa. "If you were going to sic the FBI or the guards on me," she said, "you'd have done it by now."

As he set the teapot down, she noticed a thin, straight four-inch scar on his hand, perhaps from a knife fight that hadn't gone as well as hers had last night.

"You're not the dilettante you've pretended to be," he

said, lifting his cup and taking a sip as he eyed her over the rim. "You didn't learn your fighting skills from reading a handbook. Who taught you?"

"I frequently travel on my own, and I decided it would be smart to take self-defense classes. But I do have the SAS handbook." She sat back. "You're not smiling, Will."

"I woke up worried about you."

"Ah. Maybe I should have given you the sofa instead. I slept just fine. Nothing to worry about." She slathered jam on a chunk of scone and indulged, relishing the sweet, rich taste. "It'll be back to mesclun soon. You and Simon are obviously good friends, but that's not why you followed me here."

"Do you have friends, Lizzie?"

"You mean in addition to my four cousins and Norman?"

Will still didn't smile. "Correct."

"Yes, I have friends, although I've neglected most of them lately." She leaned back and studied him as he placed his cup in its saucer and broke off a piece of his scone. "No jam, no butter? You're an ascetic."

"I wasn't the one who engaged in hand-to-hand combat last night."

"Combat? When you put it that way…" But Lizzie couldn't maintain her light mood, feigned as it was. "I'm not that hungry, having had a full Irish breakfast at midnight. How long have you known Simon?"

Will deliberated a moment. "Two years."

"Norman got very curious when he found out Simon was hanging out with you in London. Did you know he was working undercover, or did you think he was a former FBI agent with a grudge against Director March?"

"Simon and I didn't discuss Norman Estabrook."

"Then MI6 isn't interested in him?"

Will gave her a slight smile. "Very clever, Lizzie. What are your plans for today?"

"Defying jetlag. Past that, I don't know." She abandoned her scone for her coffee, not meeting his eye as she said, serious now, "I asked Michael Murphy about one of your countrymen last night. I saw your reaction, Will, and I think he's why you're here in Dublin. You know him, don't you?"

"As I indicated," he said, picking up his teacup again, "you're playing a dangerous game."

Lizzie didn't relent. "Who is he?"

"A ghost."

"Another spook?"

He sighed. "I never said…"

"You didn't have to. This man showed up in Las Vegas a few days before Norman's arrest. Is he SAS? Special Branch? A fugitive?"

"He's a killer. Eddie O'Shea ran into him on the Beara Peninsula last week. Simon and Keira weren't there."

Lizzie absorbed this new information and felt a sting of regret that Eddie and his brothers had had their quiet lives disrupted. But they seemed capable of handling anything. "Did this man arrange the attack on Keira?"

"Whatever he did, Lizzie, you must stay away from him. As capable as you are, you can't best him. If you know anything about him, tell me now."

"At least give me his name."

Will steadied his gaze on her, the blue, green and gold of his eyes melding into a gleam of black. "His name is Myles."

She stifled an involuntary gasp at the pain in his voice. "He's your friend," she said. "Will—"

"I haven't seen the man you and Eddie O'Shea described myself." His words were measured, everything about him under control. "I could be wrong."

"We only talked for a few minutes. He joined me at the hotel bar and asked me for a bottle of water and…" Lizzie paused, remembering that strange encounter in Las Vegas. "He told me to behave."

There was an edge of sadness to Will as he smiled. "That sounds like Myles. Had he and Estabrook already met?"

Lizzie nodded. "He—Myles, the Brit—went up to Norman in the middle of his poker game. No one else at the table seemed to know him. I couldn't hear what he and Norman said to each other, but it seemed important. That's one reason why I remember him."

"There's another reason?"

She didn't look away but instead met Will's gaze straight on. "I was trying to remember everything."

"Why, Lizzie? This was before Estabrook's arrest. Were you aware of his illegal activities?"

She smiled easily. "I should take the Fifth on that one. That's the Fifth Amendment. Bill of Rights. U.S. Constitution—"

"Lizzie. We're not discussing one of your hotel luxury excursions."

Didn't she know.

"I'm sorry," he said immediately. "That was patronizing."

"I shouldn't have gone vapid hotel heiress on you."

"Which you're not."

"No, I'm not. Will, if your friend Myles is helping Norman exact his revenge, Abigail Browning is in serious trouble, isn't she?"

"For the past two years, I've thought Myles was dead."

"Until you heard me describe him last night. That's why you let me leave, isn't it? You didn't want me stuck for hours with garda detectives. You wanted to talk to me yourself. Have you told the FBI?" But Will's expression startled her, and she almost knocked over her coffee. "I see now. Simon, you, Myles. Comrades in arms?"

"You see too much, Lizzie." Will lifted the teapot again and changed the subject as he refilled his cup. "What's your relationship with Estabrook?"

She decided to answer. "He thinks I understand him."

"Do you? Did he discuss his intentions for revenge with you?"

"Not specifically. I just happened to be with him in Montana when he threatened to kill Simon and Director March. I can't always tell what's bravado and fantasy with Norman and what he actually plans to do. He's grandiose and, at the same time, very smart and very calculating. I'd hoped his lawyers and a brush with incarceration would straighten him out, and he'd accept that violent revenge was a fantasy. But I also doubted that would happen. He's taken it on as his next death-defying challenge."

Will settled back in his chair. "Lizzie…"

But she'd gone far enough. She gave him a bright smile. "All of a sudden, Lord Davenport, you look very much like a man who never puts jam and butter on his scones." She noticed Justin in the doorway and waved to him. "You met my cousin Justin last night. I practically grew up with him and his three older brothers. My father traveled frequently. Still does."

"Your mother—"

"My mother died when I was a baby. Ripple effects, Will." Lizzie got to her feet, laid her napkin next her plate. "So much of life is about ripple effects. Drop a stone into a pond, and you don't always know what and who will be affected as the ripples make their way across the water. Take your time with your tea. Justin will help you with whatever you need. I have a flight to catch."

"Be careful, Lizzie."

She beamed a smile at him. "I'm always careful."

He didn't move to get up. "I suspect we have different ideas about what that means."

She was aware of him watching her as she walked across the restaurant to her cousin. "Run interference for me," she said to him. "I need a head start on our Lord Davenport. You won't be able to outmaneuver him, so don't try. Just buy me some time."

Justin straightened, obviously up to the job. "What if he's scheduled to take the same flight as you to Boston?"

"No worries," she said, heading for the lobby. "Lord Davenport will fly first-class. I'll be in coach."

Justin Rush, who bore a detectable resemblance to his cousin in the shape of his nose and eyes, sat across from Will and started telling family secrets.

A delaying tactic.

"Lizzie's a worry," the youngest Rush said. "From what my parents and older brothers tell me, she always has been. Whit's the eldest. He's named after our paternal grandmother, who was a Whitcomb. Then Harlan— Lizzie's dad is a Harlan, too, named after our grandfather Rush, who talked our grandmother into converting her family home on Charles Street in Boston into a hotel."

"Did it require much convincing?"

"Almost none. She'd discovered rats and roaches in the butler's pantry." Justin reddened. "There aren't any there today, of course."

"Of course," Will said. "So it's Whit, Harlan—then Lizzie?"

"That's right. Then Jeremiah. I'm last." He smiled, a charmer. "The baby."

"I see."

"Lizzie spent a lot of time with us and our grand-mother Rush growing up, but she traveled with her father, too. Do you know she's as good at five-card stud as she is at ordering wine in a five-star restaurant?"

"And she plays bridge," Will said.

"By herself. She tell you it anchors her mind? Personally, a pint of Guinness does the job for me. How well do you know her?"

"We only met last night."

"Where? Not Dublin, not from the state of her shoes, at least. Were you tramping through stone circles and fighting Irish bulls with her in West Cork?"

Will wondered when word of the attack on Keira would reach Justin Rush in Dublin, or if it had and he was just more adept at dissembling than his cousin. "I ran into her in a West Cork pub."

Justin looked momentarily awkward and glanced toward the door, as if he hoped Lizzie would be there to take him off the hook. He turned back to Will. "Lizzie's a free spirit, but she's a hard worker, too. She's worked at every one of our hotels just like the rest of us. She's very good at her job. My dad would fire her if she wasn't."

"But she's been on a bit of a hiatus this past year, hasn't she?"

"Sort of." The red spread to her young cousin's neck. "She got mixed up with that cretin Norman Estabrook. I know it's wrong of me, but I hope his plane—never mind. I won't say it out loud."

"Where does Lizzie's father live? Boston?"

"Uncle Harlan avoids Boston whenever possible."

"And Ireland, too, I gather," Will said.

He noticed a wince of genuine discomfort as Justin's expression softened. "It's because of the memories."

"Lizzie's mother?"

Justin feigned great interest in a pepper grinder.

Will persisted. "What happened to her?"

"She died in a freak accident when Lizzie was a baby—here in Dublin, as a matter of fact. She was Irish herself. She was here to visit her family."

"She came without Lizzie?"

He nodded.

"And without her husband?"

Another awkward nod. "It was eight years before I was born. She flew to Dublin for a five-day visit and tripped on a cobblestone on Temple Bar. She hit her head. They say she died instantly." Justin cleared his throat and lifted his gaze from the pepper grinder. "Just one of those things."

It didn't sound like just one of those things, but Will could see Justin had said all he planned to say on the matter, and possibly all he knew. "Where does your uncle Harlan live, then, if not Boston?"

"His official residence is Las Vegas, but I doubt he's there half the year. He's on the board of the family biz, but he doesn't have an active role these days. He spends most of his time traveling and gambling."

"I understand Lizzie travels a great deal. Does she also gamble?"

"Not with money. She's a risk-taker, but she's tight with a buck. She's debating whether to rent or tear down the old Rush family place in Maine. No one else wanted it, but she loves it—the location, anyway. The house itself is a wreck." Justin Rush shrugged, clearly reluctant to share so much information about his cousin, but he had his marching orders and needed to hold Will's interest and stall him. "Lizzie says it's unpretentious."

Will smiled, imagining Lizzie wringing costs out of a renovation project with carpenters and architects. She'd have her way. But he steered Justin back to the more immediate concerns at hand. "Do you know Norman Esta-brook yourself?"

"I've met him. I carried his bags."

"When he stayed here a year ago this past April," Will said.

"What, do you know *everything* already?"

"Not at all. How did Mr. Estabrook strike you?"

"I didn't really notice him. I was here on spring break. I had my hands full not to drop bags on the toes of hotel guests. I've improved since then. Mr. Estabrook had some adventure in the works—I think he hiked the Skelligs, but I'm not sure. He had quite an entourage with him. Ran me ragged."

"Do you consider Lizzie part of his entourage?"

Justin looked slightly annoyed as well as protective. "Lizzie would never be part of anyone's entourage."

"But she was here then, in Dublin," Will said.

"Yes. On her own—not with him. That's when they met." Justin picked up a crumb of his cousin's abandoned scone. "They were never more than just friends. And if you're going to ask if she has a boyfriend, I'm not going to tell you."

His tone suggested she didn't, which pleased Will more, undoubtedly, than was smart. "Do you remember anyone else from Mr. Estabrook's entourage?"

"Nope."

"Did he stay here again after that April visit?"

"Not that I know of." Justin glanced down at his crumb, then up again, his eyes showing more maturity. "Is Lizzie in trouble?"

"I don't know. I hope not."

"She can kick butt with the best of them. She's prac-ticed on all of us. She bloodied my brother Jeremiah's nose last New Year's."

"Your family was gathered for New Year's? Where?"

"Vegas. All of us, including Uncle Harlan."

"Your hotel's very comfortable," Will said, rising, "and you did your job. You delayed me."

Justin got to his feet. "You wanted to learn more about Lizzie."

Will saw the unease in the young Rush's expression. "Justin, is your family worried about her?"

"Doesn't much matter, does it? Lizzie thinks she's on her own."

Will had his own experience with worried family members left behind, but he was a professional officer. Lizzie Rush, clearly, was not. He said quietly, "I'm not going to hurt her."

"But will you help her?"

"If I can. If she'll let me."

"Sometimes I think she likes living dangerously."

"Perhaps she's merely trying to do what she can to help with a difficult situation and leave her family out of it." Will didn't wait for a reply. "You've given your cousin sufficient time to get to the airport. It's a pleasure to meet you, Justin. If you're ever in London, look me up."

He frowned, scrutinizing Will a moment, then sighed. "I don't start work until later. Come on, I'll drive you to the airport myself. You're chasing Lizzie to Boston, right?"

"I already have a flight arranged."

"Your own plane?"

Will didn't answer.

"Oh, that's good—you flying a private jet across the Atlantic and Lizzie stuck in coach with her deck of cards." Justin laughed. "That'll teach her to sneak off."

En route to the airport, Will learned a few more tidbits. Lizzie's full name was Elizabeth Brigid Rush. Her mother was born Shauna Morrigan. "There are family rumors about Aunt Shauna," Justin said. "My brother Jeremiah is convinced she spied on the Boston Irish mob."

"This was before she married your uncle?"

"Jeremiah thinks so. Who knows? There are family rumors about Uncle Harlan, too." Justin grinned as he pulled into the airport. "*Now* I've gone too far. For all I know, you're a British spy."

Indeed, Will thought, deciding he liked Justin Rush.

Chapter 17

Boston, Massachusetts
8 a.m., EDT
August 26

Bob felt the metal bars under the thin mattress as he rolled onto his back, reminding him that he'd spent the night on the pullout sofa in his niece's attic apartment in the Garrison house. Sunlight streamed through lace curtains Keira had bought in Ireland. He draped an arm over his eyes to block out the sun and slumped deeper into what passed for a bed. His feet hung off the end. He hadn't wanted to sleep. He'd still be at BPD headquarters now if Tom Yarborough hadn't all but put a gun to his head and dragged him to Beacon Hill.

Yarborough had probably gone right back to work.

Bob adjusted his position and got another poke in the back. Everyone had offered him a place to stay. Theresa, Lucas Jones, even Yarborough. Hell, the mayor and the commissioner would have put him up for the night if he'd asked. Easier to stay in his niece's vacant apartment with her pictures of Irish fairies and cottages, her books of folktales and poetry.

Simon and March had an FBI detail looking after their

safety. Neither liked it or had wanted to sleep any more
than Bob had. Simon, in particular, wanted to chase Estabrook on his own, but not only did he have a giant
target painted on his back, he would be more help to
Abigail working the investigation than going solo. He
knew Estabrook, his contacts, how he thought, places he
liked, places he'd been or had talked about. If he could
hide millions for drug traffickers, he could hide himself.

Someone would have paged or called or shouted up the
stairs if Estabrook or his plane had turned up, but Bob
checked his messages, anyway.

Nothing.

He walked to the window in his undershorts and pulled
back the Irish lace curtains, grimacing when he saw that
the protective detail the commissioner insisted be put on
his chief homicide detective was still down there. Waste
of manpower as far as Bob was concerned. He'd rather
have them out looking for Abigail and the bombers, but
he didn't have a choice.

He headed for the bathroom and took a shower, using
Keira's almond soap, which wasn't as girlie as he'd
feared. He'd managed to grab a couple changes of clothes
out of his apartment. They didn't smell too sooty to him,
but they might to someone else. Not his problem.

Yarborough met him downstairs. He was as straight-
backed as ever but looked raw around the edges. He'd
never say the tension was getting to him, but Bob
wouldn't, either. "Morning, Lieutenant. You sleep?"

"Like a baby. You?"

"Some."

Bob squinted across Beacon at the Common, all
dappled shade on a sunny summer morning. It'd be
another hot day. "Did you find Abigail and just not want
to wake me?"

"No. Sorry."

The guy had no sense of irony. Bob turned back to him. "What's going on? Why are you here?"

Yarborough rubbed the back of his neck. He was a cool, controlled type, but right now, he looked miserable. "Fiona refused police protection this morning and cleared out of her mother's house. She's over eighteen. We can't force her."

"I can. Where is she?"

Yarborough didn't answer.

"You don't know, or you don't want to tell me?"

"ATF wants to put her under surveillance."

"My daughter?"

"Yeah."

"Why?"

"They think she could have seen something here yesterday morning and she just doesn't realize it."

"Big difference between protection and surveillance," Bob said, stony. "The feds don't call the shots when it comes to my family. Where's Fi now?"

"I don't know. In my opinion—" Yarborough abandoned his thought. "Never mind."

Bob glared at him. "In your opinion, what?"

Yarborough sighed and looked out at the Common. "I got the feeling when we interviewed her that she's holding back."

"What do you mean, holding back? Holding back what?"

The younger detective didn't flinch at Bob's tone. "I don't know. Lucas thought so, too." Like Bob wouldn't kill him if Lucas agreed. "We think she's got something on her mind, but she's not sure it's relevant. She's afraid of getting someone into trouble or wasting our time."

Bob didn't respond as he considered what Yarborough was saying.

Yarborough rubbed the side of his mouth with one finger. "I'm not criticizing her."

"Yeah. It's okay. I'm not armed. Not yet." Bob fished out his cell phone and tried Fiona's number, but he got her voice mail. He left a message and tried texting her. "I hate these damn buttons. My fingers are too big. I can't see the screen." He messed up and had to start over. "Fi's fast, but little Jayne—she's a whiz. Her teacher has the students leave their cell phones in a box when they come to class. Eleven years old, and they all have cell phones. Where's the money coming from? When I was a kid, we had one phone in the house. It was a big deal when the first family on the street got an extension."

"It's called progress, Lieutenant," Yarborough said.

"It's called kids texting their friends spelling words and the capital of Wisconsin. Or don't kids take tests anymore?" Bob managed to type in "call me" and hit some other damn button to send the thing. "I'm going to the hospital to visit Scoop. Ten to one Fiona's there. Any update on his condition?"

Yarborough was expressionless. "He's alive." He looked at Bob in the uncompromising way he had. "I'll drive you over there."

No way of talking him out of it. Bob gestured to the uniformed officers. "Tell them to go to work."

"Lieutenant—"

"Never mind. I'll do it."

Yarborough raised a hand, stopping him. He walked over to the cruiser, said a few words, then rejoined Bob. "Let's go," he said tightly.

"So, if someone jumps out of the bushes with a gun and tries to shoot me, you're diving in front of the bullet?"

"I'm shooting the bastard first. You're on PTSD watch, you know."

"Posttraumatic stress disorder doesn't happen in a day. It's normal to have the yips right after a crisis."

"The yips, Lieutenant?"

"Sleeplessness, flashbacks, startle response. Not that I have any of that. I told you, I slept like a baby—"

"Bob. Stop, okay? I know."

He grinned at the younger detective. "Is that the first time you've called me by my first name? Honest, Yarborough, we might make a human being out of you yet."

Yarborough clamped his mouth shut, a muscle working in his jaw as he got out his keys and walked to his car. He unlocked the passenger door. "I keep wondering where Abigail spent the night."

"No point going down that road."

"She's good, but…" Yarborough yanked open the door and stood to one side for Bob to get in. "It's okay. I checked for bombs already."

"You're a ray of sunshine, Yarborough."

"Always aim to please the boss."

Bob got rid of him when they arrived at the hospital. There were enough cops there for him to get a ride to BPD headquarters if he needed one, and Yarborough was clearly itching to do something besides escort him around town.

And Bob was right. He found his eldest daughter shivering in the corridor outside Scoop's hospital room. Scoop had been moved out of ICU to a regular room, another positive sign. It wasn't the air-conditioning that had Fiona shivering. If anything, the temperature was on the warm side. She was on edge. Bob wasn't thrilled with her for refusing police protection, but he melted when he saw her. Uniformed officers were posted outside Scoop's room and drifting past her while she mustered courage to go in and see him.

Scoop's family was there. His colleagues from internal

affairs. Bob wasn't going to embarrass Fiona—or himself—by treating her like a two-year-old, but she had to go back under police protection. Just because she was over eighteen didn't mean she didn't have to listen to his common sense advice.

She tried to smile. "This is worse than any performance anxiety I've experienced," she said, her arms crossed tight on her chest. "Performing is nothing compared to facing a man who nearly died saving your life."

"Scoop won't look at it that way," Bob said.

"I don't care how he looks at it. It's what happened."

"I know, Fi."

A white-coated doctor who didn't look much older than Fiona came out of Scoop's room. "You can go in now," she said. "He's awake."

Fiona nodded without speaking.

The doctor headed for the nurses' station. When his daughter still didn't move, Bob said, "Scoop will want to see you and know you're okay."

She blinked back tears. "He saved my life," she said again.

Bob had talked to Theresa last night, and she'd told him Fi had been repeating those words ever since they'd left his burned-up house.

"Maybe you saved his life, too. If you hadn't been there, he might have gone for the porch and Abigail when the bomb went off. Instead he grabbed you and dived for cover." Bob nodded to the doorway. "Go on in, Fi. Just talk to him a few minutes."

She nodded, and Bob gritted his teeth as he watched his daughter enter the small room and walk up to one side of Scoop's bed. Scoop was on his side, bandaged, bruised, stuck with IVs. He had his own clicker for pain medication.

"Hey, Scoop," Fiona said, her voice clear and strong now. "How're you feeling? Don't talk if it hurts."

"I'm getting there. You?"

Standing just outside in the hall, Bob could barely hear him.

"Just some bumps and bruises," Fiona said. "I'm fine. We're all fine."

Bob knew that Tom Yarborough and Lucas Jones would have asked her not to mention Abigail to anyone, even to Scoop, not just to keep him from worrying about her but to maintain tight control over the investigation.

"I just wanted to say hi and thank you," she added, her voice a little less strong.

"Don't thank me, Fi. I should have spotted the bomb." Scoop sounded weak, drugged, but lucid. "Before it went off. You got a detail on you?"

"I'm okay."

"Fiona."

Bob grinned to himself. Good for you, Scoop, he thought.

"I said no." She was defensive now. "I don't want a protective detail. I don't need one. The bomb wasn't meant for me."

"Abigail," Scoop said.

Bad move, Bob thought. She should have lied and told him she had a protective detail. Even drugged and fighting pain, Scoop would have his cop instincts. As an internal affairs detective, he was used to penetrating lies told by men and women trained to see through them. He was the best in the department at detecting any type of lie.

Fiona sniffled. "Sorry, Scoop, I didn't hear you. I should leave. You should be with your family. I'm taking it easy today. I'm heading over to the Garrison house to practice."

"Good. Play an Irish tune for me."

"I will. I'll play something fun. Something happy."

But Scoop didn't respond, and Bob saw he'd drifted off. Fiona withdrew, bursting into tears when she reached her father. He tried to hug her, but she jerked away. The officers watched her closely, and he could tell they knew she was his daughter. So could she, and it just irritated her more.

Better irritated than sobbing and shivering.

She ran down the hall. Bob didn't go after her. The foundation staff would be back to work at the Garrison house, and patrol cars would be making frequent checks.

He went in to see Scoop. "You awake?"

"No."

"You look like hell."

"Feel worse."

"They say you're going to live."

Scoop paid no attention. "While I have the energy." He licked dry, chapped lips. "Before I konk out again. There's a woman."

"There always is with you."

"That's not what I mean. Black hair. Long, straight. Little thing. Green eyes. She was on our street."

"Okay," Bob said, unimpressed.

Scoop seemed to try to focus, but his eyelids were swollen from the fluids being pumped into him. "Day before the bomb. She stopped in front of the house. Said she had shin splints."

"She got your attention?"

"Yeah. I wondered…" He licked his lips again, his movements sluggish as he struggled to stay alert.

The man needed rest. "I'll look into it," Bob said. "A small woman with black hair, green eyes and shin splints."

Bob didn't tell Scoop, but the description also fit the woman in Ireland who'd taken on the s.o.b. sent to kill Keira. Michael Murphy continued to deny he intended to hurt anyone, but the Irish police didn't believe him. Bob didn't, either.

"Abigail was on to something," Scoop said in a slurred whisper. "She…her father…ask her."

Bob wouldn't lie to Scoop about Abigail, but he didn't have to. Scoop was out.

On his way out of the hospital, Bob dialed Theresa's cell number. "You know Fiona was just here visiting Scoop?"

"I assumed as much. She went back to her apartment first thing this morning. One way to get her out of bed early, put a police detail on her."

"It's a thought," Bob said without humor. "At least her apartment's in BPD jurisdiction. We can keep an eye on her."

Theresa got all hot. "If you're implying I should have kept her here, I tried. She's as stubborn as you are."

"You're at work today?"

"What's that supposed to mean?"

"It's just a question. Yes or no answer. Easy."

"Yes."

Bob ignored her tight, irritated tone. He didn't even blame her for being testy.

"If you have vacation days left, take them. Go to the beach with the girls."

"Fiona won't go. She and her band have paying gigs. Classes start soon. She—"

"You can make her go."

"So could you. You've got a gun, because that's what it'll take. She's nineteen, Bob. She makes her own decisions. It's time you respected that."

"I don't like her decisions."

"Well, you can't control what she does. Neither can I. We can influence but not control."

"You been to see a shrink or something?"

She swore at him, really irritated now.

"Take Maddie and Jayne to the beach, Ter. I'll deal with Fi."

"She may play harp, Bob, but she's just like you."

"Prettier."

"Thank God."

"Ter?" He sighed. "I'm sorry."

She disconnected without a word.

Yarborough appeared out of nowhere and fell in beside him. Bob frowned. "I thought you were doing something useful."

"I decided I didn't want to leave you alone," Yarborough said, almost kindly, and nodded toward his car. "Come on. I'll take you wherever you want to go."

"The crime scene."

"The—"

"That would be my house, Tom."

He looked uncomfortable for a half beat. "Okay. Let's go."

"Abigail ever mention a small, black-haired woman to you?"

"No, why?"

"You ever see one?"

"Like, two million every time I get on the subway."

"She's got green eyes, too. And shin splints."

Yarborough was staring at him as if he might have to make a detour to the psych ward, but he said, still kindly, "You can tell me about her on the way to Jamaica Plain."

Which was when Bob knew he looked as sick and worried as he felt. But it didn't matter. He had to stay focused and do his job.

"Abigail's strong," Yarborough said, all reassuring. "She'll—"

"I'm getting my gun."

The younger detective looked relieved. "Good idea."

Chapter 18

Off the New England coast
Mid-day
August 26

Norman Estabrook entered the stateroom with Fletcher two steps behind him. The billionaire looked more rested, and he wasn't wearing his porkpie hat. His light brown hair needed a trim. Abigail sat up on the sectional. She was nauseated but so far had managed to keep her food down. The wet bar was well-stocked with gourmet items, but she'd have loved a plain piece of toast.

"You're pale," Estabrook said. "Are you getting enough to eat?"

"Plenty."

"Did you sleep?"

She nodded. Fitful sleep, pacing, jumping jacks, pool, a shower. She'd done what she could to maintain her energy and stay attuned to her surroundings, the voices outside her door, the comings and goings of the small boat. She'd tried to use her worsening seasickness to her advantage and let it remind her she was still alive and still wanted to feel good and enjoy life.

"Have you ever met Lizzie Rush?" Estabrook asked abruptly.

His question took Abigail by surprise, but she answered truthfully. "No, I haven't."

"But you've heard of her?"

"Her family. They own the Whitcomb Hotel in Boston."

"She stayed with me through my arrest and my discovery of Simon's betrayal. I haven't heard from her since the FBI took her away. I imagine your father got to her."

Abigail walked over to the pool table and rolled a solid blue ball into a trio of other balls. It knocked against a yellow one, bounced off the side of the table and stopped at the edge of a pocket. "I wouldn't know," she said without looking at either man. "Believe it or not, my father hasn't discussed your case with me."

"If you think referring to me as a 'case' will give you the upper hand, Detective, or irritate me, or make me feel bad, you're wrong. I know I matter to your father." Estabrook picked up the eight ball. "Lizzie grew up without a mother. Did you know that?"

"I'm not familiar with her background." That, Abigail thought, tapping in her blue ball with the tip of her finger, was an outright lie.

Estabrook massaged the eight ball. "She's just a few years younger than you. While you were growing up with a mother and father, Lizzie was being shuffled back and forth among various relatives. Her father traveled frequently for his work with the Rush hotels. She would stay with her uncle and aunt and their four sons in Boston, and her grandmother in Maine. Lizzie was a motherless little girl, Detective Browning."

"You seem to know a lot about her."

"I know a lot about everyone I have as a guest in my home."

But Simon had fooled him, and that grated. "What happened to Lizzie's mother?" Abigail asked, although she knew the answer to her question. Not the whole answer. Only her father would know the whole answer.

She was aware of Fletcher waiting by the door with his arms crossed on his chest. He managed somehow to look both bored and impatient.

Estabrook set the eight ball back on the table and gave it a sharp spin. "Lizzie's mother was Irish. Shauna Morrigan Rush. She died in Dublin when Lizzie was seven months old. Her death was ruled an accident—a freak fall—but who's to say? It's daunting to think about the little things that can have such an impact on our lives. One wrong move on an unfamiliar cobblestone street, and your daughter's an orphan."

Abigail subtly held on to the edge of the table as she tried to control another wave of her persistent nausea. "Do you have plans for Lizzie? Is she helping you?"

"All in good time."

Whatever her role, Lizzie Rush wasn't his equal, not in his eyes. Her father was. Simon? Estabrook, Abigail thought, would take special pleasure in exacting his revenge on Simon Cahill.

Estabrook turned abruptly to Fletcher. "Continue."

"I need you to leave," the Brit said.

"As you wish," he said coolly.

Fletcher lowered his arms to his sides and walked over to Abigail. He put his finger on her chin and tilted her bruised cheek toward the light. "The swelling's down a bit."

"I think so, too. How did you and Estabrook meet?"

"We had tea together at Buckingham Palace."

"For all I know you're telling the truth. You seem like a practical sort. What do you want out of this?"

"Money."

"I have access to money. We can work out our own deal."

"You're feeling sick," he said.

"I've turned green, have I?"

"More chartreuse."

"Ugly color, chartreuse, but to each his own. I hope being pregnant isn't this bad." She gave him a faltering smile. "I want kids. Do you have any?"

His eyes went flat. "No."

There was something there. A loss, a chance missed. "Give up Norman in exchange for cash and a safe exit back to whatever hole you crawled out of. There'll be a reward for my safe return."

"Mr. Estabrook has access to hundreds of millions of dollars. What do you suppose the FBI or Boston police would pay for you? Your fiancé comes from a wealthy family, but compared to Mr. Estabrook? I don't think so, love. Sorry."

"We can set you up with a new identity. He'd never find you. In your line of work, you must have enemies hunting you. You can make a fresh start."

"I've made my choices."

Abigail rolled a yellow ball from one end of the pool table to the other, without it hitting any other balls. "What does Estabrook want?"

Fletcher didn't hesitate. "To kill the people who tried to destroy him."

"It's not that simple, and I think you know it. And no one tried to destroy him. He broke the law." She stood up from the pool table. "He's become more and more obsessed with thwarting my father, hasn't he?"

"I'm afraid I'm not particularly interested in his motives."

"He appreciates an adversary as strong as he is. He sees himself as a special person, and he wants special adversaries—such as the director of the FBI."

Fletcher picked up a pool cue and examined the array of balls on the table.

"You're obviously not stupid," Abigail said. "Anyone taking the risks you've taken would want to be well paid."

"You're making assumptions that perhaps you shouldn't."

Without a doubt, but she said, "You should listen to me."

He got down low, sized up the array of balls on the table. "You're aching to shoot me and dump me overboard, aren't you, love? I can't say I blame you."

"I wouldn't dump you overboard. I'd let your body fall into the ocean if the bullets took you in that direction. Norman's, too." She walked to the end of the table, watching as Fletcher lined up his cue on a solid red ball. "I heard a smaller boat coming and going again. Have you kidnapped anyone else?"

He made his shot, crisp, clean, two solid-colored balls pivoting into pockets. But he didn't answer her.

"Is Lizzie Rush on board?" Abigail asked. "Are we on our way to meet her somewhere? Maine, maybe? Estabrook mentioned her grandmother had a house there."

Fletcher walked around the table, standing close to Abigail as he sized up another shot. "You know more about Miss Rush than you let on to Mr. Estabrook."

"Not much more. Simon Cahill met Estabrook at a Fast Rescue fund-raiser held at the Rush family's hotel in Boston last summer. My fiancé is the founder and director of Fast Rescue. But you know that already, don't you?"

Fletcher leaned far over the table and angled his cue sharply. "It's good that you didn't lie about that one, love," he said, making another perfect shot.

"I'm not the one with something to hide. For example, kidnapping a police officer." She fought more seasickness, bile rising in her throat. "Not going to tell me Estabrook's plan for me, are you?"

"There is one. Have no doubt of that."

"You don't sound very enthusiastic." Abigail stepped back away from the table, giving him room for another difficult shot. "You don't like this, do you? You're a professional, and Norman's a brilliant, narcissistic, crazed amateur. He's off the reservation, isn't he?"

"Perhaps you should vomit and get it over with."

She ignored his remark. "If you had your way, what would you do, put a bullet in my head and dump me overboard?"

"No profit in that, love." He tapped a ball into a side pocket. "Does talking keep you from vomiting?"

She almost smiled. "So far, so good."

Eyeing the remaining balls on the table, he said, without looking at her, "There's a way you can help me. If you do, I'll help you when the time comes."

"What can I do for you?"

Fletcher positioned his cue for another shot. "You can tell me what you know about Will Davenport."

This was a surprise. "He's a friend?"

"Once upon a time."

Abigail considered her answer and decided there was little risk to the truth. "I'm sure I know less about him than you do. He and Simon were friends before Simon hooked up with Fast Rescue. I've never met Davenport, but I understand he's a wealthy British noble, a former military officer. I don't know the details, but I suspect he and Simon didn't meet over tea and crumpets."

"Correct. They did not."

"Simon worked in counterterrorism before he went undercover after Estabrook. I've wondered if he was on to some kind of drug-terrorism connection there. What about you, Fletcher? How do you know Davenport?"

He fired off another shot without answering.

"You were with the good guys?"

"I was with them. I wasn't one."

His hard, quick shot sent balls banging into each other, richocheting off the sides of the table.

Abigail maintained her composure. "Davenport provided assistance—voluntarily—with the Ireland end of a case we wrapped up earlier this summer involving a serial killer."

"Then Will hasn't been to Boston?"

"Not that I'm aware of."

"I believe you. Now," Fletcher said, moving around the table, his tone unchanged, "tell me about Fiona O'Reilly."

He caught Abigail totally off guard, which, she realized, had been his intention. She couldn't stop herself. The images of the previous day and her fear for Fiona were too much. Bile rose in her throat, and she stumbled. Fletcher moved fast, grabbing her, half carrying her to the bathroom, shoving her in front of the toilet. She vomited until she had nothing left inside her, then dry heaved for a few more minutes.

Finally, spent, eyes tearing and bloodshot, hands shaking, she splashed herself with cold water and looked at her reflection. She was bruised, ashen. "Owen," she whispered. "Give me strength. I love you so much."

When she turned, Fletcher was in the doorway. "I have to leave for a while," he said, impassive. "We can talk later. I'll let you get some sleep."

When she was alone again, Abigail lay down flat on the carpeted floor next to the pool table and closed her eyes.

In through the nose for eight.

Hold for eight.

Out through the mouth for eight.

"Again," she said, ignoring the tears trickling down her temples into the carpet.

In for eight. Hold for eight.

Out for eight.

Chapter 19

Boston, Massachusetts
4:15 p.m., EDT
August 26

Fiona O'Reilly relaxed slightly when she entered the Whitcomb Hotel on Charles Street, her small lap harp in a soft case over one shoulder, and saw Jeremiah Rush in the lobby. The hotel was so elegant with its antiques and shining brass, but Jeremiah, she thought, was amazing.

And she desperately wanted to relax.

She'd practiced for hours in the drawing room at the Garrison house. Owen wasn't around, but the foundation's staff was back at work and police cars stopped by. Tom Yarborough, Abigail's partner, came into the drawing room at one point and asked her if she'd remembered anything else about yesterday. She'd said no and resumed practicing. Now she wondered if she shouldn't have. If she should have just told him. But what if she was wrong? What if she was just being stupid? *Hundreds* of people had been on Beacon Street yesterday who could have planted the bomb in Owen's car. The man she'd seen...

She lowered her harp off her shoulder. She was proud of herself for having screwed up the courage to visit Scoop. Seeing him so vulnerable was awful, but she'd done it. She hadn't chickened out. Turning down police protection hadn't made her afraid. The opposite. The prospect of bodyguards, even police bodyguards, scared her more than being on her own. She was an adult now and could decide for herself. She felt empowered.

She pulled herself out of her thoughts and greeted Jeremiah. "I'm here early. I hope you don't mind."

"Of course not." He got up from the dark wood desk, rumored to have belonged to his great-something-grand-father Whitcomb, and walked around to her. "I heard about the fire at your father's house yesterday. How is everyone? Are you okay? Were you there?"

"I was there but I wasn't hurt. It was pretty frightening. I didn't sleep much last night, but I practiced most of the day. That always helps. I've been working on a Mozart concerto for flute and harp." She gave Jeremiah what even felt like a strained smile. "Of course I slipped in a few Irish tunes."

He frowned at her. He wore a light tan suit that didn't have a single wrinkle. He was working reception right now, but he seemed willing to do a variety of jobs. Fiona had seen him running a vacuum last week. "I can tell you've been through an ordeal," he said. "I saw on the news one of the detectives was badly hurt—"

"Scoop. His real name's Cyrus Wisdom. He's doing much better today. I'm not supposed to talk about the fire while it's still under investigation." That was the response Lucas Jones had suggested she give to any questions. He'd strictly forbidden her from talking about Abigail. Fiona made herself smile again. "I came here to get away from everything for a while."

"Whatever we can do, let us know."

"Thanks." She changed the subject. "I thought I'd work some on planning our Ireland trip."

"My brother Justin's there now," Jeremiah said, heading back behind the desk. "He's a bellman at our Dublin hotel. He's a natural. I swear he'd stay a bellman if our dad would let him. Mum wouldn't care. She just wants us to be happy."

Fiona's mother had said that morning she just wanted Fiona and her sisters to be safe. Happy would be nice, too, she thought, suddenly feeling depressed.

Jeremiah opened a side drawer in the desk and pulled out a stack of brochures and an Ireland guidebook. "I've been collecting these for you. There's a brochure on our Dublin hotel."

"Does it serve tea on Christmas Eve?"

"Sure does." He came back around to Fiona and handed her the stack. "Are you sure you're okay? You look—"

"I'm fine," she said quickly, realizing she was about to cry. She brushed a stray tear and tried to smile. "Is your brother in Dublin cute?"

"He thinks so."

Fiona laughed, but more tears escaped, and she thanked Jeremiah and took the steps down to Morrigan's. It was at ground level, with full-size windows looking out on Charles Street. She found herself eye-to-eye with a dirty-faced toddler in a stroller. He waved at her, and she waved back, instantly feeling better.

She set her harp on the small stage. She and her friends had performed at Morrigan's a half-dozen times over the summer. Her father didn't know. She thought he'd object. Scoop and now Abigail knew, but Fiona hadn't asked them not to tell her dad. Then it'd seem like she was keeping it a secret instead of just not having gotten around to telling him.

She sat at a table under a window with her brochures and ordered a Coke Zero. She wasn't sure which friends would show up, but it didn't matter. They all could play more than one instrument and would manage with whatever they had. Morrigan's patrons always seemed to enjoy her ensemble's performances.

She opened up one of the brochures to a photograph of a country lane that reminded her of her cousin Keira's paintings. Fiona knew something terrible had happened in Ireland, too, but no one would tell her anything except that Keira was safe.

Keira was as excited as Fiona was about their trip to Ireland and had said she couldn't wait to take her younger cousin to Irish pubs for live music. "You can join in, and we can get your dad and Simon to sing—just not my mum and me." Keira's mother, Fiona's aunt Eileen, had come home from studying in Ireland in college pregnant with Keira. She'd had some kind of mad, mysterious affair in the same ruin, apparently, where Keira had found her Celtic stone angel. The angel had disappeared, but Fiona had no doubt her cousin had seen it. Keira believed that whatever had happened to it, it was where it was meant to be.

As Fiona finished her Coke, a man she didn't recognize walked over to the stage area and pointed to her harp. "It looks like an angel's harp," he said in a British accent.

Fiona felt a shiver in her back. She'd just been thinking about Keira's stone angel. "There are several different kinds of harps," she said.

"And can you play all of them, Miss O'Reilly?"

Now the hairs on her arms and the back of her neck stood on end, and her breathing got shallow and her mouth went dry. But she didn't move.

The man pulled out the chair across from her and sat down. "It's all right, love. I'm a friend."

"I've never met you. I'll scream if you try anything."

He smiled, winked at her. "You do that, love. Scream loud. How was your harp practice at the Garrison house?"

"How—"

"It's a beautiful day for a stroll, isn't it?"

Fiona thought she'd pass out. To calm herself, she looked up at a poster of the brightly painted Georgian doors of Dublin. They were already on her list of sights to see at Christmas.

"Have a sip of your drink," the Brit said.

"It's not alcoholic. I'm under twenty-one."

There were several people in the bar. Jeremiah was just up the stairs. Fiona reminded herself she wasn't alone. Feeling more in control, she focused on the man across from her. "You followed me?"

"Yes, love. I can follow you anytime, anywhere. You'll never know if I'm there or not there." He leaned back in his chair. "When and where did you last see Simon Cahill?"

"Why do you want to know?"

"He's an old friend."

"I don't believe you. Did you have anything to do with the fire at my dad's?"

His eyes narrowed on her, and he leaned toward her. "I asked you a question, love. Best you answer."

"Yesterday. At my dad's." Fiona wanted to sound strong and defiant but thought she sounded weak, afraid. She cleared her throat. "It was after the fire. Late. That's when I saw Simon last."

The Brit had gray eyes that seemed to see right through her. "You're telling the truth," he said, satisfied. "That's smart. What about Director March?"

"I just got a glimpse of him yesterday. I didn't talk to him."

"And your friend Lizzie Rush?" He paused, watching Fiona. "When did you see her last?"

"She's not—I barely know her."

"When, love?"

She didn't want to tell him anything more.

"I can ask someone else. Her cousin up—"

"No, don't," Fiona broke in. "Leave Jeremiah alone. It was a few days ago. I don't remember the exact day."

"Here?"

"Yes." Fiona gulped in a breath, sweating now. "I have no idea where she is now. My friends and I perform here on occasion. I don't know the Rushes at all, really."

The Brit smiled. "Like your Irish music, do you? Well, Miss O'Reilly, I have a different sort of job for you." He pointed up at the window behind her, toward the street. "I want you to go back to the Garrison house. Call no one. Tell no one. Do you understand?"

Fiona nodded, her heart pounding.

"There's an alley off a side street just before you reach the house. Don't go into it. Stop and call your copper dad and tell him to come and have a look. Will you do that for me, love?"

"Yes."

Fight to escape. That was what her dad had taught her. He'd also taught her not to leave one crime scene for another. "It almost never works out," he'd said, "but use your fear as your guide. Let it help you."

The Brit reached across the table and tucked a finger under her chin, forcing her to meet his eye. "A man is in grave danger. Only you can get him help in time."

"Who is it?"

He ignored her. "When you speak with your dad, tell him Abigail is alive and unharmed. Will you do that for me, too, love?"

"Abigail," Fiona said. "Where—"

He tapped her chin with one finger. "Now, don't start.

Just listen and do as I say. Tell your dad that he and his colleagues in law enforcement have an imaginative and dangerous enemy."

"You."

"I'm no one's enemy." He sat back again, his eyes hard. "No one's friend, either. Can you remember what I just said, love?"

"Yes. Yes, I can remember."

"There you go. Don't follow me. Don't have anyone else follow me." He nodded toward the street. "Lizzie Rush will be arriving very soon from Ireland. If you see her in time, she can go with you."

"How do you know she—"

He winked. "You'd be surprised what I know."

"I didn't see you yesterday. No one did."

"I know. Now you have seen me, but it's all right. I'm not going to hurt you. I especially enjoyed your Irish music. Special quality it has, doesn't it? Even for a Londoner like myself."

"What do you want with Abigail?"

"Nothing. I'm her only hope. I must leave now. If you do anything to interfere, she'll be dead before nightfall. You need to stay calm and do as I ask." The Brit stood up, looming over Fiona as he reached a hand out to her. "On your feet on three. Count with me. It'll help you focus. One. Two. Three."

She got up without his assistance. Should she scream? Kick him? Create a scene? If a man was dying…

She raised her chin to the Brit. "My sisters are under police protection."

He smiled. "You will be now, too. Alley. Your dad. Abigail. You can remember?"

"Why are you doing this?"

"It's important not to leave loose ends."

Fiona didn't breathe or speak as he trotted lightly up the steps and back out to Charles Street.

A cab pulled up to the hotel and a small, black-haired woman got out.

Lizzie Rush. As promised.

Chapter 20

Lizzie headed toward the Whitcomb lobby, shaking off the pummeled feeling she always had after the long flight across the Atlantic. It was late afternoon in Boston, late evening in Ireland, but she wasn't quite on either clock. She figured she'd need the five hours she'd gained heading west from Dublin. She didn't know how long she'd have before Will turned up. Based on the text message she'd received from Justin when she landed, probably not long: Brit to Boston. Right behind you.

Justin wasn't one to waste words.

Spending the night in the same suite as a British intelligence agent was one thing. Having him following her was another, but Lizzie had an advantage in Boston. She knew the city and had family there, and Will didn't. She'd contemplated him, her situation and her options while playing one solo game of bridge after another on her little tray table.

How did Will Davenport fit into whatever was going on, and where was he now?

Was he trouble?

"*Everyone's* trouble," she muttered, quoting her father, even as she welcomed the familiar surroundings of the Whitcomb's classically appointed lobby.

A dour-looking Sam Whitcomb, in actuality a firebrand privateer during the American Revolution, stared down at her from his oil portrait above the unlit marble fireplace. Henrietta wanted to replace him with one of Keira Sullivan's wildflower watercolors.

Lizzie focused on the situation at hand, smiling at her cousin Jeremiah as he stood up from his desk. "I cut my trip to Ireland short," she said.

"Justin's already filled me in," Jeremiah said, shaking his head. "Lizzie. What's going on? All hell's broken loose in Boston. I've never seen so many cops on the streets."

"I noticed. What do you know?"

"Nothing. Fiona O'Reilly's here. Cops are mum on the details about the fire at her father's place and the evacuation at the Garrison house. Your friend Norman Estabrook's disappeared, too. You know that, right?"

"Yes, but I'm not in contact with him."

"The FBI hasn't been in touch?"

Lizzie shook her head. No need to mention that she'd been in touch with John March herself. "I haven't spoken to Norman since his arrest."

Jeremiah seemed faintly reassured. "But you're back here because Simon Cahill and FBI Director March are in town, aren't you?" Her cousin narrowed his eyes on her. "Lizzie…"

Of all her cousins, Jeremiah was the one most tuned in to the history between March and her mother, but Lizzie dodged his question. "I'm not involved in Norman's legal case, Jeremiah. I wish I'd never had anything to do with him."

"I don't blame you. I imagine most of his friends feel the same way. What are you going to do now?"

"Pick up my car and head to Maine."

Go to Maine, she'd decided on her flight across the Atlantic. Figure out what she could do to help find Norman and leave the rest of her family out of it. John March might give her time, but if Scoop Wisdom had provided her description to his BPD colleagues, they could already be after her. Best, she'd reasoned, to stick to her cover story and go about her business as if she had nothing to hide. She'd gone to Ireland to hike the Beara Way and pop in on Simon Cahill, only to end up in the middle of a knife fight. It made perfect sense that she'd come straight home and head to her house in Maine.

Whether or not Norman thought she was an ally—believed she hated John March as much as he did—Lizzie had no doubt he would expect her to head to Maine.

Jeremiah touched her shoulder and looked past her. "Fiona…"

Lizzie turned as Fiona O'Reilly stumbled on the steps up from Morrigan's and hesitated, very pale, barely breathing. She stared at Lizzie a split second before bolting down the main steps and out to Charles Street.

"I wonder what just happened," Jeremiah said. "A man joined her downstairs. I've never seen him here before. He just left."

"What did he look like?" Lizzie asked.

"Brown hair, fit—not that he did push-ups on the floor, but I wouldn't want to take him on in a bar fight."

Lizzie felt the same shiver of coolness she'd experienced last night questioning Michael Murphy. "Was he British?"

"I didn't hear him myself. Lizzie, we're not talking about Lord Davenport, are we?"

She shook her head. "For one thing, Will's blond. Put hotel security on alert. I'll go after Fiona."

Her cousin took a sharp breath. "Should we call the police? Fiona's father—"

"Yes. Call Lieutenant O'Reilly and tell him something's up with her." Lizzie thought quickly. She didn't like keeping Jeremiah in the dark, but there was no time. "I owe you an explanation, but right now I need to go after Fiona. Keep her here if she returns."

"*I* should go."

She managed a smile. "My father taught me the tricks of the trade, not you." But her smile faded. "If the man who was with Fiona shows up again, don't confront him. Don't go near him. He's dangerous, Jeremiah."

"Who is he?"

"My guess? A British spy."

Her cousin rolled his eyes. "You think my golden retriever's a spy."

"He *is*, but of a different sort."

The humor helped break the tension, just enough to give her energy. Wishing she had on the shoes she'd worn last night in the stone circle instead of her flats, Lizzie headed out to Charles Street and up past a knot of college students and tourists to the intersection at Beacon Street. She spotted Fiona running in the direction of the Garrison house in what appeared to be blind panic.

Cursing her shoes, Lizzie took off after her on the uneven sidewalk. "Fiona, hold on," she called as she closed in on the teenager.

Fiona didn't break her stride. "I have to hurry."

"Why? Jeremiah told me a man joined you just now." Lizzie kept her voice calm. "Fiona, what did he say to you?"

"Did you see him? He thinks we're friends. I told him I hardly know you. It's true. He said not to follow him."

She slowed slightly, clearly terrified. "You didn't try— you didn't send Jeremiah—"

"No one's following him."

"He knew you'd come. He told me a man's in danger and I should go to the alley by the Garrison house and— and—" Already close to hyperventilating, she gulped in more air as they continued up Beacon Street. "And then call my dad."

"Did this man threaten you?"

"He implied Abigail's life depends on my cooperation. There's a man dying. What if it's someone I know—one of Dad's detectives, one of my friends? We practice at the Garrison house. We—"

"Don't speculate." Lizzie tried to penetrate Fiona's mounting panic. "Let's just figure out what to do."

Fiona was marginally calmer as she glanced at Lizzie. "He said you could go with me."

"All right. Let's do this together."

Fiona slowed her pace and walking now, still breathing hard, turned onto a side street that led up onto Beacon Hill. She stopped at the entrance to a narrow alley that ran behind two elegant brick mansions.

"This must be it." She had her cell phone clutched in one hand. "He told me to call my dad and not go in the alley."

Lizzie peered into the alley. "He didn't say I couldn't go in, did he?"

Fiona shook her head, already dialing her cell phone.

"I'll stay in sight. I'm not leaving you, Fiona."

"I'll be okay."

Lizzie stepped into the alley, which dead-ended at a tall stockade fence. She expected to hear a moan, ragged breathing, a cry for help, but there was nothing. She glanced back at Fiona, who was holding herself together as she talked on her phone, and took another two steps.

A car was parked along the fence. She walked around it, past a stack of empty flower pots. The sounds of Beacon Street traffic fell away, blocked by the two big houses.

She stopped abruptly, hearing flies. Placing a hand on the car's hood, cool in the shade, she leaned forward and saw a man was on the ground, slumped against the fence.

Even from a distance of a few yards, Lizzie could see he was dead.

Fiona, off the phone now, started into the alley. Lizzie shook her head at her. "Don't, Fiona. You don't need to see this."

But Fiona covered her mouth with her wrist and kept coming. Mindful that she was in what was now a crime scene, Lizzie edged closer to the dead man. She had to be sure she hadn't made a mistake and he was alive.

No mistake. He'd been shot—obviously—in the left temple. He was middle-aged and slightly overweight, dressed in dark chinos and a dark polo shirt, with a gash on his right forearm, as if someone had fingernail-clawed him.

Fiona gasped, "Is he—"

"He's dead, Fiona."

She dropped her wrist from her mouth. She'd stopped shaking, but her face was ashen. Her blue eyes were fixed on the dead man.

Lizzie felt her heart jump. "Fiona, do you know who this is?"

"No—I mean, I don't know his name. We never…" She motioned back toward Beacon Street. "I saw him on the street when I arrived at the Garrison house yesterday morning. He was walking across from the Common. I didn't talk to him."

"Was he alone?"

She nodded. "He said hi to me. He—" She squinted, as if digging deep to remember more. "He had a messenger bag with him. I remember thinking it looked heavy. It…he…"

"You couldn't have known what would happen," Lizzie said quietly.

"He must have had the bomb in the bag. I could have stopped him. If Owen hadn't been warned, he'd have— the bomb would have gone off." Fiona stopped suddenly, focusing on Lizzie. "I wasn't supposed to say that. About the bomb."

"It's okay," Lizzie said. "I already figured it out."

"The man…the Brit…he…"

Fiona broke off, turned and fled, tripping, gagging, back out to the street. Lizzie ran after her, slowing when she saw that Will Davenport had intercepted Fiona. He had an arm wrapped around her waist as she covered her mouth with both hands and cried.

"It's all right." He spoke firmly, but his tone was reassuring. "You're safe."

Fiona took a step back, and Will let her go. "The man who…" She was hyperventilating again. "He had an English accent. I think it was English. He said I…" She gulped in a breath and mumbled, "My dad will be here any second."

Lizzie understood Fiona's fear and tried to reassure her. "This is Will Davenport. He and Simon Cahill are friends."

"I'm sorry I frightened you," Will said gently.

"There's a man dead in the alley," Lizzie told him. She heard sirens. The police would be there soon. "The Brit I ran into in Las Vegas and Eddie O'Shea ran into at his pub is in Boston. He told Fiona to come here. He knew I was headed back from Ireland." Lizzie gave Will a hard look. "Did you tell him?"

"No, Lizzie." He didn't look tired or even rumpled after his long flight, but his expression had taken on a studied control, a certain distance. "I told you this morning. For the past two years, I've believed Myles to be dead."

"Then you haven't been lying to me?"

"I have not."

"Who is he? Who is this Myles?"

"You've just seen for yourself." Will's eyes were flinty. "Myles Fletcher is a killer."

Fiona, listening to every word, cried out in shock but didn't move.

Lizzie glanced back toward the alley. "Yes. I did just see for myself. Are you going after him?"

Fiona gasped and grabbed Will's wrist. "No! You can't! He said—he said not to follow him. He said he's Abigail's only hope." She was close to hysteria. "Please."

"All right, then." Will gently extricated himself from her hold. "I won't go after him."

Lizzie's head was spinning, and she felt ragged from jetlag, adrenaline, fear, being cooped up on a plane for hours with nothing to do but play cards and think. She turned to Will. "Now that Myles Fletcher has surfaced, I imagine you and your MI6 and SAS friends will want to figure out what he's up to."

Will ignored her and addressed Fiona. "How long ago did you see this man?"

"A few minutes. Ten, fifteen. Please, you can't…"

"I'll do as you ask and not go after him. We'll wait here together for your father."

"He called me 'love,'" Fiona whispered.

Will's eyes shut briefly, but Lizzie saw the pain in them. She was touched by his gentleness with Fiona but knew what she had to do. "I haven't witnessed anything." She looked once again down the alley, as if part of her expected the dead man to walk out and say it was all a joke, a bit of makeup and sheer nerve. But she knew it wasn't. "I'm no good to anyone if I'm stuck here explaining myself to the police."

Will didn't respond immediately. Lizzie gave him a moment. Finally he said, "You work for John March."

She skimmed the back of her hand along his jaw, rough with stubble. Sexy. A reminder he wasn't a Prince Charming out of a fairy tale. "Find me," she said, her voice hoarse, then shifted her attention to Fiona. "I have to go. You're safe with Will."

The sirens blared closer now. Lizzie bolted up the side street. Will didn't follow her. She cut down pretty residential Chestnut Street, running past classic Beacon Hill homes with their black iron fences, brass-fitted doors and wreaths of summer flowers. She came to Charles Street at the bottom of Chestnut, and fighting tears of her own, ducked into the Whitcomb. Without saying a word, she headed straight through the lobby past Jeremiah and down a half-dozen steps to the rear exit.

Her cousin reached her before she could get the back door open. With Whit and Harlan Rush as older brothers, Jeremiah had learned to stay cool in a crisis. "Lizzie, what's going on?"

She knew she had to give him the basic facts. She owed him that much. "Fiona and I just found a man shot to death up by the Garrison house. The Brit who was with her earlier told her where to find him."

"What can I do?"

"The police will be here any minute. I have to go, Jeremiah. I can't stay." She raked a hand through her hair as she considered her options. "You can find me a car. I can't take mine—or yours. The police…" She didn't finish.

"Take Martha's. Martha Prescott. She's Mum's new assistant." He unlocked a drawer to a small cupboard, pulled a set of keys from a series of hooks and handed them to

Lizzie without hesitation. "Gray Honda on Mount Vernon. The only free space will be the driver's seat." He smiled through his obvious worry. "Martha's a slob."

Lizzie started to thank him, but he just shoved her out the door into the narrow alley behind the hotel. The Rushes might not get everything right, she thought, but they could be counted on in a pinch.

She ran between parked cars and a Dumpster out to Mount Vernon Street, finding the gray Honda halfway up to Louisburg Square. It had a Beacon Hill resident's sticker in the back windshield, and every available space beyond the driver's seat was loaded with fabric samples, empty soda cans, CDs, paperbacks, magazines, torn envelopes. Martha Prescott, indeed, was a slob, but apparently also incredibly creative and good at her job. Anyone who worked for Henrietta Rush would have to be.

The car had a full tank of gas, and Lizzie was quickly on her way.

As she pulled onto Storrow Drive, her cell phone rang. She checked the screen, recognized her father's Las Vegas number and almost didn't answer. "Don't distract me," she said as cheerfully as she could manage. "I'm in traffic."

"Dublin?"

"Boston. Storrow Drive."

Her father sighed. "I just got off the phone with a Boston detective named Yarborough. A real s.o.b. He's threatening to fly out here. Lizzie, tell me what's going on?"

"It's complicated."

"So? I'm playing solitaire. Clock. Ever play clock? My eyes are bleeding it's so boring. I've got time. Take me through it. Start to finish."

"There is no finish. Not yet."

"All right. Start to where we are now."

"The two Brits. Will Davenport and the one I asked

you about who was in Las Vegas in June—I think they're both from your world."

"What world would that be?"

"Dad, I can't...I have a name for the one we saw in Vegas. Myles Fletcher."

"I'll see what I can do."

She hesitated. "John March is in town."

Her father sighed again. "Terrific. Have you seen him?"

"No. I'm trying to get out of here." She squeezed into the left lane, heading for I-93 North. "Dad, I just found a dead man."

"Damn, Lizzie."

"I think he planted at least one bomb yesterday." Was it only yesterday? "John March's daughter is missing." She slowed in the crush of traffic. "Dad, I can help."

"Lizzie. Oh, Lizzie."

"Norman's obsessed with March. I didn't see it at first. I only saw it in the last days before his arrest."

"Lizzie."

"I know March investigated my mother's death." She fought back more tears. "I haven't wanted to tell you. I understand how painful—"

Her father cut her off. "Does Estabrook know about March and your mother?"

"He never said so, but—yes." She eased onto the interstate, speeding up as she escaped the twists and turns of Storrow Drive. "I'm sure he knows. I didn't realize it at the time, but I think that's why he made the call threatening Simon and Director March in front of me. He assumes I hate March."

"So will the cops. Once they put the pieces together, you'll look as obsessed with John March as this bastard Estabrook is."

"That's why I'm not sticking around."

Silence. "That's not why."

Lizzie pictured her handsome father moving a card to the six o'clock position, a glass of Scotch at his side. He never drank Irish whiskey.

"You're in deep, Lizzie," he said. "You have been all along, haven't you?"

She didn't answer.

Another sigh. "I'm heading to Boston as soon as I finish my game of clock. I'll run interference with the feds. I'll stay as long as you need me."

"You hate Boston."

"Not as much as I hate Ireland."

She managed a smile. "Thanks, Dad."

But he was serious. "You're hoping Estabrook comes after you, aren't you?"

"If I knew what he was going to do, where he was, I'd tell the FBI."

"You're an amateur, Lizzie."

"So is Norman. He'll use Abigail Browning to get what he wants. Then he'll throw her away."

"I could call Detective Yarborough and have him stop you."

"You won't."

"No." Her father didn't speak for a moment. "I have a picture of my mother as a little girl playing dress-up in the drawing room at the hotel in Boston. She has on an Edwardian gown she found in the attic. She's standing on a chair, giggling in front of a mirror. Imagine your grandmother giggling."

"Dad…"

"She did her best, Lizzie. We all did."

"You did great. All of you. I miss Gran, too." Lizzie tried to concentrate on her driving. "If you don't get cold feet and actually do head out here, I should warn you that cousin Jeremiah has put his wild youth behind him. He's a tough taskmaster these days. He'll throw you out if you don't behave."

Her father laughed. "Sounds like a challenge."

She sobbed out loud when she hung up, but her hand was steady as she dialed the number John March had given her over a year ago.

He answered immediately. "Where are you?"

"My name's Lizzie," she said, her voice cracking as she finally told him the truth. "Lizzie Rush. But you know that now, don't you?"

"You misled me. I thought you were a professional."

"Was I even on your list of suspects?"

"No."

"You could have hesitated," she said, making an attempt at levity.

"I want you to come in. Now. Help us." He took in a breath. "Lizzie, let me help you."

"I was with Norman in June when he called Simon and threatened to kill the two of you. I knew he meant it. I knew he would turn violent." The late afternoon sun beat down hard on the busy road. "I should have found a way to stop him. He has your daughter because I didn't."

"You work for a chain of luxury boutique hotels. It's not your job—"

"Don't ever let my aunt and uncle hear you call our hotels a chain."

"Lizzie. Stop. Come in."

She stayed in the middle lane of I-93. "Did you try to stop my mother? She was your informant, too, wasn't she?"

"You're operating on assumptions and suppositions." His tone was more mystified and worried than harsh. "You've done your part. More than you should have. Your efforts helped us arrest major, dangerous drug traffickers."

"Norman's free."

"Not because of you. Stand down."

"Thirty years ago, you let my mother go to her death, didn't you? You regret it now."

"I regretted it then."

"Did you warn her of the danger she was in? Did she ignore you? Did you ignore—" Lizzie took a breath, gripping the steering wheel of her borrowed car. "Never mind."

"You are not to endanger yourself. You are not to interfere with this investigation. I'll sit down with you when this is over and answer every question you have about your mother." March paused, then added, "Every question I can answer."

Lizzie knew what she had to do. She'd figured out on the flight from Dublin, before Fiona and Myles Fletcher and the dead man in the alley—before Will had turned up.

Her eyes were dry now. "I'd love to sit down with you and talk about my mother. Until then, Director March, the rules are the same. Norman can't know I've been helping you. He can't know I'm not on his side. He won't just kill me if he finds out what I've done. He'll kill your daughter."

"This isn't your fight," March said.

"It is now. Keep your guys and the BPD off my case."

"Let me help you, Lizzie. Not the FBI. Me. Abigail's father."

His anguish brought fresh tears to her eyes. "You know that won't work. I'm not doing anything crazy. I'm just going about my business the same way I have for the past year."

"I was your age when your mother died. Looking back, I know now how young I was. How young she was. And your father."

"Then she didn't trip on a wet cobblestone, did she?"

"I've made mistakes. Don't become one of them."

"There's one thing you can do for me. If Norman finds out what I've done and comes after my family—"

"We'll protect them, Lizzie. You have my word."

"You know you don't need to protect my father, don't you?"

March didn't answer.

"He's mad right now as it is. If he sees a bunch of FBI agents coming at him—" Lizzie didn't finish her thought. "He's not retired. He just pretends to be. He's the reason I was able to lead you to believe I was a professional."

"We can protect you, too."

"I hope you find your daughter. More than anything."

"Thank you," he said, his voice strangled now. "Lizzie—"

But she hung up on the director of the FBI, moved to the far right-hand lane and tossed her cell phone out the window. It was an inconvenience, but she didn't want the feds, the BPD or a bunch of spies pinging the number and finding her.

Chapter 21

Will kept his emotions in check, as much for his own sake as Fiona O'Reilly's, but there was no longer any question. Myles Fletcher was alive. Near. In Boston. Perhaps watching the police arrive at the murder scene.

Will had asked Fiona to repeat everything Myles had said to her. "It's important," he'd told her. "I can help in a way the police can't."

Fiona had complied. She was calmer now, hugging her arms to her chest as police cruisers descended on Beacon Street. "Your friend killed the man in the alley, didn't he?"

"Your father and his detectives will determine who is responsible. What you must do now is to be sure you've told me all you know."

She stared down at the pavement as if looking for ants.

Will knew he couldn't let her off the hook. "You've had a terrible scare, Fiona. It's understandable you don't want to do anything to distract investigators and send them in the wrong direction."

"Abigail's missing. Every minute..." She squinted up at him. "Every *second* counts."

On his cab ride into Boston from the airport, Will had called both Simon and Josie for updates, but there was still no sign of Abigail Browning, Norman Estabrook or his plane. He couldn't give Fiona false comfort. She was the daughter of an experienced detective and would see right through it.

"Good detectives prefer to have as much information as possible," he said. "They want to rely on their own experience and training to decide what's worthwhile and what isn't."

"I know," Fiona said, not combative, just stating the facts. As traumatized as she was, Will could see a similar inner strength he had observed in her cousin, Keira.

"What are you holding back?"

"Abigail…" Fiona curled her fingers into tight fists. "She stopped by the pub at the Whitcomb Hotel the night before last. Morrigan's. My friends and I were performing. We were wrapping up our final set. I could see she was uptight about something. She pulled me aside after we finished and told me it wasn't a good idea for me to be there."

"At the hotel?"

Fiona nodded. "She said she'd explain later but I should just…" The teenager sucked in a breath, fighting her own emotions. "She said I should trust her."

"What did you say to her?"

"Nothing. I didn't argue with her. I ignored her. I thought she didn't want me there because Morrigan's is a bar and I'm under twenty-one and a cop's daughter. When I saw her—" Fiona again stared down at the pavement. "I avoided her yesterday. Before the bomb went off. I was snotty. I didn't want to talk to her. Now…"

"You feel guilty," Will said.

Tears spilled down her cheeks, and she sobbed silently

as two police cruisers screeched to a halt at the alley, followed immediately by an unmarked police car. A red-headed man who had to be Fiona's father leaped out and trotted straight for her.

"Dad," Fiona whispered, using both hands now to wipe her tears.

A stiff, serious younger man got out from behind the wheel, joined uniformed officers and headed into the alley.

Bob O'Reilly was apoplectic when he reached his daughter. "I thought you played the damn harp so you wouldn't get yourself mixed up in a murder investigation." He sighed, his blue eyes—the same shade as Fiona's, as Keira's—filled with fear and guilt. "Fi... hell. You okay?"

She brushed her tears with the back of her wrist and nodded.

O'Reilly turned to Will. "Lord Davenport, I presume."

"Yes, Lieutenant. I'm sorry we're meeting under such difficult circumstances."

"Yeah, so am I. Simon's on his way." O'Reilly shifted back to his daughter. "Tell me what happened."

Fiona repeated her story. Will listened for additional details but heard nothing that made him doubt it was Myles who'd sat across from a nineteen-year-old musician and told her how to find a man he knew to be dead, presumably whom he'd killed himself. Possibly he was in fact Abigail Browning's only hope, but that didn't mean he was on her side.

Will let the questions come at him. Why was Myles Fletcher involved with Norman Estabrook? Had the man Will had once trusted and considered a friend become a cutthroat mercenary? Was Myles now on no one's side but his own?

Had he never been on anyone's side but his own?

When Fiona finished, Bob O'Reilly had the look of the veteran detective he was. "Where's Lizzie Rush now?"

"She left." Fiona gave Will a sideways glance before turning back to her father. "She stayed cool. The whole time, Dad. She tried to keep me from seeing…the man."

"She a friend of yours?"

"I only…no."

He narrowed his eyes on his daughter. "What were you doing at the Whitcomb Hotel, Fi?"

"My ensemble performs there. I didn't tell you—" A touch of combativeness sparked in her blue eyes. "I knew you wouldn't approve."

"I don't," her father said bluntly. He nodded to the unmarked car. "Go sit in the air-conditioning. Get off your feet."

"Dad—"

"Go on, kid." He touched a thumb to a stray tear on her cheek. "I'll be right here. I'm not going anywhere."

"That man…the one who was killed…"

"We'll figure out what happened to him. Go." O'Reilly struggled for a smile. "See if you can find some harp music on the radio."

Will noticed her reluctance as she headed for the unmarked car, but he decided it had more to do with her desire not to miss anything than to remain with her father.

O'Reilly took a pack of gum from his pocket and tapped out a piece. He unwrapped it, balled up the paper in one hand and shoved it into his pocket with the rest of the pack. A ritual, Will realized.

The detective chewed the gum as he studied Will. "You know this guy, our killer Brit?"

"I didn't see him, Lieutenant O'Reilly."

"That's not what I asked."

Will said nothing. He wasn't in a position to explain

his history with Myles Fletcher to this American detective. At the same time, Will didn't want to do anything that would impede the investigation into the murder in the alley and any connection the dead man or Myles had to Abigail Browning's disappearance.

"Here's the thing," O'Reilly said. "After thirty years as a cop, I often know when someone's lying or not telling me everything—unless it's one of my daughters. Want me to ask again?"

Will shook his head. "There's no need. Your daughter described a man I thought I knew."

"But now that he's put a bullet in some guy's brain, you're thinking maybe you didn't know him after all. His name?"

Will looked back at the car where Fiona sat alone in the back seat, the door still open. "Myles Fletcher."

"Who is he?"

"I told you—"

"No, you didn't. What's he do for a living? Is he a British noble? Does he go fishing a lot in Scotland? Does he know Simon Cahill?" O'Reilly worked hard on his gum. "I can rattle off a dozen other questions if you want or you can just tell me."

Will thought of Lizzie going into the alley on her own and finding a man shot to death by someone he should have dealt with himself two years ago.

He knew now what he had to do. "My assistant, Josie Goodwin, can help you." He kept his tone professional, without emotion. "Simon knows how to reach her. She'll be more precise and thorough than I can be."

"She in London?"

Will met the detective's eye. "Ireland. With your niece."

"Great," O'Reilly said sarcastically. "Just great. Did this Fletcher character send that thug after Keira?"

"I don't know."

"Another nonanswer. Does Fletcher know Abigail Browning, John March or Simon Cahill?"

"Lieutenant…"

"Norman Estabrook?"

"If you'll allow me, Lieutenant O'Reilly, I suggest you speak with Director March."

"All right. I'll do that." The detective's tone was cool, suspicious—and careful. As if he knew he didn't want to go too far and end up having his hands tied. "What do you know about the black-haired woman who helped my niece in the wilds of Ireland last night?"

He waited, but Will didn't fill the silence. He had anticipated that Boston law enforcement would have Lizzie's description by now. Undoubtedly, she had, too.

"I talked to Eddie O'Shea," O'Reilly continued. "He described her. American. Small, fast, black hair, green eyes. Knows how to fight—she took on an armed killer. The Irish cops are trying to find out who she is, where she went."

"Again—"

"Talk to March. Talk to anyone but you." O'Reilly pointed a thick finger at Will. "Eddie says you were there, and you let this woman go."

"Your niece is safe, Lieutenant, thanks to her."

"And a big black dog and no doubt fairies, too. I'm glad for that."

Fiona slipped out of the car and stood by the open door.

Her father didn't stop. "I saw Scoop Wisdom in the hospital. He's all cut up. A mess. He managed to describe a suspicious woman he saw on our street the day before our house blew up. Small, green eyes, black hair. Even with all the pain dope in him, Scoop remembered her. Who is she?"

Will maintained a steady gaze on the senior law enforcement officer. "Again, you'll want to speak with Director March."

Before O'Reilly could respond, Fiona approached him. "Dad." She remained calm, but she was very pale. "Dad…I…"

Her father stared at her. "You know?"

"The woman—she—"

The detective groaned half to himself. "Ah, hell. Are we talking about Lizzie Rush? The woman who just helped you—"

"Her family owns the hotel on Charles Street."

"The Whitcomb. Yeah, I know. Why—"

"I told you, my ensemble plays there. We've been playing there all summer. The Rushes are nice people."

"The Rushes are…" O'Reilly glared at his daughter. "How well do you know them?"

Fiona looked miserable. "I didn't meet Lizzie until a few weeks ago. Her cousin Jeremiah has been helping me plan our trip to Ireland. He said Lizzie had worked there. Dad, I know she's not responsible for the bombs. She can't be."

"What did you two talk about besides Ireland?"

"I told her everything. I told her about Keira and Simon, and you and Aunt Eileen and the serial killer, and Ireland—the story about the stone angel. I told her that Keira and Simon borrowed a boat from Simon's friend, a British lord, and…Dad, I'm sorry."

O'Reilly looked as if he couldn't decide between hitting something or grabbing his daughter and running. "Relax, Fi." His tone softened as he unwrapped another piece of gum. "You didn't tell Lizzie Rush anything she couldn't have found out on her own."

"I feel like a blabber."

"Lizzie's easy to talk to," Will said quietly. More police cars descended on the scene. Yellow tape was going up. Onlookers were arriving. He knew he had to make his stand now. "I can find her, Detective, but not if I'm caught up with your people."

Bob O'Reilly was clearly a man under monumental strain, but he remained focused. "This Fletcher character?"

"I can find him, as well."

"Does Simon go way back with him?"

"No, he doesn't. Lieutenant, you know if I don't leave now, I won't be able to without a lot of time and fuss."

The detective put the fresh piece of gum in his mouth. "Go."

The Whitcomb was smaller, narrower and more traditionally furnished than the Rush hotel in Dublin, but equally high-end and individual. A man who bore a striking resemblance to Justin Rush walked into the lobby from a side door. This would be Jeremiah, Will remembered. The third-born of the four Rush brothers and Lizzie's cousin.

"Lord Davenport, right?" Jeremiah nodded to a door behind him. "Through there. Down the steps. Out back."

"Thank you," Will said.

He followed Jeremiah's instructions and found himself in an alley with broken pavement, parked cars and Simon Cahill standing in front of a large Dumpster. Unlike his fellow FBI agents who'd begun to arrive farther up Beacon Street as Will had left, Simon wore jeans and a polo shirt.

Will descended the steps. "I wondered if you might find your way here. Has Lizzie—"

"She took off before I got here. Abigail's partner called me. Tom Yarborough. You'll meet him—he'll see to it."

"He's the detective who was with Lieutenant O'Reilly just now?"

Simon gave a curt nod. "He said you let Lizzie go."

"I did," Will admitted.

"Yarborough's ready to take her, you and me into custody. Her father, too."

"Is the tension getting to him?"

"Not a chance. He's just that way." Simon's expression was more that of an FBI agent than a friend as he eyed Will. "Myles Fletcher is alive?"

"Apparently so. He killed that man in the alley and arranged for Fiona O'Reilly to find him. I've been trying to think how he could have become involved with Estabrook."

"He could have figured out you and I were friends, discovered I was working for Estabrook and watched and waited for his chance."

"His chance for what? Money? Action? To get back at us, perhaps? Me for damaging his relationship with his friends in Afghanistan. You for saving my life."

"I could believe money and action," Simon said. "Not revenge. The Myles Fletcher you described to me is too pragmatic to indulge in revenge."

Will felt the humid heat of the afternoon and smelled asphalt, gasoline fumes and, faintly, garbage. As immaculate as the Whitcomb was, he and Simon were nevertheless in an alley. Will shut his eyes, launching himself back two years. He saw Philip and David fighting for their lives. For his life. For the life of the man who'd betrayed them.

And yet...none of what had happened had ever made sense to him. Will had fought alongside Myles Fletcher. They'd trained together, gone drinking together. They'd tracked enemy fighters together, disrupted ambushes, cleaned out caches of weapons, called in close-air support—whatever their various missions had required.

"Will..."

He opened his eyes, focusing again on Simon. "You're right. Myles is too much a professional to take the risks he did today purely for revenge. He's doing a job."

Simon walked toward the hotel. There were terra cotta pots of red geraniums on each step up to the back door. "The Lizzie Rush I know is elegant, personable, attractive and smart, but she's not anyone I'd remotely imagine taking on a knife-wielding thug." He turned to Will. "Or you. She's under your skin, isn't she?"

He sidestepped the question. "How did you see her role with Estabrook?"

"They were friendly, not in a romantic way. She wasn't involved in his riskier adventures. She'd organize a hike in the Grand Canyon, a whale-watching trip, a kayaking tour of the Maine coast—the normal stuff people want to do."

"And all the while, she was gathering information on Estabrook and his friends and passing it on to John March."

Simon leaned over and straightened one of the flowerpots. "I knew we had an anonymous source. An important one. But Lizzie…" He shook his head. "She never was on my radar."

Will stared at the geraniums. How had he let his life become so complicated? He could see his mother walking in his garden in Scotland, not far from her home village. She'd never imagined herself marrying his father. What had Lizzie thought as a little girl, playing out here in this alley? Had she ever imagined finding a man murdered up the street?

"Lizzie's father is an intelligence officer who taught her his tradecraft," Will said. "She knew how to keep you and Director March from discovering her identity. When did you first meet her?"

"Last summer, here at the Whitcomb. That's when Norman hired me. I was in Boston for a Fast Rescue dinner, and he was a guest at the hotel. He and Lizzie were already friends."

"With your search-and-rescue expertise, you were in the perfect position to go undercover." Will toed a bit of broken asphalt. "As we've seen in the past two days, Lizzie is brazen and resourceful. Does she know March?"

Simon looked uncomfortable.

"This isn't about my own history with Director March," Will said. "I'm trying to ascertain the facts. When did you become aware March had a source?"

"Last summer. We didn't want to endanger whoever it was by getting too close. We both assumed we were dealing with a professional. Of the possibilities—Lizzie Rush wasn't even on the list."

"*Could* she be affiliated with an intelligence agency?"

Simon sighed. "I think she is exactly what she appears to be."

"She's playing with fire," Will said. "But she could also be the one who can lead us to March's daughter."

"I'd trade myself for Abigail in a heartbeat." Simon's guilt was palpable as he continued. "So would her father. She got caught in the middle. This isn't her fight."

"Why kidnap her but try to kill Keira?"

"Norman's making us suffer. That's all I know. We have to find him, Will. His plane didn't evaporate into thin air. Owen Garrison will find it." Simon plucked a dried, brown leaf from a geranium and smiled sadly as he looked at Will. "Scoop's influence."

"Simon...I'm sorry. But you must understand. You are not responsible for Norman Estabrook's actions."

"Could we have this wrong, Will? What if Fletcher is working for the drug cartels and not for Norman?"

"Regardless who is paying him, Myles is working for himself."

Simon crumpled up the dead leaf. "According to Tom Yarborough, the dead man Lizzie and Fiona found had a deep scratch on one arm. We know Abigail got a piece of whoever kidnapped her yesterday. There was blood at the scene. If he was the one who grabbed her and Fletcher killed him—"

"Fiona had seen him. She'd have remembered eventually. It's not the sort of risk Myles would take. He could simply have handled a problem and tried to mislead us at the same time."

"So he shot a man in the head for a reason instead of just because he could?"

"Fair enough, Simon. Nonetheless, I doubt Myles would get in the middle of a scheme for violent revenge, even a well-paying one. If he's working for Estabrook, there's likely another reason." Will regretted he hadn't arrived in Boston in time to deal with Myles himself, but hadn't that been his old friend's plan? Myles had known Lizzie had left Dublin that morning—and undoubtedly knew that Will had, too. He pushed back his fatigue and worry, forcing himself to continue. "Simon, Myles and Estabrook can't discover Lizzie is an FBI informant."

"I know. If they do, she goes onto Norman's hit list right up there with March and me."

Will pictured Lizzie sitting across from him at their lace-covered table in Dublin. He could see the intensity and the light green color of her eyes, the shape of her mouth as she'd tried to put her fight in the stone circle behind her and decide what to do about him. He'd checked on her during the night, her duvet half off, her skirt and T-shirt askew as she'd slept on the sofa.

"Will? I'm losing you again."

He heard the concern in his friend's voice. "I need to

leave now, Simon. I trust you, and I trust Josie. I'll keep an open mind when it comes to everyone else."

"Right, Will," Simon said, skeptical, but he managed a quick smile. "You've always wanted a woman who could put a knife to your throat."

The back door to the hotel opened, and Jeremiah Rush jumped down the half-dozen steps in a single bound. "Two detectives are here to interview the staff and anyone who might have seen the Brit who scared the hell out of Fiona O'Reilly. I thought you'd want to know. My dad's on his way. He's not wild about a killer showing up here."

Simon eyed the younger Rush. "Do you know where your cousin went?"

"Lizzie?" Jeremiah instantly looked uncomfortable.

"That would be the one, yes."

"She's like a sister to my brothers and me. Her father's a great guy, but he was on the road so much…" Jeremiah shoved a hand through his tawny hair and gave a quick laugh, obviously trying to divert the FBI agent in front of him. "We all think he's a spy."

Will almost smiled. "So your brother Justin said this morning in Dublin."

Jeremiah's hand fell to the back of his neck, then his side, as if he was feeling cornered, torn by what he knew and what he feared. "You two…" He motioned first to Will, then to Simon. "Lord Davenport, Special Agent Cahill. How do I know I can trust you?"

"We're not a danger to your cousin," Will said.

"The people you hang out with are."

"What about the people she hangs out with?" Simon asked sharply.

A ferocity came into Jeremiah's eyes, one that Will had seen in his cousin. "I hope Norman Estabrook ends up dead or in a holding cell by nightfall."

Simon didn't react to Jeremiah's emotion. "Your family has resources, contacts. Are you looking for Estabrook yourselves? What about your uncle? What's he up to?"

"Uncle Harlan? I have no idea. We all want to do whatever we can to help." Jeremiah was clearly worried—and angry. "I thought Lizzie had hooked up with a rich eccentric and was having a little fun for herself. Estabrook held a New Year's Eve bash for his friends at our hotel in Las Vegas. Lizzie didn't want me to go, but we were having our own family party and I dropped in on him and his friends."

"I remember," Simon said.

Jeremiah fastened his gaze on the FBI agent. "I should have thrown him off the roof that night. Uncle Harlan would have helped me make it look like an accident."

Simon's brow went up, obviously as uncertain as Will whether Jeremiah Rush was serious. The entire Rush family defied stereotype, and not one of them was to be underestimated.

Will didn't want to come under the scrutiny of the Boston detectives now on-site. They might not be as amenable to letting him go about his business as Bob O'Reilly had been. They could easily conclude the lieutenant had been under duress, considering his daughter had just encountered a killer and a murder victim, and wasn't thinking straight. Even with Simon, an FBI agent, at his side, Will could find himself with a long night of explaining ahead.

He turned again to Jeremiah. "Justin mentioned that Lizzie intends to renovate your family home in Maine. Is she headed there now?"

Jeremiah hesitated, and Simon said quietly, "We're on your cousin's side."

"Maybe so," Jeremiah said, "but that doesn't mean

she won't throw *me* off the roof for telling you. I don't know for sure, but, yes, I think she's gone to Maine. She has her own place there. It's about as big as a butler's pantry, but she loves it." He dipped a hand into a trouser pocket and produced a set of keys. "Take my car." He nodded toward a side street at the end of the alley. "Go that way. You'll avoid the BPD."

Simon didn't argue or intervene as Will took the keys.

Jeremiah looked more worried, even afraid, than he likely would want to admit. "Lizzie's father trained her well. He gave the rest of us some pointers, but she had— I guess you'd call it an aptitude. She has a good sense of her limits. I hope she'll be safe in Maine. I hope this bastard Estabrook doesn't think she'll go along with him just because of her mother. I hope," he added, energized now, "she's not the key to finding him."

Simon plucked another dried geranium leaf and crunched it to bits between two big fingers. "What about her mother, Jeremiah?"

Jeremiah Rush obviously realized he was about to step into a bottomless pit, into dangerous layers of history, family, secrets, powerful men. Will could see Lizzie as she'd sipped brandy in Ireland and questioned the man who'd tried to kill Keira Sullivan. Lizzie had been born into this complicated world. She knew how to navigate it, just as Will knew how to navigate his world.

"From what I understand," Jeremiah said carefully, "Aunt Shauna was a daredevil with a keen sense of justice." He gave Simon a pointed look. "Just like Lizzie."

Simon studied the younger Rush a moment. His eyes were as green as the Irish hills where the woman he loved was being protected. "Walk out to the street with Will and give him directions to Lizzie's place in Maine. I'll see to the detectives." He turned to Will. "Stay in touch."

Without waiting for a response or pressing for more information, Simon ascended the steps back into the hotel. Jeremiah did as requested, and in ten minutes, Will was navigating a sleek, expensive sedan and the impossible Boston traffic as he found his way north to Maine.

And, he hoped, to Lizzie.

Chapter 22

Boston, Massachusetts
7:15 p.m., EDT
August 26

Fiona looked gaunt and stressed but also relieved to be back in her element. Bob watched as she and her friends set up in the bar of the Rush-owned boutique hotel on Charles Street. As far as he could tell, "boutique" meant small and expensive. He'd teased his daughter that he thought it meant a place that sold cute clothes, but she wasn't ready to be teased. Play music, yes. Music had been her escape as well as her passion since she'd first crawled up onto a piano stool as a tot.

Bob had peeled himself away from the crime scene up on Beacon, but it was in good hands. He needed to be here, nursing a glass of water at this same table where a killer had sat across from his daughter. Lucas Jones and Tom Yarborough had questioned Fiona thoroughly. Afterward, Lucas had told Bob, "I should have asked her when she'd last talked to Abigail," and Yarborough had told him, "She should have told us about seeing Abigail," which summed up the differences between the two detectives. Bob had felt their suspicion drift over him like a living thing. Yarborough had even said out loud that he thought Bob was holding back on them.

Which he was. He'd kept most of his chat with Lord Davenport to himself. While not a rule-breaker by nature or conviction, Bob had learned to rely on his instincts when it came to bending the rules to get things done. Right now, they had a mess on their hands, with no trace of Abigail or word—a single crumb of hope—from her kidnappers.

He had to stop himself from picturing her and Owen in their small backyard, teasing Scoop about his garden and compost pile. For seven years, Abigail had focused on her work and finding her husband's killer, living her life, a part of it always on hold. Then last summer, she and Owen fell for each other. They had some things to work out—houses, families, kids, careers—but they were the real thing, good together.

Now this.

Fiona's friends were all as young as she was, nervous about the murder and the fire but determined to play, to be there for her. "Can you guys sing 'Johnny, I Hardly Knew You'?" Bob called to them. "I used to sing that one as a kid."

"Sing it with us, Dad," Fiona said, her cheeks pinker now, even if only from the exertion of setting up.

Fiona had been after him to sing with her band since she'd discovered he had an okay voice. He hadn't hid it from her. He just wasn't that much for singing. He let them get through a few numbers on their own, then got up and sang with them. The upscale crowd seemed to enjoy themselves, like he was authentic or something— the Boston Irish cop singing an Irish tune.

When the band took a break, Fiona eased back toward him. "I'm sorry for all this, Dad."

"I'm putting a detail on you. Deal with it."

She nodded, not meek or acquiescent. Accepting. As if she knew he was making sense.

Relieved, Bob checked out one of the brochures she'd left on the table when she'd made her mad dash up Beacon Street, after her visit from Myles Fletcher. He hoped by their December trip things would be quieter in their lives, back to normal. They'd been magnets for trouble lately. Theresa was right, he thought. When Fiona was six, he'd had more control. His sister had told him he had to let his daughters grow up. Like he had any choice?

He noticed the brochure was of the Rush hotel in Dublin. "My grandmother used to make these little mince pies at Christmas. Melt in your mouth." He smiled at his daughter, probably his first real smile since the bomb had gone off yesterday afternoon. "Maybe they'll serve them at tea in Dublin."

"The Rush hotel there serves a Christmas Eve tea," Fiona said eagerly.

Great, he thought.

"It's within walking distance of Brown Thomas."

"What's that?"

"An upscale department store on Grafton Street."

"You've been memorizing maps of Dublin?"

She blushed. "You only live once, Dad."

He admired her resiliency but knew she had to process the ordeal of the past two days. And it wasn't over. They didn't have Abigail. Scoop was in shreds in the hospital but would be okay. Keira was under police protection in Ireland. March's wife in D.C. Bob's own family here in Boston.

The bad guys were unidentified and at large.

"Have you identified the man who…" Fiona lost the color that had started back in her cheeks.

Bob understood what she was asking. "We're still working on a name."

"I saw the scratch on his arm, Dad. He helped kidnap Abigail, didn't he?" Fiona flinched as if she'd been struck. "Sorry. Lucas and Detective Yarborough said I shouldn't say that out loud."

"It's okay, kid."

"What if he left her tied up somewhere?"

"He didn't work alone. Almost certainly."

"I'm sorry I didn't say anything about seeing her here."

"Abigail didn't say anything, either, Fi. Whatever she was worried about, she probably didn't think it was that big a deal—nothing to make someone set a bomb on her porch."

But had Abigail come here specifically to tell his daughter to back off playing at the hotel?

If so, why?

He had about a million questions whose answers he suspected involved Lizzie Rush. She'd come to Jamaica Plain the afternoon before Abigail's evening visit here to the Whitcomb and Morrigan's. The next day, Lizzie Rush and Keira had called from Ireland about the bomb.

"If the man who was killed helped kidnap Abigail," Fiona said thoughtfully, dropping into a chair opposite Bob, "why did the Brit kill him? If he's a bad guy, too?"

"We can sit here and tick off all the possibilities. They had a spat. The Brit decided the other guy was reckless. The Brit got greedy and wanted the other guy's cut of whatever they're getting paid."

"Or he *didn't* kill him."

"My point is, we don't know. That's why we keep plugging away at the facts and evidence."

"Simon's friend Will must—"

"Do you know 'Whiskey in the Jar?'"

Fiona rolled her eyes in a way—not a bad way—that reminded him of her mother. "Of course, Dad. You've heard me play it a hundred times."

"I've never sung it with you."

But she wasn't giving up. "The Brit—Fletcher—could have killed that man in self-defense, couldn't he?"

"Yes. Whatever happened, Fi, you didn't cause it."

"I'm in the middle of it."

"That's ending now."

For once, she didn't argue. "How's Keira?"

"I only talked to her a few minutes before you called me. She's no happier about being under police protection than you are. She knows it has to be done. Simon has to concentrate on doing his job."

"Scoop…it was hard to see him this morning."

"You were brave to go to the hospital on your own like that. He's doing better. He'll make it." Bob tried to soften his voice, but heart-to-heart talks with his daughter—with anyone—made him squirm. "Fi, Scoop's a good guy. The best. But he's a lot older than you. In another five years, maybe it won't seem like so much, but right now—you should stick with guys closer to your own age. These losers here. The fiddle player. He's not bad, right?"

She made a face. "Dad, Scoop's just a friend."

"Yeah? What about the fiddle player?"

"Him, too. Besides, Scoop's got a thing for Keira."

"You see too much. Play your music."

She returned to her friends on the small stage and picked up her harp. They had a half-dozen different instruments among the three of them and would switch off depending on the number. They all could sing.

Bob walked up to the lobby to Lizzie Rush's cousin Jeremiah at the reception desk. Tom Yarborough and Lucas Jones had already interviewed him and said he was smart, clever and creative. Too creative, Yarborough had said, convinced the kid knew more than he was admitting.

He wasn't lying, just parsing his answers—which Yarborough always took as a challenge.

"Talk to me about Abigail Browning," Bob said to the young Rush.

He scooped a few envelopes to stack. "She was here last week and again two nights ago."

"She? Not they?"

"Correct. She was alone both times."

"Irish music night?"

"Every night is Irish music night, but her first visit was in the afternoon. She had tea."

"Formal tea or like a tea bag hanging out of a cup?"

"Something in between."

"What about your cousin?"

"My cousin?"

Playing dumb. "Lizzie. The one who just found a dead guy up the street."

Jeremiah maintained his composure. "She's often in Boston. Our hotel offices are here."

"Right. So how much has she been in town since June?"

"On and off. Not so much in July. Almost constantly in August. She was working with our concierge services on new excursions. That's her area of expertise. But she spent time on her own."

"Spying on Abigail?"

He paled a little and gave up on his stack of envelopes. "I didn't say that."

"Okay, so back to Abigail. How did you recognize her?"

"Garrisons have stayed here. They book rooms at the hotel for their annual meeting and various functions for the Dorothy Garrison Foundation and Fast Rescue. Abigail's been here for those, but she's also John March's daughter." Jeremiah stopped himself, as if he knew he'd gone too far.

Bob tilted his head back. There was something about the way Jeremiah had said March's name. "You know Director March?"

"Not me. Not personally."

"But you've seen him," Bob said, getting now what Yarborough meant about dealing with Jeremiah Rush. If all the Rushes were like him, Yarborough would go crazy. "When?"

"He comes here once a year. It's a long-standing tradition."

"What, he got married at the Whitcomb or something? He and his wife have their anniversary dinner here every year?"

"No." The kid looked as if he wished he'd kept his mouth shut. "He has a drink at Morrigan's."

"He comes alone?"

"Yes, always."

"When?"

"Late August, so around now."

"Whoa. How long has this been going on?"

Jeremiah glanced at his desk. "I should get back to work. Reporters have been calling—"

"They'll keep calling, don't worry. So, how long?"

"I shouldn't have said anything."

"Well, you did. How long, Mr. Rush?"

The kid licked his lips. "At least thirty years. Since before I was born."

Thirty years ago, March was a BPD detective, and Bob was a twenty-year-old kid in South Boston, the son of a cop who wanted nothing more than to be a homicide detective. "What's this tradition about?"

"I don't know for a fact, but whatever it's about, it's always struck me as a private matter."

"Something to do with Lizzie or her dad?"

Jeremiah rubbed a smudge on his desk.

"You have an idea," Bob said, no intention of backing off.

"An idea," he said, "isn't fact."

"Do you Rushes ever tell the whole story about anything?"

"Fiona's excited about her trip to Ireland," Jeremiah said with a fake smile. "My dad wants to invite her and her party to something special at our hotel there—depending on what she wants to do."

"Shop, listen to music and have high tea. She talk to Lizzie about Ireland?"

"Some. Maybe. I don't know."

"When I was a kid, your pub downstairs was this WASP bastion. When did you decide to convert it to an Irish pub and call it Morrigan's?"

Jeremiah looked as if he wanted to melt into the woodwork. He gave up on the smudge. "It was after Lizzie's mother died. Her name was Morrigan."

"And what happened to her?"

This time, the kid didn't flinch. He seemed to know Bob had him now and he might as well give up the rest. "She tripped on a cobblestone in Dublin."

"Dublin," Bob said.

"It was an accident," Jeremiah Rush said.

Before Bob could drag the rest out of the kid, syllable by syllable if necessary, John March walked into the lobby, surrounded by FBI agents.

His teeth clenched, Bob kept his eyes on the young Rush. "You have a quiet room where Director March and I can talk?"

"Yes. The police watching your daughter—"

"Aren't moving. The rate things are going, people will like having a police presence. Won't hurt business."

"We all just want Fiona and her friends to be safe."

Jeremiah Rush seemed perfectly sincere. He pointed to the stairs that curved up to a balconied second floor. "Please feel free to use the Frost Room."

"Named after a relative or the weather?"

"The poet."

While March stood back, not saying a word, Bob suggested the FBI director's entourage go up and sweep for bombs, bugs, spies, God knew what. He took the half flight of stairs down to Fiona and told her and the officers on her detail where he'd be. He said on the mezzanine level with Director March. He didn't say he'd be prying the truth out of an old friend accustomed to keeping his mouth shut.

He returned to the lobby level, and he and March headed up to the elegant, wood-paneled Frost Room. Most of its furnishings looked as if they'd been carted up from the old bar. Musty books on shelves, dark oil paintings of dour men, pewter Paul Revere could have made. Somehow, the place managed not to be stuffy. But Bob didn't want to try to figure out the Rushes and their approach to hotel decorating.

He turned to his old friend, standing over by a coat of arms. "Ever think you'd be a knight in shining armor?"

March shook his head. "No."

"Me, neither," Bob sighed. "You haven't been straight with me, John."

"I've told you what I know."

"Nah. That's never the case with you. You've told me what you thought was relevant. You haven't asked too much about Will Davenport. Our Brit. You know him."

It wasn't a question, but March said, "I know that he and Simon are friends, but Davenport and I have never met."

A careful answer. "He's a lord. Son of a British noble—a *marquess* or something. Sounds like it should be a woman, doesn't it?"

March gave him the barest flicker of a smile, his dark eyes racked with emotional pain. "Bob, whatever I can do to find Abigail—whatever you think I can tell you—just say it."

"We're both on edge," Bob said with some sympathy. "Can Davenport find Abigail?"

"He'll do what he can to help. For her sake, and for Simon's."

"Not for yours," Bob said.

The FBI director kept his gaze steady. "No. I suspect he believes I withheld—personally withheld—information that ended in tragedy for his men."

"What do you believe about him?"

"The same."

"The other Brit?"

"I don't know who he is."

"Cagey answer, John. The fine print reads: you don't know but you have an idea."

"My speculation won't help you."

March abandoned the armor and walked over to a wall of books. Several were collections of Robert Frost poetry. Bob noticed that the FBI director's suit was expensive and neatly pressed, but the man inside it seemed to shrink into its folds.

"There are days I wish I'd become a poet," March said, turning away from the shelves. "You, Bob?"

"Nope. I like being a cop and asking tough questions. What do you know about Lizzie Rush?"

"We're putting the entire Rush family under FBI protection."

It was an indirect answer, yet filled with meaning. Bob saw it now. "How long has she been an informant for you?"

"I didn't know it was her until today."

"Because you didn't want to know. How long?"

"A year."

Bob gave a low whistle. "Anonymous?"

"She's good, and she didn't want to be found out. She created a story…persuaded me that pursuing her identity would put her at increased risk. Her help was critical but not asked for."

"Regular?"

"Intermittent. I thought she was a professional."

"Just not one of yours."

"I doubt we'd know about her now if she hadn't interceded with Keira and warned you yesterday."

"Abigail checked into Estabrook's Boston connections. She didn't like his threat against you and Simon." And Simon's relationship with her father had thrown her for a loop, even if she was trying to be big about it. Bob wasn't going there. March knew. "Lizzie Rush isn't here."

"I don't know where she went. She called me after she and your daughter—"

"Did you ask her where she was going, what her plan was?" Bob sighed, knowing the answer. "You people give me a headache. I'm going to find your daughter, John. I want to know why that thug who's now dead up on Beacon Street grabbed her instead of letting her get blown up. If your relationship with the Rush family has anything to do with what's going on, you need to tell me about it."

March ignored him. "Keep me informed."

"Go back to Washington. Stay out of my investigation."

"Get some rest, Bob. Where did you sleep last night?"

"Keira's apartment."

"Have you heard from her?"

"Yeah, sure. A little Irish fairy flew in my window last night and whispered in my ear."

March didn't so much as crack a smile.

Bob pointed a finger at him. "You keep too many secrets."

"Part of the job."

"Not all of them."

Bob kissed Fiona goodbye and left the Whitcomb as Theresa was arriving. She refused even to look at him, but he didn't care. She and the girls—all three daughters— were going back to her house in Lexington and staying there, under police protection, until they all had a better fix on what was going on. The rest didn't matter. Let Theresa blame him.

He helped himself to a handful of smoke-flavored nuts on his way out and went back to the hospital. Alone. No detail. No Yarborough with the suspicious looks.

Scoop still had his morphine clicker, but he seemed more alert.

"Your black-haired woman is named Lizzie Rush," Bob said. "While you were pulling weeds and talking compost, did Abigail mention her?"

Scoop thought a moment. "No."

"Fiona tell you about playing Irish music at the Rush hotel on Charles—the Whitcomb, Morrigan's Bar?"

"Yeah. Never occurred to me it was dangerous."

"No reason it should have. Why didn't I know? I could have gone to hear them play. I'm busy, but I'm not a total jerk. I like to keep track of what my kids are doing. Support them."

Scoop's puffy eyes narrowed. "You okay, Bob?"

"Yeah, sure. I just need to do something about my life. Same old, same old. Nothing to worry about. You just focus on getting better."

But Scoop was tuned in to people, and he said, "Fiona

didn't mean to leave you out. She says she normally doesn't like family in the audience."

"Scoop, forget it. It's okay." Bob felt lousy for letting a guy in stitches, on morphine, see him crack, even a little. "Did Abigail say anything to you about Fiona, Morrigan's, the Rushes?"

"Not a word. Does she know, even? Fiona tells me things she doesn't tell you two."

"No kidding. Yeah, she knows."

"Abigail was onto something and not talking."

Bob grunted. "What else is new?"

"I can tell...Bob. Hell. What's going on?" Scoop shifted position, which seemed to be a major effort. "Let me out of here."

"The doctors'll spring you as soon as you can walk without spilling blood all over the floor. Until then—"

But Scoop had already drifted off. Bob sat there, watching him sleep. He was used to bouncing ideas off Scoop and Abigail, and now he didn't have either one of them.

Before he could get too pathetic, he drove to BPD headquarters in Roxbury. He'd pull himself together and work the investigations, see what his detectives had on Abigail, the bombs, the dead guy. The task force was set up in a conference room, with maps, computers, charts, timelines.

Nobody talked to him. He must have had that look.

He got Tom Yarborough over in a corner next to a table of stale coffee. "Don't start on me," Bob said. "Just listen. I need you to work on Norman Estabrook's Boston connections."

"The Rush family?"

Bob sighed. The guy was always a step ahead. "You've already started?"

"Just a toe in the water. I wonder what'd happen if we

typed Harlan Rush into the system. He's Lizzie Rush's father. He's a reprobate gambler in Las Vegas—except when he's not."

"Think the feds would storm the building if we get too close to him?"

"Maybe not the FBI."

CIA. Terrific. More Washington types meddling in his investigation. "We'd get a visit by humorless spooks with big nasty handcuffs?"

"Cop or no cop, Lieutenant, I don't want to piss off this guy. Harlan Rush is a player. He's still in the game."

Harlan's daughter, Lizzie, was obviously a chip off the old block. "You've talked to him," Bob said.

Yarborough nodded.

"Good work."

"I'm not sure it gets us any closer to Abigail."

Chapter 23

Lizzie took the stairs up to the wraparound deck of her small house built on the rocks near the mouth of the Kennebunk River. The tide was going out, pleasure craft and working boats still making their way to the harbor. She let herself into her house—one main room with very little separation of space—and opened up the windows and doors, the evening breeze pouring in through the screens. She walked out to the deck and shut her eyes, listening to the sounds of the boats and the ocean at dusk.

The rambling house her grandfather Rush had built was two hundred yards up the rockbound shore. After an architect friend had walked through it with her, he'd sent her a book of matches in lieu of a plan for renovations. Lizzie loved Maine, but her father avoided it, just as he did Dublin and, to a lesser extent, Boston. "The water's always too cold," he'd say. But memories haunted him here, too. Nostalgia not just for what had been but what might have been.

Lizzie was ten when she'd first fantasized her father

was a spy and fifteen when she knew he was one. He always deflected her questions without giving a direct answer, even as he taught her how to defend herself, how to spot a tail, shake a tail, do a dead drop—how to *think* in such terms.

Only when she went to Ireland herself was Lizzie certain that her mother hadn't tripped on a cobblestone after all, and the circumstances of her death—his inability to stop it—were why her father had taught her how to jab her fingers into a man's throat. "Don't be bound by dogma," he'd say. "Never mind niceties or rules when you're in a fight for your life. Trust your instincts. Do what you have to do to get out alive."

Lizzie opened her eyes, noticing a cormorant swooping low over the calm water. Her grandmother, famous for her frugality, had spent as much time as she could in Maine during her last years. She liked her crumbling house the way it was, liked the memories it conjured up for her.

"Sitting here by myself, the memories are like a warm, fuzzy blanket," she'd told her only granddaughter. But that was a rare display of sentimentality for Edna Whitcomb Rush, and in the next breath, she'd said, "Tear this place down when I'm gone. It's the location I love."

Lizzie had smiled. "It's magical."

"Ah, you have your mother's romantic soul."

"Do you believe she tripped on a cobblestone, Gran?"

It was a question Lizzie had asked before, but her grandmother only answered it then, at the very end of her long, good life. "I'll ask her when I see her in heaven, Lizzie, but no. No, I never believed your mother simply tripped and fell. But," her grandmother had continued, some of her old starch coming back into her voice, "I do believe that whatever happened to her, justice was rendered. Your father would have seen to that."

"What was she like?"

"She was very much like you, Lizzie."

The sound of a car pulled her out of her thoughts and drew her attention to the gravel driveway down to her left. She walked to the railing and leaned over as a familiar sedan pulled to a stop behind the one she'd borrowed from Martha Prescott.

Jeremiah's car.

Jeremiah who now owed her, Lizzie thought as she watched Will Davenport get out on the driver's side and look at the darkening horizon. She waited, but no one else appeared.

At least he'd come alone.

She remained on the deck, listening to his even footsteps on the stairs. When he came around to her, she put both hands on the back of an old Adirondack chair she'd collected from her grandmother's house farther up the rocks. "You got here even faster than I anticipated."

"Does that surprise you?"

"No. Not even a little." It was true, she realized. "You're more rugged looking up close. I can picture you humping over remote mountains with a heavy pack and a big gun."

He smiled, walking toward her. "I see your imagination and flare for dramatics are at work again."

"Ha. SAS and MI6 equal heavy pack and big gun." She frowned. "Jeremiah told you where to find me? I have blabbermouth cousins."

"Who adore you and whom you adore in return."

"Serves me right for using them to run interference."

But she saw the strain of the past day at the corners of his eyes as he squinted out at the Atlantic, seagulls crying in the distance, out of sight. "Is this your place, or does it belong to your family?"

"It's mine. My great-grandfather Rush was a Maine fisherman. His son did well and married a Whitcomb from Boston, and he came back here and built a big—but not *too* big—house. I own it, too. No one else in the family wanted it after my grandmother died two years ago."

Will turned and leaned against the railing, his back to the ocean, the evening breeze catching the ends of his hair. His eyes were more blue-green now, dark, observant. "Maybe they wanted you to have it."

Lizzie dropped her hands from the chair and stood next to him on the railing, facing the water. "I hadn't thought of it that way. My family—I love them all, Will." She watched a worn lobster boat cruise toward the river harbor. "My parents planned to raise me here. Then my mother died, and my father—well, things changed."

"Things always change."

She glanced sideways at him. "How much do you know about me?"

That slight smile again. "Not nearly enough."

She hadn't expected the spark of sexuality in his eyes, but it was there. And it pleased her even as it unnerved her. "I looked up your family in *Burke's Peerage and Gentry.*"

"You were in London in July," he said.

"Josie's been busy following my trail?"

"Very. I spoke to her on my drive up here."

"I imagine the FBI will want to talk to her."

"I gave them her number."

"Supposedly you were in Scotland fishing when I was in London. I was careful to stay off any spy radar. I met people at a hotel bar where you and Simon often meet for a drink, and I walked past your sister's wedding dress shop. I never saw her—I wouldn't do that." Lizzie shrugged, stood back from the deck railing. "I was just the hotelier on a London holiday."

"I never knew," Will said.

"That was the idea. I didn't get close enough for you to find out."

"You should have."

Lizzie turned and faced him. "Maybe you should go back to Boston and join forces with Simon and the rest of the FBI, do what you can from there to find Myles Fletcher."

"It's Abigail Browning we need to find. Myles isn't important compared to her safety."

"Will…this place is my refuge. I've never…" She paused, tried to smile. "I've had my cousins over for lobster rolls, but otherwise this is where I come to be alone."

"I get your meaning, Lizzie. I'm invading your space."

"'Invading' is too strong. I had ants once. Now, that was an invasion—"

He touched a finger to the corner of her mouth. "I can see you battling ants." He trailed his fingertip across her lower lip. "Are you all right, Lizzie?" he asked softly.

"Sure. Yes." Her heartbeat quickened, but she tried to ignore its meaning. That she was reacting to this man. That she'd lost all objectivity with him. "I'm not the one lying dead in an alley or recovering from shrapnel wounds or—" But she squeezed her eyes shut at sudden images of where Norman could have Abigail Browning, what he could be doing to her. She tried to block them as she opened her eyes. "I don't want him to hurt her."

Will tucked his fingers under her chin and raised it so that she was meeting his eye. "Whatever happens won't be your doing. Guilt gets us nowhere." He lowered his mouth to hers and kissed her softly. "I've been thinking about doing that for some time now."

Lizzie smiled. "Long plane ride across the Atlantic."

"I started wondering what it would be like to kiss you when you pretended not to recognize my name at Eddie O'Shea's pub. When I saw you take on Michael Murphy—" Will kissed her again "—I knew it would be only a matter of time."

"Very bold of you."

This time, their kiss took on an urgency, nothing soft or tentative about it. She responded, putting a hand on his arm to steady herself. She was tired and raw emotionally, and all she wanted to do was to feel his arms around her, his mouth on hers.

"Kissing you is everything I imagined it would be," he said.

"I hope what you imagined was good."

He laughed. "Very good, just not sufficient." His eyes sparked as he stood back from her. "I want more than a kiss."

"Will—"

"Also only a matter of time, wouldn't you say, Lizzie?"

She hoped so. Every nerve ending she had wanted it to be so. But she said lightly, "You are very bold, indeed, Lord Davenport."

"A point to remember."

He turned to face the ocean, and Lizzie shook off the aftereffects of their kiss as best she could and reminded herself who was standing next to her. What did she know about this man and why was he really here? "Maybe being attracted to each other is inevitable after all the adrenaline of the past twenty-four hours. Heightened senses and all that."

Will seemed amused. "I was attracted to you before the adrenaline set in."

Now she felt warm. She looked out at the water.

Lights were coming on at the inns and houses down toward the river.

"Does Estabrook know about this place?" Will asked, back to business.

"Yes."

"You think he'll come here."

"I think he knows *I'll* come here."

"Lizzie, you can't deal with Norman Estabrook on your own any longer. No one would ask that of you."

"What if I told you he kidnapped Abigail because of me? What would you say then?" She narrowed her gaze on him. "What would you ask me to do?"

He didn't hesitate. "The same. You're not a criminal, nor are you a law enforcement officer."

"Did John March tell you to keep an eye on me?"

His expression darkened slightly. "I don't work for March."

"Did the queen tell you? Your friend the prime minister?" Lizzie didn't wait for an answer. "You're after Myles Fletcher."

"I'm here because I want to help you."

She noticed the air was cool, almost chilly, with nightfall. Maine's too-short summer was coming to an end. "Thank you."

Will said nothing.

"I kayaked out here with Norman last summer. If only…"

"It's too easy to lose ourselves in regrets," Will said. "And not helpful."

"Maybe a drug cartel hired your friend Fletcher to deal with Norman—crash his plane, manipulate him, drag him out and shoot him. Whatever. Maybe yesterday and today weren't Norman's doing. If that's the case, we're clueless about who really does have Abigail."

Lizzie watched seagulls perch on the tumble of barnacle-covered rocks below the tideline. She shook off any doubt. "No. It's Norman."

"You've become accustomed to keeping secrets. Not telling anyone what you know. Not trusting anyone." Will eased his arms around her, locking his eyes with hers. "You're not alone, Lizzie."

She smiled at him before there was no turning back. "Fat chance of that with the feds, BPD and MI6 after me." She gave him a quick kiss. "Come on. I can at least make you dinner," she said, yanking open a screen door, and he followed her into her little house. He seemed as comfortable there as he probably did in London, Scotland, the home of his father, the marquess, or wherever else he happened to be at a given moment.

He walked over to a wall covered with family photographs she'd framed herself. "How did you get involved with Estabrook in the first place?" he asked, his back to her. "His other friends didn't know he had criminal dealings. Why did you?"

"Curiosity," she said, pulling open the refrigerator and frowning at the sparse contents. "For once I was responsible and tossed everything before I left. I don't even have a pint of wild blueberries to offer you."

"When were you here last?"

"A couple weeks ago. I don't need to be in an office every day. I did a little poking around—my trip to London, for example—but I figured I'd keep a low profile until Norman was tried and convicted. Once I realized he was about to make a deal…" She opened a cupboard, sighing as she glanced back at Will. "I have steel-cut oats, a couple of cans of kidney beans and salsa. Cooking's not exactly my long suit."

He pointed to the top photograph on the wall display and glanced back at her. "Your father?"

"Can you recognize a kindred spy soul?" She shut the cupboard and tried another. "Unopened spices and boxes of cornstarch aren't very helpful, now, are they? How do you suppose I ended up with two boxes of cornstarch?"

"One does," Will said with a smile, leaving the photos and taking a seat on a bar stool.

Lizzie shut that cupboard, too. "For a long time I didn't know who was good, bad, possible law enforcement, or if I was completely off base about Norman. But March stayed in touch. That was a clue. I didn't take crazy risks. I met a half dozen of Norman's drug-cartel friends, at least that I'm aware of...sexy, macho guys who like high living and adventures and are very, very violent. They prey on other people's weaknesses for their own pleasure and profit."

"When did you first run into them?"

"At a resort in Costa Rica. I took their pictures and e-mailed them to the FBI."

"To John March, you mean."

"Yes." She looked at Will and felt a rush of relief that she'd made the admission, even if he already knew and didn't need her confirmation. "For personal reasons. But we've never met. I've only seen him from a distance." It was the truth, if also a dodge. "I understand money, but I'm not in Norman's league. I latched onto bits and pieces of what he was up to."

"Did you tip off March in the first place?"

She shook her head, abandoning her efforts to muster together a dinner for two. "I wondered that myself, but no. He was already onto Norman. Simon took the big risks and got the most damning information against him. I did what I could to point whatever investigation might be going on in the right direction."

"Norman trusted both you and Simon," Will said.

"In different ways, but Norman has an unusual idea of trust. Relationships are entirely on his terms. He's the sun in his universe. Everyone else is a tiny planet that revolves around him. I was an especially tiny planet—but desirable to have around. That was helpful."

"Attractive, elegant, vivacious Lizzie Rush."

She gave a mock bow. "Compliment accepted with gratitude, especially considering you've now seen me in a knife fight and up to my knees in mud and manure."

"An image I shall never forget."

She managed a laugh, but she couldn't sustain it. "Norman's father was a police officer, just a regular guy. From what I've been able to put together, Norman felt inferior to him, vulnerable even as he was embarrassed that his father never rose up through the ranks."

"Going up against John March and the FBI makes him feel important. Why did you stay in, Lizzie? A year's a long time."

"I couldn't unring the bell. Once I knew, I knew. And I was in a position to help. I wasn't with Norman all the time. Not as much as Simon. I provided names, faces, numbers. I was careful. I didn't want March to know it was me. If something went wrong, I knew he'd blame himself."

"You never approached Simon or tried to find out if he was someone you could trust?"

"I couldn't let myself trust anyone."

But Will's changeable eyes narrowed on her, and she felt a surge of heat, as if he could see through her, straight to her secrets, her fears.

"There's more, Lizzie. Isn't there?"

She avoided his eyes as she came around the counter and sat upon a bar stool next to him. "How's Josie

Goodwin? I figure she's MI6, too. Has she provided a complete dossier on me by now?"

"It's not complete."

"Does she know I love the smell of lavender?"

A chilly breeze blew through the little house. Will was very still next to her. "Do you?"

"I never knew why until I went to Ireland for the first time in college. I was on my own—my father would never go with me. I was standing in a lace shop and picked up a sachet filled with dried lavender, and I smiled and cried and laughed. I had an emotional meltdown there in the shop. I knew it was because of my mother. She loved lavender, too."

"Growing up without her must have been difficult," Will said.

"I didn't know any different. I'd watch other girls with their mothers..." Suddenly restless, Lizzie eased off the bar stool. "I love my family. My father's a mystery to us all. My uncle and aunt are kind and hard-working, totally dedicated to the hotels and to my cousins. And to me. But you know all this, don't you, from Josie?"

"Some." Will gave her a near-unreadable smile. "Josie is very thorough and dogged. I, on the other hand, am not."

"I don't know nearly enough about you. London, Scotland, lords and ladies. Made your own money, or at least that's what the U.K. government wants the rest of us to believe."

"Lizzie..."

She'd gone too far, and if he kissed her again, she was lost. "I could see what's in the freezer, or we could walk down to the river and have lobster rolls."

He got up from the bar stool, standing close to her, and tucked a few strands of her hair behind her ears. "I believe I've met my match," he said, a sadness coming into his eyes even as he smiled.

They sat at an outdoor table covered in red-checked vinyl. Tourists at nearby tables in the popular roadside diner glanced at Will as if they suspected he might be someone. Like British nobility, Lizzie thought, amused. "Forget cholesterol and calories," she said, "and order a cup of clam chowder, a lobster roll and wild blueberry pie—warm, with ice cream."

"With a salad?"

"Sure. You can order a salad."

He smiled. They resisted the lobster rolls and ordered clam chowder and salads.

Lizzie pushed back the fatigue from her long two days. "How did you and Simon become friends?"

"He saved my life two years ago."

"Because of Myles Fletcher," she said.

Will leaned back, tapped a finger on a white square of the tablecloth. "You see too much, Lizzie."

"My father taught me to be observant."

"I led a team into a remote area of Afghanistan. We— *I* trusted Myles. He betrayed us. Until yesterday, I had every reason to believe he'd been captured and executed by his terrorist friends."

"Your team," Lizzie said, feeling an overwhelming sense of dread. "What happened to them?"

Will leveled his gaze on her. "They were killed in action."

"What were their names?"

"David Mears and Philip Billings. They were the best men the U.K. has to offer. The best men I've ever known."

Lizzie was aware of a car passing on the street by their table and the smell of scallops as a waiter came out with a tray, but her mind was in Afghanistan, a place she'd never been, with men she'd never met. Finally she said, "I'm sorry."

"I'd have died in their place."

She knew he meant it. "People are loyal to you, aren't they? Josie Goodwin. Your men."

"Not Myles. I led Josie to him." Will spoke without bitterness, without flinching from the truth. "I led David and Philip to their deaths."

"You don't want to trust or be trusted anymore, do you, Will? No one to disappoint or to owe." Lizzie leaned over the table, aware now only of the man across from her. He was emotionally self-contained and mission-oriented, but he was also, in his own way, tortured by the past. "I'd love to see you really laugh one day."

"Lizzie—"

"You need to know what Fletcher's been up to the past two years. And you need to find out what really happened in Afghanistan. The answers you thought you had are looking a little muddy right now. Am I right?"

"I like clarity," he said with a small smile.

A couple at another of the roadside tables laughed loudly, enjoying their late-summer vacation. Lizzie had pulled on a sweatshirt before leaving the house, but she still felt chilly. "Did John March have a role in what happened in Afghanistan?"

Will hesitated ever so slightly. "I suppose since I've told you this much, I might as well…" He sighed and looked away from her a moment. "Simon found me in the cave where I was trapped. I assume he was there because of March. David and Philip were already dead. Myles had already been captured. Simon had only an ax and a rope with him, but you've seen him."

"He's built like a bull. Do he and March know about Myles Fletcher?"

"Yes. Most certainly."

This time, Lizzie noticed a trace of bitterness in his tone. "Fletcher will try to kill you if he gets the chance, won't he?"

"He'll make the chance."

"Because you know he's alive," Lizzie said.

"Because if everything I've believed for the past two years is true, I know what he did." Will looked across the narrow street at a flower shop and a pretty gray-shingled inn. "In a way, I hope if Myles wants me dead it's because he can't tolerate having us know he's alive. Dead, he could still pretend he didn't betray us."

"It would say he still has something of a conscience." Lizzie reached across the table and took his hand briefly. "It would also say he knows you won't rest until you find him. You're handsome and elusive, Lord Davenport, and I do believe I'm falling for you. It's not just adrenaline and jetlag, either."

He smiled. "We'll see."

"Would your family be horrified?"

"Delighted. I've become something of a worry."

Their bowls of chowder arrived, thick, steaming. Lizzie tore open a packet of oyster crackers and dumped them into her soup. "My cousin Whit makes the best chowder of the lot of us. Are your MI6 and SAS comrades after Fletcher? The House of Lords? The prime minister? I hear you're mates."

Will managed to look something between exasperated and amused.

Lizzie shrugged. "Just trying to inject a touch of humor into a humorless situation. Are you a magnet for Fletcher?" She studied him. "You hope so. Do you suspect Norman has ties to some of the same people you ran into in Afghanistan?"

"Anything's possible."

"Ripple effects. Did you look for Fletcher after Simon saved your life?"

"Night and day for weeks."

"I guess he didn't want to be found. He's as dangerous as you say, isn't he?"

Will's expression didn't match their quaint, cheerful surroundings. "Myles can't have been in charge of every aspect of what happened yesterday in Boston and Ireland. Otherwise, the outcome would have been quite different."

"You mean he doesn't make mistakes. At least not that kind. He's a professional."

"You obviously have a sixth sense for…"

"Spies?"

This time, he smiled at her humor. "Eat your soup, Lizzie."

After dinner, they walked up to the rambling house her grandfather had built on the rocks above the Atlantic. There was no sign anyone was there now or had been since her last visit. Some days Lizzie wanted to renovate the house for the mother she'd never known and other days just to tear it down and start from scratch with a new house, fresh memories. Her aunt had asked her if Norman was in her sights and had been openly relieved when Lizzie had said no. Her aunt hadn't known then of his association with violent international criminals. She'd objected to him because of his personality. "He's self-absorbed, Lizzie. You wouldn't make a good trophy. You want a partnership, at the very least. You'd love to have a soulmate, but life doesn't always provide one. You might have to look under a few rocks and kiss a few toads."

Henrietta was as near to a mother as Lizzie had ever known, even more than her grandmother, but neither woman had ever tried to be something she wasn't. Successful, creative, not bound by clocks and routines, Henrietta Rush was a devoted wife and mother of four sons. The daughter of the Whitcomb's head maintenance man, she'd met Bradley Rush when she hand-delivered a list of a hundred things her father thought the hotel was doing wrong. The two of them still lived in the same drafty Victorian north of Boston. Lizzie considered it home as much as anywhere. When she was growing up, her father had maintained an apartment in Boston because it was convenient for him to leave her with his brother and wife when he had to be away for weeks at a time and couldn't take her with him.

When she left for college, he moved to Las Vegas.

"I was supposed to grow up here," Lizzie said, Will close to her in the dark. She could hear the wash of waves down on the rocks. "Then my mother died, and my father—I think that's when he gave up on leaving the CIA or whatever alphabet agency he works for."

"Do you believe your mother died because of his work?"

"I believe I don't have all the facts about her life or her death."

Will stayed close to her as they made their way back to her little house. The tide had shifted and was just starting to come in, bringing with it the cool night breeze and smells of the ocean.

Lizzie was intensely aware that Will would be sleeping close by again tonight. "I'm just enough on Irish time to be exhausted," she said.

"Taking on a killer and finding a man shot to death can't help."

"I didn't think. I just acted."

"You fight well." He nodded to her small living area. "Do you train here?"

"Sometimes. I almost took out a window in July with my kicking."

He stood in front of her, looking at her as if he wanted to push back all her defenses and see into her soul.

Which was just nonsense. She had to stay focused and couldn't indulge in romantic fantasies. But he took her hand into his and she leaned into him, letting herself sink against his chest.

He put his arms around her, and she lifted her head from his chest so that she could see his face. "When you walked into Eddie O'Shea's pub..." She wasn't sure she could explain. "There's something about that village. It's as if I was meant to be there, sitting by a fire reading Irish folktales. When I was in London, I thought you were just another spy. Of course, I didn't actually see you."

He smiled. "You didn't get this close."

"Too dangerous." She eased her hands up his arms, hard under the soft, light fabric of his sweater. "Way too dangerous."

"I don't know if I want to disabuse you of your romantic notions about me."

"You mean that you're as sexy—"

His kiss stopped her midsentence and took her breath away, a mix of tenderness and urgency. Lizzie tightened her grip on him just to keep herself on her feet. The ocean breeze gusted through the screens, hitting her already sensitized skin, and she let her arms go around him. There was nothing soft or easy about him.

"I'm breaking all my rules with you," he whispered.

"You're used to discipline and isolation."

"My father left broken hearts in his wake. I learned at an early age the dangers of romantic entanglements."

"*Entanglements.* Scary word."

He kissed her again, lifting her off her feet, and she gave herself up to the swirl of sensations—ocean, seagulls, wind, wanting—and relished the taste and feel of him, imagined him carrying her to her bedroom, and making love to her for the rest of the night. She knew it wouldn't happen. Not tonight.

Will pulled away, or she did, and they turned toward the water.

Lizzie cleared her throat and adjusted her shirt. "Our focus is rightly on Abigail, Norman, Fletcher and what we can do to help the situation."

Will pivoted around to her, his eyes dark and serious now. "Not *we*, Lizzie."

"You're a British citizen. You shouldn't be sneaking around southern Maine on your own, either."

"Lizzie—"

"I know what you're saying, but right now I'm here, and I'm safe. I hope the FBI and BPD find Abigail and arrest Norman tonight. I'd love to wake up tomorrow morning with nothing more dangerous on my mind than a trip to the lobster pound."

"I'd like that, too, but whatever's happened by morning, you need to leave Myles and Estabrook to real professionals."

"And if I'm in the wrong place at the wrong time as I was with Norman and his friends in the drug cartels? Then what?" She smoothed the back of her hand along his rough jaw and didn't wait for an answer. "You've a job to do. I won't get in your way. But I really am falling for you. Tall, fair, handsome and loyal—and you can walk through an Irish pasture and hardly get a bit of manure on your shoes."

He grabbed her hand and pulled her to him and kissed her, nothing tentative or gentle about him now. He kept her close, smiled as he spoke. "You Rushes don't do anything by half measures, do you?"

This from a man who fought terrorists.

He kissed her on the forehead. "Hiking the Beara Way. One day…" He dropped his arms from her and stood back. "Go to bed, Lizzie. I'll stay out here. I'm not going anywhere, and I have no intention of taking advantage of a woman about to fall asleep on her feet."

"Will…"

"We have time."

"I hope so. You must be tired yourself."

"I slept on my flight. I didn't have a deck of cards to distract me, and I had the comforts of a private jet."

She gave a mock protest. "I was in coach with a toddler kicking the back of my seat, and you—"

He laughed softly. "Next time perhaps you'll think twice before you slip out on me."

Chapter 24

Fiona had left her full-size, classic harp in the corner of the Garrison house first-floor drawing room, in front of Keira's sketch of the Christmas windowbox in Dublin. Bob plucked a string. Fiona had shown him how, but it made a twangy sound, nothing like the rich, full sound she could produce. He'd walked up from Charles Street. The joint task force was meeting at BPD headquarters in a little while. He'd be on his way there soon. They were making progress, but they still didn't have Abigail or her captors.

Yarborough materialized in the foyer door. "Lieutenant?"

Bob resisted biting the guy's head off and turned from the harp. "Yeah, what's up?" Even he could hear the fatigue in his voice.

Yarborough, who'd been glum all night, was almost perky. "We have an ID on the dead guy, a South Boston thug named Walter Bassette. Lucas and a couple precinct detectives are on their way over to his apartment."

Bassette. Bob liked having a name. It was something solid. "Good work, Yarborough."

"I didn't have anything to do with it. I'm just telling you."

Credit where credit was due. He was ambitious, but he was also fair.

"We're checking if Bassette was in Ireland recently, called there, met someone from there. Having a decent lead…" Yarborough shrugged, not getting himself too excited. "It helps."

"The bombs weren't sophisticated, but these bastards had to get the materials from somewhere and put them together somewhere." Bob looked at Keira's sketch of the Dublin windowbox. "Someone had to hire Murphy, the guy in Ireland. If it was Bassette—" He broke off with a sigh and shifted back to Yarborough. "Who has Abigail now? What was Bassette doing in that alley?"

Yarborough rubbed the side of his nose and didn't answer. Bob recognized the tactic for what it was. The younger detective was giving him time.

Bob felt his stomach go south on him. "Bassette knew Fiona saw him. He'd talked to her. He came there to kill her."

"Don't think about it. He's out of the picture, and she's under protection. No one's getting near her." Yarborough walked into the empty room. "Abigail's spent a fair amount of time here this summer. I think she's trying this place on for size to see if it might work for her and Owen. Turn it back into a residence. She comes over and does paperwork while he does his thing. Sometimes Fiona and her friends are here practicing."

"Tom?"

He got a little red. "I don't know. Maybe there's something here we missed."

"I'll check it out," Bob said.

Bob saw past Yarborough's arrogance to his worry, but it wasn't a place either wanted to go. Bob liked being

emotionally repressed and figured Yarborough was a
fellow traveler on that score.

"I'll see you back at headquarters," Yarborough said.

"You getting any sleep?"

"There's time for that." He gave Bob a quick grin. "Us
younger guys can go a few days without sleep."

"Go to hell, Yarborough."

"Do you need a ride? I can stay—"

"Nah. I'm all set. Go."

After Yarborough left, Bob paced, his footsteps
echoing on the hardwood floor. Teams had gone through
Abigail's desk at BPD headquarters, her computer, her
car, the remnants of her apartment. They'd only swept the
Garrison house for bombs. They hadn't searched it.

He walked up the stairs to the second-floor offices of
the Dorothy Garrison Foundation. It focused on gardens
and oceans—the things Owen's sister had loved most.
Bob couldn't imagine losing one of his daughters at any
age, but at fourteen?

He looked for any files or work Abigail might have left
there and, tucked on a bookcase, found a laptop labeled
with her name.

Yarborough wasn't easy, but he had good instincts.
Bob took another flight of stairs up to Keira's apartment.
She and Abigail were just getting to know each other.
Simon had given her and Owen an early wedding present
of one of Keira's paintings, which Abigail loved. Bob
figured Owen didn't care one way or the other, provided
she was happy.

And now they didn't know if she was even alive.

He forced back the thought before it could take hold
and noticed Keira's apartment door was ajar.

Simon stood in the doorway with his Glock in one
hand. "Hey, Bob."

"I'm glad I didn't have to shoot you," Bob said wryly, then sighed. "Too damn much time on a desk. I'm getting stale. Then again, I'm brains not brawn these days. You here alone?"

A twitch of his mouth. "I think so."

Meaning Simon had shaken his detail. "Bet your FBI friends aren't happy about that." Bob stepped past him into the little apartment. "A big target on your back—don't stand too close, okay?"

"I'm not staying."

"Anything from Owen?"

Simon holstered the Glock. "They've expanded the search for Norman's plane. Owen's focused on his mission."

Simon nodded to the laptop under Bob's arm. "What's that all about?"

Bob shrugged. "Probably wedding dress searches."

"Let's have a look."

They pushed aside books on fairies and folklore and a box of art supplies and opened up the laptop on Keira's table. Bob had taken a liking to Simon. His wanderlust niece wouldn't have trouble coping with an extended stay under the Irish guards. She'd have trouble being without him.

Even Bob, with his limited computer skills, had no trouble spotting a desktop file labeled "Rush hotels" on Abigail's laptop.

He clicked on it, and up popped her notes, links and downloaded descriptions of each of the Rushes' fifteen boutique hotels.

Simon's eyes narrowed. "Looks as if Abigail was onto Lizzie Rush."

Bob kept clicking. Nothing was password-protected. He found a copy of an old *Boston Globe* article about the death of Harlan Rush's Irish wife, Shauna Morrigan, in Dublin when their daughter was a baby.

Simon leaned over and scanned the article. "John March flew to Dublin and consulted with Irish investigators about what happened. There's a quote from him about what a tragedy her death was."

"Ireland's a long way to go for an Irish citizen who tripped and fell, even if she was married to a rich Bostonian." Bob clicked on another file and gave a low whistle. It was another *Globe* article. "Simon, look at this."

He was all FBI agent as he read the article over Bob's shoulder about the deaths of Shauna Morrigan's parents and brother in a car accident on their way to identify her body. Apparently they were so distraught, they missed a curve and drove off a cliff.

"Another 'tragedy,'" Simon said under his breath.

Bob knew he had to take the laptop in. "Come with me to BPD headquarters," he told Simon. "We'll open up the files. I know this bastard Estabrook wants you dead, but you're hard to kill. I figure I'm safe with you."

"No," Simon said. "You go on."

Bob saw what Simon had in mind and shook his head. "You shouldn't do this."

"I haven't said what I'm going to do."

"Going solo *will* get you killed, Simon."

But Bob didn't argue with him and instead walked back down the two flights of stairs and out into the summer night. He looked up at the dark sky and thought of Abigail last summer, tearing up the journals she'd kept for the seven long years after her husband's death, burning them in the backyard charcoal grill.

When he arrived at BPD headquarters, Bob avoided everyone and went into his office and pulled up the file on Shauna Morrigan Rush. She'd died in August, two months after Deirdre McCarthy's body had finally washed ashore in Boston. It had been hard times in the city, particularly dark and violent days in South Boston. March's work with the BPD to bring down the mob had helped catapult him to the position he now held.

Where exactly did an Irishwoman married to a wealthy Boston Rush fit into March's rise?

Bob thought of his friend having a drink alone at Morrigan's every August.

He became aware of March in the doorway and looked up from his computer. "So, Johnny," Bob said, settling back in his chair. "It's time you told me all you know about Shauna Morrigan Rush and just how obsessed her daughter is with you."

Simon touched Keira's colored pencils, her paintbrushes, the Irish lace at her windows, allowing them to bring her closer to him.

But Owen called from Montana, breaking the spell. "We found Estabrook's plane. He didn't crash. He landed safely on a private airstrip on an isolated ranch owned by one of his hedge-fund investors."

"Where are you?"

"Standing on the airstrip. No one else is around. Looks as if someone met him and drove him out of here. The FBI's on the way. They can pick up the trail from here." Owen's voice was professional, but he took in a breath. "Estabrook had help, Simon. He had this thing planned. All he had to do was pull the trigger."

"That's the way he does everything. He doesn't tie his shoes in the morning without a plan."

"He could be anywhere by now. He has the money, the connections, apparently the will."

It wasn't exhaustion Simon heard in his friend but barely suppressed fear and anger. "We were mindful of that when we launched the investigation into his activities last summer. I went deep for that reason. Norman wants John and me, Owen. Abigail's his leverage."

"She's been preoccupied the past couple weeks. I thought it was the serial killer case, but I've been out of town a lot lately." He was silent a moment. "That can't continue. It won't continue."

"You and Ab will work that out when you're back together. You two are lifers." Simon wondered if it was Owen or himself he was trying to reassure. "None of us will rest until we find her."

After they hung up, Simon headed outside. The heat had gone out of the air with nightfall. Lucas Jones motioned to him from an unmarked car. Simon hesitated, then went over to the open window on the driver's side.

"Walter Bassette flew into Shannon Airport in Ireland two weeks ago," Lucas said. "Get in, Simon. I know what you're thinking, but taking off on your own right now won't help anyone. You can do more good working with us."

"If that changes, I'm gone."

"If that changes, you can take the keys to my car." Lucas managed a grin. "I made sure it's got a full tank of gas before I came over here."

Everyone was in the big conference room at BPD headquarters when the call came to March's personal cell phone a few minutes before 5:00 a.m.

Simon watched the FBI director—his friend— follow Norman Estabrook's orders and put the call on speakerphone.

"You'll never find her." Norman's voice was smug, but with a hint of nervousness, too, as if he knew he was talking to men and women who were better than he'd ever be. "Not unless I decide to give her back to you."

"Tell us what we can do for you," March said, his voice clear, steady.

"You can listen. Listen to your daughter. Here, Detective. Say hi to your daddy."

There was a pause before another voice came on the line. "This is Abigail Browning—"

"Daddy," Norman shouted in the background. "Say 'Hi, Daddy.'"

As Simon stood across the table from March, listening to the exchange, he figured everyone in the room wanted to jump through the phone and kill Norman Estabrook. He knew he did.

"Hi, Daddy," Abigail said, toneless. "How—"

The sound of a hard slap—Norman hitting her—cut her off.

She sucked in a breath. *"Bastard."*

Norman hit her again.

March's hands tightened into fists. "All right. You've made your point. What can we do for you? Let's talk."

Estabrook laughed. "What can you do for me? You can suffer, Director March. You can suffer and suffer and suffer."

He hit Abigail again, clearly a harder blow, and this time she screamed. "Beg him," Norman ordered. "Beg your daddy to come save you."

Farther down the table, Tom Yarborough got out his jackknife and worked on his nails, the muscles in his jaw visibly tight. Next to him, Lucas Jones had tears in his eyes.

Bob chewed gum. All of the dozen or so men and women in the room remained silent.

On the other end of the connection, Abigail complied with her captor's orders and sobbed and begged her father to come save her.

John March leaned forward to the phone. "I'll be there,

sweetheart," he said. "I won't let you down. I'll come now. Let me trade myself for you—"

"There." Estabrook spoke again, sniffling as he caught his breath. "My hand hurts. I've never hit anyone that hard before. It was exhilarating."

March's eyes stayed focused on the telephone. "Tell us what you want."

"I want Simon Cahill. I want you." Estabrook was smug again, not as winded. "I want your source. I know you have one. Who is it?"

"I have no idea. Whoever it is wanted to remain anonymous."

"Liar. Lies, lies, lies. You tell so many you don't know when to stop. You'll want to hunt me to the ends of the earth by the time I've finished."

"How can we reach you?" March asked.

"I'll reach *you.*"

March glanced at Simon, and he nodded, taking his cue, and spoke into the phone. "Hello, Norman. It's been a while. We should talk. You and me. Face to face."

Estabrook snorted. "I want March alive and suffering, thinking about me every minute of every day, but you, Simon. Nothing's changed. I want you dead. Dead, dead, dead."

He disconnected.

The room was quiet.

March said, "Abigail's alive. We have the call on tape."

"The screams were tactical," Lucas said. "Estabrook hurt her, but she played to it. She wanted him to think he'd gotten to her. Make him back off before he hit her harder, maybe keep his frustration from building to a breaking point."

Yarborough flipped his knife shut. "I heard a seagull in the background. Anyone else? It's not much. Damn seagulls are everywhere."

No one responded.

Simon went out into the hall. March followed. "Lizzie Rush is your source, John," Simon said. "You knew her mother. What the hell's going on? Does Lizzie think you covered up her mother's murder for your own ambition?"

"Did you?" Bob asked, coming out into the hall.

March looked at him. "No."

Bob shrugged. "Sorry, John. I had to—"

"I know you did." March's voice was tortured but controlled. "I don't know what Lizzie's personal feelings are toward me, but I believe she trusts me. We need to trust her."

"And we need to protect her," Simon added.

March gave a grim nod. "Unfortunately, she doesn't make that easy."

"She thinks she's one of us," Bob said.

"From what Will tells me," Simon said, "she has the skills and the instincts of a pro."

"That doesn't make her one." Bob looked from Simon to March before he spoke again. "If Estabrook finds out what she's done, he'll kill her."

There was nothing left to say. Simon remembered he had Lucas Jones's keys in his pocket. Without a word, he walked down the hall and out of the building.

No one stopped him.

Chapter 25

Abigail could hear seagulls. She sank onto the cracked linoleum floor of the basement room where she was now being held. Her head ached, and she could feel blood trickling down her chin from where Norman had hit her on the mouth. Amateur. He had no idea how to hit a person.

She leaned her head against the wall, listening for more seagulls as she tried to stay focused and alert.

Owen...

Two of Estabrook's men had come for her in her stateroom on the yacht and taken her at gunpoint to a fast, rigid inflatable dinghy. She was alone with them in the Zodiac as they sped across choppy waves in the cold mist. She wasn't blindfolded, so she had seen the most beautiful dawn spill across the horizon in shades of pink, purple and red. Fog hovered over the western horizon. She'd sailed the New England coast with Owen and recognized the magnificent summer homes and inns of Kennebunkport, a popular tourist and fishing village in southern Maine. She and Owen had docked there a few weeks ago and wandered its attractive streets hand in hand. They'd had lobster rolls while watching the tide ebb from the mouth of the Kennebunk River.

But even as she was allowing herself the comfort of that memory, her captors had shoved her down into the boat, and she'd vomited—flat-out seasickness, she'd told herself. Not fear or pain.

Thinking about Owen strengthened her, even as she felt tears hot in her eyes. Her face was bloody and swollen, and she was dehydrated. She had no energy left. Still, Estabrook's thugs had threatened to kill just about everyone she knew and cared about if she tried anything. They'd seemed agitated, even nervous, as if they understood they were working for someone whose tolerance for risk might exceed their own and lead them to disaster. They'd tied the Zodiac to an ancient dock in a cove not easily seen from land or sea. Getting on either side of her, they escorted her at gunpoint up a steep trail to an abandoned house built onto the hillside overlooking the ocean.

They brought her down dusty stairs to a walk-out basement and shoved her into a room furnished with an old sofa and a folding card table and chairs. Tall shelves held board games, paperback novels and comics, and the walls were covered with posters of the Hulk, Batman and various other comic-book superheroes.

Kids had hung out here, Abigail thought now as she stayed still, pain pulsing through her. This had to be the Rush family home in Maine. Lizzie Rush owned it. Where was she now? Abigail resisted the urge to speculate and instead assessed her surroundings. The room had small eyebrow windows—she'd never get out that way. She'd have to get out into the hall somehow, where she'd noticed a door that exited onto the side of the house.

She shut her eyes against a flutter of nausea and a stab

of pain. She could hear Bob telling her that one day the constant training they did would come in handy. "You'll be glad you know how to take a hit."

Glad wasn't the word she'd use, but tonight, on the phone with her father, with Norman Estabrook relishing his power over her, she'd acted with reasonable control and deliberation, falling back on her training to help get her through her ordeal. The agony and fear she'd experienced had been real, but she felt no sense of humiliation at having cried for her father. Whatever Estabrook believed about her, she knew what she'd done, and why.

Her father and anyone else listening would understand, as she would have in their place, that she'd been trying both to survive and provide them with as much information as possible about the man they were hunting.

At least now they knew she was alive, and they knew for sure who had her.

Estabrook and Fletcher entered the basement room. Fletcher had stood by while Estabrook hit her. But Abigail didn't think he'd liked it. If nothing else, the violence and the call to her father were reckless and unnecessary in the eyes of a professional. He slouched against the doorjamb, impassive while Estabrook massaged the hand he'd used to hit her. In the dim light, she saw that his knuckles were swollen.

He didn't speak to her right away as he paced in front of her, more agitated than she'd seen him in the long hours of her captivity.

"You can stop pacing, Mr. Estabrook," Fletcher said with a yawn. "Your man Bassette isn't coming back."

Estabrook spun around at him. "How do you know?"

"Because I killed him. It was necessary. He was dangerously incompetent."

"Who the hell do you think you are?"

"Sorry, mate. There was no time to ask your permission."

With a sharp breath, Estabrook splayed the fingers of his bruised hand, then opened and closed them into a fist two times before speaking again. "What about Fiona O'Reilly?" he asked, calmer.

Fletcher shrugged. "She's not a concern now that Bassette's gone."

"The police will know—"

"They'd know, regardless. They had Bassette's blood. He had a criminal record. He might as well have left a bread-crumb trail for them. Your two remaining men now understand the stakes if they get out of line." Fletcher never raised his voice or adjusted his position against the doorjamb. "I got you out of Montana, and I've kept the police away from you thus far, but I can't perform miracles. You have highly motivated law-enforcement personnel all over the world looking for you."

Estabrook nodded with satisfaction. "Good."

Fletcher's gray eyes narrowed slightly. "You must give up this quest for revenge. Cut your losses, Mr. Estabrook. Move on. I'll help you."

"I've never run from a fight."

"Simon Cahill and John March aren't fools. They're out of your reach, at least for the moment."

Estabrook sucked in another sharp breath and took a menacing step toward the Brit. "No one is out of my reach."

"Torment them from a distance if you must," Fletcher said, still impassive, "but it's my professional advice that you leave this place now. Let me get you out of here."

"I don't need your help." Estabrook bent down, peering at Abigail, her back against the wall, her legs stretched out in front of her. "I should have hit you harder."

A half-dozen retorts popped into her head. Being around Bob O'Reilly for eight years had taught her to be quick with remarks, but she knew that in this situation she had to choose her words carefully. "You hit me plenty hard enough."

Estabrook stretched his fingers and stood up straight again.

"It hurts, doesn't it?" Abigail nodded to his swollen hand. "Hitting someone. You don't expect how hard bones are. Scoop almost broke his hand once in a fight."

He ignored her. "Your new friend Keira Sullivan has the luck of the Irish. She escaped her serial killer in June and two nights ago in Ireland she escaped—well, she escaped an idiot, obviously."

"Bassette's work," Fletcher said from the doorway.

"Ah." Abigail tasted blood in her mouth but tried not to react to Estabrook's taunts. "Hired the wrong man in Ireland, did you?"

"Keira's luck will run out in due course," Estabrook said, completely calm now. "I'm patient. I didn't become a successful hedge-fund manager by being impatient. In a way, it's just as well my man failed. Simon was already in Boston."

"You didn't send one incompetent man to kill both him and Keira—"

"No. I didn't."

His smirk, the way he studied her, made Abigail sick to her stomach. "You wanted Simon to find Keira's body and know you'd killed her. Monster."

He smiled knowingly. "Simon was in the room with your father when we called. They're suffering right now. Both of them. That does please me. It's sufficient for the moment."

"You should listen to Fletcher and let me go."

Abigail felt her energy draining out of her, and she focused on a crack in the linoleum, aware of Estabrook watching her, enjoying her suffering.

He examined a Spider-Man poster, torn on the edges, slightly yellowed. "Tell me, Detective, why did your father leave the Boston Police Department after Deirdre McCarthy's murder?"

Estabrook's fascination with her father was unnerving, but she reminded herself it wasn't a surprise. What *was* a surprise was his willingness to risk his freedom and his millions to bloody his hands with revenge. But it definitely was more than that. She thought Fletcher had seen it, too. Her father was a fresh challenge. A new death-defying adventure, and an excuse to commit violence himself.

Abigail kept her voice matter-of-fact. "I don't know that my father's decision to leave the department had anything to do with Deirdre McCarthy's murder."

"He didn't like the blood. The violence of murder." Estabrook moved to another superhero poster and glanced down at her. "The suffering. He wanted to be at a distance."

"It was a career move," Abigail said, taking any drama out of her father's decision. Not that she had any real idea why he'd chosen to leave the police department thirty years ago. They'd never discussed his reasoning. "He earned a law degree and decided to join the FBI. He's not God. He's just a man doing a job."

"Was he just doing his job when Simon Cahill's father was executed?"

Abigail didn't answer. Estabrook was at a Batman poster now. Bob liked to tease Owen, calling him Batman and saying he probably had a Batmobile stowed away at the Fast Rescue headquarters in Austin. She pushed back thoughts of the two of them, how they'd react to her kidnapping, the call she'd been forced to make—her cries of pain and anguish. Bob would be tight-lipped and chew one piece of gum after another as he focused on his job.

Owen would figure out what he could do. It wouldn't matter that he wasn't law enforcement.

Estabrook abandoned the posters and squatted in front of her. He seemed unaffected by the stress of the past two days—the past two months. "Was your father just doing his job when Shauna Morrigan was murdered the same summer that Deirdre McCarthy was kidnapped and tortured?"

Abigail's stomach lurched. "I don't know—"

"Shauna Morrigan was Lizzie Rush's Irish mother."

She tried to look confused. "The Rushes are in the hotel business. I've never met Lizzie, but she's got nothing to do with any of this." But Abigail didn't believe that. She ran the tip of her pinkie along her lower lip, feeling the cracks, the coagulating blood. "She's not in law enforcement. My father, Simon, Bob, Scoop. We're pros. Never mind anyone else. Deal with us."

"Lizzie loves Maine. This is her family's house. It's so simple compared to the luxury hotels they own. They pamper their guests, but not themselves." Estabrook smiled. "She's here, or she will be soon. She'll hope I've come."

"Why?"

"Lizzie knows, at least deep down, that I can help her find peace. She knows I can help her confront her anger through decisive action."

"You want her as your minion," Abigail said tiredly.

"Very good, Detective." Estabrook smiled nastily at her. "You do remember your lessons on evil. There's only one Lucifer. One devil." He turned abruptly to Fletcher. "See to Detective Browning. Then find Lizzie and bring her to me. She has a cottage farther down the rocks. She loves to spend time there alone. With all that's gone on—" He inhaled through his nose. "She'll be there."

Fletcher stood up from the door. "You should listen to me, mate. Vengeance is a temporary high. When it's over, you've nothing to show for it. You're left with an empty hand."

"I don't plan for it to end with this one flurry of activity. I'm looking to a new beginning. A new way of life." Estabrook started for the door, all business now. "Are you any closer to learning who informed on me to the FBI?"

Fletcher shrugged. "What difference does it make now? Because you couldn't resist making that call tonight, the FBI knows you have Detective Browning. They're not going to be diverted, thinking your friends in the drug cartels could be responsible."

"I could have been forced to hit her under duress."

"Perhaps, but it's not what you want. You want John March to know you're responsible for his daughter's predicament. You want him to know you have her and can do as you please with her. And that, mate," Fletcher said as he approached Abigail, "is what will get you killed or sentenced to a long stretch in prison."

Estabrook licked his injured knuckles. "You knew my arrest was imminent when you came to me in Las Vegas, didn't you? You said you'd get me out if I got into trouble. You already knew I couldn't trust Simon and didn't tell me."

Fletcher glanced back at him. "You're right. I didn't tell you. It would have made no difference. I was already too late to warn you properly. The FBI had you nailed."

"You wanted money."

"You didn't have to hire me. You did because you understood that our interests are aligned."

"Something you should keep in mind now," Estabrook said stonily.

Once Estabrook was gone, Fletcher handed Abigail a folded black bandanna. "You're dehydrated. Try to keep some water down."

She took the bandanna and dabbed it to her bloody

face. She studied the pencil markings on the wall, names written next to them:

Whit. Harlan. Lizzie. Jeremiah. Justin.

Children's heights.

"I want children," Abigail whispered. "Do you, Mr. Fletcher?"

He didn't respond as he put a hand down to her.

She let him pull her to her feet, listening for seagulls and picturing herself with Owen on Mount Desert Island, farther up the Maine coast, walking on the rocks pregnant with their first child. Grief welled up inside her. After all this time, what if she didn't live to have babies? What if Owen…

"You'll be reunited with him soon, love. Your man, Owen, is searching for Mr. Estabrook's plane in Montana. He's not one to sit tight." Fletcher winked at her. "He'd be proud of you."

"Have you ever been in love?"

"Me?" He gave her a sexy grin. "Count on it."

As he turned from her, Abigail saw an ache in his gray eyes. She hadn't imagined it or wished it there. Whoever he was, whatever game he was playing, Myles Fletcher had his own secrets and regrets.

And he was more alone in the world than she was.

Chapter 26

Near Kennebunkport, Maine
6:25 a.m., EDT
August 27

Will stood out on Lizzie's deck in the gray of the southern Maine early morning. Fog had overspread the coast and stolen away the expansive view of the water. He had endured an interminable night on her sofa, the doors and windows open to the breeze and the sounds of seabirds, boats, a nearby chattering red squirrel. He'd have enjoyed the atmosphere of the little ocean house more if he'd been in Lizzie's bed.

With her, of course.

She was down by an evergreen, gnarled from its exposure to the ocean winds and salt spray, clinging to the edge of the rocks above the water. She'd slipped outside while he was in the shower. A signal, he'd thought, that she'd slept as fitfully as he had—and that she was as worried about Abigail Browning as he was and hoping she'd made the right decision in coming to Maine. Lizzie was no more patient with feeling useless than he was.

She was an innocent civilian, he reminded himself. A hotelier, even if one who'd made sacrifices and taken dangerous risks to expose a criminal network and bring a wealthy, resourceful man to justice.

Josie Goodwin had texted him from Ireland asking him to call her. Will dialed her now as he watched Lizzie pick up a small rock and fling it into the fog.

"Our friends in the garda would prefer I not call you," Josie said when she picked up. "But I am ignoring their wisdom."

"Where are you?"

"At Aidan O'Shea's farmhouse. It's a delight. Two sheep just wandered up to me among the roses. I had tea with Keira this morning. The guards objected letting me see her at first, but I persuaded them."

Will smiled. "Of course you did. What have you learned?"

"Keira can draw scary pictures as well as beautiful ones, and Michael Murphy had helpers. He's cooperating. He led the guards to an isolated house near the old copper mines. He and two friends planned to take Simon there after he'd discovered Keira's body in the stone circle."

"They were to hold him for Estabrook," Will said.

"Yes. He wanted to witness Simon's grief and then kill him himself, with his own hands."

Will stared into the fog. He could hear a seagull, invisible in the distance. Lizzie had moved to the other side of her tree. "I want this bastard, Josie."

"So do I. We're not alone. The guards, Keira and I have become great friends. But there's more, Will. Before her death, Shauna Morrigan Rush tipped off the Americans to an FBI agent working with the Boston Irish mob...." When Will didn't respond, Josie added, "That would be Lizzie Rush's mother, Will."

"Who tripped on a cobblestone on Temple Bar."

"And whose family died in a tragic car accident when

they rushed to Dublin after hearing the news of her death. The Boston police sent a detective to Ireland to look into Shauna's death."

Will gripped his phone. "John March."

"Indeed," Josie said. "Shortly after he returned from Dublin, he exposed the identity of an FBI agent who had dealings—imagine this—with the Boston Irish mob. The Irish ruled the deaths of Shauna and her family accidents."

"Undoubtedly March didn't tell them all he knew."

"Does he ever tell anyone all he knows?"

It wasn't a question Will was meant to answer. Below him, Lizzie's hair seemed as black as the rocks that ran up and down the immediate coastline. The famous beaches of southern Maine were farther to the north and south. He envisioned exploring tide pools with her in some vague and no doubt unrealizable future.

"Will? Are you there?"

He understood the concern he heard in Josie's voice. He wasn't one for a wandering mind, in part because he was so disciplined about avoiding romantic entanglements, particularly on the job.

But was he, really, on the job right now?

"March attracts tragedy," Will said.

"No one goes through life without facing tragedy, but a man with *his* life is bound to face more than his share. Director March is a complex and honest man," Josie said, unusually thoughtful and introspective. "He's had to make difficult choices, and he has secrets. They come with the work he does, and he's been at it a long time."

"What do you suppose we'll be doing in thirty years, Josie?"

Her bright laugh broke through their somber mood. "I'll be having tea with other toothless old women and telling tales about my days working with a handsome nobleman. They'll think I've gone daft and won't believe a word." She quickly returned to the serious matters at hand. "Will, if Shauna Morrigan was killed because she was an informant for March, then your Lizzie Rush has reason to hate him."

"Estabrook must know. Her past could be the reason he befriended her in the first place. He could have been drawn to the drama of it initially, and as his obsession with March grew—"

"He could want Lizzie as his ally in fighting March," Josie interjected, "or perhaps as a prize of some sort— the motherless child wronged by a powerful and ambitious man. Estabrook's a very twisted human being, Will. It's not easy to get inside his thinking."

"Lizzie knows, or at least suspects, what he's up to," Will said. "That's why she's here. She hopes he'll come to her."

Josie didn't respond at once. "From what I've managed to get out of our Irish friends, Shauna Morrigan was very good. Regardless of how she died. Sometimes, despite our best efforts, things don't work out the way we mean them to."

Will stiffened as he noticed two men emerge from the trees and fog on the path along the edge of the rocks and approach Lizzie.

A dark-haired man touched her arm, and she turned to him.

Will peered through the gloom, recognizing the man's movements, his posture. "Josie, I have to go."

"He's there, isn't he?"

But Will had disconnected.

Lizzie called up to him on the deck. "I'll be back soon."

She went with the two men.

With Myles Fletcher.

They ducked behind the evergreen and disappeared up the path, in the thick fog.

Will bolted for the stairs, but Simon was on the top step, blocking the way. "Hold on, Will," he said, putting up a hand. "Think."

"Simon, it's Myles. I can't let him—"

"We won't let anything happen to Lizzie. You, me, we're here for her."

"You're an FBI agent. You have procedures you need to follow."

"Listen to me, Will. Norman doesn't know Lizzie is March's source. March didn't even know until yesterday. I sure as hell didn't have a clue." Simon came up onto the deck, its wood shiny and wet from the damp air. "She's been playing this game for months."

"Not with Myles she hasn't."

"Norman forced Abigail to talk to her father last night." Simon turned to Will as he stood in front of the railing. "It was bad."

Will understood what his friend was saying and didn't need him to describe the call in detail. "I'm sorry, Simon. I can only imagine how painful that must have been for March—for you." He walked over to the railing. A red squirrel scampered up the tree where only moments ago Lizzie had been throwing rocks into the water. Had she seen the men on the path? Could she have called for his help sooner, run back to the house—kept them from taking her? "I know how Myles thinks. I know his tactics."

"And you want him," Simon said.

"Simon, we must do this my way or Lizzie and Abigail Browning are almost certainly dead."

"What about Fletcher? Is there a chance—"

"Is there a chance we can trust him? It makes no difference. Whether Myles is with us or against us—or only looking after himself—doesn't affect what we must do now."

"All right." Simon gave a grim smile. "Lucky I came armed."

"Simon," Will said, "you don't have to do this."

"Does Lizzie have a weapon?"

Will pictured her lithe, small body in jeans and a sweatshirt down on the rocks. He wished he'd shut her up in the fog with him and left Norman Estabrook, Myles Fletcher and their violence to the Americans.

Simon frowned. "Will…"

"No. No weapon. She has her wits, and her father trained her well. She's managed to keep her secrets for months from you, John March and a brilliant, wealthy risk-taker." Will looked down at the rocks and water. The squirrel chattered, out of sight. A seagull landed on a large boulder and stared up at the deck as if he had answers, knew all the secrets of his coastline. "Lizzie guessed Estabrook would come here."

"Maybe she hoped he would." Simon pulled open a door. "I'll alert SWAT and get them moving."

"On our direction. Not a moment sooner."

"Sure, Will. We'll make sure they get here in time to save our asses or put us in body bags."

Chapter 27

Boston, Massachusetts
7:02 a.m., EDT
August 27

Bob sat across from John March at a table under a window in Morrigan's. It was very early, and the bar was closed, the liquor bottles still put away for the night. Jeremiah Rush, who seemed to be perpetually on duty, hadn't stopped the FBI director—or Bob—from going downstairs. March was alone. He'd shaken his protective detail, told them to go to hell, threatened to shoot them— Bob didn't know what.

None of them had slept. Him, March, Lucas Jones, Tom Yarborough. Who knew where Simon was. Hearing Abigail tortured on the line with her father didn't sit well with any of them.

"It's too early to drink," Bob said. "You should at least have a cup of coffee."

"I just wanted to be alone for a few minutes. Here, where…" March cleared his throat without finishing his thought.

"We're never alone, John. Our ghosts are always with us."

March's eyes showed a fear no man should know. "Lizzie Rush. Abigail…" He sighed heavily and nodded to the empty bar. "It all started here thirty years ago."

Bob didn't know what good drifting into the past would do. "We've made progress in the past few hours. Not much. Some."

"You shouldn't have come here, Bob." March abruptly snapped up to his feet. "Don't follow me," he said, making it an order, and started for the half flight of stairs.

Bob's head throbbed. John March had never made anyone's life easy. It wasn't why he was on the planet. Resisting the temptation to sit there and wait for the bar to open, order Irish whiskey and not move for the rest of the day, Bob forced himself to get to his feet.

If he wasn't breaking federal laws, March had no authority over him.

Bob headed up the stairs after the FBI director. Given what she knew about her mother's death—what any of them knew except March himself—Lizzie Rush had good reason to hate him, at least to be a little or a lot obsessed with him. She was up on the board as a person of interest, potentially in cahoots with Norman Estabrook and guilty as hell.

Except no one really believed that.

Jeremiah Rush was standing behind his desk, directing a middle-aged couple to the Freedom Trail. Without breaking eye contact with them, he gave a subtle nod toward a hall behind him.

Two minutes later, Bob took the hotel's back steps to a narrow alley, one of the countless nooks and crannies he was always surprised to find on Beacon Hill.

March was eyeing a shiny dark blue BMW.

Bob motioned to the expensive car. "Going to steal it, John?"

"I want to trade my life for hers." March didn't meet

Bob's eye, the only indication—other than being there in the first place—that the strain of his daughter's kidnapping had gotten to him. "Let Estabrook torture me instead."

"Come on, will you?" Bob said, nearly knocking a pot of geraniums off the bottom step. "Cut me a break. I lose the FBI director in Boston, and they'll zap my pension for sure."

March's shoulders slumped, but only for a second before he straightened again. Even now, after hearing his kidnapped daughter scream in agony, cry for her daddy, he didn't have a thread or a hair out of place. But anyone who thought he was unaffected would, Bob knew, be making a mistake.

March blew out a breath at the overcast sky. "It was hard enough to shake my detail, but you, O'Reilly. Hell." He looked over at his longtime friend. "Fill me in."

Bob was relieved to have the emotions out of the way. "The dead guy, Bassette, was local. You know that. He hired a couple of guys from Chicago—Estabrook's old stomping grounds. One of them must have sneaked into our yard and planted the bomb on Abigail's porch. Cops. You'd think we'd sew up the place, but only so much you can do. They could have thrown the bomb over the fence and killed Scoop and Fiona outright."

"Bob—"

"You don't need Estabrook to torture you. You're torturing yourself. I know. I've been doing the same thing, blaming myself for Fiona having to sit there with Scoop bleeding all over her. For what she saw yesterday in that alley." Bob bent over and righted the flowerpot. He had no idea why. He sighed. "It gets us nowhere. The blame."

"I'm sorry, Bob. For Fiona. She's a good kid. She—"

"Why are you sorry? What did you do to her?"

The FBI director barely cracked a smile, and Bob

suddenly remembered them standing on a South Boston
street years ago. March, ten years older, handsome, had
been on the move, and Bob, just a kid, had been a cop's
son who didn't want his friend up the street to be dead.
Every night, he'd prayed for Deirdre McCarthy to come
home to her mother. Things hadn't worked out that way,
and now, thirty years later, he could feel that awful, hot,
violent summer reaching out to him and the man a few
yards from him, sucking them back into a time and a
world they both had tried to forget.

Bob felt ragged and out of control, even as he was determined to get through the day. Do his job. Find Abigail.
Arrest her kidnappers.

March looked as if he'd crumble if anyone touched him.

"You know Abigail wants a wedding?" Bob dug out
another pack of gum. "She's not waiting anymore. She's
marrying her rich Garrison. I'll be invited. Who knows
where it'll be."

"Owen's a good man," March said, choking back his
emotion.

"He didn't grow up like we did. None of them did." Bob
worked a piece of gum out of the pack. "Then there's Keira.
Ten to one she and Simon will be getting married. She's
already dragging me on that Christmas trip to Ireland. Hell,
John. These women are going to break my bank."

March had tears now in his dark eyes. "Are you at
peace with your past, Bob?"

Bob grinned at him. "Never."

"I keep hearing her scream."

"I know. We all do, but it's worse for you. Be glad her
mother didn't get that call." Bob peeled off the wrapper
and stuck the gum in his mouth. "Because I'm your
friend, John, I'm going to tell you this. Kathryn wants to
take you to a spa retreat."

"A spa—Bob, what are you talking about?"

He chewed his gum. "She told Abigail on her last trip to Boston. I was up on my porch, and I overheard them talking down by Scoop's garden. I can see you in a bathrobe, drinking herbal tea, waiting for your massage—"

"All right, enough." March sighed up at the sky again. "We're not as young as we used to be."

"So? Who cares? We know what we're doing now. Right?"

"Does anyone ever—"

"You're giving me a headache, John. I figure we have ten minutes, tops, before that prick Yarborough lands on us. You know damn well he's on our trail. He's not going to let us off Beacon Hill."

March managed a weak grin. "Whose job does he get first, yours or mine?"

"He can have mine. I'm moving to Ireland to sing in pubs." Bob saw now what he and March had to do. Maybe March had already seen it, and he'd just been letting the younger police lieutenant come to the same conclusion on his own. Or maybe Bob was taking the lead this time. It didn't matter. "Lizzie Rush's old man taught her well, but let's go find her and her new Brit friend, Lord Davenport. You and me."

The back door to the hotel opened, and a tawny-haired, middle-aged man in wrinkled khakis walked down the steps. Clearly a Rush, he looked at the two men in the alley as if he knew exactly who they were. "Lizzie's her mother's daughter." The newcomer was tanned and leathery, his tone cool, controlled—but he radiated an intensity that told Bob that this man, too, had a loved one in harm's way. "I took the red-eye from Vegas. I hate flying. Fill me in, or do I need to kidnap Boston's chief homicide detective and the director of the FBI?"

Harlan Rush, Lizzie Rush's father, could do it, too. Bob balled up his gum wrapper and shoved it in his pocket as he looked to March. "John?"

March didn't hesitate. "We go."

Harlan dangled a set of keys from his hand. "My nephew said we could borrow his dad's car. It's that one right there. Lucky, huh? You don't need to steal it after all."

"Licensed to carry concealed?" Bob asked him.

Harlan headed past Bob for the BMW. "I'm licensed to carry a cruise missile to shove up Norman Estabrook's flabby butt."

Bob figured, who was he to argue?

He climbed into the leather backseat of Bradley Rush's sedan, Harlan Rush at the wheel, next to him, the former BPD detective who'd investigated his Irish wife's death.

"I hope by the time we get to Maine," Bob said as Rush started the car, "we find out Abigail is safe and sound here in Boston, and we can all have fried clams."

The two men in front made no comment.

"Yeah," Bob said on a breath. "Let's go."

Chapter 28

"I love cormorants," Lizzie said as she ambled along the narrow path above the rocks. "I can watch them endlessly."

Neither of the two men with her responded. Myles Fletcher had stayed next to her, even if it meant he had to veer off the path, into pine needles or onto the rocks. The second man, silent and obviously less fit, walked a few steps ahead of them. Both men were armed with nine-millimeter pistols, Fletcher's holstered at his waist, his partner's in his right hand.

Lizzie hadn't left her house with so much as a butter knife. She'd tried reaching for a fist-size rock, but Fletcher had calmly touched her shoulder and shaken his head, effectively changing her mind.

She nodded to the ocean, calm and gray in the fog. "It's a beautiful spot, isn't it? I know you can't see much today. I used to walk this path with my grandmother." She tried to adopt the breezy style she'd had with Norman—oblivious, personable, as if she had no concerns about being escorted to him by armed guards and wasn't a woman who'd send information anonymously to the FBI. "She'd tell me if she had her way, she'd die out here, watching a cormorant dive for food."

Fletcher stepped over an exposed spruce root. "Did she?"

"No. She died in the hospital."

Fletcher eased back onto the path. His manner was detached, but he was clearly on high alert. "You miss her."

"I do, but it's okay. You'd want someone to miss you if you died, wouldn't you?"

"I don't know that I would, love."

He and his partner must have seen Will on the deck and Simon's arrival. Fletcher, at least, would know he had an SAS officer and FBI agent after him. Lizzie would concentrate on finding Abigail Browning and giving them a chance to act. Her father had lectured on being tentative. "Be bold. Be decisive. Especially if lives are at stake."

She noticed the man ahead of them had picked up his pace. She looked up at Fletcher. "Quite a difference between here and Las Vegas, isn't there?"

He glanced down at her. "Quite."

"What did you do, look up Norman in Las Vegas and offer your services? Did you know he was about to be arrested?"

"Keep up," Fletcher said.

"No problem. Is Norman here or on a boat? He came here last summer in a yacht he'd leased. Gorgeous. I had dinner with him on it, a real step up from my sit-on-top ocean kayak." She tripped on a sharp, exposed rock but righted herself before Fletcher could take her arm. "How much is Norman paying you to create the mayhem of the past couple days?"

"He's a wealthy man."

Lizzie resisted a smart remark and kept to her role. "Norman knew I'd come, and I have. We should hurry."

She gestured back toward her little house. "I gather you and Will go way back."

A glint of humor came into Fletcher's gray eyes. "That's why I'm staying out of his line of fire."

"He's not armed."

Fletcher laughed outright. "He's a man of many talents, our Lord Davenport."

The path curved uphill along the edge of a steep cliff. Seagulls swarmed onto the rocks below, their familiar cries and the rhythmic wash of the tide helping Lizzie to control her breathing. If she hyperventilated, Norman and his men would see through her. She'd walked this route hundreds of times since she was a child. Her grandmother would point out landmarks, plants, birds, the occasional seal, dolphin or whale. Edna Whitcomb Rush hadn't been a demonstrative woman—no hugs and kisses from her—but she'd been loving in her own way.

"Estabrook will leave us to hold off the FBI and whoever else turns up," Fletcher called to his partner. "Are you okay with that, mate?"

The thug paused and shrugged. "I don't plan to stick around for a tactical team to get here, but we do what we have to." He was American, in his early thirties. He gestured at Lizzie with his gun. "I say we kill this one and the detective and clear out. They'll only slow us down."

Lizzie was careful not to react, but now she knew. Abigail Browning was here and she was alive.

Fletcher didn't look as if he cared one way or the other what happened to her or to Lizzie. "Do you suppose Estabrook has an escape route for himself?" he asked his colleague. "One that doesn't include us?"

"He pays me before he leaves. That's it. I don't care what he does after that."

"All right, then," Fletcher said, impassive. "We're on the same wavelength."

The other man increased his lead over them. They veered off the path onto the overgrown yard of the shingled house that the first Harlan Rush, Lizzie's grandfather, had built. He'd died when she was small, but she had a vague memory of his taking her out in a rowboat, staying close to the shore as he told her stories. He'd loved the sea. "Take everything else away from him," her grandmother had said, "and if Harlan could still get to the ocean, he'd be a happy man."

It had mystified her that their older son, his father's namesake, preferred the dry desert of Las Vegas. But there were reasons for that, Lizzie thought.

She angled a look up at Fletcher. "Will believed in you, didn't he?"

The ex-SAS officer didn't meet her eye. "Will believes in honor, duty and country."

"And you don't?"

They continued through tall, wet grass on the soft ground, past a dense row of beach roses, entangled with wild blackberry vines, but he didn't answer.

"I know what I'm doing and why," Lizzie said, falling a few steps behind him. "Do you know the same about yourself?"

"Listen, love." Fletcher waited for her to catch up. He draped an arm over her shoulders and leaned in close to her. He was self-confident, amused. "I'd enjoy a nice chat with you, but not now. All right?"

"Why did you kill that man in Boston?"

His eyes held hers an instant longer than was comfortable. "Necessity."

Lizzie took a breath. "He was about to kill Fiona O'Reilly, wasn't he?"

Fletcher kept his arm around her as they crossed the lawn to stone steps that led up the hill to the front of the house. His partner had gone on ahead. "You don't give up, do you?" He spoke without humor now. "I had no other choice. Whatever side I'm on, that's a fact."

"Norman hired him. He got him working on his hit list without your knowledge."

"Mr. Estabrook is a very independent man, love. As you know."

"You scared the hell out of Fiona."

"All right, then. I scared her. She's agreed to police protection, now, though, hasn't she?" He dropped her arm from Lizzie's shoulders. "How is Lord Davenport these days?"

"Handsome. Those changeable eyes of his." Lizzie went ahead of Fletcher and started up the steps, but he met her pace. "I think he might be my Prince Charming."

Fletcher's mouth twitched. "He'll find you, love." He smiled, enigmatic, a man very much in control. "I think Will's been looking for you his entire life."

Her heart jumped. "You're—"

"If you want to get Abigail Browning and yourself out of here alive, you must do exactly as I say." His gray eyes leveled on her, but he maintained the same detached manner she'd first noticed back at the bar in Las Vegas. "Do you understand?"

"You want me to trust you."

"I don't give a damn if you trust me. I want you to follow my lead."

Lizzie hesitated, imagining this man and Will on a secret mission together. She understood now how Will had trusted Fletcher—how shocking it must have been to believe that trust had been betrayed. How devastating. Right now, standing in the fog above the oncoming tide, she wanted to put her life in Myles Fletcher's hands.

"I'll do as you say," she said, "but if I'm making a mistake and you're not—"

"It won't matter. You and Abigail will be dead." He grinned and winked at her. "You're good, love, but I'm better."

"I came with you because I can help."

His gaze narrowed on her. "I know."

Lizzie felt a coolness in the small of her back as they followed a walkway around to a side entrance. "How long have you known?"

"You're Harlan Rush's daughter."

"So," she said carefully, "since Las Vegas. You tried to warn me."

"And you paid no attention." Fletcher wasn't one to be distracted by the past. He stayed next to her, close, serious. "Estabrook wants the identity of John March's source. I've pointed him in the direction of someone in his financial empire. Right now, he's still completely fascinated with you."

"Because of my mother," Lizzie said half to herself.

"You and Detective Browning mustn't leave with him. Whatever else happens, that can't. Clear?"

Lizzie nodded. "Where's Abigail now?"

"Locked in a room in the basement—"

"Put me down there," she said, then gave him a quick smile. "There isn't a room in this house my cousins and I can't get out of."

"You were an incorrigible child?"

"We're a resourceful family."

His eyes were half-closed. "You are still to take my lead."

"Norman has a backup plan. He always does. I can find out what it is."

"You can get Abigail Browning and hide while I do my job."

"Let Will and Simon help you—"

"Off we go, love." Without waiting for a response, he grabbed her by the elbow and shoved her up the steps. "Mr. Estabrook, get yourself together. We need to leave. Now. Simon Cahill and Will Davenport are here." Fletcher kept his grip on Lizzie as they entered the mudroom. "I have your rich-girl landlady."

Norman appeared in the doorway, rubbing his thumb on the swollen knuckles of his right hand. "Good," he said, pleased, without even glancing at Lizzie. "We make our stand now."

Maintaining his grip on Lizzie's arm, Fletcher shook his head. "They'll have called in a tactical team."

"Then we'll just have to deal with Simon and Davenport before SWAT can get here. I want them both. Special Agent Cahill and his princely friend."

"These men know what they're doing. They won't let us see them, much less get off a shot at them." Fletcher's tone was professional, still somewhat deferential to Norman's authority. "My advice is to leave Miss Rush and Detective Browning and get out of here."

"I know what I'm doing, too," Norman said, petulant. He shifted his attention to Lizzie, finally acknowledging her presence. "It's good to see you, Lizzie. I knew you'd come to Maine. This house…" His gesture seemed to take in the entire property. "The very walls cry out with what might have been if John March hadn't caused your mother's death."

"Where's his daughter now?" Lizzie asked. She wriggled in Fletcher's grasp, and he let her go. "I can't help it, Norman. She had the life I didn't. A father *and* a mother."

"We have her now, Lizzie."

She noticed a flicker of distaste—of *hatred*—in Fletcher's eyes before his detached manner took hold again.

"I want to see her," Lizzie said.

"I'll take Miss Rush downstairs," Fletcher said. "She and Detective Browning can chat about her father while we deal with Cahill and Davenport. No argument, Mr. Estabrook. We do this my way here on out or I walk now."

"All right. Lock Lizzie in with our detective." Norman smiled and brushed his fingertips across her cheek. "Detective Browning needs to know the impact her father's had on your life. Tell her. Make her understand it's his fault she's in this predicament."

"I thought I hid it from you…how much I hate John March."

Norman gave her a supercilious little laugh. "You could never hide anything from me. You're refreshingly transparent. I'll come for you." He tucked a strand of hair behind her ear in a possessive but asexual manner. "You're special to me, Lizzie. You have been right from the start."

"Same here, Norman. You're special to me." She ignored the sudden dryness in her mouth. "You've transformed my life."

Fletcher took her by the arm and led her down the basement stairs. The man who'd helped him collect her in the first place unlocked the door to the old rec room. He waited in the hall while Fletcher brought her inside.

Abigail was sitting on the floor with her back against the wall, her face, especially her mouth and left cheek, swollen and bloody, scabs forming on the deeper cuts. Lizzie stifled a gasp and turned to Fletcher, grabbed his wrist. "Tell Norman he's proved his point," she said in a low voice. "There's nothing unique about killing Abigail now. If he leaves her, he'll have even more power over her father. March will know what Norman could have done, that it was in his power to do more."

"Power through restraint."

"Exactly."

"Will do, love." Fletcher winked at her. "I'm thinking more in terms of putting a bullet in the bloody bastard's head at the first opportunity."

"But you need him," Lizzie said. "Why? If you're MI6—"

"A fiction."

"Colloquial expression. The Secret Intelligence Service isn't a fiction. Neither is the Special Air Service. Even if you're freelancing, you're on a mission. You disappeared in Afghanistan. Are you after some drug lord-terrorist connection?"

His eyes darkened to a hard slate color. "I have to go. A boat's on the way to the old dock here. I need it not to be scared off by shots. I'll try to keep Simon and Will from coming to your rescue too soon. In the meantime, find a nice hiding place." He glanced at Abigail and then winked again at Lizzie. "Be good, love."

At the click of the lock in the door after he left, Abigail let out a low moan of pain and sat up straighter. "I look worse than I feel."

"I hope so."

"You're Lizzie Rush." Abigail struggled to focus, one eye markedly less swollen than the other. "My father looked into your mother's death in Ireland. It was ruled an accident."

"It wasn't," Lizzie said.

Abigail nodded. "No, it wasn't."

Following Fletcher's lead, Lizzie concentrated on the immediate problem, quickly explaining the situation to the detective. "I told Myles I can get us out of here."

"Myles…" Abigail swallowed visibly. "Fletcher. He's an interesting character. There are at least two other men in addition to him and Estabrook. A third—I think he's dead."

"Yes. Fiona O'Reilly and I found him yesterday. It's a long story. Let's focus on getting out of here before Norman pays us a visit. Can you stand?"

She nodded, allowing Lizzie to help her to her feet. "You obviously have something in mind."

Lizzie smiled. "My cousins and I used to pretend we were prisoners on a pirate ship."

"And this room was the ship? There's an exit?"

"Sort of." She pulled the ratty couch away from the wall and pointed to a knee-high door. "It goes under the stairs to the laundry room. My cousins and I would...well, we liked our adventures. You'll have to crawl."

"I can do it. I should have found this myself. The laundry room—there's an exit just outside the door, isn't there?"

"It leads right into my grandmother's hydrangeas."

"If Estabrook or his men catch us—"

"We end up back here playing cards," Lizzie said lightly.

Abigail tried to smile. "My optimism took a hit along with my face." She studied the door a moment. "I'll go first. If I run into problems, get back here and blame me."

Lizzie didn't argue with her and squatted to unlatch the door. "I wonder if the adults in our lives realized the door was here and wanted to encourage a certain amount of creativity and rebellion in my cousins and me." She looked up at Abigail. "I'm not promising we won't happen upon mice, dead or alive."

"I heard mice running in the walls." Abigail got down low and peered into the pitch-dark crawl space. She gave Lizzie a beleaguered smile. "I figured they were better company than the rats upstairs."

She got on all fours and went through the small opening. Lizzie pulled the couch back as close to the wall as she could, but it wasn't enough—Norman and his men would know exactly what had happened the minute they entered the room. She shut the door behind her, anyway, as she ducked into the crawl space. She breathed in dust and in the darkness, thought she really did hear a mouse scurrying. But she moved fast, making her way to another small door, which Abigail had left open.

Lizzie emerged in the laundry room. It was equipped with an old washer and dryer, a freezer and a wall of hooks and shelves. Abigail, panting and ashen, held a pair of large, rusted garden shears. "I'd rather have my Glock. Stay behind me, Lizzie. Let me—" Abigail frowned as Lizzie grabbed her grandmother's old walking stick. "What are you doing?"

Lizzie held the stick at her side, felt its worn, smooth wood as her eyes misted. "My gran...I can see her now, walking in her garden. She was so proud of her delphiniums." She shook off the memories. "I'm pretty good with a *bo*."

"You know martial arts?"

"Harlan Rush arts," Lizzie said with an attempt at a smile.

"We can do some damage with garden shears and a walking stick, but they've got automatics." Even bruised, Abigail looked like the experienced homicide detective she was. "Nothing crazy, okay?"

They eased out into the hall. Lizzie pulled open the door, wincing at every noisy creak it made, and they slipped outside, into the fog, squeezing along the edge of the six-foot hydrangeas that grew on the hillside. She shut the door tightly behind her.

Abigail was clearly done in, fresh blood oozing from a cut on her cheek. Lizzie smelled the hydrangeas in the damp air and fought an urge to hide under their low, thick branches. But she knew what she had to do. "You're hurt, and you've been through hell," she said softly. "Let me do this, Abigail. Norman thinks I'm on his side—"

"No. We stay together."

She touched Abigail's shoulder. "Fletcher needs something from Norman. It's important, and I can get it. If he gets away now, we'll never find him. He'll win. He *will* be your father's nemesis."

"I can't let you—"

"I'll at least buy you all time. I won't take unnecessary risks. Here." Lizzie pointed Abigail to an old wood bench hidden among the hydrangeas. "I knew I didn't have these bushes cut back for a reason. They'll hide you."

Abigail sank onto the bench. "Stay here with me."

"There's no way Fletcher can do this alone. Norman trusts me. If I don't do what I can now—" Lizzie didn't finish. "Make sure Will and Simon know Fletcher's one of the good guys. Another reason for you to stay behind. We don't want a friendly-fire incident."

"No, but—"

Lizzie straightened with her walking stick and smiled. "Don't make me knock you out. I'm trusting you and our fairy prince, Prince Charming and dark lord to come save me."

"Simon, Davenport and Fletcher." Abigail smiled weakly. "Very amusing. You can take my garden shears."

"Take a look around at all the overgrown stuff. Do you think I'm any good with garden shears?"

Lizzie didn't wait for an answer and walked out from the cover of the hydrangeas toward the stone steps. She couldn't see anyone through the fog and continued down the sloping yard. She debated calling out for Norman, but she spotted him by himself next to the wild blackberries and roses above the rocks.

She waved and ran toward him. "Norman! Abigail just almost killed me! She used me as a hostage—I'm sorry. I took off. I didn't know what else to do."

"Where is she now?"

"She's gone upstairs. She's looking for you. She thinks she can take on your men."

"She'll learn otherwise."

"Norman…" Lizzie caught her breath. "This is for real, isn't it?"

His eyes were cold, and beads of sweat glistened on his upper lip. "Very real," he said. "And whether or not you're lying, Lizzie, you're mine now."

Fog enveloped the coastline in its shroud of gray. Abigail shivered as she crept toward the sounds of the ocean, staying in the cover of overgrown shrubs and gnarled, drooping evergreens. She ached and she was sick, but she would do what she could to distract and divert Estabrook and his men—anything to back up Lizzie Rush.

Her teeth chattered now.

Simon materialized through the fog as he came up from the rocks. He lowered his pistol when he saw her. A tall, light-haired man, also armed, came up beside him. Simon's British friend, Will Davenport.

Lizzie's Prince Charming.

Abigail fought back a surge of emotion. "Estabrook has Lizzie Rush."

Simon took in her injuries with a quick scan. "We'll take care of her, Ab."

Her cut, swollen lip cracked painfully as she gave him the barest of smiles. "Ab. Hell, Simon." She focused and described the situation to the two men. "Lizzie's trying to stall Estabrook. She thinks Fletcher needs information from him. He's—I don't know what he's doing. Estabrook has two other men. Hired guns."

Will squinted toward the water, into the gray, then turned to Abigail. "Myles has been alone long enough."

He seemed to struggle a moment. "Lizzie's as stubborn and independent as he is."

Abigail hugged her arms to her chest, the damp air making her ache even more. "I'm sorry I couldn't stop her," she whispered.

"No one's been able to stop her for a year," Simon said.

Will looked at him. "I have to go."

Simon straightened, a federal agent taking charge. "Will—hell. Fletcher's a British agent, isn't he?"

"Now. Yes. I didn't know."

"You two can at least try not to kill anyone else on U.S. soil."

Without comment, Will headed back past the evergreen and down toward the water, disappearing in the fog.

Abigail put a hand out to Simon. "Give me a gun. I'm not going after these bastards with garden shears," she said, tossing them to the ground.

He smiled grimly as he handed her his pistol, retrieving another from his holster.

Abigail felt marginally better having a gun in her hand. "We need to hold off on firing as long as we can. If Norman thinks he's lost…" She knew she didn't need to finish. She glanced toward the water, almost invisible now in the fog. "Simon…can you at least clue me in?"

"Afghanistan," he said.

It was enough. Drugs, terrorism. Whatever the specifics, the Brits were on the case.

So, undoubtedly, was her father.

And Lizzie Rush.

Chapter 29

A fine mist was falling now, collecting on Lizzie's hair and shoulders. She saw a Zodiac tied to the ancient dock her grandmother had meant to have removed. But her husband had built it with their two sons, and it had stayed.

Norman walked behind her with a nine-millimeter pistol pointed at her back. He'd pulled it from under his lightweight jacket. As far as Lizzie knew, none of his exploits over the past year had included guns, but how much did he need to know about shooting? He just had to pull the trigger.

He hadn't taken her walking stick from her. She used it now to navigate a steep, eroded section of the familiar path down to the dock. "Where are we going?" she asked.

"Trust me, Lizzie." When they reached the bottom of the path, he moved in front of her and steadied his gaze on her. "You do trust me, don't you?"

"Sure, Norman, I trust you, which I'd say even if you didn't have a gun in my face. Will you put that thing away?"

He lowered the pistol but didn't holster it. He was breathing rapidly, almost panting as he peered up toward the house, invisible in the gray. "I can't see through this fog."

"Going on a boat probably doesn't make much sense in these conditions."

Irritation sparked in his eyes as he focused back on her. "You're not to worry."

"I can't help it." Lizzie hoped she was striking the right note—not too combative but not too meek, either of which Norman would hate. "Where are your men? The Brit and the other two?"

"They'll meet us here. Again, you're not to worry. I'll deal with them."

Lizzie tried not to show any reaction, but she'd never experienced such cold hatred. It was even worse than what she'd seen in him when he'd called Simon from Montana and threatened to kill him and John March. Norman had clearly nursed his anger and sense of betrayal in the two months since his arrest, holding on to that moment when he'd learned Simon Cahill wasn't a former FBI agent and didn't despise John March.

"What happened?" she asked. "Did Abigail Browning come after you the second you were set free because you dared to threaten her father?"

"*I* came after *her*."

"Oh. I see. You meant what you said when you told Simon you wanted to kill him and her father."

"I always mean what I say."

"You want them to suffer first," Lizzie said.

Norman smiled. "Yes."

Lizzie realized she hadn't needed Fletcher to have told her not to get into a boat with Norman. She leaned on her grandmother's walking stick at her side and tried to keep him talking. "You know I was supposed to be raised here, don't you?"

"Of course. I know everything about you. You don't have to pretend anymore, Lizzie." Mist glistened on his hair and made his pasty skin shine. "It will be ironic, poetic even, for March's daughter to die here."

His eyes were so frigid, his hatred so deep, that Lizzie could only manage a nod as she heard a boat close by in the fog.

Norman's gaze was still on her. "It will be just as poetic for you to die here if you've betrayed me."

"How would I betray you? Have your bed at one of our hotels short-sheeted?"

He almost smiled. "I've always loved your sense of humor. I have had so little to laugh about this summer, but that's about to change."

Lizzie ignored the chill she felt and pointed to his bruised hand. "Did you do that defending yourself against March's daughter? I saw how beat up she looked—"

"Lizzie, Lizzie. She didn't attack *me*. I attacked *her*." He stepped onto the dock. "Everything changed in June when I realized what had been done to me. John March went from being an amusing challenge to figure out—to thwart—to…" He paused, inhaled through his nose. "It's a deadly battle we're in now."

"You didn't just come up with this plan in June," she said, pretending to be impressed—a small planet circling his brighter, smarter-than-everyone sun. "Did a part of you hope March was investigating you?"

"He's a compelling adversary, and I plan for everything."

"Those friends of yours the feds were after…well… It's not for me to say, but why didn't you tell me what you were up to?"

"Reasons of operational security."

"Fletcher came to you in Las Vegas. I saw him—"

"He helped me get out of Montana," Norman said curtly.

Lizzie glanced at the gun in his hand. It was a pricey Sig Sauer. He didn't have his finger on the trigger. "When we became friends, was it because of my personal history with March?"

"You tell me, Lizzie. Was it?"

She felt an involuntary shiver. "My mother…"

"Help me. Be at my side. That's what I want and need from you now. Do you for a moment believe the FBI has everything on me? That I…" He spoke with an intensity that reminded her he had made billions for himself and his investors. He was focused, driven and very intelligent. "My work in hedge funds taught me the value of secrecy and discretion. You want John March to suffer, don't you, Lizzie? For what he did to your mother."

Ignoring how cold she felt, she nodded. "Yes."

"That's good. None of this is personal for me. My motives are more pure—more interesting—than hatred and revenge. I need you to have those simpler emotions. I have a powerful, secretive man obsessed with me, Lizzie. An equal. A man who will know I have killed people he cared about. I refuse to submit to his authority. I'll be out here forever."

The silhouette of a small speedboat materialized in the fog beyond the dock, and he glanced out to the water. "We must hurry."

"I'm not the risk-taker you are, Norman." Lizzie added a note of uncertainty to her voice, as if she needed his strength, cleverness and certainty. "Tell me where we're going. Please."

"A yacht's waiting to take us away from here." He shrugged and added, almost as an afterthought, "I have powerful allies."

"What yacht? I gather you came here by boat. Is this a different—"

"I assume that yacht's compromised. This one is registered to a company of mine that no one knows about.

You're her inspiration." He looked back at Lizzie and raised his free hand to her. "You're my ally. My number-one helper."

Lizzie caught her breath as she realized that Myles Fletcher had to be after the yacht. "I want to help you... but...I'm nervous. This yacht. What's it like? Where—"

"Your mother loved lavender. You told me. Think of her out there waiting for you. *Lavender Lady.*" Norman was gentle with her now, reassuring and yet still smug. "Don't be afraid. We'll win. March. Simon. I'll be an enemy like they've never had."

The speedboat slowed as it approached the dock. Lizzie could see a man at the wheel and another seated in the stern, armed with an assault rifle.

She pretended to be confused. "We're not going in the Zodiac?"

"Don't be afraid, Lizzie," Norman whispered.

"What about your men at the house? The Brit and the other two—"

"They'll deal with Simon and his friend Will Davenport. I told them they'll receive bonuses if Simon finds Abigail dead." Norman wiped his brow with the back of his gun hand, wistful. "I thought I wanted to take her with me, but I'm bored with her. I should have killed her myself so that I could tell her father what it was like to feel her blood dripping down my arms."

"Simon and your three men and you and me..." Managing to ignore the shiver in her back at Norman's words, Lizzie frowned as if she were still trying to understand his plans. "We won't all fit in the boat, will we?"

The change in Norman's expression gave her his answer.

"You're having them killed. The men in the boat will do it."

"I need a fresh team."

If she got into the boat with these men, Lizzie knew, she'd be lost. Will, Simon, Fletcher, March—they'd never find her.

And they'd never find *Lavender Lady*.

The rocks, trees, fog and steep hillside all offered cover and concealment, but only if she could get away from Norman before he and the thugs in the boats figured out she wasn't on their side.

"I'm not going with you," she said.

Her words startled him, and in that split second, Lizzie acted, smashing the walking stick onto his hand with the gun. He dropped the weapon and cried out in pain and shock.

The gun skittered across the dock and into the tide.

Norman lunged for her, but Lizzie leaped out of his path onto the rocks. She knew every tide pool, boulder and stone in the cove.

The man in the back of the boat jumped out onto the dock with his rifle pointed in her direction. She ducked for cover behind a large, square boulder, just as she heard a movement on the hill in the thick fog above her.

Myles Fletcher dropped down from behind a windswept spruce tree and leveled an assault rifle of his own at the man on the dock. "Drop your weapon now."

The man didn't obey and tried to get off a shot, but Fletcher was faster and fired. Norman yelled, a squeal of rage and terror as he tried to get his footing on the wet rocks. Fletcher ignored him. At that moment, billionaire, thrill-seeking Norman Estabrook might as well have been a tiny hermit crab.

In the next instant, Will burst out from the spruce tree and bounded onto the dock, pistol pointed at the second man in the speedboat. "You. Hands in the air."

The man complied and raised both his hands above him.

A three-shot burst rang out farther up on the hill, but

neither Fletcher nor Will seemed concerned that it was anything but friendly fire.

Will addressed Fletcher but kept his eyes—and gun—on the man in the boat. "Do you need him on the boat or off?"

"Off. You're bloody relentless, Lord Will." Fletcher sighed, rifle pointed at Norman, who was still thrashing for balance on the rocks. "I've been trying to stay a step ahead of you for two years."

"Myles. My God." Will stepped onto the dock and spared a half glance toward the rocks. "Lizzie?"

"I'm okay. I think I stepped on a starfish." She climbed over the tumble of rocks to Norman, still thrashing for his balance. "Don't move or one of the Brits will shoot you." She checked him for additional weapons but found none. "You had everything, Norman. Money, adventure. Friends. But they weren't enough. Now you're alone in this world, and it's your own doing."

He hissed at her. "A hotelier. A Rush. You're one of John March's people. You betrayed me. I will kill you one day, Lizzie." He spoke coldly, as if he hadn't lost. "Slowly. With my own hands."

Lizzie stood on a dry boulder. "John March is a good man, and you're exactly what you're afraid you are."

"Not one of the big boys," Abigail said, appearing at the bottom of the steep path.

Norman breathed in with a snarl and started to charge for her, but she leveled a pistol at him. "Don't," she said.

He stopped, debated a fraction of a second and dived for her and her gun.

Simon was right behind her on the path and fired at the same time Abigail did.

If Norman made a sound as he fell, Lizzie didn't hear

it over the echo of the gunfire, the whoosh of the tide moving on and off the rocks behind her.

Abigail collapsed onto her knees and vomited among the rocks. Fletcher stepped off and put an arm around her, helping her to her feet. "Might not just be seasickness, love," he said. "Ever think of that?"

She stared at him. "What?"

He winked. "You'll make a hell of a mum." He walked past Norman's body to Lizzie, no humor in his gray eyes now. "Don't look at him. He's gone. A pity, in a way. He'd rather be off to hell than in prison."

"You're right. He…" Lizzie shivered in the cool, damp air. "I did what I could."

"I know, love. I wouldn't have let him shoot you." Fletcher grinned suddenly. "Not with Lord Davenport on the premises. He's besotted with you."

Down the dock, the man on the boat refused Will's order to disembark and scoffed. "You won't shoot an unarmed man."

"Watch this," Fletcher said, amused, beside Lizzie.

In the next instant, Will leaped onto the boat, nailed the man with the butt of his gun and sent him sprawling into the cold Maine water.

Fletcher smiled at Lizzie. "Now he's off the boat. You're just as handy with your walking stick." His eyes matched the color of the fog as he nodded toward the water. "Estabrook has a yacht waiting for him offshore. It's not the same one he took here from Boston."

"I know," Lizzie said.

Simon took charge of the man in the water, and Will approached his fellow Brit. "Its name?" he asked.

Fletcher looked at him. "I'd kill for its name."

The dripping thug walked down the dock, his hands held high, Simon behind him. He glanced down at the body of his partner. "We were just transportation. We didn't know where we were headed from here."

"And killers," Simon added.

"You've been onto a terrorist plot," Will said to Fletcher.

"For two years. It's a bad one. The name of the yacht gets me closer to stopping it." Fletcher settled his gaze on his friend. "I couldn't prevent what happened in Afghanistan. David and Philip. You. There was nothing I could do except carry on. It was necessary for you to think I was dead. A traitor."

"You latched on to a drug-terrorism connection. It led you to Estabrook."

"I tipped off March. Anonymously, but I think he sensed it was me. He didn't ask."

Abigail glanced at them from the dock. "My father won't ask a question if he doesn't want to know the answer."

Fletcher nodded. "Smart man." He turned back to Lizzie and Will. "Afghanistan wasn't March's fault, either. Or yours, Will. I found out about the attacks in Boston too late to do anything but try to mitigate the damage. I didn't know about the attack in Ireland."

"You were there," Will said.

"I'd contemplated talking to Simon myself, but he wasn't in the village. I came to my senses." Fletcher's gray eyes sparked with amusement. "If I wasn't talking to Special Branch, I wasn't talking to the bloody FBI."

"You had to remain a ghost. Whatever I can do," Will said, "I am at your disposal. You're not alone."

Fletcher grinned. "As if I have a choice."

Lizzie contained her emotions. "You were right. Norman was headed to a yacht. He had it all planned. I was to be his…" She took a breath, not looking at his body. "The boat's name is *Lavender Lady*."

"*Lavender*—"

"My mother loved lavender," Lizzie whispered.

"The man was a manipulative, controlling bastard who relished the thought of being John March's nemesis, with you at his side," Fletcher said. "You've helped this past year more than you know. I promise you. We'll catch the rest of these bloody bastards."

"I'll do what I can—"

"What you can do is keep Lord Will busy and off my tail." He turned to his friend. "Take care of Josie."

"She'll hate the idea," Will said, but his humor didn't reach his eyes. "She's been muttering about killing you for two years even when she thought you were dead. She said we should find your body, dig you up and kill you again."

Fletcher's grin broadened. "That's my girl."

He ran onto the dock, jumped in the speedboat and took off into the fog.

Lizzie began to shake. Will turned to her, easing his arms around her, and they held each other as the last sounds of the boat carrying his friend faded in the distance.

Chapter 30

When Bob saw Lizzie Rush for the first time, standing on a rock with the tide swirling at her feet and Will Davenport not taking his eyes off her, he decided he might as well give up. Things had happened in his city in the past thirty years that he didn't know about and never would, and most of them involved John March.

He, March and Harlan Rush had arrived just as the Maine SWAT guys were sweeping the property for bombs, bodies, thugs and weapons, but Lizzie, Simon, the two Brits and a beat-up Abigail had the situation under control.

All the Maine guys found was a .22 revolver in a sugar canister.

The old lady who'd lived her last years here had been as self-reliant as her offspring.

Paramedics were still trying to talk Abigail into letting them strap her to a stretcher. She'd collapsed in her father's arms when she saw him, but she was back on her feet now, reenergized, ready to argue with anyone or anything.

And puking. Bob could take her fat lip better than the vomit.

He watched Davenport walk up the hill from the water. The fog was burning off, creating a glare. The investigation was just getting started. Two thugs dead and two thugs captured. One dead billionaire.

One missing Brit.

"I used to wonder what kind of people lived in these big old houses on the ocean," Bob said to Davenport as he walked up the hill. "Now I know. You meet Harlan yet? Lizzie's pop?"

"Briefly," the Brit said.

"He's one of you. American, but a spook."

Davenport's hazel eyes settled on Bob. "He says he's a semiretired hotelier."

Bob held up a hand. "Don't start with me." He nodded to the horizon as the sun burned white through the last of the gray. "I gather your Brit friend got away."

"So he did."

"He's one of you, too."

"British, you mean," Davenport said.

Bob knew the drill. They were all supposed to pretend the missing Brit was one of the bad guys.

Myles Fletcher was another damn spy.

"He killed Walter Bassette," Bob said.

"In self-defense, after he discovered Bassette planned to kill your daughter and confronted him." Davenport shrugged as he, too, stared out at the water. "She stopped quarreling about being under police protection, didn't she?"

"Hell of a wake-up call."

"Myles isn't subtle, but he's effective."

Bob saw Davenport's expression change, soften—if that was possible—as he lowered his gaze down to a knot of Maine state troopers and feds. At first, Bob didn't get it. Then he saw Lizzie Rush break off from the law enforcement types and head up the hill in their direction, her black hair shining in the mist-filtered sunlight. She was soaked up to her knees in seawater, but Bob had no doubt she was up to handling a British lord, spy and SAS officer who was falling in love with her.

"If you'll excuse me," Davenport said.

As he started to her, John March and Harlan Rush eased in next to Bob, and none of them spoke for a moment as they watched the two young people embrace.

"You know," Harlan said finally, "when I taught Lizzie how to fight, I wasn't thinking she'd be defending herself against a gun-toting billionaire out here on the damn rocks."

"What were you thinking?" Bob asked him.

His eyes, the shape of his daughter's if not their light green, shone with the mix of pain and happiness that, Bob had decided, was memory. "I was thinking I didn't want to lose her."

"She's as brave and as beautiful as her mother, Harlan," March said.

Rush didn't argue. "She doesn't like secrets."

"Neither does Abigail."

"A different generation."

Bob frowned at the two men. "Who the hell has secrets anymore these days? My kids know everything."

March shrugged and seemed almost to manage a smile. "We all have our wars to fight." Lizzie and Will joined them, and March went on briskly. "We boarded *Lavender Lady* a few minutes ago. We didn't find Fletcher or any sign he'd been there."

Bob spoke up. "He got what he needed and disappeared. A ghost."

Harlan Rush and Davenport—two bona fide spooks— didn't say anything. Neither did March, who, Bob figured, knew when a lizard crawled out from under a rock anywhere in the world.

Lizzie stayed close to her Brit as she addressed John March. "I could have done things differently this past year."

But before March could respond, her father rolled his eyes. "Lizzie. Damn. What did I teach you?"

She smiled at him. "How to block a punch from Cousin Whit."

"After that."

She sighed. "Don't look back with regret."

"Right. Look back to learn, but since you're never doing this again, spying on some lunatic billionaire, there's nothing to learn. So there's no need to look back at all."

But Bob knew she would. They all would. Abigail, terrorized by a man obsessed with her father. Scoop, bloodied. Fiona and Keira, traumatized.

They'd recover. What other choice did they have?

Lizzie turned her pale green eyes to the FBI director. "Norman believed you destroyed the life I could have had."

"Maybe I did," March said.

"Do you think you'd be the FBI director today if you had?"

"Doubtful. Your father would have arranged an accident for me. Payback." But March's rare display of humor didn't take. "Lizzie, your father was prepared to trade himself for you and Abigail. I was, too."

"Two of us for one of you?"

"Two for two."

Harlan Rush's eyes misted. "Whatever it took."

Bob decided he'd had enough and scoffed at Lizzie. "Shin splints. What crap. You should have knocked on our door and talked to Scoop, Abigail and me. Leveled with Scoop when he caught you."

She didn't look the least bit intimidated by him. "I didn't have any information you didn't have. You might have prevented me from going to Ireland. Then what?"

"Keira would have had to rely on her Irish fairies."

"Maybe she did," Lizzie said.

"Don't start with me."

She grinned at him and Bob was pretty sure he saw her Brit kiss the top of her head. Maybe it was just a brush of his lips.

Who the hell knew anymore.

But Bob saw Owen Garrison walking across the yard and said, "Batman arrives."

Owen spotted Abigail sitting on the stretcher down by the dock and broke into a run. No one tried to stop him.

Bob glanced at March and quickly averted his eyes. It wasn't that he didn't want to see the director of the FBI was crying. It was that the man deserved a moment.

Harlan Rush crossed his arms on his chest, looking as at home on the Maine rocks as he probably did at a poker table in Las Vegas. He nodded toward Davenport, still with an arm around Lizzie as they walked back toward the water, and said to Bob, "His grandfather was a good man. I ran into him during the Cold War from time to time in my misspent youth. Funny how things work out. Does our Lord Davenport spend a lot of time fishing in Scotland?"

"Apparently," Bob said.

"That's what his grandfather used to do, too." The old spook sighed. "I don't know if it's occurred to Lizzie, but we Rushes don't have a hotel in London or Scotland."

"You should open one," Bob said. "It'd give her something to do while she and Davenport think up how to get into trouble again."

Chapter 31

Owen took Abigail's hand and led her into a large, spacious apartment in the renovated building on the South Boston waterfront that was to be the new headquarters for Fast Rescue. She stood at the tall windows overlooking the harbor. Jeremiah Rush had set aside rooms for everyone at the Whitcomb on Charles Street, and the E.R. doctor had told her to rest. But she'd wanted to come here.

"There are two apartments here that we can choose from," Owen said, staying close to her, "or we can renovate the house on Beacon Street. I don't care where we live. I just want to be with you."

She leaned against him. "We're lucky. We have each other. We have friends, families…"

Owen seemed to understand what she meant. "Norman Estabrook made his choices, Abigail. So did the men with him."

She thought of Myles Fletcher coming to her on the yacht that first time and had to fight back tears. Was he safe now? Was he safe ever?

"Abigail…"

"I'm not going to feel sorry for myself over what happened. It wasn't good, but…" She smiled at this man she loved. "I'm here with you now, and that's enough. I knew you were there for me. With me. The whole time."

"I'd have traded places with you in a heartbeat."

"Maybe things worked out the way they were meant to." She watched a large yacht sailing out into the harbor. "I was so sick on that damn boat. I tried not to let myself think I might be pregnant. But when Fletcher said it, I knew."

She felt Owen's arm tighten around her, but he didn't speak. The doctor in the E.R. had confirmed that she was pregnant. Four weeks. They'd have a spring baby.

"I loved Chris with all my heart. If he'd lived…" Abigail thought of the man she'd married and lost so long ago. "The memory of him is good. He'll be a part of my life forever."

"I know, babe," Owen said. "I'm glad for that."

She turned to him. "I love you."

"Then let's have a wedding."

"Will Davenport offered us the use of his house in Scotland. Anytime. Owen, I don't want to wait another second, never mind months…even days…"

Owen smiled. "Good, because I told Will to cut the grass. We're coming. I can't wait any longer, either."

She touched his mouth with her fingertips. "My cuts and bruises are superficial. I'll be fine…"

He kissed her on the forehead. "Just being with you is enough." He held her and smiled again. "Bob's going to Ireland with his daughters and Keira for Christmas. Telling him he's invited to a wedding in Scotland—"

"Oh." Abigail's face hurt, but it felt good to laugh. "This'll be fun."

* * *

Will spoke to Josie from the Garrison house on Beacon Hill. Simon was pacing in the near-empty drawing room, periodically pausing to stare at Keira's sketches of the Dublin windowbox and her Celtic stone angel.

"Did he die a clean death this time?" Josie asked.

"He's a phoenix, our Myles."

"Our?"

Silence. She knew now. There was no more doubt.

"I'm still in Ireland," she said, her voice cracking, "but Arabella and I are having tea upon my return to London. Your baby sister is quite worried about you."

"Tell her to get her needle and thread ready."

"You and Lizzie Rush?"

His heart almost stopped, but he said, "Abigail Browning and Owen Garrison are having their wedding at my house in Scotland in a few days."

"Ah. Well, then."

Simon obviously couldn't stand it any longer and took the phone. "Hello, Moneypenny. Any chance you can get me to Ireland? I want to leave in the next ten seconds."

Will smiled. Knowing Josie Goodwin, she had a plane already waiting at the Boston airport for him.

Chapter 32

The doctors had sprung Scoop sooner than they'd expected, and Bob found him at their burned-out triple-decker, out back inspecting his garden. He was bandaged and clearly in pain, but he stood up with a squished tomato. "Bastard firefighters trampled my tomatoes. That was uncalled for."

"They were dragging your sorry butt out from behind the compost bin."

Scoop sighed. "My apartment's got so much smoke and water damage, they're going to have to gut it."

"Whole building."

"You can supervise. Where are you going to live?"

"Keira's apartment for now," Bob said. "The lace curtains have to go. I don't care if it's Irish lace."

"What about her?"

"She has plans."

Scoop was silent a moment. "Simon."

Bob winced inwardly. What a dope he'd been. Fiona had tried to tell him it wasn't her. It was his niece. "Scoop..."

"They're good together."

Scoop wasn't exactly up to it, but nothing would stop him from heading with Bob to Morrigan's Bar at the Whitcomb Hotel on Charles Street. Simon had left for Ireland. Jeremiah Rush and a couple other Rushes were there, including Jeremiah's father, Bradley, and his uncle, Harlan, the spook.

Lizzie showed up late. Nobody knew where her Brit was, or at least no one was saying.

Fiona was pink cheeked and happily playing Irish tunes with three of her musician friends. She saw Scoop and blushed, and Bob's heart broke, but he knew she'd be okay.

John March appeared on the steps for a few seconds before turning around and heading back toward the lobby. Lizzie got up and quietly followed him. Her father stayed put.

Making peace with the past, Bob knew from experience, wasn't the easiest thing to do.

Theresa arrived with Maddie and Jayne. "We got through this one," his ex-wife said and gave Bob's hand a little squeeze. "Thank you."

"I didn't do much."

"You didn't get killed."

"All in a day's work."

They sat at a booth together, and Bob was off his guard for that split second that put him back in the past, and he saw what he could have had if he hadn't been such a jerk. But Theresa and their daughters looked happy, and he figured the least he could do was not to saddle them with his regrets.

At a break, Fiona joined them with more Ireland brochures and printouts. "The Rush hotel in Dublin is now officially on our Christmas itinerary. I made reservations for us to have Christmas Eve tea there. It's expensive."

"What a surprise," Bob said.

"Jeremiah has a brother in Dublin. His name's Justin. He's just twenty-two."

"So long as they serve those little buttery mince pies my grandmother used to make, I'm good. And sing Christmas carols." Bob smiled as Jayne crawled onto his lap. "I like Christmas carols."

Lizzie found John March alone at a quiet table in the Whitcomb's elegant second-floor restaurant. He had a bottle of good Irish whiskey. He poured her a glass as she sat across from him. "I met your mother here before you were born. Before she'd met your father. I was a young cop. She was a pretty Irish girl who happened to know some very bad people. She stayed here."

"Good taste," Lizzie said, but her mouth was dry, her hands trembling. She'd stood up to Norman Estabrook and his killers, but this, she thought—talking to a tortured man about the mother she never knew—was almost too much for her.

"She was in Irish tourism development," March said. "Except, of course, she wasn't."

"It was a good cover for her intelligence work."

"She knew what she was doing, Lizzie. She went up against very dedicated, very bad people." He looked away. "I wish I could have saved her. If you hate me…"

"I don't. I never have, even when I suspected that I didn't know everything about her death. I'd have loved to have known my mother. I'd love to have her at my side if I ever get married and have babies of my own—"

"Lizzie." His dark eyes, so like his own daughter's, filled with tears. "I'm so sorry."

"I had a wonderful, interesting upbringing, with a truly loving family. My mother has remained unreal to me, but the choices I faced this past year, the decisions I made, dealing with someone like Norman, have brought me closer to her, helped me to understand her better."

"She loved you and your father with all her heart."

"And you, Director March?"

He didn't flinch at her question. "I could have fallen in love with her. Maybe I did. We met just before Kathryn and I started dating. But then pretty, black-haired, green-eyed Shauna Morrigan ran into Harlan Rush here at the Whitcomb, and that was that."

"My father knew she was a spy?"

"He wasn't a part of what she did. She had IRA contacts in Boston. That's how I hooked up with her. After you were born, she quit. But it was too late."

"Who killed her and her family?"

"An FBI agent with ties to the Boston Irish mob was responsible. I'd been on his trail. She got me closer to him. He found out. He thought killing her would keep me from him. He gave her up to her enemies in Ireland. It didn't matter that she'd retired. They killed her and her family." March drank more of his whiskey. "We cooperated with the Irish in order to save lives."

"So that's why their deaths were ruled an accident. What happened to this corrupt FBI agent?"

"He died in a South Boston gunfight. The shooter was never found." March polished off his whiskey and set the glass down firmly. "Rough justice. They were violent, turbulent times, Lizzie. We got those mobsters, but others took their place."

"Do you think she knew she'd been murdered?" Lizzie looked down at the amber liquid in her glass. "Or did she believe she fell?"

"I think she loved you and your father, and the rest of it isn't where I would dwell."

"I wanted you to have answers."

"People do. You're not alone. The older I get, the fewer answers I have. I wish I'd known your mother was in danger. I wish I'd saved her. After she died, everyone just wanted to save you, her little baby she loved so much."

"I knew I didn't have the whole story." Lizzie tried to smile through her tears. "Tripped on a cobblestone outside an Irish pub and fell to her death. Ha. What about Simon's father?"

"Brendan Cahill was a friend. He was killed ten years after your mother."

"Ripple effects," Lizzie said, giving the man across from her a long look. "You have a lot of secrets, Director March."

"So I do."

"Thank you for being there for me this past year."

"Lizzie…" He sighed, less tortured. "Abigail and Owen want you at their wedding. It's in Scotland in five days. The Davenport castle."

"Will says it's a house."

"You can tell me what you think when you see it. In my world, it's a castle."

"You mean you've been there?"

He shrugged. Another secret. "You should get your father talking sometime. He has tales to tell about British lords and ladies."

She laughed. "I'll bet he does."

"He loved your mother, and she loved him. Most of all they both loved you. Maybe the rest doesn't matter anymore. Live your life, Lizzie. Don't put it on hold because of the past." He leaned back, eyeing her as she rose. "And stay in touch."

On her way out of the restaurant, she noticed a framed photograph she'd never seen before of her parents hand in hand on the rocks in Maine, her mother visibly pregnant, both of them smiling as they looked out toward the ocean.

"Your father hung it there this morning," Jeremiah said next to her.

"Where is he now?"

"It's Uncle Harlan. Who knows?"

Chapter 33

Beara Peninsula, Southwest Ireland
4:00 p.m., IST
August 29

Lizzie sat at what she now considered her table by the fire in Eddie O'Shea's pub. She had Keira's book of Irish folktales opened to an illustartion of trooping fairies. She sighed. "I wish I could draw."

"You have other talents," Eddie said, sitting across from her. His dog, settled on the hearth, kept staring at her as if he knew she'd been kissed a by British lord and didn't approve.

"This place feels different than it did the night I was here," Lizzie said.

Eddie reached down and patted the dog. "I'd hope so. Simon's returned. He'll be here soon to start up an argument." The barman seemed to relish the idea. "Have you heard his Irish accent?"

"I understand it's very good."

"Not to a real Irishman."

Lizzie laughed. "Keira will be happy to see him, now that the guards are satisfied she's safe." She turned to another illustration, one of a beautiful fairy princess and a handsome fairy prince. "Imagine loving someone that much. Having someone love you that much."

"There are rules about weddings in Ireland, but I have a feeling Keira and Simon will figure them out." Eddie sat up straight, and the dog rolled onto his side close to the fire. "Your mum was Irish."

"Yes, she was. When I lived in Ireland, I found the cottage where she was born. It's been abandoned, but it's structurally sound, tucked in a quiet, isolated valley not that far from here."

"A magical valley?"

Lizzie smiled at the Irishman across from her and decided he wasn't as skeptical about the wee folk as he liked to pretend. "I have an open mind. I'd like to take Keira there. Maybe it'll inspire a painting. We can find old stories."

"You've a new friend in Keira."

"I hope so. I'm also good at wishful thinking."

Eddie kept his eyes on her. "You've fallen for your Brit, haven't you? Well, your mother fell for a Yank."

"You like Will. My Irish ancestors—"

"They'd want you to be happy. I hear there's no Rush hotel in London."

"Imagine that."

"Convenient, wouldn't you say?"

Josie Goodwin entered the pub and walked behind the bar, helping herself to a bottle of expensive whiskey. She collected a glass and headed to Lizzie's table. Eddie rose and gave her his seat.

"I've become very fond of the Beara Peninsula," Josie said, setting down her glass and opening the bottle. "Should I have brought you a glass?"

Lizzie shook her head. "I've a weakness for Eddie's blackberry crumble."

"Ah. Who doesn't."

Josie poured her whiskey and, after taking a sip, produced a handwritten invitation to Abigail and Owen's wedding in Scotland, along with arrangements for transportation. "And I wasn't sure if you'd have time to shop, so I've a dress for you, too. I've had it sent to Scotland. It's pale blue, flowing, I'm sure just the right size. Your auntie's a dear. Your cousin Justin in Dublin put me in touch with her." Josie took a breath and another swallow of her drink. "How are you? It's all a bit of a crush, I know, but that's how these people are. Will and his American friends. I expect you'll fit right in."

"I love weddings," Lizzie said.

"I expect you do. Will's delayed, but he plans to arrive in time for the ceremony. Whatever's between you is more than the heat of the moment." She pursed her lips, as if debating how much to say. "His family's complicated."

Simon had come into the pub. The local men moaned but were obviously delighted to see him. They exchanged a few good-natured barbs as he dragged a chair over to Lizzie's table and joined her and Josie by the fire. "All families are complicated, Josie." It seemed to be a familiar exchange between them, but he was serious as he addressed Lizzie. "March should have told me about his connection to you. I should have found out on my own. I shouldn't have left you out there alone for so long."

"I was never alone," Lizzie said. "I'd only to give Director March my name, and I'd have had help. I knew that, even when I was most convinced I was on my own."

"This was a tough mission from start to finish. Norman was manipulative and deceptive, but even he didn't have all the pieces."

"Did John March?"

It was Josie who answered. "One never knows."

Simon reached over and tapped the wedding invitation. "Time to sing and dance." His deep green eyes sparked with mischief. "I haven't a clue whether Will knows how to do either."

"As a matter of fact," Josie said, "I don't, either."

Simon smiled. "You'll have to find out, Lizzie, and tell us."

She felt a surge of heat that, she knew, had nothing to do with the fire and everything to do with the thought of dancing in Scotland with Will Davenport. "Is that a challenge, Special Agent Cahill?"

He got to his feet. He truly was a bruiser of a man. "Designed to appeal to the daredevil in you." His eyes were warm now, a promise in them. "You'll be among friends in Scotland."

The local men teased him, and he them back. He was affable and well liked, but he didn't linger. He headed out, and Lizzie rose, restless, uncertain, suddenly, why she'd even come here.

She thanked Josie, who'd given up on her whiskey and was providing Eddie O'Shea with precise instructions about the blackberry crumble she was ordering.

Lizzie followed Eddie's dog out to the pretty village street. The spaniel trotted ahead of her and turned, tail wagging. Hugging her Irish sweater close to her, she let him lead her onto the lane along the ancient wall above the harbor.

As they turned onto the dirt track, she saw a woman running across the field from the stone circle, and recognized Keira Sullivan.

Simon was by the fence, the barren hills quiet except for the intermittent bleating of sheep. Lizzie stopped, and the springer spaniel wandered back down to her in the fine, gray mist. Together they watched as Simon climbed over the fence. Keira cried out as she spotted him and started to run, and he scooped her up into his arms.

They held on to each other as if they'd never let go.

"Soulmates," Lizzie whispered, and she and the dog headed back down the lane.

When she reached the village, she had a panicked text message from Justin in Dublin.

Help. Uncle Harlan is here.

She called her cousin. "Lizzie," Justin said, still worked up, "Uncle Harlan's taking me to the Irish village where your family's from. I'm touched, I swear I am, but I have a feeling he's going to teach me how to survive a night in an Irish ruin. And he wants to drive."

"Maintain situational awareness, and you'll be fine."

"Situational—Lizzie!"

She laughed. "I'm going to a wedding."

Chapter 34

Highlands of Scotland
3:00 p.m., BST
September 2

Will Davenport's "house" was a stunning Regency period mansion in the Scottish highlands. Lizzie found Abigail Browning on a path that meandered through the extensive gardens. The detective, more or less healed from her ordeal, was in her element. "I'm so glad you're here," she said. "The Davenports have been so generous. Will's sister, Arabella, had a rack dress that fits me. Will arranged for a private plane so that Scoop could make it. I don't know how he did it. Josie Goodwin said she'll have an ambulance on call. He looks awful, but he says it's because he spent hours trapped on a plane with Bob complaining about another cross-Atlantic trip. My folks are here. The Garrisons. I don't know how a small wedding got so big so fast." She caught herself. "I'm talking a mile a minute."

Lizzie smiled. "It's a special day. Your family and friends are all delighted to see you happy and well."

"It's perfect. And I've never..." Her dark eyes, no longer filled with pain and fatigue, settled on Lizzie. "Thank you for saving my life."

"Myles Fletcher wouldn't have let you be killed."

"He'd have done what he could, but you had instincts and information and doggedness. They're what made the difference. Without you, Estabrook…" She made a face. "Never mind. Let's not ruin a perfect day by mentioning him."

"Your father—"

"He arrived last night. And here comes my mother. She's so nervous, she's making me nervous."

"She's had a rough time."

Abigail grimaced. "I love her, and I don't take her for granted—"

"No, it's all right. Go let her fuss over you. Be a mum and daughter."

Lizzie wandered the grounds until a few minutes before the ceremony started in a large, airy room with tapestries on the walls and giant urns of hydrangeas. She was seated next to Arabella Davenport, who had her brother's hazel eyes. She whispered to Lizzie, "Will is due back any moment."

He arrived in time for the ceremony and stood in back, elegant, reserved, well mannered and thoroughly sexy. Their days apart hadn't changed anything, not for her. She was as attracted to him as ever. It hadn't been a passing fancy fueled by the danger and fears they'd faced together.

And he couldn't dance. Neither could Lizzie.

"Your family, Will. They're proud of what you do?" She stumbled in his arms, righted herself. "Or don't they know?"

"My sister…but the rest…no."

An answer without answering.

Out of the corner of her eye, Lizzie saw Simon dancing with Keira, keeping her off her feet most of the time. "Now, Simon can dance."

"He can, indeed. Philip Billings could, too. David and

Myles and I were always surprised…." Will smiled at her, holding her close. "They were right, Billings and Mears. About you. I've met my match."

"Will—"

But he spun her toward glass doors that led to the gardens. "Tell me what you want, Lizzie."

"I want to live in a castle with a handsome prince and grow hollyhocks and lavender."

"With the occasional holiday to save someone?"

"I suppose I'll have to work, too. I have to find somewhere in the U.K. to locate a hotel."

"An adventure in its own right." He bent down to whisper in her ear. "Let's skip the dancing. I've two left feet, as you can see."

"You're faking it. You can dance as well as any Jane Austen hero."

He walked with her onto a cool terrace, fragrant with roses. "I've told everyone I'll be fishing here for the next few weeks. I thought you might like to see where."

"I don't fish."

"You don't fish and you don't dance. Just what will we do to amuse ourselves?"

He took her to a small stone cottage on a stream amid fir trees.

Sweeping her into his arms, he carried her into the bedroom and lowered her to the soft sheets and undressed her to the sounds of the stream. He worked slowly, patiently, or at least deliberately.

Lizzie shivered at the feel of his breath, his hands, on her bare skin. "Can you fall in love with someone in such a short time?"

"I can," he said, his hands warm on her bare skin. "I've been waiting for you my whole life."

"My Prince Charming."

He smiled, smoothing his palms over her hips. "You're not going to turn into a Sleeping Beauty, are you?"

She sank deeper into the soft bed. "Not for a while."

A breeze floated over her, adding to the sensations of his touch, his kisses. She slipped her hands under his warm sweater and spread her fingers over the muscles of his back, felt his shudder of pleasure.

He shed his clothes and came to her again. She sank into the soft bed and lost herself in the feel of him. Touching him, caressing him, kissing him, until she was quivering and hot. She led him into her, their eyes locking as he whispered her name. He moved inside her, and she was gone, pulling him deep, crying out for him as his own urgency mounted.

Days they had ahead of them…

He seemed to read her mind and held her tight. "We're just beginning," he said, and that was the last either spoke for a long time.

Later, they dressed warmly and walked along the stream, holding hands in the cool late-summer air. Lizzie leaned against him, and suddenly the pressures of the past year—its secrets and dangers—seemed far away.

When they returned to the cottage, they found a basket on the doorstep, with a bottle of champagne…and a sprig of lavender.

Lizzie looked at Will and squeezed his hand.

Myles Fletcher.

Will took the basket inside without a word. He opened the champagne and filled two glasses, handing one to her as he slipped one arm around her.

"To friends in harm's way," he said.

They touched their glasses together, and Lizzie whispered, "May they always know they're not alone."

* * * * *

Dear Reader,

As I type this note to you, I'm just back from the southwest Irish coast, where I wrote portions of *The Whisper*, the follow-up to *The Mist*. Writing in an Irish pub, with a Guinness and a witty Irish barman for company, was a special experience as well as great fun.

In *The Whisper*, Boston detective Scoop Wisdom is convinced another officer was involved in the bomb blast that almost killed him. He meets Sophie Malone, an archaeologist haunted by a terrifying night she spent in an Irish cave. Scoop suspects Sophie isn't telling him everything…and he's right.

Check out the sneak peek of *The Whisper* on the next pages, and look for it on bookshelves in late June!

While in Ireland, I took pictures of some amazing rainbows. You can see them on my Web site, as well as enter my monthly draw and find the latest details about what I'm up to.

For their help with my many questions while writing *The Mist*, I'd like to thank Gregory Harrell; Fire Chief Stephen Locke of Hartford, Vermont; Hilda Neggers Stilwell; and Dave and Margie Carley. A special thank-you to Denis Burke for the Irish stories.

I keep adding to my collection of books on all things Irish, and I highly recommend *Beara: The Unexplored Peninsula* by Francis Twomey and Tony McGettigan (Woodpark Publications); the Ordnance Survey's *The Beara Way*

(Wayfarer Series); *The Stone Circles of Cork & Kerry* by Jack Roberts (Bandia Publishing); and *Irish Folktales*, edited by Henry Glassie (Pantheon Books). Enjoy!

Please e-mail me anytime at Carla@CarlaNeggers.com, or write to me at P.O. Box 826, Quechee, VT 05059. I'd love to hear from you.

Take care, and happy reading,

Carla Neggers

Excerpt from THE WHISPER
Carla Neggers

Scoop Wisdom opened his backpack, got out his water and took a long drink. He had unfinished business. It had been gnawing at him ever since he'd gotten off painkillers and IVs, but he hadn't felt it as acutely as he did now, here, sitting on a cold, damp rock in a remote, isolated Irish ruin.

He needed to find out who had planted the bomb that had almost killed him a month ago in Boston.

Maybe, Scoop thought, the spiral of violence over the summer had started here in June, on the night of the summer solstice, with fairies and magic and a serial killer obsessed with his own ideas of sin and evil. Maybe it was here he could put them to rest.

He shifted his position on the rock. He heard a splash of water in the stream just outside the ruin and stiffened.

"I know, I know." It was a woman's voice, American. Amused. "You're coming with me, and there's not a thing I can do to stop you."

Scoop got up from his rock, stood in the entrance of the ruin and peered through the mist as a woman with wild red hair arrived a split second ahead of a big black dog. Even in the gray light, he saw that she had bright blue eyes and freckles—a lot of freckles. She looked trim and fit, comfortable with the Irish weather and terrain.

"I saw your footprints in the mud," she said cheerfully.

Scoop nodded at the dog. "He seems tame."

"At the moment, yes."

A warning? Not that she looked nervous, but Scoop wouldn't blame her if she did. They were out in an isolated pasture, and even before the scars of the bomb blast, he'd looked, according to his friends and enemies alike, ferocious with his thick build, shaved head and general take-no-prisoners demeanor. No one would mistake him for a leprechaun or a fairy prince.

She was finishing up an apple, and she tossed the core across the stream into the dense undergrowth. Even in the mild southwest, brushed by the Gulf Stream, its climate mild and wet, the greenery was turning brown, the flowers of summer fading.

"You're the detective who saved that girl's life in the bomb blast last month." The woman paused a moment, her expression suggesting a focused, intelligent mind. "Wisdom, right? Detective Cyrus Wisdom?"

Scoop was instantly on alert, but he kept his tone even. "Most people call me Scoop, which some don't think is much better than Cyrus, but that's my name. And you would be?"

"My name's Sophie. Sophie Malone. I'm from Boston. That's how I know about the bomb." She glanced into the ruin, her eyes narrowed. "Do you believe in fairies, Detective Wisdom?"

"Only when I'm standing in an Irish ruin with a scary black dog."

And a smart, pretty redhead. But Scoop decided to keep that part to himself. It was as if fairies had put a spell on him the moment he'd laid eyes on Sophie Malone and the black dog.

Definitely time to go back to Boston and be a cop again.

NEW YORK TIMES
AND *USA TODAY*
BESTSELLING AUTHOR

CARLA NEGGERS

When Emile Labresque's research ship sinks, killing five people on board, Emile, his granddaughter, Riley St. Joe, and the captain barely survive. But a year later, when the captain's body washes up on a beach, Emile is suspected of murder.

Riley is determined to clear her grandfather's name and turns to the only person willing to help: John Straker, an FBI special agent who is compelled to help Riley because of his friendship with the old man.

Riley and Straker are from different worlds, but they have something in common: a determination to save Emile's life…and a passion that's hard to ignore.

ON FIRE

Available wherever books are sold.

MIRA®

www.MIRABooks.com

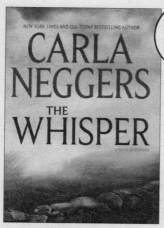

NEW YORK TIMES AND USA TODAY BESTSELLING AUTHOR

CARLA NEGGERS

THE **WHISPER**

A NOVEL OF SUSPENSE

$24.95 U.S./$27.95 CAN.

$2.00 OFF

New York Times and **USA TODAY**
Bestselling Author

CARLA NEGGERS

Look for Carla's next book, another gripping story you won't be able to put down.

THE **WHISPER**

Available June 29, 2010,
wherever books are sold!

$2.00 OFF   the purchase price of
THE **WHISPER** by Carla Neggers

Offer valid from June 29, 2010, to July 13, 2010.
Redeemable at participating retail outlets. Limit one coupon per purchase.
Valid in the U.S.A. and Canada only.

52608966

5 65373 00082 3   (8100)0 11643

MCN0410CPN

International Bestselling Author
M. J. ROSE

**Hypnosis opens the door to the past…
but what happens if the truth on the other side
is something you can't live with?**

A modern-day reincarnationist is hell-bent on finding tools
to aid in past life regressions no matter what the cost—
in dollars or lives.

Everything rests on the shoulders of Lucian Glass, special agent
with the FBI's Art Crime team, who himself is suffering from a
brutal attack, impossible nightmares and his own crisis of faith.

If reincarnation is real, how can he live with who he was
in his past life? If it's not, then how can he live with who
he has become in the present?

The HYPNOTIST

Available April 27, 2010, wherever books are sold!

www.MIRABooks.com

MMJR2675

REQUEST YOUR FREE BOOKS!

2 FREE NOVELS
FROM THE SUSPENSE COLLECTION
PLUS 2 FREE GIFTS!

YES! Please send me 2 FREE novels from the Suspense Collection and my 2 FREE gifts (gifts are worth about $10). After receiving them, if I don't wish to receive any more books, I can return the shipping statement marked "cancel." If I don't cancel, I will receive 3 brand-new novels every month and be billed just $5.74 per book in the U.S. or $6.24 per book in Canada. That's a saving of at least 28% off the cover price. It's quite a bargain! Shipping and handling is just 50¢ per book in the U.S. and 75¢ per book in Canada.* I understand that accepting the 2 free books and gifts places me under no obligation to buy anything. I can always return a shipment and cancel at any time. Even if I never buy another book, the two free books and gifts are mine to keep forever.

192 MDN E4MN   392 MDN E4MY

Name _____ (PLEASE PRINT) _____

Address _____ Apt. # _____

City _____ State/Prov. _____ Zip/Postal Code _____

Signature (if under 18, a parent or guardian must sign)

Mail to **The Reader Service:**
IN U.S.A.: P.O. Box 1867, Buffalo, NY 14240-1867
IN CANADA: P.O. Box 609, Fort Erie, Ontario L2A 5X3

Not valid for current subscribers to the Suspense Collection
or the Romance/Suspense Collection.

Want to try two free books from another line?
Call 1-800-873-8635 or visit www.morefreebooks.com.

* Terms and prices subject to change without notice. Prices do not include applicable taxes. N.Y. residents add applicable sales tax. Canadian residents will be charged applicable provincial taxes and GST. Offer not valid in Quebec. This offer is limited to one order per household. All orders subject to approval. Credit or debit balances in a customer's account(s) may be offset by any other outstanding balance owed by or to the customer. Please allow 4 to 6 weeks for delivery. Offer available while quantities last.

Your Privacy: Harlequin Books is committed to protecting your privacy. Our Privacy Policy is available online at www.eHarlequin.com or upon request from the Reader Service. From time to time we make our lists of customers available to reputable third parties who may have a product or service of interest to you. If you would prefer we not share your name and address, please check here. ☐

Help us get it right—We strive for accurate, respectful and relevant communications. To clarify or modify your communication preferences, visit us at www.ReaderService.com/consumerchoice.

MSUSI0

NEW YORK TIMES AND USA TODAY
BESTSELLING AUTHOR

HEATHER GRAHAM

Ten years ago, Chloe Marin escaped death when a party
she attended turned into a savage killing spree. Chloe's
sketch of one of the killers led to two dead cult members,
closing the case to the cops.

Now, working as a psychologist and police consultant, Chloe
joins forces with Luke Cane, a British ex-cop-turned-P.I., to
investigate the disappearance of a model. But when Chloe
discovers a gruesome mass murder at the modeling agency,
eerily similar to the one she witnessed a decade ago, she
fears the real killers were never caught and now she's their
target—and that she won't be able to cheat death again.

THE
KILLING EDGE

Available wherever books are sold.

MIRA®